Fiction of the Eighties

a decade of stories from TriQuarterly

Edited by Reginald Gibbons and Susan Hahn

A special issue of *TriQuarterly* magazine

Northwestern University / 1990

TriQuarterly 78 Spring/Summer 1990

Editor
Reginald Gibbons

Associate Editor
Susan Hahn

Managing Editor
Kirstie Felland

Executive Editor
Bob Perlongo

Special Projects Editor
Fred Shafer

Assistant to the Editor
Gwenan Wilbur

Design Director
Gini Kondziolka

TriQuarterly Fellow
Belinda Edmundson

Editorial Assistants
**Jo Anne Ruvoli,
Amy Rosenzweig**

Readers
**Campbell McGrath,
Anne Calcagno**

Advisory Editors
**Hugo Achugar, Robert Alter, Michael Anania, Cyrus Colter,
Rita Dove, Gloria Emerson, Richard Ford, George Garrett,
Gerald Graff, Francine du Plessix Gray, Michael S. Harper,
Bill Henderson, Maxine Kumin, Grace Paley, Michael Ryan,
Alan Shapiro, Ellen Bryant Voigt**

TRIQUARTERLY IS AN INTERNATIONAL JOURNAL OF WRITING, ART AND CULTURAL INQUIRY PUBLISHED AT **NORTHWESTERN UNIVERSITY.**

Subscription rates (three issues a year)—Individuals: one year $18; two years $32; life $250. Institutions: one year $26; two years $44; life $300. Foreign subscriptions $4 per year additional. Price of single copies varies. Sample copies $4. Correspondence and subscriptions should be addressed to *TriQuarterly,* **NORTHWESTERN UNIVERSITY,** 2020 Ridge Avenue, Evanston, IL 60208. Phone: (708) 491-3490. The editors invite submissions of fiction, poetry and literary essays, which must be received between October 1 and April 30; manuscripts received between May 1 and September 30 will not be read. No manuscripts will be returned unless accompanied by a stamped, self-addressed envelope. All manuscripts accepted for publication become the property of *TriQuarterly,* unless otherwise indicated. Copyright © 1990 by *TriQuarterly.* No part of this volume may be reproduced in any manner without written permission. The views expressed in this magazine are to be attributed to the writers, not the editors or sponsors. Printed in the United States of America by Thomson-Shore, typeset by Sans Serif. ISSN: 0041-3097.

National distributor to retail trade: B. DeBoer, 113 East Centre Street-Rear, Nutley, NJ 07110 (201-667-9300). Distributor for West Coast trade: Bookpeople, 2929 Fifth Street, Berkeley, CA 94710 (415-549-3030). Midwest: ILPA, P.O. Box 816, Oak Park, IL 60303 (708-383-7535); and Ingram Periodicals, 1117 Heil Quaker Blvd., La Vergne, TN 37086 (800-759-5000).

Reprints of issues #1–15 of *TriQuarterly* are available in full format from Kraus Reprint Company, Route 100, Millwood, NY 10546, and all issues in microfilm from University Microfilms International, 300 North Zeeb Road, Ann Arbor, MI 48106.

Copyrights and Acknowledgments

Contents

3

Cover design by Gini Kondziolka

Preface

When a literary magazine lasts more than five years or so, it begins to define itself as a span of attention rather than an instance of it. Now twenty-five years old, TriQuarterly began by offering its readers, among other things, an uncommon richness of short fiction, and in its middle years was devoted almost exclusively to that form. In the 1980's, the particular responsiveness of the best short fiction to the conditions of life around author and reader seemed to us very characteristic of the era in this country—somewhat private, but with a more readily apparent "background reality," as Czeslaw Milosz calls it, than what one sees in lesser work.

The 1980's ended perhaps sometime around the middle of 1989, when the 1990's were announced by the tumultuous first steps of progress toward the democratization of political power, especially in China, Eastern Europe and now, at the beginning of 1990, in South Africa. Whether those steps were crushed, as in China, or blocked repeatedly as they have nearly always been in Central America, they set a new social tone in the global village, where refugees and emigrés have turned up everywhere on the planet with their double task of acculturating themselves to a new place, and of acculturating new places to themselves— whether they are Russian Jews in Israel, or Hmong in Minneapolis. This new social tone is undoubtedly in some part the effect of many unnoticed cultural preparations that were made for it, especially in the way writers imagined the ways in which the life with which they were familiar might be different.

The record of short fiction in the decade preceding this new tone, as that record was preserved in one American literary magazine, is especially interesting for several reasons. While the latest trends in literary

7

criticism and theory were sweeping aside the claim for the very existence of such a creature as an author, and questioning the reliability of any statement about the things and events and persons outside language, the short story – call it naive if you wish, or perhaps you will want to call it responsive – made use of the full bag of fictional tricks precisely in order to keep up the sleight of hand of literary illusion. Karl Shapiro has remarked that to the poet, although language is a game, the poem never is. The germ of truth in "the death of the author" and the "deconstructive turn" seem to have been well known, and well exploited in terms of art, by imaginative writers before they were taken to be ultimate terms by later critics.

And imaginative writing seems to be registering far more accurately and usefully than current literary criticism the range of human experience, feeling, thought and projected possibility as these are actually experienced. In the 1980's, short fiction seems to have satisfied a good number of reasonably sophisticated readers that this era, like earlier ones, asked of its writers that they attempt an artistic response to the events and atmospheres, the persons and parties, the endeavors and toxins, the despairs and hopes, the loves and hates, around them. Emerson remarked that every age requires a new confession – which we might interpret to mean that as the circumstances of life continue to unfold and alter, so these circumstances are continually putting into a new light the artistic resources and strategies already discovered and employed – making some seem less useful, others newly invigorated, and creating conditions for the invention of entirely new ones, as well. And just as the recent changes set in motion in the social and political world, while surprising for their speed, did not arise out of nothing but rather out of all sorts of unnoticed or suppressed preparations, so whatever it is that short fiction will do in the 1990's (in whatever degree of responsiveness to events, to the protean and continuing changes in language and in the way literature is perceived, and to developments in the publishing industry) so these changes in short fiction, and perhaps in contemporary writing generally, will come out of preparations laid down already in the 1980's.

While *TriQuarterly* cannot claim to have brought together the full range of fictional strategies of the decade just ended (for that wasn't our purpose as we went along), we can hope that the works we selected for publication during the decade, and especially those selected in a further refinement of judgment for this volume, do give a view of the short story, and of the purposes to which it has been turned, that effectively characterizes the decade artistically. And it does seem worth pointing

8

out—again—that much of what is most interesting to readers, most fruitful to understanding, most engendering of artistic possibility and accomplishment, in what writers are doing, continues to lead a half-hidden life in the literary magazines and journals, rather far from both the wider reach of commercial publishing and the very tight grasp of current academic literary criticism. Not for the sake of new trends in themselves, but for the sake of the very variety of imagination, technique, materials and voices, the literary magazines persist in the lovely folly of their existence, with the odds heaped against them by lack of money, difficulty of distribution, entanglements of sponsorship, relative scarcity of subscribers and the indifference or hostility of other spheres of literary culture.

But as a span of attention, over a period of years, a literary magazine is the best reminder that the dizzying variety of expression that makes up the whole of literary culture does not tend ineluctably toward throwing out, from the crest of the highest wave of each period, some few great writers and their works, who land on the beach where readers are waiting, despite our having been taught that this is what it does. There is rather a moving current, moiled by a good number of eddies and undertows, as well. This current is in constant motion forward with time, and the natural life of literary expression is the simultaneous life of a very great number of writers and works—new, remembered and freshly recovered—in conversation with each other and with the age. There may be a kind of "natural" selection of literary texts that determines which will survive, but no more than in real life does this selection guarantee that there are inherent virtues in the survivors that have led to their survival. The great and awestriking virtue of cultural expression, however, is that unlike extinct species, lost literary works, when rediscovered, gain a "second life," as Eugenio Montale called the life of art in those who keep it alive.

The most accurate representation of all this writing—both historically in this century and in our time as well—and the best guarantee of the survival of some of it, is the range of literary magazines, which convey to us the variety and sheer quantity of work at any given moment. There seems to have been such variety ever since the beginning of print culture, if not before; and of course it's this variety that is experienced by the writer and by his or her contemporaries, not the firmly established, unquestionably canonized, relatively few figures who make up the later academic short list for thorough study.

So in a university backyard, so to speak (and grateful to be there), we raise a little banner called *TriQuarterly* three times a year; and this year

9

we bring back into view some of the short fiction that had its first life in the 1980's. We do so with pleasure and hope. We are pleased that *TriQuarterly* has attained its maturity and then some; we are grateful for the contributions of many remarkable writers, generous donors and supporters (whose contributions have financed not only the production of the magazine but also the payment of writers), and the home provided for the magazine by its parent institution. We have enjoyed being able to present new writing in such a way as to please the writer and instruct, entertain and move the reader. We have been especially pleased to have been able, in the last ten years, to present new writing by both American writers and also writers from abroad. We hope that the magazine will continue another twenty-five years, with the help of writers, readers and friends, and that it will remain as lovely a folly as ever.

It might try a reader's patience to claim that we wanted this collection to be longer, but we did. We have excluded all excerpts from novels, in order to try to get at what it is that the short story does that is different from a novel or a piece of a novel. And in order to get down to a size we could afford to produce and a reader could manage to hold in one hand, we have reluctantly omitted many other fine pieces.

So now, please turn the page to where the art begins. Join us in the experience of this ability that men and women persist in cultivating and refining in order to shape, with a peculiar and unique memorableness, certain moments of shared consciousness in which the language we speak creates the illusion of life, and in so doing, helps to establish the value of life.

Reginald Gibbons and Susan Hahn
Northwestern University
March 1990

Where Is Everyone?
Raymond Carver

I've seen some things. I was going over to my mother's to stay a few nights, but just as I came to the top of the stairs I looked and she was on the sofa kissing a man. It was summer, the door was open, and the color TV was playing.

My mother is sixty-five and lonely. She belongs to a singles club. But even so, knowing all this, it was hard. I stood at the top of the stairs with my hand on the railing and watched as the man pulled her deeper into the kiss. She was kissing back, and the TV was going on the other side of the room. It was Sunday, about five in the afternoon. People from the apartment house were down below in the pool. I went back down the stairs and out to my car.

A lot has happened since that afternoon, and on the whole things are better now. But during those days, when my mother was putting out to men she'd just met, I was out of work, drinking, and crazy. My kids were crazy, and my wife was crazy and having a "thing" with an unemployed aerospace engineer she'd met at AA. He was crazy too. His name was Ross and he had five or six kids. He walked with a limp from a gunshot wound his first wife had given him. He didn't have a wife now; he wanted my wife. I don't know what we were all thinking of in those days. The second wife had come and gone, but it was his first wife who had shot him in the thigh some years back, giving him the limp, and who now had him in and out of court, or in jail, every six months or so for not meeting his support payments. I wish him well now. But it was different then. More than once in those days I mentioned weapons. I'd say to my wife, I'd shout it, "I'm going to kill him!" But nothing ever happened. Things lurched on. I never met the man, though we talked on the phone a few times. I did find a couple of pictures of him once when I was going through my wife's purse. He was a little guy, not too little, and he had a mustache and was wearing a striped jersey, waiting for a kid to come down the slide. In the other picture he was standing against a house—my house? I couldn't tell—with his arms crossed, dressed up, wearing a tie. Ross, you son of a bitch, I hope you're O.K. now. I hope things are better for you too.

The last time he'd been jailed, a month before that Sunday, I found out from my daughter that her mother had gone bail for him. Daughter Kate, who was fifteen, didn't take to this any better than I did. It wasn't that she had any loyalty to me in this—she had no loyalties to me or her mother in anything and was only too willing to sell either one of us down the river. No, it was that there was a serious cash-flow problem in the house and if money went to Ross, there'd be that much less for what she needed. So Ross was on her list now. Also, she didn't like his kids, she'd said, but she'd told me once before that in general Ross was all right, even funny and interesting when he wasn't drinking. He'd even told her fortune.

He spent his time repairing things, now that he could no longer hold a job in the aerospace industry. But I'd seen his house from the outside; and the place looked like a dumping ground, with all kinds and makes of old appliances and equipment that would never wash or cook or play again—all of it just standing in his open garage and on his drive and in the front yard. He also kept some broken-down cars around that he liked to tinker on. In the first stages of their affair my wife had told me he "collected antique cars." Those were her words. I'd seen some of his cars parked in front of his house when I'd driven by there trying to see what I could see. Old 1950's and 1960's, dented cars with torn seat covers. They were junkers, that's all. I knew. I had his number. We had things in common, more than just driving old cars and trying to hold on for dear life to the same woman. Still, handyman or not, he couldn't manage to tune my wife's car properly or fix our TV set when it broke down and we lost the picture. We had volume, but no picture. If we wanted to get the news, we'd have to sit around the screen at night and listen to the set. I'd drink and make some crack to my kids about Mr. Fixit. Even now I don't know if my wife believed that stuff or not, about antique cars and such. But she cared for him, she loved him even; that's pretty clear now.

They'd met when Cynthia was trying to stay sober and was going to meetings three or four times a week. I had been in and out of AA for several months, though when Cynthia met Ross I was out and drinking a fifth a day of anything I could get my hands on. But as I heard Cynthia say to someone over the phone about me, I'd had the exposure to AA and knew where to go when I really wanted help. Ross had been in AA and then had gone back to drinking again. Cynthia felt, I think, that maybe there was more hope for him than for me and tried to help him and so went to the meetings to keep herself sober, then went over to cook for him or clean his house. His kids were no help to him in this regard. Nobody lifted a hand around his house except Cynthia when she was there. But the less his kids pitched in, the more he loved them. It was strange. It was the opposite with me. I hated my kids during this time. I'd be on the sofa with a glass of vodka and grapefruit juice when one of them would come in from school and slam the door. One afternoon I screamed and got into a scuffle with my son. Cynthia had to break it up when I threatened to knock him to pieces. I said I would kill him. I said, "I gave you life and I can take it away."

Madness.

The kids, Katy and Mike, were only too happy to take advantage of this crumbling situation. They seemed to thrive on the threats and bullying they inflicted on each other and on us—the violence and dismay, the general bedlam. Right now, thinking about it even from this distance, it makes me set my heart against them. I remember years before, before I turned to drinking full time, reading an extraordinary scene in a novel by an Italian named Italo Svevo. The narrator's father was dying and the family had gathered around the bed, weeping and waiting for the old man to expire, when he opened his eyes to look at each of them for the last time. When his gaze fell on the narrator he suddenly stirred and something came into his eyes; and with his last burst of strength he raised up, flung himself across the bed, and slapped the face of his son as hard as he could. Then he fell back onto the bed and died. I often imagined my own deathbed scene in those days, and I saw myself doing the same thing, only I would hope to have the strength to slap each of my kids and my last words for them would be what only a dying man would have the courage to utter.

But they saw craziness on every side, and it suited their purpose, I was convinced. They fattened on it. They liked being able to call the shots, having the upper hand, while we bungled along letting them work on our guilt. They might have been inconvenienced from time to time, but they ran things their way. They weren't embarrassed or put out by any of the activities that went on in our house either. To the contrary. It gave them something to talk about with their friends. I've heard them regaling their pals with the most frightful stories, howling with laughter as they spilled out the lurid details of what was happening to me and

13

their mother. Except for being financially dependent on Cynthia, who still somehow had a teaching job and a monthly paycheck, they flat-out ran the show. And that's what it was too, a show.

Once Mike locked his mother out of the house after she'd stayed overnight at Ross's house . . . I don't know where I was that night, probably at my mother's. I'd sleep over there sometimes. I'd eat supper with her and she'd tell me how she worried about all of us; then we'd watch TV and try to talk about something else, try to hold a normal conversation about something other than my family situation. She'd make a bed for me on her sofa—the same sofa she used to make love on, I supposed, but I'd sleep there anyway and be grateful. Cynthia came home at seven o'clock one morning to get dressed for school and found that Mike had locked all the doors and windows and wouldn't let her in the house. She stood outside his window and begged him to let her in— please, please, so she could dress and go to school, for if she lost her job what then? Where would he be? Where would any of us be then? He said, "You don't live here any more. Why should I let you in?" That's what he said to her, standing behind his window, his face all stopped up with rage. (She told me this later when she was drunk and I was sober and holding her hands and letting her talk.) "You don't live here," he said.

"Please, please, please, Mike," she pleaded. "Let me in."

He let her in and she swore at him. Like that, he punched her hard on the shoulders several times—whop, whop, whop—then hit her on top of the head and generally worked her over. Finally she was able to change clothes, fix her face, and rush off to school.

All this happened not too long ago, three years about. It was something in those days.

I left my mother with the man on her sofa and drove around for a while, not wanting to go home and not wanting to sit in a bar that day either.

Sometimes Cynthia and I would talk about things—"reviewing the situation" we'd call it. But now and then on rare occasions we'd talk a little about things that bore no relation to the situation. One afternoon we were in the living room and she said, "When I was pregnant with Mike you carried me to the bathroom when I was so sick and pregnant I couldn't get out of bed. You carried me. No one else will ever do that, no one else could ever love me in that way, that much. We have that, no matter what. We've loved each other like nobody else could or ever will love the other again."

We looked at each other. Maybe we touched hands, I don't recall.

14

Then I remembered the half-pint of whisky or vodka or gin or Scotch or tequila that I had hidden under the very sofa cushion we were sitting on (oh, happy days!) and I began to hope she might soon have to get up and move around—go to the kitchen, the bathroom, out to clean the garage.

"Maybe you could make us some coffee," I said. "A pot of coffee might be nice."

"Would you eat something? I can fix some soup."

"Maybe I could eat something, but I'll for sure drink a cup of coffee."

She went to the kitchen. I waited until I heard her begin to run water. Then I reached under the cushion for the bottle, unscrewed the lid, and drank.

I never told these things at AA. I never said much at the meetings. I'd "pass" as they called it: when it came your turn to speak and you didn't say anything except "I'll pass tonight, thanks." But I would listen and shake my head and laugh in recognition at the awful stories I heard. Usually I was drunk when I went to those first meetings. You're scared and you need something more than cookies and instant coffee.

But those conversations touching on love or the past were rare. If we talked, we talked about business, survival, the bottom line of things. Money. Where is the money going to come from? The telephone was on the way out, the lights and gas threatened. What about Katy? She needs clothes. Her grades. That boyfriend of hers is a biker. Mike. What's going to happen to Mike? What's going to happen to us all? "My God," she'd say. But God wasn't having any of it. He'd washed his hands of us.

I wanted Mike to join the army, navy, or the coast guard. He was impossible. A dangerous character. Even Ross felt the army would be good for him, Cynthia had told me, and she hadn't liked him telling her that a bit. But I was pleased to hear this and to find out that Ross and I were in agreement on the matter. Ross went up a peg in my estimation. But it angered Cynthia because, miserable as Mike was to have around, despite his violent streak, she thought it was just a phase that would soon pass. She didn't want him in the army. But Ross told Cynthia that Mike belonged in the army where he'd learn respect and manners. He told her this after there'd been a pushing and shoving match out in his drive in the early morning hours when Mike had thrown him down on the pavement.

Ross loved Cynthia, but he also had a twenty-two-year-old girl named Beverly who was pregnant with his baby, though Ross assured Cynthia he loved her, not Beverly. They didn't even sleep together any longer, he told Cynthia, but Beverly was carrying his baby and he loved all his

15

children, even the unborn, and he couldn't just give her the boot, could he? He wept when he told all this to Cynthia. He was drunk. (Someone was always drunk in those days.) I can imagine the scene.

Ross had graduated from California Polytechnic Institute and gone right to work at the NASA operation in Mountain View. He worked there for ten years, until it all fell in on him. I never met him, as I said, but we talked on the phone several times, about one thing and another. I called him once when I was drunk and Cynthia and I were debating some sad point or another. One of his children answered the phone and when Ross came on the line I asked him whether, if I pulled out (I had no intention of pulling out, of course; it was just harassment), he intended to support Cynthia and our kids. He said he was carving a roast, that's what he said, and they were just going to sit down and eat their dinner, he and his children. Could he call me back? I hung up. When he called, after an hour or so, I'd forgotten about the earlier call. Cynthia answered the phone and said "Yes" and then "Yes" again, and I knew it was Ross and that he was asking if I was drunk. I grabbed the phone. "Well, are you going to support them or not?" He said he was sorry for his part in all of this but, no, he guessed he couldn't support them. "So it's no, you can't support them," I said, and looked at Cynthia as if this should settle everything. He said, "Yes, it's no." But Cynthia didn't bat an eye. I figured later they'd already talked that situation over thoroughly, so it was no surprise. She already knew.

He was in his mid-thirties when he went under. I used to make fun of him when I had the chance. I called him "the weasel," after his photograph. "That's what your mother's boyfriend looks like," I'd say to my kids if they were around and we were talking, "like a weasel." We'd laugh. Or else "Mr. Fixit." That was my favorite name for him. God bless and keep you, Ross. I don't hold anything against you now. But in those days when I called him the weasel or Mr. Fixit and threatened his life, he was something of a fallen hero to my kids and to Cynthia too, I suppose, because he'd helped put men on the moon. He'd worked, I was told time and again, on the moon project shots, and he was close friends with Buzz Aldren and Neal Armstrong. He'd told Cynthia, and Cynthia had told the kids, who'd told me, that when the astronauts came to town he was going to introduce them. But they never came to town, or if they did they forgot to contact Ross. Soon after the moon probes, fortune's wheel turned and Ross's drinking increased. He began missing work. Sometime then the troubles with his first wife started. Toward the end he began taking the drink to work with him in a thermos. It's a modern operation out there, I've seen it—cafeteria lines, executive dining rooms, and the like, Mr. Coffees in every office. But he brought his own thermos to work, and after a while people began to know and to talk. He was laid off, or else he quit—nobody could ever give me a straight answer when I asked. He kept drinking, of course. You do that. Then he commenced working on ruined appliances and doing TV repair work and fixing cars. He was interested in astrology, auras, I Ching—that business. I don't doubt that he was bright enough and interesting and quirky, like most of our ex-friends. I told Cynthia I was sure she wouldn't care for him (I couldn't yet bring myself to use the word "love" about that relationship) if he wasn't, basically, a good man. "One of us," was how I put it, trying to be large about it. He wasn't a bad or an evil man, Ross. "No one's evil," I said once to Cynthia when we were discussing my own affair.

My dad died in his sleep, drunk, eight years ago. It was a Friday night and he was fifty-four years old. He came home from work at the sawmill, took some sausage out of the freezer for his breakfast the next morning, and sat down at the kitchen table, where he opened a quart of Four Roses. He was in good enough spirits in those days, glad to be back on a job after being out of work for three or four years with blood poisoning 'and then something that caused him to have shock treatments. (I was married and living in another town during that time. I had the kids and a job, enough troubles of my own, so I couldn't follow his too closely.) That night he moved into the living room with his bottle, a bowl of ice cubes and a glass, and drank and watched TV until my mother came in from work at the coffee shop.

They had a few words about the whiskey, as they always did. She didn't drink much herself. When I was grown, I only saw her drink at Thanksgiving, Christmas, and New Year's—eggnog or buttered rums, and then never too many. The one time she had had too much to drink, years before (I heard this from my dad who laughed about it when he told it), they'd gone to a little place outside Eureka and she'd had a great many whiskey sours. Just as they got into the car to leave, she started to get sick and had to open the door. Somehow her false teeth came out, the car moved forward a little, and a tire passed over her dentures. After that she never drank except on holidays and then never to excess.

My dad kept on drinking that Friday night and tried to ignore my mother, who sat out in the kitchen and smoked and tried to write a letter to her sister in Little Rock. Finally he got up and went to bed. My mother went to bed not long after, when she was sure he was asleep. She said later she noticed nothing out of the ordinary except maybe his snoring seemed heavier and deeper and she couldn't get him to turn on

17

his side. But she went to sleep. She woke up when my dad's sphincter muscles and bladder let go. It was just sunrise. Birds were singing. My dad was still on his back, eyes closed and mouth open. My mother looked at him and cried his name.

I kept driving around. It was dark by now. I drove by my house, every light ablaze, but Cynthia's car wasn't in the drive. I went to a bar where I sometimes drank and called home. Katy answered and said her mother wåsn't there, and where was I? She needed five dollars. I shouted something and hung up. Then I called collect to a woman six hundred miles away whom I hadn't seen in months, a good woman who, the last time I'd seen her, had said she would pray for me.

She accepted the charges. She asked where I was calling from. She asked how I was. "Are you all right?" she said.

We talked. I asked about her husband. He'd been a friend of mine and was now living away from her and the children.

"He's still in Richland," she said. "How did all this happen to us?" she asked. "We started out good people." We talked a while longer; then she said she still loved me and that she would continue to pray for me.

"Pray for me," I said. "Yes." Then we said good-bye and hung up.

Later I called home again, but this time no one answered. I dialed my mother's number. She picked up the phone on the first ring, her voice cautious, as if expecting trouble.

"It's me," I said. "I'm sorry to be calling."

"No, no, honey, I was up," she said. "Where are you? Is anything the matter? I thought you were coming over today. I looked for you. Are you calling from home?"

"I'm not at home," I said. "I don't know where everyone is at home. I just called there."

"Old Ken was over here today," she went on, "that old bastard. He came over this afternoon. I haven't seen him in a month and he just shows up, the old thing. I don't like him. All he wants to do is talk about himself and brag on himself and how he lived on Guam and had three girlfriends at the same time and how he's traveled to this place and that place. He's just an old braggart, that's all he is. I met him at that dance I told you about, but I don't like him."

"Is it all right if I come over?" I said.

"Honey, why don't you? I'll fix us something to eat. I'm hungry myself. I haven't eaten anything since this afternoon. Old Ken brought some Colonel Sanders over this afternoon. Come over and I'll fix us some scrambled eggs. Do you want me to come get you? Honey, are you all right?"

18

I drove over. She kissed me when I came in the door. I turned my face. I hated for her to smell the vodka. The TV was on.

"Wash your hands," she said as she studied me. "It's ready."

Later she made a bed for me on the sofa. I went into the bathroom. She kept a pair of my dad's pajamas in there. I took them out of the drawer, looked at them, and began undressing. When I came out she was in the kitchen. I fixed the pillow and lay down. She finished with what she was doing, turned off the kitchen light, and sat down at the end of the sofa.

"Honey, I don't want to be the one to tell you this," she said. "It hurts me to tell you, but even the kids know it and they've told me. We've talked about it. But Cynthia is seeing another man."

"That's O.K.," I said. "I know that," I said and looked at the TV. "His name is Ross and he's an alcoholic. He's like me."

"Honey, you're going to have to do something for yourself," she said.

"I know it," I said. I kept looking at the TV.

She leaned over and hugged me. She held me a minute. Then she let go and wiped her eyes. "I'll get you up in the morning," she said.

"I don't have much to do tomorrow. I might sleep in a while after you go." I thought: after you get up, after you've gone to the bathroom and gotten dressed, then I'll get into your bed and lie there and doze and listen to your radio out in the kitchen giving the news and weather.

"Honey, I'm so worried about you."

"Don't worry," I said. I shook my head.

"You get some rest now," she said. "You need to sleep."

"I'll sleep. I'm very sleepy."

"Watch television as long as you want," she said.

I nodded.

She bent and kissed me. Her lips seemed bruised and swollen. She drew the blanket over me. Then she went into her bedroom. She left the door open, and in a minute I could hear her snoring.

I lay there staring at the TV. There were images of uniformed men on the screen, a low murmur, then tanks and a man using a flamethrower. I couldn't hear it, but I didn't want to get up. I kept staring until I felt my eyes close. But I woke up with a start, the pajamas damp with sweat. A snowy light filled the room. There was a roaring coming at me. The room clamored. I lay there. I didn't move.

19

Coyote Holds a Full House in His Hand

Leslie Marmon Silko

He wasn't getting any place with Mrs. Sekakaku. He could see that. She was warming up leftover chili beans for lunch, and when her niece came over, they left him alone on the red plastic sofa and talked at the kitchen table. Aunt Mamie was still sick, her niece was telling her, and they were all so worried because the doctors at Keams Canyon said they'd tried everything already and old man Ko'ite had come over from Oraibi and still Aunt Mamie was having dizzy spells and couldn't get out of bed. He was looking at the same *Life* magazine he'd already looked at before, and it didn't have any pictures of high school girls twirling batons, or plane crashes, or anything he wanted to look at more than twice, but he didn't want to listen to them because then he'd know just what kind of gossip Mrs. Sekakaku found more important than him and his visit.

He set the magazine down on his lap and traced his finger over the horse's head embossed on the plastic cushion. It was always like that. When he didn't expect it, it always came to him, but when he wanted something to happen, like with Mrs. Sekakaku, then it shied away.

Mrs. Sekakaku's letters had made the corner of the trading post where the mailboxes were smell like the perfume counter at Woolworth's. The Mexican woman with the fat arms was the postmaster and ran the trading post. She didn't approve of perfumed letters and she used to pretend the letters weren't there, even when he could smell them and see their pastel edges sticking out of the pile in the general-delivery slot. The Mexican woman thought Pueblo men were great lovers. He knew this because he heard her say so to another Mexican woman one day while he was finishing his strawberry soda on the other side of the dry-goods section. In the summer he spent a good number of hours there watching her because she wore sleeveless blouses that revealed her fat upper arms,

20

full and round, and the tender underarm creases curving to her breasts. They had not noticed he was still there, leaning on the counter behind a pile of overalls. ". . . the size of a horse" was all that he had heard, but he knew what she was talking about. They were all like that, those Mexican women. That was all they talked about when they were alone. "As big as a horse" – he knew that much Spanish and more too, but she had never treated him nice, not even when he brought her the heart-shaped box of candy, having carried it on the bus all the way from Albuquerque. He didn't think it was his being older than her; she was over thirty herself. It was because she didn't approve of men who drank. That was the last thing he did before he left town; he did it because he had to. Liquor was illegal on the reservation, so the last thing he did was have a few drinks to carry home with him, the same way other people stocked up on lamb nipples or extra matches. She must have smelled it on his breath when he handed her the candy because she didn't say anything and she left the box under the counter by the old newspapers and balls of string. The cellophane was never opened, and the fine gray dust that covered everything in the store finally settled on the pink satin bow. The postmaster was jealous of the letters that were coming, but she was the one who had sent him into the arms of Mrs. Sekakaku.

In her last two letters Mrs. Sekakaku had been hinting around for him to come see her at Bean Dance time. That was after Christmas when he had sent a big poinsettia plant all the way to Second Mesa on the mail bus. Up until then she had never answered the parts in his letters where he said he wished he could see the beautiful Hopi mesas with snow on them. But that had been the first time a potted plant ever rode into Hopi on the mail bus, and Mrs. Sekakaku finally realized the kind of man he was. All along, that had been the trouble at Laguna: nobody understood just what kind of man he was. They thought he was sort of good-for-nothing, he knew that, but for a long time he kept telling himself to keep on trying and trying.

But it seemed like people would never forget the time the whole village was called out to clean up for feast day and he sent his mother to tell them he was sick with liver trouble. He was still hurt because they didn't understand that with liver trouble you can walk around and sometimes even ride the bus to Albuquerque. Everyone was jealous of him and they didn't stop to think how much it meant to his mother to have someone living with her in her old age. All they could talk about was the big COD that came to the post office in his name and she cashed her pension check to pay for it. But she was the one who had told him,

"Sonny Boy, if you want that jacket, you go ahead and order it." It was made out of brown vinyl, resembling leather, and he still wore it whenever he went to town. Even on the day she had the last stroke, his two older brothers had been telling her to quit paying his bills for him and to make him get out and live on his own. But she always stood up for him in front of the others, even if she did complain privately at times to her nieces, who then scolded him about the bills from the record club and the correspondence school. He always knew he could be a lawyer; he had listened to the lawyers in the courtrooms of the Federal Building on those hot summer afternoons when he needed a cool place to sit while he waited for the bus to Laguna. He listened and he knew he could be a lawyer because he was so good at making up stories to justify why things happened the way they did. He thought correspondence school would be different from Indian school, which had given him stomach aches and made him run away all through his seventh-grade year. Right after that he had cut his foot pretty bad, chopping wood for his older brother's wife—the one who kept brushing her arms across his shoulders whenever she poured coffee at the supper table. The foot had taken so long to heal that his mother agreed he shouldn't go back to Indian school or chop wood any more. A few months after that, they were all swimming at the river and he hurt his back in a dive off the old wooden bridge, so it was no wonder he couldn't do the same work as the other young men.

When Mildred told him she was marrying that Hopi, he didn't try to stop her, although she stood there for a long time like she was waiting for him to say something. He liked things just the way they were down along the river after dark. Her mother and aunts owned so many fields they expected a husband to hoe them, and he had already promised his mother he wouldn't leave her alone in her old age. He thought it would be easier this way, but after Mildred's wedding, people who had seen him and Mildred together started joking about how he had lost out to a Hopi.

Hopi men were famous for their fast hands and the way they could go on all night. But some of the jokes hinted that he himself was as lazy at lovemaking as he was with his shovel during spring ditch cleaning, and that he would take a girlfriend to the deep sand along the river so he could lie on the bottom while she worked on top. Later on, some of the old men took him aside and said he shouldn't feel bad about Mildred, and told him about women they'd lost to Hopis when they were all working on the railroad together in Winslow. Women believed the stories about Hopi men, they told him, because women liked the sound of those stories, and the women didn't care if it was the Hopi men who were making up the stories in the first place. So when he finally found himself riding the Greyhound bus into Winslow on his way to see Mrs. Sekakaku and the Bean Dance he got to thinking about those stories about Hopi men. It had been years since Mildred had married that Hopi; and her aunts and her mother kept the man working in their fields all year round. Even Laguna people said "Poor thing" whenever they saw the Hopi man walking past with a shovel on his shoulder. So he knew he wasn't going because of that—he was going because of Mrs. Sekakaku's letters and because it was lonely living in a place where no one appreciates you even when you keep trying and trying. At Hopi he could get a fresh start; he could tell people about himself while they looked at the photos in the plastic pages of his wallet.

He waited for the mail bus and drank a cup of coffee in the café across the street from the pink stucco motel with a cowboy on its neon sign. He had a feeling that something was about to change because of his trip, but he didn't know if it would be good for him or bad. Sometimes he was able to look at what he was doing and to see himself clearly two or three weeks into the future. But this time when he looked, he only saw himself getting off the bus on the sandy shoulder of the highway below Second Mesa. He stared up at the Hopi town on the sand rock and thought that probably he'd get married.

The last hundred feet up the wagon trail seemed the greatest distance to him and he felt an unaccustomed tightness in his lungs. He knew it wasn't old age—it was something—something that wanted him to work for it. A short distance past the outside toilets at the edge of the mesa top, he got his breath back and their familiar thick odor reassured him. He saw that one of the old toilets had tipped over and rolled down the side of the mesa to the piles of stove ashes, broken bottles, and corn shucks on the slope below. He'd get along all right. Like a lot of people, at one time he believed Hopi magic could outdo all the other Pueblos, but now he saw that it was all the same from time to time and place to place. When Hopi men got tired of telling stories about all-nighters in Winslow motels, then probably the old men brought it around to magic and how they rigged the Navajo tribal elections one year just by hiding some little painted sticks over near Window Rock. Whatever it was he was ready for it.

He checked his reflection in the window glass of Mrs. Sekakaku's front door before he knocked. Gray hair made him look dignified; that was what she had written after he sent her the photographs. He believed in photographs, to show to people as you were telling them about yourself and the things you'd done and the places you'd been. He always carried a pocket camera and asked people passing to snap him outside the fancy bars and restaurants in the Heights, where he walked after he had a few drinks in the Indian bars downtown. He didn't tell her he'd never been inside those places, that he didn't think Indians were welcome there. Behind him he could hear a dog barking. It sounded like a small dog but it also sounded very upset and little dogs were the first ones to bite. So he turned, and at first he thought it was a big rat crawling out the door of Mrs. Sekakaku's bread oven, but it was a small, gray wirehaired dog that wouldn't step out any farther. It must have known it was about to be replaced because it almost choked on its own barking. Only lonely widows let their dogs sleep in the bread oven, although they always pretended otherwise and scolded their little dogs whenever relatives or guests came. "Not much longer, little doggy," he was saying softly while he knocked on the door. He was beginning to wonder if she had forgotten he was coming, and he could feel his confidence lose its footing just a little. She walked up from behind while he was knocking; that was something he always dreaded because it made the person knocking look so foolish—knocking and waiting while the one you wanted wasn't inside the house at all but was standing right behind you. The way the little dog was barking, probably all the neighbors had seen him and were laughing. He managed to smile and would have shaken hands, but she was bending over petting the little dog running around and around her ankles. "I hope you haven't been waiting too long! My poor Aunt Mamie had one of her dizzy spells and I was over helping." She was still looking down at the dog while she said this and he noticed she wasn't wearing her perfume. At first he thought his understanding of the English language must be failing—that she had really only invited him over to the Bean Dance, that he had misread her letters when she said that a big house like hers was lonely and that she did not like walking home alone in the evenings from the water faucet outside the village. Maybe all this had only meant she was afraid a bunch of Navajos might jump out from the shadows of the mesa rocks to take turns on top of her. But when she warmed up the leftover chili beans and went on talking to her niece about the dizzy spells, he began to suspect what was going on. She was one of those women who wore Evening in Paris to Laguna feast and sprinkled it on letters, but back at Hopi she pretended she was somebody else. She had lured him into sending his letters and snapshots and the big poinsettia plant to show off to her sisters and aunts—and now his visit, so she could pretend he had come uninvited, overcome with desire for her. He should have seen it all along, but the first time he met her at Laguna feast, a gust of wind had showed him the little roll of fat above her garter and left him dreaming of a plunge deep into the crease at the edge of the silk stocking. The old auntie and the dizzy spells gave her the perfect excuse and a story to protect her respectability. It was only two-thirty, but already she was folding a flannel nightgown while she talked to her niece. And here the whole bus ride from Laguna he had been imagining the night together—fingering the creases and folds and the little rolls while she squeezed him with both hands. He felt it lift off and up like a butterfly moving away from him, and the breathlessness he had felt coming up the mesa returned. He was feeling bitter—that if that's all it took, then he'd find a way to get that old woman out of bed.

He said it without thinking—the words just found his mouth and he said, "Excuse me, ladies," straightening his belt buckle as he walked across the room, "but it sounds to me like your poor auntie is in bad shape." Mrs. Sekakaku's niece looked at him for the first time all afternoon. "Is he a medicine man?" she asked her aunt, and for an instant he could see Mrs. Sekakaku hesitate and he knew he had to say, "Yes, it's something I don't usually mention myself. Too many of those guys just talk about it to attract women. But this is a serious case." It was sounding so good that he was afraid he would start thinking again about the space between the cheeks of the niece's ass and be unable to go on. But the next thing he said was they had a cure that they did at Laguna for dizzy spells like Aunt Mamie was having. He could feel a momentum somewhere inside himself. It wasn't hope because he knew Mrs. Sekakaku had tricked him, but whatever it was, it was going for broke. He imagined the feel of grabbing hold of the tops of the niece's thighs, which were almost as fat and would feel almost as good as the tops of Mrs. Sekakau's thighs. "There would be no charge; this is something I want to do especially for you." That was all it took because these Hopi ladies were like all the other Pueblo women he ever knew—always worrying about saving money, and nothing made them enemies for longer than selling them the melon or mutton leg they felt they should get for free as a love gift because all of them, even the thin ones and the old ones, believed he was after them. "Oh, that would be so kind of you! We are so worried about her!" "Well, not so fast," he said, even though his heart was racing. "It won't work unless everything is just so. All her clans-

25

women must come to her house, but there can't be any men there, not even outside." He paused. He knew exactly what to say. "This is very important. Otherwise the cure won't work." Mrs. Sekakaku let out her breath suddenly and tightened her lips, and he knew that any men or boys not in the kivas preparing for Bean Dance would be sent far away from Aunt Mamie's house. He looked over at the big loaf of fresh oven bread the niece had brought when she came; they hadn't offered him any before, but now, after she served him a big bowl of chili beans, she cut him a thick slice. It was all coming back to him now, about how good medicine men get treated, and he wasn't surprised at himself any more. Once he got started he knew just how it should go. It was just getting it started that gave him trouble sometimes.

Mrs. Sekakaku and her niece hurried out to contact all the women of the Snow Clan to bring them to Aunt Mamie's for the cure. There were so many of them sitting in rows facing the sick bed—on folding chairs and little canvas stools they'd brought just like they did for a kiva ceremony or a summer dance. He had never stopped to think how many Snow Clan women there might be, and as he walked across the room he wondered if he should have made some kind of age limit. Some of the women sitting there were pretty old and bony, but then there were all those little girls; one squatted down in front of him to play jacks and he could see the creases and dimples of her legs below her panties. The initiated girls and the women sat serious and quiet with the ceremonial presence the Hopis are famous for. Their eyes were full of the power the clanswomen shared whenever they gathered together. He saw it clearly and he never doubted its strength. Whatever he took, he'd have to run with it, but the women would come out on top like they usually did.

He sat on the floor by the fireplace and asked them to line up. He reached into the cold, white juniper ashes and took a handful, and told the woman standing in front of him to raise her skirt above her knees. The ashes were slippery and they carried his hands up and around each curve, each fold, each roll of flesh on her thighs. He reached high, but his fingers never strayed above the edge of the panty leg. They stepped in front of him one after the other, and he worked painstakingly with each one, the silvery white ashes billowing up like clouds above the skin they dusted like early snow on brown hills—and he lost all track of time. He closed his eyes so he could feel them better—the folds of skin and flesh, the little crevices and creases—as a hawk must feel canyons and arroyos while he is soaring. Some thighs he gripped as if they were something wild and fleet like antelope and rabbits, and the women

26

never flinched or hesitated because they believed the recovery of their clan sister depended on them. The dimple and pucker at the edge of the garter and silk stocking brought him back and he gave special attention to Mrs. Sekakaku, the last one before Aunt Mamie. He traced the ledges and slopes with all his fingers pressing in the ashes. He was out of breath and he knew he could not stand up to get to Aunt Mamie's bed; so he bowed his head and pretended he was praying. "I feel better already. I'm not dizzy," the old woman said, not letting anyone help her out of bed or walk with her to the fireplace. He rubbed her thighs as carefully as he had the rest, and he could tell by the feel that she'd probably live a long time.

The sun was low in the sky and the bus would be stopping for the outgoing mail pretty soon. He was quitting while he was ahead, while the Hopi men were still in the kivas for the Bean Dance. He graciously declined any payment, but the women insisted they wanted to do something, so he unzipped his jacket pocket and brought out his little pocket camera and a flash cube. As many as could squeeze together stood with him in front of the fireplace and someone snapped the picture. By the time he left Aunt Mamie's house he had two shopping bags full of pies and piki bread.

Mrs. Sekakaku was acting very different now: when they got back to her house she kicked the little gray dog and blocked up the oven hole with an orange crate. But he told her he had to get back to Laguna right away because he had something important to tell the old men. It was something they'd been trying and trying to do for a long time. At sundown the mail bus pulled onto the highway below Second Mesa, but he was tasting one of the pumpkin pies and forgot to look back. He set aside a fine-looking cherry pie to give to the postmaster. Now that they were even again with the Hopi men, maybe this Laguna luck would hold out a little while longer.

Dillinger in Hollywood

John Sayles

You know how they get after New Year's when the visits dry up and the TV is bust and there's steamed chicken for lunch three days in a row? It was one of those weeks, and Spurs Tatum starts in after rec therapy, before we could wheel them out of the dayroom.

"Hoot Gibson held my horse," says Spurs. "I took falls for Randolph Scott. I hung from a wing in *The Perils of Pauline*. And Mr. Ford," he says, "Mr. Ford he always hired me on. You see a redskin blasted off a horse in one of Mr. Ford's pictures, like as not it's me. One-Take Tatum they called me, before the 'Spurs' thing took."

We'd heard it all before, every time there was a western or a combat picture on the TV, every time a patient come in with a broken hip or a busted rib, all through the last days when the Duke was dying in the news. Heard how Spurs had thought up most of the riding stunts they use today, how he'd been D. W. Griffith's drinking buddy, how he saved Tom Mix's life on the Sacramento River. It was hot and one of those weeks and we'd heard it all before so I don't know if it was that or the beating he's just taken at Parcheesi that made old Casey up and say how he used to be John Dillinger.

His chart said that Casey had been a driver on the Fox lot long enough to qualify for the Industry fund. I told him I hadn't realized he'd done any stand-in work.

"The bird who done the stand-in work," says Casey, "is the one they potted at the Biograph Theater. I used to be Johnnie Dillinger. In the flesh."

He said the name with a hard g, like in "finger," and didn't so much as blink.

Now we've had our delusions at the Home, your standard fading

28

would-of-been actresses expecting their call from Mr. De Mille, a Tarzan whoop now and then during the full moon, and one old gent who goes around mouthing words without sound and overacting like he's on the silent picture screen. Generally it's some glorified notion of who they used to be. Up to this point Casey's only brag was he drove Joe DiMaggio to the airport when the Clipper was hitched to Monroe.

"If I remember right," says Spurs, giving me an eye that meant he thought the poor fella had slipped his tracks, "if I'm not too fuzzy on it, I believe that Mr. Dillinger, Public Enemy Number One, departed from our midst in the summer of '34."

"You should live so long," says Casey.

Now I try to give a man the benefit of a doubt. With Spurs I can tell there's a grain of fact to his brags because I was in the wrangler game myself. I was riding broncs in Santa Barbara for their Old Spanish Days and this fella hires me to stunt for some rodeo picture with Gig Young in it. He says I take a nice fall.

The pay was greener than what I saw on the circuit, so I stuck in Hollywood. See, I could always *ride* the sumbitches, my problem came when it was time to get *off*. What I had was a new approach to tumbling from a horse. Whereas most folks out here bust their ass to get *into* pictures, I busted mine to get *out*. Some big damn gelding bucked me before I'd dug in and I landed smack on my tailbone. The doctor says to me—I'm laying on my stomach trying to remember my middle name—the doctor comes in with the X rays and he says, "I don't know how to tell you this, Son, but you're gonna have to learn to shit standing up."

If they'd known who I was *Variety* would of headlined "Son Bishop Swaps Bridle for Bedpan." Horses and hospitals were all I knew. Over the years I'd spent more time in emergency rooms than Dr. Kildare. So it was hospitals, and pretty soon I drifted into the geriatric game. Your geriatrics and horses hold a lot in common—they're high-strung, they bite and kick sometimes, and they're none of them too big on bowel control. Course if a geriatric steps on your foot it don't take a wood chisel to peel it off the floor.

It's a living.

So Spurs I can back sometimes, though I'm sure he didn't play such a starring role in the invention of the saddle. With Casey I had to bring it up at report.

"He thinks he's a dead gangster?" says Mrs. Goorwitz, who was the charge nurse that night.

"No, he thinks he's an old man in a Hollywood nursing home. He says he *used* to be John Dillinger."

"In another life?"

"Nope," I answered her, "in this one."

We had this reincarnated character in here once, claimed to have been all the even-numbered King Louies of France from the second right up to Louie the Sixteen. I asked how he ended up an assistant prop man at Warners and he said after all that commotion his spirit must of needed the rest.

"I thought he was shot," says Mrs. Goorwitz.

"At point-blank range," I tell her. "They couldn't of missed."

Mrs. Goorwitz was a bit untracked by the news. She hates anything out of its place, hates waves, and many's the geriatric she's hounded to death for holding a book overdue from the Home library. She pulled Casey's chart and studied it. "It says here his name is Casey Mullins."

"Well that's that, isn't it?"

"Confused behavior," says Mrs. Goorwitz as she writes it into the report. "Inappropriate response. Watch carefully."

The only thing that gets watched carefully in this joint is the time-punch at two minutes till shift change, but I figured I might save Casey some headache.

"Maybe he's just lying," I tell her. "To work up a little attention."

"Did he say anything else?"

She was on the scent now and threatening to go practice medicine on somebody any minute.

"Not a whole lot," I tell her. "But if we breathe a word to the Feds he claims they'll find us off Santa Monica Pier with our little toes curled up."

"This bird Jimmy Lawrence, a very small-time character," says Casey, "he had this bum ticker. A rheumatic heart condition, congenital since birth. We dated the same girl once is how I got to know him. People start coming up to say, 'Jeez, you're the spittin' image of Johnnie Dillinger, you know that?' and this girl, this mutual friend, tells me and I get the idea."

After he let the Dillinger thing out Casey got very talkative, like he had it stewing in him a long time and finally it blows out all at once. I'd be in this room tapping the catheter bags on these two vegematics, Kantor and Wise, and it would be just me and this fella Roscoe Baggs who was a midget listening. Roscoe had been in *The Wizard of Oz* as a Munchkin and was a very deep thinker. He reads the kind of science-fiction books that don't have girls in loincloths on the cover.

"This girl has still got the yen for me," says Casey, "so she steers Lawrence to a doctor connection who tells him two months, maybe three, and it's the last roundup. The guy is demolished. So I make him this offer—I supply the dough to live it up his final days and he supplies a body to throw to the authorities. You could buy Chicago cops by the job lot back then so it was no big deal arranging the details. Hard times. Only two or three people had to know I was involved.

"Well the poor chump didn't even know how to paint the town right. And he kept moaning that he wanted us to hold off till after the Series, onnaconna he followed the Cardinals. That was the year Ripper Collins and the Dean brothers tore up the league."

"Just like Spangler," says Roscoe. "Remember, he wanted to see a man walk on the moon? Held off his cancer till he saw it on television and the next day he went downstairs."

Downstairs is where the morgue and the kitchen are located.

"One step for mankind," says Roscoe, "and check-out time for Spangler. You got to admire that kind of control."

"Another hoax," says Casey. "They staged the whole thing in a little studio up the coast. I know a guy in video."

I told Casey I'd read where Dillinger started to run when he saw the cops outside the picture show. And how his sister had identified the remains the next day.

"He turned chickenshit on me, son. We hadn't told him the exact date, and there he is, coming out from the movies with a broad on each arm and all of a sudden the party's over. What would you do, you were him? And as for Sis," says Casey, "she always done what she could to help me out.

"The day after the planting we send in a truck, dig the coffin out, pour in concrete and lay it back in. Anybody wants another peek at the stiff they got to drill a mine shaft."

It sounded reasonable, sort of. And when the shrink who comes through twice a year stopped to ask about his Dillinger fixation Casey just told him to scram. Said if he wanted his brains scrambled he'd stick his head in the microwave.

I did some reading and everything he said checked out pretty close. Only I couldn't connect Casey with a guy who'd pull a stunt like that on the Lawrence fella. He was one of the nice ones, Casey—never bitched much even with his diabetes and infected feet and his rotting kidneys and his finger curling up. A stand-up character.

The finger was curling up independent from the others on his right hand. His trigger finger, bent like he was about to squeeze off a round.

"It's like the *Tell-Tale Heart*," says Roscoe one day. I'm picking up dinner trays in the rooms and Roscoe is working on four chocolate puddings. They had put one on Casey's tray by mistake and I didn't have the time to spoon the other two down Kantor and Wise.

"The what?" asks Casey.

"It's a story. This guy kills an old man and stuffs him under the floorboards. When the police come to investigate he thinks he hears the old man's heart beating under the boards and he cracks and gives himself away."

"So what's that got to do with my finger?"

"Maybe your finger is trying to blow the whistle on your life of crime. Psychosomatic."

"Oh." Casey mauled it over in his mind for a minute. "I get it. We had a guy in the can, kilt his wife. Poisoned her. At first everybody figured she'd just got sick and died, happened all the time in those days. But then he starts complaining to the cops about the neighborhood kids— says they're writing nasty stuff on the sidewalk in front of his place: 'Old Man Walsh croaked his wife with rat bait,' stuff like that. So the cops send a guy to check it out on his night rounds. The cop's passing by and out comes Walsh, sleepwalking, with a piece of chalk in his hand. Wrote his own ticket to the slammer, right there on the sidewalk, onnaconna he had a leaky conscience."

It had been bothering me so I took the opening to ask. "Do you ever feel bad? About things you done back then?"

Casey shrugged and looked away from me and then looked back. "Nah," he says, "What am I, mental? This guy Walsh, he was AWOL."

AWOL is what we call the senile ones. Off base and not coming back.

"Hey Roscoe," says Casey, "why'd this telltale character kill the old man in the first place?"

"Because this old man had a big eye. He wanted to kill the big eye."

Just then Spurs wheels in looking to vulture a loose dessert.

"I wonder," says Casey, "what he would of done to a fat head?"

It seemed to make him feel better, talking about his life as Dillinger. Kept him up and alert even when his health took a big slide.

"Only reason I'm still percolating," he'd say, "is I still got my pride. They beat that into me my first stretch."

I told him I'd never heard of beating pride into somebody.

"They beat on you one way or the other," he says. "The pride comes in how you stand up to it."

I went on the graveyard shift and after two o'clock check I'd go down to chew the fat with Casey. Roscoe slept like the dead and the two veggies were on automatic pilot so it didn't make any difference how loud we were. Casey was a hurtin cowboy and his meds weren't up to knocking him out at night. We'd play cards by the light from the corridor sometimes or sometimes he'd cut up old scores for me. He told me about one where their advance man posed as a Hollywood location scout for a gangster movie. When they come out of the bank holding hostages the next day, sniping at the local shields, the townspeople just smiled and looked around for cameras.

He didn't have much to say on his years driving for Fox. He only hung on because of what he called the "fringe benefits," which mostly had to do with women.

"Used to be a disease with me," he'd say. "I'd go two days without a tumble and my eyeballs would start to swoll up, my brains would start pushing out my ears. Shut me out for three days and I'd hump anything, just anything. Like some dope fiend."

When I asked how he'd dealt with that while he was in the slammer he clammed up.

He was still able to wheel himself around a bit when Norma took up with him. Norma had bad veins and was in a chair herself. She'd been in the silents in her teens, getting rescued from fates worse than death. Her mother was ninety and shared a room with her. The old vulture just sat, deaf as a post, glaring at Norma for not being Mary Pickford. Norma had been one of the backgammon crowd till word spread that Casey thought he was John Dillinger. She studied him for a week, keeping her distance, eavesdropping on his sparring matches with Spurs Tatum, watching how he moved and how he talked. Then one day as the singalong is breaking up she wheels up beside him. Norma's voice had gone deeper and deeper with the years and she filled in at bass on "What a Friend We Have in Jesus."

" 'All I do is dream of you,' " she sings to Casey, " 'the whole night through.' "

"That used to be my favorite song," he says.

"I know," says Norma.

It give me the fantods sometimes, the way they'd look at each other like they known one another forever. Norma had been one of those caught up by the press on Dillinger when he had his year in the headlines. A woman near thirty years old keeping a scrapbook. She had picked up some work as an extra after her silent days were over, but it never came to much. She still had a shoe box full of postcards her mother had sent out every year to agents and flacks and producers—a grainy blowup of Norma in a toga or a buckskin shift or a French peasant outfit. Norma Nader in *Cimarron*. Norma Nader in *The Pride and the Passion*. Norma Nader in *The Greatest Story Ever Told*. They were the only credits she got in the talkies, those postcards, but her mother kept the heat on. I'd find Norma out in the corridor at night, wheels locked, watching the light coming out from her room.

"Is she in bed yet?" she'd ask, and I'd go down and peek in on Old Lady Nader.

"She's still awake, Norma."

"She always stood up till I come home, no matter what hour. I come in the door and it's not 'Where you been?' or 'Who'd you see?' but 'Any work today?' She had spies at all the studios so I could never lie about making rounds. Once I had an offer for a secretary job, good pay, steady, and I had to tell them sorry, I got to be an actress."

Casey had his Dillinger routine down pretty well, but with Norma along he was unstoppable.

"Johnnie," she'd say, "you 'member that time in St. Paul they caught you in the alleyway?" or "Johnnie, remember how Nelson and Van Meter were always at each other's throats?"—just like she'd been there. And Casey he'd nod and say he remembered or correct some little detail, reminding her like any old couple sharing memories.

I'd come on at eleven and they'd be in the dayroom with only the TV for light, Casey squirming in his chair, hurting, and Norma waiting for her mother to go to sleep, holding Casey's hand against the pain. We had another old pair like them, a couple old bachelors were crazy for chess. One game could take them two, three days. Personally I'd rather watch paint dry.

Usually some time around one o'clock Norma would call and we'd wheel them back to their rooms. I'd park Casey by the window so he could watch the traffic on Cahuenga.

By the time I got back on day shift Casey needed a push when he wanted to get anywhere. He could still feed himself and hit the pee-jug nine times out of ten, though we were checking his output to see what was left of his kidneys. This one morning we had square egg for breakfast, which is the powdered variety cooked up in cake pans and cut in little bars like brownies. If they don't get the coloring just right they'll come up greenish and they wiggle on your fork just like Jell-O. Even the blind patients won't touch them. Usually our only taker is this character Mao, who we call after his resemblance to the late Chinese head Red. Mao is a mongoloid in his mid-thirties whose favorite dishes are square egg and thermometers. Already that morning a new candy striper had

34

given him an oral instead of a rectal and he'd chomped it clear in half. Now she was fluttering around looking for Mr. Hellman's other slipper.

"I looked in his stand and under his bed," she says to me, "and all I could find is the right one."

"He doesn't have a left one," I tell her.

"Why not?"

"He doesn't have a left leg."

"Oh." The candy stripers are good for morale but they take a lot of looking after.

"Next time peek under the covers first."

"Well I started to," she says, "but he was flipping his—you know—his *thing* at me."

"Don't you worry, honey," says Spurs Tatum. "Worst comes to worst I'd lay odds you could outrun the old goat."

"When they give us this shit in the state pen," says Casey so's everybody in the dayroom could hear him, "we'd plaster the walls with it."

The candy striper waggles her finger at him. "If you don't care for your breakfast, Mr. Mullins, I'm sure somebody else would appreciate it."

"No dice," says Casey. "I want to see it put down the trash barrel where it can't do no harm. And the name's Dillinger."

"I'm sure you don't mind if somebody shares what you don't want. I mean what are we here for?" Lately we've been getting candy stripers with a more Christian outlook.

"What we're *here* for," says Casey, "is to die. To die. And some of us," he says looking to Spurs, "aren't doing much of a job of it."

Casey was on the rag that morning, with a bad case of the runs his new meds give him and a wobbling pile of square egg staring up at him. So when the candy striper reaches to give his portion over to Mao, Casey pushes his tray over onto the floor.

"You birds keep swallowin' this shit," he calls out to the others, "they'll keep sending it up."

Mao was well known for his oatmeal tossing. You'd get two spoonfuls down him and he'd decide to chuck the whole bowl acrost the room. Or wing it straight up so big globs stuck to the ceiling. The old-timers liked to sit against the back wall of the dayroom afternoons and bet on which glob would loosen and fall first. So when Mao picked up on Casey and made like a catapult with his plate there was chunks sent scattering clear to the bingo tables.

"Food riot!" yells Roscoe, flicking egg off his fork, aiming for old oatmeal stains on the ceiling. "Every man for himself!" he yells and then goes into "Ding-Dong the Witch Is Dead."

I didn't think the old farts had it in them. It was like being inside a popcorn popper, yellow hunks of egg flying every which way, squishing, bouncing, coffee sloshing, toast Frisbeeing, plates smashing, orange juice showering while Mrs. Shapiro, stone blind and AWOL for years, is yelling "Boys don't fight! Don't fight, your father will get crazy!"

The rec therapist is a togetherness freak. They sing together, they make place mats together, they have oral history sessions together. So somebody starts throwing food the rest of them are bound to pitch in. When there was nothing left to toss they calmed down. We decided to wheel them all back to their rooms before we cleaned out the dayroom.

"I'm hungry," says Spurs. "Crazy sumbitch made me lose my breakfast. Senile bastard."

"Shove it, cowboy," says Casey. "In my day we'd of used you for a toothpick."

"In my day we'd of stuck you in the bughouse. Dillinger my ass."

Casey didn't say a thing but Norma wheeled up between them, a big smear of grape jelly on her cheek.

"John Dillinger," she said, "was the only one in the whole lousy country was his own man, the only one that told them all to go hang and went his own way. Have some respect."

I never learned if she really thought he was Dillinger or if they just shared the same interest like the chess players or the crowd that still reads the trade papers together. When Norma went AWOL it was like her mother called her in from the playground. She left us quick, fading in and out for two weeks till she give up all the way and just sat in her chair in her room, staring back at her mother.

"I'm sorry," she'd say from time to time. No word on why or what for, just stare at Old Lady Nader and say, "I'm sorry."

Casey tried to pull her out of it at first. But it's like when we have a cardiac arrest and we pull the curtain around the bed—even if you're right in the room you can't see through to know what's happening.

"You remember me?" he'd say. "You remember about Johnnie Dillinger?"

Usually she'd just look at him blank. One time she said, "I seen a movie about him once."

For a while Casey would have us wheel him into Norma's room and he'd talk at her some but she didn't know who he was. Finally it made him so low he stopped visiting. Acted like she'd gone downstairs.

"You lose your mind," he'd say, "the rest of you ain't worth spit."

Mrs. Goorwitz got on his case then and tried to locate relatives. None to be found. What with the way people move around out here that's not so unusual. Casey's chart was nothing but a medical record starting in 1937. Next Mrs. Goorwitz loosed the social worker on him, Friendly Phil, who ought to be selling health food or real estate somewhere. Casey wasn't buying any.

"So what if I am crazy?" he'd say to Phil. "Delusional, schizo, whatever you wanna call it. I can't do squat one way or the other. What difference does it make if I was Dillinger or Norma was Pearl White or Roscoe was the King of Poland? You're all just a bag a bones in the end."

He went into a funk, Casey, after Norma faded—went into a silence that lasted a good month. Not even Spurs could get his goat enough to argue. He spent a good part of the day trying to keep himself clean.

"I'm on the cycle," he whispered to me one day. "I'm riding the down side."

The geriatric racket is a collection of cycles. Linen goes on beds, gets dirtied, down the chute, washed, dried and back onto the beds. Patients are checked in downstairs, up to the beds, maintained a while and then down to the slabs with them. Casey even found a new cycle, a thing in the paper about scientists who had learned how to make cow flops back into cow food.

"I don't want to make accusations here," says Casey one day, pointing to his lunch, "but what does *that* look like to you?"

The day came when Casey lost his control, racked up six incontinents on the report in one week. His health was shot but I tried to talk Mrs. Goorwitz out of it when she handed me the kit. He had a thing about it, Casey.

"A man that can't control his bowels," he'd say, "is not a man."

He knew what was up when I started to draw the curtain. Roscoe scowled at me from across the room and rolled over to face the wall. Kantor and Wise lay there like house plants. It was midnight and they'd given Casey some heavy meds with his dinner. He looked at me like I come to snuff him with a pillow over his face. He was too weak to raise his arms so I didn't have to put the restraints on.

"It has to be, Casey," I told him. "Or else you'll be wettin' all over yourself."

I washed my hands with the soap from the kit.

"If they ask why I done it, the banks and all," he whispers, "tell them I was just bored. Just bored crapless."

I took the gloves out of their cellophane and managed to wriggle into them without touching my fingers to their outside. I washed Casey and laid the fenestrated sheet over so only his thing stuck through. If the

37

stories about Dillinger's size are true, Casey was qualified. The girls on the evening shift called it "The Snake." I swabbed the tip of it, unwrapped the catheter tube, and coated it with K-Y.

"You been white to me, son," says Casey. "I don't put no blame on you."

"I'm sorry."

"Don't ever say that," says Casey. "Don't ever say you're sorry. Do it or don't do it but don't apologize."

I pushed the catheter tube down till it blocked at his sphincter, wiggled it and it slipped past. It was the narrowest gauge but still it's a surprise that you can fit one into a man. I stuck the syringe into the irrigation branch and shot the saline up till the bulb was inflated in his bladder. I gave a tug to see if it was anchored. Casey was crying, looking away from me. His eyes had gone fuzzy, the way fish eyes do after you beach them. I hooked the plastic tubing and the piss-bag to the catheter.

"I used to be somebody," said Casey.

I had a long weekend, and when I came back on I didn't get a chance to talk with him. Mrs. Goorwitz said in report how he'd been moved to Intensive Care. On my first check I found him looking like the pictures of the Biograph shooting—blood everywhere, hard yellow light. Something had popped inside and he'd bled out the mouth. He had pulled the catheter out, bulb and all, and he was bleeding down there. We put sheets on the floor and rolled him sideways across the bed on his belly so he drained out onto them. It takes a half hour or so.

I traced him back through the medical plan at Fox and ran into nothing but dead ends. Usually I forget about them once they go downstairs but Casey had gotten his hooks in. There at Fox I found an old fella in custodial who remembered him.

"Always taking the limos for joyrides," he said. "It's a wonder he didn't get his ass fired."

I brought the subject up at the nurses' station one night—how maybe he could of been—and they asked me how much sleep I'd been getting. So I don't know one way or the other. Roscoe, he's sure, he's positive, but Roscoe also thinks our every move is being watched by aliens with oversized IQ's. I figure if they're so smart they got better things to occupy their time.

One day I'm tube-feeding some vegematic when out in the corridor I hear Spurs Tatum giving his brag to a couple recent admissions that come in with their feet falling off.

38

"Hoot Gibson held my horse," says Spurs. "I took falls for Randy Scott. John Wayne blew me off a stagecoach. And once," he says, "I played Parcheesi with John Herbert Dillinger."

Hunters in the Snow

Tobias Wolff

Tub had been waiting for an hour in the falling snow. He paced the
sidewalk to keep warm and stuck his head out over the curb whenever
he saw lights approaching. One driver stopped for him, but before Tub
could wave the man on he saw the rifle on Tub's back and hit the gas.
The tires spun on the ice.

The fall of snow thickened. Tub stood below the overhang of a building. Across the road the clouds whitened just above the rooftops, and
the streetlights went out. He shifted the rifle strap to his other shoulder.
The whiteness seeped up the sky.

A truck slid around the corner, horn blaring, rear end sashaying. Tub
moved to the sidewalk and held up his hand. The truck jumped the curb
and kept coming, half on the street and half on the sidewalk. It wasn't
slowing down at all. Tub stood for a moment, still holding up his hand,
then jumped back. His rifle slipped off his shoulder and clattered on the
ice; a sandwich fell out of his pocket. He ran for the steps of the building.
Another sandwich and a package of cookies tumbled onto the new
snow. He made the steps and looked back.

The truck had stopped several feet beyond where Tub had been standing. He picked up his sandwiches and his cookies and slung the rifle and
went to the driver's window. The driver was bent against the steering
wheel, slapping his knees and drumming his feet on the floorboards. He
looked like a cartoon of a person laughing, except that his eyes watched
the man on the seat beside him.

"You ought to see yourself," said the driver. "He looks just like a beach
ball with a hat on, doesn't he? Doesn't he, Frank?"

The man beside him smiled and looked off.

"You almost ran me down," said Tub. "You could've killed me."

"Come on, Tub," said the man beside the driver. "Be mellow, Kenny was just messing around." He opened the door and slid over to the middle of the seat.

Tub took the bolt out of his rifle and climbed in beside him. "I waited an hour," he said. "If you meant ten o'clock, why didn't you say ten o'clock?"

"Tub, you haven't done anything but complain since we got here," said the man in the middle. "If you want to piss and moan all day you might as well go home and bitch at your kids. Take your pick." When Tub didn't say anything, he turned to the driver. "O.K., Kenny, let's hit the road."

Some juvenile delinquents had heaved a brick through the windshield on the driver's side, so the cold and snow tunneled right into the cab. The heater didn't work. They covered themselves with a couple of blankets Kenny had brought along and pulled down the muffs on their caps. Tub tried to keep his hands warm by rubbing them under the blanket, but Frank made him stop.

They left Spokane and drove deep into the country, running along black lines of fences. The snow let up, but still there was no edge to the land where it met the sky. Nothing moved in the chalky fields. The cold bleached their faces and made the stubble stand out on their cheeks and along their upper lips. They had to stop and have coffee several times before they got to the woods where Kenny wanted to hunt.

Tub was for trying some place different; two years in a row they'd been up and down this land and hadn't seen a thing. Frank didn't care one way or the other; he just wanted to get out of the goddamned truck. "Feel that," Frank said. He spread his feet and closed his eyes and leaned his head way back and breathed deeply. "Tune in on that energy."

"Another thing," said Kenny. "This is open land. Most of the land around here is posted."

Frank breathed out. "Stop bitching, Tub. Get centered."

"I wasn't bitching."

"Centered," said Kenny. "Next thing you'll be wearing a nightgown, Frank. Selling flowers out at the airport."

"Kenny," said Frank. "You talk too much."

"O.K.," said Kenny. "I won't say a word. Like I won't say anything about a certain baby-sitter."

"What baby-sitter?" asked Tub.

"That's between us," said Frank, looking at Kenny. "That's confidential. You keep your mouth shut."

Kenny laughed.

"You're asking for it," said Frank.

"Asking for what?"

"You'll see."

"Hey," said Tub. "Are we hunting or what?"

Frank just smiled.

They started off across the field. Tub had trouble getting through the fences. Frank and Kenny could have helped him; they could have lifted up on the top wire and stepped on the bottom wire, but they didn't. They stood and watched him. There were a lot of fences and Tub was puffing when they reached the woods.

They hunted for over two hours and saw no deer, no tracks, no sign. Finally they stopped by the creek to eat. Kenny had several slices of pizza and a couple of candy bars; Frank had a sandwich, an apple, two carrots, and a square of chocolate; Tub put out one hard-boiled egg and a stick of celery.

"You ask me how I want to die today," said Kenny. "I'll tell you, burn me at the stake." He turned to Tub. "You still on that diet?" He winked at Frank.

"What do you think? You think I like hard-boiled eggs?"

"All I can say is, it's the first diet I ever heard of where you gained weight from it."

"Who said I gained weight?"

"Oh, pardon me. I take it back. You're just wasting away before my very eyes. Isn't he, Frank?"

Frank had his fingers fanned out, tips against the bark of the stump where he'd laid his food. His knuckles were hairy. He wore a heavy wedding band, and on his right pinky was another gold ring with a flat face and "F" printed out in what looked like diamonds. He turned it this way and that. "Tub," he said, "you haven't seen your own balls in ten years."

Kenny doubled over laughing. He took off his hat and slapped his leg with it.

"What am I supposed to do?" said Tub. "It's my glands."

They left the woods and hunted along the creek. Frank and Kenny worked one bank and Tub worked the other, moving upstream. The snow was light, but the drifts were deep and hard to move through. Wherever Tub looked, the surface was smooth, undisturbed, and after a time he lost interest. He stopped looking for tracks and just tried to keep up with Frank and Kenny on the other side. A moment came when he realized he hadn't seen them in a long time. The breeze was moving from him to them; when it stilled he could sometimes hear them arguing but that was all. He quickened his pace, breasting hard into the drifts, fighting the snow away with his knees and elbows. He heard his heart and felt the flush on his face, but he never once stopped.

Tub caught up with Frank and Kenny at a bend in the creek. They were standing on a log that stretched from their bank to his. Ice had backed up behind the log. Frozen reeds stuck out, barely nodding when the air moved.

"See anything?" asked Frank.

Tub shook his head.

There wasn't much daylight left, and they decided to head back toward the road. Frank and Kenny crossed the log and started downstream, using the trail Tub had broken. Before they had gone very far, Kenny stopped. "Look at that," he said, and pointed to some tracks going from the creek back into the woods. Tub's footprints crossed right over them. There on the bank, plain as day, were several mounds of deer sign.

"What do you think that is, Tub?" Kenny kicked at it. "Walnuts on vanilla icing?"

"I guess I didn't notice."

Kenny looked at Frank.

"I was lost."

"You were lost. Big deal."

They followed the tracks into the woods. The deer had gone over a fence half buried in drifting snow. A no-hunting sign was nailed to the top of one of the posts. Frank laughed and said the son of a bitch could read. Kenny wanted to go after him, but Frank said no way—the people out here didn't mess around. He thought maybe the farmer who owned the land would let them use it if they asked, though Kenny wasn't so sure. Anyway, he figured that by the time they walked to the truck and drove up the road and doubled back it would be almost dark.

"Relax," said Frank. "You can't hurry nature. If we're meant to get that deer, we'll get it. If we're not, we won't."

They started back toward the truck. This part of the woods was mainly pine. The snow was shaded and had a glaze on it. It held up Kenny and Frank, but Tub kept falling through. As he kicked forward, the edge of the crust bruised his shins. Kenny and Frank pulled ahead of him, to where he couldn't even hear their voices any more. He sat down on a stump and wiped his face. He ate both the sandwiches and half the cookies, taking his own sweet time. It was dead quiet.

When Tub crossed the last fence into the road, the truck started moving. Tub had to run for it and just managed to grab hold of the tailgate and hoist himself into the bed. He lay there panting. Kenny looked out the rear window and grinned. Tub crawled into the lee of the cab to get out of the freezing wind. He pulled his earflaps low and pushed his chin into the collar of his coat. Someone rapped on the window, but Tub would not turn around.

He and Frank waited outside while Kenny went into the farmhouse to ask permission. The house was old, and paint was curling off the sides. The smoke streamed westward off the top of the chimney, fanning away into a thin gray plume. Above the ridge of the hills another ridge of blue clouds was rising.

"You've got a short memory," said Tub.

"What?" said Frank. He had been staring off.

"I used to stick up for you."

"O.K., so you used to stick up for me. What's eating you?"

"You shouldn't have just left me back there like that."

"You're a grown-up, Tub. You can take care of yourself. Anyway, if you think you're the only person with problems, I can tell you that you're not."

"Is something bothering you, Frank?"

Frank kicked at a branch poking out of the snow. "Never mind," he said.

"What did Kenny mean about the baby-sitter?"

"Kenny talks too much," said Frank. "You just mind your own business."

Kenny came out of the farmhouse and gave the thumbs up, and they began walking back toward the woods. As they passed the barn, a large black hound with a grizzled snout ran out and barked at them. Every time he barked he slid backward a bit, like a cannon going off. Kenny got down on all fours and snarled and barked back at him, and the dog slunk away into the barn, looking over his shoulder and peeing a little as he went.

"That's an old-timer," said Frank. "A real graybeard. Fifteen years, if he's a day."

"Too old," said Kenny.

Past the barn they cut off through the fields. The land was unfenced, and the crust was freezing up thick, and they made good time. They kept to the edge of the field until they picked up the tracks again and followed them into the woods, farther and farther back toward the hills. The trees started to blur with the shadows, and the wind rose and needled their faces with the crystals it swept off the glaze. Finally they lost the tracks.

Kenny swore and threw down his hat. "This is the worst day of hunting I ever had, bar none." He picked up his hat and brushed off the snow. "This will be the first season since I was fifteen that I haven't got any deer."

"It isn't the deer," said Frank. "It's the hunting. There are all these forces out here and you just have to go with them."

"You go with them," said Kenny. "I came out here to get me a deer, not listen to a bunch of hippie bullshit. And if it hadn't been for Dimples here, I would have, too."

"That's enough," said Frank.

"And you . . . you're so busy thinking about that little jailbait of yours, you wouldn't know a deer if you saw one."

"I'm warning you," said Frank.

Kenny laughed. "I think maybe I'll have me a talk with a certain jailbait's father," he said. "Then you can warn him, too."

"Drop dead," said Frank and turned away.

Kenny and Tub followed him back across the fields. When they were coming up to the barn, Kenny stopped and pointed. "I hate that post," he said. He raised his rifle and fired. It sounded like a dry branch cracking. The post splintered along its right side, up toward the top.

"There," said Kenny. "It's dead."

"Knock it off," said Frank, walking ahead.

Kenny looked at Tub and smiled. "I hate that tree," he said, and fired again. Tub hurried to catch up with Frank. He started to speak, but just then the dog ran out of the barn and barked at them. "Easy, boy," said Frank.

"I hate that dog." Kenny was behind them.

"That's enough," said Frank. "You put that gun down."

Kenny fired. The bullet went in between the dog's eyes. He sank right down into the snow, his legs splayed out on each side, his yellow eyes open and staring. Except for the blood, he looked like a small bearskin rug. The blood ran down the dog's muzzle into the snow.

They all looked at the dog lying there.

"What did he ever do to you?" asked Tub. "He was just barking."

Kenny turned to Tub. "I hate you."

Tub shot from the waist. Kenny jerked backward against the fence and buckled to his knees. He folded his hands across his stomach. "Look," he said. His hands were covered with blood. In the dusk his blood was more blue than red. It seemed to belong to the shadows. It didn't seem out of place. Kenny eased himself onto his back. He sighed several times, deeply. "You shot me," he said.

"I had to," said Tub. He knelt beside Kenny. "Oh, God," he said. "Frank. Frank."

Frank hadn't moved since Kenny killed the dog.

"Frank!" Tub shouted.

"I was just kidding around," said Kenny. "It was a joke. Oh!" he said, and arched his back suddenly. "Oh!" he said again, and dug his heels into the snow and pushed himself along on his head for several feet. Then he stopped and lay there, rocking back and forth on his heels and head like a wrestler doing warm-up exercises.

Frank roused himself. "Kenny," he said. He bent down and put his gloved hand on Kenny's brow. "You shot him," he said to Tub.

"He made me," said Tub.

"No, no, no," said Kenny.

Tub was weeping from the eyes and nostrils. His whole face was wet. Frank closed his eyes, then looked down at Kenny again. "Where does it hurt?"

"Everywhere," said Kenny. "Just everywhere."

"Oh, God," said Tub.

"I mean where did it go in?" said Frank.

"Here." Kenny pointed at the wound in his stomach. It was welling slowly with blood.

"You're lucky," said Frank. "It's on the left side. It missed your appendix. If it had hit your appendix, you'd really be in the soup." He turned and threw up onto the snow, holding his sides as if to keep warm.

"Are you all right?" asked Tub.

"There's some aspirin in the truck," said Kenny.

"I'm all right," said Frank.

"We'd better call an ambulance," said Tub.

"Jesus," said Frank, "what are we going to say?"

"Exactly what happened," said Tub. "He was going to shoot me but I shot him first."

"No, sir!" said Kenny. "I wasn't either!"

Frank patted Kenny on the arm. "Easy does it, partner." He stood. "Let's go."

Tub picked up Kenny's rifle as they walked down toward the farmhouse. "No sense leaving this around," he said. "Kenny might get ideas."

"I can tell you one thing," said Frank. "You've really done it this time. This definitely takes the cake."

They had to knock on the door twice before it was opened by a thin man with lank hair. The room behind him was filled with smoke. He squinted at them. "You get anything?" he asked.

"No," said Frank.

"I knew you wouldn't. That's what I told the other fellow."

"We've had an accident."

The man looked past Frank and Tub into the gloom. "Shoot your friend, did you?"

Frank nodded.

"I did," said Tub.

"I suppose you want to use the phone."

"If it's O.K."

The man in the door looked behind him, then stepped back. Frank and Tub followed him into the house. There was a woman sitting by the stove in the middle of the room. The stove was smoking badly. She looked up and then down again at the child asleep in her lap. Her face was white and damp; strands of hair were pasted across her forehead. Tub warmed his hands over the stove while Frank went into the kitchen to call. The man who had let them in stood at the window, his hands in his pockets.

"My partner shot your dog," said Tub.

The man nodded without turning around. "I should have done it myself. I just couldn't."

"He loved that dog so much," the woman said. The child squirmed and she rocked it.

"You asked him to?" said Tub. "You asked him to shoot your dog?"

"He was old and sick. Couldn't chew his food any more. I would have done it myself but I don't have a gun."

"You couldn't have anyway," said the woman. "Never in a million years."

The man shrugged.

Frank came out of the kitchen. "We'll have to take him ourselves. The nearest hospital is fifty miles from here and all their ambulances are out anyway."

The woman knew a shortcut, but the directions were complicated and Tub had to write them down. The man told where they could find some boards to carry Kenny on. He didn't have a flashlight, but he said he would leave the porch light on.

It was dark outside. The clouds were low and heavy-looking and the wind blew in shrill gusts. There was a screen loose on the house, and it banged slowly and then quickly as the wind rose again. They could hear it all the way to the barn. Frank went for the boards while Tub looked for Kenny, who was not where they had left him. Tub found him farther up the drive, lying on his stomach. "You O.K.?" said Tub.

"It hurts."

"Frank says it missed your appendix."

"I already had my appendix out."

"All right," said Frank, coming up to them. "We'll have you in a nice warm bed before you can say Jack Robinson." He put the two boards on Kenny's right side.

"Just as long as I don't have one of those male nurses," said Kenny.

"Ha ha," said Frank. "That's the spirit. Get ready, set, over you go," and he rolled Kenny onto the boards. Kenny screamed and kicked his legs in the air. When he quieted down, Frank and Tub lifted the boards and carried him down the drive. Tub had the back end, and with the snow blowing into his face he had trouble with his footing. Also he was tired and the man inside had forgotten to turn the porch light on. Just past the house Tub slipped and threw out his hands to catch himself. The boards fell and Kenny tumbled out and rolled to the bottom of the drive, yelling all the way. He came to rest against the right front wheel of the truck.

"You fat moron," said Frank. "You aren't good for diddly."

Tub grabbed Frank by the collar and backed him hard up against the fence. Frank tried to pull his hands away, but Tub shook him and snapped his head back and forth and finally Frank gave up.

"What do you know about fat?" said Tub. "What do you know about glands?" As he spoke, he kept shaking Frank. "What do you know about me?"

"All right," said Frank.

"No more," said Tub.

"All right."

"No more talking to me like that. No more watching. No more laughing."

"O.K., Tub. I promise."

Tub let go of Frank and leaned his forehead against the fence. His arms hung straight at his sides.

"I'm sorry, Tub." Frank touched him on the shoulder. "I'll be down at the truck."

Tub stood by the fence for a while and then got the rifles off the porch. Frank had rolled Kenny back onto the boards and they lifted him into the bed of the truck. Frank spread the seat blankets over him. "Warm enough?" he asked.

Kenny nodded.

"O.K. Now how does reverse work on this thing?"

"All the way to the left and up." Kenny sat up as Frank started forward to the cab. "Frank!"

"What?"

"If it sticks, don't force it."

The truck started right away. "One thing," said Frank, "you've got to hand it to the Japanese. A very ancient, very spiritual culture and they can still make a hell of a truck." He glanced over at Tub. "Look, I'm sorry. I didn't know you felt that way, honest to God, I didn't. You should have said something."

"I did."

"When? Name one time."

"A couple of hours ago."

"I guess I wasn't paying attention."

"That's true, Frank," said Tub. "You don't pay attention very much."

"Tub," said Frank, "what happened back there—I should have been more sympathetic. I realize that. You were going through a lot. I just want you to know it wasn't your fault. He was asking for it."

"You think so?"

"Absolutely. I would have done the same thing in your shoes, no question."

The wind was blowing into their faces. The snow was a moving white wall in front of their lights; it swirled into the cab through the hole in the windshield and settled on them. Tub clapped his hands and shifted around to stay warm, but it didn't work.

"I'm going to have to stop," said Frank. "I can't feel my fingers."

Up ahead they saw some lights off the road. It was a tavern. Outside in the parking lot were several jeeps and trucks. A couple of them had deer strapped across their hoods. Frank parked and they went back to Kenny. "How you doing, partner?" said Frank.

"I'm cold."

"Well, don't feel like the Lone Ranger. It's worse inside, take my word for it. You should get that windshield fixed."

"Look," said Tub, "he threw the blankets off." They were lying in a heap against the tailgate.

"Now look, Kenny," said Frank, "it's not use whining about being cold if you're not going to try and keep warm. You've got to do your share." He spread the blankets over Kenny and tucked them in at the corners.

"They blew off."

"Hold on to them then."

"Why are we stopping, Frank?"

"Because if me and Tub don't get warmed up we're going to freeze solid and then where will you be?" He punched Kenny lightly in the arm. "So just hold your horses."

The bar was full of men in colored jackets, mostly orange. The waitress brought coffee. "Just what the doctor ordered," said Frank, cradling the steaming cup in his hand. His skin was bone white. "Tub, I've been thinking. What you said about me not paying attention, that's true."

"It's O.K."

"No. I really had that coming. I guess I've just been a little too interested in old number one. I've had a lot on my mind—not that that's any excuse."

"Forget it, Frank. I sort of lost my temper back there. I guess we're all a little on edge."

Frank shook his head. "It isn't just that."

"You want to talk about it?"

"Just between us, Tub?"

"Sure, Frank. Just between us."

"Tub, I think I'm going to be leaving Nancy."

"Oh, Frank. Oh, Frank." Tub sat back. "What's the problem? Has she been seeing someone?"

"No. I wish she was, Tub. I wish to God she was." He reached out and laid his hand on Tub's arm. "Tub, have you ever been really in love?"

"Well . . ."

"I mean *really* in love." He squeezed Tub's wrist. "With your whole being."

"I don't know. When you put it like that."

"You haven't, then. Nothing against you, but you'd know it if you had." Frank let go of Tub's arm. "Nancy hasn't been running around, Tub. I have."

"Oh, Frank."

"Running around's not the right word for it. It isn't like that. She's not just some bit of fluff."

"Who is she, Frank?"

Frank paused. He looked into his empty cup. "Roxanne Brewer."

"Cliff Brewer's kid? The baby-sitter?"

"You can't just put people into categories like that, Tub. That's why the whole system is wrong. And that's why this country is going to hell in a rowboat."

"But she can't be more than . . ." Tub shook his head.

"Fifteen. She'll be sixteen in May." Frank smiled. "May fourth, three twenty-seven P.M. Hell, Tub, a hundred years ago she'd have been an old maid by that age. Juliet was only thirteen."

"Juliet? Juliet Miller? Jesus, Frank, she doesn't even have breasts. She doesn't even wear a top to her bathing suit. She's still collecting frogs."

"Not Juliet Miller—the real Juliet. Tub, don't you see how you're dividing people up into categories? He's an executive, she's a secretary, he's a truck driver, she's fifteen years old. Tub, this so-called baby-sitter, this so-called fifteen-year-old has more in her little finger than most of us have in our entire bodies. I can tell you this little lady is something special."

Tub nodded. "I know the kids like her."

"She's opened up whole worlds to me that I never knew were there."

"What does Nancy think about all of this?"

"Nothing, Tub. She doesn't know."

"You haven't told her?"

"Not yet. It's not so easy. She's been damned good to me all these years. Then there's the kids to consider." The brightness in Frank's eyes trembled and he wiped quickly at them with the back of his hand. "I guess you think I'm a complete bastard."

"No, Frank. I don't think that."

"Well, you *ought* to."

"Frank, when you've got a friend it means you've always got someone on your side, no matter what. That's how I feel about it anyway."

"You mean that, Tub?"

"Sure I do."

Frank smiled. "You don't know how good it feels to hear you say that."

Kenny had tried to get out of the truck but he hadn't made it. He was jackknifed over the tailgate, his head hanging above the bumper. They lifted him back into the bed and covered him again. He was sweating and his teeth chattered. "It hurts, Frank."

"It wouldn't hurt so much if you just stayed put. Now we're going to the hospital. Got that? Say it: 'I'm going to the hospital.'"

"I'm going to the hospital."

"Again."

"I'm going to the hospital."

"Now just keep saying that to yourself and before you know it we'll be there."

After they had gone a few miles, Tub turned to Frank. "I just pulled a real boner," he said.

"What's that?"

"I left the directions on the table back there."

"That's O.K.. I remember them pretty well."

The snowfall lightened and the clouds began to roll back off the fields, but it was no warmer and after a time both Frank and Tub were bitten through and shaking. Frank almost didn't make it around a curve, and they decided to stop at the next roadhouse.

There was an automatic hand dryer in the bathroom and they took turns standing in front of it, opening their jackets and shirts and letting the jet of hot air breathe across their faces and chests.

"You know," said Tub, "what you told me back there, I appreciate it. Trusting me."

Frank opened and closed his fingers in front of the nozzle. "The way I look at it, Tub, no man is an island. You've got to trust someone."

"Frank . . ."

Frank waited.

"When I said that about my glands, that wasn't true. The truth is I just shovel it in."

"Well, Tub . . ."

"Day and night, Frank. In the shower. On the freeway." He turned and let the air play over his back. "I've even got stuff in the paper towel machine at work."

"There's nothing wrong with your glands at all?" Frank had taken his boots and socks off. He held first his right, then his left foot up to the nozzle.

"No. There never was."

"Does Alice know?" The machine went off and Frank started lacing up his boots.

"Nobody knows. That's the worst of it, Frank, not the being fat—I never got any big kick out of being thin—but the lying. Having to lead a double life like a spy or a hit man. This sounds strange but I feel sorry for those guys, I really do. I know what they go through. Always having to think about what you say and do. Always feeling like people are watching you, trying to catch you at something. Never able to just be yourself. Like when I make a big deal about only having an orange for breakfast and then scarf all the way to work. Oreos, Mars bars, Twinkies, Sugar Babies, Snickers." Tub glanced at Frank and looked quickly away. "Pretty disgusting, isn't it?"

"Tub. Tub." Frank shook his head. "Come on." He took Tub's arm and led him into the restaurant half of the bar. "My friend is hungry," he told the waitress. "Bring four orders of pancakes, plenty of butter and syrup."

"Frank . . ."

"Sit down."

When the dishes came, Frank carved out slabs of butter and just laid them on the pancakes. Then he emptied the bottle of syrup, moving it back and forth over the plates. He leaned forward on his elbows and rested his chin on one hand. "Go on, Tub."

Tub ate several mouthfuls, then started to wipe his lips. Frank took the napkin away from him. "No wiping," he said. Tub kept at it. The syrup covered his chin; it dripped to a point like a goatee. "Weigh in, Tub," said Frank, pushing another fork across the table. "Get down to business." Tub took the fork in his left hand and lowered his head and started really chowing down. "Clean your plate," said Frank when the pancakes were gone, and Tub lifted each of the four plates and licked it clean. He sat back, trying to catch his breath.

"Beautiful," said Frank. "Are you full?"

"I'm full," said Tub. "I've never been so full."

Kenny's blankets were bunched up against the tailgate again.

"They must have blown off," said Tub.

"They're not doing him any good," said Frank. "We might as well get some use out of them."

Kenny mumbled. Tub bent over him. "What? Speak up."

"I'm going to the hospital," said Kenny.

"Attaboy," said Frank.

The blankets helped. The wind still got their faces and Frank's hands but it was much better. The fresh snow on the road and the trees sparkled under the beam of the headlight. Squares of light from farmhouse windows fell onto the blue snow in the fields.

"Frank," said Tub after a time, "you know that farmer? He told Kenny to kill the dog."

"You're kidding!" Frank leaned forward, considering. "That Kenny. What a card." He laughed and so did Tub. Tub smiled out the back window. Kenny lay with his arms folded over his stomach, moving his lips at the stars. Right overhead was the Big Dipper, and behind, hanging between Kenny's toes in the direction of the hospital, was the North Star, pole star, help to sailors. As the truck twisted through the gentle hills, the star went back and forth between Kenny's boots, staying always in his sight. "I'm going to the hospital," said Kenny, but he was wrong. They had taken a different turn a long way back.

53

Walking Out

David Quammen

As the train rocked dead at Livingston he saw the man, in a worn khaki shirt with button flaps buttoned, arms crossed. The boy's hand sprang up by reflex, and his face broke into a smile. The man smiled back gravely, and nodded. He did not otherwise move. The boy turned from the window and, with the awesome deliberateness of a fat child harboring reluctance, began struggling to pull down his bag. His father would wait on the platform. First sight of him had reminded the boy that nothing was simple enough now for hurrying.

They drove in the old open Willys toward the cabin beyond town. The windshield of the Willys was up, but the fine cold sharp rain came into their faces, and the boy could not raise his eyes to look at the road. He wore a rain parka his father had handed him at the station. The man, protected by only the khaki, held his lips strung in a firm silent line that seemed more grin than wince. Riding through town in the cold rain, open-topped and jaunty, getting drenched as though by necessity, was – the boy understood vaguely – somehow in the spirit of this season.

"We have a moose tag," his father shouted.

The boy said nothing. He refused to care what it meant, that they had a moose tag.

"I've got one picked out. A bull. I've stalked him for two weeks. Up in the Crazies. When we get to the cabin, we'll build a good roaring fire." With only the charade of a pause, he added, "Your mother." It was like a question. The boy waited. "How is she?"

"All right, I guess." Over the jeep's howl, with the wind stealing his voice, the boy too had to shout.

"Are you friends with her?"

"I guess so."

"Is she still a beautiful lady?"

"I don't know. I guess so. I don't know that."

"You must know that. Is she starting to get wrinkled like me? Does she seem worried and sad? Or is she just still a fine beautiful lady? You must know that."

"She's still a beautiful lady, I guess."

"Did she tell you any messages for me?"

"She said . . . she said I should give you her love," the boy lied, impulsively and clumsily. He was at once embarrassed that he had done it.

"Oh," his father said. "Thank you, David."

They reached the cabin on a mile of dirt road winding through meadow to a spruce grove. Inside, the boy was enwrapped in the strong syncretic smell of all seasonal mountain cabins: pine resin and insect repellent and a mustiness suggesting damp bathing trunks stored in a drawer. There were yellow pine floors and rope-work throw rugs and a bead curtain to the bedroom and a cast-iron cook stove with none of the lids or handles missing and a pump in the kitchen sink and old issues of *Field and Stream*, and on the mantel above where a fire now finally burned was a picture of the boy's grandfather, the railroad telegrapher, who had once owned the cabin. The boy's father cooked a dinner of fried ham, and though the boy did not like ham he had expected his father to cook canned stew or Spam, so he said nothing. His father asked him about school and the boy talked and his father seemed to be interested. Warm and dry, the boy began to feel safe from his own anguish. Then his father said:

"We'll leave tomorrow around ten."

Last year on the boy's visit they had hunted birds. They had lived in the cabin for six nights, and each day they had hunted pheasant in the wheat stubble, or blue grouse in the woods, or ducks along the irrigation slews. The boy had been wet and cold and miserable at times, but each evening they returned to the cabin and to the boy's suitcase of dry clothes. They had eaten hot food cooked on a stove, and had smelled the cabin smell, and had slept together in a bed. In six days of hunting, the boy had not managed to kill a single bird. Yet last year he had known that, at least once a day, he would be comfortable, if not happy. This year his father planned that he should not even be comfortable. He had said in his last letter to Evergreen Park, before the boy left Chicago but when it was too late for him not to leave, that he would take the boy camping in the mountains, after big game. He had pretended to believe that the boy would be glad.

55

The Willys was loaded and moving by ten minutes to ten. For three hours they drove, through Big Timber, and then north on the highway, and then back west again on a logging road that took them winding and bouncing higher into the mountains. Thick cottony streaks of white cloud hung in among the mountaintop trees, light and dense dollops against the bulking sharp dark olive, as though in a black-and-white photograph. They followed the gravel road for an hour, and the boy thought they would soon have a flat tire or break an axle. If they had a flat, the boy knew, his father would only change it and drive on until they had the second, farther from the highway. Finally they crossed a creek and his father plunged the Willys off into a bed of weeds.

His father said, "Here."

The boy said, "Where?"

"Up that little drainage. At the head of the creek."

"How far is it?"

"Two or three miles."

"Is that where you saw the moose?"

"No. That's where I saw the sheepman's hut. The moose is farther. On top."

"Are we going to sleep in a hut? I thought we were going to sleep in a tent."

"No. Why should we carry a tent up there when we have a perfectly good hut?"

The boy couldn't answer that question. He thought now that this might be the time when he would cry. He had known it was coming.

"I don't much want to sleep in a hut," he said, and his voice broke with the simple honesty of it, and his eyes glazed. He held his mouth tight against the trembling.

As though something had broken in him too, the boy's father laid his forehead down on the steering wheel, against his knuckles. For a moment he remained bowed, breathing exhaustedly. But he looked up again before speaking.

"Well, we don't have to, David."

The boy said nothing.

"It's an old sheepman's hut made of logs, and it's near where we're going to hunt, and we can fix it dry and good. I thought you might like that. I thought it might be more fun than a tent. But we don't have to do it. We can drive back to Big Timber and buy a tent, or we can drive back to the cabin and hunt birds, like last year. Whatever you want to do. You have to forgive me the kind of ideas I get. I hope you will. We don't have to do anything that you don't want to do."

"No," the boy said. "I want to."

"Are you sure?"

"No," the boy said. "But I just want to."

They bushwhacked along the creek, treading a thick soft mixture of moss and humus and needles, climbing upward through brush. Then the brush thinned and they were ascending an open creek bottom, thirty yards wide, darkened by fir and cedar. Farther, and they struck a trail, which led them upward along the creek. Farther still, and the trail received a branch, the another, then forked.

"Who made this trail? Did the sheepman?"

"No," his father said. "Deer and elk."

Gradually the creek's little canyon narrowed, steep wooded shoulders funneling closer on each side. For a while the game trails forked and converged like a maze, but soon again there were only two branches, and finally one, heavily worn. It dodged through alder and willow, skirting tangles of browned raspberry, so that the boy and his father could never see more than twenty feet ahead. When they stopped to rest, the boy's father unstrapped the .270 from his pack and loaded it.

"We have to be careful now," he explained. "We may surprise a bear."

Under the cedars, the creek bottom held a cool dampness that seemed to be stored from one winter to the next. The boy began at once to feel chilled. He put on his jacket, and they continued climbing. Soon he was sweating again in the cold.

On a small flat where the alder drew back from the creek, the hut was built into one bank of the canyon, with the sod of the hillside lapping out over its roof. The door was a low dark opening. Forty or fifty years ago, the boy's father explained, this hut had been built and used by a Basque shepherd. At that time there had been many Basques in Montana, and they had run sheep all across this ridge of the Crazies. His father forgot to explain what a Basque was, and the boy didn't remind him.

They built a fire. His father had brought sirloin steaks and an onion for dinner, and the boy was happy with him about that. As they ate, it grew dark, but the boy and his father had stocked a large comforting pile of naked deadfall. In the darkness, by firelight, his father made chocolate pudding. The pudding had been his father's surprise. The boy sat on a piece of canvas and added logs to the fire while his father drank coffee. Sparks rose on the heat and the boy watched them climb toward the cedar limbs and the black pools of sky. The pudding did not set.

"Do you remember your grandfather, David?"

"Yes," the boy said, and wished it were true. He remembered a funeral when he was three.

"Your grandfather brought me up on this mountain when I was seventeen. That was the last year he hunted." The boy knew what sort of thoughts his father was having. But he knew also that his own home was in Evergreen Park, and that he was another man's boy now, with another man's name, though this indeed was his father. "Your grandfather was fifty years older than me."

The boy said nothing.

"And I'm thirty-four years older than you."

"And I'm only eleven," the boy cautioned him.

"Yes," said his father. "And someday you'll have a son and you'll be forty years older than him, and you'll want so badly for him to know who you are that you could cry."

The boy was embarrassed.

"And that's called the cycle of life's infinite wisdom," his father said, and laughed at himself unpleasantly.

"What did he die of?" the boy asked, desperate to escape the focus of his father's rumination.

"He was eighty-seven then. Christ. He was tired." The boy's father went silent. Then he shook his head, and poured himself the remaining coffee.

Through that night the boy was never quite warm. He slept on his side with his knees drawn up, and this was uncomfortable but his body seemed to demand it for warmth. The hard cold mountain earth pressed upward through the mat of fir boughs his father had laid, and drew heat from the boy's body like a pallet of leeches. He clutched the bedroll around his neck and folded the empty part at the bottom back under his legs. Once he woke to a noise. Though his father was sleeping between him and the door of the hut, for a while the boy lay awake, listening worriedly, and then woke again on his back to realize time had passed. He heard droplets begin to hit the canvas his father had spread over the sod roof of the hut. But he remained dry.

He rose to the smell of a fire. The tarp was rigid with sleet and frost. The firewood and the knapsacks were frosted. It was that gray time of dawn before any blue and, through the branches above, the boy was unable to tell whether the sky was murky or clear. Delicate sheet ice hung on everything, but there was no wetness. The rain seemed to have been hushed by the cold.

"What time is it?"

"Early yet."

"How early?" The boy was thinking about the cold at home as he waited outside on Ninety-sixth Street for his school bus. That was the cruelest moment of his day, but it seemed a benign and familiar part of him compared to this.

"Early. I don't have a watch. What difference does it make, David?"

"Not any."

After breakfast they began walking up the valley. His father had the .270, and the boy carried an old Winchester .30-30, with open sights. The walking was not hard, and with this gentle exercise in the cold morning the boy soon felt fresh and fine. Now I'm hunting for moose with my father, he told himself. That's just what I'm doing. Few boys in Evergreen Park had ever been moose hunting with their fathers in Montana, he knew. I'm doing it now, the boy told himself.

Reaching the lip of a high meadow, a mile above the shepherd's hut, they had not seen so much as a magpie.

Before them, across hundreds of yards, opened a smooth lake of tall lifeless grass, browned by September drought and killed by the frosts and beginning to rot with November's rain. The creek was here a deep quiet channel of smooth curves overhung by the grass, with a dark surface like heavy oil. When they had come fifty yards into the meadow, his father turned and pointed out to the boy a large ponderosa pine with a forked crown that marked the head of their creek valley. He showed the boy a small aspen grove midway across the meadow, toward which they were aligning themselves.

"Near the far woods is a beaver pond. The moose waters there. We can wait in the aspens and watch the whole meadow without being seen. If he doesn't come, we'll go up another canyon, and check again on the way back."

For an hour, and another, they waited. The boy sat with his hands in his jacket pockets, bunching the jacket tighter around him, and his buttocks drew cold moisture from the ground. His father squatted on his heels like a country man, rising periodically to inspect the meadow in all directions. Finally he stood up; he fixed his stare on the distant fringe of woods and, like a retriever, did not move. He said, "David."

The boy stood beside him. His father placed a hand on the boy's shoulder. The boy saw a large dark form rolling toward them like a great slug in the grass.

"Is it the moose?"

"No," said his father. "That is a grizzly bear, David. An old male grizzly."

The boy was impressed. He sensed an aura of power and terror and authority about the husky shape, even at two hundred yards.

"Are we going to shoot him?"

"No."

"Why not?"

"We don't have a permit," his father whispered. "And because we don't want to."

The bear plowed on toward the beaver pond for a while, then stopped. It froze in the grass and seemed to be listening. The boy's father added: "That's not hunting for the meat. That's hunting for the fear. I don't need the fear. I've got enough in my life already."

The bear turned and moiled off quickly through the grass. It disappeared back into the far woods.

"He heard us."

"Maybe," the boy's father said. "Let's go have a look at that beaver pond."

A sleek furred carcass lay low in the water, swollen grotesquely with putrescence and coated with glistening blowflies. Four days, the boy's father guessed. The moose had been shot at least eighteen times with a .22 pistol. One of its eyes had been shot out; it had been shot twice in the jaw; and both quarters on the side that lay upward were ruined with shots. Standing up to his knees in the sump, the boy's father took the trouble of counting the holes, and probing one of the slugs out with his knife. That only made him angrier. He flung the lead away.

For the next three hours, with his father withdrawn into a solitary and characteristic bitterness, the boy felt abandoned. He did not understand why a moose would be slaughtered with a light pistol and left to rot. His father did not bother to explain; like the bear, he seemed to understand it as well as he needed to. They walked on, but they did not really hunt.

They left the meadow for more pine, and now tamarack, naked tamarack, the yellow needles nearly all down and going ginger where they coated the trail. The boy and his father hiked along a level path into another canyon, this one vast at the mouth and narrowing between high ridges of bare rock. They crossed and recrossed the shepherd's creek, which in this canyon was a tumbling free-stone brook. Following five yards behind his father, watching the cold, unapproachable rage that shaped the line of the man's shoulders, the boy was miserably uneasy because his father had grown so distant and quiet. They climbed over deadfalls blocking the trail, skirted one boulder large as a cabin, and blundered into a garden of nettles that stung them fiercely through their trousers. They saw fresh elk scat, and they saw bear, diarrhetic with late berries. The boy's father eventually grew bored with brooding, and showed the boy how to stalk. Before dusk that day they had shot an elk.

An open and gently sloped hillside, almost a meadow, ran for a quarter mile in quaking aspen, none over fifteen feet tall. The elk was above. The boy's father had the boy brace his gun in the notch of an aspen and take the first shot. The boy missed. The elk reeled and bolted down and his father killed it before it made cover. It was a five-point bull. They dressed the elk out and dragged it down to the cover of large pines, near the stream, where they would quarter it tomorrow, and then they returned under twilight to the hut.

That night even the fetal position could not keep the boy warm. He shivered wakefully for hours. He was glad that the following day, though full of walking and butchery and oppressive burdens, would be their last in the woods. He heard nothing. When he woke, through the door of the hut he saw whiteness like bone.

Six inches had fallen, and it was still snowing. The boy stood about in the campfire, amazed. When it snowed three inches in Evergreen Park, the boy would wake before dawn to the hiss of sand trucks and the ratchet of chains. Here there had been no warning. The boy was not much colder than he had been yesterday, and the transformation of the woods seemed mysterious and benign and somehow comic. He thought of Christmas. Then his father barked at him.

His father's mood had also changed, but in a different way; he seemed serious and hurried. As he wiped the breakfast pots clean with snow, he gave the boy orders for other chores. They left camp with two empty pack frames, both rifles, and a handsaw and rope. The boy soon understood why his father felt pressure of time: it took them an hour to climb the mile to the meadow. The snow continued. They did not rest until they reached the aspens.

"I had half a mind at breakfast to let the bull lie and pack us straight down out of here," his father admitted. "Probably smarter and less trouble in the long run. I could have come back on snowshoes next week. But by then it might be three feet deep and starting to drift. We can get two quarters out today. That will make it easier for me later." The boy was surprised by two things: that his father would be so wary in the face of a gentle snowfall and that he himself would have felt disappointed to be taken out of the woods that morning. The air of the meadow teemed with white.

"If it stops soon, we're fine," said his father.

It continued.

61

The path up the far canyon was hard climbing in eight inches of snow. The boy fell once, filling his collar and sleeves, and the gun-sight put a small gouge in his chin. But he was not discouraged. That night they would be warm and dry at the cabin. A half mile and he came up beside his father, who had stopped to stare down at dark splashes of blood.

Heavy tracks and a dragging belly mark led up to the scramble of deepening red, and away. The tracks were nine inches long and showed claws. The boy's father knelt. As the boy watched, one shining maroon splotch the size of a saucer sank slowly beyond sight into the snow. The blood was warm.

Inspecting the tracks carefully, his father said, "She's got a cub with her."

"What happened?"

"Just a kill. Seems to have been a bird. That's too much blood for a grouse, but I don't see signs of any four-footed creature. Maybe a turkey." He frowned thoughtfully. "A turkey without feathers. I don't know. What I dislike is coming up on her with a cub." He drove a round into the chamber of the .270.

Trailing red smears, the tracks preceded them. Within fifty feet they found the body. It was half-buried. The top of its head had been shorn away, and the cub's brains had been licked out.

His father said "Christ," and plunged off the trail. He snapped at the boy to follow closely.

They made a wide crescent through brush and struck back after a quarter mile. His father slogged ahead in the snow, stopping often to stand holding his gun ready and glancing around while the boy caught up and passed him. The boy was confused. He knew his father was worried, but he did not feel any danger himself. They met the trail again, and went on to the aspen hillside before his father allowed them to rest. The boy spat on the snow. His lungs ached badly.

"Why did she do that?"

"She didn't. Another bear got her cub. A male. Maybe the one we saw yesterday. Then she fought him for the body, and she won. We didn't miss them by much. She may even have been watching. Nothing could put her in a worse frame of mind."

He added: "If we so much as see her, I want you to pick the nearest big tree and start climbing. Don't stop till you're twenty feet off the ground. I'll stay down and decide whether we have to shoot her. Is your rifle cocked?"

"No."

"Cock it, and put on the safety. She may be a black bear and black bears can climb. If she comes up after you, lean down and stick your gun in her mouth and fire. You can't miss."

He cocked the Winchester, as his father had said.

They angled downhill to the stream, and on to the mound of their dead elk. Snow filtered down steadily in purposeful silence. The boy was thirsty. It could not be much below freezing, he was aware, because with the exercise his bare hands were comfortable, even sweating between the fingers.

"Can I get a drink?"

"Yes. Be careful you don't wet your feet. And don't wander anywhere. We're going to get this done quickly."

He walked the few yards, ducked through the brush at streamside, and knelt in the snow to drink. The water was painful to his sinuses and bitterly cold on his hands. Standing again, he noticed an animal body ahead near the stream bank. For a moment he felt sure it was another dead cub. During that moment his father called:

"David! Get up here right now!"

The boy meant to call back. First he stepped closer to turn the cub with his foot. The touch brought it alive. It rose suddenly with a high squealing growl and whirled its head like a snake and snapped. The boy shrieked. The cub had his right hand in its jaws. It would not release.

It thrashed senselessly, working its teeth deeper and tearing flesh with each movement. The boy felt no pain. He knew his hand was being damaged and that realization terrified him and he was desperate to get the hand back before it was ruined. But he was helpless. He sensed the same furious terror racking the cub that he felt in himself, and he screamed at the cub almost reasoningly to let him go. The boy did not think to shout for his father. He did not see him or hear him coming.

His father moved at full stride in a slowed laboring run through the snow, saying nothing and holding the rifle he did not use, crossed the last six feet still gathering speed, and brought his right boot up into the cub's belly. That kick seemed to lift the cub clear of the snow. It opened its jaws to another shrill piggish squeal, and the boy felt dull relief on his hand, as though his father had pressed open the blades of a spring trap with his foot. The cub tumbled once and disappeared over the stream bank, then surfaced downstream, squalling and paddling. The boy looked at his hand and was horrified. He still had no pain, but the hand was unrecognizable. His fingers had been peeled down the palm like flaps on a banana. Glands at the side of his jaw threatened that he would vomit, and he might have stood stupidly watching the hand bleed if his father had not grabbed him.

He snatched the boy by the arm and dragged him toward a tree without even looking at the boy's hand. The boy jerked back in angry resistance as though he had been struck. He screamed at his father. He screamed that his hand was cut, believing his father did not know, and as he screamed he began to cry. He began to feel hot throbbing pain. He began to worry about the blood he was losing. He could imagine his blood melting red holes in the snow behind him and he did not want to look. He did not want to do anything until he had taken care of his hand. At that instant he hated his father. But his father was stronger. He all but carried the boy to a tree.

He lifted the boy. In a voice that was quiet and hurried and very unlike the harsh grip with which he had taken the boy's arm, he said:

"Grab hold and climb up a few branches as best you can. Sit on a limb and hold tight and clamp the hand under your other armpit, if you can do that. I'll be right back to you. Hold tight because you're going to get dizzy." The boy groped desperately for a branch. His father supported him from beneath, and waited. The boy clambered. His feet scraped at the trunk. Then he was in the tree. Bark flakes and resin were stuck to the raw naked meat of his right hand. His father said:

"Now here, take this. Hurry."

The boy never knew whether his father himself had been frightened enough to forget for that moment about the boy's hand, or whether his father was still thinking quite clearly. His father may have expected that much. By the merciless clarity of his own standards, he may have expected that the boy should be able to hold onto a tree, and a wound, and a rifle, and with one hand. He extended the stock of the Winchester toward the boy.

The boy wanted to say something, but his tears and his fright would not let him gather a breath. He shuddered, and could not speak. "David," his father urged. The boy reached for the stock and faltered and clutched at the trunk with his good arm. He was crying and gasping, and he wanted to speak. He was afraid he would fall out of the tree. He released his grip once again, and felt himself tip. His father extended the gun higher, holding the barrel. The boy swung out his injured hand, spraying his father's face with blood. He reached and he tried to close torn dangling fingers around the stock and he pulled the trigger.

The bullet entered low on his father's thigh and shattered the knee and traveled down the shin bone and into the ground through his father's heel.

His father fell, and the rifle fell with him. He lay in the snow without moving. The boy thought he was dead. Then the boy saw him grope for the rifle. He found it and rolled onto his stomach, taking aim at the sow grizzly. Forty feet up the hill, towering on hind legs, she canted her head to one side, indecisive. When the cub pulled itself up a snowbank from the stream, she coughed at it sternly. The cub trotted straight to her with its head low. She knocked it off its feet with a huge paw, and it yelped. Then she turned quickly. The cub followed.

The woods were silent. The gunshot still echoed awesomely back to the boy but it was an echo of memory, not sound. He felt nothing. He saw his father's body stretched on the snow and he did not really believe he was where he was. He did not want to move: he wanted to wake. He sat in the tree and waited. The snow fell as gracefully as before.

His father rolled onto his back. The boy saw him raise himself to a sitting position and look down at the leg and betray no expression, and then slump back. He blinked slowly and lifted his eyes to meet the boy's eyes. The boy waited. He expected his father to speak. He expected his father to say *Shinny down using your elbows and knees and get the first-aid kit and boil water and phone the doctor. The number is taped to the dial.* His father stared. The boy could see the flicker of thoughts behind his father's eyes. His father said nothing. He raised his arms slowly and crossed them over his face, as though to nap in the sun.

The boy jumped. He landed hard on his feet and fell onto his back. He stood over his father. His hand dripped quietly onto the snow. He was afraid that his father was deciding to die. He wanted to beg him to reconsider. The boy had never before seen his father hopeless. He was afraid.

But he was no longer afraid of his father.

Then his father uncovered his face and said, "Let me see it."

They bandaged the boy's hand with a sleeve cut from the other arm of his shirt. His father wrapped the hand firmly and split the sleeve end with his deer knife and tied it neatly in two places. The boy now felt searing pain in his torn palm, and his stomach lifted when he thought of the damage, but at least he did not have to look at it. Quickly the plaid flannel bandage began to soak through maroon. They cut a sleeve from his father's shirt to tie over the wound in his thigh. They raised the trouser leg to see the long swelling bruise down the calf where he was hemorrhaging into the bullet's tunnel. Only then did his father realize that he was bleeding also from the heel. The boy took off his father's boot and placed a half-clean handkerchief on the insole where the bullet had exited, as his father instructed him. Then his father laced the boot on again tightly. The boy helped his father to stand. His father tried a

65

step, then collapsed in the snow with a blasphemous howl of pain. They had not known that the knee was shattered.

The boy watched his father's chest heave with the forced sighs of suffocating frustration, and heard the air wheeze through his nostrils. His father relaxed himself with the breathing, and seemed to be thinking. He said,

"You can find your way back to the hut."

The boy held his own breath and did not move.

"You can, can't you?"

"But I'm not. I'm not going alone. I'm only going with you."

"All right, David, listen carefully," his father said. "We don't have to worry about freezing. I'm not worried about either of us freezing to death. No one is going to freeze in the woods in November, if he looks after himself. Not even in Montana. It just isn't that cold. I have matches and I have a fresh elk. And I don't think this weather is going to get any worse. It may be raining again by morning. What I'm concerned about is the bleeding. If I spend too much time and effort trying to walk out of here, I could bleed to death.

"I think your hand is going to be all right. It's a bad wound, but the doctors will be able to fix it as good as new. I can see that. I promise you that. You'll be bleeding some too, but if you take care of that hand it won't bleed any more walking than if you were standing still. Then you'll be at the doctor's tonight. But if I try to walk out on this leg it's going to bleed and keep bleeding and I'll lose too much blood. So I'm staying here and bundling up warm and you're walking out to get help. I'm sorry about this. It's what we have to do.

"You can't possibly get lost. You'll just follow this trail straight down the canyon the way we came up, and then you'll come to the meadow. Point yourself toward the big pine tree with the forked crown. When you get to that tree you'll find the creek again. You may not be able to see it, but make yourself quiet and listen for it. You'll hear it. Follow that down off the mountain and past the hut till you get to the jeep."

He struggled a hand into his pocket. "You've never driven a car, have you?"

The boy's lips were pinched. Muscles in his cheeks ached from clenching his jaws. He shook his head.

"You can do it. It isn't difficult." His father held up a single key and began telling the boy how to start the jeep, how to work the clutch, how to find reverse and then first and then second. As his father described the positions on the floor shift the boy raised his swaddled right hand. His father stopped. He rubbed at his eye sockets, like a man waking.

"Of course," he said. "All right. You'll have to help me."

Using the saw with his left hand, the boy cut a small forked aspen. His father showed the boy where to trim it so that the fork would reach just to his armpit. Then they lifted him to his feet. But the crutch was useless on a steep hillside of deep grass and snow. His father leaned over the boy's shoulders and they fought the slope for an hour.

When the boy stepped in a hole and they fell, his father made no exclamation of pain. The boy wondered whether his father's knee hurt as badly as his own hand. He suspected it hurt worse. He said nothing about his hand, though several times in their climb it was twisted or crushed. They reached the trail. The snow had not stopped, and their tracks were veiled. His father said:

"We need one of the guns. I forgot. It's my fault. But you'll have to go back down and get it."

The boy could not find the tree against which his father said he had leaned the .270, so he went toward the stream and looked for blood. He saw none. The imprint of his father's body was already softened beneath an inch of fresh silence. He scooped his good hand through the snowy depression and was startled by cool slimy blood, smearing his fingers like phlegm. Nearby he found the Winchester.

"The lucky one," his father said. "That's all right. Here." He snapped open the breach and a shell flew and he caught it in the air. He glanced dourly at the casing, then cast it aside in the snow. He held the gun out for the boy to see, and with his thumb let the hammer down one notch.

"Remember?" he said. "The safety."

The boy knew he was supposed to feel great shame, but he felt little. His father could no longer hurt him as he once could, because the boy was coming to understand him. His father could not help himself. He did not want the boy to feel contemptible, but he needed him to, because of the loneliness and the bitterness and the boy's mother; and he could not help himself.

After another hour they had barely traversed the aspen hillside. Pushing the crutch away in angry frustration, his father sat in the snow. The boy did not know whether he was thinking carefully of how they might get him out, or still laboring with the choice against despair. The light had wilted to something more like moonlight than afternoon. The sweep of snow had gone gray, depthless, flat, and the sky warned sullenly of night. The boy grew restless. Then it was decided. His father hung himself piggyback over the boy's shoulders, holding the rifle. The boy supported him with elbows crooked under his father's knees. The boy was tall for eleven years old, and heavy. The boy's father weighed 164 pounds.

The boy walked.

He moved as slowly as drifting snow: a step, then time, then another step. The burden at first seemed to him overwhelming. He did not think he would be able to carry his father far.

He took the first few paces expecting to fall. He did not fall, so he kept walking. His arms and shoulders were not exhausted as quickly as he had thought they would be, so he kept walking. Shuffling ahead in the deep powder was like carrying one end of an oak bureau up stairs. But for a surprisingly long time the burden did not grow any worse. He found balance. He found rhythm. He was moving.

Dark blurred the woods, but the snow was luminous. He could see the trail well. He walked.

"How are you, David? How are you holding up?"

"All right."

"We'll stop for a while and let you rest. You can set me down here." The boy kept walking. He moved so ponderously, it seemed after each step that he had stopped. But he kept walking.

"You can set me down. Don't you want to rest?"

The boy did not answer. He wished that his father would not make him talk. At the start he had gulped for air. Now he was breathing low and regularly. He was watching his thighs slice through the snow. He did not want to be disturbed. After a moment he said, "No."

He walked. He came to the cub, shrouded beneath new snow, and did not see it, and fell over it. His face was smashed deep into the snow by his father's weight. He could not move. But he could breathe. He rested. When he felt his father's thigh roll across his right hand, he remembered the wound. He was lucky his arms had been pinned to his sides, or the hand might have taken the force of their fall. As he waited for his father to roll himself clear, the boy noticed the change in temperature. His sweat chilled him quickly. He began shivering.

His father had again fallen in silence. The boy knew that he would not call out or even mention the pain in his leg. The boy realized that he did not want to mention his hand. The blood soaking the outside of his flannel bandage had grown sticky. He did not want to think of the alien tangle of flesh and tendons and bones wrapped inside. There was pain, but he kept the pain at a distance. It was not *his* hand any more. He was not counting on ever having it back. If he was resolved about that, then the pain was not his either. It was merely pain of which he was aware. His good hand was numb.

"We'll rest now."

"I'm not tired," the boy said. "I'm just getting cold."

"We'll rest," said his father. "I'm tired."

Under his father's knee, the boy noticed, was a cavity in the snow, already melted away by fresh blood. The dark flannel around his father's thigh did not appear sticky. It gleamed.

His father instructed the boy how to open the cub with the deer knife. His father stood on one leg against a deadfall, holding the Winchester ready, and glanced around on all sides as he spoke. The boy used his left hand and both his knees. He punctured the cub low in the belly, to a soft squirting sound, and sliced upward easily. He did not gut the cub. He merely cut out a large square of belly meat. He handed it to his father, in exchange for the rifle.

His father peeled off the hide and left the fat. He sawed the meat in half. One piece he rolled up and put in his jacket pocket. The other he divided again. He gave the boy a square thick with glistening raw fat.

"Eat it. The fat too. Especially the fat. We'll cook the rest farther on. I don't want to build a fire here and taunt Momma."

The meat was chewy. The boy did not find it disgusting. He was hungry.

His father sat back on the ground and unlaced the boot from his good foot. Before the boy understood what he was doing, he had relaced the boot. He was holding a damp wool sock.

"Give me your left hand." The boy held out his good hand, and his father pulled the sock down over it. "It's getting a lot colder. And we need that hand."

"What about yours? We need your hands too. I'll give you my—"

"No, you won't. We need your feet more than anything. It's all right. I'll put mine inside your shirt."

He lifted his father, and they went on. The boy walked.

He moved steadily through cold darkness. Soon he was sweating again, down his ribs and inside his boots. Only his hands and ears felt as though crushed in a cold metal vise. But his father was shuddering. The boy stopped.

His father did not put down his legs. The boy stood on the trail and waited. Slowly he released his wrist holds. His father's thighs slumped. The boy was careful about the wounded leg. His father's grip over the boy's neck did not loosen. His fingers were cold against the boy's bare skin.

"Are we at the hut?"

"No. We're not even to the meadow."

"Why did you stop?" his father asked.

"It's so cold. You're shivering. Can we build a fire?"

"Yes," his father said hazily. "We'll rest. What time is it?"

"We don't know," the boy said. "We don't have a watch."

The boy gathered small deadwood. His father used the Winchester stock to scoop snow away from a boulder, and they placed the fire at the boulder's base. His father broke up pine twigs and fumbled dry toilet paper from his breast pocket and arranged the wood, but by then his fingers were shaking too badly to strike a match. The boy lit the fire. The boy stamped down the snow, as his father instructed, to make a small ovenlike recess. He added more deadwood. Beyond the invisible clouds there seemed to be part of a moon.

"It stopped snowing," the boy said.

"Why?"

The boy did not speak. His father's voice had sounded unnatural. After a moment his father said:

"Yes, indeed. It stopped."

They roasted pieces of cub meat skewered on a green stick. Dripping fat made the fire spatter and flare. The meat was scorched on the outside and raw within. It tasted as good as any meat the boy had ever eaten. They burned their palates on hot fat. The second stick smoldered through before they had noticed, and that batch of meat fell in the fire. The boy's father cursed once and reached into the flame for it and dropped it and clawed it out, and then put his hand in the snow. He did not look at the blistered fingers. They ate. The boy saw that both his father's hands had gone clumsy and almost useless.

The boy went for more wood. He found a bleached deadfall not far off the trail, but with one arm he could only break up and carry small loads. They lay down in the recess together like spoons, the boy nearer the fire. They pulled fir boughs into place above them, resting across the snow. They pressed close together. The boy's father was shivering spastically now, and he clenched the boy in a fierce hug. The boy put his father's hands back inside his own shirt. The boy slept. He woke when the fire faded and added more wood and slept. He woke again and tended the fire and changed places with his father and slept. He slept less soundly with his father between him and the fire. He woke again when his father began to vomit.

The boy was terrified. His father wrenched with sudden vomiting that brought up cub meat and yellow liquid and blood and sprayed them across the snow by the grayish-red glow of the fire and emptied his stomach dry and then would not release him. He heaved on pathetically. The boy pleaded to be told what was wrong. His father could not or would not answer. The spasms seized him at the stomach and twisted the rest of his body taut in ugly jerks. Between the attacks he breathed with a wet rumbling sound deep in his chest, and did not speak. When the vomiting subsided, his breathing stretched itself out into long bub-bling sighs, then shallow gasps, then more liquidy sighs. His breath caught and froth rose in his throat and into his mouth and he gagged on it and began vomiting again. The boy thought his father would choke. He knelt beside him and held him and cried. He could not see his father's face well and did not want to look closely while the sounds that were coming from inside his father's body seemed so unhuman. The boy had never been more frightened. He wept for himself, and for his father. He knew from the noises and movements that his father must die. He did not think his father could ever be human again.

When his father was quiet, he went for more wood. He broke limbs from the deadfall with fanatic persistence and brought them back in bundles and built the fire up bigger. He nestled his father close to it and held him from behind. He did not sleep, though he was not awake. He waited. Finally he opened his eyes on the beginnings of dawn. His father sat up and began to spit.

"One more load of wood and you keep me warm from behind and then we'll go."

The boy obeyed. He was surprised that his father could speak. He thought it strange now that his father was so concerned for himself and so little concerned for the boy. His father had not even asked how he was.

The boy lifted his father, and walked.

Sometime while dawn was completing itself, the snow had resumed. It did not filter down soundlessly. It came on a slight wind at the boy's back, blowing down the canyon. He felt as though he were tumbling forward with the snow into a long vertical shaft. He tumbled slowly. His father's body protected the boy's back from being chilled by the wind. They were both soaked through their clothes. His father was soon shuddering again.

The boy walked. Muscles down the back of his neck were sore from yesterday. His arms ached, and his shoulders and thighs, but his neck hurt him most. He bent his head forward against the weight and the pain, and he watched his legs surge through the snow. At his stomach he felt the dull ache of hunger, not as an appetite but as an affliction. He thought of the jeep. He walked.

He recognized the edge of the meadow but through the snow-laden

71

wind he could not see the cluster of aspens. The snow became deeper where he left the wooded trail. The direction of the wind was now variable, sometimes driving snow into his face, sometimes whipping across him from the right. The grass and snow dragged at his thighs, and he moved by stumbling forward and then catching himself back. Twice he stepped into small overhung fingerlets of the stream, and fell violently, shocking the air from his lungs and once nearly spraining an ankle. Farther out into the meadow, he saw the aspens. They were a hundred yards off to his right. He did not turn directly toward them. He was afraid of crossing more hidden creeks on the intervening ground. He was not certain now whether the main channel was between him and the aspen grove or behind him to the left. He tried to project from the canyon trail to the aspens and on to the forked pine on the far side of the meadow, along what he remembered as almost a straight line. He pointed himself toward the far edge, where the pine should have been. He could not see a forked crown. He could not even see trees. He could see only a vague darker corona above the curve of white. He walked.

He passed the aspens and left them behind. He stopped several times with the wind rasping against him in the open meadow, and rested. He did not set his father down. His father was trembling uncontrollably. He had not spoken for a long time. The boy wanted badly to reach the far side of the meadow. His socks were soaked and his boots and cuffs were glazed with ice. The wind was chafing his face and making him dizzy. His thighs felt as if they had been bruised with a club. The boy wanted to give up and set his father down and whimper that this had gotten to be very unfair; and he wanted to reach the far trees. He did not doubt which he would do. He walked.

He saw trees. Raising his head painfully, he squinted against the rushing flakes. He did not see the forked crown. He went on, and stopped again, and craned his neck, and squinted. He scanned a wide angle of pines, back and forth. He did not see it. He turned his body and his burden to look back. The snow blew across the meadow and seemed, whichever way he turned, to be streaking into his face. He pinched his eyes tighter. He could still see the aspens. But he could not judge where the canyon trail met the meadow. He did not know from just where he had come. He looked again at the aspens, and then ahead to the pines. He considered the problem carefully. He was irritated that the forked ponderosa did not show itself yet, but not worried. He was forced to estimate. He estimated, and went on in that direction.

When he saw a forked pine it was far off to the left of his course. He turned and marched toward it gratefully. As he came nearer, he bent his head up to look. He stopped. The boy was not sure that this was the right tree. Nothing about it looked different, except the thick cakes of snow weighting its limbs, and nothing about it looked especially familiar. He had seen thousands of pine trees in the last few days. This was one like the others. It definitely had a forked crown. He entered the woods at its base.

He had vaguely expected to join a trail. There was no trail. After two hundred yards he was still picking his way among trees and deadfalls and brush. He remembered the shepherd's creek that fell off the lip of the meadow and led down the first canyon. He turned and retraced his tracks to the forked pine.

He looked for the creek. He did not see it anywhere near the tree. He made himself quiet, and listened. He heard nothing but wind, and his father's tremulous breathing.

"Where is the creek?"

His father did not respond. The boy bounced gently up and down, hoping to jar him alert.

"Where is the creek? I can't find it."

"What?"

"We crossed the meadow and I found the tree but I can't find the creek. I need you to help."

"The compass is in my pocket," his father said.

He lowered his father into the snow. He found the compass in his father's breast pocket, and opened the flap, and held it level. The boy noticed with a flinch that his right thigh was smeared with fresh blood. For an instant he thought he had a new wound. Then he realized that the blood was his father's. The compass needle quieted.

"What do I do?"

His father did not respond. The boy asked again. His father said nothing. He sat in the snow and shivered.

The boy left his father and made random arcs within sight of the forked tree until he found a creek. They followed it onward along the flat and then where it gradually began sloping away. The boy did not see what else he could do. He knew that this was the wrong creek. He hoped that it would flow into the shepherd's creek, or at least bring them out on the same road where they had left the jeep. He was very tired. He did not want to stop. He did not care any more about being warm. He wanted only to reach the jeep, and to save his father's life.

He wondered whether his father would love him more generously for having done it. He wondered whether his father would ever forgive him for having done it.

If he failed, his father could never again make him feel shame, the boy thought naively. So he did not worry about failing. He did not worry about dying. His hand was not bleeding, and he felt strong. The creek swung off and down to the left. He followed it, knowing that he was lost. He did not want to reverse himself. He knew that turning back would make him feel confused and desperate and frightened. As long as he was following some pathway, walking, going down, he felt strong.

That afternoon he killed a grouse. He knocked it off a low branch with a heavy short stick that he threw like a boomerang. The grouse fell in the snow and floundered and the boy ran up and plunged on it. He felt it thrashing against his chest. He reached in and it nipped him and he caught it by the neck and squeezed and wrenched mercilessly until long after it stopped writhing. He cleaned it as he had seen his father clean grouse and built a small fire with matches from his father's breast pocket and seared the grouse on a stick. He fed his father. His father could not chew. The boy chewed mouthfuls of grouse, and took the chewed gobbets in his hand, and put them into his father's mouth. His father could swallow. His father could no longer speak.

The boy walked. He thought of his mother in Evergreen Park, and at once he felt queasy and weak. He thought of his mother's face and her voice as she was told that her son was lost in the woods in Montana with a damaged hand that would never be right, and with his father, who had been shot and was unconscious and dying. He pictured his mother receiving the news that her son might die himself, unless he could carry his father out of the woods and find his way to the jeep. He saw her face change. He heard her voice. The boy had to stop. He was crying. He could not control the shape of his mouth. He was not crying with true sorrow, as he had in the night when he held his father and thought his father would die; he was crying in sentimental self-pity. He sensed the difference. Still he cried.

He must not think of his mother, the boy realized. Thinking of her could only weaken him. If she knew where he was, what he had to do, she could only make it impossible for him to do it. He was lucky that she knew nothing, the boy thought.

No one knew what the boy was doing, or what he had yet to do. Even the boy's father no longer knew. The boy was lucky. No one was watching, no one knew, and he was free to be capable.

The boy imagined himself alone at his father's grave. The grave was open. His father's casket had already been lowered. The boy stood at the foot in his black Christmas suit, and his hands were crossed at his groin, and he was not crying. Men with shovels stood back from the grave, waiting for the boy's order for them to begin filling it. The boy felt a horrible swelling sense of joy. The men watched him, and he stared down into the hole. He knew it was a lie. If his father died, the boy's mother would rush out to Livingston and have him buried and stand at the grave in a black dress and veil squeezing the boy to her side like he was a child. There was nothing the boy could do about that. All the more reason he must keep walking.

Then she would tow the boy back with her to Evergreen Park. And he would be standing on Ninety-sixth Street in the morning dark before his father's cold body had even begun to grow alien and decayed in the buried box. She would drag him back, and there would be nothing the boy could do. And he realized that if he returned with his mother after the burial, he would never again see the cabin outside Livingston. He would have no more summers and no more Novembers anywhere but in Evergreen Park.

The cabin now seemed to be at the center of the boy's life. It seemed to stand halfway between the snowbound creek valley and the train station in Chicago. It would be his cabin soon.

The boy knew nothing about his father's will, and he had never been told that legal ownership of the cabin was destined for him. Legal ownership did not matter. The cabin might be owned by his mother, or sold to pay his father's debts, or taken away by the state, but it would still be the boy's cabin. It could only forever belong to him. His father had been telling him *Here, this is yours. Prepare to receive it.* The boy had sensed that much. But he had been threatened, and unwilling. The boy realized now that he might be resting warm in the cabin in a matter of hours, or he might never see it again. He could appreciate the justice of that. He walked.

He thought of his father as though his father were far away from him. He saw himself in the black suit at the grave, and he heard his father speak to him from aside: *That's good. Now raise your eyes and tell them in a man's voice to begin shoveling. Then turn away and walk slowly back down the hill. Be sure you don't cry. That's good.* The boy stopped. He felt his glands quiver, full of new tears. He knew that it was a lie. His father would never be there to congratulate him. His father would never know how well the boy had done.

He took deep breaths. He settled himself. Yes, his father would know somehow, the boy believed. His father had known all along. His father knew.

He built the recess just as they had the night before, except this time he found flat space between a stone bank and a large fallen cottonwood trunk. He scooped out the snow, he laid boughs, and he made a fire against each reflector. At first the bed was quite warm. Then the melt from the fires began to run down and collect in the middle, forming a puddle of wet boughs under them. The boy got up and carved runnels across the packed snow to drain the fires. He went back to sleep and slept warm, holding his father. He rose again each half hour to feed the fires.

The snow stopped in the night, and did not resume. The woods seemed to grow quieter, settling, sighing beneath the new weight. What was going to come had come.

The boy grew tired of breaking deadwood and began walking again before dawn and walked for five more hours. He did not try to kill the grouse that he saw because he did not want to spend time cleaning and cooking it. He was hurrying now. He drank from the creek. At one point he found small black insects like winged ants crawling in great numbers across the snow near the creek. He stopped to pinch up and eat thirty or forty of them. They were tasteless. He did not bother to feed any to his father. He felt he had come a long way down the mountain. He thought he was reaching the level now where there might be roads. He followed the creek, which had received other branches and grown to a stream. The ground was flattening again and the drainage was widening, opening to daylight. As he carried his father, his head ached. He had stopped noticing most of his other pains. About noon of that day he came to the fence.

It startled him. He glanced around, his pulse drumming suddenly, preparing himself at once to see the long empty sweep of snow and broken fence posts and thinking of Basque shepherds fifty years gone. He saw the cabin and the smoke. He relaxed, trembling helplessly into laughter. He relaxed, and was unable to move. Then he cried, still laughing. He cried shamelessly with relief and dull joy and wonder, for as long as he wanted. He held his father, and cried. But he set his father down and washed his own face with snow before he went to the door.

He crossed the lot walking slowly, carrying his father. He did not now feel tired.

The young woman's face was drawn down in shock and revealed at first nothing of friendliness.

"We had a jeep parked somewhere, but I can't find it," the boy said. "This is my father."

They would not talk to him. They stripped him and put him before the fire wrapped in blankets and started tea and made him wait. He wanted to talk. He wished they would ask him a lot of questions. But they went about quickly and quietly, making things warm. His father was in the bedroom.

The man with the face full of dark beard had telephoned for a doctor. He went back into the bedroom with more blankets, and stayed. His wife went from room to room with hot tea. She rubbed the boy's naked shoulders through the blanket, and held a cup to his mouth, but she would not talk to him. He did not know what to say to her, and he could not move his lips very well. But he wished she would ask him some questions. He was restless, thawing in silence before the hearth.

He thought about going back to their own cabin soon. In his mind he gave the bearded man directions to take him and his father home. It wasn't far. It would not require much of the man's time. They would thank him, and give him an elk steak. Later he and his father would come back for the jeep. He could keep his father warm at the cabin as well as they were doing here, the boy knew.

While the woman was in the bedroom, the boy overheard the bearded man raise his voice:

"He what?"

"He carried him out," the woman whispered.

"What do you mean, carried him?"

"Carried him. On his back. I saw."

"Carried him from where?"

"Where it happened. Somewhere on Sheep Creek, maybe."

"Eight miles?"

"I know."

"*Eight miles?* How could he do that?"

"I don't know. I suppose he couldn't. But he did."

The doctor arrived in half an hour, as the boy was just starting to shiver. The doctor went into the bedroom and stayed five minutes. The woman poured the boy more tea and knelt beside him and hugged him around the shoulders.

When the doctor came out, he examined the boy without speaking. The boy wished the doctor would ask him some questions, but he was afraid he might be shivering too hard to answer in a man's voice. While the doctor touched him and probed him and took his temperature, the boy looked the doctor directly in the eye, as though to show him he was really all right.

The doctor said:

"David, your father is dead. He has been dead for a long time. Probably since yesterday."

"I know that," the boy said.

Jonathan
Jay Neugeboren

Arthur Borofsky slept in the front seat of the car, his head against his father's side. They had left their home, outside Putney, Vermont, at five-fifteen in the morning. It was now six-thirty, and the sun was just beginning to come up over the horizon of snow-covered hills. Daniel Borofsky shifted slightly, withdrawing his right arm from under his son's back. He was pleased that Arthur, home from Dartmouth for the Christmas vacation, had offered to drive down with him to New York to visit Daniel's brother Jonathan. Daniel had last visited his brother in early June, five months before. That five-month period was the longest, in the thirty-four years since Jonathan had first been hospitalized, that the two brothers had ever been apart.

Arthur slipped down slightly, so that his head rested against his father's hip. Daniel ruffled his son's curly brown hair and smiled. There were no other cars on the highway, and Daniel loved the deserted landscape, the stillness. He thought of the nights, more than forty years before, when, after the rest of the family was asleep, he had tiptoed into the kitchen and sat at the kitchen table and written his first stories. He remembered balancing his old Underwood typewriter on top of a stack of towels, to muffle its sound. He remembered, above all, how still the apartment was, and how good he'd felt to be conjuring up voices and stories where nothing had existed before—voices and stories that, once they were down on paper, neither his mother nor his sisters could ever take away from him. He remembered Jonathan's smile—sweet Jonathan!—when the two of them would sit in bed together and Daniel would read aloud from the drafts of the stories he was working on.

A copy of Daniel's latest book, *Two Rabbis*, inscribed "With deepest love to Jonathan, who's been there and knows," lay on the back seat, along with a twine-wrapped package: two new sets of underwear, a pair of gray corduroy trousers, cookies that Janet had baked, a new toothbrush, three packs of Chesterfield cigarettes, and chewing gum.

Arthur stirred and sat up. "I'll drive," he said, rubbing his eyes.

"You don't mind?"

"I don't mind," Arthur answered. "I told you before."

Daniel reached across the front seat of the car impulsively, and took his son's hand. "I appreciate this, Arthur. Really. It means a lot to me."

Arthur pulled his hand away. "You don't have to thank me so much," he said.

Daniel shrugged. "Well. You know Janet thinks I shouldn't go—that I go so often only because I still feel . . ."

"Yeah," Arthur said. "I know all about it, with you and Mom." He leaned his head against the window, looking away from his father, at the snow.

"But tell me something," Daniel said. "If you'd had a brother or sister— if Mother had been willing to have another child—I know it's too late now, but just supposing—do you think it would have made a difference?"

"Oh Christ," Arthur sighed. "Here we go round the mulberry bush. Just don't, O.K., Dad? Just don't start in with all that psychological crap again. Do us both a favor." He looked into his father's face and his voice shifted and was, for a moment, less cold. He spoke deliberately, as if he'd practiced the words and memorized them. "Look. I told you before to stop worrying so much about me, O.K.? That would be a big help. Mom's never been as fragile as you like to think, and neither am I. O.K. I'm not like Uncle Jonathan and neither is she. O.K. I'm not—"

"I never said you were, did I? I just—" Daniel stopped, then smiled. "Why don't we just forget the whole thing, all right?"

"Fine with me."

But Daniel knew that in his heart he didn't want to forget anything. When Arthur had offered to come with him, he had hoped that, alone in the car, they would be able, at last, to talk easily with each other. He'd hoped, now that Arthur had left home and was on his own, that they would somehow be more comfortable with each other. He'd hoped, he now realized, even as he chided himself for his foolishness, that they would somehow be able suddenly to open to one another and to talk about all the things Daniel had always longed to talk about with his son.

There were so many memories Daniel wished he could give to Arthur, and he didn't really believe there would ever be enough time. The new

79

book, like the others before it—except that this one was based, consciously, on Jonathan and Daniel's life—was only a beginning, he told himself. Less than a beginning. What he wanted to do, he knew, was to be able to give Arthur enough memories so that Arthur would know that he did understand the fears Arthur lived with. What he wanted, he knew, was to be able to have both Arthur and Jonathan—the two men he loved most in the world—read his new book so that they would then see how much he cared, how much he loved them. And when they'd both read the story, he imagined, maybe then things would loosen up. Maybe then they'd be able to sit around together and talk for as long as they wanted about their childhoods. Maybe then they'd be able to talk at last about the times, when they were boys together, that he and Jonathan would go to Uncle Harry's apartment and sleep outside on his fire escape. Maybe then they'd all be able to talk about that hot summer night in August 1937, when Daniel was eleven and Jonathan was only six. Maybe then they'd even be able to talk about the time, many years later, when Jonathan's doctors asked if Daniel were willing to let Jonathan come live with him and Janet, were he to leave the hospital, and Daniel had said no.

He pulled to the side of the road, and, not speaking, got out, walked around in front of the car, and let Arthur slide across into the driver's seat. He watched his son's face as they drove, hoping, he knew, to see something there that he longed to see—relaxation, tenderness, love; hoping, he knew, that Arthur might turn sideways and smile at him in the way that, a few minutes before, he had smiled down on him. But Arthur, his head set slightly forward, his neck and mouth stiff, kept his eyes on the road. What Daniel wanted, above all, he knew, was to be able to tell Arthur, in detail—if he could ever truly remember the details—of the night Jonathan had slept with him on the fire escape and had fallen over the edge and landed on his head.

Daniel could hear the sound of the subway trains going by, on the elevated platform next to his Uncle Harry's building. He could remember when he spent nights wondering if a train, coming around the curve toward Throop Avenue, would ever continue in a straight line and soar through space, above the street and sidewalk, crashing into the side of his uncle's building. Again, as he had more than forty years before, he imagined the trains heading west from Brooklyn, toward wide horizons and noiseless cities. It was the very sound of the trains, he thought, that had, after Jonathan's fall, caused him to run away from home. He had imagined the trains steaming silently through beautiful cornfields and across lush green valleys. The red of the grass seemed to him to be blotting the prairies with wine stains. The wheat fields stretched before him, rippled by a gentle wind, like the ocean itself. He had imagined himself coming to new cities where families of wealthy Jews took him in and taught him trades and nurtured the hope that, when he came of age, he would want to marry their beautiful daughters . . .

He stayed away for less than a week, and got no farther than Newark. He lived on peanuts and raisins and halvah, and he spent most of his time riding the subways from one end of the city to the other, changing trains only when he thought a conductor was becoming suspicious of him. At night he slept in parks, and on trains, and in subway stations. Tired and hungry and humiliated, he returned home on a Friday evening, for Shabbos, to find that Jonathan was still in the hospital. His mother accused him again, as she had in the first instant—while she sat on the pavement clutching his brother's head against her blood-soaked lap—of having dropped Jonathan over the side.

"Are you still going for therapy?" Daniel asked.

"Yeah, I'm still going," Arthur said sullenly. His eyes darted sideways, toward his father. His shoulders sagged slightly. "So what else is new?"

"Look, Arthur," Daniel said. "I know you don't want to talk about it with me—you don't even want me to ask—but if we hide this from each other, then—"

"Let's not and say we did, O.K.?"

"Let's not what?"

"Let's not go round the mulberry bush." Arthur sighed again. "Look. The doctor thinks I don't need to see him once a week even any more. Maybe every other week during spring semester. He seems pleased with my progress. But he says I still have a hard time trusting anyone. O.K.? It's why I fly off into such fits sometimes, like when—"

"I didn't mean to intrude. I just wanted to know if you were still going."

"Bullshit. You want to know everything."

Daniel shook his head. He waited, then spoke very gently. "Not really, Arthur. You're on your own now. I do wish things weren't so hard for you sometimes, but I don't—"

"You mean well, right? Like your famous mother and sisters you're always talking about—my grandmother and aunts, of blessed memory."

"Of blessed memory," Daniel repeated. He laughed then. "I like your style," he said.

"Me too," Arthur said morosely, but Daniel saw the straight line of Arthur's thin mouth break slightly, toward a smile. "I guess."

81

"Did I ever tell you about the time Jonathan bit Momma—your grandmother—on the lip?"

Arthur turned toward his father. He smiled brightly. "No kidding?"

"Do you want to hear?"

Arthur turned back, his smile gone. "I suppose. If you want to tell me."

"It was in the same hospital he's in now. I'd take the train and bus in from the city, where your mother and I were living then—you weren't born yet; this was twenty, twenty-one years ago—and I'd always meet Momma and Poppa in the main lobby. Every Tuesday evening. We'd go for a family therapy session together once a week . . ."

Sunlight filtered onto the tiled walls through enormous barred windows. Dr. Teitleman, who was very old and spoke with a heavy German accent, and a man named Mr. Gordon, a student doing his internship, sat next to each other at one end of the long room. "What I want to do," Daniel offered, "is to write my next book about a mental hospital. But before I did I thought I'd ask if you thought it would hurt Jonathan in any way. Because if it would . . ."

Silence.

"What I mean is, it wouldn't be about Jonathan—but it would be set in a place something like this, and people might not understand and would assume . . ."

Silence.

"My basic idea is that it would be about two mad rabbis, one who's in and one who's out, and how they change places and nobody knows the difference. That's my basic idea. But before I started, I thought I'd ask if you thought it would hurt Jonathan in any way . . ."

"How do you feel about your brother's question?" Mr. Gordon asked.

"I like it," Jonathan said. "I think it's wonderful."

"The question?" Daniel asked. "Or the idea?"

Jonathan laughed. "Very good, Daniel. You're very sharp tonight. Didn't I tell you how smart he was? Didn't I show you his book? When it comes to smart, my big brother is tops, believe me."

"It's a sick idea," their mother said. "What do you think, Isaac?" She turned to her husband. He shrugged. "I'll tell you what I'm thinking, since you asked me," she went on. "I don't see why my son can't wait until Jonathan is well—why should other people have to know? Answer me that? Why can't Daniel write a different book if he's so worried about his brother?"

Dr. Teitleman turned to Jonathan. "Yes?" he asked.

"I love you, Momma," Jonathan said. "I love you so much."

Jonathan walked across the room, arms extended. His mother smiled at the doctors, proud to show them that they would now see how her son felt toward her. Jonathan bent over, touched her cheek—how handsome he looked to Daniel, the sunlight caressing his young face!—and when he kissed his mother, she screamed. Jonathan stood. His mother's lip was bleeding. Jonathan was beaming.

Their mother sat there, her hand over her mouth, while Daniel, as horrified as he was pleased, found himself laughing. "I don't understand it at all," their mother was saying, the blood dripping down her chin. "That's what I mean. I just don't understand it at all—why he does things like that—and I come here hoping you could explain it to me. That's why I come here, but all you do is sit and ask how I feel and how Daniel feels and how Jonathan feels. So why do I come back? Isaac?"

Their father shrugged. "That was a terrible thing he just did," he said, and he gave his wife his handkerchief. She asked the doctors again why her son did such things.

Jonathan smiled. "I'm sorry," he said. "It's just something I've always dreamed of doing and I wanted to be sure not to forget to do it before I left." Jonathan waited. Daniel said nothing. "Did I tell you that? That the doctors say I can leave soon? I told them that when I got out I could come into the city and live with you and Janet, Daniel, because . . ." Jonathan stopped. He looked at Daniel. "Can I come live with you, Daniel? The doctors said they thought it would be a good idea."

"Mr. Borofsky?"

"No," Daniel heard himself say. "No. Not now."

"Good," Jonathan said.

"I'm sorry. But I just don't think it would be good for either of us to live together again. It would—"

"Listen. You don't have to justify to me, brother," Jonathan said. "I understand, believe me. A man like you, what with—"

"No," Daniel said. "The answer is no. If—"

"You're doing the smart thing for once in your life," their mother said to Daniel. She blotted her lip with the handkerchief. "You'd have to have your head examined to let him out now, with the way he's acting." She laughed. "So tell me, if you know so much, why is he here in the first place? Is he alive? Is he dead?" She tapped on the side of her head with her fist. "I bang my head against the wall sometimes, trying to understand, do you hear me? My child is alive—my child is dead! That's what I cry out, but who listens?"

"I'm sorry," Daniel said to Jonathan. "I wish . . ."

Jonathan laughed. "And how about me? If you're sorry, how do you think a man in my position feels? Have you thought about that for a while?"

"How do you feel, Jonathan?" Mr. Gordon asked. "Tell us."

"Ask him how *he* feels," Jonathan replied. "He gave the answer. I was willing to try, wasn't I? Despite everything." He stepped toward his mother. "Don't hurt your head over me, Momma."

"What am I saving it for?"

Jonathan laughed and clapped his hands. "Did you hear, Daniel? Did you hear what she said?" He turned to the doctors. They showed nothing.

"Your brother has his own life to live, Jonathan," Dr. Teitleman said.

"That's what they all say. But I don't believe it for a minute—and neither does he."

"Is my child alive? Is my child dead?" their mother asked. "Once he was a beautiful child. He was so good, doctors—he was so talented. And now he's here. What did I do?"

"You were too good to me, Momma," Jonathan whispered. He winked at Daniel. "That was your trouble. When you're too good to children they crap all over you."

She sniffed in. "I'm sorry," Daniel said again. "But in the first place, Janet and I only have a small two-room apartment, and she's been—well-nervous herself sometimes lately. And then too—even if things were different with us, what with my writing and the way Jonathan sometimes feels about it and about me, I just . . ."

"Could you tell us maybe how you feel about writing this new book?" Mr. Gordon asked. "That might be helpful. That was the question you brought to us today, wasn't it? Perhaps if you could explain—"

"I don't know," Daniel said. "It's why I'm asking you. It seemed a simple question when I came here: yes, write it—no, wait a while. Why can't you answer yes or no?"

"Do you feel you could not write it if Jonathan were living with you?"

Their mother took the handkerchief from her lip and showed the spots of blood to the doctors. "I don't understand things. Explain to me. Why does he do such things if he loves me? He was never like this when he was a child. He was a very loving child." She glanced at Daniel. "More than him. That one was always—how do you say?—a cold fish."

"She's right," Jonathan said. "That's what Momma always called my big brother. A cold fish."

"I could just as easily write a different book now, if you think that would be best," Daniel offered. "Then after he was well—after he was out of here—then I could write this book. But what I meant was that I thought it would probably be better if, when Jonathan gets out and sets up his own life, he could feel that it hadn't happened because of *me* somehow. So that if he came to live with me, you see . . ."

"Yes?" Dr. Teitleman asked, stroking his chin. "You feel that you are in need perhaps of our permission to write this book, yes?"

"No," Daniel said quickly. "Look. I was just asking for your opinion, O.K.? Why can't you just give me your real opinion? Why . . .?"

"You seem to be feeling very angry, Mr. Borofsky. You are feeling as if, perhaps, we have to accuse you of something?"

Jonathan's head was on Daniel's lap. "I'd really like to be in your new book," he said, "but I just thought it over and I decided I agree with you about us not living together. I can find a place by myself. Or maybe I could move in with Momma again, or with one of our beloved sisters. You need your privacy for your writing, Daniel. A great man like you! But I understand that. I really do."

"You haven't answered the question, Mr. Borofsky. Perhaps if you could try to tell us how you feel about what your brother says . . ."

"You don't have to answer their questions," Jonathan said. "What do they know, after all? I'm the patient, right? And speaking of patience, how's your lip, Momma darling?"

"I always said it," Daniel heard himself telling the others then, "didn't I? That his bite was worse than his bark—"

He and Jonathan laughed together. He stroked Jonathan's hair. They embraced. The doctors stared at them, showing nothing.

The three men sat on Jonathan's cot together. Jonathan looked awful. His eyes were almost closed, his face was puffed and splotched, his skin was pasty. Although he was five years younger than Daniel, Daniel felt as if he were sitting next to a man much older than himself, like the kind of little old Jewish man their father had always sat with in *shul*. Jonathan rocked back and forth, shoulders hunched. Daniel looked at Arthur, who sat up stiffly, with a straight back, and he thought of the moment in *Two Rabbis*, when, after being apart for only three months, the rabbi comes to the mental hospital to visit his son and, standing ten feet away, does not at first recognize him.

Daniel talked about Janet, about the vegetable garden they'd had the summer before, about the fact that the Book-of-the-Month Club had chosen *Two Rabbis* as an alternate selection. He asked Arthur to tell Jonathan about Dartmouth and Arthur shrugged and said that he liked college, that he liked his courses, that he thought he would major in biology and be a pre-med. Jonathan patted Arthur on the arm. He untied the package and put the items into his locker. He tried to light a cigarette but his hands trembled too much and Daniel lit it for him. He took the book from Daniel and, without opening it or looking at the inscription, put that into his locker too. He handed Arthur a little black silk purse.

"Here, sonny boy," he said. "Chanukah *gelt*."

"Thanks, Uncle Jonathan."

"The purse was Momma's." Jonathan, his eyes now closed, began singing the sentence to himself. "The purse was Momma's, but were we . . .? The purse was Momma's, can't you see . . .?"

"I wrote the book," Daniel said.

"So who den?" Jonathan asked, his nose close to Daniel's. "You were the writer, right? And I was the brother. And this is the son. You were the writer, but the purse was still Momma's."

"It's the book I wanted to write," Daniel continued. "That I asked about that time you wanted to come and live with us."

Jonathan pinched Arthur's cheek. "And where would this dollink have slept? You did the right thing, Daniel. You always did the right thing. I wanted you to know I forgot about what you didn't do for me years ago. You'd rather write than be president, right? So you bring presents instead of writing."

"I hope you'll read it," Daniel said. "I hope you'll like it, Jonathan."

Jonathan giggled. He put his arm around Arthur's shoulder and led him from the room. "Listen," he said. "It's best this way, me living here. You know how I always put it, from way back, so your father would understand. 'Out of sight,' I said, 'means out of mind.'" He stopped and waited. "Do you get it?" he asked. "Out of sight—out of mind."

He leaned on Arthur. Daniel walked behind them. They stopped and Jonathan introduced Arthur to some other patients. A tall man, his hair in curlers, a purple scarf around his wrist, was banging his head against a soda machine. In the lounge, patients sat and watched television. Jonathan and Arthur joined them. Jonathan offered his new pack of cigarettes to the other patients, going to each of them, saying their names, introducing them all to Arthur, the son of his famous brother.

Jonathan let his head rest against Arthur's shoulder. Daniel saw Arthur raise his arm—hesitate—and then put it around Jonathan's shoulder, easily and gently. What was he feeling? Daniel turned away. An old man asked him for directions to the Staten Island Ferry. Daniel smiled, but said nothing. The man cursed him in Yiddish and left. Daniel read the notices on the bulletin board—letters from the director and staff, rules and regulations, therapy schedules, bus schedules, menus.

Jonathan touched his arm. "I told him I'm too old to go to college, so he doesn't have to worry that I'd want to move in with him. But tell me something, Daniel: what's it like to have a son? Our father had two sons, but where did it ever get him? Can you please tell me that . . .?"

Jonathan started crying. He walked away from them. Daniel walked after him and put his arms around him. Jonathan let his head rest against his brother's chest. "Poppa used to come here and give me chocolate bars even though Momma told him not to, did I ever tell you? He gave the guards money so they wouldn't beat me up, in the old days. But we never spoke, Daniel." Jonathan looked around and motioned to Arthur. He put his arms around both of them and whispered: "Do you think maybe Poppa was so quiet because his tongue wasn't right? Do you remember when I tried to chew my tongue up, Daniel?" Daniel nodded. "But listen. Maybe Poppa's tongue wasn't right from the time he licked Momma's shoes. What do you think?"

Daniel tried to pull away, but Jonathan held on to his collar. "When did he ever do such a thing?" Daniel asked.

Jonathan leaned back and laughed. "You mean you don't remember such a scene and yet you have the nerve to think you can write a book about us? Oh Daniel—sometimes you worry me!" He patted his brother on his arm, then put one arm into Daniel's and one into Arthur's and led them along the corridor. "But listen. It wasn't such a big deal, I suppose, but I remembered it one day years ago when I was talking with a nice young woman therapist they gave me, and what I said was that in our home my father used to grovel a lot—he was a *maven* on groveling—and that he used to kiss our mother's feet. And do you know what happened then? I said the words and laughed, and then I got hit with this very clear picture of Poppa down on his knees on the living-room rug, showing Momma how much he loved her after a fight, and he was licking the soles of her shoes and kissing them and Momma was beaming. It made her very happy." He stopped. "Remembering that scene helped me get out that time. It was what we call in the trade, a breakthrough. You're sure you don't remember, Daniel?"

"Just calm down a little," Daniel said. He led Jonathan back to his room and sat him on the cot. Jonathan closed his eyes, stuck his hands between his thighs, and rocked back and forth, humming to himself. "You know, sometimes I think maybe it would be better if I didn't come so often," Daniel offered. "That maybe it's too hard on you. What I mean is, this is your home now, Jonathan. And to receive me here . . ."

Daniel heard his heart thump. "I mean, I think I know what you must feel, how hard—"

Jonathan sat up straight. "*Never!*" he said. "Never! Maybe in your books you can get into other people's heads, Daniel, but not in my head. There are no books there. You never loved me as much as Momma wanted you to. You never—"

"You're babbling," Daniel said sharply.

"Drop dead," Jonathan replied. He looked up and smiled. He beckoned to Arthur, who was standing in the doorway. "Ah," he said. "Now I feel better. Much better." He looked at his brother. "Did you see how angry your father got with me, and for what, I ask you?" He patted the cot, beside him, and Arthur sat. "But listen, I put on a little act sometimes, but it really does stink here. I'm not as crazy as I think I am. After all, I'm insane, right? That means I'm sane. I'm *in* sane, no?"

Arthur laughed. "I like the way you put things, Uncle Jonathan."

"In our family we always had a way with words, and your father got most of them. But who's counting, right? I'm glad you came, but you should go before I get too nervous." He giggled. "I don't take my medication," he whispered. "I hide it and then spit it into the toilet bowl, but don't tell on me."

He took his brother's hand. "So what else did you bring me, darling?"

"Nothing."

"Yourself," Jonathan said. "When I say what did you bring me, you're supposed to say you brought me yourself. Haven't you ever been in therapy?"

"I brought you myself," Arthur said, giggling, raising a hand to cover his mouth, "because I'm in therapy."

Jonathan shook his head. He patted Arthur's hand. "That's too bad, sonny boy. Your father should know better. I mean, I know you want to please me—but I'm sorry to hear it. Listen, Daniel. When you speak to Poppa, you tell him I forgive him, all right?"

"Poppa's dead."

"You'll know how to get in touch with him. I'll leave it to you. Money buys anything." He smiled. "Not to worry, yes? Tell him I said that, the way he always did. Not to worry."

"But I'm not in a hospital, Uncle Jonathan," Arthur explained. "I'm just seeing this shrink once a week or so, that's all. It's all right. Really. I don't mind. He's a good guy. We get along."

Jonathan put a finger to his lips, as if to indicate that he would say no more. He clasped his hands upon his lap. He rocked back and forth and then his eyes began to close and his mouth to open. His jaw stiffened;

his arms rose. Arthur took his uncle by the shoulder and shook him. "Really, Uncle Jonathan, I'm not sick or anything. I just— I just—"

"Shh," Daniel said, softly. "It's O.K., Arthur. It's just the medications. I've seen it happen before. It's just the medications."

They stood inside the main lobby with other visitors, putting on their coats. "Come," Daniel said. "We'll go to the bathroom and then start back. We can stop on the turnpike for some supper and we'll be home by midnight. So Janet won't worry."

Arthur nodded. They walked into the men's room and stood at adjacent urinals. Daniel looked around, as if expecting to see somebody he knew. Without the book and the package he'd come in with, he felt for a moment as if he'd forgotten something. He smiled. He zipped up his fly and waited for Arthur. He remembered watching his father, after a session, rushing to the urinal. Was it after the time Jonathan had bitten their mother's lip? He remembered screaming at him: *Why don't you ever say anything? Why do you just sit there like a goddamn fucking lump?* He remembered lifting his father up and shoving him against the tiled wall. He remembered how surprised he was then—how light his father had felt, how weightless.

He let his father go. It was a hot July day. His hands were moist; his shirt stuck to his back. He'd apologized to his father and said something about how upset he still was to see his brother where he was, about how he sometimes wondered what good it did for all of them to come every Tuesday night. But his father only sneered at him, triumphantly, as if Daniel's rage had proven something he had always suspected about his son.

In the lobby his mother chastised his father for taking so long. She said something about how much better Jonathan looked, about how she really didn't mind giving up her Tuesday nights if only it would be a help to him. She kissed Daniel on the cheek and told him what a good brother he was—how most brothers would never make the long trip in from the city week after week the way he did. Daniel remembered how enraged he'd felt, to be praised by her in this way. But he'd said nothing. They walked from the building, his father trailing behind, and when Daniel looked back and stopped to wait for him, he'd seen the round dark stain: his father had wet his pants.

They left the turnpike near New Haven and ate at a Howard Johnson's. Arthur asked a lot of questions about Jonathan, about what he'd been like as a child, and Daniel found that he enjoyed talking about

Jonathan, about things they'd done together when they were boys. He spoke for a long time about the walks he and Jonathan would take together in Prospect Park—anything, he realized, to get out of the house and stay away as long as possible in those years—and about how, in the park and the zoo and along Flatbush Avenue and Eastern Parkway, he had been able, holding such a cute younger brother by the hand, to strike up conversations with girls more easily than when he was by himself.

Arthur also asked about when things had changed with Jonathan—about his first breakdown, about the effect of his fall on his illness, about why Daniel felt he was the way he was, and about whether he would ever get well. Daniel answered all the questions, slowly and deliberately. He said that he did not believe Jonathan would ever get well.

On the way home, Arthur fell asleep again, close to his father. He held the silk purse in his fist. Daniel thought of the times when, as a boy, he would wake in the middle of the night, or toward morning, and carry Jonathan from his crib to his own bed. Whenever, through the years, he had wanted to conjure up the tender feelings they'd shared, he thought of those nights. He had never, despite many women, touched skin that was softer than his brother's skin. Remembering Jonathan in this way, he believed, was what enabled him to feel what Arthur must have often felt, not having a brother.

Daniel looked at his son, and in his head he could see Jonathan, hiding under their bed, dressed in a blouse, skirt, and high heels. He smiled. He could hear his sister Rivka, yelling about the police and about her friends and about the clothing she never got back. She screamed that she would break his head for him again! In her dresser drawers, where her clothing had been, she would find chocolate bars and balls of string and paper clips. And Jonathan—beautiful, talented Jonathan! beautiful Jonathan with the golden curls!—he could see Jonathan roaming the neighborhood, playing his violin on street corners and in candy stores, dressed like a gypsy in Rivka's clothes. The pennies people tossed at his feet he would bring home to his mother, hoping to save her from unhappiness and poverty.

Daniel remembered the way his mother smiled when Jonathan gave her the pennies. Her face was radiant. "And him?" he remembered her saying once, laughing and waving a hand at their father: "Him? What does that one ever bring me?" Daniel remembered how angry he'd felt—murderously so—watching his mother embrace his brother and cover his face with kisses. He remembered how he had stared at his father and vowed to himself that he would never be like him.

Daniel touched his son's cheek with the back of his hand, very gently. Arthur opened his eyes. "Are we home?" he asked.

"Shh," Daniel said. "No. You can go back to sleep."

"Oh yeah," Arthur said, and, smiling, he snuggled closer to his father and closed his eyes.

Prize Tomatoes

Anne Rosner

All right, everyone at attention. There's been ample time since watering for revival. Beans! Pick up those bottom leaves. New tomato plants, stand up! That's it. Erect stems, leaves perpendicular. Remember, I have plans to enter tomatoes in the county fair this year. So you must work very hard. You all look beautiful. I'm proud of the effort you've all put forth this evening. Thank you and good night.

I'm lingering. Going into the house seems an undeserved sentence. I glance around the familiar landscape. New townhouses loom, a smug wall, to the east. The lights of a new shopping center reflect in the darkening sky. Turning westward, I can see a large field stretching away into a line of trees. When I face this way, the neighborhood of large homes retains its air of remoteness that I loved when our house was first built.

The twilit sky holds me, and I, standing in the purity of the sun's last rays, could be only another briefly drawn streak, like the evening clouds.

A door slams at the house. I know without turning that my daughter, Barbara, will be standing on the porch looking worriedly toward the garden. "Dad." Her voice is carried on the soft air.

I wave, smiling a smile she can't see from the porch. But this casual smile prepares me to walk to the house. Light, light step. Easy, loose gait. The picture of a man returning from engaging in a modest interest. She'll wait, my sentinel daughter, until she sees that I'm going into the house.

Barbara, her husband, Dick, and their two children had been contemplating a move when I went into the hospital three years ago. It was decided that it would work out well for everyone if she and her family

92

moved into my house when I came home from the hospital. Shaky and acutely mindful of the emptiness of the big house, I had not resisted, had indeed been grateful for the arrangement.

I approach the porch. Barbara says, "It's getting dark. I was afraid you might get chilled."

"Yes," I agree, "I think I will get a sweater."

An anxious flash across her eyes. "You're going to come back from your room, aren't you, Dad?" she asks. "There's a very good play on television tonight. I thought we could all watch it."

Dr. Hooper, the psychiatrist, has told her that I'm not to spend too much time alone.

"That sounds great," I say. "I'll just get the sweater and be back out."

Barbara retreats to the living room. I enter my bedroom, sighing in resignation because I'll have to postpone looking through the new seed catalogue that came in the mail today until everyone is in bed. Although Dr. Hooper has released me from his care, he and his advice hang about the house like iron-willed specters.

The children are both out for the evening. Dick, Barbara, and I settle into our tacitly appointed places before the television. The play proves to be avant-garde, hard to follow. My mind wanders. I think about the cabbage. Just the under-leaves seem a bit ragged. I remind myself to question Mr. Miggs about a possible culprit. Not cabbage worms, I know, because those are easy to see. Maybe—.

"Dad, did you notice the way these sets have been designed for the scene changes? Isn't that clever?"

I start. No need to panic. Calm, cool. Maybe just a nod will do. I nod. She buys it. I try again to concentrate on the show. Lucky Dick has fallen asleep, unnoticed. God, I'm weary of Barbara's concern.

She's tired tonight. Dark smudges have appeared under her eyes. She's relaxed and forgets to hold her chin up. The telltale sag in her jawline touches me.

She was more frightened than my other two children, I think, when I went to the hospital. She's more frightened still by the changes in the man who came home from the hospital.

I've overheard her on the phone, explaining to her friends, explaining to herself what happened. "It was Mother's death. It simply undid him. You know how devoted they were."

It's true what she says. Peg's death had much to do with it, but not in any way she might imagine. It wasn't as if we were young. Peg was sixty-three and I was sixty-five. That was four years ago last winter.

The devotion? Well, I'll concede a mutual respect. If there was devotion, it was the formal and dutiful devotion of habit—until the end, that is.

Peg died of a peculiar slow-growing form of cancer. We knew she had it for five years. She bore it with the serenity of people who have been forced to acknowledge their own deaths. I bore it, barely believing in its existence.

Almost precisely a year before she died, Peg told me one evening, in nothing more than a conversational tone, "Walter, there's something that's bothered me for more than thirty years. I think I'd feel better if you knew."

"What is it?"

"I had an affair when we were living in Shreveport." Then she laughed very girlishly and shrugged.

"With whom?" I asked.

"You didn't know him."

"For how long?"

"Two years."

I said, "Peg, I can't believe this. Then you were in love with him."

"I thought I was at the time," she said. Then she reached out and touched my arm. "Walter, I've never had any regrets about being married to you. Can you understand that?"

I jumped up and strode about the room, slamming the fist of one hand into the palm of the other. I wonder if I harbored some notion of beating up my wife's lover. I don't remember. All I remember is the gesture. I said, "I'll have to think about this."

For several days, I sorted through the feeling her confession had raised in me. There was an odd quality to my sense of betrayal in that it seemed to have so little to do with the other man. He seemed only a part, but certainly not the cause, of my agitation.

No, the element in it that ached with the persistence of a stubborn thorn was that I would have been absolutely certain that Peg was incapable of having the affair in the first place. It was a breach of trust, to be sure, but that seemed too small to describe the abyss that opened between us.

In those days after her confession, I had no reason to doubt her ability to have carried the secret for thirty years without my slightest suspicion. If I had been the sort of man then who doubted his own perceptions, I might have thought she had never told me, so unchanged was her customary equanimity. Freshly wounded, I saw her calm dignity as an added treachery.

The incident might have slipped silently below the surface of our lives, like so many things in the past, had I not pinpointed the source of my pain.

We were sitting at a late supper one night. Peg said, "Do you think Charlotte would like to come away with us this summer?"

I glanced up from my plate. Her face, lit by the one lamp in the room, was suddenly vivid, like a blurry photo coming into sharp focus. With a stupefying panic I realized that I didn't know this woman who had borne my three children, who had slept beside me for most of my life, who had been the one constancy in my life. And now she was dying.

I blurted, "I've had a couple of affairs myself." That lay flatly over us a moment. What a foolish thing to say. I tried again.

"What I mean is, it doesn't matter—your affair. I want—. I want—."

"You want what, Walter?"

I couldn't put my mouth around the enormity of what I wanted. "I want to talk" was the best I could do.

We lay awake most of the night, uncertain where to begin: haphazardly evoking memories, questioning each other. Toward morning, I held her, already so thin from the voraciousness of her illness. Her fragility was terrifying in its awful mortality. Peg, Peg. Peg o' my heart, did I sing to you as a young man?

Each time together then brought surprises: the joy of discovering each other without the expectancy of first love, deepened by the chill breath of Peg's measured time.

I loved her for the first time, was bound to her in parts of myself I had never known. Later, when she lay in the hospital, her skin tugged firmly, quite youthfully over her face by the rapacious disease, when tears were no longer strange to me, I cried, "Peg, all the years we wasted together. That loss is unbearable to me."

She said, "We couldn't have done this at any other time. We were far too much the sort of people that we were."

She offered it as comfort, I know, but it resounded down the empty well of my soul and continued to echo long after she died.

So Barbara was right in thinking that her mother's death had caused the eventual darkness that descended over my life. With Peg gone, I became the only one who heard those echoes.

The show ends. Barbara stirs in her chair, nudges Dick awake. I'm free to go now. We've all done our duty.

She rises. I sit quietly, not to appear too eager. "Well, Dad, I'll see you in the morning. Are you going to watch more television?"

"No, I don't think so," I say with a well-placed yawn. "I'm going to go to bed."

Good night. Good night.

In my room, I quickly search out the new seed catalog and position the lamp for the best light.

Fruit trees, shrubs. I'm idly flipping the pages. Flowers require slightly more attention. Maybe next year I'll try some flowers.

I linger for a moment over the red grapes. I've considered an arbor—not so much from any particular fondness for grapes but because of memories of sitting in the opulent shade of my grandmother's arbor as a boy. Yes, grapes might be interesting.

The vegetable section begins. I glance at the clock and listen for sounds in the house. The children when they come home will see my light, but fortunately they are teenagers—an age when whatever I do holds so little interest as to be invisible.

I pore over each picture, read the printed section underneath. I'm convinced that the people who compose the written information are rabid gardeners, too. Who but a gardener could describe rhubarb in such terms: "blushing red, clear through to the heart," "full shapely leaves"?

I'm captured by the catalog, entranced by the possibilities presented in the glossy pictures of potatoes, corn, and . . .

The doorknob has turned so softly that I don't know Barbara is there until she speaks. "Dad, it's three o'clock."

I shove the catalog guiltily into a shelf in the night table. Easy, easy. "I'm just going to bed, Barbara," I say. "You could have knocked." That, as Dr. Hooper would say, is a reasonable demand.

"I'm sorry," she says. "I thought you had fallen asleep with your light on."

She remains in the doorway in uncomfortable silence. Then says, "I don't like to check up on you." She's pleading because she really doesn't like it. "But you know Dr. Hooper spoke to us very specifically about your getting enough rest."

"I'm old enough to decide when to go to bed."

"Dad," she says, "I know I annoy you, but I don't know what else to do to get you to take care of yourself."

I wonder if she means she annoys me in general. During the bleak time right before I went to the hospital, Barbara confronted me tearfully, "You have always loved Charlotte better than me," and I—too raw, too naked in my despair to lie to her—said nothing. She remembers, I know.

"I'm fine," I say.

She hesitates, then says in a rush, "The garden scares me. It reminds me of the CB."

"It wasn't a CB," I say and turn from her.

"O.K., Dad, O.K. Will you promise you'll go to bed?"

"Yes," I say, and climb obediently into bed after she leaves.

The earth smell blowing through the window makes me anxious to be in the garden in the morning. I'm only slightly sleepy. Old men don't need much sleep.

I think of the radio. It wasn't a CB. It was a ham outfit. I built it myself from a kit. At first my son, John, and Barbara had been quite happy about my interest. Good therapy, Dr. Hooper had pronounced.

Barbara, uneasy as my keeper, was grateful for the time I spent with the radio, I suppose.

It was a wonderful radio. I could send signals nearly anywhere in the world, and because night is the best time for reception and transmission, I was many times bent over my set, headphones over my ears, when the sun came up. I slept most of the day, saw Dr. Hooper once a week, and operated my radio at night.

I should have seen it coming—the end of my radio. Dr. Hooper was very insistent that I talk about something besides the radio when I saw him. That made the sessions all the more arduous, as I thought of little else.

Especially after Cecelia. I contacted her in the Philippines. The signal was amazingly clear. Her voice held all the lush mystery of her home. Its cadence described a tropical fragrance around my room. Her English was quite good, and I began to call her every night.

She was twenty, a student of philosophy at the University of Manila. For her I played the experienced older man, seasoned and unsurprised by life. "How wise you are, Walter," she said many times, and I would chuckle comfortably. The distance between us secured the fraud.

Because she loved Aristotle particularly, I studied him, searching for ideas to intrigue her. I must have done enough because she spent a great deal of time with me nearly every night.

The evenings with the family seemed interminable. I paced. I checked my watch, sat restlessly watching television—waiting for the time to pass.

There were times when it was difficult to reach her, but with the patience of love I turned the dials for as long as it took, straining to hear her voice, however faint.

I don't know what happened. She was young, after all. Perhaps she simply lost interest. Perhaps her radio had been damaged in some way, but weeks went by and I couldn't reach her. I did everything I knew to do. I checked with the shop where I had bought the kit, but nothing helped.

My agitation became apparent. I was aware of low-voiced telephone conversations. Barbara was alerting the rest of the family. Even sensing their growing concern, I couldn't control the panic of my loss.

One early morning, after a night of frantic searching for Cecelia, I rose to the window and began to shout in desperation, "Cecelia, Cecelia. Oh please, Cecelia."

Barbara and Dick crashed into the room—Barbara shaking visibly at the sight of my tear-stained face, Dick circling me warily.

Dr. Hooper was called, medication secured. I began to see him three times a week.

I disliked going to see Dr. Hooper. In fact, I probably dislike Dr. Hooper. He has a sharp nose that points downward, seeming always to be calling attention to his shoes. He is a hard-faced man who makes much of small things. As though seeing him three times a week weren't punishment enough for alarming my family, he neatly disposed of my radio as well.

"Walter, you must see what this radio has meant to you," he said. "Your need for communication was served without your having to risk any real intimacy. That is why it became such an obsession. Because you need the communication.

"I think, and I have told the family the same thing, that it's fine for you to enjoy the radio, but you must put it into balance with the rest of your life."

But I didn't enjoy the radio any more. I had seen the radio as a great benevolent spider spinning a shining web over the world at the touch of my fingers. After Dr. Hooper, it became only a perverse instrument of a crazy old man. It gathered dust in my room until my grandson dismantled it for parts.

At last, I'm sleepy. Ah, Cecelia, why did you leave me?

Barbara and Dick are off to work, the children still sleeping. In the garden the lettuce holds the dew in its fluted depths. Last year tiny black insects riddled the leaves with holes. Mr. Miggs suggested planting radishes in their rows "to draw them devils off the lettuce." This year the leaves are unblemished and the little bugs reside, apparently oblivious to the lettuce, on the tough, useless radish leaves.

I kneel, carefully sliding my fingers along the stem of a weed that has grown hidden within the lettuce leaves, then shoved its imprudent head above them. It grows there among the cultivated plants. I place my fingers as close to the ground as possible. Otherwise the stem will break off from the root and the weed will put out another shoot within days. Broken off at the ground, weeds enlarge in the root to return tougher than ever. I must pull up the entire root.

I give a light tug. It remains fixed. I exert more pressure. The root begins to give. Rolling my wrist, I give it a final yank. Too hard. It comes out, the stem broken. You son of a bitch, I'll get you. I thrust my hand into the lettuce, gently pushing the leaves aside, and see the end of the weed. It has broken right at the ground. I dig with my fingers around the shaft, losing a lettuce leaf in the process. All right, now I'm angry. I'm going to get you if I have to stay out here all day. With only my fingertips, I get a sturdy hold and pull. Hah! there you are. That's the end of you.

Inspection, inspection everybody. Corn, you have a goal—knee-high by the Fourth of July. Kale, recovering nicely from an insect attack. And my beauties, the tomatoes, are in flower, yellow blossoms dotting the dark green vines. I have such plans for you at the fair this year.

"Dad?"

I turn. My younger daughter, Charlotte, stands at the edge of the garden. She is the baby and the rebel of the family. I smile in welcome.

"You look so peaceful out here," she says.

Her remark makes me love her very much.

"Hello, dear." I embrace her.

She has been dieting again. Her face is gaunt beneath a deep tan.

"Come on," I say, "I'll get you a cup of coffee."

"No, no, you go on with what you've been doing."

She teases me—the only one of the three who dares to do that. "So what are you doing today, Farmer Brinkman?"

"I'm pea picking. I'm going to freeze them."

She seldom visits when Barbara is here. Their views of the world have been irreconcilable since childhood.

She sees where I'm going to work and sits down at the end of the row. Because the sun has risen in the sky, I roll my shirtsleeves up. The harsh sunlight shines on my arms; the scars on the inside of my wrists are as bright as lightning. Charlotte sees. She winces with an almost impercep-tible shudder.

I'm told that Charlotte was the one who found me, lying on the blood-soaked bed. So much blood, they all agreed, and yet I didn't die.

I wanted to die. There was no fear when I slid the razor painlessly across my wrists—just a relief as though it made no difference whether that red flow emptied onto the crisp white sheets or remained encased in my veins.

I pull my gloves from my pocket, slip them on, adjust them over my wrists. Charlotte and I are relieved.

She talks of a recent trip to Bermuda she has made. I haven't been there in a long time and don't care to go. The pea pods strike the pail with hollow thuds.

Later, in the kitchen, the blancher sends up great clouds of steam. I'm proud to have my daughter know that I'm efficient about the business of preserving food.

Charlotte shells peas, admires their sweet odor, and we make each other laugh. It's a wonderful day.

The grandchildren, Carrie and Mike, straggle sleepily into the kitchen and stay. They too love Charlotte. She makes us all laugh with a story of a drunken man on a plane trying to pick her up. She uses words which make me flinch, and that makes me laugh all the more.

Carrying several plastic bags for her freezer, Charlotte kisses us all and leaves.

At dinner that evening my son, John, drops by. I know Barbara has told him she is worried about me. She and her family are silent as John and I talk.

"So, how're you doing, Dad?" he asks.

"Fine, John. How are you?"

"Oh, I'm fine," he says, with an "of course" just barely unspoken.

"Barbara tells me you're getting pretty hung up on this garden of yours."

"I enjoy it. I wouldn't say I was hung up on it," I answer evenly.

"Hey, you know what I think?" he says as though the idea has just occurred to him. "It would be good for you to get back to work. That's what you need. Will you consider it?" John and I have had this conversation many times.

"No, I will not."

"For God's sake, why not? You're wasting away with nothing to do."

Mike, still warmed, I suppose, by the camaraderie of the morning in the kitchen, says, "Maybe he's tired of being a corporate robber."

"Michael," Dick and Barbara admonish in unison. Mike looks to me for affirmation. I can't meet his eye, nor can I claim his romantic motive. I can't explain to John why I won't return to work – John who loves the family business with all the devotion I imbued in him, loves it just as I did, building from the sturdy foundation my father had laid.

I have no words to tell him how that which had been central to my life had moved so irretrievably to the periphery, how the finely honed heavy machinery parts manufactured there no longer seem to have much to do with me.

John runs the business with a competence I don't question, and I am satisfied.

No, John, no. He leaves defeated by an old man's stubbornness.

Barbara and I are alone at the table. She regards me sharply. "Dad, will you at least think about what John said?"

"I have thought about it. A lot. I'm not going back to work."

"Why not?" Her voice rises.

"Because I don't want to."

"Dad—"

"I don't want to discuss it." I rise from the table and pick up a light jacket.

"I'm going out now," I say, walking toward the door.

"Where?" she demands.

"To visit a friend," I reply shortly, slamming the door behind me.

I walk down the long driveway and turn left toward the shopping center.

If I hurry, I can catch the nine-thirty bus. Mr. Miggs will be riding home from work now. I quicken my pace and am soon at the shopping center. I can see a bus in the distance. It pulls to the curb and picks up the large crowd of people there. My bus comes into view several minutes later. I reach the corner as it stops, step aboard, and drop my money into the coin box as the doors close behind me with a pneumatic sigh.

I look expectantly toward the back of the bus. Mr. Miggs is there. He doesn't sit in the back because he is black, he has assured me, but because that's the best vantage point for watching the other passengers. "You can see everybody without turning your head," he explains. "People don't like it if they think you're watching them."

Mr. Miggs waves and smiles. He is tall and reedlike. He is missing half his upper teeth. The remaining teeth are strong and large. The even division of the missing and existing teeth gives his dignified face a comic aspect. Despite his children's embarrassment he refuses to wear the dentures they have bought for him.

I place my hand on the back of each seat to keep my balance. I sit down next to Mr. Miggs, who welcomes me as always: "Good evening, Mr. Brinkman. How are you tonight?"

Our friendship is contained within the bus. He rides the bus home from work each evening and I catch it at nine-thirty at my stop, riding to the end of the line in the city where he gets off. Then the bus turns around, and I ride home alone. I don't know where Mr. Miggs lives.

Tonight as we ride through the night into the city, we talk of our dead wives. When I leave the bus, I'm pleasantly lost in memories of my college days and meeting Peg.

I met Mr. Miggs two years ago, shortly after the demise of my radio. I was buoyed in my loss by the drug Dr. Hooper prescribed for me. It was a comfortless tranquility. The mild summer evenings hung heavily without the radio and I began to take long walks.

I discovered the new shopping center to be a place of constant activity. I enjoyed strolling there or sitting on a bench watching the crowds.

One night, feeling particularly aimless, I was attracted by the self-contained mobility of the passing buses. I boarded a bus to the city on impulse.

Almost immediately, I regretted it. As I stepped aboard, I was hit by a wave of heavy, still, hot air. The driver intoned in a weary voice, "Air conditioning's broke. Got fans but no cooling."

Unable to think of a graceful retreat, I paid and sat down. There were few people on the bus. Two young boys jostled each other and made faces out the windows. A young woman cradled a small child, tired and irritable in the heat. I was touched by her patience as he squirmed and whined smudging the window with his restless hands. In the rear seat, an elderly black man sat nearly immobile, his eyelids lowered. I might have thought he was dozing off except that the eyes visible below the lids were as alert and sagacious as the hawks' that occasionally perch atop our fence. He divided his attention among the passengers with a judicious liveliness.

I was not, however, too interested in my fellow passengers because the bouncing of the bus and the closeness of the air seemed to collect inside my head. We passed several empty stops. I felt dizzy and nauseous. I leaned forward, resting my head on the back of the next seat. A fuzzy panic grew as I felt more and more faint.

Disoriented and weak, I was only vaguely aware of a hand on my shoulder. "You all right?" The black man's face was blurry as he leaned over me. The nausea had reached my throat. Afraid to speak, I shook my head.

"Driver, driver, open a window. You got a sick man back here," the black man called with authority.

The bus lurched and the driver called irritably, "Windows don't open no more. Goddamned bus is supposed to be air conditioned."

"Well, it ain't. So stop the bus."

The bus came to a halt and the doors swung open. With the first rush of air into the bus, I began to feel better.

"Can you walk?" he asked.

"I think so."

He supported my elbows. I was conscious of the tautness of the muscles in his thin arms.

"We get you out in the air, you perk right up," he said, guiding me toward the door.

The driver shouted, "I can't wait for you. You hear me, you two?"

"Don't worry about us," my new friend called.

"Please," I said, much revived, "I don't want you to miss your bus."

"That's all right. I catch another one. Us old mens has got to stick together."

We found a bench at the nearest bus stop and sat down. We were in a rundown, black neighborhood at the very outskirts of the city.

"I'm very grateful to you," I said, "but I'm fine now. Please take the next bus."

He studied my face with the same keenness I had noticed on the bus. "You better let me call your family come and get you. You awful pale. I don't know if you be all right." We both glanced around the shabby neighborhood surrounding us, and began to laugh.

"You awful pale. You awful pale. Oh my," he chortled.

Serious again, he repeated, "You let me call your family. I wait 'til they come."

The thought of Barbara swooping down in all her frantic concern was chilling.

"Oh no, I can't do that. I can't call my children. They don't even know where I am tonight. They'll just—" I stopped, hearing how foolishly fearful of my children I must sound.

"Yes, children," he said, "can sure be vexatious when you get old. I think they don't ever forget all them times you made them mad when they was little ones. They just been waiting for us to get old and weak. Then they got the upper hand. It funny how it go like that."

"It is funny, isn't it?" I said, delighted by his understanding. "My name is Walter Brinkman," I said, extending my hand.

"Good evening, Mr. Brinkman. I'm Mason Miggs."

And for all of our friendship we have retained this formality. We decided that I should take a cab. With an air of abashment, Mr. Miggs went to a phone booth to call the son with whom he lived, to explain his lateness. "They worry, you know," he said, shrugging. "Then they make a racket." I knew he would lie about his lateness to his son, just as I would lie to Barbara.

As Mr. Miggs and I waited, he mentioned that he rode the same bus every evening. The next night, wishing only to thank him again, I boarded the nine-thirty bus. It surprised me to find that Mr. Miggs and I seemed to have so many things to talk about. His wry humor and enthusiasm were compelling. After that first evening, I have found myself more and more often riding the bus simply to visit with Mr. Miggs. He seemed unconcerned that I ride the bus with no particular destination.

Now, two years later, my family still knows nothing of Mr. Miggs. I tell them I visit Stan Garrity, an old friend whose face I barely remember.

Good, the cabbage is heading. The middle leaves turn inward and press against each other to form the concise heads. How do you know to perform this way? Why not turn outward to create leafy branches like the kale?

I'm going to learn to make sauerkraut this year. There's always more cabbage than we can possibly eat fresh.

The tomatoes cling to the vines like small, green fists. The fruit is well formed, the skin smooth. They are Chesapeake variety, well suited to this soil. It seems as though one plant is producing particularly well. I reach down into the wire hoops that support them to trim the yellow leaves.

It's time for a pep talk, tomatoes. You will represent all of us assembled here at the county fair! You will compete for ribbons. I fully expect to see a blue ribbon laid across the best of you. It's something you should be striving for, going to the fair. Enough said. I have confidence in you.

Last year at the fair, laid on the long tables in the produce exhibits, were squash, green beans heaped on white paper plates, fiery red peppers and waxy green ones, potatoes, pumpkins, pungent onions, precisely rowed ears of corn, fat red tomatoes, and so many more. Some could only boast of size, ostentatious and grotesque. Oh, but the serious competitors—perfection of their kind. This year mine will be there, too.

Yes, I'll start with one entry but in a prestige event: tomatoes, the crown of any garden.

I pace the garden, smiling, snapping my fingers in anticipation.

"Dad?" Barbara so soon? I check my watch. It's early. Puzzled, I go into the house.

"Hi, you're home early," I say.

Barbara purses her lips in exasperation. "Oh Dad, did you forget? The party is tonight."

Uh oh. A weak chuckle. "I'm sorry. It did slip my mind."

"Did you at least check the liquor when it came, as I asked you?"

"Yes, yes, I did do that. All accounted for." I resist an urge to salute. Barbara wouldn't laugh.

"Thanks," she says, kissing me on the cheek. "I'm sorry I barked at you. I feel a little overwhelmed right now."

"Sure. Well, look, let me help."

"Would you? I could really use it."

Barbara organizes well. We work together smoothly with little conversation.

I'm glad to help her, comfortable in her company until she begins to tidy the living room.

She takes a copy of a news magazine and lays it atop a carefully arranged stack of magazines on the coffee table. The magazine is six years old. Inside, there is an article on my business with a picture of me interposed in the column.

I reread it not long ago. It describes me as "dynamic, inexhaustible." It goes on to say that, "at sixty-three, there is no sign of the energetic Walter Brinkman releasing the reins of absolute power he holds at *Brinkman International*."

Barbara has several copies of these magazines. She continues to display them for reasons I refuse to dwell upon.

She often tells Dick when she thinks I don't hear her, "He's just lost his confidence, that's all. In no time at all he'll be wise, wonderful Dad again." She tells him as though Dick needed the reassurance.

Every time she says it, I want to shout at her, just as I want to shout at her now: "That man is dead. What's more, I don't mourn him. He crept out in the blood that stained the bed. There was so little of him left by then. Indeed, he had unraveled to a sad, gray tatter, that man, and left me behind to pay his debts."

But I'm not brave enough to tell my children this late in their lives that I was wrong about so many things; that, as sincere as my certainty was, it served me so poorly when I needed it.

I had wanted to protect them, to arm them, as any parent does. As Peg observed, I was too much the sort of person that I was to have done any differently. Nevertheless, I'm frightened for their vulnerability, frightened that they have shaped their lives around the wisdom of a man who thought the only vanity he need be forgiven was his pleasure in looking well in a dinner jacket.

Barbara starts out of the room, saying over her shoulder, "I invited the Garveys. I thought you'd enjoy seeing them." I wouldn't, but say nothing.

When she is gone, I take the magazine and slip it out of sight.

Later at the party, the magazine has reappeared on the table. I sit, with a smile I'm hoping is friendly and relaxed. My dinner jacket, it seems to me, drapes unevenly across my chest.

Frank Garvey is pushing a conversation along with the rugged determination of loyalty to an old friendship.

"So, when are you going back to work?" he asks.

"I'm not going back."

"Ho well, you've got something going. I know you, Walter. You're the man who said he'd never retire." He is jovial and pokes me in the chest.

Without a trace of compassion, I say, "You're right. No retirement for me, Frank. I've taken up gardening, in fact."

He recovers quickly, "No kidding? You'll be interested in this then. We're having our place landscaped."

Then he pins me to the chair with a lengthy story of the laying of the piping to a new fountain he and his wife have had sent from Italy.

Despite his best efforts, long silences fall. Finally, I allow my chin to drop gradually onto my chest; a reasonable picture of a man caught in a doze. I peer through slitted lids as Frank's back recedes. He's no less relieved than I, I'm sure, to be done with the conversation.

"Dad." Barbara touches my shoulder.

"Oh, I'm sorry." I shake my head. "I must have dropped off."

"Are you tired?"

"Yes. If you don't mind, Barbara, I'll go to bed now. The party can probably get along without me. Everyone seems to be having a good time."

Barbara isn't pleased. "Well, if you feel you simply can't stay awake, go ahead."

I pretend I don't hear the pique in her voice. "Thanks, dear. I'll see you in the morning."

I walk straight through the house and out of the back door.

The air is pleasant. I walk toward the closing shopping center. I look at my watch—nine-twenty. I can catch the bus.

The bus and I arrive at the corner at the same moment. I board and approach Mr. Miggs at the back of the bus. He gestures toward my dinner jacket. "You going to a dance?"

I laugh, unembarrassed. I know Mr. Miggs will relish my escape from the party as much as I do.

"My daughter was giving a party. She insisted I put in an appearance. There didn't seem to be much to say to anyone."

Mr. Miggs nods, smiling. "Yes, yes," he says, "they put you out for looks, just like the cookies.

"Before I had my heart attack, they'd let me drink at their parties. When I used to get to dancing, and they all stand around and say, 'Ain't that something, that old man do them funny dances?' but back of that, they saying, 'That old man a fool. He too old for all of that.' "

"Then if you don't get up and dance, they say, 'Ain't that sad and he used to be so lively.' " We laugh.

"They don't want you to be old, they just want you to act old," he says, "or leastways how they see old before they get there. That's because they don't know about being old."

"No, they don't."

"But that's all right," he says slyly, "because they don't know the bad of it but they don't know the good of it either. Like how you get to loving little things you wouldn't have thought much about when you was a young man."

"Little things like my garden," I add.

"And like my job," he says. "Anyway, getting old going to take them by surprise just like it did you and me."

Mr. Miggs works, although his children don't want him to. They don't like his working because of his heart condition, but they more especially don't like his job. Yet every weekday afternoon he rides out of the city into the suburbs to a house where he was a gardener until the heart attack made him unable to handle the heavy work. Mr. Miggs often speaks of his illness. I never speak of mine.

On his job now, he stays in the kitchen, drinking coffee and reading the paper, until nine, when the man who has hired him comes home from work. The man's wife is afraid to be alone in the house, and she can't find a man who will stay past five. Mr. Miggs says she will call through the kitchen door, "Mason, Mason, what is that noise?" He has only to call back, "That's the dog" or "Only the wind," and she is comforted.

His children, all professionals whom he worked to educate, are ashamed of his job.

It's the having somewhere to go every day that's important enough for him to resist all his children's threats and cajolery. He explains, "The days, they don't just run together, all the same, no more. You know how they can do.

"And as for the children, I give in a lot of times because I'm plain too

107

tired to fight. But everybody know when enough is enough. Then you can't give no ground."

Because the bus is more crowded than usual tonight, Mr. Miggs and I must share the rear seat with three teen-aged girls who comb their hair and giggle. We lower our voices. He asks after the garden as one might inquire after relatives.

Everything is doing well, I tell him, but I'm worried about late blight in the tomatoes. I hate to think of the disfigurement the disease could cause so close to the fair.

He consoles me, "You don't get that unless you got a real wet summer. We ain't had that. They be fine. You listen to me because I know."

He shakes a long finger at me. "You got a good garden. All them things you bring me taste just fine. I don't get no flavor from the things in the grocery stores. Back home when I was a child, my mama always had a garden. When she'd start canning and line all them jars up in the cupboard, why, we thought we was rich." His eyes have a faraway look. "Yes, I always did love a garden and yours is a fine one. I can tell."

"It is, Mr. Miggs," I say. "I wish you could see it. Perhaps you could . . ."

I stop. Buoyed by his compliments, I have nearly invited Mr. Miggs to my house. I shudder, picturing Barbara at the sight of him. He would hear as well as I the warning bells behind her politely impassive face.

I feel a sharp twist of anguish at having hurt my friend. But he says without rancor, "Mr. Brinkman, it might surprise you, but it wouldn't be easy for me to take you home either. You see, they'd all start, 'What that white man want with you?' because they'd never think you and me could be friends. And when you look at it, it is peculiar. So it's all right because I know how it is."

A heaviness settles in me that lingers after we say goodbye. Mr. Miggs forgives what I cannot.

The fair is two weeks away. The garden pulses with a common breath in its full-blown extravagance. The plants enfold the nighttime dampness in their dense depths, releasing it in steady clouds when the morning sun lies in shadowless lengths along the rows. The cabbage heads are tight-skinned and shiny, like bald men. The stems of the string beans stagger beneath the weight of the pods. The cucumber vines greedily creep over every available inch of soil. The cornstalks tower above the rest of the garden, shaking their long, thin leaves like nervous fingers.

I've decided to have a greenhouse built this fall. The winter won't press so heavily this year.

108

A greenhouse! I have plans that I've copied from a library book: glass for the life-giving sunlight, water, and heat. With cold frames outside, I can plant well into December.

In the fall, I'll have a greenhouse. After the fair, when I'm not so busy, I'll call a builder.

The tomatoes are tinged a faint red. They're round, their pulp pressing evenly against the skin. They're prize tomatoes, for certain. Their pungent odor rises in the heat. In untangling several vines, my hand is yellow to the wrist from the fine powder under the leaves. Prize tomatoes, going to the fair.

I make excuses to go out in the evenings. Barbara is anxious. I tell her I visit Stan Garrity. Instead, Mr. Miggs and I ride the bus—he with a protective arm encircling a large bag of canned vegetables I have brought for him, and I exuberant and talkative about the fair.

Barbara is attentive to me. I see the mental picture she does when she regards me. "Out again tonight, Dad?" she asks, her eyes fixed to draw an answer larger than her casual question demands.

I'm careless, too excited by the fair to conceal it. I hear my laugh—a loud, sharp bark that makes her jump. I walk to my garden, rubbing my hands, thinking of the fair. I leave the house without explanation to meet Mr. Miggs, sometimes in defiance, sometimes only because I've forgotten the danger in alarming Barbara.

The sun slants low in the sky. Tomorrow is the fair, and this evening I select the tomatoes I will take.

I stoop in the garden, poking a sure hand through the wide wire hoops around the tomato plants. I carefully pull six from the vine. I chose these six, weeks ago, while they were still green. None is a disappointment. My eye was that sure! How beautiful you are, your symmetry, your uniform color. Six glossy, red globes, the pick of the vines. The jewels of my garden.

I lay them in a small basket beside me, delicately and gently, so as not to bruise them. They're perfect. They're . . .

"Dad." Barbara stands by the garden, her arms folded ominously.

"I ran into Stan Garrity in the supermarket today," she says. "He said he hasn't seen you in years."

"Oh, really? It doesn't seem that long. Old age showing up, I guess."

"Where are you going in the evenings?" she demands.

I stand, staked by the resolution of her stare. "I don't think that at my age I should have to account for my whereabouts," I say in a voice braver than I feel.

"I would agree with you, except for the-the-the trouble you've had. I'm responsible for you and I think you owe me this much just to put my mind at ease."

"Good God, Barbara, I'm not running a diamond-smuggling operation or patronizing the local ladies of the evening."

"You're not going to tell me, are you?" she says and the idea that she expects that I will not tell her crystallizes a decision I hadn't made.

"No."

"I'm sorry to hear that," she says, starting for the house. I feel a pang of fear at the genuine regret in her voice.

That fear pricks at me as I lift the basket. I worry that leaving tonight will antagonize her further, but Mr. Miggs must see the tomatoes that will go to fair. Cradling the basket tenderly under one arm, I walk toward the shopping center to meet the bus.

On the bus, Mr. Miggs examines each tomato with meticulous scrutiny. He pronounces them all as fine as any he's seen. I'm ready for the fair.

I'm awake before first light this morning. I don't rise until I hear the rest of the family. Sleeplessness is a bad sign, Dr. Hooper has told us all.

In the clarity of the early morning, I see the threat of Barbara's anxiety. With the fair nearly here, I'm afraid I've waited too long to mollify her. I lay my plans. The tomatoes wait atop my dresser.

"What are you going to do today?" Barbara asks at breakfast.

"I'd planned to go out for a while. Might play a little golf. I'm rather tired of the garden just now."

Bingo! Right on target. Barbara leans over to kiss me. "Oh, that sounds wonderful. Have a good time."

"I will," I say, chiding myself for considering Barbara so formidable.

Later, I walk the rows of the garden, touching a leaf here and there, and thinking of the fair. I took the tomatoes there this morning to enter them into exhibit for tonight's judging. I placed them in a basket and covered them with a small towel. I've seen people carrying their pets in just such a way. Traveling in the opposite direction that I take with Mr. Miggs, I took a bus ride to the fairgrounds in the next town.

What a place, the fair! So early in the morning and already a large cow was being coaxed and pushed into a stall by two children who barely rose above her flank. A nanny goat bleated in an alarming human wail when her kid was taken from the truck before her. Pigs grunted as they slammed their ponderous bodies against the slats of their pens. Roosters crowed, people shouted, the horses in the vans moved restlessly in the excitement. The rides on the midway sat hunched and silent, great metallic beasts. A wondrous place, the fair.

Although I stayed as long as I dared, I couldn't wait long enough to see the tomatoes put into exhibit. It would be late in the day, I was told, and I've promised myself that Barbara shall have nothing to fault in my behavior. Just as I have my plan, so I know does she: to be sprung into action at the first sign of what she deems craziness.

When she comes home from work, she will find me in the house, reddened from the sun and speaking of a pleasant golf game.

I stay home in the evening and play canasta with Dick and Barbara. She says several times, "Isn't this nice, Dad? Isn't this fun?" I heartily agree each time.

I'm badly beaten in the game because although I didn't see the tomatoes put into exhibit, I know how they must look. The exhibits are all displayed on the starkness of white paper plates. Perhaps the tomatoes reflect a pinkness on the plate from the lights overhead. People walk by the tables, and how the tomatoes must shine. Of the ones I saw brought in, surely none were better than mine.

I don't dwell on the image as I can't appear distracted to Barbara. I'm very tired when I go to bed.

The next day I run some errands for the family. This takes longer than I expect. There is not time to go to the fair without risking being late for dinner. Even with so much to do, time passes with the perversity I remember from waiting for Christmas as a child. By dinner time, the anticipation has compressed into a solid warmth in my chest.

The judging begins at six-thirty. If I leave right after dinner, I'll arrive just in time. The children aren't home for dinner. An extra burden of conversation falls on me. I'm holding my own and Barbara seems relaxed.

Slowly, deliberately, fork to mouth and back to plate; again fork to mouth and back to plate until the plate is empty. I thank Barbara for the meal, then say offhandedly, "I think I'll take a little walk." It's a quarter to six.

Barbara's head snaps up, "Where are you going?" There's a hard edge to her voice that warns me to be very cautious. Dick looks away. This is it.

"I'm going to the shopping center," I say, starting for the door. "I have a few things I want to pick up."

"I'll drive you up."

"I'd rather walk, Barbara."

"No." Her eyes never leave my face.

The bubble of excitement explodes into anger. "You can't keep me here," I shout.

Dick rises and comes toward me. "Now, take it easy, Walter. We think it's best if you stay around the house for awhile, until you get yourself calmed down."

"I was perfectly calm until my daughter began treating me like a ten-year-old."

I take a step toward the door. Dick catches my arm firmly. "Come on, Walter." He is pleading.

"Dad," Barbara says, "you haven't fooled me for one minute in the last few days. This garden has been exactly like the CB."

"It wasn't a CB, goddamnit!" I shout.

"Whatever. I want you to see Dr. Hooper again. In the meantime, I want you to stay home where the people who love you can protect you."

"Protect me from what?" Dick still grips my arms.

"From yourself, for right now. I'm not going to stand by and allow you to slide into—into what we had before."

"This isn't the same thing, I swear to you." I'm seized by desperation at the implacability of her expression.

"Dad, people who have your—problem often don't recognize it themselves."

"I simply won't stand for this," I say. "I'm leaving." The pressure of Dick's hand on my arm increases. He guides me to a chair and presses my shoulder until I sit down.

"Who are you, Dick, Barbara's goon?" My cheeks are hot with humiliation. Dick is embarrassed. "I'm sorry, Walter. I wish it were different."

"Dad, listen please." Barbara sits opposite to me at the table. "I'm going to stay home from work tomorrow. Then you and I will go to see Dr. Hooper. He's told me that we could have an appointment at a moment's notice."

I'm defeated, too uncertain that what they say is untrue. "All right." I rise. "I'm going to my room now, if that's permitted these days."

"Of course, Dad. Listen—" I go to my room.

I sit on the edge of my bed, blank, drained, a crazy, old man, not to be trusted out alone. My eyes scan the room and come to rest on the basket that carried the tomatoes to the fair.

No, by God, they're not going to do this. Mr. Miggs is right. Everybody knows when enough is enough. I pace around the room, hot with rage. Then I hurriedly pick up the phone and dial. It rings so many times. At last, "Hello?"

"Charlotte, Charlotte," I say, "you must help me."

Charlotte laughs in confusion. "Dad, slow down. What is it?"

"I made plans to go out tonight for something very important, and Barbara has refused to allow me out, if you can imagine anything so absurd. She even has Dick acting like some sort of henchman. He was actually muscling me around."

Charlotte is wary. "I can hardly believe that. Why?"

"You know how Barbara is. Because I haven't been to the country club and don't socialize with people she considers acceptable, she thinks I'm off the track again. Once her mind's set, well, you know how she is." I feel only a faint pang of shame for exploiting my daughters' rivalry.

"What do you want me to do?" she asks.

"Come plead my case for me."

"Be right there." She hangs up.

I stand by the window, watching the road in front of the house. Car after car goes by. Charlotte doesn't live far away but it's a long time until she pulls into the driveway. It's seven-thirty.

I leave my room and let her in the back door. "Thanks for coming, honey," I say. Barbara enters the room behind me.

Charlotte is brisk. "What's going on here, Barbara? Dad says you've refused to let him go out. Who in the hell gave you that right?"

Barbara's face reddens. "How dare you come marching in here, telling me what to do about Dad? You see him only when it suits you. You've refused to even listen to anything I've tried to tell you about him. You know nothing about what's been going on around here. If you were here, you'd know he's—he's having trouble again."

"And you're a psychiatrist, I suppose," Charlotte says. "What wild, strange things is he doing?"

Dick appears behind Barbara as she says, "He's obsessed with that garden, Charlotte. He disappears at night until all hours, and won't tell me where he's going."

"I'm home by eleven every night," I say, quietly.

Charlotte laughs. "He gardens and he stays out until eleven. Yes, indeed, Barbara, that's certainly bizarre behavior. I think you're the one that's crazy."

Barbara's voice chokes with rage. "I don't expect you to understand. You weren't even in the country when we had the CB incident a couple of years ago."

"It wasn't a CB," I say, almost to myself.

Charlotte clicks her tongue in disgust, and turns to me. "Come on, Dad. I'll take you where you want to go."

"Oh no, you don't," Barbara screams. "Dick."

113

"Just let them go," Dick says. "This is ridiculous."

Barbara wheels on him. She is utterly betrayed. "Dick, do something. Call the police."

Dick starts toward us, reluctantly. "Charlotte, come on, now. Leave Dad here with us. We'll take care of him."

Charlotte's feet are planted in a combative stance. Her eyes gleam with the joy of the contest. "Stop right there, fucker," she says.

Dick stops as though she has pointed a gun at him. He sputters, "There's no need for that sort of language."

"Oh," shrieks Barbara.

Charlotte turns again to me. "Where do you want to go, Dad?"

"To the fair. To the fair, James," I crow.

She takes my hand and we hurry out to her car. It's a small sports car. The top is down. As we speed up the road, the wind catches our hair and waves it like banners around our heads. I laugh in great hiccoughs of exhilaration. Charlotte is perhaps now a little doubtful, but she drives me to the fairgrounds. She stops at the gate, saying, "I can't stay. Can you get home?" I assure her I can.

"O.K.," she says. "Take care of yourself, will you, or Barbara will have my head on a platter."

"I'm fine, honey."

I walk through the fairgrounds. The sun is setting. Throngs of people walk between the buildings housing the livestock. The animals are quiet here at the end of the day. They have given over the activity to the people. The aroma around the pens, however, attests to their presence.

The rides on the midway scream and thunder, streaking into the darkening sky in garish bolts, then plummeting again toward the ground.

I push through the crowds toward the produce display building. I'm caught again in the celebration of the fair. I think the excitement I feel is a premonition that I won't miss the tomato judging.

Closer, closer. I can see the wide doors propped open and a flow of people issuing through them. It's not over. It can't be. I glance again at my watch. It's 8:35.

I hurry toward the door. I question a man I've seen descend the ramp of the building. "Is the produce judging over?"

"Yes," he says, "they just finished."

Feeling hot tears pressing my eyelids, I retreat into the shadow of the building. These tears are ludicrous, of course. Here I am hiding in the shadows from a crowd of strangers, and weeping. Over what? Six tomatoes!

The tomatoes. The way they looked lying in the basket in the garden; round and perfect. Yes, perfect. I wasn't there for the judging, but then I didn't need to be. The judges saw the tomatoes, turned them over, looked with knowing eyes.

I walk slowly toward the door. I'm afraid now to know, afraid of being wrong in my judgment of the tomatoes. I reach the door and, squaring my shoulders, walk into the vast, harshly lit room. The tomato exhibits are set on a central table. I can see them from the door. There are ribbons laid across some of them. Some are blue ribbons. One in each class of tomato.

When I reach the table, I walk alongside as I imagine a disinterested observer might. I turn over several ribbons in other classes, read the names of the exhibitors: "Tomato-Rutgers—Henry Ames." Henry has taken a second place. "Tomato-Hybrid Red—Lucille Banks." Lucille has taken a blue ribbon.

The Chesapeakes—my class—are set near the end of the table. I hesitate, then turn over the white ribbon, third place. My name isn't there. I turn over the red ribbon, second place, thinking, "Second would be nothing to be ashamed of." My name isn't there.

I inspect the losers. Some I know aren't mine. Their flaws are too obvious. My hand trembles as I reach for the blue ribbon. I turn it over and read, "Tomato-Chesapeake—Walter Brinkman."

Prize tomatoes! My tomatoes! Blue-ribbon tomatoes!

I lay the ribbon down on the plate and touch the tomatoes gently. I feel light, as though my body were no more than air. I smile. I want to laugh out loud, to clap my hands, point out the tomatoes to who ever passes by. Mr. Miggs, I wish that you were here.

Mr. Miggs. I check my watch. I'm only a stop or two above his stop. There's plenty of time to catch his bus. I take a last look at the tomatoes, the ribbon. Tomorrow I'll come with a camera. Goodbye, my beauties.

I walk slowly. I consider going home, but Barbara's enraged face is far too vivid. I stop, stand gazing into the trees at the edge of the fairgrounds. The sun has sunk below the horizon. The sky behind the trees, still softly lit in gold, casts a long shadow behind me.

A strange peace settles over me as the sky fades into gray. I feel whole again, for the first time since Peg's death—not the same, to be sure, but no less than I was before. A man who has raised prize tomatoes must know something, something of great value perhaps. Surely I have something yet to teach my children. I, still with much to learn from the pain that disassembled and rearranged me, am different but not lost.

Oddly, Barbara's anger has lost its threat. The worst she can do is to send me back to Dr. Hooper, and he, after all, doesn't know everything. He wouldn't know a prize tomato if he saw one.

I begin to walk toward the gate. Ah, Barbara, I do love you. With effort, we could be friends, you and I. I believe I have the courage now to try to explain to you some of what has happened to me. I was quite a persuasive man at one time; perhaps I still am. Who knows? You may find you can love me just as well now as before. Ours are primal ties that go far beyond appearances. We'll test those ties, Barbara, I promise.

Yes, I'll ride the bus home, talk to Barbara tonight. But first I have one more thing to do.

My strides feel long and strong. The bus stop is an easy distance away. The bus pulls up just as I reach the curb. I climb aboard and take the seat at the back.

Mr. Miggs will be surprised to see me already on the bus. So much has happened and we have so little time to talk.

The familiar jostling of the bus seems to heighten my exhilaration. I watch the lights glide over the windows as we near Mr. Migg's stop.

Through the window I see him rise from the bench, his back erect. Boarding the bus, he blinks in the glare. As he turns toward the back, he spots me. His half-and-half grin splits his face.

Unable to wait until he sits down, I say as he approaches, "Mr. Miggs, next Saturday you must come to see my garden and stay to dinner afterward. I won't take 'no' for an answer."

He halts, his hand clutching the back of a seat in the rocking aisle of the bus. "Well, I'll be," he says, "then I guess you better call me Mason."

Domestic

Frederick Barthelme

Marie watches her husband from the porch of their bungalow, leaning against the open screen door as he digs in their backyard. The sun is out and warm, although it is fall, and late afternoon. They have been married eight years.

"Albert," she asks, "why are you doing that?" She is not entirely sure what it is that he is doing, but has asked that question already with unsatisfactory result, so she has opted for the question of motive.

"Why?" Albert says. He always repeats her questions.

He has been digging in the yard since eleven that morning, without a break, and his wife has come out of the house to ask him if he would like an early dinner. He straightens and pushes the long-handled spade into the dirt. "Marie, I am doing this because this is what I like, this is something I like, digging this hole. There are too few things in this life that are in and of themselves likable, and for me this is one of them. This is valuable to me and from this I derive pleasure. You might say I enjoy working with my hands, although that isn't the whole thing, not by a long shot." Albert stops to wipe his brow with a dime-store neckerchief, then turns to look at the hole he has dug, to gauge his progress. "Did you have something in mind?" he asks, turning back to his wife.

"Why don't you come have dinner now," Marie says, waving a fly away from her face.

He points to the sky and reaches for his shovel. "Got some light yet," he says. "Best use it."

Marie suddenly feels stupid for having suggested dinner at four o'clock in the afternoon, feels angry, feels that her husband has made a fool of her again, in another one of the small ways that he so often makes a fool

117

of her, and she snaps, "Well, I don't like it, frankly," and goes back inside.

After watching him from the kitchen window for a few minutes, Marie climbs the hardwood stairs and flops on the king-size bed in their bedroom, on her back, her arms outstretched. Even with her arms and legs spread, she is swallowed up in the huge mattress, enveloped by it, unable to touch the edges. She looks straight up at the ceiling and tries to imagine a great battle from the Middle Ages pictured there—horses, and cannon, and armor—but sees instead a lone knight in black mail astride an equally black horse, riding backward, bent over inspecting the rump of the animal. "Oh Lord," she says, and she rolls off the bed and reaches for the telephone. She calls her mother.

"What're you doing, Mama? How are you? I haven't talked to you in such a long time."

"I talked to you Thursday, Peaches. Is something wrong between you and Albert?"

"Mama! You always think that. And don't call me Peaches, please."

"Marie," her mother says, "you didn't call me two thousand miles across this great continent to ask me the time of day in the middle of the afternoon on the long-distance telephone, I know that don't I?"

"Albert is digging in the backyard is why I called," Marie says. "I don't know why—it isn't even Saturday."

"Your father dug, Peaches."

"This is different, Mama. And don't call me Peaches."

"So you called me now when the rates are high to tell me that your husband and the father of your eventual child is in the backyard digging a hole? Is that all you have to say to me? And you want me to believe that nothing is wrong in your marriage?"

Marie looks out the upstairs window at the bent white shoulders of her husband, watches as he hoists a small mound of dirt, gazes at the shovel's attenuated arc. "It's a serious problem, Mama, or I wouldn't have called. You know what happened to Papa."

"That was different, Peaches. Your papa went a little crazy, that's all. I suspect it ran in the family. When he bought the P-38 for the neighborhood kids, when he cut the hole in the roof of the den, remember? There were reasons, there were explanations—Papa was always up to some good. And by the way, have you asked about me yet? How I am and what I'm doing out here all alone on this barren coast? No you have not. Maybe if you had brought that Albert out here last summer like I asked you to I could have straightened him out and you wouldn't have

118

this terrible problem you have right now, which, if I may say, doesn't sound all that terrible from this distance."

"Thank you, Mama," Marie says.

"Don't start with me, young lady," her mother says. "I'm just trying to help. A mother has an investment in a daughter as you might well learn one day if that Albert ever gets his head out of the clouds and gets down to business like a real man."

"I have to go now, Mama," Marie says.

"Of course you do, Peaches. You should've gone before you called, if you get my meaning. And by the way thank you very much I'm getting along fine. Mr. Carleton is coming over this evening and we're going to walk down by the water and maybe take in a movie at the Showcase, if you want to know, just by way of information."

"Mr. Carleton?"

"Yes. And if you want my advice you'll stop your whimpering and get out there with a shovel of your own, if you see what I mean."

Albert and Marie live in a small suburb near Conroe, Texas, and all of their neighbors own powerboats which, during the week, clutter the driveways and front lawns. Albert and Marie do not own a powerboat, although Albert does subscribe to *Boats & Motors*, a monthly magazine devoted largely to powerboating. Marie is small, freckled, delicate, blond. Albert is overweight.

That evening, when he finishes digging and comes inside for dinner, Marie presses the question of the hole. "I can't stand it anymore, Albert," she says. "You took a day off from work and you spent the whole day outside digging a hole. If you don't explain this minute, I will leave you."

He looks at her across the dinner table, fatigue and discomfort on his face in equal measures, then pushes an open hand back over his head, leaving some strands of hair standing straight up in a curious peak. Finally he looks at the pork chop on his dinner plate and says, "I love the work, Marie. I love the product. For many years I have been interested in holes—how many times have I pointed out a hole to you when we drive to the store? A hole for telephone equipment, or for a gas line, or for the foundation of a great building? And, of course, I need the exercise, don't I? Marie, there are many wonderful holes in life—dogs dig holes, as do other animals; pretty women dig small holes on weekend afternoons—can't you understand?"

"I think you're being foolish, Albert," she says, twisting a silver chain around her fingers until the tips of the digits turn purple. Then she unwinds the chain and twists it again, on new fingers. "You may even be silly. Still, you are my husband, and even though you have not provided me with any children, I love you. What are you going to do with this hole when you get it dug?"

Albert's eyes go suddenly very dark, flashing. "Ha!" he says, thrusting himself out of his chair, his arm at full extension, his fork teetering between the tips of his fingers. "You see? *You* are the foolish one! *You* ask stupid questions! And this pork has turned." With that he slaps the fork flat onto the table and rushes upstairs to the bedroom, slamming the door behind him.

Marie sighs deeply and continues the meal alone, chewing and thinking of Albert's fingernails which looked to her like tiny slivers of black moon.

In the morning, after Albert has gone to work at the airline, Marie takes her coffee to the hall table where she sits staring at the telephone for a long time. The hands of the electric clock on the table fly around the clock's face, making a barely audible whir.

An airplane passes overhead, through the clouds.

In the distance there is a siren.

Marie begins to cry, falling forward on the table, her arms folded there and cradling her head. Between sobs she whispers, "I don't want my husband to dig this hole, I don't want my husband to dig this hole. . . ."

The telephone rings. It is her friend Sissy, now a secondary school teacher in Vermont. Marie begins to tell Sissy the story of Albert and the hole, but is unable to make her objection clear, and Sissy responds unsympathetically. Marie is surprised that she isn't clearer about why she is upset by Albert's behavior, and instead of listening to Sissy, she gazes at Albert's university diploma which is framed and mounted above the hall table and wonders why she can't explain herself more clearly.

Finally she says, "I don't know why this upsets me so much, it's silly really." But she has interrupted Sissy's explanation of Albert's behavior, and Sissy insists on finishing the explanation.

"A metaphor," Sissy says, "works in a lot of ways to release the feelings of an individual, opening that individual to expressions which are, for some reason, closed to him. Albert may simply be depressed, and the physical digging is for him a model of the emotional digging that's going on, see what I'm saying? Reflects his disaffection, or something. Maybe he's bored?"

"I see what you mean," Marie says, and she marks another minute gone on the pink pad in front of her, a horizontal stroke crossing four vertical strokes.

"Why don't you dig some too?" Sissy asks. "Seems like that'd be more to the point."

"I've been thinking about that," Marie says.

"Don't think," Sissy says. "Do." Then, her voice rising with relief and new interest, she says, "We're on strike up here, that's why you caught me at home. I know it's terrible for the kids, but business is business, right? Besides, they're probably grateful."

"Strike?"

"Yeah," Sissy says. "We're going to bury the bastards if they don't pay up. There've been promises—it's real complicated, but we're up against the school board and an old jerk named Watkins who'd just as soon see us work for room and board. Anyway, we've been out three weeks and no end in sight. I've got a little money tucked away, so it's all right. Maybe you ought to get a job yourself, give you something to take your mind off old Albert. I mean, you never worked at all after we finished school, did you?"

"I worked in that hospital," Marie says.

"Oh that. That wasn't work, darling, that was recreation. Try getting an office job these days. Maybe you should take a graduate course? Or pottery, pottery's always good."

When Albert returns from work he goes directly into the yard to work on the hole. Marie watches him from the porch for a few minutes, then goes outside and sits in the passenger seat of their Plymouth station wagon, with the door closed, watching her husband. When, after twenty minutes of sustained digging, he stops to rest, she leans out the car window and says, "You're making this to hurt me, aren't you? I know. I know you, Albert."

"Maybe you're right," he says, looking at the hole. "About knowing me, I mean."

He climbs out of the hole and Marie gets out of the car and they walk to the house together, side by side, their arms bumping into each other as they walk. He is thirty-nine years old; she is younger.

"I want to watch television tonight," he says. "And then make love. What do you say?"

"You're not trying to hurt me?"

"No I'm not," he says, and he links arms with her and together they turn to survey the yard.

"But," she says, "then . . . why a hole?"

"It'll be beautiful," he says. "Just wait."

Marie glances at the neighbor's crisp green bushes, then nods tentatively. "It's hard to understand, you know."

They stand for a moment together on the concrete steps of the porch, then go into the house. Albert washes his hands in the kitchen sink while Marie burns the toughest hairs of the chicken they will have for dinner.

"Why can't we refurbish an old house like everybody else?" she asks. "Or refinish furniture together?"

Albert looks at her and grins. "I lied about the television," he says, and he reaches for her with his hands still soapy, staggering across the kitchen Frankenstein fashion.

She glares at Albert as hard as she can, then giggles and runs up the stairs very fast. At the landing she stops and leans over the rail and shouts, "I'm not having a baby, Albert!"

She slams the bedroom door and Albert, who has followed her from the kitchen still acting out his monster role, allows his shoulders to slump, and sighs, and moves on up the stairs. He taps on the bedroom door with a knuckle. "Marie?" he calls through the door.

"What if it rains, Albert?"

"What?"

"My mother doesn't like you," Marie shouts. Then, a little less loudly, "Sissy likes you, but Sissy's ugly."

"What? Who's Sissy?"

"But you can't dig that hole anymore or I will not do anything you want me to do," she says, still shouting as he enters the room.

"What are you talking about?" he asks.

"Promise me that you won't," she says. "Promise it's all over."

"Oh, Jesus," Albert says. "Forget the hole for shit's sake; it's just a hole. Jesus."

"Maybe it's just a hole to you, but it's more to me; it's something I don't want you to do—promise, Albert, please."

Marie is on the bed, her knees up under her chin held tight by her arms. She isn't smiling. Albert stands in the doorway with one hand still on the knob. "I just want to see what's under there," he says.

"You don't mean that," Marie says.

"I'm going downstairs to watch television," Albert says.

Much later, Marie tiptoes down the stairs to see what Albert is doing. He is asleep on the couch in front of the television set, and, seeing him asleep, Marie squats on the stairs and weeps.

The following morning Marie eats a late breakfast alone on the porch, staring at the hole through the screen door. It is a cool day, cooler than yesterday, and she feels the closeness of winter, sees it in the graying sky, smells it in the scent of the morning air. The leaves on the trees seem darker to her, as if mustered for a final battle with the season. Taking a fresh cup of coffee in her striped mug, she goes down the steps into the yard. She walks in circles around the hole there, sipping her coffee and surveying the perimeter of their property—the fragment of an old stone fence, a willow, some low bushes with unremarkable fat leaves. The lot is a little more than half an acre—large, Albert has said, for this particular development.

At first she gives the hole a wide berth, almost ignoring it, but as she completes her third circle, she bears in toward it, stopping a few feet from its edge at a point on its perimeter farthest from the house. The hole, she observes, is about five feet in diameter and four feet deep. The sides are cut at ninety degrees to the horizontal and the bottom of the hole is very flat. Albert's spade is jammed into the spreading pile of dirt that borders the hole on the side away from the driveway. She drops to her knees in the still-damp grass of the lawn and mutters, "Not very prepossessing," then leans forward over the edge of the hole, looking to see what's inside. "Nothing," she says, "just nothing." She tosses the dregs of her coffee into the hole and watches the coal-colored earth turn instantly darker as it absorbs the liquid. "I don't know what Albert is so smug about," she says self-consciously. "Just a damn hole in the ground, for Christ's sake." Marie walks forward on her knees and then pivots her legs over the edge and into the hole. Now she realizes that the hole is a little deeper than she had thought, that it is very nearly five feet deep. Standing in the hole she can barely see over its edge and her coffee mug, which is now only inches from her nose, looms very large. She bends to inspect the wall of the hole and finds there only ordinary dirt and a few small brown worms, working their ways across what is for them a suddenly brighter terrain. Above her the sky is going very dark, and the rain is no longer a suggestion, it is a promise. This makes her excited and nervous at once—like a child, she is seduced by the prospect of passing the rainstorm outside, in the splashing mud of the hole, in the cold of water on her skin; like an adult, she is apprehensive about getting out of the hole, about tracking the mud into the house, about the scrubbing that now seems inevitable. She looks at her hands, then her arms, then her feet and knees—all muddied—and her pink dressing gown, which is marked and smudged in a dozen places. "Oh my," she mutters. "I suppose I'd better not." But she doesn't make an effort to climb out of the hole, and instead sits down abruptly on the bottom, leaning her back against the dirt wall.

The rain comes. Fitfully at first, the few surprisingly large droplets slapping into the hole with what is to Marie a charming music. Then the storm is upon her and suddenly her gown is soaked through, showing darker brown where the cloth is stuck to her skin. Under her legs she feels a puddle beginning to form, then sees it, its surface constantly agitated by the rain. She pops the shallow water with the flat of her hand and the dark splashes stain her gown, and she laughs, and she wipes thick strands of her hair away from her face with a wet palm, laughing and splashing the water all about her, and then she begins to sing, in a very wonderful voice, "The Battle Hymn of the Republic," because it is a song she has always wanted to sing.

Going to the Dogs

Richard Ford

My wife had just gone out West with a groom from the local dog track, and I was waiting around the house for things to clear up, thinking about catching the train to Florida to change my luck. I already had my ticket. It was on the dinette, in my wallet.

It was the day before Thanksgiving, and all week long there had been hunters parked down at the gate: pickups and a couple of old Chevys sitting empty all day — mostly with out-of-state tags — occasionally, two men standing beside their car doors drinking coffee and talking. I hadn't given them any thought. Gainsborough — who I was thinking at that time of stiffing for the rent — had said not to antagonize them and let them hunt unless they shot near the house, and then to call the state police and let them handle it. No one had shot near the house, though I had heard shooting back in the woods and had seen one of the Chevys drive off fast with a deer on top, but I didn't think there would be any trouble.

I wanted to get out before it began to snow and before the electricity bills started coming, and since my wife had sold our car before she left, getting my business settled wasn't easy, and I hadn't had time to pay much attention.

Just after ten o'clock in the morning there was a knock on the front door. Standing out in the frozen grass were two fat women with a dead deer.

"Where's Gainsborough?" the one fat woman said. They were both dressed like hunters: one had on a red plaid lumberjack's jacket and the other a greenish camouflage suite. Both of them had the little orange cushions that hang from your back belt loops and get hot when you sit on them. Both of them had guns.

125

"He's not here," I said. "He's gone back to England. Some trouble with the government. I don't know about it."

Both fat women were staring at me as if they were trying to get me in better focus. They had green and black camouflage paste on their faces and looked like they had something on their minds. I still had on my bathrobe.

"We wanted to give Gainsborough a deer steak," the one who had spoken first said and turned and looked at the dead deer, whose tongue was out the side of his mouth and whose eyes looked like a stuffed deer's eyes. "He lets us hunt and we wanted to thank him in that way," she said.

"You could give me a deer steak," I said. "I could keep it for him."

"I suppose we could do that," the one who was doing all the talking said. But the other one, who was wearing the camouflage suit, gave her a look that said she knew Gainsborough would never see the steak if it got in my hands.

"Why don't you come in," I said. "I'll make some coffee and you can warm up."

"We *are* pretty cold," the one in the lumberjack's jacket said and patted her hands together. "If Phyllis wouldn't mind."

Phyllis said she didn't mind at all, though it was clear that accepting an invitation to have coffee had nothing to do with giving away a deer steak.

"Phyllis is the one who actually brought him down," the pleasant fat woman said when they had their coffees and were holding their mugs cupped between their fat hands, sitting on the davenport. She said her name was Bonny and that they were from across the state line. They were big women in their forties with fat faces, and their clothes made them look like all their parts were sized too big. Both of them were jolly, though—even Phyllis when she forgot about the deer steaks and got some color back in her fat cheeks. They seemed to fill up the house and make it feel jolly. "He ran sixty yards after she hit him and went down when he jumped the fence," Bonny said authoritatively. "It was a heart shot, and sometimes those take time to have effect."

"Ran like a scalded dog," Phyllis said, "and dropped like a load of shit." Phyllis had short blond hair and a hard mouth that seemed to want to say hard things.

"We saw a wounded doe, too," Bonny said and looked aggravated about it. "That really makes you mad."

"The man may have tracked it, though," I said. "It may have been a mistake. You can't tell about those things."

126

"That's true enough," Bonny said and looked at Phyllis hopefully, but Phyllis didn't look up. I tried to imagine the two of them dragging a dead deer out of the woods and it was easy.

I went out to the kitchen to get a honey pull-apart I had put in the oven, and they were whispering to each other when I came back in. The whispering, though, seemed good-natured, and I gave them the honey pull-apart without mentioning it. I was happy they were here. My wife is a slender, petite woman who bought all her clothes in the children's sections of department stores and said they were the best clothes you could buy because they were made for hard wearing. But she didn't have much presence in the house; there just wasn't enough of her to occupy the space — not that the house was so big, in fact it was very small — a prefab Gainsborough had had pulled in on a trailer. But these women seemed to fill up everything and to make it seem like Thanksgiving was already here. Being that big never seemed to have a good side before. But now it did.

"Do you ever go to the dogs?" Phyllis asked with part of her pull-apart in her mouth and part floating in her mug.

"I do," I said. "How did you know?"

"Phyllis says she thinks she's seen you at the dogs a few times," Bonny said and smiled.

"I just bet the quinellas," Phyllis said. "But Bon will bet anything, won't you, Bon? Trifectas, daily doubles, anything at all. She doesn't care."

"I sure will," Bon said and smiled again and moved her orange hot-seat cushion from under her seat so that it was on top of the davenport arm. "Phyllis said she thought she saw you with a woman there once, a little, tiny woman who was pretty."

"Could be," I said.

"Who was she?" Phyllis said gruffly.

"My wife," I said.

"Is she here now?" Bon asked, looking pleasantly around the room as if someone were hiding behind a chair.

"No," I said. "She's on a trip. She's gone out West."

"What happened?" said Phyllis in an unfriendly way. "Did you blow all your money on the dogs and have her bolt off?"

"No." I didn't like Phyllis nearly as well as Bon, though in a way Phyllis seemed more reliable if it ever came to that, and I didn't think it ever could. But I didn't like it that Phyllis knew so much, even if the particulars were not right on the money. We had, my wife and I, moved up from the city. I had some ideas about selling advertising for the dog track

127

in the local restaurants and gas stations and arranging coupon discounts for evenings out at the dogs that would make everybody some money. I had spent a lot of time, used up my capital. And now I had a basement full of coupon boxes that nobody wanted, and they weren't paid for. My wife came in laughing one day and said my ideas wouldn't make a Coke fizz in Denver, and the next day she left in the car and didn't come back. Later a fellow had called to ask if I had the service records on the car—which I didn't—and that's how I knew it was sold, and who she'd left with.

Phyllis took a little plastic flask out from under her camouflage coat, unscrewed the top, and handed it across the coffee table to me. It was early in the day, but I thought what the hell. Thanksgiving was the next day. I was alone and about to jump the lease on Gainsborough. It wouldn't make any difference.

"This place is a mess," Phyllis said and took back the flask and looked at how much I'd had of it. "It looks like an animal starved in here."

"It needs a woman's touch," Bon said and winked at me. She was not bad-looking, even though she was a little heavy. The camouflage paste on her face made her look a little like a clown, but you could tell she had a nice face.

"I'm just about to leave," I said and reached for the flask, but Phyllis put it back in her hunting jacket. "I'm just getting things organized back in the back."

"Do you have a car?" Phyllis asked.

"I'm getting antifreeze put in it," I said. "It's down at the BP. It's a blue Camaro. You probably passed it. Are you girls married?" I asked. I was happy to steer away from my troubles.

Bon and Phyllis exchanged a look of annoyance, and it disappointed me. I was disappointed to see any kind of displeasure cloud up on Bon's nice, round features.

"We're married to a couple of rubber-band salesmen down in Petersburg. That's across the state line," Phyllis said. "A real pair of monkeys, if you know what I mean."

I tried to imagine Bonny's and Phyllis's husbands. I pictured two skinny men wearing nylon jackets, shaking hands in the dark parking lot of a shopping mall in front of a bowling-alley bar. I couldn't imagine anything else. "What do you think about Gainsborough?" Phyllis asked. Bon was just smiling at me now.

"I don't know him very well," I said. "He told me he was a direct descendant of the English painter. But I don't believe it."

"Neither do I," said Bonny and gave me another wink.

"He's farting through silk," Phyllis said.

"He has two children who come snooping around here sometimes," I said. "One's a dancer in the city. And one's a computer repairman. I think they want to get in the house and live in it. But I've got the lease."

"Are you going to stiff him?" Phyllis said.

"No," I said. "I wouldn't do that. He's been fair to me, even if he lies sometimes."

"He's farting through silk," Phyllis said. "Just like Commander McCann."

Phyllis and Bonny gave each other a knowing look. Out the little picture window I saw it had begun to snow, just a mist, but unmistakable.

"You act to me like you could use a good snuggle," Bon said, and she broke a big smile at me so I could see her teeth. They were all there and white and small. Phyllis looked at Bonny without any expression, as if she'd heard the words before. "What do you think about that?" Bonny said and sat forward over her big knees.

At first I didn't know what to think about it. And then I thought it sounded pretty good, even if Bonny was a little heavy. I told her it sounded all right with me.

"I don't even know your name," Bonny said and stood up and looked around the sad, little room for the door to the back.

"Henderson," I lied. "Lloyd Henderson is my name. I've lived here six months." I stood up.

"I don't like Lloyd," Bonny said and looked at me up and down now that I was up, in my bathrobe. "I think I'll call you Curly, because you've got curly hair. As curly as a Negro's," she said and laughed so that she shook under her clothes.

"You can call me anything you want," I said, and felt good.

"If you two are going into the other room, I think I'm going to clean some things up around here," Phyllis said. She let her big hand fall on the davenport arm as if she thought dust would puff out. "You don't care if I do that, do you, Lloyd?"

"Curly," said Bonny, "say Curly."

"No, I certainly don't," I said and looked out the window at the snow as it began to sift over the field down the hill. It looked like a Christmas card.

"Then don't mind a little noise," she said and began collecting the cups and plates on the coffee table.

Without her clothes on Bonny wasn't all that bad-looking. It was just as though there were a lot of heavy layers of her, but at the middle of all

129

those layers you knew she was generous and loving and nice as anybody you'd ever meet. She was just fat, though probably not as fat as Phyllis if you'd put them side by side.

There were a lot of clothes on my bed and I put them all on the floor, but when Bon sat on the cover she sat on a metal tie tack and some pieces of loose change and she yelled and laughed, and we both laughed. I felt good.

"This is what we always hope we'll find out in the woods," Bonny said and giggled. "Somebody like you."

"Same here," I said. It wasn't at all bad to touch her, just soft everywhere. I've often thought that fat women might be better because they don't get to do it so much and have more time to sit around and think about it and get ready to do it right.

"Do you know a lot of funny stories about fatties?" Bonny said.

"A few," I said. "I used to know a lot more, though." I could hear Phyllis out in the kitchen, running water and shuffling dishes around in the sink.

"My favorite is the one about driving the truck," Bonny said.

I didn't know that one. "I don't know that one," I said.

"You don't know the one about driving the truck?" she said, surprised and astonished.

"I'm sorry," I said.

"Maybe I'll tell you sometime, Curly," she said. "You'd get a big kick out of it."

I thought about the two men in nylon jackets shaking hands in the dark parking lot, and I decided they wouldn't care if I was doing it to Bonny or to Phyllis, or if they did they wouldn't find out until I was in Florida and had a car. And then Gainsborough could explain it to them, along with why he hadn't gotten his rent or his utilities. And maybe they'd rough him up before they went home.

"You're a nice-looking man," Bonny said. "A lot of men are fat, but you're not. You've got arms like a wheelchair athlete."

I liked that. It made me feel good. It made me feel reckless, as if I had killed a deer myself and had a lot of ideas to show to the world.

"I broke one dish," Phyllis said when Bonny and I were back in the living room. "You probably heard me break it. I found some Magic Glue in the drawer though, and it's better than ever now. Gainsborough'll never know."

While we were gone, Phyllis had cleaned up almost everything and put away all the dishes.

130

She had on her camouflage coat now and looked like she was ready to leave. We were all standing in the little living room, filling it, it seemed to me, right up to the walls. I had on my bathrobe and felt like asking them to stay over. I felt like I could grow to like Phyllis better in a matter of time, and maybe we could eat some of the deer for Thanksgiving. Outside, snow was all over everything. It was too early for snow. It felt like the beginning of a bad winter.

"Can't I get you girls to stay over tonight?" I said and smiled hopefully.

"No can do, Curly," Phyllis said. They were at the door. Through the three glass portals, I could see the buck lying outside in the grass with snow melting in his insides. Bonny and Phyllis had their guns back over their shoulders. Bonny seemed genuinely sorry to be leaving.

"You should see his arms," she was saying and gave me a wink. She had on her lumberjack's jacket again and her orange cushion was fastened to her belt loops. "He doesn't look strong. But he is strong. Oh my God! You should see his arms," she said.

I stood in the door and watched them. They had the deer by the horns and were pulling him off down the road toward their car.

"You be careful, Lloyd," Phyllis said. Bonny smiled over her shoulder.

"I certainly will," I said. "You can count on me."

I closed the door.

I stood in the little picture window and watched them walk down the road to the fence, sledding the deer through the snow, making a swath behind them. I watched them laugh when they stood by the car, watched them drag the deer under Gainsborough's fence and haul it up into the trunk and tie down the lid with string. The deer's head stuck out the crack to pass inspection. Then they stood up and looked at me in the window and waved, each of them, big wide waves. Phyllis in her camouflage and Bonny in her lumberjack's jacket. And I waved back from inside. Then they got in their car, a new blue Pontiac, and drove away.

I stayed around in the living room most of the afternoon, wishing I had a TV, watching it snow, and being glad that Phyllis had cleaned up everything so that when I cleared out I wouldn't have to do that myself. I thought about how much I would've liked one of those deer steaks.

It began to seem after a while like a wonderful idea to leave, just call a town cab, take it all the way in to the train station, get on for Florida, and forget about everything, about Tina on her way to Phoenix with a guy who only knew about greyhounds and nothing else.

But when I went to the dinette to have a look at my ticket in my wallet, there was nothing on the dinette but some change and some matches, and I realized it was only the beginning of bad luck.

Prayer for the Dying

Willis Johnson

The day Yakov Kaputin died he managed to make the nurse understand that he wanted to see Father Alexey. Yakov had lived in America for thirty years but he did not speak English. He scribbled a faint, wiggly number on the paper napkin on his lunch tray and pointed a long knobby finger back and forth between the napkin and his bony chest. "You want me to call, do you dear?" the nurse asked in a loud voice that made Yakov's ears ring. Yakov could not understand what she said but he nodded, "*Da.*"

When the telephone rang Father Alexey was just dozing off. It was July. Crickets were chirring in the long dry grass outside his window. The priest was lying in his underwear listening to a record of Broadway show tunes on the new stereo his mother had bought him. His long beard was spread out like a little blanket on his chest. The window shade was down and a fan was softly whirring.

He thought it was the alarm clock that rang and tried to turn it off.

"Mr. Kaputin wants you to come to the hospital," the nurse said with finality, as if announcing some binding decision from above.

He did not know how long he had slept. He felt shaky and unfocused.

"I can't," he said.

"Is this the Russian priest?"

"This is Father Alexey." His voice seemed to echo far away from him. "I'm busy just now."

"Well, we're all busy, dear," the nurse said. She paused as if waiting for him to see the truth in that and do the right thing.

"What is it this time?" Father Alexey said with a sigh.

"I just came from him," the nurse began to converse chattily. ("That's better now," her tone seemed to say.) "He's a real sweetheart. He wrote your number down. He didn't touch his lunch, or his breakfast. I don't think he feels well. Of course we can't understand a word he says, and he can't understand us . . ."

"He never feels well," Father Alexey said irritably. "You usually do not feel well when you have cancer."

"Well," the nurse said indignantly. "I've called. I've done my duty. If you don't want to come . . ."

Father Alexey sighed another large sigh into the receiver. He hated the hospital. He hated the way it smelled, the way grown men looked in little johnny coats, the way Yakov's bones were all pointed. Besides that, it was very hot out. During the entire morning service not even the hint of a breeze had come in the door of his little church. In the middle of a prayer he had thought he might faint. He had had to go into the Holy of Holies and sit down.

"It's not a matter of 'not wanting,'" he said pointedly. "I'll have to adjust my schedule, and that's not always easy. I don't know when I can be there. I have to try to find a ride."

He lay for a while longer with the fan blowing on him, his hands clasped on his soft white stomach. The sheet under him was clean and cool. He looked tragically at the window shade. It was lit up like a paper lantern.

Father Alexey lived next to the church in an old house with a cupola, fancy molding and derelict little balconies. A rusty iron fence tottered around the unmowed yard. Once every seven or eight years one or two sides of the house got a coat of paint. The different shades of paint and the balusters missing from the little balconies gave the house a patched, toothless look. On rainy days water dripped down the wall next to Father Alexey's bed. He complained to Mr. Palchinsky, the president of the Union of True Russians, which owned the house. Mr. Palchinsky got the Union to provide each room with a plastic bucket. Father Alexey would have tried to fix the roof himself but he did not know how to do it. Yakov said he knew how to do it but he was too old to climb a ladder and besides they did not have a ladder.

Yakov's room was next to Father Alexey's. Each night after the old man said his prayers he would say good night to the priest through the wall.

Father Alexey did not always answer. Yakov was a nice man but he could be a pain. He was always talking, telling stories about himself. Yakov in the forest, Yakov in the Civil War, Yakov in the labor camp, Yakov tending flower beds for some big shot in White Plains. Father Alexey knew them all. And whenever he made an observation with which Yakov did not agree, Yakov would say, "You're young yet. Wait a while. When you're older, you'll see things more clearly."

The priest knew it was one of the things people in town said about him: he was young. He tried to look older by wearing wire-rimmed glasses. He was balding, and that helped. Not that it was a bad thing to say, that he was young. If people really wanted to be disparaging—as when the Anikanov family got mad at him because he forgot to offer them the cross to kiss at their mother's memorial service—they went around reminding their neighbors that he was not Russian at all but an American from Teaneck; if they knew about his mother being Polish they called him a Pole; they brought up the fact that he once had been a Catholic. If they wanted to truly drag his name through the mud, they called him a liberal, even though he almost always voted Republican.

Yakov had been in the hospital before, once when he had his hernia and once for hemorrhoids. This time, even before they knew it was cancer, he sensed he wouldn't be coming home. He was, after all, almost ninety years old. He carefully packed his worn suit, the photographs of his wife, his Army medal, some old books that looked as if they had been rained on, into cardboard boxes which he labeled and stacked in his room. He left an envelope with some money with Father Alexey and also his watering pail for his geraniums. When the car came he didn't want to go. Suddenly he was afraid. Father Alexey had to sit with him in his room, assuring him it was all right, he was going to get well. He carried Yakov's suitcase out to the car. Yakov was shaking. When Father Alexey waved goodbye the old man started to cry.

The hospital was in the city, fifteen miles away. Once a week the senior citizens' bus took people from the town to the shopping center, which was only a mile from the hospital, and you could get a ride if there was room. But if you did not have a car and it was not Thursday, you had to call Mikhail Krenko, the dissident. He had a little business on the side driving people to the city for their errands.

Krenko worked nights on the trucks that collected flocks from the chicken barns. He had arrived in town one day after jumping off a Soviet trawler. It was said that he offered a traffic policeman two fresh codfish in exchange for political asylum. People suspected he was a spy. They were almost certain he had Jewish blood. Why else, they asked each other, would the Soviets have given him up so easily? Why had he come to live in a godforsaken town that did not even have a shopping center?

Krenko was a short man with limp yellow hair and a round face like a girl. He chewed gum to cover the smell of his liquor, sauntered with his hands in his pockets and did not remove his hat upon entering a house, even with an ikon staring him in the face. In the churchyard one Sunday people overheard him call Mr. Palchinsky *Papashka*—"Pops." Anna Kirillovna Nikulin told of the time she rode to the city with him and he addressed her as Nikulina—not even *Mrs.* "Here you are, Nikulina," he said, "the drugstore."

Some female—an American; young, by the sound of her—answered when Father Alexey dialed his number.

"He's in the can," she said.

"Well, would you call him please?" he said impatiently.

"O.K., O.K., don't have a kitten."

She yelled to Krenko. "I don't know—some guy having a kitten," she said.

When Krenko came on the telephone, the priest said as sarcastically as he could, "This is Father Alexey—the 'guy' from your church."

"Hey, you catch me hell of time, with pants down."

"I called you," Father Alexey replied stiffly, "because one of my parishioners happens to be very ill."

He hung his communion kit around his neck and went to wait for Krenko in the sparse shade of the elm tree in front of the house. Only a few branches on the old tree still had leaves. In some places big pieces of bark had come off. The wood underneath was as dry and white as bone.

Across the street was the town's funeral home. Sprays of water from a sprinkler and a couple of hoses fell over the trim green grass and on the flowers along the walk. Father Alexey held his valise with his holy vestments in one hand and in the other his prayer book, a black ribbon at the prayers for the sick. He could feel the sweat already running down his sides.

He thought how it would be to strip off his long hot clothes and run under the spray, back and forth. He saw himself jumping over the flowers. He could feel the wet grass between his toes. Setting down his valise, he took off his hat and wiped his face and bald head with his handkerchief. He fluttered the handkerchief in the air. In a minute it was dry.

Then from behind him a window opened and he heard Mrs. Florenskaya call. He pretended not to hear. He did not turn around until the third time.

"Oh, hello, Lidiya Andreyevna," he said, holding the bright sun behind his hand.

"Somewhere going, *batiushka?* the old woman asked in her crackly voice.

"Yes," the priest said reluctantly.

"Good," Mrs. Florenskaya said. *"Ich komme."*

The Union of True Russians had bought the house as a retirement home (it had been a fine, sturdy house, the home of a sea captain; the church next door had been the stable for his carriage horses) and at one time all the rooms and flats had been occupied. Everyone was gone now, dead or moved away—mostly dead. The whole parish had grown older all at once, it seemed. Now with Yakov in the hospital, Father Alexey was alone in the old house with Mrs. Florenskaya. Every day she shuffled up and down the empty, echoing hallway in her worn slippers and Father Alexey would hear her crying. In nice weather she cried out on the porch. The first time he heard her—it was shortly after he had arrived to take over the parish a year ago (his predecessor, Father Dmitri, had started to drink and was transferred back to New York)—Father Alexey had run upstairs to see what was wrong. Mrs. Florenskaya listened to his beginner's Russian with a happy expression on her face, as if he were trying to entertain her. Then she had replied in a mixture of English and German, although he didn't know any German, that a bandit was stealing spoons from her drawer.

He no longer asked.

After a minute the front door opened and the little woman came spryly down the stairs carrying a cane which she did not seem to need. A paper shopping bag and an old brown purse hung from one arm. She was wearing a kerchief and a winter coat.

"Where going *Sie*, little father?" She came into the shade and smiled up at him.

When he told her about Yakov, she sighed heavily. "Old people just closing eyes," she said. Her chin started to wobble.

"Aren't you hot in that coat, Lidiya Andreyevna?" he asked.

She pulled a wadded tissue out of her pocket. *"Sie* young man, *Sie* can *arbeiten.* I am old." She wiped her nose, then lifted her chin in the air. "I *arbeiten* in Chicago," she said proudly. "In fine hotel."

Father Alexey looked down the empty street.

"He's late," he said.

"Ja," the old woman said emphatically, as if he had confirmed all she had said. "Many *zimmer* taken care of; wash, clean, making beds."

A short distance from where they stood the road dropped steeply to the river. Father Alexey could see the far bank and the dark pines of the forest beyond. The sky was blue and still. The leaves were motionless on the trees, as if they were resting in the heat. Above the brow of the hill, Father Alexey saw two heads appear then slowly rise like two plants pushing up into the sun. The heads were followed by two bodies, one long, one square. They came up over the hill and came slowly in the heat toward the priest and Mrs. Florenskaya. They were dressed for the city, the woman in a dress with flowers, the man in a suit and tie. The woman was the long one. The man was sheer and square like a block of stone. As they drew near, the man took the woman's arm in his thick hand and stopped her short of the shade. They looked back down the street. The man checked his watch.

Bending around the priest, Mrs. Florenskaya peered at them with curiosity.

"Good heavens," she said at last in Russian, "why are you standing in the sun? Come here, dearies, with us."

The man gave them half a smile. "It's all right," he said as if embarrassed. But the woman came right over.

"Thank you," she said as if the shade belonged to them. "That hill! We had to stop four times. Stepanka, come join these nice people." She took him by the arm. "Now that's much better—no?"

Father Alexey introduced himself and said in Russian that the weather was very hot.

"Fedorenko," the man said but he did not offer his hand. He added in English: "My wife."

"*Ach, Sie sprechen Englisch!*" Mrs. Florenskaya said delightedly. "I, too!"

From time to time Father Alexey ran into them in the market or on the street. The man was Ukrainian, the woman Byelorussian. The woman would always smile. Once in a while the man nodded stiffly. On Sundays Father Alexey would see them pass by on their way to the Ukrainian church.

"Are you waiting for someone?" the man's wife asked, continuing the English. "We're supposed to meet Mr. Krenko here."

"He was supposed to be here ten minutes ago," the priest said.

"We're going to do a little shopping," the woman informed them. "Stepan's not allowed to drive. It's his eyes. They wouldn't renew his license. We're going to get some glasses for him. He doesn't want them. He thinks they'll make him look old."

"Not old," her husband said sharply. "Don't need it. What for spend money when don't need it?"

"You see?" she said hopelessly.

As they waited the sun grew hotter. They inched closer together under the tree. They could see the heat coming up from the road and

137

from the black shingles of the roofs that showed above the hill. Mrs. Fedorenko fanned her face. Mrs. Florenskaya unbuttoned her coat. They stared longingly at the glistening spray of water across the way. There was a rainbow in the spray and the water glistened on the green grass and on the flowers and on the lawn sign on which the undertakers had painted in gold an Orthodox cross beside the regular Christian one.

Finally they heard an engine straining. Up over the hill through the waves of heat came Krenko's car. It was a big car, several years old, all fenders and chrome. Upon reaching level ground it seemed to sigh. It came up to them panting.

Krenko pushed open the front door.

"You're late," Father Alexey told him. With a look of distaste, he set his valise with his holy vestments on Krenko's zebra-skin seat. Mr. and Mrs. Fedorenko climbed into the back, followed by Mrs. Florenskaya, who nudged Mr. Fedorenko into the middle with her bony hip.

"Where is she going?" Krenko said.

"Ask her," the priest shrugged.

"Never mind," Mrs. Florenskaya said.

"Not free, you know. Cost you money."

"Ja. Everything all time is money."

"Ten dollars," Krenko said.

"Ja, ja."

"You have?"

Mrs. Florenskaya took a rag of a bill out of her pocketbook and waved it angrily under Krenko's nose. She put it back and snapped her purse. "Everything is money," she said. Tears suddenly rolled out from under her eyeglasses.

"Crazy old woman," Krenko muttered.

"May we go?" Father Alexey said.

They drove around the block onto the main street of the town. On the street was the market, the bank, the hardware store, the laundromat, the boarding house where old people who did not belong to the Union of True Russians lived, and a variety store where they sold pizzas. Part way down the hill Krenko stopped and blew the horn.

"Another passenger, I presume?" Father Alexey said.

"Make it when sun is shining," Krenko winked.

From a door marked "Private" stepped Marietta Valentinova, the famous ballerina who lived over the hardware store. A white cap with green plastic visor kept the sun from her small severe face. Krenko got out and opened the front door, giving her a mock bow, which she ignored.

She had been at the St. Vladimir's Day service that morning at Father Alexey's church. Several members of the parish were named Vladimir, so there had been a good attendance in spite of the heat, more than a dozen. St. Olga's Day a few days earlier had not been nearly so successful, but then there was only one Olga in town, and she was sick and couldn't come. Marietta Valentinova had stood in her usual place in the center, where she was in range of any idle chatter, which she would silence at once with a scalding look. She also kept an eye on the ikon candles. She did not like to let them burn down more than halfway, and all during the service she was blowing them out and removing them from their holders. People who had lit the candles complained about it to each other but none dared say anything to her. On Sundays or saints' days, it didn't matter, she put a dollar in the basket. No one had ever seen her take back change. But she was very severe.

"Good afternoon, Marietta Valentinova," Father Alexey said. "*Ya yedu v gospital.*"

The ballerina glanced at his valise. One corner of her small red mouth lifted slightly. "I thought you have been looking thin," she teased him in English. "That's the trouble with being monk: no wife to feed you."

"It's Yakov Osipovich," he said, reddening.

"Well," she said, "shall you move over or must I stand in sun all day?"

"Maybe you get in first, lady," Krenko said. "With such little legs you fit better in middle."

"I will thank you to pay attention to your own legs. And also your manner. Who do you think you are, blowing that horn?"

"Like joking with her," Krenko winked when the priest got out to let the ballerina in.

"How about the air conditioning?" Father Alexey said when Krenko got back behind the wheel.

"O.K. First got to put up all windows," Krenko said. Then he turned a switch. Air blew out from under the dashboard.

"I think that's the heat," said Father Alexey.

"Is O.K.," Krenko said. "Got to cool up."

They drove to the bottom of the hill and turned up along the river. The water lay flat and colorless between banks of colorless clay. Soon they were in the woods. The road ran over the tops of hills and down to streambeds filled with rocks. The undergrowth was dense and tangled and they could not see the river. They passed a farmhouse with a barn home squatted like a gypsy, its children and its trash strewn round the yard.

The air was blowing out, but the car was stifling. They were squeezed together, Father Alexey with his valise on his lap. Marietta Valentinova smelled Krenko sweating. She moved a fraction closer to the priest, who had pulled out his handkerchief and was wiping his face.

"If I don't get some air, I am going to faint," Marietta Valentinova said.

Krenko moved the switch another notch. The hot air blew out harder.

"Sometimes takes couple minutes," he said.

"In a couple of minutes we will be cooked," the ballerina said. "Can't you see I'm dying?"

"Hold it!" Krenko said. He felt under the dashboard. "Now is coming."

Father Alexey wiggled his small white fingers in the air blowing on his knees. It was still hot.

"*Now* is coming," Krenko said confidently.

"Open a window," the ballerina commanded.

"You going to let air condition out . . ."

"Did you hear me?" she said in a voice so severe that everyone at once rolled down his window.

"Thank God," said the priest as the hot wind blew in on them. They put their hands out into it, groping for a current of coolness.

After a while Mrs. Fedorenko said, "It was very hot in New Jersey, too. That's where we lived."

"Hot like hell," Krenko agreed, although he had never been to New Jersey. "Here is not hot."

"I am very glad to hear that this is not hot," the ballerina said. She held a hanky over her mouth as they passed a chicken barn.

"More hot in California," Mr. Fedorenko said. "I been all over United States. Many Ukrainian people live in California. Many Russian, too," he added for the benefit of the ballerina who had cocked her ear toward him, showing him her profile, the raised eyebrow. "And many Ukrainian. Not same thing."

"Do tell us about it," the ballerina said haughtily. To Marietta Valentinova there was no such thing as a Ukrainian. That was modern nationalist nonsense. What was the Ukraine?—*Malorossiya*, Little Russia. They were all Russians.

"You are from New Jersey, *batiushka?*" Mrs. Fedorenko asked to change the subject.

140

"Yes. It is very hot in New Jersey. I haven't been to California."

"I in Chicago *arbeiten*," Mrs. Florenskaya said.

"You were saying something about the *malorossy*, I believe?" the ballerina said.

"Not Little Russians, lady. Ukrainian."

"All right, Stepanka. Did you hear? *Batiushka* also lived in New Jersey."

Mr. Fedorenko folded his heavy arms. "Don't call us *malorossy*."

"I don't call you anything," the ballerina smiled coldly.

"No?" Mr. Fedorenko pushed forward his big chin. "What are you calling ten million Ukrainians? The ones Russia starved?"

"If you are speaking of the Soviet Union, I'll thank you not to call it Russia," the ballerina said. "I even hate to say that word—*soviet*."

"O.K.," Krenko said, "long time ago—O.K.?"

"I have a question," Father Alexey said.

"You too," said Mr. Fedorenko accusingly. His face was very red.

"Me too, what?"

"Stepanka," Mrs. Fedorenko implored.

"I see you Four July parade. See you turn away when Ukrainian club marching. You don't remember, huh?"

"I didn't turn away."

"I wouldn't blame you if you did," the ballerina said. "I certainly would."

"I didn't."

"That's enough, Stepanka."

"Maybe I just looked somewhere else," the priest said. "There is a big difference between looking somewhere else at a given moment and turning away."

"Of course there is," Mrs. Fedorenko assured him.

"I know how is seeing," her husband said.

"All right, Stepanka. What were you going to ask before, *batiushka*? You had a question."

"I don't know," the priest said dejectedly. After a moment he said, "I guess I was going to ask why everyone is speaking English."

"You're absolutely right," Mrs. Fedorenko said. "You need to learn." And then she said something in Russian, or Ukrainian, or Byelorussian, which Father Alexey did not quite catch. In the conversation that followed, he heard many words he knew but there were many words in between—they spoke so quickly—which he could not understand.

Then there was silence.

He looked around and saw the others looking at him.

"*Nu?*" the ballerina said.

"*Shto?*" he asked.

"*Shto ti dumayesh?*"

"*Shto?*"

"Heavens, my dear Father Alexey," the ballerina changed to English. "We are talking about poor Mr. Kaputin. Haven't you been listening?"

"Of course I've been listening."

"Well, then?"

"Well, what?"

"Is he getting better? You did say you were going to see him?"

"Yes, of course, Marietta Valentinova. I know. I understand." He had picked out Yakov's name in the wash of words but assumed they were talking about the old man's geraniums. Yakov grew them in his window box. They were big and healthy flowers, all from pinchings from other people's flower pots, and it was the thing people saw when they walked past the house. Father Alexey shifted the valise on his lap. His clothes were stuck to him.

"The nurse said he wasn't feeling well," he said. "Who knows what that means? Last time they said the same thing and I went all the way there and there was nothing wrong with him. He was fine. He just wanted someone to talk to. I walk in and he says, 'I'm glad you came, *batiushka*. Have you paid my electric bill? I think I paid it before I came here, but I can't remember.' I told him everything was taken care of. 'That's good,' he says. 'I was worried. So how are you, *batiushka*? It's hot out, isn't it?' "

"How sweet," the ballerina said.

"Sweet? It cost me—the church—ten dollars."

"Don't blame me," Krenko said. "They don't give the gas away yet."

There were more farms, more rocky fields and unpainted houses that tilted one way and another. Then more woods broken by raw-cut clearings full of stumps and weeds and plastic toys and house trailers on cement blocks.

Of the farms and houses, Father Alexey could almost pick which was Russian, which American. None of the people in them had money, you could see that easily enough, but the American ones almost seemed to be the way they were out of stubbornness. There was something in a savage, defiant way willful about the broken porches, the rusty machinery outside the barns. The Russian yards were unkempt only with weeds and overgrown grass and the woods coming closer and closer. They had little gardens, just tiny patches, with flowers and a few vegetables. Father Alexey started to get depressed.

"Did you ever think," he said, looking out the window, "that you would be here?"

No one said anything.

"Are you speaking to me?" Marietta Valentinova said.

"Yes. To anyone."

"Think I would be here? Of course not. Who would?"

"Then why did you come?"

"We're getting personal, I see." But she wasn't angry.

"I'm sorry. I was just thinking . . ."

"You want to know? All right, I came for my health."

Mr. Fedorenko gave a guffaw. His wife pulled at his sleeve.

"It's true. Why would I leave New Jersey? I had a nice apartment. When I danced I got good write-ups. You should see the people who came to my ballets. You could barely find a seat. And it wasn't a small auditorium in that school, either. Only thing, the air was no good for my health. All that pollution. So where does a Russian go? You've got to have a church. So you go where there are Russians. At least there there were people with intelligence," she added over her shoulder. "Not like this godforsaken place."

"How many people lived in New Jersey!" Mrs. Fedorenko said before her husband could say anything. "We like it here, though," she said, patting Mr. Fedorenko's thick square hand. "We've had enough big things—the war, DP camp. After the camp we went to Venezuela. On Monday morning you turned on the radio and if there was a revolution you didn't have to go to work. Too many things. Here it's small and quiet. And Stephan always wanted to live near a river. He says that way you will never starve."

"I live in this place eighteen year," declared Mrs. Florenskaya. "*Achtzehn jahr*," she added for Father Alexey's benefit. "All in this old house."

"Eighteen years," said the ballerina sadly. "I couldn't stand this place so long." But she already had been in the town more than half that.

Father Alexey calculated. Eighteen years ago he was nine years old. It was a whole year in his life, but all he could remember of being nine was being in the fourth grade and Sister Rita St. Agnes being his teacher, a stern little woman with thick black eyebrows who had seemed to take to him after his father died. "The boy with the laughing eyes," she called him affectionately. Sometimes he looked into the mirror to see why she called him that. The eyes belonged to a bald, not very old person who was expected to be full of answers for people far older than he, people who were afraid of getting sick and of nursing homes and hospitals and

143

what was going to happen to them. He dispensed answers like the holy water he flung on heads and shoulders at a feast-day procession. Answers for death and fear and sadness and stolen spoons. And in all his life he had only lived in New Jersey with his mother and in the monastery in New York and now in a little town no one had ever heard of. How could he know?

In another eighteen years he would be forty-five. How much would he know then? Would he see things more clearly, as Yakov said? Krenko, the ballerina might still be around. Krenko probably would be in jail, he thought with some satisfaction, or in the real estate business or some scheme, making money one way or another. The ballerina would be an old woman if she were still alive. The others would surely be dead. Most of the people in the parish would be dead.

He was becoming more and more alone in the world.

The shopping center was on a long broad avenue that ran between the interstate and the city. It once had been a road of fine old houses with wide porches and broad lawns and beds of marigolds and tulips. A few remained. Dentists and lawyers had their offices in them. The rest had been torn down for the fast-food restaurants, gas stations and bargain stores that lined the road like a crowd at a parade. Krenko drove into the shopping center parking lot from the back road that came up from the river and discharged his passengers in front of the K mart. He'd be back in two hours, he said.

Father Alexey let the ballerina out and got back in the front seat. His cassock was wet and wrinkled where the valise had been.

"Look like you piss yourself," Krenko said and laughed.

In the hospital Father Alexey carried his valise in front of him to hide the wet place. Two teenaged girls snickered behind him on the elevator. A small boy who got on with his mother gawked up at him all the way to the seventh floor. "Hey, mister—you look like something," the boy said when the elevator stopped.

Father Alexey marched to the nurses' station and set his valise down hard. Then he remembered the wet place and covered it with his prayer book.

"You're here for Mr. Kaputin?" asked the nurse who was there.

"Yes," Father Alexey said curtly. "Are you the one who called?"

"No, Mrs. Dinsmore has gone." She came into the corridor. She was a tall woman with narrow shoulders and a tired face. Even before she said anything, Father Alexey knew that Yakov was going to die.

"The doctor has been in," she said.

He followed her to the room. Yakov was asleep, long and gaunt under the sheet. There was a thick sweet smell in the room. Yakov's bones looked as if they might pop through his face. With each breath his mouth puffed out like a frog's. On the stand beside his bed was an ikon of the Holy Mother of Kazan and a vase with daisies whose petals were falling off.

Father Alexey touched the old man's arm. His eyes blinked open. For a while he stared up at the priest. "It's you," he said.

"How are you feeling, Yakov Osipovich?" the priest asked in Russian.

"I saw my mother." Yakov's voice was hoarse and old. He took a long time between his words.

"Where did you see her?"

"She went away. There are fewer Russians, *batiushka* . . ."

He began to talk incoherently, something about apples in his father's orchard. The words came out in pieces that did not fit, as if something had broken inside of him.

The nurse brought a glass of tea. Father Alexey cooled it with his breath.

"Here, Yakov Osipovich," he said, raising the old man's head. The tea rose halfway up the glass straw, then sank back into the glass.

"Try again, Yakov Osipovich. Pull harder."

"Shall I try?" the nurse asked.

Father Alexey took his communion kit from around his neck. "I don't think it matters," he said.

The nurse went out quietly, leaving the door ajar.

Father Alexey arranged articles from his kit and others from his valise on the stand beside Yakov's bed and put on his holy vestments. He took the ribbon from the place he had marked in his book, then turned through the pages to the prayers for the dying.

He read quietly, occasionally making a cross over the old man's head. Yakov gazed up at him in silence and a kind of wonder, his mouth agape.

The priest softened a piece of bread in a little wine.

"Yakov Osipovich," he said, "are you sorry for your sins?"

The old man looked from the priest's face to the hand with the bread. Then his eyes closed. The priest shook him. "Yakov Osipovich," he said. "Say yes."

He tried to put the bread into Yakov's mouth but the old man's teeth were clenched. He slipped the bread between Yakov's lips, tucking it back into his cheek. Eventually Yakov's mouth began to move. He chewed fast, as if he were hungry.

Yakov opened his eyes just once more. Father Alexey was putting his things away. He heard Yakov's voice behind him. The old man was looking at him calmly.

"How did you come?" he said.

The priest came and sat beside him. "I found a ride. Are you feeling better?"

"Then you have to pay."

"Don't worry about it, Yakov Osipovich."

"Well, I'll straighten it out with you later, *batiushka*."

Krenko was parked outside the emergency door in a place marked "Doctors Only."

"You make me wait long time," Krenko said. Father Alexey could smell liquor on him.

"I'm sorry."

"Not me, I don't care. But little dancing lady going to be mad like hell."

Marietta Valentinova sputtered at them half the way home. Tiny drops of saliva landed on the dashboard. Father Alexey watched them evaporate, leaving little dots. At last she stopped. They became aware of his silence.

"*Batiushka?*" Mrs. Fedorenko said.

After a while Krenko said, "Well, you got to go everybody sometimes."

"Where going?" Mrs. Florenskaya said.

"Mr. Kaputin," Mrs. Fedorenko told her gently.

"*Ja, alles,*" the old woman said, "*alles kaput, Mein man, meine kinder. Alles* but me."

The sun was gone from the window shade when Father Alexey got back to his room and lay down on his bed. It was still light, it would be light for a while yet. He turned on his fan to move the air and looked at the wall through which Yakov had said good night. He heard Mrs. Florenskaya upstairs in the hallway. She was starting in again.

The priest switched on the stereo with the record from the afternoon. But he could still hear her.

"Christ," he said, and turned up the volume.

The Student

David Plante

She wondered if it was because she had been for only a month in Tulsa, Oklahoma, that, driving in the morning from her apartment to the university campus, the sight of a small clapboard house with a porch and a large tree in the front yard and a chest of drawers in the shade of the tree would make her go past slowly with the wonder of where she was and what the house and the tree and the chest of drawers had to do with one another, because they didn't *seem* to make sense. In her office, she concentrated hard on what her graduate student said. His name was Ken.

He said, "Women are mysterious. Don't you think, Dr. Langlais? As a woman, don't you think so?"

She said, "Mysterious in what way?"

"In their largeness."

"What?"

He wore a denim shirt and dungarees and a worn leather belt; he sat slouched back in the chair, boots extended.

"I don't know what you mean," she said.

"Well, women are—" His hands on his thighs were large; he raised them and indicated space. "Women are like that—"

Frowning, she stared at a square of white paper on her desk.

"Look," Ken said, his voice higher, "my wife lives out in New Mexico, and sometime I'll be going out there for a long weekend, and I wondered if you'd like to come with me."

"To New Mexico?"

"You said in class that this is your first time out West, and I thought, 'Well, why not ask her if I can show it to her?'"

She didn't know why she shouldn't say, immediately, yes or no. Perhaps she couldn't because she didn't quite know what he meant. Then it occurred to her that if he said, "Bullshit," she'd wonder what he meant.

"Thanks," she said.

"Then you'll come."

"No, I didn't say I'd come."

"Why not?"

"I'm not sure I'll be free."

"I could go whenever you are."

She thought: Am I frightened to go?

He stood. His belt was slung low; he tucked his shirt into his jeans and moved the big buckle to settle his belt more firmly down on his hips. His large body was powerful.

She said, "I'll let you know."

"You do that," he said.

He always sat further away from the seminar table than the other students, so he wrote in his notebook with his arms stretched out, the sleeves of his denim shirt rolled up; he never leaned forward. During the seminars, he wore gold-rimmed spectacles which magnified his eyes fixed on Helen Langlais as she spoke. Whenever she glanced at him it would come to her that he knew something she did not know which she wanted to know; she would pause, then look beyond him out of the seminar-room window to a tree.

He sometimes stopped by her office, just because he was passing, and asked, "Do you know when you'll be coming to New Mexico?"

"I don't know if I'll ever be able to," she answered.

Once he was in her office, she didn't want him to leave; and though she wanted him to know that, she couldn't exactly tell him. There should have been a way. She wouldn't have minded if he knew about her strong sense of him. She wouldn't have minded his knowing everything about her, and she'd have answered any question he asked; but he never asked her questions about herself. That was probably because she was his professor. As he stood halfway between her desk and the doorway, waiting perhaps for her to speak, she said, with a sudden small rush through her, "I left the East because I wanted to get away from my husband," and this, she thought, would allow him to ask any number of questions, but he said, "Oh," and shifted his books from one hip to the other. "I wanted to be free," she said. "Freedom's everything," he said. "Yes," she said. He said, "Freedom really is everything," and, again, she said, "Yes," because she didn't know what else to say. He left her office, and she tried to think of what she could have said which would have kept him.

In October, it was warm, and when he stopped by her office he was perspiring, so his shirt was wet under the arms and clung to his chest.

She said, "In the last three times I've seen you, you haven't asked me if I can make it to New Mexico." She smiled, but puckered her lips as to contain the smile.

His smile parted his lips and showed his teeth. "You'll come?"

She kept her lips puckered.

"That's great," he said. "That's really great."

His truck was parked against the green, after-sunset sky at the end of the wide parking lot.

"We're going in a truck?" she asked.

"Do you mind?"

"Mind?" She laughed. "No. I've never been in a truck before."

Stretched over the back of the truck was a tarpaulin; he unfastened it just enough to flap it open and place her suitcase inside, then he refastened it. He opened the door for her.

Up in the cab, she imagined she was seeing the city, as they drove through, as from a high, wide distance. The skyscrapers of the city were lit against the still-pale green sky. The truck curved down from an elevated highway and went straight for that sky.

"Do you want a beer?" he asked. "There's a cooler at your feet."

It was filled with crushed ice and cans of beer, and she took a cold, wet can out, opened it, passed it to Ken, and took one for herself.

She watched him drive with one large veiny hand on the steering wheel while he held the can of beer in his other and took swigs. His eyes stared ahead, and she caught herself wondering what he could possibly be thinking.

He said, suddenly, "There's a lot I've been wanting to talk to you about."

"Is there?" she asked.

"A lot."

He drank the last of his beer down and threw the can out of the window.

"Well, where do you want to begin?" she asked.

"Oh, we don't have to begin in any one place."

"Don't we?"

After she swigged down the last of her beer, she, with a sense of giving in to something beyond her, threw it out the window. The one can made her light-headed.

"I think," she said, "I'm going to concentrate on beer."

"Then I'll have another one too," he said.

The night air blew in through the cab windows.

With another half can drunk, Helen Langlais asked, "Does your wife know I'm coming?"

"No," Ken said.

"I had an idea that you didn't tell her."

"She won't mind. She's spacious."

The image came to Helen of a huge woman, so huge she sat, all day, in a big chair, and, because of her hugeness, she couldn't care about anything.

"Still," Helen said, "you might have told her."

"Honest, she won't mind. I have a special relationship with her, so she accepts everything I do. She's that way."

"Everything?"

"Yes, sir."

"Well, what about—?" An activity occurred to Helen which she thought Ken's wife might object to, if she objected to anything, but Helen wasn't quite light-headed enough to express that. She said, rhetorically, "What about if you took her money away and gave it to someone else?"

"She wouldn't mind about that. There are other things more important than that."

"Are there?"

"Come on," Ken said, "you know. You're ironical, Dr. Langlais, and I like the irony in you, but I know, deep down, you're not."

"Perhaps I'm not," she said. "Perhaps not."

"I know you're not."

Lit up in the vast outside darkness were grain elevators and oil derricks.

Helen threw her empty can out. He threw his out. She opened two more.

Because of the shaking cab, the beer dribbled from her lips; she wiped it away with the back of a hand. More beer dripped from her chin onto her blouse when she drank, and she let it drip.

"And supposing you were unfaithful to your wife?" she asked.

"That doesn't matter to her."

"And if she were unfaithful to you?"

"That wouldn't matter to me, either."

150

She said, "I left my husband because he was unfaithful to me. Not only that, he was giving all the money he should have been sharing with me to her. I guess I thought all of that was very important."

She wanted to talk to Ken about her husband and the woman. She wanted to tell him what had happened, but, in his silence, she knew he did not want to know. Then, maybe, she didn't want to talk to him about what had happened, but wanted to ask him, if he and his wife didn't feel it was important to be faithful to one another, whether they weren't, from time to time—

She asked, "What's your wife's name, or don't you call one another anything?"

"Her name's Betsy."

"Betsy," she said.

I wonder how fat Betsy is? Helen thought.

"All right," she said, "I give up. Tell me what you both consider really important."

"Come on," he said. "You know nobody can talk about things like that. Not really."

She was reminded that he was not a very good student; she gave him B's when she should have given him C's.

"I can't imagine what it is you've been wanting to talk to me about," she said.

"Oh, the time will come."

"I'll look forward to it then," she said. "And I count on Betsy not minding."

Ken laughed loud; his head raised, the tendons in his neck stood out and while he laughed he watched the road. Then he went silent and watched the road as if he had become fixed on it.

Great flames raging from the top of a pipe lit up a round area of weeds and scrub, apparently floating in the darkness.

"What's that?" Helen asked.

"A newly drilled well burning off gas."

She looked back at it as they passed.

They drank beer and drove in silence for hours. The windows were shut against the cold. All about them, the black horizon was low, and seemed to be lower than the road they were traveling on; below the horizon were many small green lights.

In open blackness, Ken stopped the truck. He said, "Let's get out." Helen was drunk, she realized, when she took the long step down from the cab to the earth. Ken shut off the headlights. She heard him call,

"Come round here," and she followed his voice round to the front of the truck, where she saw him standing, a large dark body in the darkness. She stood by him and imagined she felt a warmth emanate from him; chilled, she crossed her arms and stood a little closer to him. He said, "We've come into what used to be No Man's Land." She glanced around, then up into the starry sky.

Hour after hour, they drove through the Oklahoma Panhandle, through what, in the memory of some people living there, had been, Helen thought, a land without police, without jails, without court-houses, a flat, open place where laws did not apply. The truck shook her. She fell asleep, then woke, over and over, and each time she woke she was not sure where she was. The head and shoulders of Ken Haggard, dimly lit by the headlights, reassured her; she woke once cold, but with a suffused sexual longing, and she wondered what Ken might do if she put her arm over his shoulders and pressed her face against his neck. She yawned. "Where are we?" she asked. He said, "Still in the Panhandle." She hugged herself. Wind was blowing, and clouds of dust, like mist, drifted slowly across the highway, and from time to time tumbleweed. Jackrabbits bounded from the darkness into the truck lights and bounded out. Helen thought: And if I were to be lawless towards him, and do something, right now, which he perhaps imagines I myself could never imagine doing— She yawned again, closed her eyes, and fell asleep.

She woke when the truck stopped. Ken was getting out. They were parked before a gasoline pump, and beyond the pump was a station, lit inside by long neon tubes, and at a desk before the wide window was a fat girl reading a magazine. "It'll be freezing out," Ken said to Helen; "maybe you should stay in the cab." "No," she said, "I'll get out." The cold wind hit her when she opened the door; outside, the wind reached her bones, and she turned at different angles to it. "You go inside the station," Ken said; "I'll take care of the gas." Shivering, she walked across the space to the station building, and pushed against the door, not sure if it was all right simply to enter without first making a sign to the girl; Helen was a little surprised that the door was unlocked and gave in with a shove. Inside was the smell of kerosene heating; the fat girl at the desk sat by a heater, and she said to Helen over her magazine, "Come over here and get yourself warm," so Helen, smiling, went to the heater, and the girl put the magazine down.

"Where you from?" the girl asked.

Helen didn't know what to say. "We've been traveling all night."

The girl laughed. "That's not such a long time."

"No, I guess not."

The girl picked up the magazine and lowered it when Ken came in.

He said to her, in a loud voice, "Hey, skinny," and the fat girl laughed. Helen stood aside as Ken and the girl talked in louder and louder voices, and laughed.

Now and then there shone, on the low, dark horizon before them, what seemed the aureole of a small sunrise, and, after a long time, glaring headlights rose, and a huge, interstate transport truck approached them, coming very fast; outlined in tiny yellow and red lights, it appeared suddenly and disappeared with a shudder in the pickup truck, then the highway was empty for another long period.

Ken's voice was low. "How're you?"

"All right, I guess."

"You're not sure."

"No, not entirely sure."

What it was that she wanted was to press close to the body of some-one. That was all. She didn't feel the need to talk to anyone. She felt the need to be against a body, like Ken's. She wished she could stretch out her arms and legs far; she pressed her elbows back and stuck out her breasts to breathe in deeply, then out.

After a while, Ken said, "We're in New Mexico."

It was still dark.

"There aren't any lights on the horizon," Helen said.

"No," Ken said.

The black horizon began to rise, to mount into black ridges and hills. Motionless deer stood in the road, staring into the lights of the truck; they jumped away only when Ken, slowing down, flicked the lights to low beam. Mountains rose with the rising dawn.

Clutching her coat about her, Helen, with a little shiver, woke to the light.

Ken drove through dark gorges up into mountains, and on the top of the highest mountain, called Eagle's Nest, he turned off the highway onto a sandy lay-by and stopped. Far below was a lake, and mountains beyond, and over the mountains the sun appeared.

"Do you want to get out?" Ken asked.

"Yes," she said.

In the bright morning cold, they, side by side, watched the sun expand into the sky. Helen leaned a little towards Ken, and she sensed him lean towards her; she had to strain to keep her tense balance, expecting him, she felt, to reach out and put his arm about her, but he didn't. The

153

sunlight clearly revealed waves on the wind-buffeted lake, and tall pines by the lake shore, and wooden houses among the pines.

"Let's go home," Ken said.

They drove down through gorges with yellow aspens, the narrow road following a rushing stream, and out on the flat they drove along a straight road from where the mountains and mesas spread out from one another, so the continuing flat was visible between them, and in the spaces appeared other, distant mountains and mesas. The sky was empty.

Ken turned off the tarmac road onto a dirt road, and the truck bounced in the holes.

They did not seem to approach the mesas and mountains, which, instead, spread out further and further from one another. There were no valleys. The windshield became layered with fine dust. Through it Ken pointed to an adobe house with a pickup truck parked outside it, in the middle of a vast plain.

"Your wife lives out here alone?" Helen asked.

"No. She lives with our son. We've got a three-year-old son."

It was as if Helen had been expecting him to be taking her to a place where they would be alone and then found other people there who made everything she had imagined possible impossible.

The slamming of their truck doors gave way to a great autumnal silence.

The house had unpainted wooden-plank shutters, shut; the plank door with a rope handle was shut too.

Ken called, "Betsy."

He stood away from the house.

Again, he called, "Betsy."

With a little thrill of apprehension, Helen saw the door open, and there, in what must have been a long white nightgown, a tall, skinny woman appeared, her hands over her eyes to protect them against the blaze of light.

From his distance, Ken called, "How're things?"

"They're all right," the woman called back.

"I've brought a friend, Dr. Langlais, from the university."

"That's all right," the woman said.

"Is it all right if we come on in?"

"It's all right."

Ken smiled at Helen. "Everything's going to be all right," he said.

Betsy went back into the house, then Ken, with her suitcase, gestured to Helen to follow. It was dim in the low room. Betsy stood on the other side of a round wooden table.

"Were you asleep?" Ken asked his wife.

"I was. I was up late last night."

"For a good reason, I hope."

"A good enough reason."

"That's good," Ken said.

"I'm going to go back to bed," Betsy said.

"I think we'll go to bed, too," Ken said to Helen. "Wouldn't you like an hour's sleep, Dr. Langlais?"

"I'm awake," she said.

"Well, you can take a walk if you like."

"I'll walk a little," Helen said, "then I'll sleep a little."

"That's all right," Betsy said.

"Where'll we put Dr. Langlais?" Ken asked.

"Well, I don't know," Betsy said. "You can give her your room if you want."

"And where will I sleep?"

"You can sleep in the kid's room."

"He's not here?"

"No. I'm not sure where he is. Tom and Sally took him off a couple of days ago to stay with them and their kid, so he may be there. Then, they may have gone off with him to some other people's kids,"

"That's nice," Ken said. "I was looking forward to being with him, but it's nice he's with other kids."

"It's all right," Betsy said.

Ken said to Helen, "We called our son Liberty. He was born right here in this house. We didn't register his birth because we wanted him to be totally free."

Betsy looked at Helen. She smiled. She said, "You do just what you want here."

"Thank you," Helen said.

"Now I'm going to bed."

Ken showed Helen to his room, with a thick beamed ceiling and cracked walls, and a small window. He turned down the Indian blanket from his narrow bed to reveal rumpled sheets.

"I guess it hasn't been changed since I last slept here," he said.

"That doesn't matter," she said.

He hesitated, as if now were the moment he'd been waiting for to tell her everything he wanted to tell her; taller than she, he looked over her head, and she turned to see what he was looking at.

155

"Well," he said, "I'm going to go to sleep."

"Just at the time we should be waking up," she said.

He smiled at her. "We'll stay up all night again."

Alone, she left the house and walked along the dirt road until she came to apple trees. Among the apple trees were deer. Helen walked among the trees and the slender deer seemed to watch her until she got almost within reaching distance, then, their long necks rigid, they bounded away. She picked a ripe apple and, eating it, returned to the house and her room, or Ken's. As she lay on the rumpled sheets, she wondered if it was meaningless to wonder why Ken and Betsy, husband and wife, did not have the same bedroom.

It was long after noon when she got up. The dry air burned in her sinuses. She covered the bed with the Indian blanket and went out. There was no one in the living room. On the wooden table was a pile of stones, shaped like cubes, and a glass of water. Helen wandered about the room, then went outside. One of the trucks—the one which she imagined belonged to Betsy—was gone. Helen walked all round the house, the dry cold air was still as it was inside, then entered, and found Ken at the table stacking the stone cubes.

"I didn't know you were up," he said.

"I took a walk," she said.

He sat back. "Well, what would you like to do?"

She, too, sat at the table. "Is it up to me to say?"

"Sure."

"I want to eat."

"Then we'll go eat."

"Of course," she said, "unless you think it isn't important."

"Come on," he said.

She knew that she shouldn't ask where Betsy had gone.

The little town was made of one-story, plank and corrugated iron, some adobe, buildings. The restaurant had a CLOSED sign in the window, but Ken knocked on the door and an old woman opened. As they ate, Helen saw that Ken's mind was not on her, or the burritos.

On the way back, Ken bought five packs of beer. Helen helped him carry them to the truck, then into the house.

She sat at the end of a long broken sofa, by a kerosene stove which Ken lit. He also lit a kerosene lamp and put it on the wooden table.

With her first beer, Helen said, "Betsy was annoyed, after all, that I came."

"Oh no," Ken said. "No, she wasn't."

"I felt she was."

156

"No, no."

"I don't know if you'd tell me."

Ken smiled, as from a long distance; he was sitting on a high-backed wooden chair, his hands on his thighs. The can of beer was at his feet, and he had to lean far over to reach for it; after he drank, he replaced it on the floor.

He said, "I thought you'd be the one person to understand the relationship I have with Betsy."

"What've I said or done that makes you think that?"

"Well, you know so much."

She sat into the deep sofa.

"You've been so many places, done so many things—"

She kept her eyes on him, aware of him looking at her body slouched into the sofa, though perhaps he wasn't looking at it. She threw her shoulders back.

She thought: I'm going to make love with him.

"There's something large about you," Ken said.

Helen laughed. "Which part of me?"

"I don't mean that. I don't mean, any part of you. I mean, altogether large."

"I think you're completely wrong about me, but I'm not going to stop you thinking anything you want."

"Thanks."

She tucked two fingers between buttons on her flannel shirt and touched skin.

"A person should love everyone," Ken said.

"He should."

"Betsy taught me that."

Helen hoped Betsy had gone far in her truck, and she imagined the space of hours alone with Ken in which, by a gradual deduction of the vast generalities to particulars, she would reduce love to lovemaking; it would take a lot of calculated talk, but Helen knew, as Ken's teacher, she'd do it, she'd convince Ken of the particular.

She said, "But how can you know what love is unless you know it with one person?"

"You're playing with me again."

"Perhaps. But perhaps not."

"It's all over," he said.

"All over?" She looked around the room.

"I love everybody," he said.

"Do you?"

157

"I do."

She opened her mouth and held it open and touched the tip of her tongue to the roof of her mouth. "Do you love me?"

"Of course I love you, Dr. Langlais."

"Can you tell me what that means? Can you tell me what it means when you say about someone that you love him or her?"

He emptied a can of beer and got up to go to the cooler in the kitchen for another; he stood at the door, opening the can, and said, "It means so much."

"No," Helen said, "I'm not going to take that as an answer."

Then he came across the room and sat on the sofa next to her, and she felt a small fear.

"What answer do you want?" he asked.

"I ask the questions," she said. "You give me the answers."

"You may not approve of the answers."

"If I don't, I simply fail you."

"It must be difficult being a teacher, grading students."

"Not so difficult."

"But don't you hate giving out grades?"

"No, I like it."

He leaned towards her. In the dim light, the features of his face appeared simplified, and she had a vivid sense of the solidity and weight of his head. His voice was low. He said, "To love a person is to give that person all the freedom in the world." They were looking at one another. Slowly, she raised a hand, but just as she was about to reach forward to his head he drew away, and she quickly jerked her hand back and touched her own cheek, then ran her fingers through her hair.

Ken got up. "What would you like to do?" he asked.

"Oh," she said, "let's see. How about going to the moon? I'd like to go to the moon."

"You're being ironical again."

"I guess I am." She sat up, raised her arms and lowered them, and said, "I'll do anything you want."

"All right," he said.

The dance hall had stuck all over its low ceiling shreds of red, blue, white crepe paper, and strings with broken balloons hung down. At one end of the hall, on a platform, two men and a woman played electric guitars and sang over amplifiers, their voices resonant in the hall, empty but for Helen and Ken on a bench at a table, two glasses and a pitcher of beer before them. Helen was sure Ken was thinking about his wife and his son, and she also was sure that if she said he was, he would say, "No, oh no." Into the dance hall came a couple, a young man and woman, both wearing boots, slim denims, checkered shirts, and stetsons, the brims rolled; they danced, and as they danced they glided through arc upon arc over the bare wooden floor, to the song about lost love. As she watched them, Helen felt tears rise to her eyes, and she had no idea why.

The second truck was not at the house when they returned.

"I think I'll go to bed," Helen said.

"You do what you want," Ken answered.

She left the door to her room open, and she heard Ken moving about the living room, then heard him go into the room next to hers, his son's room; he didn't shut the door, as she could hear him undress and get into bed. She wondered if he had left the door open on purpose, but she didn't know on what purpose. Unable to sleep, she lay listening for sounds from his room. She thought she heard him, from time to time, turn over in his bed, and whenever he did, she did, and she tried to do it so he would hear to let him know she was awake; the sheets came untucked. When she heard him groan a little, she waited for a while, then groaned, too, and waited for him to; a long while later he groaned again, and she groaned right away and waited, listening. She heard him get up and her body went rigid. The toilet flushed. She raised her head to stare out her doorway, but she couldn't see into the living room; then a kerosene lamp was lit, and she saw him, in his underpants, walk about the room. She didn't move. Her body urged her up, and she was on the fine point of getting up, her back raised, but she remained motionless. He was cut off from view, then reappeared, closer to the door, and she rose higher on her elbows, about to say, "Ken," but he went past, and she lay down, her eyes open.

In the Cemetery Where
Al Jolson Is Buried

Amy Hempel

for Jessica

"Tell me things I won't mind forgetting," she said. "Make it useless stuff or skip it."

I began. I told her insects fly through rain, missing every drop, never getting wet. I told her no one in America owned a tape recorder before Bing Crosby did. I told her the shape of the moon is like a banana—you see it looking full, you're seeing it end-on.

The camera made me self-conscious and I stopped. It was trained on us from a ceiling mount—the kind of camera banks use to photograph robbers. It played our image to the nurses down the hall in Intensive Care.

"Go on, girl," she said, "you get used to it."

I had my audience. I went on. Did she know that Tammy Wynette had changed her tune? Really. That now she sings "Stand By Your *Friends*"? Paul Anka did it too, I said. Does "You're Having *Our* Baby." He got sick of all that feminist bitching.

"What else?" she said. "Have you got something else?"

Oh yes. For her I would always have something else.

"Did you know when they taught the first chimp to talk, it lied? When they asked her who did it on the desk, she signed back Max, the janitor. And when they pressed her, she said she was sorry, that it was really the project director. But she was a mother, so I guess she had her reasons."

"Oh, that's good," she said. "A parable."

"There's more about the chimp," I said. "But it will break your heart."

"No thanks," she says, and scratches at her mask.

160

*   *   *

We look like good-guy outlaws. Good or bad, I am not used to the mask yet. I keep touching the warm spot where my breath, thank God, comes out. She is used to hers. She only ties the strings on top. The other ones—a pro by now—she lets hang loose.

We call this place the Marcus Welby Hospital. It's the white one with the palm trees under the opening credits of all those shows. A Hollywood hospital, though in fact it is several miles west. Off camera, there is a beach across the street.

She introduces me to a nurse as "the Best Friend." The impersonal article is more intimate. It tells me that *they* are intimate, my friend and her nurse.

"I was telling her we used to drink Canada Dry Ginger Ale and pretend we were in Canada."

"That's how dumb *we* were," I say.

"You could be sisters," the nurse says.

So how come, I'll bet they are wondering, it took me so long to get to such a glamorous place? But do they ask?

They do not ask.

Two months, and how long is the drive?

The best I can explain it is this—I have a friend who worked one summer in a mortuary. He used to tell me stories. The one that really got to me was not the grisliest, but it's the one that did. A man wrecked his car on 101 going south. He did not lose consciousness. But his arm was taken down to the wet bone—and when he looked at it—it scared him to death. I mean, he died.

So I didn't dare look any closer. But now I'm doing it—and hoping I won't be scared to death.

*   *   *

She shakes out a summer-weight blanket, showing a leg you did not want to see. Except for that, you look at her and understand the law that requires *two* people to be with the body at all times.

"I thought of something," she says. "I thought of it last night. I think there is a real and present need here. You know," she says, "like for someone to do it for you when you can't do it yourself. You call them up whenever you want—like when push comes to shove."

She grabs the bedside phone and loops the cord around her neck.

"Hey," she says, "the End o' the Line."

161

She keeps on, giddy with something. But I don't know with what.

"The giveaway was the solarium," she says. "That's where Marcus Welby broke the news to his patients. Then here's the real doctor suggesting we talk in the solarium. So I knew I was going to die.

"I can't remember," she says, "what does Kübler-Ross say comes after Denial?"

It seems to me Anger must be next. Then Bargaining, Depression, and so on and so forth. But I keep my guesses to myself.

"The only thing is," she says, "is where's Resurrection? God knows I want to do it by the book. But she left out Resurrection."

She laughs, and I cling to the sound the way someone dangling above a ravine holds fast to the thrown rope.

We could have cried then, but when we didn't, we couldn't.

"Tell me," she says, "about that chimp with the talking hands. What do they do when the thing ends and the chimp says, 'I don't want to go back to the zoo'?"

When I don't say anything, she says, "O.K.—then tell me another animal story. I like animal stories. But not a sick one—I don't want to know about all the seeing-eye dogs going blind."

No, I would not tell her a sick one.

"How about the hearing-ear dogs?" I say. "They're not going deaf, but they are getting very judgmental. For instance, there's this golden retriever in Jersey, he wakes up the deaf mother and drags her into the daughter's room because the kid has got a flashlight and is reading under the covers."

"Oh, you're killing me," she says. "Yes, you're definitely killing me."

"They say the smart dog obeys, but the smarter dog knows when to disobey."

"Yes," she says, "the smarter *anything* knows when to disobey. Now, for example."

She is flirting with the Good Doctor, who has just appeared. Unlike the Bad Doctor, who checks the IV drip before saying good morning, the Good Doctor says things like "God didn't give epileptics a fair shake." He awards himself points for the cripples he could have hit in the parking lot. Because the Good Doctor is a little in love with her he says maybe a year. He pulls a chair up to her bed and suggests I might like to spend an hour on the beach.

"Bring me something back," she says. "Anything from the beach. Or the gift shop. Taste is no object."

The doctor slowly draws the curtain around her bed.

"Wait!" she cries.

162

I look in at her.

"Anything," she says, "except a magazine subscription."

The doctor turns away.

I watch her mouth laugh.

*   *   *

What seems dangerous often is not—black snakes, for example, or clear-air turbulence. While things that just lie there, like this beach, are loaded with jeopardy. A yellow dust rising from the ground, the heat that ripens melons overnight—this is earthquake weather. You can sit here braiding the fringe on your towel and the sand will all of a sudden suck down like a hourglass. The air roars. In the cheap apartments onshore, bathtubs fill themselves and gardens roll up and over like green waves. If nothing happens, the dust will drift and the heat deepen till fear turns to desire. Nerves like that are only bought off by catastrophe.

"It never happens when you're thinking about it," she observed once.

"Earthquake, earthquake, earthquake," she said.

"Earthquake, earthquake, earthquake," I said.

Like the aviaphobe who keeps the plane aloft with prayer, we kept it up till an aftershock cracked the ceiling.

That was after the big one in '72. We were in college; our dormitory was five miles from the epicenter. When the ride was over and my jabbering pulse began to slow, she served five parts champagne to one part orange juice and joked about living in Ocean View, Kansas. I offered to drive her to Hawaii on the new world psychics predicted would surface the next time, or the next.

I could not say that now—next. Whose next? she could ask.

Was I the only one who noticed that the experts had stopped saying if and now spoke of when? Of course not; the fearful ran to thousands. We watched the traffic of Japanese beetles for deviation. Deviation might mean more natural violence.

I wanted her to be afraid with me, but she said, "I don't know. I'm just not."

She was afraid of nothing, not even of flying.

I have this dream before a flight where we buckle in and the plane moves down the runway. It takes off at thirty-five miles an hour, and then we're airborne, skimming the tree tops. Still, we arrive in New York on time. It is so pleasant. One night I flew to Moscow this way.

She flew with me once. That time she flew with me she ate macadamia nuts while the wings bounced. She knows the wing tips can bend thirty

163

feet up and thirty feet down without coming off. She believes it. She trusts the laws of aerodynamics. My mind stampedes. I can almost accept that a battleship floats, and everybody knows steel sinks.

I see fear in her now and am not going to try to talk her out of it. She is right to be afraid.

After a quake, the six o'clock news airs a film clip of first-graders yelling at the broken playground per their teacher's instructions.

"*Bad* earth!" they shout, because anger is stronger than fear.

*   *   *

But the beach is standing still today. Everyone on it is tranquilized, numb or asleep. Teenaged girls rub coconut oil on each other's hard-to-reach places. They smell like macaroons. They pry open compacts like clamshells; mirrors catch the sun and throw a spray of white rays across glazed shoulders. The girls arrange their wet hair with silk flowers the way they learned in *Seventeen*. They pose.

A formation of low-riders pulls over to watch with a six-pack. They get vocal when the girls check their tan lines. When the beer is gone, so are they—flexing their cars on up the boulevard.

Above this aggressive health are the twin wrought-iron terraces, painted flamingo pink, of the Palm Royale. Someone dies there every time the sheets are changed. There's an ambulance in the driveway, so the remaining residents line the balconies, rocking and not talking, one-upped.

The ocean they stare at is dangerous, and not just the undertow. You can almost see the slapping tails of sand sharks keeping cruising bodies alive.

If she looked, she could see this, some of it, from her window. She would be the first to say how little it takes to make a thing all wrong.

*   *   *

There was a second bed in the room when I returned. For two beats I didn't get it. Then it hit me like an open coffin.

She wants every minute, I thought. She wants my life.

"You missed Gussie," she said.

Gussie is her parents' 300-pound narcoleptic maid. Her attacks often come at the ironing board. The pillowcases in that family are all bordered with scorch.

"It's a hard trip for her," I said, "How is she?"

"Well, she didn't fall asleep, if that's what you mean. Gussie's great— you know what she said? She said, 'Darlin' just keep prayin', down on your knees.'"

She shrugged. "See anybody good?"

"No," I said, "just the new Charlie's Angel. And I saw Cher's car down near the Arcade."

"Cher's car is worth *three* Charlie's Angels," she said. "What else am I missing?"

"It's earthquake weather," I told her.

"The best thing to do about earthquakes," she said, "is not to live in California."

"That's useful," I said. "You sound like Reverend Ike: 'The best thing to do for the poor is not be one of them.'"

We're crazy about Reverend Ike.

I noticed her face was bloated.

"You know," she said, "I feel like hell. I'm about to stop having fun."

"The ancients have a saying," I said. "'There are times when the wolves are silent; there are times when the moon howls.'"

"What's that, Navajo?"

"Palm Royale lobby graffiti," I said. "I bought a paper there. I'll read to you."

"Even though I care about nothing?" she said.

I turned to page three, to a UPI filler datelined Mexico City. I read her "Man Robs Bank With Chicken," about a man who bought a barbecued chicken at a stand down the block from a bank. Passing the bank, he got the idea. He walked in and approached a teller. He pointed the brown paper bag at her and she handed over the day's receipts. It was the smell of barbecue sauce that eventually led to his capture.

The story made her hungry, she said, so I took the elevator down six floors to the cafeteria and brought back all the ice cream she wanted. We lay side by side, adjustable beds cranked up for optimal TV viewing, littering the sheets with Good Humor wrappers, picking toasted almonds out of the gauze. We were Lucy and Ethel, Mary and Rhoda in extremis. The blinds were closed to keep light off the screen.

We watched a movie starring men we used to think we wanted to sleep with. Hers was a tough cop out to stop mine, a vicious rapist who went after cocktail waitresses.

"This is a good movie," she said, when snipers felled them both.

I missed her already; my straight man, my diary.

A Filipino nurse tiptoed in and gave her an injection. She removed

165

the pile of Popsicle sticks from the nightstand—enough to splint a small animal.

The injection made us sleepy—me in the way I picked up her inflection till her mother couldn't tell us apart on the phone. We slept.

I dreamed she was a decorator, come to furnish my house. She worked in secret, singing to herself. When she finished, she guided me proudly to the door. "How do you like it?" she asked, easing me inside.

Every beam and sill and shelf and knob was draped in black bunting, with streamers of black crepe looped around darkened mirrors.

*   *   *

"I have to go home," I said when she woke up.

She thought I meant home to her house in the Canyon, and I had to say No, *home* home. I twisted my hands in the hackneyed fashion of people in pain. I was supposed to offer something. The Best Friend. I could not even offer to come back.

I felt weak and small and failed. Also exhilarated. I had a convertible in the parking lot. Once out of that room, I would drive it too fast down the coast highway through the crab-smelling air. A stop in Malibu for sangria. The music in the place would be sexy and loud. They would serve papaya and shrimp and watermelon ice. After dinner I would pick up beach boys. I would shimmer with life, buzz with heat, vibrate with health, stay up all night with one and then the other.

Without a word, she yanked off her mask and threw it on the floor. She kicked at the blankets and moved to the door. She must have hated having to pause for breath and balance before slamming out of Isolation, and out of the second room, the one where you scrub and tie on the white masks.

A voice shouted her name in alarm, and people ran down the corridor. The Good Doctor was paged over the intercom. I opened the door and the nurses at the station stared hard, as if this flight had been my idea.

"Where is she?" I asked, and they nodded to the supply closet.

I looked in. Two nurses were kneeling beside her on the floor, talking to her in low voices. One held a mask over her nose and mouth, the other rubbed her back in slow circles. The nurses glanced up to see if I was the doctor, and when they saw I wasn't, they went back to what they were doing.

"There, there, honey," they cooed.

166

*   *   *

On the morning she was moved to the cemetery, the one where Al Jolson is buried, I enrolled in a Fear of Flying class. "What is your worst fear?" the instructor asked, and I answered, "That I will finish this course and still be afraid."

I sleep with a glass of water on the nightstand so I can see by its level if the coastal earth is trembling or if the shaking is still me.

What do I remember? I remember only the useless things I hear—that Bob Dylan's mother invented Wite-out, that twenty-three people must be in a room before there is a fifty-fifty chance two will have the same birthdate. Who cares whether or not it's true? In my head there are bath towels swaddling this stuff. Nothing else seeps through.

I review those things that will figure in the retelling: a kiss through surgical gauze, the pale hand correcting the position of the wig. I noted these gestures as they happened, not in any retrospect. Though I don't know why looking *back* should show us more than looking *at*. It is just possible I will say I stayed the night. And who is there that can say I did not?

Nothing else gets through until I think of the chimp, the one with the talking hands.

In the course of the experiment, that chimp had a baby. Imagine how her trainers must have thrilled when the mother, without prompting, began to sign to the newborn. Baby, drink milk. Baby, play ball. And when the baby died, the mother stood over the body, her wrinkled hands moving with animal grace, forming again and again the words, Baby, come hug, Baby, come hug, fluent now in the language of grief.

The Texas Principessa

William Goyen

Who would've dreamed that I would get the Palazzo? Well let me try and stay on what you asked me about before we were so rudely interrupted—by me. That ever happen to you? Start out to tell one thing and get off onto another? Well let me try and stay on what you asked me about. Welcome to the Palazzo.

The Texas Principessa had married a Naples prince of an old line. Hortense Solomon (we called her Horty) was herself of an old line—of dry-goods families. Texas Jews that had intermarried and built up large stores in Texas cities over the generations. Solomon's Everybody's Store was an everyday word in the mouths of Texas people and an emporium—which was their word—where Texas people were provided with everything from hosiery to clocks. The Solomons, along with the Linkowitzes, the Dinzlers and the Myrons, were old pioneers of Texas. They were kept to their faith by traveling rabbis in early days, and later they built synagogues and contributed rabbis and cantors from their generations—except those who married Texas Mexicans or Texas Frenchmen. These, after awhile, melted into the general mixture of the Texas population and ate cornbread instead of bagels and preferred barbecue pork and tamales to lox and herring. That ever happen to you? Let's see, where was I?

Oh. The Naples prince, Renzi da Filippo, did not bring much money to the marriage because the old line of da Filippos had used up most of it or lost it; or had it taken from them in one way or another—which was O.K. because they had taken it from somebody else earlier on: sometimes there is a little justice. That ever happen to you? Renzi was the end of the line. Someone who was the end of a line would look it, wouldn't you think so? You could not tell it in Renzi da Filippo, he looked spunky enough to *start* something; he was real fresh and handsome in that burnt

168

blond coloring that they have, sort of toasted—toast-colored hair and bluewater eyes and skin of a wheaty color. He was a beauty everyone said and was sought after in Rome and London and New York. Those Italianos! About all he had in worldly goods was the beautiful Palazzo da Filippo in Venice, a seventeenth-century hunk of marble and gold that finally came into his hands. Had Hortense Solomon not given her vows to Renzi in wedlock, Palazzo da Filippo might have gone down the drain. It needed repair in the worst kind of way—all those centuries on it—and those repairs needed a small fortune—which Horty had a lot of. As soon as the marriage was decided upon, there was a big party. The Prince was brought to Texas and an announcement party was thrown, and I mean *thrown*, on the cold ranch river that flowed through the acres and acres of hot cattleland owned by the Solomons. The gala stirred up socialites as far as Porto Ércole and Cannes, from which many of the rich, famous and titled flew in on family planes. Horty Solomon— which was very hard for Italians to say so they called her La Principessa di Texas—started right in with her plans for fixing up the Palazzo. The plans were presented in the form of a little replica of the Palazzo used as a centerpiece for the sumptuous table. Two interior decorators called The Boys, favorites of Horty's from Dallas, exhibited their color schemes—a lot of Fuchsia for Horty loved this favorite color of hers. "You're certainly not going to redecorate that Palazzo" (they said Palazzo the way she did, so that it sounded like "Plotso"), "you're certainly not going to furnish it out of Solomon's Everybody's Store!" The Boys declared to Horty as soon as they heard of her plans to redo the Plotso da Filippo. "Nor," said they, "are you going to make it look like a West Texas ranch house. We're using Florentine silk and Venetian gold, with rosy Fuchsia appointments!"

When Palazzo da Filippo was in shape, the Texas relatives poured in. The Palazzo was crawling with them, young and old. The Palazzo could have been a big Texas house. Black cooks and maids from East Texas mingled with Italian servants. The Venetians loved it. "Viva la Principessa di Texas!" they cried. Those Italianos!

Here I must inform you something of which you were asking about, that on his very wedding night in a villa in Monaco (the beautiful Prince gambled on his wedding night) the beautiful Prince Renzi burst a blood vessel in his inner ear and succumbed (the newspapers' word for it). He just plain died in his wedding bed is what it was. You were asking about how he died. Vicious talk had it that the only stain on the nuptial (newspapers' word)—only stain on the nuptial sheets came from the Prince's ear. Crude. The poor bride, who had been married before—a big textile man from Birmingham, Alabama – was stunned. Poor Horty. Tragedy dogged her, as you well can see. I myself have never experienced the death of a husband but I have experienced two divorces and let me tell you they are similar, they are like a death. They are no fun. My last divorce was particularly nasty. Thank God there was no issue, as the Wills said. Both my husbands were without issue. Issue indeed. That's a joke for the last one, who issued it to Old *Granddad* instead of me – mind as well say it; and excuse the profanity – that one had little issue except through his mouth . . . when he threw up his Bourbon. Crude, I know. But that's mainly the kind of issue *he* had. That ever happen to you? Let's see where was I. Oh. Anyway, this left me in London, quite penniless; tell you why I was in London some other time. Don't have time for that garden path now – it's a memory lane I choose at the moment to take a detour from. But the thing of it is, this is how Horty Solomon got the Palazzo da Filippo, which is what you were asking me about: under the auspices of a sad circumstance – a broken blood vessel leading to death; but a tragedy leading to a new life for her. And for me, as you will soon hear the story (that you were asking about). Anyway, Horty went on with her plans for the Palazzo, now all hers.

As I said somewhere – I can't tell a story straight to save my life, my mind races off onto a hundred things that I remember and want to tell right then, don't want to wait. That ever happen to you? *Anyway*, as I said somewhere, Texans flooded into the canals of Venice because of the Principessa: *Venezia* was half Texas some days – and loved it. And if you've ever heard a Texan speaking Italian, you won't believe the sound of it. Big oilmen came to the Palazzo and Texas college football players – Horty had given them a stadium in Lampasas (they called her Cousin Horty) – Junior League ladies, student concert pianists (Horty was a patron of the Arts, as you will see more about), and once a Rock group – they had that Grand Canal jumping, and some seventeenth-century tiles *fell*, I can tell you. And maybe something from even earlier, a Fresco or two from the Middle Ages. And talented young people who wanted to paint or write came over to the Palazzo, to write in or paint in, or practice a musical instrument in; and they accepted. See what she did? Palazzo da Filippo jived, that was the word then; it was in the nineteen-fifties. That joint jumped, as they said.

I said back there that I was going to tell you why I was in London. Or did I? Can't remember. Just try to remember something with all this noise around here. Italians are noisy, sweet as they are – singing and calling on the Canals. Now where was I? Oh. London. Well, forget London for the time being – *if* I haven't already told it to you. Just keep

London in the back of your mind. Now where was I? Oh. Well, you have asked me to tell you what you are hearing—the story of the Texas Principessa, my old schoolmate and lifelong pal, that you asked about. After the Prince's death, Horty pulled herself together and got the Palazzo together—a reproduction of Palazzo da Filippo was engraved on Renzi's tombstone *with* Horty's changes incorporated (which, of course, I thought was rather nifty, wouldn't you)—and Horty pleaded with me in April by phone and cable to come stay. "Come and stay as long as you want to, stay forever if you're happy in the Palazzo; just come on," Horty said, long distance, to me in London. Horty loved to have people in the house. This doesn't mean that she always loved being with them. Sometimes I've seen it happen that a motorboat would arrive and disburse a dozen guests and a week later depart with the same guests and not one of them had ever *seen* the Principessa. Horty would've confined herself off in her own apartment in the far right top wing and there remain in privacy. Simply did not want to have anything to do with them, with her guests. "That's Horty," everyone said. They'd had a grand time, gone in the Principessa's private motorboats to Torcello, to lunch at the Cipriano, to cocktails at other palazzos, been served divine dinners with famous Italians at the da Filippo. But no Horty. She usually—she was so generous—gave expensive presents to her guests to get them to forgive her. Once she gave everybody an egg—a sixth-century—B.C.!—egg of Chinese jade. Amounted to about a dozen eggs. Somebody said the retail value of those eggs was about one hundred and fifty dollars apiece. Where was I? Oh.

Well this was in April and May I came. Horty at once announced to me that there was no room for me at the Palazzo! She was getting crazy over painters. She'd become more and more interested in painting, Horty did, but that's no surprise because she always seemed to possess a natural eye and feeling for painting, not so curious for an heiress to generations of garment salesmen, even though you might so comment. For Hortense Solomon inherited good taste and a tendency for her eye to catch fine things when she saw them. Though there were Brahma bulls leering through the windows of the Solomon ranch in West Texas, what those bulls saw inside was fine china and Chippendale, silver and crystal and satin and silk. Those bulls saw the handiwork of a chic decorator and an elegant collector; not every bull sees *that*. So a seventeenth-century palazzo in Venice was not so far a cry for Horty to fix up.

Well, here was I living over at the Cipriano where Horty, who couldn't do without me till I got there and then banished me—to a terrific suite, I

171

must say, and footed by her—and here was I coming across the Canal every day to observe the goings on at the Palazzo. Frankly I was glad to have me a little distance from the commotion. Well-known artists came to live in the Palazzo da Filippo and to set up studios there and in the environs. Horty patronized them. Gave them scholarships as she called them. A few were very attractive, I must say, some very young—Horty's eye again. The Venetians adored La Principessa di Texas. They appreciated her for unscrewing the horse's outfit from the horse sculpture in her garden on the Grand Canal when the Archbishop passed in his barge on days of Holy Procession. The Principessa had commissioned the sculpture of a beautiful horse possesed of some wild spirit, with a head uplifted and long mouth open in an outcry. On it sat a naked man, again possessed of some wild spirit, seemed like, and his mad-looking head was also raised up in some crying out. You did not see the rider's outfit but the horse's was very apparent, and the Principessa commissioned the sculptor—a then-unknown but handsome sculptor—to sculpt one that was removable. Which seems to apply to a lot of men that I have known—where was it? A lot of them seem to have removed it. Put it in a drawer someplace. Or mind as well have. Where was I? Oh yes. The horses's outfit. On high holy procession days the Texas Principessa could be seen on her knees under the belly of the horse with grasping hands, making wrenching movements. The Italians coined a phrase for it. When they saw her going at the horse as if she were twisting a light globe, they said to each other that La Principessa di Texas was "honoring the Archbishop." The community generally appreciated her decency for doing this; some felt that the Archbishop should give her a citation. And a few called her a castrator—in Italian of course—castratazionera, oh I can't say it right but you know what I mean; and of course a few from home in Texas said she was a dicktwister—had to put their nasty mouths into it. Crude. Where was I? Oh. An American painter came to visit Horty one afternoon. He was showing in the Biennale, which is what they call the show of paintings that they have every year. Horty and the painter drank and talked about his painting. When the Principessa turned around from making *another* double martini for the American painter—she hardly gave it to him when she had to whirl around and make another one—*pirouette* is what you had to do when you made drinks for that man. Unless you just made a whole jug and gave it to him. Anyway, she whirled to find him urinating in the fireplace. The Principessa was so impressed with the American painter—imagine the audacity!—that famous summer afternoon that she asked him to stay. He stayed—over a year, it turned out—and you can see some of his paintings in the Palazzo gallery; they have become very sought-after and the painter very famous—though dead from alcoholism not so many years after that. More proof of the ability of discovery that the Principessa had, which is what an article about her recently said. And of the tragic cloud that kept lurking over her life. Even with all her money and the good that she did people, that cloud lurked. And of course it got her, as you well know.

Because Horty's dead. As you well know. Which is what I started out to tell you the details about when you asked me. Well, it was when we were lunching on the terrazzo of the Palazzo. One of those gold June days that Venice has. I'll go right into it and not dwell on it: Horty was bitten by something, some kind of terrible spider, and blood poisoning killed her before we knew it. Guess where the spider was? In a peach. Living at the core of a great big beautiful Italian peach from the sea orchards of the Mediteranean. Horty cried out and fainted. We'd all had a lot of champagne. By the time we got her to the hospital she was dead. Doctor said it was rank poison and that Horty was wildly allergic to it. When she broke the peach open out sprung the horrible black spider. I saw it in a flash. And before she knew it, it had stung her into the bloodstream of her thigh, right through pure silk Italian brocade. I'll never eat a peach again, I'll tell *you*. All Venice was upset. The Archbishop conducted the funeral himself. Horty'd left quite a few *lire* to the Church. We forgot to unscrew the horse's outfit, but when the funeral procession passed by, all the gondoliers took off their hats. Those Italianos!

And I am the new Principessa—except of course I am not a Principessa. But the Italians insist on calling me the new Principessa. The Palazzo is mine. Who ever dreamed that *I* would get the Palazzo? When the will was opened back in Texas they read where Horty had given the place to me! I almost had a heart attack. The will said "to my best friend." But what in the world will I do with a Palazzo? I said. I have not the vast fortune that Horty had. But you have all the paintings of the famous dead American, they said. Sure, the family have all fought me for the paintings of the dead American painter. Just let somebody find something good and everybody else tries to get it. Like a bunch of ants. That ever happen to you? They couldn't care less about the Palazzo. But the paintings are something else. The Museum has offered half a million dollars for one. I will not sell yet. And that man that peed in the fire died drunk and broke. Ever hear of such a thing? But they say the pollution is just eating up the paintings. *And* the Palazzo. So far *I'm* safe, but I wonder for how long? And the very town is sinking. Venice is a little lopsided. I don't know where to go. I hardly know how I got here. Sometimes I think, who am I, where am I? That ever happen to you? But the Texas Principessa is a saint in Venezia. Better not say anything in this town against Horty, I'm telling you. Those Italianos speak her name with reverence and the Archbishop says her name a lot in church. I have offered the horse to the Church, without outfit, but the Archbishop suggested—he's so cute, with a twinkle in his eyes, those *Italianos!*—the Archbishop suggested that *il cavallo* stay where it is. Because it is an affectionate monument for the townspeople, particularly the gondoliers. They point it out to tourists. I hear they're selling little replicas near the Vatican. The sculptor is very upset. He's made many more sculptures (not of horses) but nobody ever paid much attention to any of his other work. Isn't everything crazy? Aren't our lives all crazy? Some days I can't believe any of it. Sometimes I want to go home but I hear Texas is just as crazy. Anyway, that's the story of Horty Solomon da Filippo, the Texas Principessa. Which is what you asked me about, isn't it?

But one more thing. Next morning after the funeral I saw below the terrazzo something sparkling in the dew, something pure silver with diamonds and rubies and emeralds—like something Horty would've worn—and I saw that it was a gorgeous web. And there in the center, all alone, was the horrible black insect that I am sure was the one that had lived at the heart of the peach that killed the Texas Principessa and brought the Palazzo to me. How could something so ugly and of death make something like that . . . so *beautiful?* I had the oddest feeling, can't describe it. That ever happen to *you?*

Well, that's the story, what you asked me. What happened.

The Third Count

Andrew Fetler

I am waiting for my sister Nina to drive up from Boston for our Saturday lunch in my house on Bay Road, an old country road near Dudleyville. For a bachelor of fifty-nine, I make good lunches, she says. I have covered the salad with Saran Wrap and put it in the fridge. She wants her lettuce crisp, with a tomato from my garden and a sliced boiled egg. Besides the salad, we will have chicken rice soup (we had chicken noodle last week), cold cuts, and toast with Diet Mazola. For dessert, fresh peaches and cottage cheese. She is dieting again.

For thirty years my sister Nina has been seeing psychiatrists and feeling better about herself. "It's a *process!*" She has discovered health foods, but won't refuse an offer of Bavarian cream pie. She has tried *est*, folk dances of many cultures (Romanian dances are fantastic), protein powders for clearing her blood, sweetened calcium tablets for her puffy eyelids, and human potential encounters for raising her consciousness. But not until Jesus saved her, a year ago, could she forgive our father for having been a Christian.

Our father, Hamilton Crail, was a successful businessman and a founding father of the Full Gospel Church in Boston. As an elder of that church he practiced a mixture of Scottish Calvinism and American fundamentalism. He struggled continually against sins of the flesh. When my sister Nina was fourteen, for example, he marched her off to his study one night for bringing the devil into our home. I don't know how she could have provoked our father. Did he catch her fondling herself, or wearing a pretty dress, or smiling while wearing a pretty dress? Shamed and bewildered in his study, she sobbed and on command croaked the Repentance Song: "Just as I am, without one plea." Appar-

175

ently not satisfied, he took her to his study again the following night, for closer questioning behind his locked door.

And then, two months after these curious interrogations in Nina's fourteenth year, she fell sick and had to be taken to the hospital. She was brought home looking pale and wilted, cured of an "infection." Our father praised the Lord, and in church, as if inspired by Nina's recovery, he stirred up the congregation against our pastor for false preaching, and had him sacked. God, our father cried from the pulpit, holding up the Bible for his authority, could not use a modernist who doubted Creation Science and tolerated immoral books in public schools. Our false pastor, moreover, had done nothing to rescue from a mental hospital a young widow, a firecracker for the Lord, who had branded the foreheads of her two children with the emblem of the cross, to protect them from demons. The widow ought not to have used a heated knife, our father allowed, but her love and faith were great.

We were happy, Nina and I and our three brothers, when we could tiptoe through the day without attracting our father's attention. We scattered when we heard him coming, or froze in guilty attitudes when his figure loomed in the doorway. We could not live up to his standards. But we were not to despair. Our sins were God's opportunities. Hamilton Crail never hugged his children, flesh revolted him, but he worried about our souls. He believed in spiritual diagrams and drew pictures of our souls—a rectangle, say, containing circles and arrows going in and out.

Silent and withdrawn since her visit to the hospital, Nina found music harder to ignore than diagrams. Sometimes, when the church choir sang, "Perfect submission, perfect delight," she was touched by the love of Jesus and wept. "Filled with His goodness, lost in His love."

My sister Nina is fifty-five years old now and very fat, and she has spent her life worrying about her weight. A year ago, at a meeting in Boston of charismatic youngsters who call themselves The Disciples, she found happiness, she tells me, that cannot be expressed in words. She gave herself to Jesus completely, without reservations—Nina insists upon her surrender by tapping her chest with her chubby fist—and in return Jesus has taken her burdens upon Himself. "The only word for it is bliss!" she says, chattering without stop—she who used to hesitate before speaking—and smiles at my wonder. She feels omnipotent, she could do anything, she declares, and looks around my living room for a mountain to move.

Nina has backslidden twice since her conversion a year ago. During these dark spells that test her faith, lasting two or three weeks, she looks miserable and mutters about her father. "He must have hated me," she says. Would I say she had been hateful as a little girl? She says he never forgave her for the "unspeakable secret" between them, which Nina has never revealed to me beyond its being her unspeakable secret. "I hope you never guess," she stammers, her intelligence lapsing strangely, and tears fill her eyes.

Poor fat Nina takes her backslidings to her overworked psychiatrist, who gives her two Valiums and sends her to The Disciples for another fix. The Disciples rally round her. Lovely youngsters with effulgent eyes. They chant and clap to the accompaniment of electric guitars and drums, and raise their hands, palms up, when the Spirit begins to move, drums beating, until Nina shudders and jiggles with hiccups, and the storefront resounds with jubilation. "I'm a Jesus junkie, there's no way without Him," she says happily, between backslidings, and has taken to quoting chapter and verse and using evangelical language not heard in our family since our father died in the Lord thirty-five years ago.

She is an honest soul, my sister, and frankly expresses doubts about The Disciples and their Apostle, who has spoken face to face with Gautama Buddha, Moses, and Jesus, and who will be translated bodily into heaven. Their Apostle sends pamphlets, tape cassettes, and instructions to his flocks from headquarters in Los Angeles. Her doubts are received with love and understanding by the joyful youngsters. They don't say much about Father, as they call their Apostle, to new converts. Her doubting is beautiful, they tell her. Her every opinion is beautiful. And after the meeting they have coffee and cake, and the elders (ages eighteen to twenty-six) organize the week's Outreach activities. Think of all the people who will be left behind, any day now. Next week, the Boston flock will divide for missionary forays into Worcester and Amherst, scheduled for the same Monday, a college holiday, and Nina has offered to transport a load of them in her Plymouth Volaré.

The minister is a twenty-six-year old sweetie from Salt Lake City, Utah, for whom the Apostle picked a darling girl from Dallas, Texas. Nina has never seen such a happy couple, so in love with each other. The girl's parents tried to have the marriage annulled, spending more money on lawyers than they ever spent on their daughter. The Apostle limits the happy couple to spiritual intercourse for two years and may separate them in different missions far from home, to deepen their God-centered commitments to each other. His missions are nursing and foster homes in thirty-eight states—God's plan is to cover all fifty—into which are funneled federal and state moneys, only the Apostle knows

177

how much and the Lord's work cannot have enough. The godless parents of that darling girl, Nina tells me with a mildly crazy look in her eyes, have not seen these kids at work, in prayer and praise.

At the meeting in their temple, a Boston storefront, Nina sits with the young minister, paper plate on her lap, Styrofoam cup in her hand, and tells him how she relapsed from her slimming diet. Does her relapse signal another backsliding? "That's beautiful," says the attentive young man, and places his hand lovingly on her fat arm. "You're a beautiful person, Nina."

All this Nina relates with a full heart, her eyes shining. Her eyes are too old for clone-like effulgence and cloud over when she gives a scared smile of hope for me as well. We should be in this thing together, she says. Our three brothers rejected Jesus, she reminds me, and look at what happened to them. All dead. "You're all I have left, Jim," she says. Jesus takes pity on her backsliding and turns His face to her again, and pulls her to His forgiving bosom, and even lets her eat if she wants to. Eat or don't eat, but don't make such a big deal of it. "Look at the flowers of the field!" she cries. What am I going to do about Jesus? she wants to know. After all His suffering for us, will I accept Him or reject Him? If I accept Him He will accept me, and if I reject Him He will reject me.

The child's garden in her soul has had a long time to grow into a jungle. Lost in those senseless mazes, Nina is at last finding a way out, or believes that a way out is being found. I am glad for her and am almost grateful to The Disciples. Better than Valium, maybe. We were five once, four boys and one girl. Now Nina and I alone are left and our Saturday lunches are the last gasps of our family.

She forgoes some of our Saturdays for The Disciples. She lends them her car and gets it returned with a bashed fender. One Saturday she joined them in a street demonstration against Moonies, followers of a false prophet who claims that Jesus was hot to get married when He was killed, a doctrine the true Apostle in Los Angeles has pronounced unbiblical, inspired by Satan, leading to such Communist godlessness as the mass suicide-murder in Jonestown, Guyana. Full proof available on request, without cost or obligation.

Nina called last Monday to say that she would be free—*free?*—to visit me this Saturday, and suggested chicken rice soup for lunch. "Father says we should eat more rice, less potatoes." So the Apostle of The Disciples is her new father. She would arrive at noon, she said, and

178

added that she had committed ten percent of her stock portfolio to The Disciples. The principal, not the income. That would come to $30,000, roughly. She sounded pleased with herself.

"The *principal?*"

"I knew you'd gasp. It's the tithe I owe them. I'm ashamed I didn't promise more. I owe them *everything!*"

Imagine owing anybody everything. Since her religious conversion, she has begun to talk like a fourteen-year-old. "Nina, you can't do that."

"I knew you wouldn't understand," she said with harrowing patience. "Just trust me, O.K.? I know what you think of The Disciples, but you're dead wrong. You're still blinded, like I was. Please don't bring it up again when I see you."

If it made me feel better, she said, the young minister talked her out of giving more than ten percent. She had to grow stronger in the Lord before her new father in Los Angeles would consider accepting her total commitment: Caesar could contest large donations in court if they were not done right. I felt a weakness in my knees and sat down by the telephone, at my kitchen table. "I'm sorry I mentioned it," she babbled. "Just fix the salad and I'll be there by noon. You know what it's like, Jim? Coming to Jesus is like coming home again!"

Right.

Ten percent to that fellow in Los Angeles—for a start. "A tithe," I said, "is a tenth of your *income*, not your *principal*, for Christ's sake!"

"I won't have you taking the Lord's name in vain!" But she allowed herself a pause, perhaps for the shadow of a doubt to cross her mind. "I don't care what a tithe is. I'd rather be dead than live without Jesus. It's called faith, if that still means anything to you. For all his faults, Father had *faith*. Now I'm sorry for every bad thought I ever had about him. I beg his forgiveness!" she began to yell. "I repent in dust and ashes! I *was* hateful! Yes, I love him! Do you hear me, Jim? I just can't hate him any more, don't you understand? I'm *tired!* I've made peace, and you're still ranting after all these years. Except now you are ranting at *me* instead of at Father."

Before The Disciples got to Nina we talked about lawn fertilizers and stock options, and walked in the woods, and came in for coffee and an oldie showing Fred Astaire and Ginger Rogers. Now Nina talks about Jesus. I had rather we talked about fertilizers and stock options again, and about a little elephant in our county.

I want to talk about a local inbred, Sloan Mudge, a spawn of incest who keeps a female dwarf elephant in his zoo. Sloan Mudge is physically and mentally deformed, and his elephant, recently acquired, resembles Nina in her obesity. I hold them in view when she talks about Jesus.

Last summer I took her out to Teewaddle Road for a look at Sloan Mudge and his dwarf elephant. Nina did not want to go, she loathes Mudge and his slithery ways. But she had not seen his elephant and came along.

Mudge sat askew on his crate, clutching a roll of zoo tickets, and greeted us with his professional "'Joy yourself, now!"

She ignored him, and she hated his dirty elephant standing in its own muck, regarding her with little eyes. Raising its trunk, it worked its prehensile lips an inch from her face. Nina would not stay another minute in that damned zoo. "Is *that* what you brought me out here for?"

On the telephone, Nina's voice quavered, suddenly plaintive. "Are you there, Jim?"

"Look," I said. "I don't mind your Disciples. They give me an idea to buy Sloan Mudge's elephant."

"What are you talking about?"

"If you can spend ten percent on Jesus, I can spend a few dollars on an elephant."

Her intake of breath was followed by a threatening silence.

"We could trade," I said. "You give me Jesus, I'll give you the elephant."

"Is that all you can feel about me now? Ridicule?"

She was crying. Kids in a Boston storefront, gone from pot to pushing an Apostle in Los Angeles, taking their guitars with them, attract a sad fat woman who has never married and loves children. They give her a Jesus-fix and she feels bright, a beautiful person with beautiful opinions. But there is a side to Nina that is not primitive: her backslidings will grow longer, darker.

"I'm sorry," she said, sniffling, when she'd had her cry. "I didn't mean that about you. God knows you're a sweetie. But listen. Are you listening?"

"I'm listening."

What she said next chilled me, as if she were offering lemonade and cyanide in Jonestown, Guyana. "Jim, you mustn't be afraid. I'm not afraid any more. I'll be with you, we'll go together. I ˉknow God will reclaim you, even if He has to break you first—remember? Father *was* right, after all."

He was right. All our brothers suffered diseases or accidents or bad marriages. The eldest was broken by all three, the second by suicide, the third by madness. Two to go, Nina and me. Hamilton Crail's ghost has been stalking his children and now has Nina cornered, a lonely woman too weary to keep running, a broken and contrite heart. In a year she will be ready to give her last stitch to The Disciples, mop floors in a barracks in Beulah, and write, when permitted contact with the doomed world, of her fears for me, and send unbelievers to hell, and pray for my salvation. It would be too awful for Nina to go alone, as the Bible threatens: sister taken, brother left behind.

In parting, Nina said on the telephone, "I'll pray for you, Jim, and I won't stop praying for you. That's all Father could ever do for us."

"Thank you very much."

"Don't *trifle* with God! I can't ever, *ever* allow you to use that tone again—praise the Lord!"

That did not sound like Nina but like the old Full Gospel Church.

Salad, cold cuts, peaches and cottage cheese—all is ready for Nina's arrival at noon. The table in my dining room is set with our father's silverware, his monogram engraved indelibly. In the kitchen I find a squat vase with narrow neck, for my glass flowers. I bought them yesterday at the Craft Fair from two scrubbed members of a commune, a man and a woman—bare feet, Levis, plaid shirt, mop of hair, torpor common to both. These two were working out their salvation by selling handmade clay pipes, ceramic medallions on thongs, glass flowers with long metal stems, and home-sewn cotton tunics piled rumpled in a dirty cardboard box. Their eyes drifted and they gave me slack-jawed smiles.

At my kitchen window I can keep an eye out for Nina's car to appear on Bay Road, while I arrange the glass flowers in the vase. Blue, green, red, and yellow—two of each. I got them for my crystal collection, glass flowers for my crystal dancer. They are supposed to sway and tinkle.

In the living room the grandfather clock Nina picked up at an auction chimes the eleventh hour, a ghostly sonority recalling the ordered days and years of a family long gone. It occurs to me, with a spasm, that I need some disorder in my house, something alive and warmer than my crystal dancer. Nina's religious estrangement is cooling the weekly warmth she used to bring. Her voice has a hard edge when she talks about Jesus. Her face looks tight. She'll end up a missionary, if I know the signs. How keep myself warm? My incontinent old Airedale had to be put away last year. How about Sloan Mudge's dwarf elephant? A little madness would be nothing new in our family.

The owner of the elephant is of a race of New England inbreds still to be seen in our parts, a stunted little man with matted hair, low forehead, yellow eyes. At today's prices he could make a good living cutting

181

firewood, but he can't stick to any one task. He sets up a stand of blackberries for the sparse traffic on his road, hires himself out to pick cucumbers at child-labor rates, patches car tires at the Mobil station in Dubleyville. Sometimes, he disappears for a month, nobody knows where. Life has taught Sloan Mudge to be secretive. Once, an alarming rumor compelled a Congregational minister to bear a gift of groceries to his shack, and ask the recluse if he kept a grown daughter chained to his bed. "Nope," said Mudge, and took the groceries. The minister did notice a fall of chain in the rubbish on the rickety porch, but no daughter in the shack or near it. "He *had* a daughter by his sister," Nina said when we gossiped, her belief unshaken. Nobody had ever seen a woman in his vicinity, and all other Mudges, young and old, were safely tucked away in Mildwood Cemetery.

Sloan Mudge put up signs for a quarter of a mile along his road, boards nailed to trees, reading "CAMPING $2" in whitewash and an arrow pointing to the sky. He had run a water pipe from his well to the camp, and clapped together an outhouse with boards from his collapsed barn. A few out-of-state explorers pulled in with their campers and were driven out by mosquitoes from Mudge's swamp. His camp fared no better the second summer, though an agent from a state agency in Boston, studying water resources, offered to drain the swamp and kill the mosquitoes. Government interference did not sit well with Mudge, but the threat may have fired his ingenuity to come up with a better idea for pulling in campers. His dream of the good life would not die, and, in the third summer of the camp's existence, below his amended, "CAMPING $4" appeared a second sign: "ZOO." I did not drive out to Teewaddle Road for a look at his zoo until two college students stopped by my house soliciting signatures for a petition to free the animals. The Society for The Prevention of Cruelty to Animals had been alerted, and legal machinery had been set in motion to close Sloan Mudge's private enterprise.

Driving out on a hot summer Saturday, when Nina was serving The Disciples, I was touched to see that in his "ZOO" signs along Teewaddle Road Sloan Mudge had not availed himself of the adman's exclamation mark. His "ZOO" stated a fact, take it or leave it. I felt instinctive sympathy for Mudge, and rejoiced at the sight of cars pulled up by the zoo entrance, a classic example of Mudge architecture: gravel dumped over a culvert.

Here, Sloan Mudge himself sat on a crate, sweating and scratching himself, wearing a new T-shirt over stained pants, and guarded the entrance with a board reading "25" propped up beside him. He looked a

182

happy man, his aches forgotten. Without raising his yellow eyes to mine, he snatched the coin from my hand before I could give it, and, turning to spy who else might be coming up the road, said, " 'Joy yourself, now!"

Seven campers and two tents showed in the trees on the swampside, striped awnings unfurled. In the foreground, a dozen locals converged around a snack wagon featuring popcorn, Fritos, hot dogs, Table Talk pies, and sodas in the drifting dust.

Setting forth on my tour, I came upon a fox in a chicken wire enclosure, lying dusty beside a dusty tin plate. The fox was being urged to move—"Move it!"—by a man who had taken his denim shirt off in the heat, his paunch hanging over his belt. "Bet this critter's dead," he guffawed, jabbing me with his elbow, and tossed his crushed beer can at the fox, just missing the tail.

The next attraction was a coughing mongrel tied by a rope to a post. Atop the post was fastened a five-inch cage made of window screening, containing a spider watching flies trying to get in. Then the path forked, offering choices. The left path took me to the birds: a pintail duck sitting in the dust, a turkey in a swarm of flies, a ring-necked pheasant with a broken tail, and two chickens and transient sparrows, all in one enclosure. Chicken wire, strung between two pines and a young elm, housed a screech owl asleep on a truncated bench. Beneath this triangular cage, small bones and droppings littered the ground, and from the hexagonal mesh of the cage floor hung bits of rodent skins.

Returning to the spider's post, I took the more traveled path to the most impressive structure in Sloan Mudge's Zoo, a massive cage of four-by-fours, spacious enough for tiger or lion, but as yet vacant. Fortified with hot dogs and sodas, the locals had preceded me to a dwarf elephant beyond.

This captive, a spiritless female and the only animal in the zoo foreign to our parts, was no larger than a donkey. She was chained by a hind leg to an iron stake driven into the ground. Behind her lay the predictable dry bucket in the dust, overturned. Children reached out to slap her lethargic trunk—"Don't get too close!"—and the man with the beer paunch stood pelting her dusty hide with popcorn, expressing the general disapproval, for in her prolonged exposure to the hot sun the little elephant ignored her visitors. In the minutes I watched, she did not rest from her comatose swaying, back and forth, each forward motion forcing her chained hind leg off the ground as she pulled the chain taut. Her trunk hung unresponsive amid flying popcorn and candy wrappers.

When I left the zoo, Mudge called from his crate, "Come again, now!"

Three months later—I had taken Nina to the zoo in the interval—the

183

SPCA succeeded in having Sloan Mudge's zoo closed and his animals impounded, including a knock-kneed pony I had missed seeing, an emaciated pony that had been kept in a narrow stall for such a long time (four years, the Dudleyville *Gazette* said) that its hooves had curled up like Turkish slippers. Mudge's domestic animals, except his coughing mongrel and spider, were taken to the university's Agricultural Station for documentation.

But for some legal reason the authorities could not impound his dwarf elephant, for which he was able to produce a dubious bill of sale. The elephant had to await separate legal action.

Yes, I am dwelling on Sloan Mudge. Arranging the glass flowers in the vase and keeping an eye out for Nina's car to appear on Bay Road, I sit at my kitchen table and dwell on Mudge. Consider. In town Mudge has been showing acquaintances his picture in the *Gazette*. How, I wonder, given his material and mental resources, did he achieve so much in so little time? A zoo, no less, with an elephant and a screech owl and other birds and beasts, and maybe a lion or tiger on the way. A good idea builds. He had actually pulled it off, his greatest idea. He had looked happy that day, snatching the coin from my hand and wishing me joy in his paradise. He and his generations of inbred artists have always run afoul of the law; it is not his fault that the law wrecked his great zoo. Tenacious, ingenious Mudge has tried. He can rest now and feel in his weary bones the tug of millennia and the deliverance that lies in extinction.

In my mind I have christened Mudge's elephant Baby. What if I offered him $2,500 for her? Would he hold out for $3,000? I foresee problems with Baby, not the least of them local publicity. But the publicity will pass and Mudge inspires. Of course Baby would be better off in the Boston Children's Zoo—or would she? I could give her my love and a good home. Her bucket would never run dry. Hell, I'd give her a whole pool to play in, in a fine expansive paddock of upright railroad ties, even if I had to dip into my stock portfolio to do it.

Apparently Mudge does have title to Baby, though how he acquired her, with what money, where, remains nobody's business but Mudge's. His bill of sale for her, an incomprehensible German "*Rechnung*" on which Mudge's name is superscribed, was pictured on page 20 of *The Boston Globe*: "*Sie erhalten auf Grund Ihrer Bestellung als Postpaket: 1 Elephas africanus pumilio.*" Signed by one "G. Hagenbeck, Hamburg," the bill shows numbers for "*Postschekkonto,*" "*Bankkonto,*" "*Girokasse,*" "*Giro-konto,*" and is originally addressed to "*Herrn, Frau, Frl., Firma* Nelly

Billiard, Philadelphia, Pa., U.S.A." Did G. Hagenbeck ship the elephant to Nelly Billiard by parcel post? Beyond the *"Elephas africanus,"* this bill of sale, in its every aspect and unimaginable connection with Mudge, or indeed with Nelly Billiard, is as unintelligible to me as my own life — those aspects and connections of my life that occupy my thoughts.

My main difficulty would be providing for Baby's comfort so late in the season. Fall is upon us, the leaves are turning, you can smell arctic regions in breezes from Canada. Winter is coming. Whoever has no house will not build one now. If I kept Baby in the garage I would need a shed for my tractor mower and workbench. I'd have to lay a drainpipe for hosing the garage floor, and run the pipe out to the septic tank. The garage would need enough insulation and heating to be warm as the Congo during snowstorms. All this needs planning, contracting, time. For this winter, I see, I would have to take Baby into my house. Needless to say . . .

Is it really impossible?

Who would consent to having a child if he foresaw in a flash all the expense and terrors which the rearing of his child would visit upon him? My sister Nina and I are vulnerable in this regard, our religion having tinted our souls with catastrophic expectations. I worry, for example, that Baby's progress through my house would punch holes in the floor, like tracks in snow. But stop and think. Look at her. This specimen of a pigmy Congo race is no larger than a donkey, which some Sicilians keep in their houses. She is no heavier than my Yamaha upright piano, which I have rolled about the house for a good acoustical spot, without cracking the floor. Baby could safely mount the two steps from garage to kitchen and find her own way to the running water, down the hall to the right.

I can see my little elephant sitting in the tub, filling her trunk with water and spraying it around the walls. I'll have the walls and doorway hung with plastic curtains, and the floor tiled toward a drainpipe, a simple job in the bathroom with its wealth of plumbing. Baby could easily climb in and out of the tub, for it is a modern tub, only twelve and one-quarter inches deep, designed for space calculated by efficiency engineers. She would not want to get out of the water, I would have to scold her through the plastic curtain, mop in hand, my view blurred by drops and rivulets on the curtains: "You've had all morning. Nina is coming. You don't want Nina catching you here, do you?"

Waiting for Nina to arrive for our Saturday lunch, I sit at the kitchen table turning the vase of prismatic glass flowers. The ceiling glitters with refracted sunlight. Outside, the wind has risen. The forecaster promised a calm day. I know a meteorologist who does not forecast; he marks the sweeping picture of the years. The prodigious elm tree on my lawn flutters in a frenzy of yellows and browns, seemingly on fire in a blizzard of elm seeds. In the light of this conflagration, Nina's car, sporting the fender bashed by The Disciples, turns into my drive at last.

"If I thought you were serious," Nina says when we have eaten the peaches and cottage cheese, "I'd commit you to a mental hospital."

She is taking my elephant fantasy more seriously than I expected. "Baby would be in the house only this winter," I say, testing Nina's credulity. "By spring I'd have the garage ready for her. The paddock would take no time at all. The big job would be the pool, but she could wait for that."

"Baby will certainly want to express her gratitude. She'll corner you one day, right there by the TV, and crush you to death."

Nina has gained weight again. She has exchanged her tweed suit for a loose batiste in penitent gray, resembling a maternity dress, too light for the season. Over her shoulders she has thrown a girlishly pink sweater, pink on gray like fall leaves awaiting winter.

A horrible thing happened when we sat down to lunch. She could not fit herself between the arms of her chair. Too fat. I hastened to substitute an armless guest chair. Seating herself precariously, she composed her face and said: "Disgusting, ain't I. Well, it's true. Why pretend?" It was a bad moment for me to go on spinning my elephant fantasy for my elephantine sister. But I would have done worse to drop the subject abruptly, after introducing it with such a toot for something a bit messy in my life.

We take our coffee to the couch in the bay window. I see the elm burning in the sun, positively on fire. Every fall Nina remarks on the turning colors, but for once I don't call her attention to my elm. A trick of light does something unpleasant to it, something other than pretty. I stand transfixed.

"Why don't you get a dog?" she says, impressing the couch enormously with her buttocks. Her body seems to be inflating before my eyes.

I sit beside her. "No dog," I say. "After Emmy"—my Airedale gone to glory—"there is no other."

"Get a cat," says Nina.

"Emmy was afraid of cats."

"You're beginning to irritate me. You're doing it on purpose, aren't you. To get back at me?"

"For what?"

"For Jesus," she says.

"I don't know Jesus. I know some people who know Jesus."

"Your joke is wearing thin. Why do you keep hammering away at it?"

"What makes you think I'm joking?"

"Because an elephant is unthinkable, even to you."

"The unthinkable can become thinkable. Jesus, for example."

"Jesus *unthinkable?*"

"Of course Jesus is unthinkable. Born of a virgin? Passing understanding. Why else would you need faith? If you can think about Jesus, why can't I think about an elephant?"

"Where in *hell*," Nina explodes, "do you propose to keep your damned elephant! In the guest room?"

"The guest room is too small. So is the sewing room."

"You considered the sewing room?" she wails. "With all my things in the sewing room?"

"I wouldn't touch your things. You can come live here any time you want."

"Bay Road," she says with a moan. "I can't live on Bay Road. I need people. How can you live on Bay Road? You must have ice in your veins, like that crystal dancer of yours. Why don't you move to Boston?"

"I'd go crazy in Boston."

"You're going crazy on Bay Road, talking about elephants."

In the bay window the wind is subsiding, the elm stands burning like an iceberg.

"I couldn't keep Baby in this room, either," I say, pushing my fantasy. "I'd have to move the couch to your bedroom and the TV to the kitchen. But where would I put the piano? The kitchen isn't big enough for the piano."

Nina rolls her eyes, an expression she reserves for my inanities.

"The dining room," I say, "is long enough, but too narrow. The den is my library. I'm not giving that up, not even for Baby. The only room left is your bedroom, Nina. It's large enough for Baby, private bath and all. Just for this winter, remember. You could have my bedroom when you stay over. I'll sleep in my den."

She is stunned.

She says, "Why do you hate me?"

"I don't hate you."

"I have nobody."

I ought to hug her now, divert her with something light, affecting, a confection on Channel 3 or a home-fried gospel song to make her clap her hands with all the people, and let her have her cry, and sniffle, and smile again. But I shall not divert her from my fantasy. She will divert herself in a moment. I am thinking of the children of Hamilton Crail, no less than of a little elephant whose keeper shows doubters a mysterious bill of sale for his authority to chain her to an iron stake. Seeing God-appropriators pelting Nina with religious popcorn, I am brightening the corner where I am. "Stand thou on that side, for on this am I!" the Full Gospel Choir used to sing in transports of self-confidence. Here is my own song, about a little elephant.

Nina recovers, going from tearful to tough in twenty seconds. "You're not hurting me, James. What I can't understand is why you should want to hurt Jesus. Because that's what you are doing. After all He has done for us! Never mind me, but Jesus *does* matter." And she quotes John 3:16 to prove that Jesus matters. "Come with me to the temple," she says, referring to the Boston storefront of The Disciples. "Just once. Your eyes will be opened."

The elm on my lawn burns icily. Shall I ask her to look? She would not see the terrible tree. She would see God's glory in the fall colors. Nina is moved by nature. "That's the glory of God," she will say. She is learning or recovering pretty ideas about God. She knows as much about God as TV evangelists and Job's comforters. She knows how loving God is, for God is Love, and, though just, He is merciful, her loving Father.

Silent, we sit on the couch, and then she is crying.

"I want to pray," she says. "Will you pray with me?"

"You go ahead."

"It's something we can do together, Jimmy."

"I'm not stopping you. Go ahead and pray."

"I want to *help* you!"

I feel a double-take. She wants to help me. I live in perpetual astonishment, in a kind of low dread that does not respond to sing-alongs sung ardently off key. Nina must have happiness, warmed and passed through many hands.

Hurt by my resistance, she sits rocking back and forth like my little comatose elephant chained to the stake. With great effort she pulls herself up from the couch, her effort so great that her eyeballs show their whites as if she's gone blind. She lumbers out between couch and coffee table and turns uncertainly, casting about for a way to kneel on the rug.

Somehow, she lands softly and stands on hands and knees, on all fours like Baby, her huge bulk breathing, her loose dress flowing in gray folds from her buttocks, revealing a blotched, liver-spotted, awesome circumference of thigh one might glimpse in the jungle.

Her pink sweater has fallen from her shoulders and lies hooked on the coffee table. She rights herself from all fours to her knees and raises her hands for praying, her body cantilevered like that of a circus elephant.

And then, horribly, our old Repentance Song breaks from her throat in her sweet little-girl voice; and I see her bewildered at fourteen, locked up with our father in his study, humiliated at his feet: "Just as I am, without one plea . . ."

But I have always loved Jesus, even as a little girl, Nina has told me since Jesus saved her, as if she were eager to please Jesus even in her memories.

"Jesus, my Lord and Savior," she says, swallowing a catch in her throat, and prays in whispers inaudible to me.

I sit on the couch studying her desolation. Thus have I known her since her fourteenth year. I can still see a vestige of that little girl in poor Nina, an outlined innocence in elbows and hands clasped in prayer. She is backsliding again and hanging on for dear life. Now and then my name rises from her slurred whispers, so she is praying for me too. Maybe I could help her by drawing the curtains: the light in which the tree stands is too harsh—too harsh altogether. I could play my stereo record of Mendelssohn's *Elijah:* "If with all your hearts ye truly seek me, ye shall ever surely find me." I'd like that myself, make no mistake. I'd need a hanky, hearing Elijah, and Nina would weep torrents and feel better, much better.

As Nina prays in her loneliness, I turn to look at the tree. The wind has fallen, the leaves are stilled, the great tree stands motionless like a crystal arrangement, not impressively colorful just now. It is a muted incandescence suffused with cold blue. I once sailed in a luxury liner dwarfed by a radiant iceberg that inclined my voyage, I know today, to this tree on my own lawn.

Yesterday, I happened to see the ruins of Sloan Mudge's Zoo. Stopping by his culvert, I got out of the car and scanned the blighted field for relics. A rank odor, sweetly putrescent, infected the air. A stark post stood where his zoo once stood. Rotting boards lay strewn about. A bit of window screening had curled and, with grass grown through, disguised itself as tumbleweed. The massive cage of four-by-fours, once intended for a miraculous lion or tiger, had vanished without a trace.

May not such a miracle live in the pilgrim's reverence, on evidence not seen?

Pilgrims not lacking. Three distinct truck tracks, made by vehicles heavy enough to churn up mud, snaked across the field to Mudge's swamp. There, where campers once camped in clouds of mosquitoes, I

189

now discerned a scattering of industrial drums, indifferently concealed from the road. The drums led the eye beside the still waters of the swamp proper, a glimmering darkness streaked with silver and foam, such as may be painted by chemical wastes.

When Mudge gets caught he will be fined $50 for polluting his own drinking water, and admonished. "Yes, sir," he will say.

I drove on but slowed down and stopped again as Mudge's shack came in view on high ground, etched against the sky. He had prospered. In his weedy yard stood a new pickup and a horse trailer. A junked car lay on its back. Within the dark proscenium of his porch, a naked light bulb shone in an uncurtained window. Beside the shack stood the wreck of a barn, somehow keeping its feet, whole sections of walls missing, the roof caved in as if smashed by a fist. In a gaping hole in the barn I saw what I had not consciously come to see, the dwarf elephant.

Or was it a pony? I got out of the car for a better look. From the road I could not make out the animal's shape in the gloom. The head seemed too large for a pony, the body too thick. I could not see her trunk or judge which way she faced. She stood under the caved-in roof, a shadow.

A shadow, polluted waters, a stark post in a blighted field, relics— Sloan Mudge never disappointed. True to his generations of inbred artists, he continued to provide. The westering sun played its light on his old sign, a board nailed to a tree by the side of the road. The sign was weathered now, hung askew, the whitewash faded but still legible: "CAMPING $4" and an arrow pointing to the sky. And below, in witness of a bygone marvel: "ZOO."

He will never knock down these joyful tidings. If a traveler should ask, Sloan Mudge will steal a look at the out-of-state license plate, shift his yellow eyes to the swamp, and in time, with hindsight and foresight, spin a myth.

I felt tired approaching my sixtieth year and was struck by the similarity between Mudge's road and mine. Too far from shopping malls, schools, and churches, both roads were shunned by home builders. Abandoned farms on Bay Road had been reclaimed by woods, while Teewaddle Road favored swamps and thickets. At twilight in October, roads more solitary than Mudge's and mine may not be seen in our parts, nor vistas more withdrawn from the human concourse. Such roads are sometimes pictured in tabloids. I could not loiter. A parked car on these desolate stretches suggested something less definable than lovers or bird watchers.

Nina's prayer smolders and goes out. It is hard to pray with an unbeliever in the room. I steady her as she reaches for the coffee table and maneuvers herself up from her knees. Having regained her feet, she pulls away from my supporting hand, recovers her pink sweater, and looks about for her overcoat.

"You're leaving?" I ask.

She is. She is going back to her friends in Boston. "I really must. We have an early meeting today."

My silly elephant fantasy has ruined our lunch. We'll not be walking in the fall colors and tart air promising winter. How pleasant it would have been, then, to come in for coffee and an oldie on TV, Basil Rathbone and Nigel Bruce this afternoon. *Great Heavens, Holmes!*

"What about *our* day?" I remonstrate. "There's a Sherlock Holmes movie today. Basil Rathbone."

"Really." She smiles in token that she has passed beyond such pabulum.

Besides losing our family hour with Sherlock Holmes, I have forfeited the moment for moderating Nina's caprice to squander $30,000 on The Disciples—her promised "tithe." Had I been sensible I might have nudged her to reconsider the sum for The Disciples. What possessed me to offer her bedroom to an elephant? I cannot reach her now, as she stands poking in her shoulder bag for the car keys.

"The chicken soup was great," she says. "Thanks for reminding me of my nothingness."

"That's not what I meant."

"That's exactly what you meant." She clasps her hands in mock gratitude. "Isn't that what you always meant—*all* of you? Didn't I get to wash the dishes while you played the piano? Nina the Moron?" And she stings herself three times with our childhood singsong: " 'Nina the moron!' "

Is that what her prayer tossed up? As I move to mollify her, she wards me off and whimpers the old incantation through gritted dentures. I can't get near her. She is spitting hellfire.

I follow Nina out to her Plymouth Volaré.

Bay Road passes through woods here and my clearing is surrounded by woods. Summer and winter, my garden (now bedded in straw) stands in shadows well after sunrise and well before sunset. From the road my house, fieldstone and wood painted white, looks neatly tucked away in the woods. When the leaves turn, an occasional tourist car slows and sometimes the driver points at my house for his passengers to see. The sky is bright now but darkness abides in the underbrush.

As I hold the car door for Nina, she falls in expertly backwards. Then she pulls her thick legs in after her, one at a time. I wonder how she avoids collisions: she drives reclining at an angle of forty-five degrees. The seat belt is not long enough for her girth. I close the car door. She fumbles with the keys and rolls down the window. Her cheek does not respond to my kiss.

"Are you really going to a meeting?" I ask.

She sits touching up her hair before the rearview.

"You treat me like a stranger," she says, adjusting a curl. Satisfied, she turns to give me a parting shot. "I wanted to talk about something important to me, and you talk about keeping an elephant in my bedroom. You think that's funny? You think it's funny telling me to trade Jesus for your damned elephant?"

"I'm sorry. It was a stupid joke. You came to talk, let's talk. Come on, get out. It's time for our walk. Then we'll have coffee and Sherlock Holmes. Won't that be fun?"

"I've had quite enough frankly," she says. The car engine sparks to life.

Reclining now in her fearful driving position, she shifts her automatic into Rear but keeps her foot on the brake pedal, hesitantly. "Giving money to The Disciples doesn't really do it, does it?" she says.

"I couldn't agree more."

"Money is not enough," she says, resolutely, and shifts back into Park. "I want to go to a Bible College. I've been thinking about Okeko in San Diego. But my friends say Okeko discriminates against fatsos. They say fatsos are cursed by God. Do you know anything about it? Is it true?"

Is this what Nina came to talk about, and I talked about an elephant?

Is it true that Okeko Bible College discriminates against fatsos, or that God has cursed fatsos, or cursed the lot of them?

"If Okeko says so," I say, "it must be in the Book."

"But that's only a human *interpretation*! Why can't they read the Bible like it's written!"

I stand looking at her. She is close to tears again. Unaccountably, Nina wears her hair short, effectively lowering her forehead to simian proportions, capped by stiff ringlets of thinning hair blasted by beauty parlors. Her hair is graying. The ringlets do not altogether conceal the curvature of her skull, when viewed against light.

"It's great your wanting to go to college," I say. "I wish you'd told me sooner. I'll find a perfect little college for you. Just don't do anything in the meantime—all right?"

"I know all about your perfect little colleges. No thanks. But find out

192

about Okeko. If I can't go to Okeko, I'll try Father. It's just that I'm not worthy of him yet."

"Worthy of Father?"

"Our Apostle," she says curtly, and seems to regret having blurted that much to an outsider. A guarded expression veils her eyes.

"Does that mean you will leave The Disciples, if you go to Okeko?"

"Why do you pretend interest? You're not interested. You haven't the faintest idea what it takes to be worthy of Father. What can you know on this deserted island of yours?"

"Are you coming next Saturday?"

"Are you inviting me?"

"Of course. Always."

"Not next Saturday," she says. "We're doing Outreach. I'll call you when I can."

So she leaves. Her car passes my roadside mailbox and glides out of my clearing into the woods.

Will she pay $30,000 to be found worthy of Father, and boil her brains into the bargain, in some Bible College that teaches Creation Science in the name of truth, *avoiding profane and vain babblings, and oppositions of science falsely so called: which some professing have erred concerning the faith?* . . . Nina would have made a good horticulturist, or a good pastry chef. She has a green thumb, can talk to plants, and her pleasure in sweets would impress an effendi in Istanbul.

Silence flows back. Bay Road is a quiet old country road, traffic having abandoned it for a better one. From the lawn bench under my elm I contemplate the empty road and hear a soft wind in the trees and the raucous slang of a blue jay, a bird whose insolence is bred by violent dislike of predators. A hawk is about, or a roosting owl. Inhaling the cool air, I return to myself on this deserted island of mine.

I have never known a man whose agonies about the sins of his children matched my father's intensity. His after-dinner Bible Hour brought the Full Gospel Church into our home every day between Sundays, and when he judged we needed more he summoned us to the living room at bedtime, or later. On such occasions, while waiting for him to appear, we sat without speaking, as ordered, and scowled accusations at each other. Who among us had transgressed?

Hamilton Crail did not account himself the most blameless man in Boston, only the most God-loving. Shortly after Nina's "infection" in her fourteenth year, his rage for glory tortured him to confess himself the Chief of Sinners.

I do not recall what else he said that night. Our family meetings were all alike, indistinguishable from church services and the Radio Gospel Hour, without the latter's pitch for a Free Gospel-Faith ("golden metal") Prosperity Cross prayed over according to God's promises in Deuteronomy and Matthew. My father had indeed prospered, he could not love God enough, and he used to conclude our family meetings with a swing of the evangelical cudgel: "Pray with me!"

What I remember lucidly is my falling into a troubled sleep after one of those meetings, a sleep that conjured up the meeting in the form of a dream. It is my dream of the event, rather than the event itself, that has stuck in my memory through the years. From time to time I dream that dream again.

In my dream, the five of us have been summoned and sit waiting in the living room for our father to appear. My two younger brothers grow restive and pull at me to climb up on a ladder-back chair. They want to sled me around the room. I mount the chair, our eldest brother watches to see if we dare, and just then the door opens and a gigantic stranger enters instead of our father.

Our summons is explained by the stranger's cropped hair and uniform of a prison guard from a 1930's melodrama. Massive neck and shoulders, blunt nose, stump of chin. He surveys the room with an air of authority. Much has happened behind the scenes last night while we slept, his manner tells us. We have all broken the law, and our father has had to go to the authorities and do his duty. The guard advances heavily into the room, an immoderate hulk suggesting restrained force, and speaks without raising his voice: "You all get ready to move, now."

He will brook no disobedience, it is clear. All except Nina rise to their feet. She slumps on the floor by the bookshelf, a dropped puppet in a pretty dress, her face that of an old woman, oddly darkened.

The guard seats himself in a Windsor chair and looks us over. His eyes rest on Nina and move on, unconcerned. Oblivious of my elevated position on the ladder-back chair, I remain standing on it, guessing that we will be marched out to a wagon and taken to our destination. I face the guard with confidence in my alacrity to obey. Hypocritical obedience is my strong suit. I will hop on one leg when ordered, fling myself to the ground when ordered. What can't I do, when ordered? I shall be a model prisoner, I shall win over the guard and get a commendation for good behavior, and maybe privileges.

"Now," says the guard, after he has scrutinized us. "When I count to three, you all start running out that door."

He will see what a good boy I am. Standing on my chair, I brace myself as for the start of a race. I want to be the first in the wagon.

"One . . . two . . ."

As the guard holds off the third count, I become aware of his watching me narrowly to see if I jump the gun. I will not jump the gun, never never. I will make for the door on the third count precisely, not a split second before or after.

I keep this promise to myself, inspired by fear of the unknown and by my need to survive. I don't jump the gun. And the third count never comes.

The guard sits scanning the room. All stand frozen like dummies.

We wait for the third count, and the guard's silence persists. My forward knee begins to tremble with the effort of holding still. I can't abandon my feeling that he is only doing his job, an elementary humanity behind the functionary must respond to my good will. I read in his eyes, as he returns my look, that he understands my sentiment. But he appraises me with an animal's vacant regard, and then I see that his skull is empty but for an implacable, unqualified, impersonal hatred, hatred without sense, directed not at transgression or transgressor but simply there like a reptile.

The third count never comes. But for a moment the pain of its not coming is transcended. My two younger brothers, ages nine and eleven, below the age of reason, one could plead, suddenly give the chair I stand on a shove, and, as I catch my balance, sled me around over the carpet, to the far end of the room and back. I feel securely fixed on the careering chair, and with the momentum gained I steer myself as on skis to the guard and come to a stop with a happy little flourish.

He leans sideways and holds me in his reptilian gaze. He can't punish me, I'm sure. Technically, I did not disobey him, I did not leave the chair, I remained standing on it, waiting for his third count, I was shoved and the chair slid about my itself.

"Having fun?" he says, and turns to the room at large. "You all accept Jesus now. There's no other way. By the time I count three it will be too late."

Who could have invented such an instrument?

The Storytellers

Fred Chappell

Uncle Zeno came to visit us. Or did he?

Not even the bare fact of his visit is incontestable. He was a presence, all right; he told stories, endless stories, and these stories worked upon the fabric of our daily lives in such manner that we began to doubt our own outlines. Sometimes, walking in the country, one comes upon an abandoned flower garden overtaken by wild flowers. Is it still a garden? The natural and the artificial orders intermingle, and ready definition is lost.

But the man who effected such transformation seemed hardly to be among us. He was a slight, entirely unremarkable man given to wearing white shirts with frayed cuffs and collars. That is, in fact, how my memory characterizes him: a frayed cuff, a shred, a nibbled husk. If he had not spoken we might have taken no more notice of him than of one of the stray cats which made our barn a sojourn between wilderness and wilderness. His hair, his face and hands, I cannot recollect. He was a voice.

The voice too was unremarkable, except that it was inexhaustible. Dry, flat, almost without inflection, it delivered those stories with the mechanical precision of an ant toting a bit of leaf mold to its burrow. Yet Uncle Zeno had no discernible purpose in telling his stories, and there was little arrangement in the telling. He would begin a story at the beginning, in the middle, or at the end; or he would seize upon an odd detail and stretch into his stories in two or three directions at once. He rarely finished a story at one go; he would leave it suspended in mid-air like a gibbeted thief or let it falter to a halt like a stalled car blocking the road. And he took no interest in our reactions. If the story was funny our laughter made no more impression upon him than a distant butterfly; when we were downcast at a sad story, he did not seem to realize it. His attention was fixed elsewhere. My father and I got the impression that he was not remembering or inventing his stories, but repeating words whispered to him by another voice issuing from somewhere behind the high, fleecy clouds he loved to stare at.

That puts me in mind of . . .

These six flat monosyllables will be spoken at break of Judgment Day; they are the leisurely herald notes which signal that time has stopped, that human activity must suspend and every attention be bent toward discovering the other leisurely country words which follow. This is the power that beginnings have over us; we must find out what comes next and cannot pursue even the most urgent of our personal interests with any feeling of satisfaction until we do find out. The speaker of these words holds easy dominion.

That puts me in mind of—Uncle Zeno said—Lacey Joe Blackman. You know how proud some folks are of what they've got—he said—cars and fine houses and such. Some folks are proud of their wonderful hunting dogs, like Buford Rhodes was, but I ain't talking about him but about Lacey Joe Blackman. Lacey Joe was proud of a watch which come down to him from his daddy and Lacey Joe kept it on him for fifty years or better, and he couldn't say how long it had been in the family before his daddy. It was real old-fashioned, a big fat bib watch in a silver casing and been around so long the silver had wore thin on it like a dime. Even when he got to be seventy-five years old, Lacey Joe was liable to tug his watch out and flip up the lid and give you the time of day, you didn't need to ask.

Lacey Joe had a well-known name as a hunter, maybe only Turkey George Palmer had killed more brutes, and Lacey Joe would go on a hunt anytime night or day, deer, bear, groundhog, you name it. Go a-hunting pissants I reckon if they was in season. They ain't much bear hunting in these parts anymore, I remember the last time Lacey Joe went.

Setback Williams had sold his big farm down on Beaverdam, as he was getting on in years, and him and Mary Sue had bought a little homestead that butted up against the Smokey National Park. No farming on it, Setback was past doing any heavy labor, but there was a little apple orchard in the back, maybe two dozen trees, and old Setback liked his apples and apple trees.

But there was a troublesome bear ranging in those acres and he liked the apples and the apple trees powerful well too. You know how it is with a bear and the apple trees, gets all excited and he'll go to sharpening his claws like a cat with a settee. Go around and around a tree ripping at the bark and pretty soon he's girdled it and that tree is doomed to die.

Setback had done already lost two trees to this bear and he didn't know what to do. Can't shoot a bear anymore even if he's on your property unless you get permission from the Park Service and they won't hardly never give permission no matter what cussedness a bear had been up to. But Setback called anyhow over there to the Ranger Station I don't know how many times and kept deviling them and finally they were out to his place and allowed as how maybe he had a problem.

What they done was put up a fence, but the Park Service won't put you up no barbwire fence because it ain't what they call rustic-like, they don't want no tourist looking at a barbwire fence. They put up a heavy peel-log fence around the orchard about six foot high, ten times as much work as a good barbwire fence, and Setback took one look at it and declared, Boys, that ain't going to keep no bear off of my apple trees. And it wasn't two days later he went out and there was a bear setting in a tree, looking down like he owned that tree and the U.S. Park Service too. Setback raised a holler and the bear scuttled down and lickety-split into the forest right over the fence. Didn't make no more of that fence than you would a plate of peach cobbler.

So he called the Rangers again and they dawdled and cussed awhile and finally come over and built another peel-log fence, never seen anything like it. This one was fourteen foot high if it was an inch and strong as a fort. Kind of awesome to look at, think about the work them fellers had put into it. But Setback wasn't nothing only suspicious, and a week later he looks out and there was that same bear up in that same tree. Like the King of England on his throne all of gold. Setback ran out and hollered and the bear jumped down and run to the fence. When he got there he stretched up like a man reaching down a jug off of a tall shelf and took hold of a middle log about seven foot high and leapt up and then he was over. It was plumb pretty to look at, Setback said, except he was so mad.

He was on the telephone in a jiffy and told them he was going to shoot that bear, National Park or no National Park, and they said, No he wasn't. He told them a man has a right to protect his property, especially the apple trees, and also besides his wife was getting scared, that bear coming in on them all the time. That was where he was stretching it because Mary Sue never took fright of nothing, stout-hearted she was. Finally they said they'd let him trap the bear as long as he used the trap they'd bring him, and he could hold it and they'd come and pick the bear up and carry it to the farthest-back part of the forest and it wouldn't wander out as far as his apple trees again. He suspicioned that wouldn't work neither, but he was willing to try anything.

The trap they brought him didn't have no teeth, smoothed off so it wouldn't hurt a bear's leg much, but it was awful big and heavy, Setback said he never seen one that big.

He pegged it in the ground out there amongst the trees. Used a locust stake must have been five foot long and a big old drag chain. Covered it over with leaves all proper.

Might be another week passed before Setback and Mary Sue heard the awfulest row and tearing-around uproar. It was the early hour of the morning, not what you call sunlight yet. Bothersome to be woke up like that, but when it come to Setback they must have caught the bear, he hustled into his clothes and went out to have a look.

But there was nothing to see but some tore-up leaves and rassled-around dirt. Not one other blessed thing. That bear had pulled that five-foot stake plumb out of the ground. Hadn't left nothing, toted off the trap, the drag chain, and the locust stake, and gone over that fourteen-foot log fence. Hard to believe his eyes, Setback said.

He was back on the phone to the Rangers again, telling them what he was going to do and them saying yessir right along. Because you couldn't leave the animal with the trap on his leg, him in pain like that. Then he called up me and five others and Lacey Joe Blackman, who still kept his bear dogs and always had such a name for bear hunting. And we met over at his place it must have been about eight o'clock in the morning.

The dogs got the scent right in a hurry, all barking to beat Joshua, and we set off in a trot. We kept an eye on Lacey Joe, him going on eighty years of age, but he was hale and spry and after a little bit we figured he would wear us down and the dogs too. Didn't have far to go, though, maybe two miles and the bear was already treed.

Might not even have been the dogs, might have treed hisself, worried kind of crazy toting that iron and wood on his leg. Whatever, he was sure enough treed, the pack yipping and jumping around the bottom of the tree.

An awful big tree too, sixty foot tall anyhow, and spindly at the top where he was at. He was right in the very tip-top, and the tree was bowed way over with him. If it wasn't a pine tree you'd think it might bust. And just enough wind to sway it, and the bear in it, that was some sight. We stood just a-looking for a long time.

Till Setback says, Well, Lacey Joe Blackman, I believe it's up to you to take the first shot. Him being the oldest, and us all thinking he was about half sand-blind and one of us would get the kill. I'll do her if that's what you want, he says, and steps out and raises up his rifle. Which we seen was an old thirty-aught-six must've belonged to Nimrod and didn't even have a front sight. We was all thinking, that bear ain't got no worries just yet, and he steps out and raised up his rifle and didn't take no aim and killed that bear stone dead. Bullet we found out later went in right between the eyes.

The bear dropped plummet. Down about thirty foot and then jerked up again. That locust stake he'd been dragging got caught crossways in the fork of a big old limb and held him up there. The tree was bending way over. And the bear hung up like that went back and forth like a pend'lum on a grandfather clock. Back and forth, and back and forth. It was a sight made us all stand there quiet as pallbearers.

And so Lacey Joe Blackman, he pulls that silver-case watch of his out and opens it up. He squints at that bear swinging back and forth and he looks down at his watch, up at the bear, down at his watch. And he says, Boys, if this-here old watch of mine is still keeping right, that bear is swinging just . . . a mite . . . slow . . .

"Just a mite slow?" My father frowned. "I don't get it. A bear is not hanging in a tree to be keeping time. What does he mean, a mite slow?"

But that was the end of the story, and the end too of Uncle Zeno's talk. He only told stories, he didn't answer questions. The voice he listened to, the voice beyond the world, gave him only stories to report; any other matter was irrelevant. Uncle Zeno turned to my father but his gaze was so abstracted that the chair my father sat in at the supper table might as well have been empty.

That was part of the trouble. Uncle Zeno lived in a different but contiguous sphere that touched our world only by means of a sort of metaphysical courtesy. So how was he able to tell stories? He seemed to absorb reality, events that took place among people, without having to be involved.

"Was Homer blind because he was a poet?" my father asked me next day. "Or was he a poet because he was blind?"

"I don't know what you mean."

"I'm thinking about Uncle Zeno," he said.

"Oh," I said.

"You remember I told you the story of the *Iliad?* Well, Homer couldn't have been a soldier, of course, because he was blind. That's how he came to know so much. If he'd been a soldier, he couldn't have told the story. If Uncle Zeno ever struck a lick of work, if he ever had any dealings with people at all, maybe he couldn't tell his stories."

I could recall vividly my father's retelling of the *Iliad.* He found a

200

magazine photograph of Betty Grable and propped it on the mantel-piece by the gilt pend'lum clock and said that Miss Grable was Helen of Troy and had been stolen away by a slick-hair drugstore cowboy named Paris. Were we going to stand for that? Hell no. We were going to round up a posse and sail the wine-dark seas and rescue her. He flung himself down on the sagging sofa to represent Achilles loafing in his tent, all in a sulk over the beautiful captive maiden Briseis. He winked at me. "These women can sure cause a lot of trouble." The account ended ten minutes later with my father dragging three times around the room a dusty sofa cushion which was the vanquished corpse of Hector.

His excitement enticed me to read the poem in a Victorian prose translation, and I found it less confusing than his redaction, its thrills ordered.

That was the trouble with my father's storytelling. He was unable to keep his hands off things. Stories passed through Uncle Zeno like the orange glow through an oil-lamp chimney, but my father must always be seizing objects and making them into swords, elephants, and magic millstones, and he loved to end his stories with quick, violent gestures intended to startle his audience. He startled us, all right, but never by the power of his stories, always by the sharpness of his violence.

He had grown jealous of Uncle Zeno's storytelling and decided he would tell a suppertime story involving a mysterious house and a haunted shotgun. But his brief tale was so perplexed that we couldn't follow it at all. We were, however, disagreeably shocked when the haunted shotgun fired because he illustrated this detonation with a swift blow of his fist on the edge of the table which caused the insert prongs of the inner leaf to break, catapulting a bowl of butter beans onto my father's shirtfront.

My mother and grandmother and I stared at him in consternation as he mumbled and began plucking beans from his lap, but Uncle Zeno, sitting directly across the table, took no notice, gazing past my father's downcast confusion into his portable Outer Space. "That puts me in mind of . . ." he began, and proceeded to tell of a haunted house of his knowledge, atop which the weather vane pointed crosswise to the wind, in which fires flamed up without human agency in the fireplaces, and the cellar resounded with a singing chorus of lost children. We turned with grateful relief from my father's predicament and were soon enrapt by Uncle Zeno's monotone narrative, which now began to include sealed doors that sweated blood, a bathtub that filled up with copper-head snakes from the faucet, a vanity mirror that gave back the images of the dead, a piano whose keys turned into fangs whenever "Roses of

Picardy" was attempted. My father too became enthralled and sat motionless among his butter beans until Uncle Zeno concluded. His ending, if that is the correct term, was, "Anyhow—"

That jerked my father awake. "Anyhow?" he cried. "What kind of climax is that? Did this Willie Hammer ever find the forbidden treasure or didn't he?"

But Uncle Zeno was not to speak again until possessed by another story, and he merely looked at my father with an expression of vacant serenity. My father gave up in disgust and began again to drop his lapful of beans into the bowl one at a time, plunk plunk plunk.

His jealousy grew. He was going to learn to tell stories that would shade Uncle Zeno's the way a mountain overtowers a hill of potatoes. He ransacked his memory, and he begged stories from the loafers down at Virgil Campbell's grocery store, and he began to delve into the volumes of fairy tales and folklore scattered about the house. He borrowed my book of Norse mythology and committed a good half of it to memory. All to no avail. My father was simply too entranced with mischief and effect, and the stories he managed to begin in leisurely fashion soon careered into wild gesticulation and ended with an unpleasant loud noise. "Wham!" he would shout. "I've gotcha!"

But he didn't have us, not in the way he wanted to, and he looked into our startled faces with an expression of expectancy quickly sagging to disappointment. "Well, maybe I left out some stuff," he would say, "but it's still a damn good story. Better than some I've heard lately."

Uncle Zeno said: That puts me in mind of Buford Rhodes and his coonhounds. Buford was a good old boy anyway you want and kind of crazy about raising coonhounds and was an awful smart hand at it. Lived out there in Sudie's Cove in a tin-roof shack with his wife and six younguns and must have been a good dozen dogs. All kinds of dogs, Walkers and Blue Ticks and Redbones and lots of old hounds with the breeding mixed in like juices in soup. One of them named Raymond, you couldn't never figure out, must have been a cross between a bloodhound and a Shetland pony. Kids rode that dog all day like a pony, he was that good-natured.

But it was the dog called Elmer that Buford was most proudest of, though Elmer wasn't much bred either, just an old sooner dog. Still he was the brightest dog anybody ever heard tell of. Buford was selling his hides to Sears and Roebuck for a dollar apiece. He'd catch them coons by the score and skin them and tack their hides up to cure. Got so after a while there wasn't a inch of wall on Buford's house or milkshed not covered with coon hides. So Buford always kept an eye out for old scrap lumber and kept piling it underneath his house to cure them hides on.

That was where Elmer's smartness come in. That dog Elmer was so smart that if Buford showed him a piece of oak board or a joint of pine siding, he'd take off and tree a coon which when the hide was skinned off and stretched would exactly fill out that length of wood. That was what made him so smart and valuable and caused Buford to think the world of him, rather have Elmer than the jewels of Sheba and the wisdom of Solomon.

But then they got into trouble one Tuesday about the middle of September. Elmer happened to wander inside the house while Buford was off somewhere and his wife had left the door open by mistake. Buford wouldn't never of let him in, ruins a good dog to lay around in a dwelling house. But Elmer wandered in this time and seen Buford's wife there ironing the laundry. He took one look at that ironing board and just lit out down the road as fast as he could go and heading west as far as you could point. Buford said later on he didn't know whether Elmer already had a coon that big somewhere he knew about or it just sparked his ambitions.

Whatever, Elmer had set hisself a journey and when Buford got home and heard what happened he took off after him. Dog like Elmer, that smart, can't afford to lose a dog like that. So Buford was traveling west now, trying to track him down, asking questions of anybody he came to, and for a long time he could tell where he'd been. Folks will remember a dog that's got something on its mind. But then the houses got scarcer and not many people to ask, and Buford was getting worried—

My father nodded sagely. "And I'll bet you're not going to tell us any more. You're just going to leave it hanging there, aren't you, Uncle Zeno?"

Uncle Zeno gazed into his placid abyss.

My father leaned over the table toward him. "Well, I've got your number now. I don't know any Willie Hammer or Lacey Joe Blackman or Setback Williams or those other people you've been telling us about. But it happens that I do know Buford Rhodes. Hired him one time to do some house painting. I know right where he lives, down there on Iron Duff, and I can drive right to his house. That's what I'm going to do, Uncle Zeno, and check your story out."

This possibility made no impression upon the old man. Why should it? We didn't care whether the story was true and Uncle Zeno didn't care about anything. But the idea that he could actually track down Buford Rhodes and talk to him seemed to give my father gleeful satisfaction.

It occurred to me that my father was preoccupied with the problem of Homer's blindness. Homer had lived in history and told his stories about real soldiers and described in grisly detail battles he could not have seen. But, like Uncle Zeno, Homer had left no trace in the world. Patient scholars were forced to debate whether the poet had actually ever lived. My father was not much interested in getting the details straight about coonhounds; he wanted to see if Buford Rhodes had ever met and talked to Uncle Zeno. The old man was living with us, eating our food and sleeping in the upstairs bedroom, but he was hardly present except as a voice. Like Homer, he was leaving no trace.

And so my father, in the disinterested pursuit of knowledge, was going to interview Buford Rhodes, the actual subject of one of Uncle Zeno's stories. Schliemann, unearthing the first traces of a Trojan site, must have felt something of the excitement my father felt.

My grandmother muttered that it seemed pure foolishness to her, traipsing down to Iron Duff for no good reason, but my father, leaning back in his chair and blowing a happy smoke ring, said, "That's just exactly where I'm headed first thing tomorrow morning."

Actually, he didn't get underway until midmorning, some five hours after rosy-fingered Eos had streaked the sky with orient pearl and gold. I realize now that he had other necessary errands to perform, but of course he wouldn't give my grandmother the satisfaction of knowing that he was doing something useful. He preferred for her to think he was off lollygagging after Uncle Zeno's story.

His absence left me with idle time and, since it was a lovely August morning and not yet sweltering, I decided to forgo reading and wander the hills of the farm until lunchtime. A favorite place for lonesome cowboy games was in a glade behind one of the farther hills on the pasture. An awesome storm had blown over a great oak there and I loved to clamber among the fallen branches and look at the jagged tears wrought in the trunk and see what new animal life had come to inhabit.

But when I arrived I found the tree already occupied. Uncle Zeno was sitting perched in a easy place on a big limb. His back was toward me and over his left shoulder protruded the end of the gnarly staff he sometimes used for walking. Never had his figure seemed so insignificant, his shoulders slumped and his head craned forward away from me so that I knew he was once again looking deep into his private void.

He was talking too, out here in the grassy knolls under the soft blue sky where there was not a living soul he could have been aware of to listen to him. I crept up as noiselessly as I could. I wanted to hear what he told himself in private, thinking that maybe the old man was revealing secrets of the earth he alone was privy to.

Here is what Uncle Zeno was saying: – but finally he was lost and he had to admit it. Hated it like poison, he'd never been lost in the woods before and he was hoping none of his buddies would ever hear about it, Buford Rhodes lost in the woods. He had give up on his good dog Elmer and he thought he'd be lucky if he could get back alive hisself. But right then he heard a baying he knew was Elmer and he begun to take heart. Happened though that he was down in a box cove with steep flanks on both sides and an anxious-looking rock-face cliff at the upper end. The sun was a-going down and the moon not coming up yet. And echoed in there till he couldn't say where the baying was coming from. He started climbing but by the time he was halfway up the mountainside Elmer lost the scent, just lost and worrying about it like Buford, but anyhow he shut up and not another sound out of him.

So now Buford was loster than before. He was going to swaller his pride and call out for help, but he seen they wasn't no use, he wasn't close to nothing but mossy rocks and sawbriars. He set down there on a rotten pine log and waited and he was feeling about as bad as a man can feel.

Didn't know how long he set there. It got cooler and the moon come up, turning the green leaves as white as snow, and it was as quiet as the bottom of a well. And then he seen somebody, or he thought he seen somebody, the moonlight deceiving. It was a Indian woman. She come at him smiling with her arms down at her sides, and he was awful happy to see her except when he tried to talk he found out she didn't speak nothing but Cherokee, which he didn't speak none of, not a speck. They tried to talk together but soon had to give it up as a bad job. She finally just reached out and took his hand and led him off with her, deeper and deeper into the woods, Buford feeling worse and worse. He was content he'd go with her wherever she wanted, he couldn't do no better.

It was a cave she lived in that she took him to and wasn't a bad cave, nice and dry, with some crevices for smoke to get out, and there was stuff to eat, berries and roots and herbs and squirrel meat. Wasn't the most comfortable place in the world but must have suited ole Buford all right because he lived there in the cave with the Cherokee woman two year or more. Turned out not such a bad life after all, because Indian women don't like for their menfolks to do no work, and Buford just laid around and let her wait on him hand and foot. Ever once in a while at night he'd hear that hound dog Elmer start up baying somewhere off in the dark and Buford would get up and go scouring around the ridges, thrashing through blackberry briars and laurel hells. But then after a few months he didn't even bother to get up and look, didn't see much point in it anymore.

Went along like that two whole years, till one morning in spring he happened to wake up just when the woman was stepping over him to poke up the fire for breakfast and he took notice of part of her he hadn't looked at close before and he wasn't what you called pleasured. Looked like a big ole crow had swallered a redbird there. He shut his eyes, and laying there with his eyes shut it come to him how awful ugly this woman was. He never thought about that before and now it started to bother him right much. After breakfast he sneaked away to a clearing where he had a favorite sandstone rock that he liked to sit on and think.

He set there and thought till he was pure gloomy. Here he was, lost in the woods and living with the ugliest woman creation ever made and he couldn't even talk to her. Well, he had plumb sunk into being a forsaken savage, all there was to it. Seemed to him there wasn't no hope for Buford Rhodes in this world anymore, he was lost to the sight of God and mankind. It was a black study he was in, but just right then when he was thinking his darkest thoughts, he heard a rustling over in the bushes—

At this point Uncle Zeno ceased. The story impulse had died in him, or maybe the story flew from this roosting-place across the world to another storyteller, Chinese or Tibetan, who sat waiting for inspiration. Uncle Zeno's audience—the white clouds and fallen tree, the blue daylight and sweet green grass—listened patiently, but the story was over for now. Yet here in the glade was the best setting for his stories, and I felt that I understood him now in a way I hadn't before. He was some necessary part of nature we hadn't recognized, seeing him only as a windy old man. But he was more than that, and different. What was he doing now that the story had ended in him? Why, he was sitting on the tree, giving audience to the story of its regal life and calamitous downfall, a story I couldn't hear. I would have to wait until Uncle Zeno was possessed by the impulse to repeat it to us.

I hoped he would never find out I'd been there to overhear him. I turned away quietly and went back to the house and made a lunch of bread and cheese and buttermilk from the icebox. I ate alone. My mother and grandmother had walked over to pay their respects to a shut-in friend, my father was down in Iron Duff playing archeologist-detective, and Uncle Zeno was in the pasture telling stories to the mica rocks and horse nettles.

After lunch I took a book of science out to the porch to read, learning that Sirius was the most luminous star in our heavens and was thought in old times to bring on madness in people and fits of poetic frenzy. I didn't care to read fiction; I'd had enough stories for a while.

My father returned about four o'clock and came into the porch to sit and chat with me. He looked haggard.

"What did you find out?" I asked him.

He rubbed the back of his neck and looked at the pine ceiling. His tone was mournful, puzzling. "Nothing," he said.

"Couldn't you find Buford Rhodes?"

"Couldn't find him, couldn't find anyone who knew him, couldn't find the least trace of him."

"Maybe you went to the wrong house. You might have forgot where he lived."

"Drove right to his front door, where he used to live. House was empty and run-down. Windows broken, doors off the hinges. Holes in the roof. Looked like nobody had lived in it for twenty years."

"Did you ask the neighbors?"

"They never heard of him. Walked down to Hipps's grocery, and nobody there ever heard of him either."

"You must have got the wrong place. Somebody would know him."

"I drove down to ask Virgil Campbell. He knows everybody that was ever in the county. At first he thought he sort of did remember a Buford Rhodes, but the more he thought about it the less he could remember."

"Maybe you got the name mixed up," I said. "Maybe the man you hired to paint had a name like that but different."

"I know Buford Rhodes," he said. "Know him anywhere. Uncle Zeno described him to a T." He snapped his fingers. "I'm glad you mentioned that. I recall I paid Buford with a check. I'll have a record in my check stubs. Paid him seventy-seven dollars exactly. Wasn't but three years ago, I'll go look that up." He rose and walked to the door.

"Where did you eat dinner?" I asked.

He gave me another harried look. "I haven't been hungry lately, Jess," he said and went in to pore through his records.

But this research, too, proved disappointing. He found a check stub for the amount of seventy-seven dollars, and its date would fit it into the period of the house painting, but he had failed to list whom he'd written the check to.

When the women returned from their errand of charity, he asked my mother about it. "See, here's the check stub," he said, waving it under her chin. "You remember Buford Rhodes, don't you?"

She backed away from the flapping paper. "We had three or four painters working about that time. I don't remember any of them."

"You'd remember Buford, though. Had the kind of beard that gives you a blue face. Always cracking jokes and talking about his hound dogs. Always had a drink or two under his belt no matter what time of day it was."

"That describes every house painter I ever met," she said.

"You ought to remember him, though. Uncle Zeno has got him down exactly. He was some kind of character."

"All I ever meet are characters," she said. "I don't believe that normal human beings show up in this part of the country."

Exasperated, he flung down the booklet of stubs and stamped on it. "How could anybody not remember Buford Rhodes?" he shouted.

"Calm down," she said. "It's not important."

But it was important to my father, and his shouting indicated the intensity of his feelings. I almost spoke up then. I almost told him that the last I'd heard Buford Rhodes was lost in the forest and living in a cave with an ugly Indian woman. I realized, however, that I'd better not speak; this information would only cause more confusion.

I was assailed by a wild thought and a goosy sensation. What if Buford Rhodes had ceased to exist upon the earth *because* Uncle Zeno told stories about him? I had entertained odd fancies since overhearing the old man this morning. What if Uncle Zeno's stories so thoroughly absorbed the characters he spoke of that they took leave of the everyday world and just went off to inhabit his narratives? Everything connected with them would disappear, they would leave no more sign among us than a hawk's shadow leaves in the snow he flies above. The only place you could find Achilles these days was in the *Iliad*. Had he ever existed otherwise? Had any of those heroes left evidence behind?

I cried out, "What about Agamemnon?"

My father gave me a peculiar look. "What about him?"

"Didn't you tell me they found his death mask? Didn't you say it was a mask made out of gold and they put it in a museum?"

He answered in a vexed tone. "That's the name they give it, but they can't really prove it belonged to Agamemnon, of course."

"Well, it ain't his," I said. "They've got the wrong man." Because now I was convinced of my notion. Homer and Uncle Zeno did not merely describe the world, they used it up. My father had said that one reason Homer was reckoned such a top-notch poet was you couldn't tell where the world left off and the *Iliad* began . . . No wonder you couldn't tell.

My theory was wild enough to amuse my father; it was just the sort of mental play-pretty he liked to entertain himself with. But I decided not to tell him about it. He was earnestly troubled by the problem of Buford Rhodes and obviously in no mood for metaphysical speculations in the philosophy of narrative. I could read that much on his face. Then he said, "Come on, Jess. We'd better get the milking chores done."

I rose and followed him willingly. I looked forward to getting the evening chores out of the way and sitting down to supper. I was hungry, with nothing but bread and cheese for lunch, and I was eager to hear Uncle Zeno tell another story. I felt like a scientist now that I'd hit upon my brilliant idea, and I wanted to watch the process at work.

Sure enough, as soon as my grandmother had got through one of her painfully detailed supper prayers, Uncle Zeno began talking, without excuse or preamble, as always.

– and out of the bushes there, Uncle Zeno said, come a gang of six kids, looked to be eight, ten years old, and dressed in washed overalls and pinafores. They kept staring at Buford and he begun to think for the first time how he might look awful strange, dirty and bearded from living in the woods so long. But he kept hisself soft-talking and gentled them kids along until they agreed to lead him back to civilization. These here kids belonged to the Sunday-school class of a hard-shell Baptist church back up that way and they'd run into Buford while they was hunting Easter eggs. Turned out he hadn't been as lost as he thought he was, no more than two miles from a little old settlement there, and the congregation had come up here for an Easter picnic. It was just that Buford's mind had been occupied, thinking about that Indian woman and worrying about his good dog Elmer that he hadn't heard bay in more than a year now. Buford just hadn't been taking no proper interest, that was all.

So the kids led him out of the woods down to the settlement and he got started on the right road a-going home. He was dreading to arrive, figured his place must have gone to rack and ruin while he was gone and his wife and children probably in the poorhouse a long time ago. He didn't know what he was going to tell folks and whether anybody would believe him or not.

But when he came in sight of his house, well, he was mighty surprised. The place was all fixed up and just a-shining, better than he ever done for it. There was a spanking new tin roof, and them old coon hides had been tore down from everywhere and the house was painted up nice and white and there was a new Ford car setting by the edge of the yard.

So he reckoned his wife had took up with another man while he was gone and they wouldn't have no use for him around there no more. But he went on up anyhow and rapped at the door. It took his wife a minute or two to recognize him but when she did she was happy fit to bust and reached out and hugged him tight and his kids run out in fine new clothes and jumped around, it was the best welcome-home you'd ever want to see.

After they settled down a little bit he got to questioning her. How come you're doing so good, with the house all fixed up and a Ford car in the front yard? And she said it was Elmer. Elmer had found his way finally back home a year ago and seen how the family was doing poorly, so he went out and got hisself a job. Buford said that was awful good news, he was proud of that dog, and what kind of job did he have? She said Elmer got him a job teaching over at the high school, arithmetic and natural science, and drawed a pretty good salary considering he didn't have no experience to speak of. And Buford said a dog that smart didn't need no experience, what he was going to do was get Elmer to show him how to smell the ground and track coon and they'd switch off, Buford would be the dog and Elmer could be the man because maybe that's the way it should have been in the first place—

"All right," my father said. "I'm glad to hear some more of that story." He kept rubbing the back of his neck. "But what I want to know is, Where does Buford live now? I've been looking for him all day and can't turn up hide nor hair. Speak, Uncle Zeno. Tell us where Buford Rhodes has got to."

But of course there was no answer. Uncle Zeno looked calmly into his vast inane, contemplating the nothingness that hung between stories. He probably wasn't aware that my father spoke to him. He lifted a slow spoonful of creamed corn to his mouth.

My father leaned back, his sensibilities sorely bruised. "No, you're not going to tell us. I know that. I wish I hadn't asked." He heaved a sorrowful sigh and looked down at his lap. "Well, now I'll tell a story," he said. "It's my turn." He leaned forward again, placing the palms of both hands flat on the table, and stared intently into Uncle Zeno's face. He looked like a bobcat ready to spring. "Once upon a time there was a pretty good old boy who never did anybody any harm. I won't say his name, but he was a pretty good old boy. It happened that he fell in love with a fine mountain girl and married into her family and they lived there in the hills and he worked the farm for them. That was all right, everything was just fine. Except that in this family there was an army of strange uncles who were always dropping by, and they were an interesting bunch, most of them. This good old boy—let's just call him Joe—got along O.K. with these strange visitors. He liked to talk to them and find out about them. He was interested, you know, in what makes people tick. . . . But there was this one weird uncle – we'll call him Uncle Z. – he couldn't figure out to save his life. Truly he couldn't. And it began to prey on his mind until he couldn't make himself think about anything but this Uncle Z. and how queer he was. . . . I'm sorry to tell you, Uncle Zeno, that I don't know the end of this story. But I think that this good old boy started worrying so much that he finally just went crazy and they carried him off to the funny farm in a straightjacket." He gazed morosely into the plate of food he had hardly touched. "But like I say, I don't really know the end of the story."

My grandmother reprimanded him, in a tone gentler than usual. "Now, Joe Robert, you don't want to be unmannerly."

He stood up. "No, of course I don't," he said. "If you-all will excuse me, I think I'll go out on the porch and have a cigarette. Maybe clear my head. I don't know what's the matter with me." He fumbled a moment with the knob, then stepped through the door and closed it.

My mother and grandmother looked at each other, and my grandmother said, "Joe Robert's acting kind of peculiar, seems to me. He ain't ailing, is he?"

"He doesn't seem to be ill," my mother said.

"It's Uncle Zeno's stories," I told them. "They get him all worked up. He wants to do something, but he don't know what to do."

"They're only stories," my mother said. "No one is supposed to do anything *about* them."

I wanted to reply, but I couldn't very well tell my mother that she didn't understand my father, that he always had to be doing things, changing the order of the world in some way, causing anarchy when he could or simple disorder if he couldn't do any better.

"Just seems peculiar to me," my grandmother said, "somebody getting all worked up about a few harmless windies." She looked at our visitor with a fond expression. "Why, Uncle Zeno wouldn't harm a fly."

The three of us looked at him, an inoffensive old man who hardly appeared to occupy the chair he sat in. He seemed ignorant of our regard, and it was clear that what she said was true. He wouldn't harm a fly.

Then his drifting abstraction formed into a voice and he began to speak again. "That puts me in mind of," Uncle Zeno said, "Cousin Annie Barbara Sorrells that lived down toward the mouth of Ember Cove. Had a right nice farm there, about a hundred acres or so, but didn't have nobody to work it, her oldest son dying when he was eight and her other boy, Luden, gone off to California on a motorcycle. But she had

211

her a son-in-law, Joe Robert his name was, and he was a pretty fair hand at farming, she didn't have no complaints to speak of, except that Joe Robert was ever the sort to dream up mischief. . . . Well, it happened one time that her boy Luden had sent Annie Barbara a present, which was a box of fancy candies he'd bought in St. Louis—"

This was too much.

Uncle Zeno was telling a story about us. I knew what he was going to say; I'd lived through those events, after all. His story focused on my father, and that fact disturbed me. My father didn't seem to get along too well with Uncle Zeno as it was, and perhaps he wouldn't be happy to hear that he was now a character in the old man's stories.

I jumped up without even saying Excuse me and went out to the porch. It was as dark as the dreams of a sleeping bear; rain clouds blocked off the starlight and there was only a dim light coming through the dining-room drapes. My father was not smoking, but just sitting in a chair shoved flat against the wall of the house.

"Are you here?" I asked.

He paused a long time before answering. "Yeah, I'm right here, Jess."

"Are you feeling O.K.?"

Another pause, and I could hear Uncle Zeno's mumble drone through the door.

"I'm all right, I guess. Maybe I'm catching a cold. I've been feeling kind of light-headed. Feel a little weak all over, like I'd lost a lot of weight in a hurry."

"Come on back in and have a piece of apple pie. Maybe it'll make you feel better."

He sat motionless. There was no wind sound, no sound at all except for the low, indistinct mutter of Uncle Zeno's story.

"Apple pie," he said softly. "Well, that's not bad medicine." He didn't move for a while yet. Finally he rose slowly from the chair. But when he took a step he walked directly into darkest shadow and I couldn't see him at all and at that moment Uncle Zeno's story concluded and all the night went silent.

Turning Out

Gayle Whittier

"Plié!" The pink and black line at the *barre* drops down.

"Relevé!" The line lifts, more unevenly.

I am scrabbling for leverage, parts of my forgetful body tilting out of art back into nature. At last, late, I rise too on a brilliant point of pain. I am upheld mostly by the sinew of my mother's gaze. From across the hall she stares fixedly through me to the ideal daughter alive only in her dangerous maternal mind. Inside my staved toe shoe, a specific pressure reopens last Saturday's blister.

"Plié!" We begin again.

The hands of the schoolroom clock on the far wall have frozen at two of twelve. If I watch they will never move. But when I look away, "Time!" Sergei dismisses us. Although we dance in spellbound, mispronounced French, we begin and end Group Ballet in a wide-awake and daily English.

"Time!" As the clock's hand darts across noon, the mothers discreetly check their watches to make sure of every paid-for minute. They smile, if at all, only at their daughters. They are as still, as grim as the face of a priestess casting bones.

My own mother wears even disappointment well. "Go *on*, Bonnie, take your toe shoes off. We haven't got all day." A towel, the admonitory smell of Lysol, come towards me. "Well, go *on*."

Turtle-shaped, my foot sticks, then springs suddenly free, the toes still invisible inside their protective "bunny pads." Worse is about to come. However gently I peel these cups away, moist strands of rabbit fur clump where my flesh has oozed or, sometimes, yielded blood. Hair by hair I draw off the whistling pain. "Ow-w."

"Shh."

"Well, it hurts."

"I know it hurts. Here," she slips me the phial of iodine powder. "Be brave." But she is gazing elsewhere. "Just look at Gillian, will you. That girl never stops."

Away from the *barre*, Gillian, our class hope, poses in command of all the eight anatomical directions of the dance. Fatigue has not touched her. Her body arches and her torso tightens for a final budburst. She unfurls upward in a perfect *entrechat*; tries the circumference of space, a *cabriole*. Then the whole staff of her body blossoms, deft porcelain, ivory, not our common stuff. She turns and returns in the gyres of an almost endless *pirouette*. Faster she spins, the boundaries of the legs going; faster, her bright hair streaks into her scarf. Faster, she revolves, *spotting*, fixing an air-mark before her. Above the blur of arms and skirt and legs, her face seems still: she has been beheaded, reassembled by magicians.

"Well, Gillian shouldn't be in Group, it's not good for morale," my mother's judgment falls.

Now Sergei has paused to watch. Our elderly pianist revives too, scattering a few rosy bars of "Amaryllis" into the blank air of the studio. Even the other students watch, observing in her the reason why they practice every day, what they will turn into if they do.

"Your *plié* will *do*," my mother turns away, "but only because you're helped by gravity. But you'll have to work on *élevation*," a great discipline in her voice as Gillian leaps, *grand jeté*, *grand jeté*, *grand jeté*. Then Madame, massively caryatid, emerges from the office in her magenta satin class dress, flamethrower hair, thighs muscular with varicose grapes. Gillian, her raddled face says, has more than *placement*, *extension*, *line*, those brief commodities: Gillian has a future.

Applause, dropped beads, and "Bravo!" dries up quickly among the odors of talcum and sweat. Gillian resumes her place among us. Madame smiles and beckons to her mother.

"Marie Ravert may be my best friend," my mother tells the walls, "but sometimes I think she's just a *stage mother* after all!" For it is understood that Gillian dances to fulfill her mother's "ambition," while I, more penitentially, dance for Grace. "Shh!" My mother strains to hear what Madame Orloff is saying. The word "exceptional" unrolls towards us; next, magic names, "New York . . . London," ascend to "Rome, perhaps," and consummate in "Paris, the Ballet Russe!" All the mothers start, look up as if they have heard their own names called.

But Mrs. Ravert's short arms crowd over her bosom. Her head bows no, no, no.

214

"You must get the money *somewhere*! *Borrow* it!" Now Madame booms whole sentences across the studio, but Mrs. Ravert's shoulders bend towards humiliation on a pulse of No, I'm afraid not, No.

"Why, the girl's a *natural*!" Madame informs everyone in earshot. "*Steal* if you have to, but get it somewhere! *Kill* for it!" she carries herself away, all Slavic extravagance. "*Kill*!"

"If there's one thing I can't stand, it's favoritism," my mother says. I sprinkle the iodine powder on my blister and wait for the reassurance of a local burn. "Bonnie, fluff your hair, it's stuck to your head."

"I can't help it."

"Group Class for *now*, then," Madame gives up on a hyperbolic gesture, you-can-see-what-I'm-up-against, to everyone who cares to watch. "But it's a *shame*!" On "shame," she turns towards us.

"Hold still while I tie it back with a ribbon, anyway," my mother says. "I wish you wouldn't twitch so."

Then it is certain. Madame is approaching us, a half-smile wired to her face. Is she going to ask *us* for Gillian's lesson money? I wonder.

"Mrs. Brent, could I see you a moment . . .?"

"We're already paid up through next month. I've got the receipt right here. . . ."

"Oh, no. No, that's not what I wanted to talk about. In my office, please? You too, Bonnie. This concerns you."

We follow her at a distance. People are leaving now, and the studio resumes its great emptiness, to be filled by other classes today and, on Wednesday nights, the Bingo games they hold here.

"I bet she's giving you the 'Sugar Plum Fairy,' what do you want to bet?" my mother hisses. "Now act *surprised*, Bonnie."

In the smaller side room, over a table strewn with snippets of costume fabric, hundreds of younger Madames look down from glossies on a red velvet board: Madame as Pierrot, with rakish melancholy, hand under chin, and painted tear; Madame as a large-featured Giselle in Black Forest bodice; and, of course, Madame as the Dying Swan.

"Mrs. Brent, I've made myself *sick* over this, just *sick*," her accent slips as she begins.

"What is it?"

"But I believe in being frank, I owe it to you, it's your investment, after all. There is"—her hand surrenders the room to fate—"no other way."

"But what's the matter?" My mother's Sugar Plum Fairy smile lingers, dead, on her face.

Madame, steadying herself, gazes into the wall of mirrors opposite us. Before them, a light oak *barre* runs prairie smooth. This is where I danced until my father "put his foot down," before I discovered, in the cheaper democracy of Group Class, the lie of my talent. This is the room for private lessons. Our glances meet in triplicate on the silver surface of the mirror.

"Where should I begin?" Madame wonders. Plunging. "It's my *sad* responsibility to tell you, Mrs. Brent . . ." the truth flows free, "that Bonnie's future in ballet is . . . well, *limited*. Believe me, I am sorry." Madame's hands ward off a protest my stunned mother cannot, as yet make. "Truly sorry."

"What exactly do you mean by 'limited'?" she asks at last.

"You know," Madame sidesteps, "even *two* years ago she was nudging the height limit for a ballerina." She smiles hurriedly. "Bonnie's not exactly prima ballerina *size*, if you see what I mean."

In the mirror, my mother sees what she means, and I do too, my random, changing flesh flashed back at us.

"Oh, she's *shot up*." My mother cannot deny it. "But she won't keep on growing, will you, Bonnie. Anyway, I have no *illusions*. She may not become a first dancer, but I'm not a *stage mother* either. As far as I'm concerned, there's nothing wrong with the *corps de ballet*."

"My dear." Madame takes my mother's hand. She clears her throat of something worse. "I'm afraid Bonnie would unbalance the line even *there*. Exactly how old *are* you, Bonnie?"

My answer and my mother's intertwine.

"I'm sure she's reached her full height. I reached *mine* early."

"Fourteen last April," I confess.

A *faux pas*. In the Dance, your exact age is never calculated. "Teen," especially, evokes panic, for everyone holds her breath as you skid across the perilous mud of adolescence, Nature finger-painting you with hormones, blurring the artful line of years of lessons. For many Mothers of the Dance, a daughter's change of heart or bone may synchronize with their darker "changes of life." We dance in a time of endings.

"Only *fourteen*!" Madame seizes on it. "What, some girls keep on growing until they're *eighteen*!"

We all close our imaginations, not quite fast enough, against the spectacle of me, a dancing giantess of eighteen, demoted, year by year, from the Ballet Russe to the sideshow.

But my mother rallies. "You don't mean to tell me that it's only a matter of *size*, do you? Didn't you say it yourself, last year, Bonnie has *talent*? How can you have talent one year and not the next?"

"All my students have talent. I never accept a student who doesn't," Madame testifies. "But talent's not the whole picture. There's structure,

216

too. With *les petits rats*, the babies, who can tell? The older ones . . . well, one needs light bones, strict muscles, a long torso, *so*, and . . ." A complicated gesture cancels me out. "Time decides. What more can I say except that I am truly, truly sorry . . .!"

The fact upon her, my mother flattens into a chair. "You mean she should *stop dancing?*"

"Did I say that? Did you hear me say that, Bonnie? Of course not?" Madame laughs palely. "Haven't I always said that Bonnie's the most . . . most *industrious* dancer I've got. She *will dance!*" Color and confusion brighten my mother's face. "She should just shift to tap, that's all."

"Tap." The sentence is pronounced. All of us know that ballet is *the* Dance, an art, unlike the dazzling, double-jointed trickery of tap dancing, or, one more fall below, acrobatic "routines" and "baton lessons."

"Oh, she'll be *striking* in tap, just look at her! Why, a few weeks of private lessons and she'll catch up in time for the Christmas recital."

"Private lessons? Oh, I don't know. . . ."

"Wouldn't you like a solo, Bonnie?"

"Who, me?"

"A solo spot," Madame promises, right hand raised to the portrait of Pavlova. "I give you my word . . . *if* she applies herself."

"A solo in five months? Is that really possible?"

Madame looks offended. "Do I know my own business or not?"

"Of course, of course. I didn't mean to suggest . . ."

"I accept your apology," Madame declares, her accent now back in place. "Now, what would be a good time for this little one's new lessons? Thursday? Friday?"

"Either. Well, Thursday."

"I hope we can fit her in." Madame consults her big ledger. "Four-thirty? Five? . . . And you can apply the Group Lessons already paid for, *of course*. Bonnie, you are a very fortunate young lady. Practice every day now, don't disappoint us."

"Oh, don't worry. I'll see that she does."

"And thank you, Mrs. Brent, thank you for being so *reasonable*. You would not believe some of the people I have to deal with!" She rolls her eyes for heavenly help.

"Stage mothers." My mother understands.

Madame starts herding us out of her office. "One of these days," she consoles my mother, "you'll have a swan there. You'll wake up and see a swan!"

We emerge beside the sign INSTRUCTION MUST BE PAID FOR IN ADVANCE. The next hour's crowd of mothers and daughters swarms around us on their way to Group Tap. Theirs is a noisy, glossy craft, carried in round red or black patent-leather hat boxes. One tiny five-year-old wears, despite the heat, a leopard-skin coat. The Mothers of Tap have hard, bright faces, red nails, lips wide with Revlon's Fire and Ice.

Mine is a small, very elegant mother who has made a lifework of her good bone structure and her Good Taste. Good Taste directs that petti-coats match skirts in one of three colors only: black, white and beige. Good Taste defines the brief season for white shoes (not before Memorial Day, not after Labor Day); it even measures and colors the rim of our company china, which may be white or cream with a "classic" gold border, but painted flowers only if they are "dainty." Daintiness, in fact, is one reason my mother has befriended Mrs. Ravert, whose humility is rubbed smooth and small like a pebble, and whose Scots accent my mother thinks "refined." Also Mrs. Ravert wrestles skittishly with many small, but manageable, worries, a good sign in a good mother. "Oh dear, I hope Gillian doesn't become too *American*. Her manners put me to shame! What do *you* think, Ida?" and "Oh dear, Gillian uses so much slang I hardly understand her! Ida, what . . .?"

The staircase clears. Marie and Gillian Ravert are waiting for us in the vacant entry below.

"Now just smile," my mother directs, sotto voce, "as if nothing's happened. There's no reason to be ashamed. Everybody knows only one or two girls ever make it."

"Only one or two will make it," Madame warns the mothers ritually. Each nods, though disbelieving that she has not earned, with her ambitious love, with the hard-saved dollar-fifties for Group or the three dollars for private lesson, a daughter's opportunity. Most of the mothers look plain and overworked, starved, like Mrs. Ravert, on American dreams. A startling number of them have, by some special curse, hatched peacocks, the challenge of uncommonly pretty daughters. Only my mother and I upend expectation. She walks, concluded, in a fading and ungiven legacy of beauty. I, it is charitably understood, am "still growing," not quite done.

"Only one or two" explains why silence so often covers the older students like a purifying snow. Yes, Barbara Cross actually tap-danced on the Ted Mack Amateur Hour, remember? And Judy Scolini *almost* got on the Ed Sullivan show with her Toy Shop ballet. But where are they now?

"I *heard* Barbara met somebody in New York, she got married."

"Is he rich?"

218

"I *heard* he's a millionaire!"

Of course. Because in every mother's mind fame flows to roses, red, red for the blood-pulse of the audience and for the passion of strangers. Millionaires all lined up outside the stage door just about to open. And if the scholarship dancer should come home quietly, failed, or pregnant, if she should be worn down to selling tickets, "Only one or two will ever make it. . . ." We have always known.

Outside Madame's studio, late summer thickens, bright and alkaline.

"I'm so embarrassed, Ida. I suppose everybody *heard*," Mrs. Ravert murmurs.

"I didn't. What did she have to say?"

"Well, she said Gillian ought to have private lessons, the way she used to." She adores Gillian with her eyes. "She says she's *talented*, a 'natural.'"

Gillian walks with us milkmaid-sweet, apple-breasted, arms a graceful birthright, joints that must move on golden pins, not bone. Her feet turn out without being commanded. She steps over the sidewalk cracks without a downward glance.

"I just don't know. What do *you* think, Ida? Do *you* think she's got talent?"

"Anybody can see that."

"What did she say to *you*, Ida? Madame."

"Exactly the same thing. Madame told us Bonnie's talented."

"You don't say!" Mrs. Ravert's amazement checks itself diplomatically.

"I do say. She's been watching her and she's decided Bonnie's got a distinct talent for tap. Fix your barrette, dear, it's slipping."

"Tap?"

"That's where the *real* money is, you know, like Eleanor Powell, vaude-ville . . ." she finds at last, "the Rockettes! Not in ballet."

"Bonnie *is* quite a strapping lassie."

"She's not big, she's statuesque. Bonnie's a long-stemmed American beauty."

"Hey, Bon." Gillian's elbow cuts into my side. "You really gonna do tap?"

"I guess so."

Gillian's jaws move up and down, *plié, relevé*, on her chewing gum while she considers this. "Well, Jeez Louise," she says.

"Of course I'm just thrilled!" my mother's voice is practicing behind us. "Tap's so much more natural. Did you know, Marie, that ballerinas never menstruate?"

"They don't? Oh, that can't be true, Ida, is that true?"

"It certainly is. I read it in the *Reader's Digest*. It's from starving themselves all the time, that's why."

"Imagine that!"

Gillian pushes me ahead of our mothers' lowered voices. By now Mrs. Ravert is or soon will be confiding how her husband came home drunk again and hit her—"right here"—her nylon glove touching her cheek as if to re-imprint it with the color of the bruise. "You ought to just *walk out*," my mother will advise, as usual. And Mrs. Ravert will agree that yes, she knows, she should leave that man, she *would* leave him if it weren't for the children, the children. . . .

Gillian walks faster. "Guess what! Guess who asked me out?"

"Who?"

"*Fred Vargulic*! He's a *senior*! It was right after Earth Science, he comes up to me, see, and he goes, 'You wanna go out next Saturday?' 'I dunno,' I says, real cool, 'why should I?' He says, 'I might take ya 'round the world, that's why!'"

"Where're you going?"

"The *drive-in*. Only my mother," she giggles, "she thinks it's a dance. They say Fred likes to French kiss." She is distracted, for a moment, by a passerby's stare. People often forget their manners in the face of such unexpected beauty.

"Bonnie! There's our bus!" my mother calls.

"So if anybody asks you, say it's a dance, O.K.?"

"O.K."

"We'll have to run for it!" my mother warns, running already. Lost girlhood strives inside her stiffening matron's body. She bunches up her skirt, against the wind. Her hair whips out weed tall, a graying ashblond paradox around her profile, fine and eroding. Still further down, pink laces of an invisible corset hold in the first dark place where once we blended into common flesh, a mother and a child. She runs awkwardly, wholly *en terre*. She runs to make me come true.

"You almost missed it, lady," the driver complains, impatient as she sorts out change. "I ain't got all day." My mother drops the exact fare for two into the slot and turns to find seats together for us.

From our window we watch Gillian, unhurried, unperturbed, ascend the steps to the bus. A veil of glances falls over her, and she smiles. The driver smiles back, turning her dollar into coins, lingering a little over her hand. The light changes to red, but no one cares. Time has paused for her.

"Beauty like that," my mother says, "it's a burden."

But I do not believe her. The faces of everyone, both genders, young and old, smile or stare in wonder at Gillian, the way sunflowers track the sun.

*   *   *

"I only hope Gillian's *grateful* for what her mother's trying to do for her. She's taking in *wash* to pay for those lessons."

"Other people's wash?"

"Yes. You've seen all those baskets of it, haven't you? Did you think it was *theirs*? Personally . . ."—she settles a summer hat on her curls—". . . I've always had a suspicion she was a *housemaid* back in Scotland. There was *some* scandal, that older husband and all . . . I bet Gillian's a *love* child!" She nods at her own thoughts. "That would explain it."

"Explain what?"

"Why she's so beautiful. I mean, otherwise it's really a *mystery*, isn't it?"

Gillian's loveliness, surely immoral, poises hummingbird static and swift in my mind. "She's going out with Fred Vargulic. He's got this awful reputation!"

"How's that?" She is asking herself whether her hat looks right.

"He puts his tongue in your mouth when he kisses. Yuk."

"There!" My mother stabs her hatpin through the straw. Below the lacy brim her face shadows with remembered beauty. "Let's get going, Bonnie, I just dread this, but we better get it over with."

That afternoon we—Gillian, her mother, me, mine—all sit on the scratchy, royal-blue, velvet seats of the Bijou Theatre while the matinee performance of *The Red Shoes* lurches, whirrs and skips from frame to frame. Before us Moira Shearer leaps up close, wafts away, at the commandment of the camera. Once, the projector jams, the picture clots to a stop, "Ohhhh!" Our disappointment brings it back in pink and purple burned spots to the exhaled relief of the mothers and Gillian's small solitary cheer. "Yeah!"

But Gillian is bored. Her flawless hand browses steadily from the popcorn box to her mouth, up and down, keeping its own time over the romantic crescendos of the movie score.

"Hey, Bon, you want some popcorn?"

"No thanks."

"Yeah, I shouldn't either. Gotta watch my figure. . . . Guess what? Didja hear about Marsha Norris?"

"No."

"She *went all the way*. Honest! I got it from Marge Donaldson and Marge, she got it from Marsh *herself*. So it's true all right."

221

"Who with?"

"Chuck Schultz. They're getting married, Marsha says, maybe this Christmas. A Christmas wedding."

"Shhh!"

"But how old is Marsha?" I ask quietly.

"She's sixteen, a girl can get married at sixteen in this state without her parents' wanting her to, it's the law. . . ."

"We are here to watch the movie, not to listen to you," my mother announces as if to strangers.

It's the dénouement. Poor Moira Shearer drops suddenly, still in her demonic shoes, before the machinery of an oncoming train. The impact jars through the women, doubling on their shocked and indrawn breaths. Mrs. Ravert cups a cry back into her mouth. "Oh, look at that, Ida!"

Against a soiled pavement the dying dancer's fractured legs splay, still *en pointe*. Wind plays at the corolla of her skirt. The pale-pink gauze of her stockings darkens to the sound of Mrs. Ravert's weeping. She is sopping up tragedy in her fresh handkerchief, saved for this moment.

"Hey, Bon, where can you get stockings like that?" Gillian nudges me. "Do you know?"

"Quiet, girls!"

Out of the dancer's legs a darkness keeps flowing. It seeps through the pearly silk of her stockings. It stains the lighter satin of the Red Shoes. Blood, but moving more gently than blood really moves, and fading from black to purple to a thoughtful blue, the color at the heart of a poppy. *"Take off the Red Shoes!"*

We leave the theater, silent, for the glare of half-deserted Sunday streets.

"Wasn't it *sad*, Ida? I thought it was very *sad*."

"There are sadder things," my mother understands.

Mrs. Ravert tries to gather all her feelings in something poetic – "She danced herself to death?" Her glance seeks out Gillian, tender, bewildered, watchful. "Oh, ballet is a cruel art, isn't it," she says, "but it's beautiful. Isn't it beautiful, Ida?"

"This sun is giving me a headache," my mother answers.

"Did I tell you, Ida, I'm taking Gillian to Scotland next year? To my sister's in Aberdeen, to study?"

"You told me, Marie."

Gillian smooths the petals of her nine-gored skirt over crinolines. She sighs, mildly exasperated, then draws me back to confide, "Bon, guess what! I got into Secretarial. Next year I get to take typing, Typing I."

"I thought you were going to Scotland, to your aunt's."

"Maybe. Maybe not." But in the shimmer of her brilliant eyes, sky color bound by darker blue, slyness cannot take hold.

"Your mother says."

"Yeah, well. My mother works real hard and everything, you know? I mean, she's really sweet. But she's not too practical, know what I mean?" She blows a pink, fruit-scented bubble. "If you take Secretarial, you can always get a job. . . ." The bubble rounds out dangerously, but just before it bursts, she sucks it back in. "I'm gonna get a job and save up for my wedding. I already got the gown picked out, *you* know," she taps her skull, "in my head. White satin, or white velvet if it's winter. My cousin, she wore blush pink. You can wear ice-blue, too, only people don't, much. Anyway, I want real lace, not fake, down here on the neckline and on the train. A *six-foot* train. Sleeves cut like so. . . ." Her hand describes a fallen triangular wing, vaguely medieval. "What about *you*, Bon? What's yours like?"

"Maybe I won't even get married."

"Sure you will. Everybody does, almost. And I wanna have three kids . . ." She pauses, almost conscious of a golden pollen of male glances. ". . . no, four, real close together, *you* know, so's they can be friends. Two girls and two boys. Well, a boy, a girl, a boy, a girl," she conceives them on her fingers. "I'm gonna call the girls Dawn and Candy. Do you like 'Dawn' and 'Candy' for names? I don't know what to call the boys, though. I guess their father can name them."

The light changes to green just as we catch up to our mothers. Sinking into the softening asphalt, we four stride forward as if to merge with our images, closing in from the plate glass window of a furniture store across the street, in Darwinian enigmas. Somehow Gillian came from her small, speckled mother, a glorious mutation. But in me my mother's silver blondness has been thrown back to mouse-brown. A triumphant moment has declined. We both know this as she walks forward in her reconstructed dignity, and I walk in my body of original sin.

"Turn, dear." I turn. "A little more." I turn a little more. Mrs. Arcangelo talks around a slipped moustache of straight pins, held tight between pursed lips. She is fitting my costume, but her mind is on her masterpiece. "It's got hundreds of tiny little rhinestones, each one I got to sew by hand. 'Starlight effect,' that's what they call it. 'Starlight.' "

"I'm sure it's beautiful." My mother fingers the expensive slipper satin of a half-made sleeve.

"*Mrs.* Ravert, she's working extra just to help pay for it. Well," the seamstress lowers her voice, "she'd have to, it's costing over *two hundred dollars!*"

"Two hundred dollars!"

"And that's not counting *my* work. Well, it makes you wonder. . . . Turn, dear." I turn for her. ". . . what with all the starving people in the world? But Mrs. Ravert says it's an investment, the girl's dancing the Dying Swan and only the best dancer gets to do it. It's in a ballet . . . now, what did she call it? Blank? A ballet blank?"

"*Blanc,*" my mother corrects. "It means all in white."

"That's right. Well, Gillian! You could put your two hands right around her waist and touch your fingers, she's such a dainty little doll. They're taking her to Scotland, to study. . . ."

"Hold still, Bonnie. You're making it harder for Mrs. Arcangelo to do her work."

A straight pin just misses me, waist level. Mrs. Arcangelo turns, too, on her massive knees, and sets her yardstick up from the floor to my thighs. "Look at that, it's not to come down another quarter-inch! When is she going to stop growing?"

It is night; my mother is tired, but, "Bonnie's a long-stemmed American beauty," she defends me. "We expect *her* to audition for the Rockettes someday. When she's older, of course."

"What's that?"

"You never heard of the Rockettes? Why, they're famous for precision kicking. All over the world."

"Mmmm."

By now I know Mrs. Arcangelo's rhythm and turn without being told.

"You have to be over five-foot-seven just to try out for them!"

"My, my." Mrs. Arcangelo sits back on her haunches, finished.

"If you ask me, that waist's still not quite long enough," my mother reflects.

"There's nothing left to let down. Just step out of it, dear."

"Careful, Bonnie, don't step on the hem."

Almost negligently, Mrs. Arcangelo picks up my shed splendor, and I stand, unmasked before myself in her oval mirror, a startled, bisquit-colored shape in a cotton slip, slouched between girlhood and whatever else is coming.

"Beautiful material," she says, "a pleasure to work on."

"That's the best satin money can buy. Bonnie, put your clothes on, you'll get sick for the recital." A suffocating cape of Blackwatch pleats snaps shut on me until, with one sharp tug, my mother lets me breathe again.

"That Ravert girl, now . . ." I emerge to see Mrs. Arcangelo sketching in air, "she's got a cap of feathers, each feather's threaded on separately with a *seed pearl* at the base. . . ."

"Put your coat on, Bonnie, It's late. When's our next fitting?"

Outside, after the bitter wind, we settle onto the cold seats of the car. She starts rummaging in her purse: makeup, bankbooks, comb.

"Where's my pocket calendar?"

"The recital's the twenty-second, Mom." Who does not know his date of execution? "Eight o'clock. The Moose Hall."

"Oh, I know *that*. But when's your next period? The twenty-fourth? Later?" she hopes.

"I'm not sure. I don't know."

"What do you mean, *don't know*? Don't you keep track?"

"What for? It always happens."

"Bonnie, you're hopeless. Now where's my calendar? I didn't leave it home, did I? Did you see me leave it somewhere, on the kitchen counter maybe?"

"I *think* it's January second."

"That's next *year*, thank heaven. You wouldn't want to ruin your costume. . . ." We swing out into the November night. "Your *father*, of course, he doesn't understand anything. Wait'll I tell him what *Gillian's* cost."

My costume has already spoiled a dinner. "*Forty-five dollars!* What the hell, do you think I'm made out of money, Ida?"

"It'll last forever."

"Sure, in the attic. Half a week's pay packed up in a goddamned box!" Above my head the swords of failure poise: an outgrown metallic-gold tutu I wore two Christmases ago, as a Marigold in the Waltz of the Flowers, also last year's tulle skirt, dirty-white, to turn into a Snowflake.

"I just don't have forty-five bucks."

"Use some of the vacation money."

"Oh, Ida."

"Please? It would make me happy."

"No, it wouldn't, but sure, go ahead, take the shirt off my back."

"I'm very surprised at you, John, denying your daughter like that. Bonnie's talented. In just four months she's gotten a solo routine."

"Solo racket."

Now every afternoon between four and five, to the ratchety Voice of Music victrola, I practice without hope. It is like lying, to drag the cargo of a half-willing body through my Military Tap, cleats scratching the linoleum, eyes on the slow redemption of the clock. Where ballet required lightness, *ballon*, tap demands crispness, firecracker smiles, "bounce." To make me bouncier, my mother bobs my hair and ties it up in rags, but within moments it too falls limp.

"More life! Put more life in it!" She drives me, a dying horse, to the outpost of performance. "All right, all right, start over. Start from bar thirty." And when the phone rings, "Tell Gillian you can't talk long, you're working on *your* routine."

"Bon, listen." Gillian's voice comes to me conspiratorily soft. "I gotta see you. I've got something to *tell*. You won't *believe* it!"

My mother replaces the needle on the record. A few vacant grooves turn while Gillilan urges, "After rehearsal tomorrow? O.K.?"

My mother gestures that time is up.

"Sure. I can't talk now."

My march starts. "Hey, is that yours?" Gillian asks, "Is that your music?" and starts singing,

> " 'Oh be kind to your web-footed friends!
> 'For a duck! may be some! body's moth-er!' "

"Bonnie, hang up."
"I've got to go."

> " 'And if you! think that this! is the end . . .
> Well it is!' "

Gillian hangs up first.

In bed that night the first black sweetness of my sleep breaks open. A dot of light is widening inside me. I lie still, as if listening, as it feathers, turns. A ribbon of cramp winds upwards through my belly. I swing out of the covers to start for the bathroom.

Outside it has been snowing, it still snows, wide steady flakes like petals falling off a peony. A seam of chill runs at the baseboard. Even the braided rugs feel cold to my bare feet. But from beyond my half-opened door quick air stirs in my parents' room. They are not asleep, but speaking softly, their voices distinct in the night darkness.

My mother's yields, "Oh, I'm not *blind*, you know. I can see it's over. Madame's right."

"Maybe she's wrong."

"She's right." The whole hall grows colder at the soft sound of weeping.

"Hey, it's not the end of the world."

At my window the georgette curtain lifts and falls in a current of thin heat. Below it, the radiator spits, then whistles. Perhaps I should make a noise, call out for somebody, stop them, my instinct for self-preservation tells me.

"You take things too hard, Ida honey. If you'd just stop wanting so many things, you'd be happy."

"Like you?"

"Well, yes, I guess I am, happy."

"No, ever since I knew you, you've been *contented* with what you have. Not like me. Sometimes it really makes me wonder."

Inside me fresh warm blood slips. Then out of a calm too good to last, her girl's voice, downy with wishes, speaks, "John," his name.

"What is it, honey? Let's get some sleep."

"John? What if we had another baby?"

"What?"

"I'd like that, wouldn't you? Wouldn't you?"

My father lengthens a silence around the house, its lonely shape in winter night. "Oh, Ida, we're too old for all that stuff."

"I am not, I'm not too old. John, we could start all over."

"Is that a threat or a promise?"

"Don't laugh at me."

"I'm not laughing, honey. Honest. Everybody likes to dream," he says. "It's nice to think about, anyway."

"I've always wanted another baby," my mother's voice rounds, rises in the darkness. "I always wanted to try again."

"Let's go to sleep now."

"John?"

"Let's go to sleep."

For a while I sit on the edge of the mattress. Brightness slips past the window shade. The dancer in the Degas poster on my walls blurs into a snowflower. At last water retreats banging down the radiator pipes, so that even the small heat vanishes. My bare feet have gone mineral-cold. I pull myself between the bedsheets, cold too now, draw my legs up into a smaller self beneath the wide, indifferent quilt.

They must be sleeping now. Blindly, my heart tells itself over and over. If I don't get up, by morning the sheet will be stained. "I always wanted to try again." If I do get up, my mind will work on what I overheard. Still bleeding, knowing it, I fall asleep.

227

"Dress" rehearsal, everyone in old leotards anyway, "Hey, Bon," Gillian leads me to the back of the auditorium, glances around for eavesdroppers, and announces, "This is *serious*. First you gotta promise never to tell. Like *swear*. . . ."

"Swear."

I gesture over my heart.

"Promise? O.K., then. *Well* . . ." She tries to delay dramatically, but her pride races forward. "*Well*, Fred and me, we went all the way the other night."

"You didn't!"

"I did." Off and on her starry eyes blink. "Well, we're really in love, you know, so it's all right and everything."

"It's *not* all right." Doesn't she know about V.D. and Pregnancy, my mother's big deterrents? "What *happened*? Did he get you drunk?"

"You shouldn't never drink," she admonishes, "it's bad for your skin." Her gum clicks and sloshes in excitement. "We just, uh, couldn't stop, *you* know." She chews faster, new juiciness.

On stage the baby swans, Beginners' Class, troop out in their soft bottoms and soft shoes, the random shoreline of our Swan Lake.

"But he won't *respect* you," the third reason Not To comes to me, "I mean, no boy really wants a girl somebody's . . ."

"Nobody's laid me, only Fred. Besides, your mother just says that so you won't. You know mothers."

Slowly I recognize that I am in the presence of an initiate, a living sourcebook. "Did you bleed much?"

"I didn't bleed at all. I bet they lie about that, too, huh? But I got worried, maybe Fred thought I'd been with somebody else, before, you know? I didn't say nothing. I just hoped he didn't notice."

From the stage Madame makes a scooping gesture toward Gillian.

"Hey, I gotta go."

"Wait. Does it hurt?"

"A little. Yeah." She half-turns her graceful back to me; it's her cue. "But, *you* know," her hand leads my glance downward to her feet, their perfect turnout, the slender pink cylinders of her toe shoes, "not as much as this. . . ."

Recital night, someone has strung dressing rooms with flannel-blanket walls behind the Moose Hall stage. Decibels of laughter and trouble travel the central aisle. Unseen nerves snap to tears. The curtain's up. Excitement burns among us.

228

"Hold still." My mother strokes solemn pigments on my face. A towel tied around the neck protects my glossy soldier's costume. Above it, her compact mirror shows me in savage colors, desiccated peachskin base, woad-blue shadow, a lipstick orange, enough to turn my teeth yellow. Not for me the wingswept ballerina's eye, the cold still red dot for a tear duct. In the small space between what my mother draws and the lines of my naked cheekbones, I feel a thin yet absolutely crucial margin, by how little I miss being beautiful. My mother's fingers move, electric with determination.

"Mom, I feel sick."

"That's just nerves. Hold still." She squints. Her sharp fingernail pares off a minute edge of paint. Up close her face terrifies my own, lipliner generous around her mouth, pores craterous with rouge. Resemblance hardens into me. "Don't look anywhere and don't blink, Bonnie, it'll smear." Then my eyes are on.

They have clamped me somehow into the white satin dress with its boy's bodice. My flesh pushes against Mrs. Arcangelo's French seams, a squash growing through rock.

"*Please* hold your stomach in." Her hands flatter her own to show me how. "If you don't, you'll look pregnant. And don't sit *down*, you might rip a seam."

"But I feel funny. Honest."

"Stage fright," she heads me off. "Everybody gets it. It's a good sign," though she knocks on the nearest wood, a cigarette stand upholding blocks, jars and sticks of makeup, its own Chinese-red lacquer peeling off.

"I think I'm getting the curse."

"Oh, you're not due for a week yet, *more*." Briefly her face clears into candor. "Please just don't get sick now, Bonnie, this means so much to me. Just keep calm, will you, and do a good job? Just this once?"

Applause, a slow match striking, comes to us through the blankets. "O.K." The aisle makes way for three belly dancers in sparkles and finger-chimes.

"Who's on now?" she whips back the flannel wall to ask them. "Nina Martin? Nina's your cue, Bonnie! You go on after Nina! Now get out there," she rights one of the purple plumes on my helmet, "and break a leg!"

Behind the hot must of the velvet curtains, I stand breathing in all the other performances of that and other nights. Overhead the pulleys creak, the curtain lifts enormously on a socket of hall. I am poised on my chalk-mark, a white X center-stage, saluting hundreds of invisible onlookers, families and friends, while the moment crawls on and on and on. In the crescent of the footlights one dead spot interrupts the ring. "Never look right at the audience!" I remember. Because if you do, your own fear and commonness stare back.

In the stage wings my mother's presence keeps getting bigger and bigger with everything she has to lose. Her hands are fixed slightly apart, as if she holds some breakable commodity, and she starts counting— numbers whisper across the boards, "One, and, two, and . . ." my march rasps in its grooves, "three, and, four AND. . ." my foot takes over from her. In a noisy rush of turns, I come alive. There is the first naked awkwardness, the fear of tripping or forgetting, then my "routine" meshes with my body, takes me in.

Gradually I dance the rows of seats into shape out of the darkness. Out of the darkness wildflower faces come up, solitary, to the now-and-then blue dart of a camera pinning me to this place and this moment forever.

Hurtling out of every turn, I sight my mother. She mouths, "Smile! Smile!" Her hand tightens my salute. Her arms are waving "Arm movements!" and with the startling gesture of a woman garrotted, "Head *up!*" By the finale she is flailing too, and as the curtains close on our farewell smile a loud, obligatory slap of applause says it is over.

"Oh, baby, I'm so proud of you!" she tells me, but she wilts into tears. I touch my own face to see if the makeup has come off. On one satin cuff an orange stain recalls my last salute.

"Now clean up and come down and sit with us . . . it's Row B, seats six and seven."

"O.K."

In my cubicle I rub my skin fiery to coldcream everything away except my simple, earlier face. Aftermath flattens out in me like the end of a birthday, like the daily texture and pallor of the street clothes I will be putting on for the rest of my life. Headed toward the audience, I walk past islands of ballerinas waiting for their cues.

"Bonnie!"

In the wings Gillian twinkles, two hundred dollars worth of light leaping and staying among the subtle rhinestones in her skirt. On her perfect, floral face worry hesitates, accepts the diminished form of puzzlement.

"Oh, Bon, am I ever scared!"

"You? *You've* got stage fright?"

"It's not that." Her eyes assess the cygnets on stage, pretending to

230

swandom in uneven bourrées. "Denise's out of step again," she says, "as usual." While I am looking, "I'm *late*, that's what's the matter."

"No, you're not. It's not even your cue."

Her violet eyes roll upward. "*Late. Late*," she repeats, " '*my aunt was coming for a visit*' and she's *late*. You *know*?"

"I bet it's the recital. It's made you nervous or something."

"Oh, no, it's not. I'm real regular, Bon. And anyways, there's other . . . signs."

"Signs?"

"Oh, Bon." She lowers her eyes in perfectly practiced shame. "I'm *expecting*."

It is the worst thing a girl could do, but even that, I sensed, you could do with talent, skill of some sort. "You're not?"

"Yeah. I'm sure. I got knocked up."

"Who?"

"Fred, who else?"

"Are you sure?"

Her glance shows damaged trust. Did I think she was one of those girls who "didn't even know the father"? Did I think she was an amateur?

"Does your mother know?"

"Bon, really. I mean, Fred and me, we'll tell her later. We're gonna get married right away, so it's O.K. Just don't say anything, promise?"

I start to cross my heart but the gesture feels foolish, childish. "But she'll find out. What about Scotland? What about the Dance?"

"Well, I'm certainly not gonna *dance* anymore!" Gillian puts on a matron's indignation.

"Oh, Gill."

"You gotta quit sometime, I mean, look at Madame." Her face pouts and she begins to cry, though carefully, a little wad of Kleenex damming up the tears to keep her mascara from flowing. "No. This is the last time."

From the stage a sharp crack of applause finishes the little swans.

"Oh, Gillian, that's awful."

"What?" The little cygnets, Beginners Class, giggle past us and she pulls back to preserve her fluted skirt.

"It's awful, you not dancing again."

"Oh. I mean, what I'm *really* worried about is maybe this could hurt the baby, mark it or something?" We hear the restless public murmur of the audience. "Well, me next," she says. "Cross your fingers, huh?"

"O.K."

Daintily Gillian pulls out a pink nubbin of gum and sticks it to the frame of the stage. A moment later she has assumed her place at center stage, legs effortlessly in the fifth position, arms *en couronne*.

In Row B I wedge past my mother's knees and sit between her and Mrs. Ravert, Seat 7, as the first bars of the Dying Swan draw a hush across the audience. On stage a wide confetti of pink and blue spotlights combine, settle on Gillian. The sweet soreness of her beauty, recognized, stirs in me, in everyone who watches. On our many drawn breaths she comes to motion.

Light plays on her rhinestones, bees on the living skin of flowers. The drafts catch and turn the feathers in her swan cap, until she trembles into something more than human, like us but also winged.

Beside me my mother holds in her disillusioned lap, eyes bravely forward, like a schoolgirl undergoing punishment both rigorous and undeserved. I reach for her in the darkness and am surprised by the readiness of her answering grip. We sit hand in hand.

From the audience a ripple, half cooing, half regret, says that Gillian, in a *temps d'ange*, has taken a bowman's arrow and now is slowly folding back into mortality.

In a few moments now she will sink into the sharp shape of a swan's outstretched throat, trembling to her silent death. The space between perfection and applause will seal her off. Then, resurrecting on the beats of acclamation, higher, higher, she will rise and curtsey, will make her *révérence* to Madame, the throats will fill up with "Encore!" until the dream cuts some other onlooker to the heart, roots there, and it begins again.

Downbent, my gaze catches the gleam of patent leather, Mrs. Ravert's cushiony small feet crammed into the pony hooves of her new shoes. She wears opaque elastic stockings, new too. Between the lapels of her Sunday suit, a cheap lace quivers. Her gloved laundress's hands are moving in small, possessed gestures to the music of her daughter's body on the stage. But I am afraid to look higher, to witness her face in all its bright intensity, the stale hair netted in a dancer's knot. Motherhood is the cruel art. If I look I will have to see her spirit burning in her eyes, the rapt and unsuspecting love of the only innocent among us.

The Last Escapade

Harry Mark Petrakis

"I'm ashamed to talk about it, even to you," his sister Naomi said. "But I'm at my wit's end about what I'm going to do with him. I had to phone you to come."

When he'd received her urgent message, he imagined it concerned their father, who was seventy-four and widowed six years since the death of his mother. He lived alone in an apartment a few miles from where Naomi lived with her husband and children. Several earlier conversations with his sister had hinted of his father's involvement with a girl. He had avoided talking to Naomi about it in the past but now he asked her if that was the problem.

"Not just a girl!" Naomi exclaimed. "A child! Keith, she's barely twenty years old! He met her . . .," she lowered her voice so the children playing in another room would not hear, ". . . in a massage parlor!"

"Maybe he just wanted a massage," Keith said.

"Oh for God's sake, Keith, spare me your academic wit! This is the most dreadful crisis we have ever had with him!"

"After all, he's in pretty good health," Keith said. "Maybe he still has an active sex drive."

"I don't want to hear about his sex drive!" she said. "I don't even want to think about what they do together! It's too disgusting! I'm sure he's giving her money and she hasn't any shame about cheating a senile old man."

"Are you sure he's giving her money?"

"He admitted it! A few times when I tried to talk to him about the danger of what he was doing, he grew impatient and flip with me and told me brazenly, he was paying her rent, gas and light!"

"That means she's not living with him."

233

"Oh God, don't even mention that possibility! If he did anything as stupid and outrageous as that I wouldn't let the children visit him again!"

"All right, Naomi," Keith tried to speak patiently. "He's seventy-four years old and he's involved with a twenty-year-old girl he met in a massage parlor. The whole business is a little sordid, I admit, but it seems to have been going on for some time. You mentioned it to me when I was here at Christmas. What makes it a crisis now?"

She rose from her chair and went to peer nervously into the dining room. The children had gone outside and she returned and sat down, leaning closer to speak to Keith in a shaken whisper.

"The girl had a baby two weeks ago!"

"Is he the father?" Keith asked.

"Don't be ridiculous!" Naomi said. "Honest to God, Keith, sometimes I think there is a streak of simpleness in you in spite of your degrees!"

"Well, other men his age have children," he protested. "There's that senator from the South, Strom Thurmond . . ."

"The baby isn't his!" she snapped. "He admits that much. He must have realized how shocked I was and he laughed, you know the nasty way he can laugh sometimes, and then brazenly told me he has been impotent for years! Can you imagine a man saying that to his own daughter? That proves he's senile!"

"Whose baby is it?"

"God only knows! One of the men she's been sleeping with, probably, some other fool she met in the massage parlor. A tart like that will never really know!"

"But if the baby isn't his child, why are you so concerned?"

"He is acting like the father!" Naomi said. "He was with her at the hospital during her delivery! My God, what if someone who knew me had seen her there?"

"A hospital is better than a massage parlor."

"Keith!"

"I'm sorry, Naomi."

"You don't seem to understand the gravity of what is taking place," she spoke in the older sister's voice he remembered her using with him for years. "Our seventy-four-year-old father, stumbling into his dotage, has taken up with a twenty-year-old girl who has had a baby! His vanity makes him act like he is the father. Can't you just see us together on one of the holidays? Bruce, the children, you and me, Father, his twenty-year-old girlfriend and the baby!"

234

"Maybe he felt obliged to help her," Keith said. "Now that she's had the baby, perhaps he won't have anything more to do with her."

"In his senility he won't be that sensible," Naomi said. "More than likely he will be reliving his own years of early marriage, pushing the baby on walks in a buggy he bought. It won't bother him that people will think he is the great-grandfather of the child."

Keith couldn't become as agitated as Naomi but he understood her concern. His father lived on a pension from the Colony Insurance Company and his Social Security and didn't have to touch the money he'd received from the sale of their house when his mother died. Some of that money had gone to Naomi when she and Bruce bought their house and his father had given Keith ten thousand dollars while he studied for his doctoral degree. But there had to be seventy to eighty thousand dollars still in the bank. The money belonged to his father to do with as he wished, but they had a responsibility to make sure the girl didn't cheat him out of it.

"What do you think we should do?" Keith asked.

"You should go and talk to him," Naomi said sternly. "You are his son and maybe you men understand this kind of perversion. Try to make him understand that what he is doing is shameful and obscene! My God, if he is impotent, what do they do together?"

He started to explain there were other diversions but Naomi cut him off with a sharp wave of her hand.

"I don't want to hear the gory details!" she said. "I just want you to talk to him!"

"All right, I'll go over and see him now."

"You better phone him first," she said. "You might find the two of them in bed." She fetched up a sigh that quivered her plump body. "Oh my God, I'm only grateful that poor Mama isn't alive to suffer this shame!"

But if his mother were still alive, Keith thought, his father would probably have never gotten involved with the girl.

He phoned his father, who seemed delighted that Keith was in town, and agreed to see him at once. He left Naomi's house after promising her he would return that evening to report to her exactly what his father had said.

The children were playing on a neighbor's lawn. As Keith walked to his car, seven-year-old Cathy sprinted over to give him a hug. Keith tousled the child's hair and told her he'd see her later.

His father lived in a pleasant residential neighborhood north of downtown, in a three-room apartment he had rented after his mother's death and the sale of their house. Keith helped him move into the apartment and understood that his father's adjustment from a large house with his mother to living alone would be difficult. He pledged he'd visit him several times each year. Somehow, his own academic and social schedule always prevented the visits. He saw his father on a few holidays and on his birthdays, which he and Naomi always spent with him. Because Naomi lived in the same city, she saw his father more than Keith but he knew neither of them had been as diligent about their visits as they should have been. As Keith drove up to park beside his father's building, he resolved that when the business of the girl was settled, he would drive in to see his father more often.

His father opened the door of the apartment and greeted Keith with a warm hug. Keith looked quickly for evidence of deterioration but his father seemed unchanged from his last visit. A tall, wiry man with gray, thinning hair and a slight paunch, the changes in him over the years seemed slight except for his ruddy complexion growing paler and his flesh more translucent. His eyes retained that keenness that had made him one of the best regional directors Colony Insurance ever had on their staff.

"Want a beer?" his father asked.

He nodded and was grateful when his father walked to the kitchen, giving him a moment to assemble his thoughts about the best way to begin. When his father returned with the beer, he took several quick swallows.

"That sure tastes good," he said. He stared nervously at his father who sat down and smiled benignly at him. "I haven't seen you in a couple of months and I just decided to drive up," he said. "The weather was nice . . ."

"Keith-O," his father interrupted him gently. "You're a bright young man with degrees in literature and English and I know you're a fine teacher. But you were never any great shakes as a liar. I've been expecting you to come. I knew your sister would call you as soon as she heard about the baby."

"You always could see through me, Dad," Keith smiled, a little flustered. "Naomi did call me. She's just concerned and hasn't been able to talk to you herself. She asked me to come and see you."

"Fair enough, son," his father said. "Your sister is a wonderful woman but she can never see beyond her outrage." He paused, raising his hand to brush at his hair. "I want to talk to you too. I think you'll appreciate

236

some of the irony in what has happened to me. I began a relationship with the basest of intentions and now I am reliving the anxieties of early fatherhood."

His father paused again, as if assembling the words to go on. From the street below a car backfired several times, the sound echoing loudly through the apartment.

"The girl, Sally," his father said, "is kind of a simple child without any wisdom about the men she becomes involved with. Now she has a baby." His father's voice was calm but when he reached to the endtable beside the chair for his pipe, Keith saw his fingers trembling. He knocked the bole gently against an ashtray. "When I first saw that red, wriggling, naked little body I was sorry for it . . . really sorry and sorry for his mother, who was still such a child, and sorry that I wasn't younger."

"If you were younger, would you marry the girl?" Keith smiled, as if to reassure his father that he was joking.

"I think I would have had more sense than that," his father said. "But if I were younger I could have helped her and kept an eye on the two of them." He paused. "We've never really had that serious a relationship. I know she doesn't really love me in the way a woman loves a man and she has deceived me about needing money for her rent or to fix her car. She might even be giving some of the money I give her for those expenses to some man. She's foolish in that way."

He tapped fresh tobacco into his pipe, a familiar gesture that reminded Keith of his years of growing up. He suddenly noticed things about his father, how his sweater was torn at the sleeve and stained at the waist, things his mother would never have allowed. His father caught him staring at him and sighed.

"I'm sorry if I'm hurting and disappointing you and Naomi," he said. "And I didn't plan for this to happen. I was lonely and feeling, you know, kind of horny . . . no matter what the young think, that can still happen often at my age. I had walked past that massage parlor at least two dozen times and, one day, I simply walked inside. I almost walked right out again except for a pleasant, matronly lady who talked to me about how natural my visit was. I gave her some money and then I went into a small room with a table like doctors have in their examining rooms. I started to unbutton my shirt, the woman had told me to undress, and then this girl came in. She was very young and blond and, when she smiled, she didn't have very good teeth. She was wearing a kind of little toga and when I saw her I started buttoning my shirt again. She must have been used to old men having second thoughts because she finished unbuttoning my shirt. When she started to unbuckle my trousers, I told her I'd do it. I felt I was exposing myself in a school yard full of children. I was conscious of how old I was and my skinny legs and I panicked. I told her I had something to do and pulled up my pants and beat it out of there like a bulldog had its teeth in my ass."

Keith was suddenly conscious that he had been listening to his father as if he were hearing him for the first time in years.

"I would never have had the courage to go back into that massage parlor," his father said, "but about a week after that first aborted visit, I was shopping in the Dominick's on Laramie and, in the produce section, I saw her. My first impulse was to run but she looked straight at me over a stack of tomatoes and recognized me. I was sure it was her when she smiled because of her bad teeth." He shrugged wryly. "We had a cup of coffee together in Burger King and talked about many things. Finally, she asked if I'd like to have her visit me and I said yes . . ."

His father drew slowly on his pipe, exhaling a tiny swirl of smoke.

"I wasn't really expecting she'd show up the following night," his father said, "but I cleaned the apartment anyway and bought crackers and cheese and a bottle of wine. She did come, dressed like a young college girl on a Saturday night date. We talked about the Cubs and the Sox and the small town in Kansas where she grew up and the first boy she loved, who left her to join the Air Force. She was a sweet girl, a little naive and simple, like I said, but uncommonly sensitive for twenty. And then, after about an hour, she got up and came over to me and gently sat down on my lap."

He paused, staring uneasily at Keith.

"Does this disgust you, Son, or make you angry?" he asked. "Would you prefer I didn't tell you anymore?"

"You don't have to explain anything to me," Keith said quickly, even as he was conscious his palms were growing moist, "but I don't mind you talking."

His father nodded with what seemed gratefulness.

"I knew that after I told Naomi about the baby, she'd call you to come and see me," his father said. "I didn't know if I'd have the courage to tell you these things and I practiced them, not because I was lying, but because I wanted to tell you honestly the things I feel, the things she made me feel. Even that first night, when we went to bed and she did a few things she thought would please me, they weren't pleasing. I was tense, frightened, ashamed. I thought of Naomi and my grandchildren and your mother. The way she would shake her head and say, 'Alfred, Alfred,' when I did something she thought absurd. All I wanted the girl to do was to get up, get dressed and leave. I wasn't even embarrassed that I was impotent. I just wanted her to get out. It wasn't until after she was gone that I recalled the wonder of the experience. The room had been dark except for a glow from the streetlight. For just a few moments she might have forgotten and thought she was truly with her lover. I thought I could tell when those moments came because there was something different, more tender and less practiced, when she touched me."

His father's voice had grown hoarser and he reached over and turned on the lamp. "Do you want another beer, Keith?" he asked. "Or shall we make a pot of coffee?"

Keith shook his head. He stole a glance at his watch, surprised that it was already five-thirty.

"There isn't much more to tell," his father said. "That was about a year ago. She'd visit me once or twice a week. Sometimes we just sat and talked, you know, the way she might have talked with her own father," he grimaced, "or her grandfather. Sometimes she'd ask me for money for her rent or for repairs on her car. She had to have some dental work done and the dentist told her he could cap her bad teeth. She didn't ask me for that money but there was such a naked pleading in her voice and eyes, like a little girl begging for something she wanted more than anything else in the world. I had the dentist fix her teeth and paid him myself."

Keith didn't ask how much that work had cost but his father understood.

"It cost about fifteen hundred dollars," his father said, "but she looked so much better and was so delighted. When she came to see me, right from the dentist's office after he'd finished, she told me she smiled at everybody she passed on the street." He laughed softly. "If I thought her gratitude would make her come see me more often, I was mistaken. Sometimes I wouldn't see her for a couple of weeks. And then, during one visit, she told me she was pregnant. She had told me before of the men she'd been involved with, one bastard after another, so even if she'd known who the father was, it wouldn't have made any difference. She had been living with one fellow and one day he kicked her out. Just like that. Then she met a mechanic who kept beating her up. She came over once with a black eye and a swollen cheek. I really bawled her out then, the way I might have if she'd been my granddaughter, and she cried a little. She broke up with him too. I'm not sure how. Maybe she found the sense to leave him."

From the street a siren wailed, the strident sound sweeping through the room. His father waited until the noise had passed.

"I don't think she has anyone now," his father said. "She's fascinated with the baby. He's like a new toy to her, a living toy, but she loves him too. I felt some of that love when I waited in the hospital with her and first saw her with the baby. He was such a beautiful little boy and in some strange, foolish way I thought of the boy belonging to me too. Since then I realize how absurd the whole business is really. She's not related to me and the baby isn't mine. But I enjoy seeing her and look forward to their visits. In the few times the three of us have been together, I feel happier than I have felt in years."

There was a long silence, his father not talking. Keith tried to think of something to say. "What is going to happen to her?" he asked finally.

"I don't know," his father said slowly. "The baby is enough for now but the day will come when she'll take up with another man, another bastard no doubt, she doesn't seem able to choose any other kind. She's young, and I suppose she'll make it through, but I worry about the baby."

He stared at Keith, who grew uncomfortable under the intensity of his father's glare.

"You know, son," his father said quietly, "I don't want to make excuses but the whole thing came about because of loneliness. I am not blaming your sister or you. You live four hundred miles away and she has her life with Bruce and her children. But when a man is alone as he grows older, you have to understand that his days and nights are different. He doesn't have the expectations he had when he was young, or the dreams, or planning for the things he hopes to do. He wakes up in the silence of the dark room and can't help thinking that it's just another night moving him closer to death. Oh, I know, there is the senior center nearby and movies and television. But I find that gathering of old people depressing and television is full of idiotic comedies and the movies show films that have nothing to do with the life I lived. I am grateful when you and Naomi and the children and I enjoy holidays and birthdays. But those celebrations pass quickly and then there are empty, lonely weeks again." His father shrugged. "I said I didn't want to make excuses but I guess I just did."

"You might go and live with Naomi," Keith said, "or come down to Carbondale with me. You know I'd love to have you."

"I'm sure you would, Son," his father smiled. "But that wouldn't work. Naomi is nervous around me now and if she had me around, day and night, no matter how hard I tried, she'd go over the brink. As for living with you, Son, when you brought a girl home to spend the night, would you ask me to go to a movie or to spend the night in the YMCA? No . . .

loneliness is a misery but when a parent lives with a son or daughter, there can't help being feelings of resentment and guilt."

"We'd never feel that way about you!" Keith said earnestly.

"I'm not saying that would be true about you or Naomi," his father said, "but it might be about many sons and daughters, even good and loving ones. I have lived alone six years since your mother's death and I'm grateful now that she died before me. This life might have been harder for her to endure because she was a woman. Can you ever imagine your mother walking into a massage parlor? I tell you something, Son, something I have come to understand in these last years and I don't say it bitterly but because it's the truth. The old are not really loved. They are tended and cared for and turned so their chairs face their favorite channel but, in our hard-sell society, they have nothing to sell anymore but a reminder that not even youth and beauty endures."

His father rose and motioned to the clock.

"It's almost six o'clock," he said. "Naomi is probably expecting you for dinner."

"Come to dinner with me," Keith said. "Naomi told me to ask you to come back with me."

"The hell she did," his father laughed. "She's so mad at me these days that she might poison my salad. You go ahead and have your dinner and, if you get a chance to talk to her alone, try to make her understand the things I told you about the girl and me."

Keith rose and hesitated a moment longer. He started to tell his father that he'd stay in town and they'd spend some time together. Then he remembered the date he had with Marcie in Carbondale the following evening.

"Let's eat together this evening anyway," he said. "I'll call Naomi and tell her you and I are having dinner together. I'll drive back to Carbondale later tonight."

His father gave his arm an affectionate squeeze.

"You stop squirming and go ahead now," he said reassuringly. "You really listened to me and I think you understand but it's got to be uncomfortable for both of us. I am relieved I got it out but I don't want to talk about it anymore and we'll strain talking about other things. Maybe on your next visit we'll spend more time together. If you didn't mind, maybe I could have Sally bring the baby up here for you to see. She likes to feel respectable and that would please her, but only if you didn't have any objections."

"That would be fine with me, Dad," Keith said.

"There's one more thing, Son," his father said. "You know I've got some money saved. Not a great deal, but money that will go to you and Naomi when I'm gone. I may want to make some provision for the baby, some money for his schooling and for other things. I hope you and Naomi will understand and won't try to cut the child out. I'm not asking you to give it all up, just to share some of it."

"It's your money, Dad," Keith said. "You do what you want with it."

"I'll leave most of it to you and Naomi," his father said. "I just feel sorry for the baby and would like to provide for him too."

On an impulse Keith moved back and embraced his father. He smelled the scents of his tobacco and the odors of food and stale coffee grounds on his sweater. He remembered then how clean his mother had always kept his father's clothing.

When he had walked down the stairs and reached his car he looked up toward the apartment windows. He wasn't sure whether his father was standing at the window, but he waved anyway. He climbed into his car buoyed by a sense of resolve he would explain everything his father had told him to Naomi.

But with every block he drove through the gathering twilight, the futility of explanation to his sister overwhelmed him. He imagined her outrage and the way she would make it appear as if he had failed her. His determination weakened until he turned his car away from the direction of Naomi's house and drove toward the Interstate. He'd phone her from a gas station and tell her he'd forgotten an important appointment he had in Carbondale for early in the morning. If she wanted to know what his father had told him, he'd say someone was waiting for the phone and he couldn't talk.

The Address

Marga Minco

"Do you still know me?" I asked.

The woman looked at me, inquiring; she had opened the door a crack. I came closer and stood on the front step.

"No," she said, "I don't know you."

"I'm the daughter of Mrs. S.," I said.

She kept her hand on the door as though she wanted to prevent it from opening further. Her face didn't betray any sign of recognition. She kept looking at me silently.

Maybe I'm wrong, I thought, maybe she isn't the one. I had only seen her once in passing, and that was years ago. It was quite likely that I had pushed the wrong doorbell. The woman let go of the door and stepped aside. She was wearing a green hand-knitted sweater. The wooden buttons were slightly faded from laundering. She saw that I was looking at her sweater and again hid partly behind the door. But now I knew that I was at the right address.

"You knew my mother, didn't you?" I asked.

"Did you come back?" said the woman. "I thought that no one had come back."

"Only I," I said. In the hall behind her a door opened and closed. A stale smell came out.

"I'm sorry," she said, "I can't do anything for you."

"I've come here especially on the train. I would have liked to speak with you for a moment."

"It's not convenient now," said the woman. "I can't invite you in. Another time."

She nodded and carefully closed the door, as though no one in the house should be disturbed. I remained on the front step for a moment.

The curtain of the bay window moved. "Oh, nothing," the woman would say, "it was nothing."

I looked at the nameplate once more. It said "Dorling," with black letters on white enamel. And on the doorpost, a little higher, the number. Number 46.

While slowly walking back to the station, I thought of my mother, who had once, years ago, given me the address. It was during the first half of the war. I had come home for a few days, and it had struck me right away that something had changed in the rooms. I missed all sorts of things. My mother was surprised that I'd noticed it so quickly. Then she told me about Mrs. Dorling. I had never heard of her before, but she seemed to be an old acquaintance of my mother's whom she hadn't seen in years. She had suddenly turned up and renewed the acquaintance. Since that time she had been coming regularly.

"Every time she leaves she takes something home with her," my mother said. "She took all the silver flatware at once. And then the antique plates which hung over there. She really had a tough job lugging these big vases, and I'm afraid that she hurt her back with the dishes." My mother shook her head with compassion. "I would never have dared to ask her. She suggested it herself. She even insisted. She wants to save all my beautiful things. She says that we'll lose everything when we have to leave here."

"Have you arranged with her that she'll keep everything?" I asked. "As though that were necessary," my mother exclaimed. "It would be an insult to agree on something like that. And think of the risk she takes every time she leaves our house with a full suitcase or bag!" My mother seemed to notice that I wasn't totally convinced. She looked at me reproachfully, and after that we didn't speak of it again.

Without paying too much attention to the road I had arrived at the station. For the first time since the war I was walking again through familiar districts, but I didn't want to go further than absolutely necessary. I didn't want to torment myself with the sight of streets and houses full of memories of a cherished time. In the train back, I saw Mrs. Dorling before me again, the way I had met her the first time. It was the morning after the day my mother had told me about her. I had gotten up late, and as I went downstairs I saw that my mother was just seeing someone out. A woman with a broad back.

"There is my daughter," said my mother. She motioned to me.

The woman nodded and picked up the suitcase which stood under the coatrack. She was wearing a brown coat and a shapeless hat.

244

"Does she live far?" I asked after seeing how laboriously she left the house with the heavy suitcase.

"On Marconistraat," said my mother. "Number 46. Do try to remember."

I had remembered. Except that I had waited quite a long time before going there. During the first period after the liberation I felt no interest at all in all that stored stuff, and of course some fear was involved. Fear of being confronted with things that had been part of a bond which no longer existed; which had been stored in cases and boxes and were waiting in vain until they would be put back in their places; which had survived all these years because they were "things."

But gradually everything had become normal again. There was bread which was steadily becoming lighter in color, there was a bed in which you could sleep without being threatened, a room with a view which you got more and more used to every day. And one day I noticed that I was becoming curious about all the possessions which should still be at that address. I wanted to see them, touch them, recognize them. After my first fruitless visit to Mrs. Dorling's house, I decided to try it a second time.

This time it was a girl of about fourteen who opened the door. I asked whether her mother was home. "No," she said, "my mother is just on an errand."

"That doesn't matter," I said, "I'll wait for her."

I followed the girl through the hall. Next to the mirror hung an old-fashioned menorah. We had never used it because it was much more cumbersome than candles.

"Wouldn't you like to sit down?" asked the girl. She held open the door to the room and I went in past her. Frightened, I stood still. I was in a room which I both knew and didn't know. I found myself among things I had wanted to see again but which oppressed me in the strange surroundings. Whether it was because of the tasteless manner in which everything was arranged, because of the ugly furniture or the stuffy air, I don't know, but I scarcely dared look around me anymore. The girl moved a chair. I sat down and stared at the woollen tablecloth. I touched it carefully. I rubbed it. My fingers got warm from rubbing. I followed the lines of the design. Someplace on the edge there should be a burn hole which had never been repaired.

"My mother will be back very soon," said the girl. "I had already made tea for her. Would you like a cup?"

"Please," I said. I looked up. The girl was setting out teacups on the tea table. She had a broad back. Just like her mother. She poured tea from a white pot. There was a gold edge just around the lid, I remembered. She opened a small box and took some teaspoons out of it. "That's a lovely little box." I heard my own voice. It was a strange voice. As though every sound in this room had another ring to it.

"Do you know much about that?" She had turned around and brought me my tea. She laughed. "My mother says that it is antique. We have lots more." She pointed around the room. "Just look."

I didn't need to follow her hand. I knew which things she meant. I kept looking at the still-life above the tea table. As a child I had always wanted to eat the apple that lay on the pewter plate.

"We use it for everything," she said. "We've even eaten from the plates which hang on the wall. I wanted to. But it wasn't anything special."

I had found the burn hole at the edge of the tablecloth. The girl looked at me inquiringly. "Yes," I said, "you get used to all these beautiful things at home, you hardly look at them anymore. You only notice when something is not there, because it has to be repaired, or, for example, because you've lent it to someone."

Again I heard the unnatural sound of my voice, and I continued: "I remember my mother once asking me to help her polish the silver. That was very long ago, and I must have been bored that day, or maybe I had to stay home because I was ill, for she had never asked me to do that before. I asked her which silver she meant, and she answered me, surprised, that she was of course talking about the spoons, forks, and knives. And that was of course the odd thing, I didn't know that the objects with which we ate every day were made of silver."

The girl laughed again.

"I bet you don't know that either," I said. I looked at her intently.

"What we eat with?" she asked.

"Well, do you know?"

She hesitated. She walked to the buffet and started to pull open a drawer. "I'll have to look. It's in here."

I jumped up. "I'm forgetting my time. I still have to catch my train."

She stood with her hand on the drawer. "Wouldn't you like to wait for my mother?"

"No, I have to leave." I walked to the door. The girl opened the drawer.

"I'll find my way." When I was walking through the hall I heard the clinking of spoons and forks.

At the corner of the street I looked up at the nameplate. It said Marconistraat. I had been at Number 46. The address was right. But now I no longer wanted to remember it. I would not go there again, for the objects which in your memory are linked with the familiar life of former times suddenly lose their value when you see them again, torn out of context, in strange surroundings. And what would I do with them in a small rented room in which shreds of blackout paper were still hanging along the windows and where in the narrow table drawer there was room for just a few dinner things?

I resolved to forget the address. Of all the things I should forget, that one would be the easiest.

Translated from the Dutch by Jeannette K. Ringold

The Chandelier

Gregory Orfalea

Mukhlis drives up Asbury Street in Pasadena and brings his green Buick to an easy, slow stop underneath the largest flowering eucalyptus in southern California. The first door cracked is that of his wife, Wardi, who gets out as she has every week for the past forty years, as if she were with child. She has not been with child for many years, but her body at center is like the large burl of a cedar and her legs are bowed as an old chair's. Mukhlis emerges from the Buick. He looks left and right for cars—a short, searing look either way. And the sun tries to plant its white seed on the center of his bald head.

Mukhlis has made a small fortune in real estate. He has apartment complexes here and there in the city, and many of his tenants are black or brown. He himself is brown, or rather almond, and his eyes, like those of many Lebanese and Syrians, are blue. He owes this hue to the Crusaders. A continent man, Mukhlis's eyes are the last blue twinkle of a distant lust.

What words there are to say, Mukhlis rarely says. His eyes and body speak—a body made to withstand. As he ascends the steps of his sister's home, the collar of his gray suit pulls taut around his neck. And his neck has the thickness of a foundation post; it welds his head to the shoulders. For years it has been bronzed by the sun. So tight is the tie and collar around his neck that his nape stands up in a welt of muscle. It is not a fat neck—nothing about the man is fat, save a slight bulge to his belly, brought on, no doubt, by forty years of Wardi's desserts, among the finest Arabic delights in Los Angeles. Mukhlis has learned it is useless to compliment her because Wardi (Rose, in English), like most Arabs, does not react to compliments; she prefers to go to great lengths to pay a compliment, instead. But not Mukhlis. He says not two

248

crooked words about Wardi's *knafi*, the bird's nest whose wafer-like shell must be rolled with the patience of Job before it is filled with pistachios as green as Mukhlis's Buick—and probably greener—then topped with a spoon of rosewater syrup.

Mukhlis kisses his sister, Matile, and booms a greeting to the air behind her in a robust voice that speaks in simple sentences and laughs silently. His large head, sapphire eyes and corded neck all shake with his laughter.

And if it is on a summer evening, with a large group of people chatting on Matile's porch, all will be aware of Mukhlis, though he will surely say the least, and when his hands come apart after having been clasped tightly on his belly for so long, people will take a drag on their cigarettes and turn in his direction.

"No one wants to work, and so the devil has his pick of the young people."

Wardi, who clasps her hands on a more bulbous belly, will nod and sip her coffee from the demitasse.

"Matile, do you have any cream?" Mukhlis asks his sister.

"Certainly, my honey," she sings. "Anything for you."

When Matile's voice sings it is to smooth over rough spots in conversation; her feigned joy or fright has saved many a wounded soul. But when Mukhlis sang—the fact that he once did sing is his most guarded secret—it was with the voice of the *hassoun*, the national bird of Lebanon, multicolored red, yellow and black, prized for its rich warble, and fed marijuana seeds by children.

Sitting among immigrants from the First World War, Mukhlis was asked to fill the gaps in all hearts over the strange Atlantic, which in Arabic is called "The Sea of Darkness." Please, Mukhlis, sing the praise to the night! Sing of the moon and its white dress! Huddled on the stoops in Brooklyn, they asked for the song of two lovers separated by a river. The one of the nine months of pregnancy, in which Mukhlis stuffed a pillow under his shirt. Sing, cousin Mukhlis, for we are tired of the dress factories, we are tired of the fish market. Sing the Old Land on the Mediterranean!

And sing he did. His voice was effortless and sweet; it was made all the sweeter by the immense power everyone knew lay under it. Then one day this unschooled tenor, this voice dipped in rosewater, simply stopped. It stopped cold when Mukhlis's mother died in a little loft above a funeral parlor in Brooklyn. It died when he covered the four long white scars of her back, from the lashes of the Turks, for the last time. No one in California has ever heard him sing.

All of this is whispered from time to time behind Mukhlis's back. None of it is spoken directly to his ears. He will not tolerate it. His usual response to any mention of the latest atrocity in Lebanon is: "How is your dog?" or "The apricots are too thick on the boughs this year. They need to be snapped off."

But today the large porch is empty, except for Matile herself and her oldest grandson, Mukhlis's great-nephew. This young man has been traveling for years. He is a restless soul, thinks Mukhlis, as they take their places on the porch—he on the legless couch, his wife on a white wrought-iron chair with a pillow of faded flowers made by Matile. The great-nephew takes to the old iron swing. What is it about this day? Mukhlis says to himself, noticing a vine in the yard. The wind is hurting the grape leaves.

Matile brings a tray of coffee and announces dinner is not too far off, and all must stay.

"It is never too far off with you, Matile," Mukhlis says, blowing over the coffee.

"You *must* stay," she sings. "I am making stuffed zucchini."

"Never mind," he says. "Have you got a *ghrabi?*"

"*Ghrabi?*" Matile stands so quickly she leaves her black shoes. And goes into a litany of food that lasts five minutes.

"No, no, no," Mukhlis punctuates each breathless pause in her list. "*Ghrabi*—just give me one."

"One!" she cries. "I have a hundred."

"One, please, is all I want."

She brings a dish piled high with the small hoops of butter, sugar and dough, each with a mole or two of pistachio.

"Eat," she says.

Wardi takes one. Mukhlis shakes his head and breaks off half a *ghrabi*.

"Isn't that delicious?" Matile asks, preempting the compliment. Mukhlis chews. "You look real good today," she smiles with a brightened face, disregarding his nodding. Mukhlis turns to the young man.

"And so, what are you doing here?"

"Looking for work," says the great-nephew, a dark, slender fellow with broad shoulders. These eyes of his, Mukhlis thinks, have a dark sparkle. He's cried and laughed too much for his age; his laugh is a cry and his cry is a laugh.

"It's time for you to get serious and stop this wandering and get a good job in business," Mukhlis says rather loudly.

"You are playing with your life. When are you going to get married?" Mukhlis gleams his crocodile smile and laughs silently. Then he

250

becomes solemn, and touches the pistachio on a *ghrabi* with a thick forefinger, taps it several times, then removes it.

"Aren't you ever really hungry, Uncle Mukhlis?"

The old realtor looks out past the stanchions of the porch, past the thickened apricots.

"Boy, have you ever seen a person eat an orange peel?"

"I've eaten them myself. They're quite good."

"No, no, boy. I mean rotten orange peels, with mud and dung on them. Have you had that?"

The great-nephew purses his lips.

"Well, I want to tell you a story. I want to tell you about hunger, and I want to tell you about disgrace."

Matile gets up again, and lets out in her falsetto, "Don't go no further till I come back."

Mukhlis disregards her and squeezes a faded pillow on the legless couch, as if he were squeezing his brain. What is it about the breeze and the light today, the crystal light? Will he go on? He does not know. His great-nephew is too silent. Mukhlis does not like silence waiting for silence. He likes his silence to be hidden in a crowd. From the dome of his almond head, he takes some sweat and smells it. Wardi continues to eat.

"I was the oldest of us in Lebanon when we lived in the mountain, but when World War I started I was still a young boy. They cut off Beirut harbor in 1914. You see, the Germans were allied with the Turks who had hold over all the Arab lands. And so the Germans became our masters for a time. When it was all we could do to steer clear of the Turks! The Allies blockaded Beirut harbor, and for four years there was no food to be had in Mount Lebanon."

At this moment Matile puts a heap of grapes in front of him.

"Nothing like this purple grape, I can assure you! These were treacherous times of human brutality. People were hungry and hunger is the beginning of cruelty. The Turks themselves would tolerate no funny business. If people refused to cooperate with them they would take it out on the children. I saw them seize a small boy by the legs and literally rip him in half. I saw this happen with my own eyes; one half of the child flew into the fountain we had in Mhciti, which is near Bikfaya. The fountain was empty, but even after the War when it had water and the remains of the child were dried up no one would drink there."

"Yi! You tell them, Mukhlis! You tell this to show what happen to us!" Matile's voice rises as she lays down a plate of goat's cheese and bread. "It was terrible."

251

"Food was so scarce people would pick up horse dung, wash it, and eat the grains of hay left. It was common to go days without eating or drinking, because the Nahr Ibrahim and the Bardowni Rivers were contaminated by dead bodies. The Germans and the Turks would throw traitors into the river . . . then there was the chandelier."

Matile clicks her tongue. "I could tell you story, boy, I could tell you story."

"Did you know 'Lebanon' means 'snow'?" Mukhlis raises his pointer finger. "It means 'white as yogurt' because the mountains are covered with snow. It was very cold in the winter, and we had to stay in. Without food, it was colder."

"What about restaurants?" the great-nephew ventures.

"Restaurant? You are an idiot, young man, forgive me for saying. Any restaurant was destroyed in the first year, any market plundered by the soldiers. We had to find food for ourselves. Each day for four years was a battle for food."

"I could tell you story." Matile puts her eyes up to the stucco ceiling of the porch and shakes her hands. "*Thoobs!* A crust of bread was so rare it was like communion. My mother she had to go away for days to trade everything we had for food on the other side of the mountain—"

"Matile, I . . ."

"—she give us a slice of bread before she leaves and she shake her finger at us and say—Matile, Mukhlis, Milhem—you don't take this all at once. Each day you cut one piece of the bread. One piece! No more. And you cut this piece into four pieces—three for you, and then you break the last one for the infants. You understand? Like one cracker a day for each of us. Little Milhem and Leila, they cry all day. They want more. They too little to understand, and the baby . . . ah! Milhem hit us for the rest of the slice of bread. I hide it under my pillow one night. And that night . . . oh I could tell you story make your ears hurt!"

Mukhlis shifts in his seat and flings out his arms. "Now, when I went off in the snow . . ."

"The chandelier, you remember."

"Yes, Matile, of course I do."

"You remember, Wardi, you wouldn't believe it."

Wardi's eyes are large as a night creature behind her thick eyeglass lenses, and she nods.

Mukhlis clears his throat loudly. "My mother gave me the last piastres we had and told me to go through the snow over the mountain to the village in the dry land, to fetch milk and bread. I was not as strong as my mother but I was strong, and so I tried. But the first day out I was shot at by a highwayman, a robber. I hid behind a rock; still he found me and stripped off my jacket and took the piastres. I was glad he did not kill me. But what was I to do? I could not go home. I continued walking until I came to the monastery. I thought I would ask the monks for some milk. They were not there."

"They die."

"Matile, please. They were not there. Perhaps they went to Greece. They were Greek monks. The place was empty. The door to the chapel opening with the wind that moved it back and forth. Inside the candles were snuffed. And the candlesticks were cold, and all the pews were covered with frost. It was winter, inside and out. Up above was a . . ."

"Chandelier!"

"Yes, Matile, a huge crystal chandelier. In all my life I have never seen one larger. Its branches were as far across as this couch, made of solid gold. Inlaid in the arms were rubies the size of your eyes, nephew! I remember standing in that chapel that day thinking how we had come to worship there with my father when I was a very young child; the chandelier was something I would worship. I would look up and its great shining light would say to me—God. This is your God, Mukhlis, here on Mount Lebanon. He brims with light and He will sit in your eyes, in your dreams. I had never thought of touching it. For one thing, it was too high. It was at least fifteen feet above my head. Well, so help the Almighty, I was hungry. And my mother was hungry. And so were my brothers . . . and my sisters. And we had not heard from our father, who was in America, for two years. Before God and man, I committed a sacrilege. The mosaics, you see, on the wall were shot out and in tatters. I crawled up the wall where the tile was gone. I crawled up that mosaic until I made it to the crossbeams of the ceiling. And I had to be very careful not to knock loose the mosaic where I was hanging—a mosaic of Our Lady it was, and who knows? Maybe my foot was in her mouth."

"How sad!" sighs Matile.

"But I hoisted myself onto the crossbeam and slid—like this, yes—slid across the beam. It was cold enough to hold my hands fast as I tried to balance. But finally I made it out over the nave of the chapel, to the chandelier."

"Yi!"

"The chandelier was held to the ceiling with tall iron nails. Carefully, carefully I put my hands through the crystal teardrops, to latch onto the gold arms. And then you know what I did, young man? I became a monkey. I swung free on that chandelier! I pulled up and heaved down on it, trying to loosen it. I yanked and yanked with the crystal hitting

253

my eyes and the rubies sweating in my hands. And I swung back and forth in the cold air. For a long time the chandelier would not loosen. It seemed like God Himself was holding onto the chandelier through the ceiling and saying to me: No you don't, Mukhlis! You do not take the chandelier from this church. This is mine, Mukhlis. This chandelier was given to the worship of the Almighty. And you—you are a puny human being who deserves to rot in hell for this.

"I am not talking about playing in the acacias. I am not talking about swinging about from those miserable apricot trees, which need to be cut back by the way, Matile."

"Anything you say, my honey."

"I am talking about a tree of crystal and gold. I am talking about food."

"Wardi, would you like more coffee, dear?"

"Matile, I am talking about food."

"So am I!"

Wardi's enlarged eyes close and her big bosom vibrates with mirth, like a dreaming horse.

"Oh it's useless. Why talk about it?" Mukhlis folds his hands, as if to tie up the story once and for all and leave everyone hanging on the chandelier.

Matile speaks with alarm: "Please, tell them, tell them. I won't get up no more. This is story you never heard the like of before. It can't be no worse!"

Mukhlis gets up, paces on the clay porch, and goes over to the apricot, breaking off a branch crowded with fruit.

"Here, Matile, here is your dessert," he spits and continues, still standing. "Finally, I heard it come loose. The plaster dust rained on my face and I heaved on this chandelier one more time. And then I fell."

Mukhlis raises his thick forearms and grips the air.

"It breaks, ah!"

"No, Matile, it does not break. Please, you are killing my story at every juncture."

She laughs and gets up for some rice pudding that is cooling in the refrigerator.

"I fall with it. I fall with it and I fall directly on my rump. This is why I walk slowly to this day, young man. Because of the chandelier. That chandelier had to become milk. It was going to save my life, our lives. What did my bones mean? Nothing. But I was a tough young fellow— not like you soft people today—and not one teardrop of that crystal was scratched. I got up, and my hip was partially cracked. But I got up. I carried the chandelier to the entrance of the church. No one was around. No one saw me do it."

"God finally let go?" the great-nephew asks, with a smirk.

"God never lets go. I yanked it out of His hands. But I could not carry the chandelier far—it weighed a ton. In the vestibule of the chapel was a small Oriental rug. I placed the chandelier on top of that, took the cord of chain, tied it around the branches of gold, and dragged the whole mess out into the snow. No, Matile, no rice pudding. For the next three days, I dragged the chandelier over the snow to get to the village over the mountain in the hot land of the Bekaa. For three days I walked and pulled it behind me."

Mukhlis stops and wipes his brow. He is sweating heavily now, even though the California air is dry.

"I was exhausted by the end of the first day. I lay down in the snow by a cedar. I did not want to damage the chandelier, so I left it on the rug and tried to sleep on the snow with as much of my body as I could against the cedar. I was so tired and fell fast asleep."

"Did you dream?" asks the great-nephew, taking a spoonful of the sweet rice pudding.

"I don't remember. No, I don't dream. Dreams are for soft times," Mukhlis grunts. "You've dropped some pudding." His listener takes up the white spot on the porch with a finger. For a while Mukhlis says nothing, and listens to them eating. His blue eyes stare out into the warm air past the apricots, past the flowering eucalyptus, to the cloudless sky.

"I awoke to the sound of licking in the dark. I felt warm breath near my face. I sat up. There were six eyes, six greenish eyes in the darkness. My blood went cold. Wolves. I got up fast, grabbed the chandelier and swung it around and around, turning inside it myself. It made a tinkling noise that was loud in the dead forest and the wolves howled and scattered back into the night. I was breathing so hard my heart felt like it would come out of me. I was much too awake now and decided to go on dragging the chandelier in the dark. All through the night the teardrops clinked against each other and the rug rubbed over the snow. My eyes have never been so wide as that night. I looked on all sides and hurried until dawn, then rested. I remember lying down by a boulder, hooking the chandelier with my arm. When it dawned, the sun sent it sparkling. It made rays of red all over the snow, and the rubies looked like drops of glistening blood. I rested a while, my eyes opening and closing, but I did not let them close completely. No, not again! The second day I met a family trudging in the snow—a mother, daughter and two babies. The mother asked if I had any milk. I said I was going to get some for the chandelier. She shook her head and kissed me on the head. Her daughter's eyes were rimmed with blue and she was shaking. She had nothing on but a nightgown and thin sweater, and her toes showed through her leather shoes. They went on—they were going to Zahle, they said. I said I thought Zahle had no food, because my mother had been there and had bought the last scoop of flour in town. The mother asked where my family lived and I told her. They said they would try and go there. I said, Please do. The mother stared at me awhile with her own blue-rimmed eyes. One baby had blue lips. The other was whimpering and breathing quickly in the daughter's arms. I went on. I went on and on, with the snow wedged in my socks and pants. That night I slept with my head inside the chandelier, my arms coiled in it, my legs twisted inside it so that if wolves came they would not want me, for they would think I was part of the chandelier. It worked. I was not bothered by wolves that night. The third day I descended from the mountain. I saw the dry lands in the distance—the rust-colored sand and rock of the Bekaa—and I broke out laughing, I was so happy. But I descended too quickly, and a thread of the rug snagged on a twig raised out of the snow. The chandelier slid off and down a smooth embankment of snow which the sun had turned into a plate of ice. I plunged down the cliff after the chandelier. But when it reached a ledge it fell. It fell about twenty feet. I cried out and rolled like a crazy dog down the snowbank and fell on my face in front of the chandelier. Luckily it had landed on snow that had not iced over, that had some shade from the ledge. I moved it slowly. One of the gold arms was bent and five or six teardrops of crystal were shattered. I turned it and stepped back. It did not look too bad if one looked from this perspective, with the broken part to the back. The rug was still above, so I fetched it and carefully laid the chandelier on it, like a wounded human being, and went on. Slow now, Mukhlis, slow now. I did not let myself be excited any more by the nearness of the Bekaa. I have never let myself be excited again because of that chandelier breaking over the ledge. That day, around four o'clock, I reached the small village my mother had told me about. The villagers there were healthy. They still had some fields producing corn and wheat and lentils, and the road to Damascus was open. When they saw me—a little runt dragging this chandelier on the dry, dusty road—they gathered around me, asking all sorts of questions. I was too tired to answer. I just said, 'Take me to a cow-farmer. Please, as soon as you can.' They led me to such a man. I said to him, 'Look, I have come from the mountain where it is very cold and no food is there. My family is starving. I will give you this chandelier for milk and anything else I can carry.' The farmer inspected the chandelier, God damn his soul. Our people! They will try to strike a deal no matter what. You may be flat on the ground, your legs chopped off, and they will throw dust in your eyes while they cheat at backgammon. This farmer held up the chandelier with the aid of another man and said, 'It is broken. It can't be worth much.' I said to him, 'Please sir. It is made of gold and rubies and crystal.' 'Where did you get it from?' he asked. I said, 'I got it from the mountain.' He nodded. He did not want to ask me the next questions. 'I'm not sure,' he said. It was then that his wife, God save her soul, slapped him on the eyes. He pushed her away. 'All right,' he said, 'Two jugs of milk and we will put a pack of bread on your back. Can you carry all that?' I said, 'Yes, yes, I can carry as much as you can give me.' And he gave me two lambskins of milk and hoisted the bread on my back. The wife put in two bags of dates and dried apricots when he wasn't looking. And she kissed me on the head.

"I stayed in that town to rest for the night. They fed me a good meal. It felt good to sleep, to sleep thoroughly. But by morning I was ready to go. I walked back up the mountain, rising from the warm air to the cold, walking back into the snow world and the dark forest. I walked steadily, though my back and pelvis were hurting. When I made it back to Mheiti in a few days, I found myself running through the worn path in the snow up to my little house – a house made of limestone blocks, a good, sturdy house in normal times. My mother spotted me through the window and came running. She shouted in a hoarse voice, 'Mukhlis! Oh Mukhlis, you've come!'"

Matile is standing rigid. She does not speak, or offer food. She watches her brother's sapphire eyes melting in their own fire.

"My mother threw me above her – *ya rubi*, she was strong – and then carried me into the house before she even saw the milk. When she did, she nearly tore it off my neck. She gave some to Matile, to my brother Milhem, and to the baby Leila. But there was the infant to go – my brother Wadie. She frantically squeezed the lambskin's tip into his mouth as he lay in his crib. It was a wooden crib. A small wooden crib. I watched her force it on him. I saw that his eyes were stunned open as if he had seen a large rock toppling on top of him. She kept squeezing the lambskin of milk until half of it was dripping out of his mouth to the floor. 'Mother!' I called to her. 'Don't, don't! You're wasting it.' She wouldn't stop. I had to pull it from her hands. She squeezed the infant's cold cheeks and then took her nails directly to the wall and clawed it. She claws it, yes. After a while she put a sheet over the whole crib."

Mukhlis looks down, then far up to the ceiling of the porch. "I never knew him."

"Ach!" Mukhlis stands slowly. "Let's go, Wardi."

"No, no." Matile wakes from her trance. "You must stay for supper."

"We can't. I must go pick up a rent."

But Matile will not be swayed. She lifts her urgent voice, as if the food were gold and they were turning their backs on precious things. Mukhlis relents while shaking his head. All move into the dining room.

They sit under the chandelier, and pass the grape leaves, the stuffed zucchini, the swollen purple eggplant. They eat in silence, the unlit chandelier struck by the California sundown. It breaks into light above the food; it breaks in pieces of light on Mukhlis's almond head. When he finishes he stands, and ticks one of the crystal droplets with the thick nail of his finger, and does not speak.

"You hear what we went through?" Matile says after they are gone. "That was not all of it." She hugs her grandson, but not long. Even before she is through crying she has opened her mammoth horizontal freezer and said, "We need more bread, more bread."

All My Relations

Christopher McIlroy

When Jack Oldenburg first spoke to him, Milton Enos leaned over his paper plate, scooping beans into his mouth as if he didn't hear. Breaking through the murmur of *o'otham* conversation, the white man's speech was sharp and harsh. But Oldenburg stood over him, waiting.

Oldenburg had just lost his ranch hand, sick. If Milton reported to the Box-J sober in the morning, he could work for a couple of weeks until the cowboy returned or Oldenburg found a permanent hand.

"O.K.," Milton said, knowing he wouldn't go. Earlier in the day his wife and son had left for California, so he had several days' drinking to do. Following his meal at the convenience mart he would hitch to the Sundowner Lounge at the edge of the reservation.

After a sleepless night Milton saddled his horse for the ride to Oldenburg's, unable to bear his empty house. As Milton crossed the wide, dry bed of the Gila River, leaving the outskirts of Hashan, the house ceased to exist for him and he thought he would never go back. Milton's stomach jogged over the pommel with the horse's easy gait. Two hours from Hashan, Oldenburg's Box-J was the only ranch in an area either left desert or irrigated for cotton and sorghum. Its twenty square miles included hills, arroyos, and the eastern tip of a mountain range – gray-pink granite knobs split by ravines. The sun burned the tops of the mountains red.

Oldenburg stood beside his corral, tall and thin as one of its mesquite logs. First, he said, sections of the barbed-wire fence had broken down, which meant chopping and trimming new posts.

Milton's first swings of the axe made him dizzy and sick. He flailed wildly, waiting with horror for the bite of the axe into his foot. But soon he gained control over his stroke. Though soft, his big arms were strong. Sweat and alcohol poured out of him until he stank.

In the afternoon Milton and Oldenburg rode the fence-line.

"Hasn't been repaired in years," Oldenburg said. "My hand Jenkins is old." Oldenburg himself was well over sixty, his crew cut white and his face dried up like a dead man's. He had bright eyes, though, and fine white teeth. Where the fence was flattened to the ground, Milton saw a swatch of red and white cowhide snagged on the barbed wire. He'd lost a few head in the mountains, Oldenburg said, and after the fence was secure they'd round them up.

"One thing I'll tell you," Oldenburg said. "You can't drink while you work for me. Alcohol is poison in a business."

Milton nodded. By reputation he knew Oldenburg had a tree stump up his ass. Milton's wife C.C. had said she'd bring their son Allen back when Milton stopped drinking. For good? he'd asked. How would she know when was for good? For all anybody knew tomorrow might be the first day of for good, or 25,500 days later he might get drunk again. For a moment Milton remembered playing Monopoly with C.C. and Allen several weekends before. As usual, Milton and Allen were winning. Pretending not to be furious, C.C. smiled her big, sweet grin. Milton and the boy imitated her, stretching their mouths, until she couldn't help laughing. Milton clicked them off like a TV set and saw only mesquite, and rocky sand, sky, and the line of fence. After his two weeks, Milton thought, he'd throw a drunk like World War Ten.

At the end of the day Milton accepted Oldenburg's offer: $75 a week plus room and board, weekend off. Oldenburg winced apologetically proposing the wage; the ranch didn't make money, he explained.

They ate at a metal table in the dining room. Milton, whose pleasure in food went beyond filling his stomach, appreciated Oldenburg's meat loaf—diced with onion, the center concealing three hard-boiled eggs. Milton couldn't identify the seasonings except for chili. "What's in this?" he asked.

"Sage, chili, cumin and Worcestershire sauce."

"Heyyy."

Inside his two-room adobe, Milton was so tired he couldn't feel his body, and lying down felt the same as standing up. He slept without dreaming until Oldenburg rattled the door at daybreak.

Milton dug holes and planted posts. By noon his sweat had lost its salt and tasted like pure spring water. Then he didn't sweat at all. Chilled and shaking at the end of the day, his body felt as if he'd been thrown by a horse. The pain gave him a secret exultation which he hoarded from Oldenburg, saying nothing. Yet he felt he was offering the man part of the ache as a secret gift. Slyly, he thumped his cup on the table and screeched his chair back with exaggerated vigor. Milton was afraid of liking Oldenburg too much. He liked people easily, even those who were not o'otham—especially those, perhaps, because he wanted them to prove he needn't hate them.

Milton worked ten-, eleven-hour days. The soreness left his muscles, though he was as tired the fourth evening as he had been the first. Thursday night Oldenburg baked a chicken.

"You're steady," Oldenburg said. "I've seen you Pimas work hard before. What's your regular job?"

"I've worked for the government." Milton had ridden rodeo, sold wild horses he captured in the mountains, broken horses. Most often there was welfare. Recently he had completed two CETA training programs, one as a hospital orderly and the other baking cakes. But the reservation hospital wasn't hiring, and the town of Hashan had no bakeries. For centuries, Milton had heard, when the Gila flowed, the o'otham had been farmers. Settlements and overgrazing upstream had choked off the river only a few generations past. Sometimes Milton tried to envision green plots of squash, beans, and ripening grains, watered by earthen ditches, spreading from the banks. He imagined his back flexing easily in the heat as he bent to the rows, foliage swishing his legs, finally the villagers diving into the cool river, splashing delightedly.

"I don't think Jenkins is coming out of the hospital," Oldenburg said. "This job is yours if you want it." Milton was stunned. He had never held a permanent position.

In just a week of hard work, good eating, and no drinking, Milton had lost weight. Waking Friday morning, he pounded his belly with his hand; it answered him like a drum. He danced in front of the bathroom mirror, swiveling his hips, urging himself against the sink as if it were a partner. At lunch he told Oldenburg he would spend the weekend with friends in Hashan.

When he tossed the posthole digger into the shed, Milton felt light and strong, as if instead of sinking fence posts he'd spent the afternoon in a deep, satisfying nap. On the way to the guest house, his bowels turned over and a sharp pain set into his head. He saw the battered station wagon rolling out the drive, C.C. at the wheel, Allen's tight face in the window.

Milton threw his work clothes against the wall. After a stinging shower, he changed and mounted his horse for the ride to Vigiliano Lopez's.

Five hours later, the Sundowner was closing. Instead of his customary beer, Milton had been drinking highball glasses of straight vodka. He felt paler and paler, like water, until he was water. His image peeled off him like a wet decal and he was only water in the shape of a man. He flowed onto the bar, hooking his water elbows onto the wooden ridge for support. Then he was lifted from the stool, tilted backward, floating on the pickup bed like vapor.

Milton woke feeling the pong, pong of a basketball bouncing outside. The vibration traveled along the dirt floor of Lopez's living room, up the couch Milton lay on. The sun was dazzling. Looking out the window, Milton saw six-foot-five, three-hundred-pound Bosque dribbling the ball with both hands, knocking the other players aside. As he jammed the ball into the low hoop, it hit the back of the rim, bouncing high over the makeshift plywood backboard. A boy and two dogs chased it.

Seeing beer cans in the dirt, Milton went outside. He took his shirt off and sat against the house with a warm Bud. The lean young boys fired in jump shots, or when they missed, their fathers and older brothers pushed and wrestled for the rebound. Lopez grabbed a loose ball and ran with it, whirling for a turnaround fadeaway that traveled three feet. He laughed, and said to Milton, "When we took you home you started fighting us. Bosque had to pick you up and squeeze you, and when he did, everything came out like toothpaste."

"Try our new puke-flavored toothpaste," someone said, laughing.

"Looks like pizza."

"So we brought you here."

Milton said nothing. He watched the arms and broad backs collide. The young boys on the sidelines practiced lassoing the players' feet, the dogs, the ball. When he finished a beer, Milton started another. Later in the afternoon he sent boys to his house for the rest of his clothes and important belongings.

When the game broke up, some of the men joined the women in the shade of a mesquite. Saddling a half-broke wild colt, the boys took turns careening across the field. Lopez drove a truckload to the rodeo arena, where a bronc-rider from Bapchule was practicing. Compact and muscular, with silver spurs and collar tabs, he rode out the horse's bucks, smoothing the animal to a canter. Two of Milton's drunk friends tried and were thrown immediately. For a third, the horse didn't buck but instead circled the arena at a dead run, dodging the lassos and open gates. From the announcer's booth Lopez called an imaginary race as horse and rider passed the grandstand again and again—"coming down the backstretch now, whoops, there he goes for another lap, this horse is not a quitter, ladies and gentlemen."

"Go ahead, Milton," Lopez said. "You used to ride."

Milton shook his head. Allen, thirteen, recently had graduated from steers to bulls. In both classes he had finished first or second in every start, earning as much money in the past months as his father and mother combined. Would there be rodeo in California? Milton wondered. In school, too, Allen was a prodigy, learning high school geometry in eighth grade. If he studied hard, the school counselor said, he could finish high school in three years and win a college scholarship. Milton didn't know where the boy's talent came from.

Tears filled Milton's eyes.

"Aaaah," Bosque said. His big hand gripped Milton's arm. They walked back to Lopez's house and split a couple of sixes under the mesquite until the men returned. Audrey Lopez and the other wives

262

prepared chili and chimuth dough while the men played horseshoes and drank in the dusk.

By the end of dinner everyone was drunk. Milton, face sweating, was explaining to Audrey Lopez, "Just a few weeks ago, Allen wins some kind of puzzle contest for the whole state, O.K.? And he's on TV. And C.C. and I have got our faces up to the screen so we can hear every word he's saying. And we can't believe it. He's talking on TV, and his hair's sticking up on the side like that, just like it always does.

"I see them so real. When C.C. plays volleyball she's like a rubber ball, she's so little and round. She *dives* for those spikes, and her hair goes flying back."

Lopez slid his leg along Audrey's shoulder. "Good song," he said. "Let's dance." The radio was playing Top Forty.

"Wait. I'm listening to this man."

"Milton talks you into tomorrow afternoon. Come on." Lopez pulled her shoulder.

Audrey shrugged him off and laid her hand on Milton's arm. "His wife and son are gone."

"Dried-up old bitch," Lopez said. "C.C.'s too old for you, man, she's way older than he is. You lost nothing."

Grabbing a barbecue fork, ramming Lopez against the wall, Milton chopped the fork into Lopez's shoulder. A woman screamed, Milton heard his own grunts as the glistening tines rose and stabbed. Lopez ducked and his knife came up. Milton deflected the lunge with his fork, the knife blade springing down its long shank. Milton shouted as the knife thudded into the wall. His little finger had bounded into the air and lay on the floor, looking like a brown pebble.

Bosque drove both men to the hospital. The doctor cauterized, stitched, and bandaged the wound, and gave Milton a tetanus shot. If Milton had brought the severed finger—the top two joints—the doctor said, he might have sewn it on. The men refused to stay overnight. When they returned to the party, couples were dancing the choti and bolero to a Mexican radio station. Gulps of vodka deadened the pain in Milton's finger. He and Lopez kept opposite corners of the living room until dawn, when Lopez pushed Audrey into Milton's arms and said, "Get some dancing, man."

Sunday Milton slept under the mesquite until evening, when he rode to the Box-J.

"That's your mistake, Milton," Oldenburg said. "Everyone's entitled to one mistake. Next time you drink you're gone. You believe me?"

Milton did. He felt like weeping. The next day he roamed the fence-line, his chest and neck clotted with the frustration of being unable to work. The horse's jouncing spurted blood through the white bandage on his finger. Finally he rode out a back gate and into the midst of the granite mountains. Past a sparkling dome broken by a slump of shattered rock, Milton trotted into a narrow cut choked with mesquite. As a boy, he would hunt wild horses for days in these ravines, alone, with only a canvas food bag tied to the saddle. He remembered sleeping on the ground without a blanket, beneath a lone sycamore that had survived years of drought. Waking as dawn lit the mountain crests, he would force through the brush, gnawing a medallion of jerked beef. Most often when he startled a horse, the animal would clatter into a side gully, boxing itself in. Then roping was easy. Once when Milton flushed a stringy gray mustang, the horse charged him instead; Milton had no time to uncoil his rope before the gray was past. Milton wheeled, pursuing at full gallop out the canyon and onto the *bajada*. Twig-matted tail streaming behind, the mustang was outrunning him, and Milton had one chance with the rope. He dropped the loop around the gray's neck, jarring the animal to its haunches. It was so long ago. Today, Milton reflected, the headlong chase would have pinned him and the horse to Oldenburg's barbed-wire fence.

The sycamore held its place, older and larger. Though encountering no horses, Milton returned three stray cattle to Oldenburg's ranch. For a month, while the slightest jolt could rupture the wound, he hunted down mavericks in the miles of ravine, painted the ranch buildings, and repaired the roofs, one-handed. Even as the finger healed, the missing segment unbalanced his grip. Swinging the pick or axe, shoveling, he would clench his right hand so tightly the entire arm would tremble. By the second month a new hand had evolved, with the musculature of the other fingers, the palm, and the wrist more pronounced. The pinky stub acted as a stabilizer against pickshaft or rope. Milton had rebuilt the fence and combed the granite mountains, rounding up another two dozen head. Oldenburg's herd had increased to 120.

In late August Milton rode beyond the granite range to the Ka kai Mountains, a low, twisted ridge of volcanic rock that he had avoided because he once saw the Devil there. Needing to piss, he had stumbled away from a beer party and followed a trail rising between the boulders. Watching the ground for snakes, Milton had almost collided with a man standing in the path. The stranger was a very big, ugly Indian, but Milton knew it was the Devil because his eyes were black, not human, and he spoke in a booming voice that rolled echoes off the cliffs. Milton shuddered uncontrollably and shriveled to the size of a spider. Afterwards he found he had fallen and cut himself. Cholla segments were embedded in his leg. The Devil had said only: "Beware of Satan within you."

The meeting enhanced Milton's prestige, and Allen was impressed, though not C.C. "You see?" she said. "What did I always tell you?"

In daylight the mountains looked like no more than a pile of cinders. Milton chose an arroyo that cut through the scorched black rubble into red slabs, canyon walls which rose over Milton's head, then above the mesquite. Chasing a calf until it disappeared in a side draw, Milton left the animal for later. The canyon twisted deeper into the mountains, the red cliffs now three hundred feet high. The polished rock glowed. Milton was twelve years old, and his brothers were fighting.

"You took my car," Steven said.

"So what," Lee said. Milton's favorite brother, he was slim and handsome, with small ears and thick, glossy hair that fell almost into his eyes. Weekends he took Milton into Phoenix to play pool and pinball, sometimes to the shopping mall for Cokes. He always had girls, even Mexicans and whites.

"I told you if you took my car I was going to kill you." Steven always said crazy things. At breakfast, if Milton didn't pass him the milk right away—"How'd you like this knife in your eye?" About their mother— "Bitch wouldn't give me a dime. I'm going to shit on her bed." He wore a white rag around his head and hung out with gangs. Now they would call him a cholo.

"So what," Lee said. "Kill me." Cocking his leg, he wiped the dusty bootheel carefully against the couch. Milton was sitting on the couch.

Steven ran down the hall and came back with a .22. He pointed it at Lee's head, there was a shocking noise, a red spot appeared in Lee's forehead, and he collapsed on the rug.

"Oh my GOD," Steven said. Fingers clawed against his temples, he rushed out the door. Milton snatched the gun and chased him, firing on the run. Steven, bigger and faster, outdistanced him in the desert. Milton didn't come home for three days. Steven wasn't prosecuted and he moved to Denver. If he returned, Milton would kill him, even twenty years later.

Milton's horse ambled down the white sand, the dry bed curving around a red outcropping. Trapped by the canyon walls, the late summer air was hot and close. The weight of Milton's family fell on his back like a landslide—his father, driving home drunk from Casa Grande, slewing across the divider, head-on into another pickup. The four children had flown like crickets from the back, landing unhurt in the dirt bank. The driver of the other truck died, and Milton's mother lost the shape of her face.

Milton felt himself turning to water. He circled his horse, routed the calf from the slit in the wall, and drove it miles to the ranch. At dinner he told Oldenburg he needed a trip to town.

"You'll lose your job," Oldenburg said.

Milton ate with his water fingers, spilling food and the orange juice that Oldenburg always served. "The lives of *o'otham* is a soap opera," he cried, trying to dispel his shame by insulting himself. "I love my boy, O.K.? But it's him who has to hold me when I go for C.C. He doesn't hold me with his strength. He holds me because I see him, and I stop. Sometimes I don't stop."

Oldenburg served Milton cake for dessert and told him to take the next day off, if he wanted.

The following morning Milton lay on his bed, sweating. In his mind were no thoughts or images save the swirls of chill, unpleasant water that washed over him. He could transform the water, making it a cold lake that pumped his heart loudly and shrank his genitals, or a clear stream immersing him in swift currents and veins of sunlight, but he could not change the water into thoughts. The green carpeting and blue-striped drapes in his room sickened him. He could have finished a pint of vodka before he knew he was drinking.

He could not imagine losing his work.

Abruptly Milton rose. In the corral he fitted a rope bridle over the horse's head. As he rode past Oldenburg, the man looked up from a bench of tack he was fussing with, then quickly lowered his head.

"I'm going to the mountains," Milton said.

He let the horse carry him into the charred crust of the canyon. The scarlet walls rose high and sheer, closing off the black peaks beyond. Tethering the horse to a mesquite, Milton sat in the sand. The cliffs seemed almost to meet above him. Heat gathered over his head and forced down on him. A lizard skittered by his ear, up the wall. A tortoise lumbered across the wash. The water rippling through Milton became a shimmering on the far wall, scenes of his life. Milton racing after Steven, aiming at the zigzagging blue shirt, the crack of the gun, a palo verde trunk catching the rifle barrel and spinning Milton to his knees. His father's empty boots beside the couch where he slept. His mother in baggy gray slacks, growing fatter. C.C.'s head snapping back from Milton's open palm. The pictures flickered over the cliff. Milton sat while shadow climbed the rock, and a cool breeze funneled through the canyon, and night fell. Scooping a hole in the sand, Milton lay face to the stone while the canyon rustled and sighed. The wind rushed around a stone spur, scattering sand grains on his face. Several times in the night footsteps passed so near that the ground yielded beneath Milton's head. Huddled, shivering, he thought his heart had stopped and fell asleep from terror. He dreamed of the cliffs, an unbroken glassy red.

Early in the morning, Milton woke and stretched, refreshed by the cool air. The only prints beside him were his own. That evening he wrote to C.C. in care of her California aunt, telling her he'd quit drinking.

When C.C. didn't respond, Milton wrote again, asking at least for word of Allen, who would have entered high school. C.C. replied, "When I got here the doctor said I had a broken nose. Allen says he has no father."

266

Milton knew he must hide to avoid drinking. When he asked Oldenburg's permission to spend a day in the granite mountains, Oldenburg said he would go, too. They camped against a rock turret. The light in the sky faded and the fire leaped up. In the weeks since the former hand Jenkins's death, Oldenburg had become, if possible, more silent. Milton, meanwhile, admitted he had been a "chatterbox," recalling high-school field trips to Phoenix fifteen years before, and rodeos in Tucson, Prescott, Sells and White River. Oldenburg, fingertips joined at his chin, occasionally nodded or smiled. Tonight Milton squatted, arms around his knees, staring into the fire. About to share his most insistent emotions with Oldenburg, Milton felt a giddy excitement, as if he were showing himself naked to a woman for the first time. Intimacy with a white man evoked stepping off the school bus in Phoenix, where buildings like great stone crystals, blanketed in dreamy smog, spilled thousands of white people into the street.

Milton told Oldenburg what C.C. had said.

"Your drinking has scarred them like acid. It will be time before they heal," Oldenburg said.

"There shouldn't be o'otham families," Milton exclaimed. "We should stop having children."

Oldenburg shook his head. After a while he said, "Milton, I hope you're not bitter because I won't let you drink. Drawing the line helps you. It's not easy living right. I've tried all my life and gained nothing—I lost both my sons in war and my wife divorced me to marry a piece of human trash. And still, in my own poor way, I try to live right." Oldenburg relaxed his shoulders and settled on his haunches.

Milton laid another mesquite limb across the fire. As the black of the sky intensified, the stars appeared as a glinting powder. Milton sipped two cups of coffee against the chill. Oldenburg, firelight sparkling off his silver tooth, wool cap pulled low over his stretched face, looked like an old grandmother. Laughing, Milton told him so. Oldenburg laughed too, rocking on his heels.

Soon after Oldenburg went to bed, Milton's mood changed. He hated the embers of the fire, the wind sweeping the rock knoll, the whirring of bats. He hated each stone and twig littering the campsite. His own fingers, spread across his knees, were like dumb, sleeping snakes. Poisonous things. He was glad one of them had been chopped off. Unrolling his blanket, he lay on his back, fists clenched. He dug his hands and heels into the ground as if staked to it. After lying stiffly, eyes open, for an hour, he got up, slung his coiled rope over his shoulder, and walked down the hillside.

Brush and cactus were lit by a rising moon. Reaching a sheer drop, Milton jammed boot toes into rock fissures, seized tufts of saltbush, to let himself down. In the streambed he walked quickly until he joined the

267

main river course. After a few miles' meandering through arroyos and over ridges, he arrived at the big sycamore and went to sleep.

Waking before dawn, Milton padded along the wash, hugging the granite. The cold morning silence was audible, a high, pure ringing. Milton heard the horse's snort before he saw it tearing clumps of grass from the gully bank, head tossing, lips drawn back over its yellow teeth. Rope at his hip, Milton stalked from boulder to boulder. When he stepped forward, whirling the lariat once, the horse reared, but quieted instantly as the noose tightened around its neck. Milton tugged the rope; the animal neighed and skipped backward, but followed.

During the next two days, Milton and Oldenburg captured three more spindly, wiry horses. Oldenburg would flush the mustangs toward Milton, who missed only once with the lasso. The stallions Milton kept in separate pens and later sold as rodeo broncs. Within a couple of weeks he had broken the mares.

Milton consumed himself in chores. Though the Box-J was a small ranch, labor was unremitting. In the fall, summer calves were rounded up and "worked"–branded with the Box J, castrated, and dehorned. The previous winter's calves, now some 400–500 pounds each, were held in side-pens for weighing and loading onto the packer's shipping trucks. The pens were so dilapidated that Milton tore them down and built new ones. Winter, Milton drove daily pickup loads of sorghum hay, a supplement for the withered winter grasses, to drop spots at the water holes. Oldenburg hired extra help for spring roundup, working the new winter calves. Summer Milton roved on horseback, troubleshooting. The fence-line would need repair. Oldenburg taught Milton to recognize cancer-eye, which could destroy a cow's market value. A low water tank meant Oldenburg must overhaul the windmill. Throughout the year Milton inspected the herd, groomed the horses, maintained the buildings, kept tools and equipment in working order.

Certain moments, standing high in the stirrups, surveying the herd and the land which stretched from horizon to horizon as if mirroring the sky, Milton could believe all belonged to him.

Every two weeks, when Oldenburg drove into Casa Grande for supplies, Milton deposited half his wages–his first savings account–and mailed the rest to C.C. These checks were like money thrown blindly over the shoulder. So thoroughly had Milton driven his family from his mind that he couldn't summon them back, even if he wished to. When, just before sleep, spent from the day's work, he glimpsed C.C. and Allen, the faces seemed unreal. They were like people he had met and loved profoundly one night at a party, then forgotten.

The night of the first November frost, soon after the wild-horse roundup, Oldenburg had asked Milton if he played cards. Milton didn't.

"Too bad," Oldenburg said. "It gets dull evenings. Jenkins and I played gin rummy. We'd go to five thousand, take us a couple of weeks, and then start again."

"We could cook," Milton said.

On Sunday he and Oldenburg baked cakes. Milton missed the pressurized frosting cans with which he'd squirted flowers and desert scenes at the CETA bakery, but Oldenburg's cherry-chocolate layer cake was so good he ate a third of it. Oldenburg complimented him on his angel food.

Oldenburg bought a paperback *Joy of Cooking* in Casa Grande. Though he and Milton had been satisfied with their main dishes, they tried Carbonnade Flamande, Chicken Paprika, Quick Spaghetti Meat Pie. Milton liked New England Boiled Dinner. Mostly they made desserts. After experimenting with mousses and custard, they settled on cakes—banana, golden, seed, sponge, four-egg, Lady Baltimore, the Rombauer Special. Stacks of foil-wrapped cakes accumulated in the freezer. The men contributed cakes to charitable bake sales. Milton found that after his nightly slab of cake sleep came more easily and gently.

The men were serious in the kitchen. Standing side by side in white aprons tacked together from sheets, Milton whisking egg whites, Oldenburg drizzling chocolate over pound cake, they would say little. Milton might ask the whereabouts of a spice; Oldenburg's refusal to label the jars irritated him. Then they sat by the warm stove, feet propped on crates, and steamed themselves in the moist smells.

As they relaxed on a Sunday afternoon, eating fresh, hot cake, Oldenburg startled Milton by wondering aloud if his own wife were still alive. She had left him in 1963, and they'd had no contact since their second son was killed in 1969, more than ten years before.

"She wanted a Nevada divorce," Oldenburg said, "but I served papers on her first, and I got custody of the boys. I prevented a great injustice." He had sold his business in Colorado and bought the ranch. "The boys hated it," he said. "They couldn't wait to join the Army."

In Hashan, Milton said, she and her lover would have been killed.

Oldenburg shook his head impatiently. "He's deserted her, certainly. He was a basketball coach, and much younger than she was."

A Pima phrase—he knew little Pima—occurred to Milton. *Ne ha: jun*—all my relations. "Here is the opposite," Milton said. "We should call this the No-Relations Ranch."

Oldenburg sputtered with laughter. "Yes! And we'd need a new brand. Little round faces with big X's over them."

"You'd better be careful. People would start calling it the Tic-tac-toe Ranch."

"Or a manual, you know, a sex manual, for fornication. The X's doing it to the O's."

Lightheaded from the rich, heavily-frosted cake, they sprayed crumbs from their mouths, laughing.

At the Pinal County Fair in May, Oldenburg entered a walnut pie and goaded Milton into baking his specialty, a jelly roll. It received honorable mention, while Oldenburg won second prize.

Milton wrote C.C., "I'm better than a restaurant."

C.C. didn't answer. When Valley Bank opened a Hashan branch in June, Milton transferred his account and began meeting his friends for the first time in a year. They needled him, "Milton, you sleeping with that old man?" His second Friday in town, Milton was writing out a deposit slip when he heard Bosque say, "Milton Oldenburg."

"Yes, Daddy just gave him his allowance," said Helene Mashad, the teller.

Bosque punched him in the shoulder and put out his hand. Milton shook it, self-conscious about his missing finger.

Bosque was cashing his unemployment check. The factory where he'd manufactured plastic tote bags for the past six months had closed. "Doesn't matter," Bosque said, "I'm living good." Before leaving, he said to come on by.

"You know what Oldenburg's doing, don't you?" Helene said, smoothing the wrinkles from Milton's check. She still wore her long, lavender Phoenix nails and a frothy perm. After years in Phoenix she'd relocated at the new branch, closer to her home in Black Butte. "Oldenburg wants to marry you. Then he'll get some kind of government project money for his Indian wife. Or he'll adopt you. Same deal."

"It's not me who's the wife or child. I run that place." Nervous speaking to a woman again, Milton rambled, boasting of his authority over hired crews, what Oldenburg called his "quick mind and fast hands" cutting calves or constructing a corner brace, his skill with new tools. Even his baking. "He has to be the wife," Milton said. "He's a better cook." Milton leaned his hip against the counter. "Older woman. He's so old he turned white. And he lost his shape." Milton's hands made breasts. "Nothing left."

They both laughed. Elated by the success of his joke, Milton asked her to dinner. Helene said yes, pick her up at six.

Milton was uneasy in Hashan. The dusty buildings – adobes, sandwich houses of mud and board, slump-block tract homes – seemed part of the unreal life that included his family. To kill time, he rode to the trading post in Black Butte, a few miles in the direction of Oldenburg's ranch, and read magazines. When he arrived at the bank, Helene slapped her forehead: she hadn't known he was on horseback. Phew, she said, she didn't want to go out with a horse. Milton should follow her home and take a bath first.

They never left her house. She was eager for him, and Milton realized

270

that as a man he'd been dead for a year. They made love until early morning. Milton lay propped against the headboard, his arm encircling her, her cheek resting on his chest. She briskly stroked his hand.

"Your poor finger," she said. "I hear Lopez has little circles in his shoulder like where worms have gone into a tomato."

"It was bad," Milton said, closing his hand.

"I can't stand the men in this town, the drunken pigs," Helene said. "I don't know why I came back."

Helene wasn't what Milton wanted, but he liked her well enough to visit once or twice a month. Because she lived outside Hashan, few people knew of the affair. They would eat dinner and see a movie in Casa Grande or Phoenix, and go to bed. Sometimes they simply watched TV in bed, or drove Helene's Toyota through the desert for miles without seeing another light.

When Milton returned from his second weekend with Helene, Oldenburg was peevish. "You drink with that woman?" he said. "You going to send her picture to your wife?" Emergencies arose that kept Milton on the ranch weekends. After selling two wild colts to a stable, Milton took Helene to Phoenix overnight. Oldenburg berated him, "The cows don't calve on Saturday and Sunday? They don't get sick? A shed doesn't blow down on Sunday?" Still the men baked together. At the beginning of the school year they entered a fund-raising bake-off sponsored by the PTO. Oldenburg won first with a Boston cream pie, and Milton's apple ring took second.

Helene transferred to Casa Grande, and Milton brought his account with her, relieved to avoid Hashan. Conversations with his friends were strained and dead. He worked; they didn't. They drank; he didn't. They had families. Milton nodded when he saw them but no longer stopped to talk.

Fridays after Helene punched out, they might browse in the Casa Grande shopping center. Milton was drawn to the camera displays, neat lumps of technology embedded in towers of colorful film boxes. The Lerners Shop manikins fascinated him—bony stick figures like the bleached branches of felled cottonwood, a beautiful still arrangement. "Imagine Pimas in those," Helene said, pointing to the squares and triangles of glittering cloth. She puffed out her cheeks and spread her arms. Milton squeezed her small buttocks. Helene's legs were the slimmest of any o'otham woman he'd known.

During the second week of October, when Milton and a hired crew had set up shipping pens and begun culling the calves, a rare fall downpour, tail end of a Gulf hurricane, struck. For six hours thunder exploded and snarls of lightning webbed the sky. The deluge turned the ground to slop, sprang leaks in the roof, and washed out the floodgates at the edge of the granite mountains. Cattle stampeded through the openings; one died, entangled in the barbed wire. When the skies cleared, Oldenburg estimated that a quarter of the cash animals, some three hundred dollars apiece, had escaped. The shipping trucks were due in two days.

The next morning, a new hired man brought further news: over the weekend, a fight had broken out at the Sundowner. The fat end of a pool cue had caught Audrey Lopez across the throat, crushing her windpipe. Her funeral was to be at two in the afternoon.

Milton stood helplessly before Oldenburg. In the aftermath of the storm, the sky was piercingly blue, and a bracing wind stung his cheeks. Oldenburg's collar fluttered.

"You have to go," Oldenburg said. "There's no question."

"You'll lose too much money," Milton said stubbornly. "The cattle are in the mountains and I know every little canyon where they run."

"There's no question," Oldenburg repeated. "The right way is always plain, though we do our best to obscure it."

The service took place in a small, white, Spanish-style church. At the cemetery the mourners stood bareheaded, the sun glinting off their hair. The cemetery was on a knoll, and in the broad afternoon light the surrounding plains, spotted by occasional cloud shadows, seemed immensely distant, like valleys at the foot of a solitary butte. Milton imagined the people at the tip of a rock spire miles in the clouds. The overcast dimmed them, and shreds of cumulus drifted past their backs and bowed heads.

Afterwards the men adjourned to the Lopez house, where Vigiliano Lopez rushed about the living room, flinging chairs aside to clear a center space. A ring of some twenty men sat on chairs or against the wall. Bosque arrived carrying three cold cases and two quarts of Crown Russe. More bottles appeared. Lopez started one Crown Russe in each direction and stalked back and forth from the kitchen, delivering beer and slapping bags of potato chips at the men's feet.

At his turn, Milton passed the bottle along.

"Drink, you goddamn Milton Oldenburg," Lopez said.

Milton said, "I'll lose my job."

"So?" Lopez shrugged distractedly. "I haven't had a job in a year. I don't need a job." Lopez had been the only Pima miner at the nearby Loma Linda pit until Anaconda shut it down. He pushed his hair repeatedly off his forehead, as if trying to remember something, then turned up the radio.

Milton sat erect in the chair, hands planted on his knees. He gobbled the potato chips. No one avoided him, nor he anyone else, yet talk was impossible. Grief surged through the party like a wave. Milton felt it in over-loud conversation, silences, the restlessness—no one able to stay in one place for long. Laughter came in fits. Over the radio, the wailing tremeloes of the Mexican ballads were oppressive and nerve-racking.

272

The power of feeling in the room moved Milton and frightened him, but he was outside it.

Joining the others would be as simple as claiming the vodka bottle on its next round, Milton knew. But he remembered standing tall in the stirrups, as if he could see over the edge of the yellow horizon, the end of Oldenburg's land, and he kept his hands spread on his knees. At the thought of vodka's sickly tastelessness, bile rose in his throat. Pretending to drink, tipping the bottle and plugging it with his tongue, would be foolish and shameful. Out of friendship and respect for Lopez, he could not leave. Their wounding each other, Milton realized, had bound him more closely to Lopez.

As night fell the men became drunker and louder. Bosque went out for more liquor. When he returned, he danced with the oil-drum cook-stove, blackening his hands and shirt.

"Hey, not with my wife," Lopez said, grabbing the drum and humping it against the wall. "Need somebody to do you right, baby," he said. The drum clanged to the floor. The men cheered. Lopez, knees bent and hands outstretched as if waiting for something to drop into them, lurched to the middle of the room. A smile was glazed over his face. He saw Milton.

"Drink with me, you son of a bitch," he shouted.

Milton motioned for the Crown Russe, a third full. "Half for you, half for me," he said. Marking a spot on the label with his finger, Milton took two long swallows and held out the bottle for Lopez. Lopez drank and flipped the empty over his shoulder. Side by side, arms around each other, Milton and Lopez danced the *cumbia*. Lopez's weight sagged until Milton practically carried him. The man's trailing feet hooked an extension cord, sending a lamp and the radio crashing to the floor. Lopez collapsed.

Milton ran outside and retched. Immediately he was refreshed and lucid. The stars burned like drill-points of light. Patting the horse into an easy walk, Milton sat back in the saddle, reins loose in his lap, and gave himself to the brilliant stillness. As his eyes adjusted to the night, he could distinguish the black silhouettes of mountains against the lesser dark of the sky. Faint stars emerged over the ranges, bringing the peaks closer. The mountains were calm and friendly, even the jagged line of the Ka kai.

That night Milton dreamed that a chocolate-colored flood swept through Hashan. The *o'otham* bobbed on the foam; from the shore others drove backward into the torrent, arms raised symmetrically by their heads. Receding, the flood left bodies swollen in the mud— Milton's brother Lee, their mother, belly down, rising in a mound. Milton, long hair fixed in the mud, stared upward. His hands were so full of fingers they had become agaves, clusters of fleshy, spiny leaves.

Peering down at him, C.C. and Allen were black against the sun, arms crooked as if for flight. Milton was glad they had escaped.

Milton woke serene and energetic, the dream forgotten. Over breakfast Oldenburg studied him intently—clear gray eyes, a slight frown—but said nothing. The penned calves were weighed and loaded onto the shipping trucks. Many remained free, and the year would be a loss.

Milton wrote C.C. of Audrey Lopez's death. "I had a big drink to keep Lopez company," he added, "but I threw it up. It was the first booze in more than a year. I don't like it any more."

Lying beside Milton the following weekend, Helene said, "Poor finger. I'll give you another one." She laid her pinky against the stub so a new finger seemed to grow. Her lavender nail looked like the fancy gem of a ring. She lifted, lowered the finger. "And Lopez with the purple spots on his shoulder like the eyes of a potato," she said. She shifted, and her small, hard nipple brushed Milton's side. "It's a wonder you two didn't fight."

"Shut up," Milton said. "His wife is dead."

"I know. It's terrible." She had worried for him, Helene said, knowing he would be at the funeral with Lopez. He should have brought her.

"I didn't want you there," Milton said. "You don't have the right feelings." He left before dawn and hadn't returned to Helene when C.C. replied.

"I was shocked to hear about Audrey," C.C. wrote. "I feel sad about it every day. Hashan is such a bad place. But it isn't any better here. At Allen's school there are gangs and not just Mexicans but black and white too."

She wrote again: "I miss you. I've been thinking about coming back. Allen says he won't but he'll come with me in the end. The money has helped. Thank you."

Milton threw up his arms and danced on the corral dirt, still moist and reddened from fluke autumn rains. Shouting, he danced on one leg and the other, dipping from side to side as if soaring, his head whirling. Oldenburg's nagging—where will they live?—worried him little. Over dinner Oldenburg suggested, "They'll live in your old place, and you can visit them on weekends. We'll have to move our baking to the middle of the week."

Milton knew he must be with the o'otham. Announcing a ride into the mountains, he saddled up and galloped toward Hashan. Because he couldn't see the faces of his family his joy felt weirdly rootless. The past year he had killed them inside. The sudden aches for Allen, the sensation of carrying C.C.'s weight in his arms from the adobe to the ranch house, were like the twinges of heat, cold and pain from his missing finger. As if straining after their elusive faces, Milton rode faster. His straw hat, blown back and held by its cord, flapped at his ear. The horse's neck was soaked with sweat.

274

Bosque's fat wife said he wasn't home. Milton made a plan for the Sundowner: after one draft for sociability, he would play the shuffle-board game. Tying up at a light pole, Milton hesitated in the lounge doorway. The familiarity of the raw wood beams crisscrossing the bare sheetrock walls frightened him. But Bosque, sliding his rear off a bar-stool, called, "Milton Oldenburg."

"C.C.'s hauling her little tail home," Milton announced. "And the boy."

"All *riiight.*" Bosque pumped his hand up and down. Milton's embarrassment at his missing finger disappeared in the vastness of Bosque's grip. Friends he hadn't spoken to in months surrounded him. "When's she coming? They going to live on the ranch? Oldenburg will have a whole Indian family now." Warmed by their celebration of his good luck, Milton ordered pitchers. His glass of draft was deep gold and sweeter than he had remembered, though flat. Others treated him in return. Someone told a story of Bosque building a scrap wood raft to sail the shallow lake left by the rains. Halfway across, the raft had broken apart and sunk. "Bosque was all mud up to his eyes," the storyteller said. "He looked like a bull rolling in cow flop." Everyone laughed.

Fuzzy after a half dozen beers, Milton felt his heart pound, and his blood. He saw them then—C.C., wings of hair, white teeth, dimpled round cheeks. Allen's straight bangs and small, unsmiling mouth. Their eyes were black with ripples of light, reflections on a pool. Milton was drawn into that pool, lost. Terror washed over him like a cold liquid, and he ordered a vodka.

"I'm a drunk," he told the neighbor on his right.

"Could be. Let's check that out, Milton," the man said.

"I never worked."

"No way," the man said, shaking his head.

"I didn't make a living for them."

"Not even a little bitty bit," the man agreed.

"Not even this much," Milton said, holding his thumb and forefinger almost closed, momentarily diverted by the game. "I hurt them."

Holding up his hands, the man yelled, "Not me."

"I tortured them. They don't belong to me. I don't have a family," Milton mumbled. Quickly he drank three double vodkas. The jukebox streamed colors, and he floated on its garbled music.

Shoving against the men's room door, Milton splashed into the urinal, wavering against the stall. He groped for the Sundowner's rear exit. The cold bit through his jacket. Milton pitched against a stack of bricks.

Waking in the dark, Milton jumped to his feet. C.C. was coming, and his job was in danger. He was foreman of a white man's ranch. Allen and C.C. would be amazed at his spread. With a bigger bank account than three-quarters of Hashan, Milton could support them for a year on savings alone. The night before was an ugly blur. But his tongue was bitter, his head thudded, he had the shakes. Cursing, Milton mounted and kicked the horse into a canter. To deceive Oldenburg he must work like a crazy man and sweat out his hangover. The fits of nausea made him moan with frustration. He kicked the horse and struck his own head.

Milton arrived an hour after sunup. Shooing the horse into the corral with a smack to the rump, he stood foggily at the gate, unable to remember his chore from the previous day. A ladder leaning against the barn reminded him: patching. He lugged a roll of asphalt roofing up the ladder. Scrambling over the steep pitch didn't frighten him, even when he slipped and tore his hands. He smeared tar, pressed the material into place, drove the nails. Every stroke was true, two per nail. Milton had laid half a new roof when Oldenburg called him.

"Come down." Oldenburg was pointing to the corral. The gate was still ajar. Milton's horse, head drooping, dozed against the rail, but the other three were gone.

Milton stood before him, wobbly from exertion, blood draining from his head.

"You lied," Oldenburg said. "You abandoned your job. The week is my time. You've been drunk. I'm going to have to let you go, Milton."

Milton couldn't speak.

"You understand, don't you?" Oldenburg said more rapidly. His eyes flicked down, back to Milton. "Do you see what happens?" His arms extended toward the empty corral.

"So I lose a day running them down."

Smiling slightly, Oldenburg shook his head. "You miss the point. It would be wrong for me to break my word. You'd have no cause to believe me again and our agreement would be meaningless."

"Once a year I get drunk," Milton burst out. "We'll put a name on it, November Something Milton's Holiday."

Oldenburg smiled again. "Once a month . . . once a week . . . I'm sorry. I'll give you two weeks' pay but you can leave any time." He turned.

"I've worked hard for you!" Milton's throat felt as if it were closing up.

Oldenburg stopped, brow furrowed. "It's sad," he said. "You've managed the Box-J better than I could. I'm going to miss our baking." He paused. "But we have to go on, Milton, don't you see? My family leaves me, Jenkins leaves me, you leave me. But I go on." He walked away.

Two long steps, a knee in the back, arms around the neck, and he could break the man in half—Milton's arms dropped. He had lost his urge for violence. Long after Oldenburg had disappeared into the open green range where the horses were, Milton stood by the corral. Then, arms over his head as if escaping a cloudburst, he ran into the adobe, packed his belongings in a sheet, and that afternoon rode the exhausted horse back to his old home.

276

To C.C. Milton wrote, "I don't have my job any more but there's plenty of money in the bank." Weeks later she replied, "Milton, I know what's going on. I can't come home to this." But she would continue to write him, she said. Milton saw no one. Pacing the house, he talked to the portraits over the TV—Allen's eighth-grade class picture, a computer-drawn black-dot composition of C.C. from the O'otham Tash carnival. He disturbed nothing, not even the year-and-a-half-old pile of dishes in the sink.

For several weeks he laid fence for a Highway Maintenance heavy equipment yard. Working with a new type of fence, chain link topped with barbed wire, cheered him. The foreman was lax, married to one of Milton's cousins, so when Milton requested the leftover spools of barbed wire, he said, "Sure. It's paid for."

Milton dug holes around his house and cut posts from the warped, gnarled mesquite growing in the vacant land. As he worked, the blue sky poured through chinks in the posts, reminding Milton pleasantly of the timeless first days repairing the line at Oldenburg's range. When he had finished stringing the wire, Milton's house was enclosed in a neat box—two thorned strands, glinting silver. Sunlight jumped off the metal in zigzag bolts. In Hashan, where fences were unknown and the beige ground was broken only by houses, cactus, and drab shrubs, the effect was as startling as if Milton had wrapped his home in Christmas lights.

Milton sat on the back doorstep, drinking beer. Discouraged by the fence, no one visited at first. But dogs still ran through the yard, as did children, who preferred scaling the fence to slithering under it. Their legs waggled precariously on the stiffly swaying wire; then they hopped down, dashed to the opposite side, and climbed out, awkward as spiders. Milton's fence became a community joke, which made him popular. Instead of walking through the gap behind the house, friends would crawl between the strands or try to vault them. Or they would lean on the posts, passing a beer back and forth while they chatted.

Keeping her promise, C.C. wrote that Allen had shot up tall. Even running track he wore his Walkman, she said. But he smoked, and she had to yell at him. Last term he'd made nearly all A's.

Milton grew extremely fat, seldom leaving the house except to shop or work the odd jobs his new skills brought him. Through spring and summer he drowsed on the doorstep. In November, almost a year after he'd left Oldenburg's, he fell asleep on the concrete slab and spent the night without jacket or blanket. The next day he was very sick, and Bosque and Lopez drove him to the hospital. The doctor said he had pneumonia.

Milton's first day in ICU, Bosque and Lopez shot craps with him during visiting hours. But as Milton's lungs continued to fill with fluids, his heart, invaded by fatty tissues from his years of drinking, weakened. Four days after entering the hospital, he suffered a heart attack.

277

In the coronary ward, restricted to ten-minute visits, Milton dreamed, feeling as if the fluids had leaked into his skull and his brain was sodden. In one dream the agaves again sprouted from his wrists, their stalks reaching into the sky. Milton gave the name *ne ha: jun* — all my relations — to his agave hands.

The next morning C.C. and Allen appeared in the doorway. Huge, billowing, formless as smoke, they approached the bed in a peculiar rolling motion. Milton was afraid. From the dreams he realized his deepest love was drawn from a great lake far beneath him, and that lake was death. But understanding, he lost his fear. He held out his arms to them.

Any Minute Mom Should Come Blasting Through the Door

David Ordan

Mom died in the middle of making me a sandwich. If I had known it was going to kill her, I never would have asked. It never killed her before to make me a sandwich, so why all of a sudden? My dad didn't understand it, either. But we don't talk about it too much. We don't talk about it too much at all. Sometimes we try. Sometimes it's just the two of us at dinner, and things are almost good. But only sometimes. Most of the time it's different. Most of the time I do things like forget to leave her place out at the table. And then we don't know what to do. Then we don't even try to talk. Three plates. Three glasses. The kitchen shines. A bright, shiny kitchen, Mom used to say. And there we are—my dad, her place, and me. And any minute Mom should come blasting through the door, all bundles and boxes, my big winter coat squaring her off at the shoulders and hips, her face smiling and wrinkled like a plant.

I should have known better.

I should have known about these things. Come on, Mom, what do you say? Is it going to kill you to make me one sandwich? Is it really going to kill you? Remember how you used to play with me? Remember? And then I undid her curlers and ran my fingers through her hair until she said all right already, what kind did I want? She looked my way, turned to my dad, and opened her bathrobe so he could get a peak just to see if the old interest was still there. But I don't think it was. What? he said. He hasn't seen this before? Make the sandwich, he said. And he let his body melt like pudding into the easy chair.

That was it. That was the last thing he said to her, I mean. Mom turned up the TV, went into the kitchen, and the next thing we knew, she was calling out for help.

Well, my dad didn't know what was going on any more than I did, so he got up from his chair, trudged across the room—making sure to scrape his feet on the carpet all the way so he could really shock her

279

good this time—and that was it. Mom was dead on the floor of the kitchen, her bathrobe open at the waist.

And I thought, Well, there's Mom dead, what now? No one thinks about that. No one thinks about what happens after you find your mother dead like that, all over the kitchen floor. But I'm telling you, that's when it really starts. That's when you have to try mouth-to-mouth on her—on your mother, for God's sake—knowing that if she does come around she'll spit up in your face, because that's what happens, but praying for it, anyway, because if she doesn't, then it's all over. That's when you've got to call an ambulance and wait for them to throw a sheet over her so they can take her away from you. That's when you've got to sit there and watch them put their hands all over her body and know they'll never believe you even tried to save her. That's when the neighbors see the flashing light in your driveway and wonder what kind of rotten son you are that you couldn't save your mother. That's when you've got your whole life to live, and all it's going to be is one excuse after another for why you didn't save her. What do you do? We didn't know, so my dad poured her on the couch, and we waited. We waited and watched TV. It was on.

But like I said, we don't talk about it too much. How can we? Mom was the talker. That's what she used to say. She used to say, "Boys, what would you do without me?" And here we are, without her. My dad and I wouldn't know how to talk to each other if you paid us, so we don't even try. Not much, anyway. What am I going to say? How's your love life? What's it like to sleep alone? He doesn't want that. He doesn't want that at all. He wants me out of the house. But he doesn't really want that, either, you know. What would he do then? Six rooms can be too many if you're not careful. I tell him this at dinner sometimes. I tell him how much he needs me. I tell him how much he cares. But he doesn't care. He cares about the kitchen, the robe, the things I did to try to save his wife. My hands. Her body. My lips. Her mouth.

"Tell me," he says, "is that really how you want to remember your mother?"

The New Moon Party

T. Coraghessan Boyle

There was a blizzard in the Dakotas, an earthquake in Chile and a solar eclipse over most of the Northern Hemisphere the day I stepped up to the governor's podium in Des Moines and announced my candidacy for the highest post in the land. As the lunar shadow crept over the Midwest like a stain in water, as noon became night and the creatures of the earth fell into an unnatural frenzy and the birds of the air fled to premature roosts, I stood in a puddle of TV lights, Lorna at my side, and calmly raked the incumbent over the coals. It was a nice campaign ploy—I think I used the term "penumbra" half a dozen times in my speech—but beyond that I really didn't attach too much significance to the whole thing. I wasn't superstitious. I wore no chains or amulets, I'd never had a rabbit's foot, I attended church only because my constituents expected me to. Of portents, I knew nothing.

My awakening—I've always liked to refer to it as my "lunar epiphany"—came at the dog end of a disappointing campaign in the coach section of a DC-10 somewhere between Battle Creek and Montpelier. It was two months before the convention, and we were on our way to Vermont to spill some rhetoric. I was picking at something the airline optimistically called Salade Madrid, my feet hurt, my digestion was shot, and the latest poll had me running dead last in a field of eight. My aides—a bunch of young Turks and electoral strong-arm men who wielded briefcases like swords and had political ambitions akin to Genghis Khan's—were daintily masticating their rubbery *coq au vin* and trying to use terms like vector, interface and demographic volatility in a single sentence. They were dull as doorknobs, dry as the dust on the textbooks that had given them life. Inspiration? They couldn't have inspired a frog to croak. No, it was Lorna, former Rose Queen and USC song girl and the sweetest, lovingest wife a man could want, who was to lift me that night to the brink of inspiration even as I saw myself swallowed up in defeat.

281

The plane dipped, the lights flickered, and Lorna laid one of her pretty white hands on my arm. "Honey," she whispered, with that soft, throbbing City-of-Industry inflection that always made me think of surf caressing the pylons of the Santa Monica pier, "will you look at that moon?"

I stabbed at my salad in irritation, a speech about Yankee gumption, coydog control and support prices for maple sugar pinwheels tenting my lap, and took a hasty glance at the darkened porthole. "Yeah?" I said, and I'm sure there was more than a little edge to my voice—couldn't she see that I was busy, worn-out, heartbroken and defeated? Couldn't she see I was like the old lion with a thorn in his paw, surrounded by wolves and jackals and facing his snaggle-toothed death in the political jungle? "What of it?" I snarled.

"Oh, I don't know," she murmured, her voice dreamy, seductive almost (had she been reading those women's magazines again?). "It just looks so old and shabby."

I squinted through that dark little porthole at the great black fathomless universe and saw the moon, palely glowing, looked at the moon probably for the first time in twenty years. Lorna was right. It did look pretty cheesy.

She hummed a few bars of "Shine On, Harvest Moon," and then turned to me with those big pale eyes—still beautiful, still enough to move me after all these years—and said, "You know, if that moon was a love seat I'd take it out to the garage and send to Bloomingdale's for a new one."

One of my aides—Colin or Carter or Rutherford, I couldn't keep their names straight—was telling a joke in dialect about three Mexican gardeners and an outhouse, another was spouting demographic theory and the stewardess swished by with a smell of perfume that hit me like a twenty-one gun salute. It was then—out of a whirl of thoughts and impressions like cream whipped in a blender—that I had my moment of grace, of inspiration, the moment that moves mountains, solves for x and makes a musical monument of the "Hymn to Joy," the moment the mass of humankind lives an entire lifetime for and never experiences. "Of course," I blurted out, upending the salad in my excitement, "yes," and I saw all the campaign trails of all the dreary, pavement-pounding, glad-handing years fall away beneath me like streamers from heaven, like ticker tape, as I turned to kiss Lorna as if I were standing before the cheering hordes on Inauguration Day.

Colin or Carter or Rutherford turned to me and said, "What is it, George—are you all right?"

"The New Moon," I said.

Lorna was regarding me quizzically. A few of the other aides turned their heads.

I was holding my plastic cup of 7-Up aloft as if it were crystal, as if it

were filled with Taittinger or Dom Perignon. "To the New Moon!" I said
with a fire and enthusiasm I hadn't felt in years. "To the New Moon
Party!"

The American people were asleep. They were dead. The great, the
giving, the earnest, energetic and righteous American people had
thrown in the towel. Rape, murder, cannibalism, political upheaval in
the Third World, rock and roll, unemployment, puppies, mothers,
Jackie, Michael, Liza: nothing moved them. Their worst fears, most
implausible dreams and foulest conceptions were all right there in the
metro section, splashed across the ever-swelling megalopic eye of the TV
screen in living color and clucked over by commentators who looked as
alike as bowling pins. Scandal and horror were as mundane as a yawn
before bed; honor, decency, heroism and enterprise were looked on as
quaint, largely inapplicable notions that expressed an inexcusable
naivete about the way of the world. In short, no one gave a good
goddamn about anything. Myself included. So how blame them when
they couldn't tell the candidates apart, didn't bother to turn out at the
polls, neither knew nor cared if the honorable Mr. P. stood for Nazi
rebirth or federally-funded electronic walkers for the aged and infirm?
I'd seen it all, and nothing stirred me either. Ultraism, Conservatism,
Progressivism, Communism, Liberalism, Neo-Fascism, parties of the
right, left, center, left-of-center and oblate poles: who cared? I didn't
even know why I was running. I'd served my two terms as a fresh-faced
ambitious young representative during the Eisenhower years, fought
through three consecutive terms in the senatorial wars, wielded the
sword of power and influence in the most armor-plated committees on
the Hill, and been twice elected governor of Iowa on a platform that
promised industrial growth, environmental protection and the eradica-
tion of corn blight through laser technology. And yet for all that I wasn't
satisfied. I guess, even at sixty-one, I was still afflicted with those hungry
pangs of ambition that every boy who can't play centerfield for the
Yankees will never wholly shake: I wanted to be top dog, kick off my
shoes in the Oval Office and stir up a fuss wherever I went, I wanted to
climb high atop the mountain and look down on the creeping, minuscule figures of queens, rock stars, matinee idols and popes. It was a cold
life in a comfortless universe, I didn't believe in God, afterlife or lepre-
chauns. I wanted to make my mark on history—what else was there?
And so I—we—came up with the issue that would take the country—
no, the world itself—by storm. From the moment of my epiphany on
that rattling, howling DC-10 I never said another word about taxes,
inflation, social security, price supports or the incumbent's lamentable
record on every key issue from the decentralization of the Boy Scouts to
relations with the Soviet Union. No, I talked only of the New Moon.
The moon *we* were going to build, to create, to hurl into the sky to take

its place among the twinkling orbs of the night and recover the dignity and economic stability of America in the process. Jupiter had twelve moons, Saturn ten, Uranus five. What were we? Where was our global pride when we could boast but one craggy, acne-ridden bulb blighting the nighttime sky? A New Moon. A New Moon Soon: it was on my lips like a battle cry.

In Montpelier they thought I'd gone mad. An audience of thirty-seven had turned out at the local ag school to hear me talk about coydogs and maple-sugar pinwheels, but I gave them a dose of the New Moon instead. I strode out onto the stage like a man reborn (which I was), shredded my prepared speech and flung it like confetti over their astonished heads, my arms spread wide, the spontaneous, thrilling message of the lunar gospel pouring from me in evangelical fervor. LUNACY, mocked the morning headlines. THORKELSSON MOONSTRUCK. But the people listened. They murmured in Montpelier, applauded lightly—hands chapped and dry as corn husks—in Rutland. In Pittsburgh, where I really began to hit my stride (I talked of nothing but the steel it would take to piece together the superstructure of the new satellite), they climbed atop tables and cheered. The American people were tired of party bickering, vague accusations and even vaguer solutions, they were sick to death of whiz-kid economists, do-nothing legislatures and the nightmare specter of nuclear war. They wanted joy, simplicity, a goal as grand as Manifest Destiny and yet as straightforward and unequivocal as a bank statement. The New Moon gave it to them.

By the time the convention rolled around, the New Moon was waxing full. I remember the way the phones rang off the hook: could we take a backseat to Fritz, throw our support to John, accept the V.P. nomination on a split-issue platform? Seven weeks earlier no one had even deigned to notice us—half the time we didn't even get press coverage. But New Moon fever was sweeping the country—we'd picked up a bundle of delegates, won in Texas, Ohio and California, and suddenly we were a force to reckon with.

"George," Colin was saying (I'm sure it was Colin, because I'd canned Carter and Rutherford to avoid the confusion), "I still say we've got to broaden our base. The one issue has taken us leagues, I admit it, but—"

I cut him off. I was George L. Thorkelsson, former representative, former senator and current governor of the Mesopotamia of the Midwest, the glorious, farinaceous, black-loamed hogbutt of the nation, and I wasn't about to listen to any defeatist twaddle from some Ivy League pup. "Hi diddle, diddle," I said, "the cat and the fiddle." I was feeling pretty good.

It was then that Gina—Madame Scutari, that is—spoke up. Lorna and I had discovered her in the kitchen of Mama Gina's, a Nashville pasta house, during the Tennessee primary. She'd made an abbacchio alla cacciatora that knocked my socks off, and when we'd gone back to

284

congratulate her she'd given me a look of such star-struck devotion I felt like the new Messiah. It seemed that the Madame (who wasn't Italian at all but Hungarian) was a part-time astrologist and clairvoyant, and had had a minor seizure at the very moment of my epiphany in the DC-10 – her left arm had gone numb and she'd pitched forward into a platter of antipasto with the word "lunar" on her lips. She told us all this in a rush of malapropisms and tortured syntax, while cauldrons of marinara sauce bubbled around her and her faintly-mustachioed upper lip rose and fell like a shuttlecock. Then she'd leaned forward to whisper in my ear like a priestess of the oracle. *Leo*, she'd said, hitting my sign on the nose, *Scorpio in the ascendant*. Then she drew up her rouged face and gave me a broad Magyar wink and again I could feel her lips moving against my ear: *A New Moon Soon*, she rasped. From that moment on she'd become one of my closest advisors.

Now she cleared her throat with a massive dignity, her heavy arms folded over her bust, and said, in that delicate halting accent that made you feel she could read the future like a Neapolitan menu, "Not to worry, Georgie: I see you rising like the lion coming into the tenth house."

"But George—" Colin was nearly whining. "Gimmicks are O.K., but they can only take you so far. Think of the political realities."

Lorna and the Madame exchanged a look. I watched as a smile animated my wife's features. It was a serene smile, visionary, the smile of a woman who already saw herself decked out in a gown like a shower of gold and presiding over tea in the Blue Room.

I turned to Colin and tersely reminded him of the political realities his late colleagues were currently facing. "We need no nay-sayers here," I added. "You're either on the bus or you're off it." He looked at me as if he were about to say something he would regret, but the Madame cut him off, her voice elevated yet soft, the syllables falling together with a kiss that cut through the confusion and the jangling of telephones like a benediction: "Promise them the moon," she said.

The convention itself was child's play. We'd captured the imagination of the country, restored the average workingman's faith in progress, given America a cause to stand up and shout about. We split the thing down the middle and I took my delegates outside the party to form the first significant rump party since the days of Henry Wallace. We were the New Moon Party and they came to us in droves. Had anyone ever stopped to consider how many amateur astrologists there were out there? How many millions who guided their every move, from love affairs to travel plans to stock purchases and the most auspicious time for doing their nails, according to the conjunction of the planets and the phases of the moon? Or how many religious fanatics and sci-fi freaks there were, Trekkies, lunatics, werewolves, extraterrestrialists, saucer nuts and the like? Not to mention women, who've had to carry that white goddess baggage around with them since the dawn of time. Well here was an issue that could unite them all. Nixon had put men on the moon, I was going to bring the moon to men. And women.

Oh, there were the usual cries of outrage and anathema, the usual blockheads, whiners and pleaders, but we paid them no heed. NASA was behind us, one hundred percent. So was U.S. Steel, the AFL-CIO, the Teamsters, Silicon Valley, Wall Street and Big Oil, and just about anyone else in the country who worked for a living. A New Moon. Just think of the jobs it would create!

The incumbent—a man twelve years my senior who looked as if he'd been stuffed with sand—didn't stand a chance. Oh, they painted him up and pointed him toward the TV monitors and told him when to laugh or cry or make his voice tremble with righteousness, and they had him recite the usual litany about the rights of the rich and the crying need for new condos on Maui, and they prodded him to call the New Moon a hoax, a technological impossibility, a white elephant and a liberal-humanist threat to the integrity of the interplanetary heavens, but all to no avail. It almost hurt me to see his bowed head, smeared blusher and plasticized hair as he conceded defeat to a national TV audience after I'd swept every precinct in the country with the sole exception of Santa Barbara, where he'd beaten me by seventeen votes, but what the hell. This was no garden party, this was politics.

Sadly, however, unity and harmony are not the way of the world, and no leader, no matter how visionary—not Napoleon, not Caesar, not Mohammed, Louis XVI, Jim Jones or Jesus of Nazareth—can hope to stave off the tide of discord, malcontent, envy, hatred and sheer seething anarchy that inevitably rises up to crush him with the force of a tsunami. And so it was, seven years later, my second term drawing to a close and with neither hope nor precedent for a third, that I found the waves crashing at my very doorstep. I who had been the most heralded chief executive in the country's history, I who had cut across social strata, party differences, ethnic divisions and international mistrust with my vision of a better world and a better future, was well on my way to becoming the most vilified world leader since Attila the Hun.

Looking back on it, I can see that perhaps my biggest mistake was in appointing Madame Scutari to my cabinet. The problem wasn't so much her lack of experience—I understand that now—but her lack of taste. She took something truly grand—a human monument before which all the pyramids, Taj Mahals and World Trade Centers paled by comparison—and made it tacky. For that I will never forgive her.

At any rate, when I took office back in January of '85, I created a new cabinet post that would reflect the chief priority of my administration—I refer to the now infamous post of Secretary for Lunar Affairs—and named Gina to occupy it. Though she'd had little formal training, she

286

knew her stars and planets cold, and she was a woman of keen insight and studied judgment. I trusted her implicitly. Besides which, I was beleaguered by renegade scientists, gypsies, sci-fi hacks (one of whom was later to write most of my full-moon addresses to the nation), amateur inventors and corporation execs, all clamoring for a piece of the action—and I desperately needed someone to sort them out. Gina handled them like diners without reservations.

The gypsies, Trekkies, diviners, haruspices and the like were apparently pursuing a collective cosmic experience, something that would ignite the heavens; the execs—from U.S. Steel to IBM to Boeing to American Can—wanted contracts. After all, the old moon was some 2,160 miles in diameter and 81 quintillion tons of dead weight, and they figured whatever we were going to do would take one hell of a lot of construction. Kaiser proposed an aluminum alloy steel filled with Styrofoam, to be shuttled piecemeal into space and constructed by robots on location. The Japanese wanted to mold it out of plastic, while Firestone saw a big synthetic golf-ball sort of thing and Con Ed pushed for a hollow cement globe that could be used as a repository for nuclear waste. And it wasn't just the big corporations, either—it seemed every crank in the country was suddenly a technological wizard. A retired gym teacher from Sacramento suggested an inflatable ball made of simulated pigskin, and a pizza magnate from Brooklyn actually proposed a chicken-wire sphere coated with raw dough. *Bake it with lasers or something*, he wrote, *it'll harden like rock. Believe me.* During those first few heady months in office the proposals must have come in at the rate of ten thousand a day.

If I wasn't equipped to deal with them (I've always been an idea man myself), Gina was. She conferred before breakfast, lunched three or four times a day, dined and brunched and kept a telephone glued to her head as if it were a natural excrescence. "No problem," she told me. "I'll have a proposal for you by June."

She was true to her word.

I remember the meeting at which she presented her findings as keenly as I remember my mother's funeral or the day I had my gall bladder removed. We were sitting around the big mahogany table in the conference room, sipping coffee. Gina flowed through the door in a white caftan, her arms laden with clipboards and blueprints, looking pleased with herself. She took a seat beside Lorna, exchanged a bit of gossip with her in a husky whisper, then leaned across the table and cleared her throat. "Glitter," she said, "that's what we want, Georgie. Something bright, something to fill up the sky and screw over the astrological charts forever." Lorna, who'd spent the afternoon redesigning the uniforms of the scouts of America (they were known as Space Cadets now, and the new unisex uniforms were to feature the spherical New Moon patch over the heart), sat nodding at her side. They were grinning conspiratorially, like a pair of matrons outfitting a parlor.

"Glitter?" I echoed, smiling into the face of their enthusiasm. "What did you have in mind?"

The Madame closed her heavy-lidded gypsy eyes for a moment, then flashed them at me like a pair of blazing guns. "The Bonaventure Hotel, Georgie—in L.A.? You know it?"

I shook my head slowly, wondering what she was getting at.

"Mirrors," she said.

I just looked at her.

"Fields of them, Georgie, acres upon acres. Just think of the reflective power! Our moon, *your* moon—it'll outshine that old heap of rock and dust ten times over."

Mirrors. The simplicity of it, the beauty. I felt the thrill of her inspiration, pictured the glittering, triumphant moon hanging there like a jewel in the sky, bright as a supernova, bright as the star of Bethlehem. No, brighter, brighter by far. The flash of it would illuminate the darkest corners, the foulest alleys, drive back the creatures of darkness and cut the crime rate exponentially. George L. Thorkelsson, I thought, light giver. "Yes," I said, my voice husky with emotion, "yes."

But Filencio Salmón, author of *The Ravishers of Pentagord* and my chief speech writer, rose to object. "Wees all due respet, Meeser Presiden, these glass globe goin to chatter like a gumball machine the firs time a meteor or anytin like that run into it. What you wan eez sometin strong, Teflon maybe."

"Not shiny enough," Gina countered, exchanging a hurt look with Lorna. Obviously she hadn't thought very deeply about the thing if she hadn't taken meteors into account. Christ, she was Secretary for Lunar Affairs, with two hundred JPL eggheads, selenologists, and former astronauts on her staff, and that was the best she could come up with?

I leaned back in my chair and looked over the crestfallen faces gathered round the table—Gina, Lorna, Salmón, my National Security Advisor, the old boy in the Philip Morris outfit we sent out for sandwiches. "Listen," I said, feeling wise as Solomon, "the concept is there—we'll work out a compromise solution."

No one said a word.

"We've got to. The world's depending on us."

We settled finally on stainless steel. Well-buffed, and with nothing out there to corrode it, it would have nearly the same reflective coefficient as glass, and it was one hell of a lot more resistant. More expensive too, but when you've got a project like this, what's a hundred billion more or less? Anyway, we farmed out the contracts and went into production almost immediately. We had decided, after the usual breast-beating, shouting matches, resignations and reinstatements, on a shell of jet-age plastic strengthened by steel girders, and a façade—one side only—of

288

stainless-steel plates the size of Biloxi, Mississippi. Since we were only going up about eighty thousand miles, we figured we could get away with a sphere about one-third the size of the old moon: its proximity to earth would make it appear so much larger.

I don't mean to minimize the difficulty of all this. There were obstacles both surmountable and insurmountable, technologies to be invented, resources to be tapped, a great and wealthy nation to be galvanized into action. My critics – and they were no small minority, even in those first few euphoric years – insisted that the whole thing was impossible, a pipe dream at best. They were defeatists, of course, like Colin (for whom, by the way, I found a nice little niche in El Salvador as assistant to the Ambassador's body-count man), and they didn't faze me in the least. No, I figured that if in the space of the eight years of World War II man could go from biplanes and TNT to jets and nuclear bombs, anything was possible if the will was there. And I was right. By the time my first term wound down we were three-quarters of the way home, the economy was booming, the unemployment rate approaching zero for the first time since the forties and the Cold War defrosted. (The Russians had given over stockpiling activities to work on their own satellite project. They were rumored to be constructing a new planet in Siberia, and our reconnaissance photos showed that they were indeed up to something big – something, in fact, that looked like a three-hundred-mile-long eggplant inscribed at intervals with the legend NOVAYA SMOLENSK.) Anyway, as most of the world knows, the Republicans didn't even bother to field a candidate in '88, and New Moon fever had the national temperature hovering up around the point of delirium.

Then, as they say, the shit hit the fan.

To have been torn to pieces like Orpheus or Mussolini, to have been stretched and broken on the rack or made to sing "Hello, Dolly!" at the top of my lungs while strapped naked to a carny horse driven through the House of Representatives, would have been pleasure compared to what I went through the night we unveiled the New Moon. What was to have been my crowning triumph – my moment of glory transcendent – became instead my most ignominious defeat. In an hour's time I went from savior to fiend.

For seven years, along with the rest of the world, I'd held my breath. Through all that time, through all the blitz of TV and newspaper reports, the incessant interviews with project scientists and engineers, the straw polls, moon crazes and marketing ploys, the New Moon had remained a mystery. People knew how big it was, they could plot its orbit and talk of its ascending and descending nodes and how many million tons of materials had gone into its construction – but they'd yet to see it. Oh, if you looked hard enough you could see that something was going on up there, but it was as shadowy and opaque as the blueprint of a dream. Even with a telescope – and believe me, many's the night I spent at Palomar with a bunch of professional stargazers or out on the White House lawn with the Questar QM 1 Lorna gave me for Christmas – you couldn't make out much more than a dark circle punched out of the great starry firmament as if with a cookie cutter.

Of course, we'd planned it that way. Right from the start we'd agreed that the best policy was to keep the world guessing – who wanted to see a piecemeal moon, after all, a moon that grew square by square in the night like some crazy checkerboard or something? This was no department store going up on West Twenty-third Street – this was something extraordinary, unique, this was the quintessence of man's achievement on the planet, and it should be served up whole or not at all. It was Salmón, in a moment of inspiration, who came up with the idea of putting the reflecting plates on the far side, facing out on the deeps of the universe, and then swinging the whole business around by means of initial-thrust- and retro-rockets for a triumphant – and politically opportune – unveiling. I applauded him. Why not? I thought. Why not milk this thing for everything it was worth?

The night of the unveiling was clear and moonless. Lorna sat beside me on the dais, regal and resplendent in a Halston moonglow gown that cost more than the combined gross product of any six towns along the Iowa-Minnesota border. Gina was there too, of course, looking as if she'd just won a fettucine cook-off in Naples, and the audience of celebrities, foreign ambassadors and politicos gathered on the south lawn numbered in the thousands. Outside the gates, in darkness, three-quarters of a million citizens milled about with spherical white moon candles, which were to be lit at the moment the command was given to swing the New Orb into view. Up and down the Eastern Seaboard, in Quebec and Ontario, along the ridge of the Smokies and out to the verge of the Mississippi, a hush fell over the land as municipalities big and small cut their lights.

Ferenc Syzgies, the project's chief engineer, delivered an interminable speech peppered with terms like photometric function and fractional pore space, Anita Bryant sang a couple of spirituals and finally Luciano Pavarotti rose to do a medley of "Moon River," "Blue Moon" and "Amore." Lorna leaned over and took my hand as the horns stepped in on the last number. "Nervous?" she whispered.

"No," I murmured, but my throat had thickened till I felt I was going to choke. They'd assured me there would be no foul-ups – but nothing like this had ever been attempted before, and who could say for sure?

"When-a the moon-a hits your eye like a big pizza pie," sang Pavarotti, "it's amore." The dignitaries shifted in their seats, Lorna was whispering something I couldn't hear and then Coburn, the V.P., was introducing me.

I stood and stepped to the podium to spontaneous, thrilling and sustained applause, Salmón's speech clutched in my hand, the shirt collar chafing at my neck like a garrote. Flashbulbs popped, the TV cameras seized on me like the hungry eyes of great mechanical insects, faces leapt out of the crowd: here a senator I loathed sitting cheek-by-jowl with a lobbyist from the Sierra Club, there a sour-faced clergyman I'd prayed beside during a dreary rally seven years earlier. The glowing, corn-fed visage of Miss Iowa materialized just beneath the podium, and behind her sat Coretta King, Tip O'Neill, Barbra Streisand, Carl Sagan and Mickey Mantle, all in a row. The applause went on for a full five minutes. And then suddenly the audience was on their feet and singing "God Bless America" as if their lives depended on it. When they were finished, I held up my hands for silence and began to read.

Salmón had outdone himself. The speech was measured, hysterical, opaque and lucid. My voice rang triumphantly through the P.A. system, rising in eulogy, trembling with visionary fervor, dropping to an emotion-choked whisper as I found myself taking on everything from the birth of the universe to Conestoga wagons and pioneer initiative. I spoke of interstellar exploration, of the movie industry and Dixieland jazz, of the great, selfless, uncontainable spirit of the American people who, like latter-day Prometheuses, were giving over the sacred flame to the happy, happy generations to come. Or something like that. I was about halfway through when the New Orb began to appear in the sky over my shoulder.

The first thing I remember was the brightness of it. Initially there was just a sliver of light, but the sliver quickly grew to a crescent that lit the south lawn as if on a July morning. I kept reading. "The gift of light . . ." I intoned, but no one was listening. As the thing began to swing round to full the glare of it became insupportable. I paused to gaze down at the faces before me: they were awestruck, panicky, disgusted, violent, enraptured. People had begun to shield their eyes now; some of the celebrities and musicians slipped on sunglasses. It was then that the dogs began to howl. Faintly at first, a primal yelp here or there, but within thirty seconds every damn hound, mongrel and cur in the city of Washington was baying at the moon as if they hadn't eaten in a week. It was unnerving, terrifying. People began to shout, and then to shove one another.

I didn't know what to do. "Well, er," I said, staring into the cameras and waving my arm with a theatrical flourish, "ladies and gentlemen, the New Moon!"

Something crazy was going on. The shoving had stopped as abruptly as it had begun, but now, suddenly and inexplicably, the audience started to undress. Right before me, on the platform, in the seats reserved for foreign diplomats, out over the seething lawn, they were kicking off shoes, hoisting shirtfronts and brassieres, dropping cummerbunds and Jockey shorts. And then, incredibly, horribly, they began to clutch at one another in passion, began to stroke, fondle and lick, humping in the grass, plunging into the bushes, running around like nymphs and satyrs at some mad bacchanal. A senator I'd known for forty years went by me in a dead run, pursuing the naked wife of the Bolivian ambassador, Miss Iowa disappeared beneath the rhythmically heaving buttocks of the sour-faced clergyman, Lorna was down to a pair of six-hundred-dollar bikini briefs and I suddenly found to my horror that I'd begun to loosen my tie.

Madness, lunacy, mass hypnosis, call it what you will: it was a mess. Flocks of birds came shrieking out of the trees, cats appeared from nowhere to caterwaul along with the dogs, congressmen rolled about on the ground, grabbing for flesh and yipping like animals—and all this on national television! I felt light-headed, as if I were about to pass out, but then I found I had an erection, and there before me was this cream-colored thing in a pair of high-heeled boots and nothing else, Lorna had disappeared, it was bright as noon in Miami, dogs, cats, rats and squirrels were howling like werewolves and I found that somehow I'd stripped down to my boxer shorts. It was then that I lost consciousness. Mercifully.

These days, I am not quite so much in the public eye. In fact, I live in seclusion. On a lake somewhere in the Northwest, Northeast or Deep South, my only company a small cadre of Secret Service men. They are laconic sorts, these Secret Service men, heavy of shoulder and head, and they live in trailers set up on a ridge behind the house. To a man, they are named Greg or Craig.

As those who read this will know, all our efforts to modify the New Moon (Coburn's efforts, that is: I was in hiding) were doomed to failure. Syzgies' replacement, Klaus Erkhardt, the rocket expert, had proposed tarnishing the stainless-steel plates with payloads of acid, but the plan had proven unworkable for obvious reasons. Meanwhile, a coalition of unlikely bedfellows—Syria, Israel, Iran, Iraq, Libya, Great Britain, Argentina, the U.S.S.R. and China among them—had demanded the "immediate removal of this plague upon our heavens," and in this country we came as close to revolution as we had since the 1770's.

Coburn did the best he could, but the following November, Colin, Carter and Rutherford jumped parties and began a push to reelect the man I'd defeated in '84 on the One Moon ticket. He was old—antediluvian, in fact—but not appreciably changed either in appearance or outlook, and he was swept into office in a landslide. The New Moon, which had been blamed for everything from rain in the Atacama to fomenting a new baby boom, corrupting morals, bestializing mankind and causing crops to grow upside down in the Far East, was obliterated by a nuclear thunderbolt a month after he took office.

On reflection, I can see that I was wrong—I admit it. I was an optimist,

I was aggressive, I believed in man and in science, I challenged the heavens and dared to tamper with the face of the universe and its inscrutable design—and I paid for it as swiftly and surely as anybody in all the tragedies of Shakespeare, Sophocles and Dashiell Hammett. Gina dropped me like a plate of hot lasagna and went back to her restaurant, Colin stabbed me in the back and Coburn, once he'd taken over, refused to refer to me by name—I was known only as his "predecessor." I even lost Lorna. She left me after the debacle of the unveiling and the impeachment that followed precipitously on its heels, left me to "explore new feelings," as she put it. "I've got to get it out of my system," she told me, a strange glow in her eyes. "I'm sorry, George."

Hell yes, I was wrong. But just the other night I was out on the lake with one of the Secret Service men—Greg, I think it was—fishing for yellow perch, when the moon—the age-old, scar-faced, native moon—rose up out of the trees like an apparition. It was yellow as the under-belly of the fish on the stringer, huge with atmospheric distortion. I whistled. "Will you look at that moon," I said.

Greg just stared at me, noncommittal.

"That's really something, huh?" I said.

No response.

He was smart, this character—he wouldn't touch it with a ten-foot pole. I was just talking to hear myself anyway. Actually, I was thinking the darn thing did look pretty cheesy, thinking maybe where I'd gone wrong was in coming up with a new moon instead of just maybe bulldoz-ing the old one or something. I began to picture it: lie low for a couple years, then come back with a new ticket—Clean Up the Albedo, A New Face for an Old Friend, Save the Moon!

But then there was a tug on the line, and I forgot all about it.

Dancing in the Movies

Robert Boswell

"Bob Marley dead," Eugene said, hand at his dick as he walked in the door, brown face yellowed from heroin, eyes puffy like a boxer's. He stared hard at me, leaned against a barstool. His shoulders made a big spread, but he was junk skinny, that all-sucked-out look. "Bob Marley *dead*," he said again, like I couldn't hear.

I wanted to call him a lemon-faced nigger, but I didn't like that ugly side and kept it quiet, even with Eugene. I got straight to the point. "You seen Dee?"

"Didn't you hear me?" He gripped at the air, making two large fists, his voice full of anger and familiarity, as if I hadn't been gone for months.

"I already heard," I said. My best friend, Lonnie, had picked me up at the bus station and given me the news. "It's all over the radio," he said. "The industrialists killed him." I felt weak, twenty hours on a Greyhound, then I hear Marley is gone. I asked Lonnie how they killed him. "Cancer," he said, "white man's disease." It had sounded like an accusation.

"Shit," Eugene said, bending close to study my face for signs of anguish. He crossed his arms to make himself bigger. "Go listen at your fucking Elton John."

I felt accused again, as if my white skin had contributed to Marley's death. I would not apologize for being white, especially not to a bonehollow junkie like Eugene. I stood and threw what was left of my beer in his face. "Where's Dee?"

For a moment his eyes sparked, but they clouded quickly. He seemed to shrink. "Shit, Freddie, why you always got a hard-on?" He wiped at his face, eyebrows. Beer ran down his fingers and dripped onto the concrete floor. "I don't know where she is. We ain't in no club."

294

"I need to find her." I sat again on the wood ladder-back chair, already regretting throwing the beer. "I need to find her, Eugene."

He turned away from me, wiping the last of the beer on his jeans, and walked to the jukebox. "Ask Wilson," he said.

Wilson was Lonnie's little brother. "Wilson's clean," I said. With Lonnie's help, Wilson had put down heroin and begun avoiding junkies, which meant he would have nothing to do with Dee. "Wilson is clean," I said again, louder.

Eugene paid no attention, slipping coins into the machine. As kids, Eugene and I had been friends, part of the neighborhood crowd that centered around Lonnie. Dee had been the only girl in the group and my girlfriend, off and on, since fourth grade. It was hard for me to remember a time I didn't love Dee. We cheated together on spelling, stole cigarettes from Quick Mart, made a wreath from oleander leaves for her mother's grave.

I knew where to find Wilson, although I didn't think he'd know where to find Dee. From noon to five Wilson sat in front of the unemployment office, hoping to find *his* girlfriend. She left him because he couldn't quit heroin. Now he was clean, but she was gone.

Eugene bent over the jukebox, ran his index finger down the song list. He looked like a Norman Rockwell parody, big and childish, black and gaunt. He reminded me of a letter from Lonnie. *I used to think junkies were like little kids*, he wrote. *They're more like dead people playing human.* I decided to look for Wilson. He, at least, would be sympathetic—we were both looking for girlfriends.

I walked out of the Bree Lounge. The rain had stopped but the sky was still hooded with clouds. Music started up inside the bar, too muffled to be recognizable. I thought it must be Bob Marley. Dee and I had seen Bob Marley once in L.A., so stoned we had to dance in our chairs. Lonnie had been with us, doing spins and dancing funk to reggae. Some song made us cry, just the sound of it, the way it moved inside. Lonnie enjoyed crying, but Dee and I weren't criers. It was Marley himself, singing with his whole body, moving like a marionette, then a dancer, that made the music into something liquid. I pictured Marley, bare to his waist, the blue light shining off his sweaty back, his dark hands on the silver microphone stand, but all I could hear was the muffled music from the Bree. I headed for the unemployment building.

Downtown was noisy as a bad movie. Vested men carrying briefcases hurried past. They looked straight ahead, their thin, high-polished shoes finding the dry spots of the sidewalk. I almost fit in, wearing my best blue slacks and olive shirt, wanting to look good when I found Dee.

In her last letter, she had written, *All the streets in Langston run the wrong way—that's why we grew up lost.* In response, I sent her a bus ticket. I didn't hear from her after that. My letters were returned.

Wilson was sitting in Lonnie's creme Coupe de Ville drinking Burgie from the can. He rolled down the window on the passenger side and yelled. "Get in before it rains some more." He put a cold Burgie in my hand. "I love the rain," he said, "but from the inside."

I nodded, drank a swallow of beer. The flower vendors were back on the corners. The thin green paper tore when they tried to pull it off the stems of the rain-flattened flowers. The women with the flowers reminded me of Dee. Because they smiled and waved the bouquets like Dee finding the phone book under a pile of magazines? Because I bought her flowers once? Lonnie told me I have a blindness for Dee; whatever I did, I was thinking how she could fit in, even if I was with my parents, who hated her, or in a class hundreds of miles from her. Then I remembered the cemetery. We had bought flowers for the graves last December, the day before I left Langston. Dee took me to where her mother, grandmother, and aunt were buried. She started crying, not because those dead women were dead, but that they didn't have any better imagination than to keep planting themselves one next to another. She had told me she wanted to be buried where everyone was a stranger. It was then she promised to come to Oregon in the summer.

Wilson was wearing a long-sleeved T-shirt and jeans speckled with white paint. He worked from six to noon, then watched the unemployment building. The flecks of paint in his hair made him look like an old man. "Any sign of Angela?" I asked.

"It's tough," Wilson said. "Paper says unemployment is up though. I'm optimistic."

I could tell from his eyes he was still clean, although I didn't know him well. I knew heroin enough to know clean, even though Dee told me that was bullshit. She said I didn't know heroin because I was straight, that I didn't know women because I was male, that I didn't know black because I was white. I just threw it back at her upside down to make her hush.

Wilson was two years younger than Lonnie and me, a junkie since he was thirteen. He used to stumble through our parties, giggling and scratching at himself. Lonnie had tried to get him to put down junk, but nothing had worked. When Wilson moved in with Angela, who was also a junkie, Lonnie bore down on her until she quit. But she couldn't endure Wilson's trying, especially when he'd get sick from shooting up again. It was her leaving that finally got him to quit. I had never felt close to Wilson before then, sharing the front seat of Lonnie's car, each of us looking for a woman who probably didn't want to be found. And something more—Wilson had been a junkie for years and quit. It gave me hope for Dee.

A Mexican woman with a sour-looking kid walked out of the unemployment building. "You think of Welfare?" I asked. The first drop of rain hit center like a huge bug splat just below the rearview mirror.

"Starting again," Wilson said. He leaned forward, looked up to the dark sky. "Welfare's a waste of time. She's too proud. Too crazy. Too stupid."

I looked at the way his long neck curved as he stared at the sky. I pictured Angela walking by, seeing Wilson craning his head up and knowing instantly that he was clean. Thinking about it reminded me of my own problems. "You know where Dee is?"

Wilson gave a short laugh. "I can't find my own woman."

"Eugene said you might know."

"Fuck Eugene." Another drop hit right above his face. "They look like stars exploding," he said, then straightened. "Why don't you just get another woman?"

I shook my head, thinking that was what Eugene wanted to say in the bar, only he would have come out and said, "Why don't you get a *white* woman?" I didn't get angry with Wilson. We both had our ugly sides. "I love Dee," I said.

"Yeah," he said, looked at the unemployment door as a man in a tie walked out. "They closing up. You need a ride somewhere?"

Wilson dropped me off at Lonnie's apartment, saying only that Dee got junk from Eugene. If I stayed close to Eugene, she would show.

Lonnie was smoking a joint. I didn't want any, even though he acted hurt and told me how wonderful it was with that effeminate twist in his voice. Everyone thought he was queer, but Lonnie was always after women and women were always after him.

"Maybe you should forget about Dee," Lonnie said, sitting with his legs crossed under him at one end of his record collection, flipping through the albums. He wore a smoke-colored shirt with a short collar and pleated beige pants, though he wasn't going anywhere and expecting no one but me.

"I love Dee." I squatted at the other end of the records. We looked for Bob Marley, moving crab-like across the floor, checking each of the albums that lined the wall. Lonnie decided he must have lent the albums out. We settled for Peter Tosh, *Equal Rights*.

The five months I had been at college, Lonnie and Dee were the only ones who had written. Lonnie's letters covered everything—from how well he was doing at work to how hard it was for his brother to quit junk. He had his own stationery—heavy, blue paper with thick and thin black lines bordering it and a big *L.W.* at the top. Dee's letters came on whatever was handy while she was high and missing me. Once she had mailed a napkin from the Bree, scribbled up and blurred from wet glass circles. Her letters were short, choppy, full of things that only made half sense. *I can't talk on telephones,* she wrote, *my throat swells up the size of testicles you seen in pictures—You love me or you just love niggers?* Her last letter said, *The birds are loose in Langston and all the streets run the wrong way, I eat drugs, Freddie.* When I had left, she'd just been fooling with heroin. With each letter she seemed more and more a junkie, until she started calling herself one. *Which your parents going to hate worser? Dee the nigger or Dee the junkie?*

"It's such a tacky love," Lonnie said. He sat, recrossed his legs, twisting his top foot behind a knee, like pretzels. "You need a cleaner love."

"I'm taking her back. I've got school housing and work study. I can afford it."

"Oh, Freddie, why on earth do you want to love Dee?" He leaned against the long fingers of his left hand, pushing his mouth into a half smile.

"Didn't say I want to. I just do."

"Huck Finn and Nigger Jim," Lonnie said.

"What's that supposed to mean?"

"It's a complex boys get where they feel they have to love what they hate." His head gave a little waggle as he said it.

"That'd explain why *you* chase after women," I said, happy for the chance to turn it upside down on him.

"You're such a clever boy," he said, flipping both hands open and spreading his fingers, then letting them fall limp at the wrists—his best fake fag gesture. "I suppose it would also explain why you hang out with me." He laughed, a giggle, and not fake. "Really, Dee and I are perfect for you: multiple outcasts."

He wanted me to laugh, forget about Dee for now, but I wouldn't buy it. "I've known you and Dee all my life."

"She smokes constantly. It's such a dirty habit." Suddenly he stood, twisting as he came out of the pretzel. "Wait here. Bob Marley may be in my closet."

"It's time someone came out of your closet," I said.

Lonnie couldn't find the album he wanted but returned with some old

Temptations. "You remember?" he asked, flashing the album cover and doing a crossover step.

When we were kids we sang backup together to Temptations and Four Tops albums, complete with steps and hand moves. Lonnie had been the best in the neighborhood and he still loved to do it. I jumped up beside him. We rocked together to get in time. "Just My Imagination" was the song and it called for finger snapping at the hips, lots of hand movements to show nothing was real. The steps were just a little box with plenty of sway. We worked well together. All that was missing was Dee to sing the Eddie Kendricks high notes. Once I thought about that, I knew I would only dance through one song. Wherever I was, Dee was what was missing.

The Bree was quiet—a couple of the regular drunks at the bar, a heavy-thighed black woman we used to call "Sisters" because she was so fat, a dog-faced junkie who knew me and had breath like turpentine, a few others sipping beer or sleeping head-down on the cheap tables. In the corner, an ugly red dog with a pointed nose was chewing his leg. Nobody was saying where Eugene might be.

I was ready to leave when Dee walked in, hair knotted back on her head and body too thin, but still beautiful in jeans and a purple blouse, baggy so her ribs didn't show. She smiled when she saw me and came straight over. Dee carried heroin in her eyes. They became milky and thick, moved too slow.

Her arms went right around me, elbows at my ribs, hands pressed against my shoulder blades. The kissing took me back to December, before I left, as if time were something people carried with them, the way some carried pictures.

"I've been looking for you," I said.

"Wilson told me." She ran her hands down then up my sides. "You look good," she said. "You got your Lonnie clothes on."

I laughed. I hadn't realized it, but everything I had on had been given to me at Christmases or birthdays by Lonnie.

"How's your college?" she said.

"I've got a place now. I want you to come back with me."

She smiled and sat at the table. "Get me a Coke."

I came back with a Coke and a beer. Dee sat, legs crossed, arms folded, leaning back and smiling, lipstick too red and smeared under her nose where she'd missed her lip.

"I mean it, Dee. This is a way out."

"Can't be." She took a big swallow of Coke.

"Why not?"

"If it was, we wouldn't know about it." Her upper lip glistened with Coke. She took another big drink, wiped her mouth with her hand. "Anyway, I don't like mixed marriages."

"Fuck that."

"They don't work, junkies and straights." She reached over and twisted one of my shirt buttons. "You'd have to take to junk."

I leaned back. The chair squeaked. Her milky eyes caught up with me. "I was thinking you could quit," I said.

Her hand moved up and down the Coke glass. "You want to consume me." She wiped the cold sweat from the glass onto her forehead, the bridge of her nose, her eyelids.

"Wilson quit."

Her hand dropped to her lap. "That's what got you all excited, ain't it?"

"Lonnie got him through it."

She glared at me, only it's her fake mean look, like Lonnie's fake fag moves, meaning just the opposite. I tilted my head to show her I knew what she was doing. It must have reminded her how long I had loved her because she went soft, showed her tongue as she smiled. Then she moved in another direction. Something came to her and her eyes flitted down to the table. "I'm one up on you," she said. "You go to college to figure out what it is *worth* getting up for." She looked up at me, thick eyes set hard against mine. "I got my reason to live."

She made me feel small, like junkies were the only full-grown people. "I tried the shit," I said, feeling stupid as soon as I said it because she knew I only snorted it. It's the needles I couldn't stand. I couldn't even look at them. But it was more than that. Junkies made me angry, especially gone junkies like Eugene, but even the clever ones, the pretty ones, the ones who could be anybody.

Dee's laugh was like a gurgle, but low enough to be a moan. "Snorting junk is like jacking off, a waste of good stuff."

I couldn't get mad at Dee. Every expression on her face was one I'd seen before, like old songs I never got tired of. "I love you, Dee."

"Love is the spike." Someone said this to her or she read it, because she just spat it out the way some people say *Dig it*, as if rehearsed. She couldn't even look at me, but I didn't know what to say or how to explain. I said what she already knew.

"I'm scared of needles."

"I'm scared of white college boys in short sleeves." She looked at me, started to look away, but I took her chin and turned her toward me.

"I want you to come with me."

"I want a Marlboro, all I've got are Kents." She lifted her purse from her lap. "Eugene smokes Kents."

"I got Luckies."

"Lucky Strikes are for lunatics."

"Then don't smoke." I leaned back. The chair squeaked again.

"I always smoke with heroin. It's what I do best. Or go with Eugene and get our shoes shined at Kressky's." She leaned way over the table, cupped my chin in her palm. "It's just like making love. That brush move through you like words move through your throat." She laughed, pulled me close, whispered as if it were a secret. "It's like dancing in the movies, when the music starts up and everyone knows their steps even though they're all strangers." She let go of my chin. "You try it. You *really* love me, then try it."

We sat without talking. I needed to convince her to leave goons like Eugene and the dog-faced black bastard at the next table, but I couldn't come up with the words. I knew what I didn't want to talk about—she was always wanting me to try the needle just once. Before she had become a junkie, when she was just using it now and then, she thought it would prove something. "You want to love me, you got to get a little dirty," she had said. I couldn't. I tried to change the subject. "Bob Marley died. Cancer."

She rocked her head without showing any emotion at all.

I needed the words to say how I had missed her, how other girls seemed plain and empty, how we could beat it if she'd just come with me. All that came in my head were the old clichés—*You have to believe in our love*—*We could make it if we believed in each other.* Dee hated those kinds of things, called them *blind talking*. I knew she wouldn't like it, but said, "You have to have some faith."

Saying this, I must have reminded her of something, maybe something she'd heard, maybe just the way I could be, my limitations. Some little recognition flashed in and she came up with one of her Dee-isms. "Faith is the wooden pistol that gets you killed."

"What's that mean?"

She bit her lower lip, looked to the right, the left. "You try it once and I'll go with you."

My throat knotted. It came down to a trade. She'd try my way if I'd try hers. She smiled at me, knowing I was too scared to do it. I decided to throw her fear back at her. "Clean?"

"Jesus, Freddie."

"You've got to quit. We can talk to Lonnie and Wilson."

"I know this shit inside out," she said, her voice flat with real anger. "Heard it in the churchhouse, heard it in the schoolhouse, heard it in the flapbox in my own house, heard it up to here." She sliced her hand across her throat. "And you telling me again? What the fuck for?" She slid her chair back and stood. "Tell me I got hands. Tell me I got feet."

"Clean," I said.

"Fuck you, Freddie. Your world's got no place to shit. You fuck it up by being there." She walked to the door, opened it, leaned on it. "This much is mine," she said.

I looked around at the wooden chairs and card table, the strung-out clowns propping up their faces with their bony fists. "You can have it," I said and looked back to Dee, but she was gone.

I caught up with her fifty yards down the street. She was crying. "Tonight," she said, arms around me again, elbows at my ribs, hands on my shoulder blades, breasts pressed tight against my chest. "We do it tonight, together, and I'll go with you."

"I can't. The whole idea. . ."

"Clean," she said. "You do it once with me, and I'll quit."

"Why?"

"No questions." She thudded my chest with the heel of her hand.

"O.K.," I said. Even as I said it, I knew I wouldn't.

Lonnie didn't answer the door, but I could hear Steel Pulse on the stereo. I tried the knob. The door was unlocked. Lonnie sat on the floor across the room, arms around his long legs, back against the off-white wall. He was wearing white pants with perfect creases and a soft, gray V-neck sweater that gathered at the waist. His eyes focused on the carpet, a blank stare that made him look older than he was and tired, really tired. Even after I closed the door, he didn't look up.

"I found Dee," I said. My stomach jerked just saying it, thinking of the needle. She needed something, like an act of faith, before she could come with me, but I had to think of an alternative, like cutting off an arm or walking barefoot through fire. I wanted to tell Lonnie all this, but he'd say Huck Finn and Nigger Jim, the more I hated her the more I'd love her. "Junkies are dead people," he told me once, while his brother lay in bed in the next room, groaning and sweating through withdrawals. "You can't invest in the dead," he'd said. "You get them back or give them up." Lonnie would want to know why I loved Dee. That was like wanting to know the why of my thoughts, the why of my walk. If my reasons for loving her were bad, I didn't care. I couldn't. Lonnie still just sat, so I said again, "I found Dee."

He nodded, staring at the carpet. His right hand went to his mouth.

I stared at the carpet where he was looking. Nothing was there. "She's going to leave with me."

He moved his head up slowly. "Angela was just here."

"Wilson's Angela?"

"She wanted to borrow money." He lowered his eyes again.

"What's the story, Lonnie?" I squatted to look at him eye to eye. He wouldn't look up. "She with Wilson now?"

His head shook slowly from side to side, eyes still down. "I didn't tell him." His long brown hands covered his eyes, then he raised his head level with mine. "I just gave her the money." He didn't move, hands over his eyes like when we were kids playing hide-and-seek. For a moment, he became a kid, nine years old. I must have become one too because I looked around the room for a couch to crawl under, a door to squeeze behind.

Just when I expected Lonnie to say *Ready or not*, he said, "You *know* what she wanted that money for," and dropped his hands. For an instant he must have seen me still as a little boy because the corners of his mouth pulled back into a surprised smile before falling back into line.

"I thought she was clean. I thought that was the whole point."

"*Was*. She said she kept getting sad." His head started shaking again, back and forth, slowly.

I thought of Wilson in the Coupe de Ville, his long neck curved up, watching the rain explode on the windshield and the people coming and going from the unemployment building. "You've got to tell your brother," I said.

Lonnie's head stopped moving. He looked me straight on. "No, I don't." His stare was so solid I could feel it on my face, like an open hand, one of Lonnie's big hands across my face. He stood. The hand lifted. "I made her promise to leave town. I wouldn't give her the money until she promised."

I stood next to him. "You trust her?"

"No, I don't *trust* her." He brushed his hand across the rear of his immaculate pants. "You want to come with me?"

"Where?"

"I'm going to get my brother and we're going to eat out, some place expensive, then maybe we'll see a movie, or come here and watch television and smoke, or anything."

"Dee and I. . ."

"Dee can't come."

I nodded. "We've got plans."

Lonnie put his arms around me, pulled me close. "You should come with us, Freddie. I'll buy you a steak."

"I can't," I said.

He leaned back, smiled. "A lobster then and I'll introduce you to a woman. Black, if you want black. I even know a very lovely paraplegic who's half Puerto Rican."

Then I surprised myself by putting my arms around Lonnie. "I love Dee," I whispered, right in his ear.

I spent the afternoon with my parents. We couldn't find much to talk about and sat in the TV room watching *Star Trek*—the crew had beamed down to a planet where everyone's dreams came true and all it did was cause them trouble. My parents had moved from the old neighborhood to a trailer park called Happy Trails Trailer Lots. All the mailbox poles looked like hitching posts. My mother said it was very quiet.

Dee had grown up less than a block from where we used to live, but she had never seen the inside of our house until we were in high school. She was quiet around my parents in a way she was with no one else. "They praying I'm a phase," she'd say, once we were out of the house. It became a routine. "Your number one phase wants to go dancing," she'd say. "This phase is getting fat and fat phases never last." One night my parents were having a party. I was in the shower when my father barged in the bathroom drunk. He pulled the curtain aside, saying we needed to talk. I tried to pull the curtain shut again, but he put his arms around me and pressed his face against my chest, even though the water was spraying all over. "Honey," he said, a name he used when he got drunk and sentimental. "She's not just black, she's a nigger. There's a difference." I hit him with the soap and he left.

He apologized the next day, the same day Dee made her biggest effort to get next to them. She told a joke about a dog that loses his tail so he has to wag his tongue. Halfway through it, my father said excuse me and left the room. Mother was ironing and never laughed, but went right into a story about a dog we used to have that died under the house and made a stink. Dee quit trying after that.

Police Woman was on after *Star Trek*. No one liked it, but the TV made it easier for us all to be in the same room. My father got out his needlepoint, which he had taken up after I left. He never wrote letters, but sent ugly needlepoint flowers or doodads and notes mentioning that Rosie Grier did needlepoint. He included the note so I wouldn't think he'd gone queer. Mother drank her beer and said an actress got her start on *The Edge of Night*.

On TV, a sniper wearing a red ski mask aimed his rifle at a woman carrying a shopping bag. Right then it hit me that I was going to have to shoot heroin or lose Dee. I couldn't do either one. The show became a marker. By the time it was over, I would have to go to Dee's and do *something*. I could see the needle pressing against the skin. A little cup in the flesh formed around the point as the needle pressed more. The skin broke, needle sank in, flesh rose around it.

I had to get Dee out of Langston without doing junk. Angie Dickinson, tied with a yellow extension cord to a chair, waggled her butt to scoot the chair across the floor, closer to the window. She was being held hostage by the man in the red ski mask. The show was almost over. I left, trusting my parents to see how Angie escaped.

Dee named the biggest vein in my arm Mississippi and pinched it out with her fingers. She sucked the last of her Pepsi out of the paper cup and set it behind her on the floor. It caught the edge of a magazine and tipped over, spilling beads of ice across the faded yellow tile. Her apartment was one little room in the back of a grocery store. Magazines littered the floor. A thin, striped mattress lay flat in one corner, partially covered by a dirty pink sheet. A TV rattled on in another corner, but I didn't look. I didn't want to see the needle. Instead, I looked at a poster, curling at the edges, hanging crooked on the wall, a picture of the earth taken from space. The world was blue, streaked with white. It looked like a great place. Paper-clipped to the poster was a photo of Dee, Lonnie and me from our trip to L.A. to see Bob Marley and the Wailers. I had my arm around Dee and Lonnie had his arm around me.

I had delayed as much as I could, talking about my classes, where we would live, my parents, *Star Trek*, how I threw beer at Eugene, Angela borrowing money from Lonnie. I tried to distract myself from the needle, couldn't; tried to think of it as walking barefoot through fire.

I pumped up my arm when she told me to. The photograph was dark. We were all smiling. She tied my arm off with a vinyl belt. I tried to remember the Wailers live. She pinched out the vein again. "Put some Bob Marley on," I said, head still turned.

"Traded all I had to Eugene."

"For what?" I asked. Instead of answering, she stuck the needle in my arm.

My arm tensed hard as wood, but the needle was already out, the belt off. Something like sleep turned in my chest, came up my throat on a wave of static, then flooded out all over. Even my fingers filled with light. "Jesus," I said.

"Our savior," Dee laughed.

I started to turn to her, but began yawning. In the TV in the blue corner: Chef Boyardi, Tony the Tiger, the Shell Fact Man, the flat yellow hat the laughing blond pressed against her breasts. Beside the set: a sour, gray apple whose skin curled around a missing piece like lips protecting teeth. A gurgle from Dee I had to laugh with. Dolphins standing straight up in the television like children choosing sides for baseball. It was like a movie, this life. The crushed cup, drained of Pepsi, had bunches of ice that looked like caviar. I said, "Caviar," and slipped a piece into Dee's mouth.

"When *you* ever seen caviar?" She was laughing.

I decided we should make love. Little legs began crawling across my cheek but I scratched them off. Dee lay back on the pink sheet, kissing me once, her lips fibrous as peaches. I couldn't get it up, even though my currents sizzled like rain on asphalt, like a scaled fish in saltwater.

"You don't need to fuck on junk," Dee said. "You don't need to do anything."

"I want to," I said. "It's Christmas," meaning we hadn't made love since I left in December. A fly landed on my face, but it was not a fly. "Is there something on my face?"

She smiled, lit a Kent 100. The smoke came inside my lungs liquid. If you listened to a smoking cigarette, it sounded like TV static, like locusts, like heroin humming through the veins inside your skull.

Dee laughed and that started me laughing. She walked from the mattress to the TV, stepping only on magazines. "Piranhas," she said and pointed to the yellow tile.

I joined her. We stepped from magazine to magazine, as if from stone to stone, above the maneaters. At the TV, she turned off the sound, abandoned the game, and walked to the stereo. She put on an album of saxophones I didn't recognize, then locked her arms around me. "You do love me," she said.

"I must," I said. My stomach started twisting. Dee led me to the bathroom. I knelt in front of the toilet but didn't vomit. We began dancing to the saxophones, slow at first, then faster, pushing off the walls to send us across the floor faster. We slid on the magazines, and that became a part of the step.

I began throwing up and that became a part of the dance too. We were both laughing. She kissed me hard. Our tongues became part of the dance. Vomit trailed across her mouth and down her cheek. We danced back to the mattress and pulled at each other's clothes. The music was over, maybe for a long time.

I kissed her breasts, bit her ribs. My fingers sank into the soft of her butt. "Freddie," she said, and I raised my head. "We can really get out?" I kissed her again, wiped the vomit from her face. "Freddie," she said again.

"We can get out," I said. "Eight hundred miles." I entered her. We made love for what may have been a long while. And all the time, inside the frenzy was the calm. Memory hovered about my head, becoming visible at intervals, like particles of dust in twilight—the alley behind the Bree where we bought pot, beneath the slide in the Woodard schoolyard where Dee and I first made love, the corner of Fifth and Main where the knobby prostitutes hawked, the vacant lot behind Mesa Drive-In where we made up dialogue for the huge silent screen, all the places we grew up lost—the men in suits and vests with high-polish shoes, the bearded transvestite who collected bottles in the basket of his bicycle, the black butcher with red slabs of meat, the abandoned Sinclair station covered with names, my name, Dee's, Lonnie's, Wilson's, Eugene's—the curtains of my parents' house drawn closed, the liquor store on Forty-ninth with the neon dinosaur, the all-night diner on Fourth Avenue, Lonnie's Coupe de Ville, the asphalt bedrooms, the unemployment building, my mother, who told me the last people who lived here didn't know how to behave.

"It's like dancing in the movies," Dee said, her hand on my chest. She laughed, looked confused. "Did I already say that?" She pulled gently at my dick. "I love you, Freddie. A lot. A very lot."

We slept.

"She just wasn't there," I said to Lonnie. The windows were starting to go dark and no sign of Dee all day. My head was clear, arm a little sore, and that grown-up feeling, age that just fell into me like a brick into a pond. Not that I liked needles or wanted junk, but I knew I couldn't tell Lonnie about heroin ever, and knowing that put a distance between us, made me feel older. "I slept late and she was just gone."

"You know where she is." He was on the floor, propping himself up with his elbows. Lonnie always sat on the floor if he had a choice.

"I know what she's doing. I don't know where she is."

Lonnie let his head drop back. He had the same long neck as his brother. He and Wilson had eaten last night across town, then drank beer at Mesa Drive-In, laughing and watching James Bond. All the tension Lonnie had the night before was gone. His brother was at a local concert in memory of Bob Marley. Lonnie believed he was safe, at least for the night. He lifted his head, smiled at me, straightened his black, pinstriped shirt. "We'll look for her," he said. "Then we'll put you both on a bus."

We drove the old streets, checked the regular spots—like the old times, me and Lonnie cruising, looking for familiar cars, waiting for something to happen. There was no sign of Dee. We decided to try the reggae concert, although neither of us thought she would have the money for it. On our way, Lonnie spotted Eugene's old Chrysler parked on a dark stretch of Thirty-second Street. We cut around and pulled up to the car.

A Mexican with long, frizzy hair lay on the hood of the Chrysler. Eugene sat behind the wheel, hand tapping the dash. Beside him, the dog-faced junkie from the Bree. "Don't stop," Eugene said as we pulled up next to the car. "We waiting here. You can't stop."

"You seen Dee?" I leaned over next to Lonnie, tried to see in the car.

"No, no, fuck." Eugene looked in his rearview mirror. Headlights appeared from around the corner, then stopped a hundred yards before reaching the cars. "She ain't here, come on." His hand hammered the dash faster.

I started to ask again, but Lonnie pulled out, U-turned so we didn't go by the other car. "Let them be," he said. "Let them rest in peace."

The headlights neared Eugene's car. A head rose from the backseat of the Chrysler. "There's somebody in the backseat," I said.

Lonnie shrugged. "Doesn't mean it's Dee. Besides, we can't stop what's going on there."

The reggae concert was in an old warehouse and sold out. From the outside, all we could hear was the bass. I tried to imagine it as part of a song, but it distorted everything. We drove again. Lonnie produced a joint. I only smoked a little. The night was dark, sky empty. I remembered something from the night before. "Let's go to the old Sinclair station," I said.

"They tore it down," Lonnie said.

We drove out on the loop we always used to take. I caught Lonnie staring at his reflection in the dark window and we laughed about that. The neon sign for the Oasis Motel read *as s Mot l*, gas gauge read under a quarter of a tank. Lonnie's car had only AM radio. All we could find was cowboy music and people talking on telephones.

Lonnie turned the radio off. He looked straight ahead, one hand pinching the crease in his pants. "I love you, Freddie," he said, "but you're not strong enough. She'll drag you down. It's dirty, Freddie. It's ugly."

I turned to him, opened my mouth to speak, and suddenly I realized why Dee had wanted me to shoot heroin. She had to see if I could be strong, if I could do the thing I hated most *for her*. It hit me so hard, I almost told Lonnie, so I would never hear Huck Finn and Nigger Jim again. Instead, I said, "I can be stronger than you think."

We turned back.

Lonnie took Fifth. It was mainly residential and good at night because there was never any traffic and no cops. He wanted to smoke another joint. I fumbled through the glove-box to find one. The yards were green all year round, trimmed straight to give them edges. I lit the joint just before we reached Fifth Street Park, a big grassy area with trees and swings. A car pulled out of the park and approached with its lights off. As it passed, I recognized Eugene and his beat-up Chrysler. I tried to see who else was in the car but couldn't make out anyone. Lonnie just shrugged.

As we drew nearer to the park, I saw a dark mound in the grass twenty yards from the street. I pointed. Lonnie stopped the car. We looked at it through the windshield. It didn't move. I couldn't tell whether the mound was a man or woman. Lonnie cut the engine. The night was perfectly quiet. Fear entered me like heroin had, turning in my chest, filling me. I hoped it was that dog-faced junkie from the Bree or the Mexican who had lain on the hood of Eugene's Chrysler or someone I had never seen or heard of. I felt like we should run to it, but we walked close to one another, very slowly.

"No," Lonnie said. "No, no."

Wilson's head twisted to the side, vomit was spattered across his chin, shoulder.

We squatted beside the body. Lonnie began crying. Neither of us wanted to touch the body, but one of his arms was wrenched behind his back. I couldn't leave him that way. I pulled on the arm at the elbow.

The arm jerked, eyelids rose. "Hey, brother," Wilson said. He smiled a goofy smile and lifted himself up on his elbows.

"Jesus," I said. "We thought you were dead."

"I puked all over Eugene's car," he said, still smiling.

Lonnie raised his hand and slapped Wilson hard. He was still crying, trembling.

Wilson just fell back. "I'm sorry," he said.

Lonnie stood, one hand over his eyes. He brought up the other to cover his mouth.

I kissed Lonnie on the cheek, a love kiss, but not a lover's kiss.

"She promised she'd leave," Lonnie said.

"You can't blame Angela for this," Wilson said, up again on one elbow. "Angela?" he called out. He turned to the dark and vacant park. "Angela?"

309

The bus out of Langston moved like a sick dog. Dee, in the window seat, looked at the same streets she'd seen all her life. The early morning light made everything look fake, like movie scenery. We went by the liquor store on Forty-ninth, the neon dinosaur flickering blue, past the grocery store Dee lived behind, still lit by its nighttime lights. Eugene was squatting next to the grocery door. His back partially covered the diagonal yellow band advertising bread. WONDER, the sign read. Dee put her head on my shoulder. "I guess this street don't owe me nothing I ain't already took."

I put my hand on her cheek. She had been sleeping on the porch of Lonnie's apartment when we pulled in. We had taken Wilson inside, then I woke her. "Eight hundred miles," she had said, high on junk but ready to go. And we were going. I tilted our seats back and closed my eyes.

"Your place have carpet?" Dee asked. "I hate carpet."

"We can pull it out," I said.

"It's a few things I can't tolerate and carpet's one."

"You don't have to talk," I said. "I'm too tired to laugh."

She kissed my cheek and we rode on, but I couldn't sleep. I didn't want to think about Lonnie and Wilson starting over again and again, or Eugene sitting in the Chrysler beating the dash, waiting for headlights. I didn't even want to think about me and Dee—it made me tired. And scared.

I tried again to hear Bob Marley, but his music just wouldn't come. I pictured him on stage in the blue light with the silver mike. Instead, I saw him skinny in some hospital bed, shitting in his sleep, his breath already the color of death, thinking It all comes down to this moment, trying to say what was left inside, what hadn't been strangled by the white hands of cancer. I tried to hear Marley's words and wondered if the vision grew soft before the mind or the mind before the vision.

Then I heard Bob Marley.

His voice was nothing like the living Marley's voice. It was flat, even, without any Jamaican accent. "Bury the swollen tongues of the dead," he said, and I understood that the faith of the living was with the dead and the faith of the dead with the living.

The bus rattled across a hole in the road, then lugged as it entered the freeway. Dee slept. The driver downshifted. We picked up speed. The sky grew light but without color, like concrete. I looked to Dee and she opened her eyes.

"Shh," she said, then fell back to sleep.

The Singing Well

Helen Norris

She was Emilu, named for two dead aunts, their names rammed together head-on like trains. And she thought as she lay on her back in the corn, racing her feet a toe at a time up the head-high stalks, letting one foot, then the other win: How you gonna handle these things that come up? Get around these grown-ups pushin' you into some kinda way you never wanted to be? But if you grew up so you could outsmart 'em, then you did what they wanted. You got yourself grown and no turnin' back. And maybe you couldn't stand it that way and waited around and hoped you would die, with cancer even, just to get it over. The way it seemed to her a lot of them did.

She was past eleven going on twelve and out of the torment of school for a while. The days of summer were long at first and then ran away like a rabbit flushed out of a blackberry bush. It scared her some, not just to be looking down the barrel of school. Eleven years old and going on twelve, she was staring right now both ways at once. She had got her feet planted plumb in the ground to keep from getting any older at all. But all the time she needed to get there. She had to know more, just to stay the same.

She knew that she was smarter than Melissa, her sister who grew up enough to get married. And smarter than Jo-Jo, who was off at their Uncle Joe's for the summer. But it wasn't sufficient. This thing coming at her was as big as a barn. Plowing her up into something else. Sometimes it was a freight train running her down. Sometimes she felt she was in there swimming and going under for the final time.

And then her grandfather came in July and she grabbed ahold of him to keep afloat.

How can you grow up when you have a grandfather like a Santa Claus

311

with his beard cut off and he calls you little daughter and feeds you peanuts one at a time?

When he got out of the truck with her father, bigger almost than she had remembered, her mother said, "Emilu, run carry that box he's got in his hand. Lord knows what's in it." Emilu ran and dropped it hard coming up the steps. It flew apart, with an old uniform falling into the nandinas. And her mother said, "Well, I might've known. Well, bring it on in."

He was in his room when she got it together. The door was ajar. She waited in the hall. When she heard silence she edged in slowly with the box in her arms. He was sitting on the brass bed all hunched over, his chin down into the front of his shirt. His chest caved in and his face was like he was sorry he came.

She said to him then, "I folded it good." They looked at one another across the years between. Her mother had said he was seventy-seven. "It's got real pretty buttons sewed on."

He must have been, easy, six foot tall and big around. Like a football player with everything on, and shoulders big and round like a bear's. He had a great head of wavy white hair that curled around and under his ears. A sunned kind of face without many lines and blue-fire eyes that were almost hidden by the shelf of his brow and the white eyebrows that went so wild they must have been raked in the wrong direction. His hands were huge and brown from the sun, with white hairs matting on the backs of his fingers. His glance wavered, then returned to her. There was something in it different this visit from last.

"Are you Melissa?" he asked.

She was surprised and even shocked at his words. "No, Grandpa, I'm Emmy." He had called her that.

"Emmy?" He looked at the mirror above the green-painted dresser. "Not Melissa?"

"No, sir. . . Melissa got married and lives in Lafayette."

His glance swept her with such a lost look that she told him again, "I'm Emmy, sir."

He was very strange. But his blue eyes beheld her without a rejection. "Emmy. . . Emmy. . ." He moved a little inside his great frame and rubbed his arm. "I'll tell you how it is."

She waited for him to tell her but he seemed to have forgotten or thought better of it. "What, Grandpa?"

His eyes circled the room. "Is this the same room I stayed in before?"

"Sure, Grandpa."

"Same mirror and all?"

"Sure it is. . . You don't remember?"

He looked at her hard. "I'll tell you how it is: I don't recall you."

She was really amazed, but she tried not to show it. "We played euchre and all. You taught me, remember? Slapjack. Every day."

He shook his head slowly. "No. No, I don't recall." He spoke so sadly that she wanted to run away. "But it seems like whoever you are. . . it seems like a good thing, you standin' here now." He smiled at her almost. "We was good friends, you say?"

"We played euchre every day."

"What did I call you?"

"Emmy. You called me Emmy, like everybody does exceptin' Mama."

"You feel right. Somehow. How old would you be?"

"Eleven last month. I was nine before."

She couldn't wait to tell her mother.

"We shouldn't have him this summer. I said so to your father. He looks healthy. I will say that. I can't deny he's a downright specimen of health." Then she flattened her lips. "But his mind. . ."

"What's wrong with it?" said Emilu.

"Well, it's gone, that's all."

Emilu was defensive. "He talks all right."

"Talks!" her mother said and turned away to run water on the beans. "Just stay out of his way."

"Why?"

Her mother flung a sideways look at her. "Folks like that get full of notions." And she left the room with the water still on.

Emilu sucked the knuckle of her finger. Her mother never came right out and answered a question. You thought you had her on the track and then she ducked into a side road.

Emilu ran out the back and circled the house. She could look through his window and see him on the bed. He hadn't moved. He seemed just the way he was two years ago. They stared at each other the way she had looked at a deer she met once that Jo-Jo had trapped and he looked at her knowing she wasn't the one did it but there he was in the fix he was in. She came in the front door and down the hall to him again.

He seemed glad she was there. She sat down at length on the chair by his bed. Then he opened his suitcase and rumpled around and came up with a bag of peanuts. He sat back on the bed and gave one to her and one to himself. They were very still while they looked at one another across their chewing.

That night before she went off to sleep she could hear him moving in the room across the hall, then a scraping sound, a sour wail of furniture being dragged across the floor. It went on for some time. She could hear her mother in the room next to hers. "My God, what's he doin'? I can't stand it, Ray." She heard her father's muffled voice. . .

And then it was daylight. The wind outside was rattling the shutters. She woke up thinking it was still the furniture being dragged around, then knowing it wasn't.

When she went to his room she saw the dresser standing slap across the corner. And now a square of dust marked the place it had been. He was sitting on the bed looking out of the window at the waving trees.

She was full of the morning. "How come you moved the dresser around in the night?"

He looked at her with haunted eyes.

"Grandpa. . . how come?"

He shook his head. "It ain't the same room," he said at last.

She started to tell him that it really was, but she stopped herself. She could hear the geese being chased by the dog. She could hear the bus passing, rounding the curve, and then taking the hill. She sat on the bed and swung her feet. "You wanta play euchre?"

He shook his head. "I don't recall it none."

"You taught me, Grandpa. I could teach you how. I remember it real good."

"Wouldn't serve. I'd fergit."

She said with pride, "I never forgot nothin' I ever knew."

He shook his head in wonder. "It goes," he said. "I can't figger where it goes, but it goes all right. . . I think when it all goes what'll I be then? What'll I be just a settin' somewhere? Sometimes it scares the livin' hell outa me."

She swung her feet. "I know ever dadblasted thing ever happen to me."

"You think so, little daughter. But there is things gittin' away from you in the night when you fergit to hold on."

She shook her head. "Not me. I got it all somewhere. In my head, I reckon."

"Course you ain't live long. There just ain't that much."

"There's a plenty, I guarantee. There is plenty done happen."

"Well, hold onto it, little daughter."

"I'm a holdin' on."

She got up and walked to the square of dust where the dresser had been. With her toe she scraped a circle and a zigzag line. "Slapjack is nothin' to it. How long you figger you can hold onto somethin'?"

"No way a tellin'. Hard to say, little daughter."

She swallowed twice. "You called me that before. . . when you were here before. You called me little daughter."

"Did I, now? I musta liked you mighty well."

"Oh, you did. You did. Better than the others. Sometimes we sung songs. On the porch. In the dark. We sung 'Old Black Joe' and 'Oh! Susannah, don't you cry for me. . .'" She was pleading now.

"I don't recall," he said.

A feeling of hopelessness swept over her. The two of them sat there locked in mourning.

"We got to start over," he told her gently. "You willin', little daughter?"

She was sad in a way she had never been before. He patted her hair. "You willin', little daughter?"

But she did not reply.

"Was you wearin' your hair a little different?" he said.

"Just the same," she said faintly and shook her brown mane. "Chopped off straight. I just can't stand it no other way."

"You willin', little daughter? It's hard," he acknowledged. "I know it ain't fair. . ."

Her voice was uncertain. "But it seems like you don't want to start over, Grandpa. I could help but it seems like you don't want to try."

He was silent for a while. "I got somethin' on my mind, little daughter, to 'tend to. . . I can't think a nothin' else. It's on me night and day."

"What is it?" she said.

"It's a misty thing now. But what's so strong is how good it was. Good. Good. If I could remember it. If I could get it back once and then tell somebody who wouldn't let go. . ."

He looked at her with something like a plea in his eyes. "That's where maybe you could come in."

"Where, Grandpa?"

"You gonna come in two ways, little mother. You gonna help me remember and then you take it from me and you don't let it go."

"So I can tell you again in case you forget?"

"No. . . no. I wouldn't need it again. Just need you to have it. Just to not let it go. Now, I'm gonna die. Someday not far away. Who cares?"

"I care, Grandpa." Then she said, disbelieving, "But someday I'm gonna die."

"Don't you think it. You gonna live forever. And if you felt yourself slippin' you could tell somebody. . . You could tell the best person you happen to know. . . like I'm tellin' you. . . when I git it back."

"Am I the best person you know?"

"You are the one best person left with any walkin'-about sense."

She swung her feet. "That ain't the general opinion around here."

"It's mine," he said.

"What about Grandma?"

"Best woman I ever knew. But she's gone, you know."

He stared out the window. "There was a thing that happen to me once. Best thing ever happen. I never told nobody, it was that good."

"You gonna tell me?"

"I'm gonna tell you if I can recall it. *If* I can recall it. If. . . if."

"If it was that good, how come you forgot it?" She was sorry she'd said it, for his face clouded over.

"I ain't entirely done that, little daughter. There's somethin' still there. But it don't come together. I hold onto one thing and somethin' else goes. . . It's gotta be the right kinda weather for holdin'. Today is no good. There's a wind a blowin'. We could work on it maybe we could tomorrow."

She listened to the sucking of wind in the eaves and beyond it the murmur of wind in the corn.

"When it blows I can't recollect one damn thing."

He did not seem to want to talk anymore. She studied a stain on the papered ceiling and decided it looked like a crow or a buzzard. After a while she got up. His eyes had gone into the cave of his brows.

"Grandpa," she said, "you gonna recollect it. I double-dog guarantee it you will."

She went outside and raced up the bank that surrounded the yard. The house was built in a wooded hollow that held a fall of rain like a bowl. She walked barefoot through the rim of corn her father had planted to hold the bank. The silk was bronzed and hung from the ears in tassels that seemed to beckon the wind. She pulled away some and stuffed it into her own two ears. She closed her eyes and between the rows wandered deaf and blind, groping for stalks, plunging, weaving one row with another. But still she could hear a bird mournfully chirping. She followed its cry. "I hear you, little bird. . . I'm comin', little bird. . . You need me, little bird." She stepped on a rock and opened her eyes. Standing on one foot, she spat on her toe and rubbed it up and down and sideways.

His door, when she passed it again, was still open and she looked inside. He was sitting in the chair. The box for the uniform was in his lap. He looked at her as if she had never left the room. "I see a well. . . But it's blowin' too hard. Too hard to tell."

At last she said, "Grandpa? What happened had a well?"

He moved his head slowly from side to side. "Hold onto it," he said.

That night before she slept she seemed to hear him singing in his room across the hall. It was a strange kind of tune. But not a tune at all, as if the notes got lost and he had to start again.

Her mother was a woman who put up food. When she was settled down into it somebody seemed to have started a war, and Emilu said the next bus that came she was climbing on. Each day was closer to the end of the world till it felt like a yell coming out of her chest. You better clear out or you'd get yourself sliced and chopped and crushed and scorched and stirred, boiled over and mopped from the stove and the floor. Her mother pink-faced, with pale hair loose and hanging in strings that had got in the jam or the succotash. "Emilu, will you hand me the mop?" And her daddy saying, "Mavis, when are we eatin'?" "Well, Ray, you see me. I can't let go. Well, fix yourself somethin'. Emilu, fix your father somethin' to eat." And Emilu saying under her breath, "This family is nuts," and thinking that for a grown-up man her father was as helpless as Barrelhead, who had to have something dumped in his dish. How come you could call yourself fully growed-up, enough to have half of your hair done gone, and couldn't slide a piece of cheese into some bread?

"I ain't gonna never get married," she said. "I double-dog guarantee it I won't."

"Suit yourself," said her mother.

"I double-dog guarantee if I did I wouldn't put nothin' up in jars. It like to ruin ever summer there is."

"Watch your tongue, Emmy," her father said.

What with living through all the fury of canning, half the time she would go what somebody present would call too far and get sent from the table before dessert. Now that her grandfather was here for the summer, her mother cut her eyes to him as Emilu rose. "I hate to have your grandfather see you like this."

"He'll have to get used to it," Emilu said. "Ever'thing around here ends up I did it."

She went to her room and lay on her bed with her feet against the headboard. Without turning over she could reach underneath and ease out the box that held her secret things. On the lid she had written "Keep out or die." She opened it on her stomach and went through all its contents. A large dead June bug, a stick of teaberry gum, and a valentine that pictured a fluffy iced cake and was inscribed underneath: "You are the icing on my cake." On the back was printed "I could devour you" and below, "Guess who" with a series of question marks. She had thought it came from Alma, but Alma said no, it was probably a boy.

She reviewed the possibility with horror and delight. She tore the gum in half and chewed out the sweet of it to make up for dessert.

Later on, she heard her grandfather moving the dresser around in his room. She got up and went to him. He had pushed it back into the place where it belonged.

He looked at her from where he stood by the window. "That woman muddies up my mind."

"You mean Mama?" she asked.

"I don't recall her," he said. "Was she here before?"

Emilu nodded.

"Well, she muddies my mind. Some women clear things. Your grandma. . . she did."

"What about me, Grandpa?"

"You clear things, little woman."

Her throat filled with pride.

"I been tryin' to get it straight."

She thought at first he meant who everyone was. But then she saw he meant the thing that had happened once. She heard her mother coming down the hall and slammed the door. She went and sat on the bed. "We gotta think about it harder."

He watched her in a kind of rich despair.

"Today is good," she said, coaxing him. "No rain. The sun is shinin'. The wind ain't blowin'."

He dropped into the chair before her. He hunched his head deep into the cave of his shoulders.

She sat and willed him to remember, holding her breath in as long as she could, plunging from one breathful into another.

"Little daughter. . ."

She sat stone-still and waited.

"There's a kinda mist. . . but I see a well. . ."

Still she waited. Then she said softly, as if she stroked a bird, "You already saw that, Grandpa." She waited again. "I got it for you."

He turned to look at her deeply. "You got it locked up tight? You won't fergit?"

She shook her head. "I got it."

She slung the hair from her eyes to see the things in his face. "Was it a real long time ago?"

"I reckon. It gits so it don't hardly matter when. It gits in your head and it don't hardly matter when it was. It's like it was in your blood," he said. "It's like it was always there."

There was pain in her chest from slowing her breath.

He began at last, "There comes a singin' in and outa my mind."

"I heard you singin' some in the night."

"It gits lost somewhere."

She smoothed his spread with a freckled hand. "It don't have to get lost with me to listen. I remember ever tune I ever heard, I guarantee. Words too." She waited for him. "Is it got some words to it, Grandpa?"

"I can't hardly say. I hear the tune, the way it went. . ."

She swung her feet and then she made them stop. "Maybe if you was to shut your eyes like it was dark."

He stared at her fiercely from under his wild brows. She could see in his eyes how it was he sailed his mind like a kite on a string and the two of them watched it soar above the house. He was seeing her now as if she was the string that he wouldn't let go. "I hear a kinda beat like a heartbeat in the ground. I hear it but I feel it."

"What is it?" she said.

"It was turnin' red."

"And singin'?" she said.

His mind caught in the branches of the sycamore behind him.

"And singin', Grandpa?"

He was caught. He was lost.

She was waiting and wishing the tree frogs would shut up their racket for once. Barrelhead the dog began to bark at the squirrels. The bus in the distance had almost made the hill. At last she said, "Grandpa?"

His eyes had never left her face.

"Do you think you might of dreamed it?"

"No! No! It happened. Don't never say that again. . . Just hold onto what I give you. Are you doin' that, Mother?"

"I got it ever bit."

Sometimes he seemed to think that she was her grandmother whom she had never known. Sometimes she seemed to be his daughter, Aunt Lou, her father's sister whose name was part of her own. She was afraid to ask. She wanted him to have her whichever way he would.

Slowly, very slowly, his eyes lost light and seemed to recede beneath the crag of his brow. A dark, baffled look came over his face. "I lost it," he said.

They sat together, grieving, hearing the guineas gone to roost in the tree.

"I lost it," he said. Over the hill the train hit the bridge with a mournful cry and beat along the trestle and echoed in the hollow.

She went out and crossed the road and climbed the hill. If a bus came by beneath she liked to practice her aim and pitch a rock at its roof.

319

There was no bus in sight. It was maybe too late. She slithered down the hill to the tracks and walked a rail. It was cold as winter ice. She had learned how to skip along the rail and never fall. She skipped to a killdeer sitting on the track and flipped a rock to make him fly. She used to put nails where the train would make them flat. Her father said it was illegal. Now she felt a mingling of yearning and defiance. In the failing light she found a lid from a snuff can tossed between the ties. She laid it on the rail and willed the train to change it into something shining that had never been before.

After supper was over she went to her room. She lay on her back with her head at the foot to keep from going to sleep, legs perfectly straight, staring into the dark. She listened to the silence in her grandfather's room. She probed her own mind for the memory he sought, thrusting to the darkness and beyond to where it lay. Then the night opened like a hole in a gunnysack and covered her head. In a moment she slept. . .

But she woke in the dark to the sound of his song. She lay still and listened. It was almost her dream. She got up and tiptoed to his door.

His singing was strange. It was not any song she had ever heard before. It had no words, just his voice, a little cracked, humming, calling the notes, as if he were lulling her back into sleep. She rubbed her eyes awake and listened intently with her ear to the door. She hummed beneath her breath until the tune was in her head. Then she slipped back to bed and sang it to herself till she had it for good. She sang it to the train and it answered her back as it skimmed the rails, making something shining for her in the dark.

The next day after lunch her mother called her to the kitchen to pick up the clean clothes and put them away.

"Emilu, I wish you'd stay away from those tracks. I knew a woman caught her foot in them once, and along came the train."

"What happened?"

"What happened! She got killed, that's what."

"Did she get it caught where the rails got hitched or under the rail or under the tie?"

"Now, how would I know? She didn't live to tell us."

"I bet she was wearin' shoes. . . I wouldn't have on shoes."

Her mother left the room with the towels. Emilu called out, "Was she kin to us?"

"No, she wasn't kin. Nobody kin to us would do a crazy thing like that."

"If she wasn't kin to us I bet it never happened. Somebody made it up to scare people off a trains."

320

Her mother appeared in the doorway. "Emilu, it's time you grew up to your age."

"I ain't got the slightest idea what that means." She looked at her toes and the bottoms of her feet.

She went out to the barn and stared a hen in the eye and shooed the red one off her nest. She took one of the three tan-colored eggs and put it in her pocket and whistled from the doorway. After a while she walked behind the sycamore tree and pulled a leaf and laid it on the ground and broke the egg into it neatly. She knelt and touched the sulfur half-moon with the tip of her tongue. Then she called to Barrelhead to come and get it.

She went looking for her grandfather and found him asleep beneath the sugarberry tree. She sat down beside him.

She watched him sleep, his white hair stirring in the breeze. Crickets were jumping from the grass to brush his great brown hand that hung from the arm of the wicker chair. He was the oldest person she had ever known, and at the same time he was like a little baby that needed a mother. Nobody but herself would pay him any mind. Her mother seemed to think he was too much trouble just to have at the table, and now she let Emilu take his breakfast to his room. And her father never talked to him hardly at all. They talked around him at the table like he wasn't there. . . She began to sing softly the song she had heard him making in the night. She sang it over and over again till after a while it seemed to be her song for singing him asleep. He woke up and listened with his eyes half closed. Then he shut them again and she thought he'd drifted off. But in a moment he said, "It was a woman done the singin'. It was like I was dreamin'. But when I come to she was singin' for real."

She listened in wonder. "Was it Grandma done the singin'?"

"No. . . no. But the moon was the brightest I ever seen."

He went to sleep again.

Her mother came to look at him and shake her head. "If it starts to rain I want that wicker chair inside."

"Mama," said Emilu, "can't you see he's asleep!"

"Well, I see that, Emilu. I don't need to be told. But if he's here for the summer we'll have to have things understood."

"I ain't got the slightest idea what that means."

"Never mind what it means. But I wish you wouldn't hang around him all the time."

"First it's the tracks and now it's Grandpa. There is more things around that I ain't got permission than there is I can do."

"Watch your tongue, Emilu."

Emilu stuck out her tongue and crossed her eyes to see it.

She had her supper and just before dark, while they sat around the table, she climbed the hill. The dark rails were now almost the color of the ground. They were like velvet ribbons you could hardly see. She skipped along one till she came to the shining round disc that caught light from the sky. The lid from the snuff can was like silver money and thin as thin. She picked it up and kissed it again and again.

She heard a mewing sound and turned to see that Barrelhead had followed her. He could sound like a cat enough to fool a kitten. "Go back," she commanded. "Barrelhead, go back." He sat down at once, blinking his eyes into the risen moon. Finally he turned and slunk away up the hill. "And don't you go blabbin' on me," she called.

Then she was walking the rail in moonlight, treading its silver. To make her free, in her mouth she held the silver disc with its faint snuff taste of honey and spice. Free of growing up. . . whatever it was.

She heard in the distance the song of the train. It was calling to her like the bird in the corn. She was nearing the trestle. Deep in the iron her bare feet knew the yielding and tremor. The hollow below her was faintly in bloom. She walked straight on as she stepped to the bridge and boarded the trestle. The rails sang out. Around the curve toward her the great beast hurtled; she saw the trees ashen in its aureole of light. It sprang to the trestle. The white rails stammered. The churning of wheels. And then the glory of the shining rails.

Sucked into thunder, she turned and ran. Buried in thunder, running in terror, reaching the end, dropping to the gulley to dwell forever in the house of thunder. She was rolling over, naked to the storm. Her heart was drowned, her life dissolving in the roar of the wheels.

She came to rest at the bottom of the gulley. She floated over the world like foam. The frogs came back, tremulous, halting, then mounting a tenor of sad betrayal, then screaming as they remembered their song. She lay very still, and after a while she pitched her trembling voice to theirs. She could not tell if she made a sound. But beneath the moon she heard the singing in the well. She herself was in the well and heard the voice spilling down. For a moment she thought that she was dead, stone-cold train-dead.

The cry rose inside her: If I got myself killed nobody could help. I'm the onliest one there is knows about the well. Not even Grandpa remembers it now.

She got up slowly and clawed her way through vines and frogs. At the top she found the silver round still clamped in her teeth. She took it out and buried it beneath a rock. . .

Her father saw her in the hall. What happened to you?"

"I fell down."

He looked her over and sighed. "You all right?"

"Sure."

He opened his bedroom door and went in.

She stopped outside her grandfather's room and listened for a time to his gentle snore. And through the door she whispered to him: "Grandpa, I outraced a train."

Then she undressed and lay down to sleep. And the thunder shook her and shook her bed. She lay on her back and crushed the pillow to her face and choked and sobbed. I almost died, God. You 'most let me die. And God said, What got into you, Emilu? And Emilu said, I wish I knew.

In the night a rising wind was raking the leaves, and she covered her head to shut it out. She knew that tomorrow he would be caved in with everything in him slipped off somewhere.

In the morning he was desolate, hollow-eyed.

She became after that a watcher of weather. Fearful, she would sniff the damp in the air. When the wind hunkered down in the hollow flinging the leaves, drumbeating the panes with fingers of rain, in another year she would have dashed through the trees, clarion with joy until they called her to shelter. Now she despaired, prowling in the hallway outside his room, gliding in to coax, "Don't worry, Grandpa. It won't last long."

But the rain ran down through the fissures in the bank to fill the bowl, and the house was a boat aground in the shallows. The pale moon floated its face in the yard for half the night. The geese honked curses from their dry retreat in a hollow oak. The watchdog guineas, gray and drenched, sat high on the branches above her window and warned of the wind in querulous tones. Below them, the tree frogs screeched their dominion of the sodden world—till daylight came.

She stole in softly with his plate of breakfast. He lay in bed. "Eat it hot, Grandpa. It will help you remember."

She sat brooding over him, warm with her tenderness, smoothing his cover. "Grandpa, there is a whole heap a little things I got locked in my mind. About the well and the singin' and the lady and all." She let her eyes stroke his bulky form. "Some other things too. All we got to do is get it together."

"I don't recollect a damn thing today."

323

"I could sing you the song."

"Give me the box, little woman." He pointed to it in the corner of the room.

She brought the box and took off the lid. He sat up and propped the pillow behind him. Then he drew from the box his uniform jacket and inched one arm into a sleeve. It was too small to cover more than half his chest.

"Did it shrink?" she asked.

He shook his head.

"You musta had it a long time ago."

He thought of it, frowning, with some surprise. "I don't recall."

"It's got real nice pretty buttons sewed on." Then she fed him some of the cereal. He ate it thoughtfully from her spoon.

"Little daughter," he said, "you got pretty ways."

"That ain't the general opinion around here."

"It's mine," he said.

He drank a little milk. "I think that woman out there wants me to leave."

"You mean Mama?"

"I don't recall her," he said.

"She ain't got such a crush on me neither, I guarantee."

They brooded together. He pulled the jacket a little more across his chest.

She swallowed on the words. "If you was to leave I wouldn't have nobody here."

He thought of it, his blue eyes circling the room. "You gonna help me, little mother. You gonna help me git it back."

She got up and closed the door and sat down again. She began to sing him softly the song of the well. He listened intently, then he hummed it to himself, breaking into a croon, his voice rising and sinking. His voice seemed to listen. And she listened with it, falling into its dream.

One day she brought his breakfast and he wasn't in his room. She put it down and waited. When he didn't return she tried the bathroom down the hall. The door was standing open. He was not inside. Her heart was in her throat. She closed the door to his room so her mother wouldn't see his breakfast on the tray. She searched for him among the trees in the hollow, with Barrelhead before her yipping at the squirrels. She looked into the corn and the wagon shed. She found him at last in the field beyond the corn on the bank of a ditch looking into the stream. He was still in his brown cotton flannel robe, with the box for the uniform beneath his arm. His white hair was like something silver in the sun. She was so glad to find him that she almost cried.

He looked up bewildered when he saw her beside him. His face was flushed in the sun. "It ain't the well," he said.

It was not an easy thing to get him back inside the house when no one was around.

After that she knew she had to think of something more than just remembering what he gave her. He hadn't told her anything new for some time. She felt him growing empty, like he was hollowed out or something. She felt her mother just about to say he was crazy and maybe couldn't stay. And she felt herself sometimes like to break in two with holding off her mother and holding onto him.

Sometimes she almost got to wishing she was older, but then it scared her to look back and see how she was different at the first of the summer. Just with minding your own business, just treading water, things got dumped on you that you maybe couldn't handle any way but growing up. She thought it was enough to make you cuss out loud. And as soon as this was over she was backing up. But it was taking all she had and then some more to help him now. She had to get him what he wanted and then he could come back every summer of her life. Or they could live somewhere else, just the two of them together.

So she lay on her bed with her feet against the wallpaper, adding to the smudge she had already made. "I hate them rotten yellow roses," she said and stomped one with her heel.

She climbed the hill and dropped down to the rock where she had buried the snuff lid the train had flattened thin. She sat on the rock and crossed her freckled legs and held the lid in her mouth. She thought she would maybe chop her hair off at the roots and give her mother a fit. And then she was crying and she didn't know why.

It was almost noon. She was getting hungry but she wouldn't go home. She sucked the lid in her mouth and thought of dipping snuff and spitting in a can, the way a black woman down the road would do, who took her spitting can with her wherever she went. . . Emilu spit into the weeds and cried.

And finally it came to her she knew about a well that used to be in a field a long way down the road. She had been there once when her daddy had bought a hound for himself. She had a drink from it then and the water had tasted like a mouth of ditch water with scum thrown in. Her father had said not to worry, it was good to drink. But Emilu had thought, You coulda sure fooled me.

And now it seemed to her a last desperate hope. She could find the place. She could head straight back to any place she'd ever been. Like a cat, her father said. "We could put Emilu in a sack and dump her off down the road. She'd turn up the next day. Melissa you can turn around once and she's lost. Not Emilu."

I got to use everything I got, which ain't all that much. She wiped her eyes on her shirt and hid the snuff lid again.

It was hard work telling him about the well. He didn't seem to listen to what she said. She seemed to be telling it all to herself. When she had finished he sat leaning over with his head in his hands.

"Grandpa, I guarantee it wouldn't hurt none to look."

He got up and went to the corner for the box and put it under his arm. "I'm ready, little daughter."

At first she was too surprised to speak. Then she said, "We gotta take that bus and we ain't got time to make it today. We gotta wait till tomorrow."

Tears sprang to his eyes.

She went to him and pulled him down into the chair. She smoothed and patted his hair like silk. "Grandpa, you got real pretty hair. It's real, real pretty, I'm tellin' you. It ain't no time at all till tomorrow gets here . . . Don't go mentionin' the bus. There is some folks around like to mess up your plans."

She found his peanuts on the dresser and they ate some together.

She had a little money for the bus. There was her grandmother on her mother's side who sent her a five-dollar bill every birthday came around. That way you could get it figured into your affairs. It had come in June and she hadn't busted into it yet. It would be enough for one way but not for coming back too. She slipped into her father's drawer and got some from the box in the corner at the back. She knew it would be the whole thing come down upon her if he found it out. Like she had robbed a train.

The bus would come by a little after two, but she got him ready early after lunch was over. She brushed and combed his hair and aimed his eyebrows in the right direction. He wanted to take along the box with his uniform, but she brought him around to taking just the jacket instead.

She put on her black leather sandals and her Easter dress that had the jacket with the braid. She thought to pack corn muffins left from lunch and stuff them into the pockets of her dress. And when her father left in the truck and her mother was sitting out in back in the swing the way she did after lunch, she took his hand and led him out to the road. She walked him down around the bend so that no one looking out could see them from the porch, and she pushed him into the shadow of an oak.

The air was empty, the way it is on summer afternoons when it's making up its mind if it intends to rain. It seemed to her the bus was a long time in coming. Then she heard it struggling with the hill. It was bearing down upon them. She stepped out to hail it and it came to a stop. She coaxed him up the steps. She had her money ready. She would not look around for fear of seeing someone who would know her. But when they were seated just behind the driver she did look down the aisle. The bus was almost empty. Three blacks, a woman and two men, were sitting in the rear. A white man halfway down appeared to be asleep.

She patted her grandfather's arm and smiled at him. His eyes were grave and trusting. She hooked her Sunday sandals on the driver's seat and stared at the back of his head and ears and tried to tell if he was kind and if he would stop where she said to stop.

He stopped the bus exactly where she pointed and never asked her a thing. But she saw him looking hard at the uniform.

There was a haze on the fields. She took her grandfather's hand and led him down a little dirt road between some burdock trees. Then the road ended and they were out in the open. She climbed through a fence and held the wire up for him. But he just stepped over with no trouble at all. There were cows ahead, mostly Jerseys. But a Guernsey bull raised his head as they passed and looked at her hard. She looked back hard and kept on going, though she was scared inside. Insects were chirring like crazy in the heat.

She found a spot beneath a tree and made him sit down. She folded his uniform and put it beside him. "I gotta find it, Grandpa. It might take a minute." She took off running.

She explored every hollow and behind every hillock. She almost panicked. She had been so sure it was there in the field. . . And then through a section of broken fence she found it. She went running back for him and coaxed him to it.

There it was in the weeds, a square of old boards greened over with moss. She tried to lift it. "It's under there, Grandpa. You lift it up. It's too heavy for me."

He stood looking down at it with deep concentration. His eyes were blue pinpoints back under his brows.

She wasn't sure that he understood. "It's the well, Grandpa. I found it. See. You take off the top and look down inside. . ." She scanned the sky for him. "It's a real good day. No wind or rainin'. It's a real good day for rememberin' things. I can remember even bein' a teeny baby. I can remember the farthest back I ever done."

He stood without moving.

Now she was pleading. "Take off the top, Grandpa. It'll be just fine." She knelt in the weeds and patted the boards.

Slowly he approached and stood looking down at her moving hands. "Lift it up, Grandpa."

He stopped and grasped the edge of one board and threw the lid back with a crash. She fell over backward into the weeds. Then she got to her knees and peered into the well. A smell of decaying vegetation rose. She looked up at his face in the sky above her. He seemed bewildered. "Sit down with me, Grandpa."

He stared out across the field and stirred and half turned. She thought he would leave. She stood up and took his hand and pulled him down beside her. She was praying to herself: God, you gotta help me get it goin'. The hardest thing there is is to get somethin' goin' that ain't started yet.

She picked up a stone and dropped it into the well and heard it strike the ground. She turned to him a stricken face. "It used to be fulla water. I had a drink out it once. . . It's done dried up, I reckon. . . And it's got fulla dirt."

But his face was changing. She could not tell what it meant. He said to her, "Little daughter. . .you gonna give me what you got saved up. You hear?"

"It's a dried-up well."

"It don't matter about the water." He was impatient now. "Give me what all you got."

She held on to the muffins in each pocket of her dress. "I got a lady singin' and a well and a beatin' in the ground and somethin' red. I got the moon." She began to sing the well song but her voice was crying. She didn't want to cry, but her voice came out crying and she had to stop. "I got you said it was the best thing ever happen. . ."

"Not at first," he said.

"How come you told me it was?"

"Not at first," he said, shaking his head from side to side. Suddenly he grabbed the jacket and threw it on his back and drew it close around his throat. "It was some kinda. . . it musta been that war. . ."

"What war was it, Grandpa?" She tried to think of the wars she had heard about in school but they all ran together and she couldn't help.

He stroked his head.

"What was they fightin' about, Grandpa?" She had to keep him talk-

328

ing. The worst was when he stopped. "I wouldn't a fought 'less they give me a reason."

"They give one," he said. "I fergit what it was."

He pulled the uniform around his throat and put it to his lips and smelled of it.

"They was runnin' through trees and outa trees. I heard shootin' in the trees. I heard Jake gittin' hit, and I turn and saw blood comin' outa his throat. Like he was tryin' to tell me somethin', 'stead a words it was blood. Me and him kep' runnin' and then he warn't there. And then I fell down and I seen I had Jake's blood all over my side. . . It warn't his, it was mine. But I didn't know it. I thought it was his. I run on further and I fell again. I fell into somethin' was a hole. . . was a well."

She heard thunder in the hills. He lifted his head. He heard it too. Now, she thought, he's gonna dry up like the well is done dried. But the words were still there. "I hear runnin'. I hear runnin'. Feet poundin' the ground. Like a heartbeat in the ground. And like all at once the sky goes away. . ."

He stopped.

"What was it, Grandpa? Did you pass clean out?"

He put the jacket to his lips. "No. . . no. It was the top for the well." He reached out and stroked it with his fingers. "She covered me up."

"Who did, Grandpa?"

He shook his head.

"Who did it, Grandpa? You gotta think real hard."

"You recollect your mother used to cover you up? 'Fore you was good asleep?"

"It wasn't Grandma. It wasn't her. It was back in that war."

"She used to sing you asleep."

She stared at him in despair. "Not Grandma. . ." She lay back on the ground.

"That woman. . . in that war."

She heard him from where she lay and was afraid to move.

"Feet was poundin' all around me." He began to moan and tore the uniform away and threw it onto the ground. "I could hear the shoutin'. And she was settin' on top a me. On top a the well. Right on top a the well. And she was singin'. It was a song. I never heard nothin' like it." He began to sing the song, at first a whisper, then loud. She could hear it way down in the pit of her stomach. And she heard how the cows were listening to it in the field.

"Then she stopped," he said. He began to cry softly.

I'm a willin' to grow up some, God, if it takes it. . .

He grew calm and wiped his eyes on the back of his hand. "They was askin' did she see me. They was talkin' foreign words, but I knew what they said. . . When you is settin' hunched up underground in the dark. . . in the wet. . . in the blood. . . and they is huntin' you down like a rabbit. . . it don't matter what kinda words. I am sayin' it don't matter what kinda words."

Then she saw him lean across the well and fall in. But not fall. He climbed inside.

She got to her knees and looked down upon him where he sat with his head against the sides and his white hair all speckled with sticks and fern. She thought it might be that he was going to die. She had never seen somebody die before, and she was aching all over with wanting him to live.

She heard him saying, "She was singin' in the dark. I never heard nothin' like it. They come back a dozen times. They was huntin' me down. But she was singin' on the well and they never look inside."

She heard his voice growing into a song. "I was young to be dyin'. I ain't grew up, and I wanted it like a drink a cold water when your tongue is dry. I seen how it was I been wastin' the world. I ain't half look at things in the field or the road or sky. I ain't half smell the hay in the rain . . . I ain't love a woman. I seen 'em in doorways and walkin' pretty, but I ain't love one. I wanted a woman and the chil'ren she give. Lyin' with her at night, gittin' up at day. . . I wanted gittin' old."

She heard the cows lowing, coming close with their lowing. Bees sang in the trees.

Wanted getting old?

But it wasn't over. For he turned his face upward and into her own. His eyes were seeking something beyond her face, beyond her help. "Long time in the dark 'fore she open me up. I thought it was sun. It was moon shinin' on me the brightest I seen. It was like her face was up in the moon lookin' down at me. It was like I been given it all right there, the rest a my life poured into that hole in the ground where I was. . . I couldn't hardly bring myself to come up then, 'cause I had it all there. I reckon I was 'fraid if I lived it out it might not be that good."

"Was it?" she said, not knowing what he meant or what she asked or why.

But it seemed to be gone. All she could see was his head sunk down and the sticks and fern and the leaves in his hair.

He stirred. "Did you git it?" he cried.

She swallowed and nodded down into the well. "I got it, Grandpa."

"It's slippin', a'ready slippin'. You got it, little daughter?"

"I got it, Grandpa." Inside she was crying, not knowing what she had. "That's good," he said. "It's yours. You keep it."

Keep what? Keep what?

Going back was hard. The sky was changing, going gray at the edges, then gray on top. By the time they were back at the road it was raining. She got him to sit on the side in the grass. She took off her jacket and put it over his head. The uniform she buttoned inside his shirt, but he didn't seem to care about it anymore. She felt it was raining down inside of her. Counting on her fingers, she guessed it would be a good five hours before the bus would return.

But long before that, her father's car lights picked them out through the mist.

"Emilu," said her mother in the front seat, turning, "I would expect from you a little more judgment."

"Shut up!" she cried, coming out of the rain. "I was helpin' Grandpa. I'll never tell what it was. Not if all my teeth rot out! Not if you lock me up forever!"

But he was the one they locked away. . .

Whatever it was he found in the well, sometimes she wished she could lock it up in the box she kept beneath her bed. A thing you have to keep in your mind, it gets shrunk up, or else it grows the way you do and blurs like a lantern held too close till, like it or not, you look away. But after a dozen summers were gone, it must have been when her child was born, she heard the cry of the thing they had found. She heard the singing inside of her.

Midrash on Happiness

Grace Paley

What she meant by happiness, she said, was the following: she meant having (or having had) (or continuing to have) everything. By everything, she meant, first, the children, then a dear person to live with, preferably a man (by *live with*, she meant for a long time but not necessarily). Along with and not in preferential order, she required three or four best women friends to whom she could tell every personal fact and then discuss on the widest deepest and most hopeless level, the economy, the constant, unbeatable, cruel war economy, the slavery of the American worker to the idea of that economy, the complicity of male people in the whole structure, the dumbness of men (including her preferred man) on this subject. By dumbness, she meant everything dumbness has always meant: silence and stupidity. By silence she meant refusal to speak; by stupidity she meant refusal to hear. For happiness she required women to walk with. To walk in the city arm in arm with a woman friend (as her mother had with aunts and cousins so many years ago) was just plain essential. Oh! those long walks and intimate talks, better than standing alone on the most admirable mountain or in the handsomest forest of hay-blown field (all of which were certainly splendid occupations for the wind-starved soul). More important even (though maybe less sweet because of age) than the old walks with boys she'd walked with as a girl, that nice bunch of worried left-wing boys who flew (always slightly handicapped by that idealistic wing) into a dream of paid-up mortgages with a small room for opinion and solitude in the corner of home. Oh do you remember those fellows, Ruthy?

Remember? Well, I'm married to one.

Not exactly.

O.K. So it's a union co-op.

But she had, Faith continued, democratically *tried* walking in the beloved city with a man, but the effort had failed since from about that age—twenty-seven or eight—he had felt an obligation, if a young woman passed, to turn abstractedly away, in the middle of the most personal conversation or even to say confidentially, wasn't she something?—or clasping his plaid shirt, at the heart's level, oh my god! The purpose of this: perhaps to work a nice quiet appreciation into thunderous heart-beat as he had been taught on pain of sexual death. For happiness, she also required work to do in this world and bread on the table. By work to do she included the important work of raising children righteously up. By righteously she meant that along with being useful and speaking truth to the community, they must do no harm. By harm she meant not only personal injury to the friend the lover the coworker the parent (the city the nation) but also the stranger; she meant particularly the stranger in all her or his difference, who, because we were strangers in Egypt, deserves special goodness for life or at least until the end of strangeness. By bread on the table, she meant no metaphor but truly bread as her father had ended every single meal with a hunk of bread. By hunk, she was describing one of the attributes of good bread.

Suddenly she felt she had left out a couple of things: Love. Oh yes, she said, for she was talking, talking all this time, to patient Ruth and they were walking for some reason in a neighborhood where she didn't know the children, the pizza places or the vegetable markets. It was early evening and she could see lovers walking along Riverside Park with their arms around one another, turning away from the sun which now sets among the new apartment houses of New Jersey, to kiss. Oh I forgot, she said, not that I notice, Ruthy I think I would die without love. By love she probably meant she would die without being *in* love. By *in* love she meant the acuteness of the heart at the sudden sight of a particular person or the way over a couple of years of interested friendship one is suddenly stunned by the lungs' longing for more and more breath in the presence of that friend, or nearly drowned to the knees by the salty spring that seems to beat for years on our vaginal shores. Not to omit all sorts of imaginings which assure great spiritual energy for months and when luck follows truth, years.

Oh sure, love. I think so too, sometimes, said Ruth, willing to hear Faith out since she had been watching the kissers too, but I'm really not so sure. Nowadays it seems like pride, I mean overweening pride, when you look at the children and think we don't have time to do much (by time Ruth meant both her personal time and the planet's time). When I read the papers and hear all this boom bellicosity, the guys out-daring each other, I see we have to change it all—the world—without killing it absolutely—without killing it, that'll be the trick the kids'll have to figure out. Until that begins, I don't understand happiness—what you meant by it.

Then Faith was ashamed to have wanted so much and so little all at the same time—to be so easily and personally satisfied in this terrible place, when everywhere vast public suffering rose in reeling waves from the round earth's nation-states—hung in the satellite-watched air and settled in no time at all into TV sets and newsrooms. It was all there. Look up and the news of halfway round the planet is falling on us all. So for all these conscientious and technical reasons, Faith was ashamed. It was clear that happiness could not be worthwhile, with so much conversation and so little revolutionary change. Of course, Faith said, I know all that. I do, but sometimes walking with a friend I forget the world.

Africa

Robley Wilson, Jr.

Married, childless, nearly sixty years old, Seth Sharp lived now where he had lived all his life, in a weathered house in New Hampshire, close by a green and oval lake, in sight on clear days of the Presidential Range of the White Mountains. It was gray, small, a frame cottage with shutters painted dirty red; it was two miles from a gravel road, three miles from the nearest neighbor, thirteen miles from the town of Lebanon. It faced northwest, took the slant light of the afternoon sun, and it was a place that suited Seth almost entirely.

Except it had never had a porch—not in the time of his parents, nor even in the time of his well-off grandparents, and Seth burned with a secret sense of deprivation. He had told his wife, when he married her and brought her to this house:

"You wait and see. I'll have a nice porch on this place."

And his wife, Agatha, had kissed him and smiled, and gone about the business of cleaning up the single bedroom so the two of them might lie respectably together.

Twenty years later he had not built the porch, but he went on promising himself he would. And to his wife:

"Aggie, next spring I am dead sure to fasten a porch onto this place."

Long winter evenings when the snow sighed outside the windows, Seth sat curled on the horsehair sofa close up to a kerosene lamp and used the fat family Bible for a desk. He drew and erased, and wrote and scratched out, and built up hazardous structures on the yellow paper under his pencils, and over the years the porch of his plans began to look more and more like the porch in his mind. He said to his wife:

"Aggie, this is the year I'm going to build her."

He was tired of having no place to sit watching the progress of the seasons, no place to put a rocking chair in the evenings, no place to puff on his pipe or breathe the woodsy air or ponder Mount Washington on clear days.

This year, on Thursday of the first week in August, Seth drove into Lebanon in his pickup, showed his sketches to the dealer at the lumber yard, and drove home at indecent speed with more than four hundred dollars worth of lumber and tarpaper piled in the truck bed. It represented all he and Aggie had managed to save throughout their marriage, and if it was not enough it was as much as he could afford. He began work immediately—though the sun had already dropped behind the mountains and shade had turned the surrounding woods cold—and succeeded in framing his porch before impossible darkness set in. At dawn the next day he threw himself out of his respectable bed, gulped a cup of thick coffee, and resumed his labors.

By working all day he was able to finish nailing in the floor joists; Saturday he laid the one-by-sixes of the flooring; Sunday he nailed the roof together and covered it with the tarpaper. He had his porch at last. It needed only steps.

That evening, while the sun still balanced at the summit of the nearest mountain, he commanded Aggie to help him drag the parlor sofa onto his porch so the two of them could sit and watch the coming of the night. Long after she had gone to bed, Seth sat on in the summer darkness, admiring the moonstruck treetops over the orange bowl of his pipe. Next morning, when he helped his wife move the sofa, spongy with dew, back into the house, he decided he would have to think about real porch furniture—chairs with thin metal legs, and perhaps one of those flimsy lounges with webbed seats and backs.

All day Monday he paced the length and breadth of the porch like a man measuring off the plot of ground for a garden or a grave. In between these tours he leaped down from the porch and admired it from a distance. Then he clambered back up and resumed his pacing. From every angle Seth took in his porch with a child's smile and a gaze of innocent respect, as if he could not quite believe his own hands capable of such a masterpiece. It had yet to be painted, and because it had no steps his wife was obliged to use only the back door, but it was a possession of his own, an extension eight feet deep and fifteen wide of his personal vision of the world; the worthiest of his ancestors had not owned such a property. He would not let the cat sleep on it, he would not let Aggie walk on it unless he was with her, and he talked of it incessantly.

"I intend to close up the front and sides with those real thin little slats," he told his wife. "I seen 'em at Murdoch's last month, all crisscross in the brochure. I'll paint the slats red to match the shutters, and the floor I'll use good deck paint on, and a good grade of house paint on the rest of it. Nothing cheap."

Then he went to the Bible and drew a sheet of yellow paper from inside the cover.

"I'm working on that pair of steps, too," he said. "They're tricky, but don't you worry."

Agatha smiled and went out the back to get to her rock garden in front of the house. She did not remind him the porch roof might want shingles; the roof was the one part of his handiwork he could not see.

Seth found a pencil and returned to his labors, less artistic than mathematical at this late stage. When his wife stopped on her way to bed, to kiss him on top of the head and steal a glance at his work, she saw a much-smeared page crowded with fractions tentatively subtracted around the geometry of his steps. He looked up at her, confident.

"Don't you worry," he said, and bowed again over the Bible.

It was nearly midnight when he folded the yellow paper in half and tucked it back inside the cover of the book. Before he joined Aggie in their bed he strolled out to the porch one last time, standing at the edge of it where the steps would be, and urinated off it to the pine-needled ground. Just for a few moments Seth realized how deep the pleasure of life could be. He gave a little jump; if the porch was not truly rock-solid, at least it did not give way. He leaned against a roof support; it felt cool against his palm. A railing. He would build a railing, too, both for appearance and strength. He took a deep breath, letting the mingled odors of pine forest, pine lumber and pungent urine make him giddy and happy.

Undressing, slipping into bed beside his wife, he realized his lips were moving. He caught himself and smiled. Here in the dark he had been looking up at the ceiling, saying, over and over, "Thank you, thank you, thank you."

He had no idea how many hours had passed when he woke up and heard rain, and for several long minutes he lay still and listened through the opened bedroom window to the sounds of the storm. It was a heavy, steady downpour, filling the woods around the house with a noise like the wind, drumming on the roof, shattering the blackness every so often with a lightning flash. The thunder came after, gradually closer and louder; Seth imagined it was the thunder that had jogged him out of sleep. At first he thought he would simply roll over – perhaps put an arm around Aggie to secure himself to the comfort of reality – and drift back into whatever quiet place he had just come from. Then he knew he was not sleepy, and that what he most wanted was to get out of bed and walk on the new porch, to enjoy this summer rainstorm from a vantage he had never had until now.

He sat up and swung his thin legs over the side of the bed. The floor under his feet was damp and cool; the light breeze that came into the room through the window washed lightly over his nakedness. He felt refreshed – because he had slept and because the touch of the cleansed air was invigorating – and the happiness he had hugged in his sleep came flooding back to him.

"By damn," he said, and was startled to hear the words. He had meant only to think them; the whisper of them in the room was a thought made actual, as if he had created something out of nothing. But of course he had done exactly that.

His wife stirred, moaned in her sleep, as he stood and made his way gingerly across the bedroom toward the kitchen. When a flicker of lightning showed him the opened doorway he moved more quickly, crossed the kitchen, and stood for a few moments at the screen door. The odor of fresh lumber filled his nostrils, widened his smile. The wetness of the rain intensified the odor, deepened it; it was as if the wood were returning to forest, growing branches and spills, recovering its pine-ness and insisting its immortality. The notion pleased Seth. At the very least, the porch would outlast him, outlast Aggie; it would be a legacy for any man who might buy this place thirty or forty years from now. He felt proud – and even understood how rare the feeling was.

He was about to step outside, to stroll the length of the porch in his bare feet, when a sound arrested him, froze him. It sounded like a moan, or a sob, or both – the sound a woman might make in her sleep. He listened. When it came again he was not sure it was a woman; it might have been an animal noise, but it was not from the surrounding woods. It was close. It seemed to be on the porch – there it was again – and now it was accompanied by a thumping, something striking the porch floor, scraping across it. Seth pushed at the door and peered out.

Nothing. Darkness. No – shadows that flickered against the trees and danced with the falling rain. He squinted, listened. Stepped out. Had he heard only the creaking of the trees, and water dripping from the eaves? He walked to the edge of the porch. Lightning flashed; it made him blink and silhouetted the treetops in front of the cottage. The thunder-clap made him blink again, and it was only as he felt the floor under him

338

tremble from the shock of the thunder that he remembered he had seen something strange in the brilliance of the light. Something on his porch. Someone.

Whoever it was lay close by the wall of the house, and Seth moved warily toward what he had seen. Now he thought it was a man. "Who is it?" he said. Then, realizing he had whispered, he talked up. "Who in hell is out here?"

He got no answer. Let me have another splash of lightning, he thought. And it came—this time dangerously close and blinding, the thunder right on top of it and a smell like a burnt-out motor filling the air. Seth's voice rose out of the noise like a different and more potent thunder:

"What is it you think you're doing?"

It was a couple, a man and a woman, and they were wrapped in each other's arms, bodies indecent, locked in what had to be lovemaking. Both were half-undressed, a piece of the woman's clothing caught at one of her ankles, the man's trousers pulled down to discover his bare thighs.

"Jesus H. and John R. Christ," Seth shrieked. In the restored darkness he stumbled toward the two, his fists clenched, kicking and cursing. It made no difference that he was barefoot, that he was more naked than they. He stood over them, kicking with both feet, hoping to hurt them more than he hurt himself. He kicked them in the direction of the near end of the porch.

"Get off!" he yelled. "Get-goddamn-off-this-goddamn-porch!"

They came apart, like the two halves of something broken, and scrambled ahead of him on hands and knees. The woman covered herself; her underwear—if that was what he'd seen—she abandoned as she tried to avoid his feet. He caught up to her over and over again, punishing her belly, her legs. The man was yanking up his pants, trying to stand, trying to talk.

"Wait a minute," he was saying. "Hold on a minute, damn it."

The words were broken. Seth punctuated them with kicks, with the closed fists he was using to pummel the man.

"Get off! Get off! Get off!"

The man, whoever he was, jumped when he got to the end of the porch—vaulted to the ground, then came back to the woman, but by that time Seth had already seized her arms, hauling her halfway to her feet and wrestling her off the porch. She gasped when she landed, the wind knocked out of her. Seth stood looking down at them.

"And don't come back. I catch you doing that stuff on my property again, I'll shoot you both." He knew there was an old shotgun some-

339

where in the closet behind the bedroom; he thought it might still fire. "Go on; get gone!"

Lightning gave him a last glimpse of them: the man pale, his hair slicked over his forehead by the downpour; the woman half-standing, supported by her lover as if she could not stay upright by herself, her mouth open to show the whiteness of her teeth, her long hair heavy with the rain. Seth watched them move away, the man helping the woman in the direction of the woods. Satisfied that he had repulsed them, he turned on his heel, picked up the scrap of woman's clothing that felt slippery in his fingers, and went into the house. Outrage had stiffened his muscles, his spine. He ached with it, hurt from it. From under the kitchen sink he drew out the bottle of bourbon Aggie kept for medicinal purposes and took a long, harsh swallow. It was like a bad dream: two filthy-minded strangers defiling his new porch.

"I'll be damned," he said out loud. The experience had so shaken him, he took a second swallow. Summer people, he thought, camping in the woods. Probably the rain had soaked their tent, dripped through onto their sleeping bag, driven them out to find new shelter. He studied the woman's underpants—shiny-white, lacy. All wet and hot and horny, he thought; what a hell of a place to pick to go at each other.

He laid the garment on the table beside the Bible. Then he took a last swig from the bottle and went back to bed.

He had scarcely crossed the muddled border of sleep when he was once more dragged back to wakefulness. He sat upright in the bed; the house clattered with violent hammerings at the screen door. A voice was calling, small behind the fists, but frantic.

"In there!" the voice cried. "In there! You! Wake up in there!"

Agatha stirred beside him. On her stomach, she raised herself to her elbows, her forehead damp against Seth's shoulder.

"What is it?" she said.

Seth shook his head, meaning ignorance, waking up. Then, as if he were possessed, he flung the sheet aside and jumped to the floor.

"That horny goat," he said; he nearly choked on the words. "He's back again." He was already at the bedroom door, turned up the lamp on the dresser, bolted naked into the kitchen.

"Make yourself decent," his wife cried. She got out of bed.

"I'll show him decent," Seth screamed, while the banging went on so loud the voices inside and out were lost in the echo of it. Behind him Agatha raised the kerosene lamp.

"Fetch that old shotgun out of the closet," Seth ordered.

340

He flung open the door. For an instant the scene was a tableau: of Agatha, her hair stringy and disheveled, looking frightened and small in a blue cotton housecoat dusted over with a print of yellow flowers; of Seth, his stark white skin hollowed between his shoulder blades and puffy over his buttocks, crouched to defend the sanctity of his porch a second time; and of a stocky, fortyish man caught in the gold of the lamplight, his eyes wild, his round face running with rain and sweat.

It was Agatha who set time moving again.

"It's Raymond," she whispered.

"What?" said Seth. He was still crouched, still ghostly simian.

"It's Raymond. It's my brother." She began walking toward the door, taking short, hesitant steps in her bare feet. "It's little brother Raymond."

Seth straightened up. "I'll be goddamned," he said.

The man lifted his arms toward the lamplight, opening his hands to his sister.

"Ag," he said hoarsely, "Ag, help us. Help her."

Agatha ran past him to the porch. The two men faced each other in the shadowy kitchen: Raymond clenching his fists, Seth open-mouthed, swaying between sleep and fierce wakefulness.

"Was that you out there before?" Seth said. "Out there going at it with that woman?"

"It was me."

Seth blinked. "I ain't seen you in twenty years," he said. "I thought you was in New Orleans or Dallas or someplace like that."

"You could have killed her," Raymond said. "Kicking her like that. We think she might be pregnant."

Agatha stood in the doorway. "There's a girl out here," she told her husband. "The poor thing looks barely alive."

Raymond raised one arm to point at Seth. "He did it."

Seth shook his head. "Hell, I didn't even have shoes on. I couldn't of done her any harm if I'd wanted to."

"Well, help me," Agatha said.

"I'll help." Raymond followed his sister to the porch.

Seth pulled a straight chair out from the table and sat, muddled. The caning was sharp on his buttocks, but he didn't need to get dressed to see what was going to happen next. He wondered if he should fetch the shotgun himself since Aggie had ignored his earlier command. Montgomery or Biloxi or Little Rock—Raymond had gone somewhere south back in the 1960's. What in hell was he doing up here in New Hampshire, lying on Seth's porch in the rain, on top of some knocked-up girl Aggie looked worried about?

Now there was more commotion at the door. Raymond's back appeared; the arms of the hurt woman dangled on either side of him as he came into the kitchen with short, shuffling steps. Then here was Aggie at the other end, holding the girl by the ankles while Raymond supported her under the shoulders. The girl looked to be unconscious.

"I never even wore shoes," Seth repeated.

"He flung her off the porch, like she was some kind of animal. She fell on all those rocks."

"Take her straight into the bedroom," Agatha said, "all the way back past the stove there." It was as if she had no interest in what had already happened, but only in what might happen next.

"You going to put her in our bed?" Seth said. He watched them pass. The woman was limp as a rag, eyes shut, head lolled to one side. Her clothes were muddy and rumpled. She was dark-skinned. Seth got to his feet.

"Hey," he said. "That's a colored girl." No one responded to him. He trailed after Agatha toward the bedroom, his right hand held out as if to take her attention. "Hey," he said to her back.

"Now now," she told him. She vanished into the bedroom; Seth stood outside the door.

"You going to put a colored in my bed? In our bed?" He heard the sound of springs, of linens pulled aside, of the exertions of Raymond and Aggie arranging their patient. He turned back into the kitchen and sat heavily in the caned chair. It made no sense—none of it. Seth knew what his mother would have said, God rest her, if she were on hand.

"It ain't proper, Aggie," he said.

She appeared in the doorway. "Heat some water," she told him, "and find me some clean towels."

He brought water up into the pump alongside the kitchen sink and filled the copper kettle. None of the towns he'd worked in—and he'd worked in five or six New Hampshire towns before marrying and settling down with Aggie—none had a single colored family in them. He set the kettle on the stove-top, rattled the grate, opened the damper to make higher heat. The alarm clock on the stove shelf over his head read five o'clock. Five o'clock in the morning; the time startled him.

"Jesus," he said under his breath. He sat down to wait for the water to boil.

Raymond came out of the bedroom.

"Where are those clean towels?" he s. id.

"Keep your shirt on," Seth said. "I'm trying to think where she keeps

342

the damned things." He got up and padded across the kitchen to the buffet. "I don't know if she wants dish towels or hand towels."

"Hand towels." Agatha stood just inside the kitchen. "Give me a couple of those big white ones in the bottom drawer."

Seth stooped over the drawer and brought out the towels. "How come we never use these?" he said.

"Because they're for company." She took them from him. "That's how it happens they're not worn out like everything else we own."

"That trash is no company," Seth said. He went back to sit at the kitchen table. The shiny underwear lay near his hand; he picked it up and fondled it.

"Why don't you put some clothes on," Agatha said. "And I don't mean those flimsy panties."

"I'll dress when I feel like it." He tossed the underpants aside. To Raymond, who had come to sit down at the other side of the table, he said: "How the dickens did a smart guy like you get tied up with a nigger?"

"She's mulatto," Raymond said. "And don't use that word around me."

"What's mulatto?"

"She's not all Negro."

"There never was one of them people all Negro, to hear them tell it." He looked at his wife, who made motions with her hands for him to stop talking. "I recollect an old nigger used to pick up beer and tonic bottles out on the Rochester road. Black as under your fingernails. He was always telling folks how he was part white — one quarter or one twentieth or one ninety-ninth. Some outlandish fraction a man couldn't take a peck of to total up to the number one. They all got that story down by heart."

"That is no story," Raymond said coolly. "Lana's half white."

"What's that name?"

"Lana. Lana Turner Windham."

Seth sat back in his chair. He looked at Agatha, then at her brother. "I'll be goddamned," he said. "I'll be god-double-damned." He stood up, walked across the kitchen, and looked into the dim room where the girl was sleeping. Then he came back to the table.

"I got to say it," he told his brother-in-law, "that you are a far sight dumber than any man who talks good ought to be, if you believe that nigger girl is any bit whiter than two ton of the Lebanon Coal Company's bituminous."

"I said she's half white. I didn't say she wasn't Negro."

"I guess you figure her name makes her half white," Seth said gleefully.

343

"I guess if I changed my name to Booker T. Washington Sharp, you'd tell it around that I was half nigger." He giggled and slapped the cover of the old Bible so hard the dust flew.

"Listen," Raymond said. The blood had gone out of his face and the force of his gripping the table turned his thumbs flour-colored. "I told you I don't like that word 'nigger.' "

"You listen!" Seth interrupted. "You listen! Nigger nigger nigger nigger nigger!" He shouted the word, dropping each 'r' so that what resounded in the small kitchen was like gibberish.

Raymond got to his feet, but Seth tasted rage as bitter as before; he went on shouting. "And while you was filthying up my new porch last night, tell me which part of that half-nigger did you think was white? The part you was plumbing?"

His brother-in-law was moving around the table toward him. Agatha stood, petrified, in front of the stove. Seth backed slowly toward the wall.

"Now I want you to get off this property and take your girl with you. If she's so white as you say she is, I ain't going to have that shoe polish she puts on to look like a nigger come rubbing off on the sheets and making laundry work for my old lady." He stopped, his back fast against the wall and no place to go. "Don't you come near me!" he shrieked. "Don't you lay a hand on me!"

Raymond had gripped him by the shoulder with one hand, and struck him across the face with the closed fist of the other.

It was a stupendous blow; it caught Seth on the cheek and it set off geysers of broken color inside his eyelids. He slid down the wall to the floor, and with his hands, which had gone cold as ice, he felt the floorboards tilt up to stand parallel with his naked body. He pushed the floor back to horizontal and sat numbly, moving his head from side to side.

"There was no call to do that," he mumbled. He opened his eyes and looked up warily. Raymond was standing over him, fists still cocked. Agatha was leaning against the stove. Neither made a move to comfort him where he sat.

"I am not going to move that girl," Raymond said, "because I don't know how badly you hurt her. I saved her life in Mississippi, and I don't intend for her to be killed in New Hampshire."

Seth stared at the floor. "I ain't keen on minding any pregnant coloreds in my house," he said sullenly.

"I'll pay you for the room, and for what food she eats."

"There's things that bother me a sight more then money."

He watched his brother-in-law kneel in front of him, his big fist hovering an inch from Seth's eyes.

"Now you attend to me," Raymond said. "I'm going into town for help, and if that girl is any worse when I come back, I will beat you within a half-inch of your scrawny life. You hear?"

Seth kept quiet, listening only to the throbbing in his head.

"And if she should by any chance die because of how you kicked her," Raymond went on grimly, "or if she miscarries, I will kill you with my bare hands. You hear that?"

Seth nodded. Raymond stood up and turned away from him.

"Are you going to fetch a doctor?" Agatha said.

"Yes."

"And a minister, too?"

Her brother almost smiled. "You want a wedding?" Raymond put his arm around her shoulders, touched her forehead with a brief kiss.

"If the baby belongs to you," his sister said. "And if you're not man and wife already."

He gave her a long, fond look. "That would make you happy," he said. Agatha beamed.

"I'd hate to tell you how long my people have lived in this state of New Hampshire," Seth said. "It's a sight longer than there's been niggers in Mississippi; I'm damn sure about that. As long as there's been niggers in Africa, maybe."

Raymond stopped at the door and said, "I don't know what that's supposed to mean." He glared at Seth, his teeth working nervously over his lower lip.

Seth shrugged and used the back of the kitchen chair to pull himself to his feet. "I guess nothing," he said dully.

He watched Raymond get down from the new porch and walk in the growing daylight straight to the pickup. Seth swore at himself for leaving the key in the ignition, cursed Raymond as the truck drove off toward town. "Live free or die," read the slogan on the license plate.

"I hope you're satisfied," Aggie said. "Fighting with your own kin."

"Your kin, not mine," Seth said. "Stealing. Fornicating. Turning against Nature."

"Go cover yourself," she said. "I declare it mystifies me, how your mind works."

All morning Agatha kept a close eye on him. When she worked outside – weeding the vegetables in the clearing beyond the outhouse, or transplanting hens and chickens in the rock garden – she asked him to keep her company, even though she could not oblige him to help with her chores. When she was inside, at the stove or the sink, he felt her looking at him over her shoulder as he sat at the kitchen table and scribbled step calculations or went through the motions of cleaning his pipe. If she went to do something in the parlor, she was back in no time.

"Just what is it you're scared of?" he said once. "Do you think I'd dirty myself?"

When she was through with her planting and cleaning, and after she had warmed up the franks and beans from Saturday's supper for Seth, Agatha sat for a while beside Raymond's Lana. Seth kept his distance, as deliberate and uninterested as he could pretend to be. In midafternoon Agatha went into the parlor and sat on the sofa with a basket of sewing. Seth watched, dividing his attention between the yellow paper—though he had done nothing new with the sketches for his porch steps; it was all a sham—and his wife. He could see that she kept looking out the window, hoping for Raymond to appear. Maybe Raymond couldn't find a doctor who'd treat a colored person. Maybe Raymond was all talk, and wouldn't even come back. He watched Aggie's face, watched her eyes, watched her hands slow over the sewing.

When she dozed, her head resting against the back of the horsehair sofa, Seth waited several minutes to be sure, then tiptoed to the doorway of Lana's bedroom. The girl, too, was asleep—at least she had her eyes closed—and unaware of him. Now that he saw her in the light she seemed younger than he had guessed she was. Twenty-five, he thought. Thirty at the most. And pretty, if you thought those people could be pretty with their thick lips and monkey bones. Yet she was not nearly so dark as he'd remembered, not so dark as he'd pictured her while he and Raymond had argued in the kitchen a few hours earlier. Lana Turner Windham was quite light, in fact—almost like a white girl who spent a lot of time in the sun. Her hands—the palms of them—would actually be white; Seth knew that. And the soles of her feet. Not bad. Maybe Raymond knew what he was doing; maybe it was true that those people had some special and secret knowledge about sex. He took a step into the room. A board creaked; the girl's eyes opened and fixed on him.

"What d'you want?" she said.

Seth stared at her. The brown skin made her eyes look enormous. "I just wanted to ask you something," he lied. What could she really know that Seth didn't?

"Ask," she told him.

"I wondered if it was true."

"If what was true?"

346

"Is it true you're pregnant from Ray."

"I maybe am," she said. "We're not sure. I'm maybe only late, or skipped."

"What color will it be?" Seth said. Now he realized he was staring at her—at a bruise on her face, just under her left eye—and lowered his eyes to her hands outside the bedsheet.

"What kind of a question is that?"

"Will it be black? Will it be white? It's an easy question. Will it be something like coffee regular, part milk and part java?"

"I don't know," she said. She turned her face into the pillow—his and Aggie's pillow—and closed her eyes as if to make him vanish.

"I don't think you're pregnant anyhow," Seth said.

"I told you," the girl said. "I'm maybe not."

"Is it true Ray saved you from being killed?"

"Yes." She said it into the pillow.

Seth hesitated; he had never met anybody who was alive because of somebody else. Then he said: "How'd he do it?"

"I don't know."

"How come you don't know? Are you stupid?"

She turned her face out of the linens. "I was real small," she said. "And no, I am not stupid."

"How old are you?"

"I'm twenty-four."

"How old were you when Ray saved your life?"

"Five years old, maybe. Or six."

Seth stared at her for several moments, sizing her up, weighing and rejecting more questions. She met his gaze coolly, squarely.

"When's the first time he took you to bed?" Seth said.

"That's his business and mine."

Seth sneered. "Monkey business," he said.

"Get out of my room," the girl said.

"It's my room," he said, "and like hell I will."

"Then shut your mouth and let me sleep." She rolled onto her stomach and pulled the pillow over her head.

"Bitch," Seth said.

Her movement had left her partly uncovered; he gazed at her bare back, at the straps of her bra—the thin verticals and the broader horizontal band of white cloth. The garment was stark against her brown skin. He thought about Raymond undressing Lana Windham whenever he felt like it. He thought of Raymond on top of her on the new porch. The two images swam in his head in a confusion of envy and anger.

347

"Bitch," he repeated.

He went out to the kitchen and sat at the table, where the bottle of whiskey, the Bible and the hurt girl's underwear were still arranged like objects in a painting. He knew if he opened the Bible to the proper chapters he would find an anger to equal his own, and a promise of vengeance from the same God who punished Sodom and Gomorrah—a God whose Justice was every whit as complex and mathematical as the correct design for the porch steps. Damned fornicators, he and God would say in unison. Trespassers. Unnatural couple. They had stolen all the pleasure the porch had given him, had upset his work on the steps. He wanted to wake Agatha, shake her off the parlor sofa as if his fury could jolt her into helping him get things back to normal. Send your damned brother back to wherever, he wanted to say. You and me, we never had any trouble by ourselves. Now we've got nothing but. Monkey-girl. Goat-man. Two freaks making a circus out of a good life.

"Old man?"

Seth turned in the chair. Monkey-girl. Lana stood unsteadily in the bedroom doorway, draped in a white sheet from her shoulders to her ankles.

"What in the hell do you want now?" he said.

"I don't feel so good. Where's your bathroom?"

He stared at her.

"What's the matter?" she said. "Haven't you got one?"

"We got one," Seth said. "I thought your kind went in the woods, like apes."

"Hey," she said, "just tell me where it is."

He gestured toward the back door. "Outside," he said. "In back."

She grimaced. "Sounds to me like you all's the ones go in the woods." She started unsteadily toward the door.

"What's the matter with you?" Seth said.

She stopped. "What do you care?"

"I don't," he said. "Why'n't you and Raymond tell us you was coming here?"

Lana looked around the room. "I don't see you got any telephone," she said.

"You could of written. Or maybe you can't."

"Ray wanted to surprise his sister."

"I'll say it was a surprise. Dirtying my new porch. . ."

"The idea was we'd wait until you and your wife woke up. We didn't want to disturb you at no three in the morning. We started off just sitting out of the rain. The rest of it—it kind of happened."

Seth closed his eyes, saw the two of them all over again. Disgust churned in him. Animals, he reminded himself.

"If you don't mind," Lana said, "I'll just go on to your outhouse." She paused, the door half-opened and the afternoon sun lighting her young face, touching the bruise on her cheek with dull color. "No electric," she said, "no plumbing, no telephone. We never lived this uncivilized since I was a little kid."

The door slapped shut, cutting off whatever hard answer Seth might have made up, and he sat, dumb, at the table. What ran through his thoughts showed on his face. The possibility of following her – or tearing away the sheet and wrestling her into the bushes, teaching her what-for. Trapping her inside the privy, locking the door from outside; let her stay there a while, breathing the decay odors, getting scared. How come you smell so bad? Raymond would say to her. Or finding a crack in the privy where he could spy in, watch her do what she was doing – see what she looked like in that white bra and no underpants, see what Raymond saw. Uncivilized! He could wait outside for her, knock her down, finish what he'd started on the porch. How do you like this? And this? I may not have much, but I don't have a dead monkey inside me.

Seth stood up from the table. He was giddy from thinking what he might do to Lana Windham, and the giddiness carried him like a drunkard into the bedroom where she had lain. The bed was a rumple of linens – the top sheet gone, the blanket thrown against the footboard, the two pillows pushed against the head. He could see the impression of her small body on the bottom sheet, could imagine her as he had seen her earlier, the white straps of the bra thin as string against her dark skin. Seth yanked at the blanket and flung it to the floor, pulled the sheet off the mattress, caught one pillow as it tumbled after the sheet and threw it toward the door that led back to the kitchen. Bitch! he thought. He kicked the bedclothes out from underfoot and went to the closet.

In the back right-hand corner he found it: a 12–gauge shotgun Agatha's father had given him thirty years before. He hauled it out into the light, took it in his right hand, rested the twin barrels across his left arm. It was unexpectedly heavy; the barrels were touched with patches of dark orange rust, and the varnished stock showed mildew like flower petals. He had never fired the gun – had not hunted with it, had not had to defend himself with it. Until today, he could not have imagined a use for it.

He managed to break the gun open, and peered into the breech; it wasn't loaded. That was all right. In a kitchen drawer there had used to be a box of shells and a narrow yellow carton of cleaning materials, and probably they were still there. That might come later. For now, he hurried out of the bedroom, trampling the linens, anxious to be at the back door before Raymond's concubine got there. Uncivilized! Perhaps he would use the gun like a club, raise it again and again until the girl couldn't get up, or perhaps he would only enjoy seeing her terrified, making her beg for mercy, listening to her promise him anything—anything—if he would let her go.

He met her halfway between the back door and the end of the path.

"You stop there," he said. "Nigger bitch."

"What's the matter with you?" she said. She hugged the sheet tight around her and stared—seemed to marvel—at the gun pointed toward her. "You crazy?"

"I want you off my property," Seth said. His mouth tasted bitter, like stale coffee. "I want you back where you came from."

"Are you going to murder me?"

"I might," he said, knowing he couldn't unless he went back to the kitchen and found the shotgun shells. "I might murder you."

She stood, swaying, watching him. She was about ten feet from him—too far to reach out and try to twist the gun out of his hands. Now would be the time she could unwrap the sheet, show herself to him, say: Look at this. Don't you want this? Now would be the time for her at least to get down on her knees and beg.

"You stupid old man," she said.

He tightened his grip on the shotgun and gestured with it toward the road, out of sight on the other side of the house.

"Get off this property," he repeated. "You're downgrading the place, making it cheap. I already got to burn your bedclothes."

"You stupid, crazy old man," Lana said. "Ray'll come back and get you good."

"I'll look out for him," he said.

"Where's my clothes?"

"You don't need clothes. Your kind don't."

She took a new grip on the sheet, careful for it not to tangle her legs. "I'll get gone," she said. "You aren't fit to kill me, old man."

"I'll see you get safe to the road," Seth said. "I'll be right behind you."

"Maybe you ought to see this first," she said. She opened the sheet so he could see her bare legs. She's doing it, Seth thought; she's offering herself. But then he saw, and his stomach turned. Blood was what she showed him—dark and dried on the inside of her legs where she had tried to wipe it away, glistening red where it was fresh on her thighs.

"What did you do to yourself?" he said hoarsely.

Lana did a clumsy pirouette, flouncing the sheet at him. "Nothing," she said. "But there's no more baby here."

Agatha was hard to rouse. When he spoke her name, she barely stirred; he had to take her by the arm and shake her. When she opened her eyes, the first thing she saw was the shotgun. It startled her awake.

"That colored girl's run off," Seth said. "Don't ask me why. I was at the kitchen figuring out those steps, and I heard the back door bang. She hightailed it into the woods."

"What's that for?" Agatha said. "That dilapidated old shotgun."

"I was thinking I ought to go out after her."

"With a gun?" Agatha set aside the sewing basket she still held in her lap. "What's Raymond going to say?"

"I don't know." It was more a question of what Raymond was going to do. "He's no brother of mine."

"He won't believe she just ran off," Agatha said. "He'll blame you."

Seth went to the sideboard and rummaged through the drawer where he had last seen the shotgun shells. Way at the back he located a box with a half-dozen dull red cartridges in it. Birdshot. The narrow yellow carton was empty, but under a rust-stained rag he found a can of light oil. He arranged the shells and the oil on the table.

"So I better be ready for him," Seth said. He sat down and opened the oil can. The cap was rusted on; when he wrenched it loose he could feel his eyeballs bulge in his head.

Agatha stood over him. "I won't have you shooting that thing," she said.

"You don't have anything to say about it," he said. "If I got to protect myself, I will."

"That shotgun belonged to my grandpa," she said.

"I know that."

"He never fired it in his whole life, and neither did my daddy. That gun's not been fired in probably forty or fifty years."

"It's whole," Seth said. "It ain't lost none of its parts, so I imagine it'll still fire when I load it and pull the trigger."

"Look how rusty it is," Agatha said. "What if it blows up in your face?"

"That's why I'm sitting her with this rag and this can of oil."

"Raymond has a strong attachment to that girl," she said.

"I had a good look at his attachment," Seth said.

"Her mother and father got killed when somebody set off a bomb.

They were in a Baptist church down South. Raymond's taken care of her ever after."

Seth nudged the muzzle of the gun under Lana's white underpants and lifted them toward the ceiling. "Pow," he said. "Pow." Both barrels.

Agatha turned away.

"Suit yourself," she said.

For a long time he worked at the shotgun, while Agatha stood at the sink, peeling potatoes for supper. Gradually the brown and orange rust disappeared and the bluish color of the barrels emerged, glowing like night sky, under his hands. Seth hoped — truly — he'd have no call to shoot the gun. What if it did explode?

"It looks sound enough to me," he told Agatha, but she seemed not to hear him.

Just at dusk the rain began, with lightning and thunder, but nothing so close as last night's storm. The drops pelted the roof and the west side of the house and streamed down the windows, blurring the woods where he had last seen Lana. He thought of the colored girl wrapped in the white sheet — how she would be drenched and cold, how the wetness would freshen the look of the blood on her legs — and he wondered if she had really miscarried Raymond's baby, or if the blood was only the ordinary curse of being a woman. You couldn't believe anything those people said; you couldn't sort out the lies from the truth. He wasn't even sure he believed the story about someone bombing a church. Who would do such a thing? Animals. Monkey-people. And she'd had the nerve to tell him he was the uncivilized one. When he sat down to the supper of stew beef and boiled potatoes, the thought of Lana Windham choked him, and he was aware that Aggie watched him with genuine alarm.

"Don't bolt your food," she said.

He ate in silence. The shotgun was leaned against the wall beside the porch door. He'd loaded it, wiped the corrosion off the brass casings and forced the shells into both breech openings. He'd tucked a couple of extra shells into the pocket of his overalls.

"Make a pot of coffee," he told Agatha, "so I can stay awake tonight."

After supper he went out to his porch, to the fresh smell of the pine lumber, his heart lifted by it. Then he thought of Raymond and Lana, and his heart dropped. For a long time he sat at the end of the porch nearest the road, his legs dangling, the shotgun across his lap. The last of the storm clouds passed; in their wake they left a thin ground fog that shimmered between him and the nearby trees under the light of a swollen moon. He half-expected Lana Turner Windham to rise from the mists and come toward him, arms outstretched, eyes popped out, moaning like a ghost. Of course, that was baloney. Driven off, afraid of what he might do to her, she would sure never appear of her own free will. And she might die out there—might drown in the weed-green lake—in which case she'd never appear at all. Seth brooded on that.

But Raymond would. Raymond would be back sometime, a doctor in tow, maybe a minister tagging along for Aggie's sake: witnesses to whatever happened. He shivered. What would Raymond do? He was not a big man, but he was a crazy one—what normal man would love a colored girl and bring her to live with whites?—and crazy men had unpredictable strengths. Look what he'd done in the kitchen. It made Seth mad to think that all this mess had started because he cared about his own property, and it made him even madder that he could not tell where the mess was going to end. These woods had always hidden him from the world. Now they hid his enemies; he could not see who or what was coming, and even if he could, there was no escape because Raymond had the truck.

He sat tensely on the raw boards, turning his face toward every small noise, hitching the shotgun from one knee to the other. It might be animals he heard in the wet leaves, or an owl waking for the night's hunt, or Lana Windham lost, or Raymond blind with rage. God knew what. In the stark moonlight he made out the shadow of Agatha's orange cat, and he raised the gun, sighting at the cat, thinking what the birdshot would do to it. Not much. He wished the shells were loaded with buckshot; he had seen what buckshot could do to a living thing, how at so close a range it could tear a squirrel or a rabbit to shreds. "Pow," he whispered, imagining the cat dead in the middle of the clearing.

He would have to let Raymond come closer than that. He would be standing as Raymond stepped down from the truck cab and came toward the porch, tracking him with the shotgun, knowing that if Raymond wanted to get at him he would have to climb up awkwardly because the steps weren't built, and in that awkward instant Raymond would be at his mercy. He would point the gun into Raymond's face; if he had to—if it was a matter of saving himself and what was important to his life—he would pull the triggers, one after the other. "Pow," he said to the darkness all around him. "Pow." Both damned barrels.

Elephant Bait

Daniel Wallace

My dearest, lovely, sweet one, Jeena,

The mailman brought me your letter today, along with my heating bill and the news that I may already be a winner.

Of course, I opened your letter first thing. And I read it. And my heart broke into one million pieces. It did. That's what you wanted and that's what's happened, words like tiny ice-picks in my heart. I can't even think about it now. I have to sit down if I accidentally think about it. The words, Jeena. The phrases. What was it? What was it you called me? "The worst man in the world." That was it. And the word *hate*. You used that word a great deal. It did everything to me, Jeena, that one word. I was nothing after I read that word. Nothing. I'm done in, Jeena. I'm all through. There is just enough left in me to write this letter, so listen to me. Please. Jeena? Listen: My heating bill for the month of January is $39.74 – a fair assessment, I think. As soon as I finish this letter I'm going to write a check for that amount, but give some thought to it, please, Jeena, before I do: at least thirteen dollars, or one-third of this bill, was spent keeping you warm and happy, baby, and no more than a dollar thirty-four was allotted to Karen, who was also cold. See: I've worked it all out, sweetheart! That's $1.34, Jeena; one dollar and thirty-four cents. Now, does that make me the worst man in the world? Does a lousy dollar thirty-four make me the worst man in the world? Especially when you think in fractions: she was one-thirteenth, sugar, of what you mean to me. We're talking the tiniest fractions when we're talking about that woman, whose name I realize now I shouldn't have mentioned, the tiniest fractions. In other words, Jeena, love, what's missing from your letter is perspective. Just look at the numbers! They speak for themselves. The scales tip to your advantage – and in a big, big way! I'm talking heat here, Jeena. I'm talking about true love.

So what is it? Wait, don't bother, I know what it is. It's what you saw, isn't it? It's that image of me and that other person, isn't it? That's what you were thinking about when you wrote that letter, isn't it? Baby, I was wondering – could you, maybe, learn to block that, my best one? Think of the mind as a blackboard and erase? I have, for the most part. I have almost entirely forgotten that nasty incident and only recall it now for the purposes of this letter. Who was that woman? What was her name? *What woman?* That's the idea. Already I've forgotten this. What I can't forget, what I'll never forget is your face the moment I saw it, the moment you walked into my small room. The expression. Never. I can't describe it but to say that it was an expression pure and amazed and innocent and unbelieving. Jeena, it's an expression I've only seen once before in my life, and it was a long time ago, but I haven't forgotten, not to this day. Have I told you about this? It was when my father, looking up from the paper he was reading, saw an elephant in the garden outside our living-room window. I kid you not, Jeena. I couldn't make this up. An elephant, big as life right there in our garden. What happened was it had escaped from the circus and was on its way to freedom, but stopped to visit our home for a moment, this elephant, big as big could be, standing right outside the window in the garden, eyes the size of eight-balls peering in at us, Father and me, one summer, Saturday afternoon. Maybe Father had expected to see – what? A blue sky? The maple? A bird on the telephone wire? He didn't see that, though. What he saw was an elephant, and what he saw gave his face the very same expression that what you saw gave yours. They are identical, Jeena! And listen to this: all Father could say when he saw it, and this is in a whisper – are you listening to me? – he said, "The azaleas, the azaleas." Twice, like that, in a whisper.

The elephant was later captured, but the garden, as Father had forseen, was in ruins.

This is serious stuff, Jeena. This is serious business. Today, however, almost twenty years later, my father and I can look back at the time the elephant trampled his garden and laugh – *laugh!* Needless to say, it wasn't funny at the time. Let me tell you. There was nothing to laugh about then. The event had its repercussions. But now we laugh. What I'm getting at is this: I'm hoping you and I can do the same thing, either look back and laugh or not look back at all.

I know what you're thinking, Jeena. I know. You're thinking a woman is not an elephant, aren't you? True, true. The thought occurred to me as well, you see – we think alike. Things would be different indeed if you had found me in bed with an elephant, and Father had seen what you had, mostly naked, standing on his azaleas.

Or would they?

Oh please be patient with me, sweetest of all things, my dear, blue-eyed Jeena, all I'm trying to make here is an analogy, that's all, a simple analogy for the sake of perspective. We thought the beast was going to thrust its trunk through the window – that is, my mother thought so. She was sure of it. See, I was on the floor, about three feet away from the casement, playing with a toy car, rolling it back and forth and making car sounds. My mother reports that I always liked to hang around the floorboards near the electrical outlets, which worried her to no end, she says to this day. That day I'm wearing shorts, tiny shoes, white socks and a dirty T-shirt. I weigh no more than a few pounds, just a little guy, Jeena, and cute! So cute. Father is in his barcalounger reading the newspaper, and Mother is in the kitchen, cooking. Remember: in a moment she'll walk into the living room, wiping her hands on a small towel, a dead smile on her face. But this is in a few seconds . . . now, oh, here she comes, she's walking into the room – there! What I want you to imagine is this: the elephant easily crashes its trunk through the living-room window. Glass shatters. He knocks over a vase of dried flowers, a table lamp – and then he sees me. Elephant bait. Ever so gently the proboscis curls around my small body, lifting me up and outward, out of the living room and my mundane childhood, safely past the jagged edge of the window and onto his back, where I sit listening to my father mutter, over and over again, "The azaleas, the azaleas," until the elephant and I are out of hearing distance, gone, gone far away, never to be seen again . . .

This never happened, of course, my tender, temporarily-bitter Jeena, but Mother, who came into the living room just in time to see that fantastic rump wobble away, thought it might have. She was not an imaginative woman, my mother, but she imagined this. Also, she heard what Father was saying, and that look on his face, she saw that, too. I'll tell you – and you'll have to take my word for this, Jeena – she became seriously, seriously upset. Upset that Father's first instinct hadn't been to jump on me, to protect me from the elephant. I am, as you know, their only child, the first having been a miscarriage and the third never arriving. Hence I was quite the precious object. Mother spoiled and adored me. I was the world to her, and when Father didn't try to save it, me, her world, she became an angry and in many ways a different woman, all in a moment.

356

Now you know Mom, Jeena. She really doesn't know how to express anger very well. She can never come right out and say something, what she means, especially at times like these. She's subtle, though, and can communicate large feelings in small ways. So she burned his toast in the morning, ironed awkward creases in his slacks, and rearranged the kitchen cabinets so that he never knew where anything was. Things like that. But never, as far as I know, did she confront him. She was never one for a confrontation. But for days, for days and days, let me tell you, she wondered about the man who sat in the barcalounger reading the paper, rustling it, grunting occasionally at an item that caught his eye. I remember her staring at him as though she were trying to remember who he was, where he'd come from and what, just what was this man doing in her living room. This was her husband, yes—but who was he? She did not know, Jeena; the man was a stranger. I could see it in her eyes as she mulled him over in her slow and certain way. This man she married—*married*, Jeena—hadn't the foresight to see what could have happened, that was the problem; he was too dull to understand *consequence*, and the meaning, if merely symbolic, of an act.

In this way, I'm afraid, I favor my father; this apple fell entirely too close to the tree. In my case, however, the worst did happen; the elephant walked away, but you used your key—which I don't for a moment regret giving you and which I found this morning in the gutter outside. That lock is a quiet one, isn't it, Jeena? I didn't even hear you turn it, but you did, and then you walked, or bounded in, rather, cold, anxious for your portion of the heat, your proper third, and saw what you saw, like Father, but unlike him saying nothing. Just looking. With that look on your face. That look I will never forget.

As to what you did see, my lovely, that could bear an explanation. K.— let's call this person K.—has a circulation disease. This is what she told me, Jeena. This disease she inherited from her mother, who inherited it from her mother, and so on. She—K.—put it this way: her blood is thick, like honey, and in the winter it flows, well, like honey in winter. Not very well. Her blood, in other words, wasn't traveling the length of her legs, and her poor feet were red, bordering on purple. The heaviest socks weren't enough to keep her toes wiggling; without blood, I don't need to tell you, the heaviest socks over the heaviest socks are no good at all. She needed stimulation, Jeena; she needed to get that flow of blood moving throughout. So when you found me with her feet in my hands—and I know where we were, baby—it was an act of kindness, if not altruism on my part, an extension, at least, of some goodwill in this wintry season.

It may have been better, if just a little, had you caught us doing something a bit more traditional, I don't know. Maybe you think we'd already gotten to that, or we're getting to it, maybe not. I don't know what good can come from nailing down this specificity. What you saw was an act of intimacy, yes. But I'd like to suggest here that you cannot leave me for holding K.'s feet in my hands, and neither does that make me the worst man in the world.

Think for a second.

Now, does it?

For the record, Jeena, queen of my heart, her feet do not compare with your own. I've often thought of your feet as perfect, the way your toes slant, and your fine bones which seem to be made of ivory.

Ivory. I'm surprised I never mentioned the elephant to you before, since it caused quite a stir in our little town. Without a doubt it was the most significant event of my childhood. We later learned that this particular elephant had escaped and been captured many times before, was, in fact, a regular occurence with this circus. But it only happened once in our little town, and the next day's headlines were fairly predictable: GENERAL MOSBY [the elephant's name] RUNS AMOK!!! And there was General Mosby's picture, about one-one-hundredth the size he was in real life. And then on page 6A, where the story was continued, there was another picture, this one of my father, standing beside his trampled azaleas. It was a grainy photo, and I still have it, I think, somewhere. In it my father is just standing there with his hands on his hips staring at the devastation. On page 6A. "Your father is the kind of man," Mom said, "who will always appear on page 6A." And the reason his picture was in the paper at all, for the first time since his marriage, was this: ours was the only yard General Mosby chose to visit. The rest of his doomed flight took place on asphalt and concrete, on the sidewalks and in the street.

Why our yard, I wonder? Why my father? He lived a quiet, unspectac-ular life making No. 2 pencils—a factory, Jeena, which made him rich, by the way. Why us? I've always wondered this. That elephant changed our lives, and as you read this (not believing a word of it, probably) remember that I've had twenty years to think it over. What happened was that for a few days my father became a celebrity in Decatur. That's the name of my hometown, Jeena: Decatur. All that town could talk about was the man on page 6A and General Mosby, and UPI ran the story and it was on the news—that last, thirty-second part of the news—

and suddenly everybody knew about Father, the elephant and his azaleas. Just everybody.

Meanwhile, Mother was burning his toast.

In other words, bright eyes, in some mysterious way, all three of us
were transfigured, changed forever, by an elephant.

The real question here is, Why didn't he shield me? He loved me. My
God, the man did love me. But if he did why were his first thoughts of
his garden and why—this is the bottom line—why did the event mean so
much to Mother? I don't believe Father even noticed her keen
displeasure—not as much as he noticed being noticed, anyway—because
today, as I told you, we can look back at the elephant and laugh. You
can imagine, Jeena, it's a story he tells quite often, so often that my
stepmother and stepbrother both know it by heart, so well that they
actually believe they were there when it happened. As for Mother, I
believe her attitude was rooted in the simple fact that Father did not rise
to the occasion. Rarely do men in Decatur have a chance to rise—acts of
heroism are not normally required of them—but some women, my
mother among them, content themselves with the thought that if the
occasion *did* present itself their men would surely rise, ascend, and
without a moment's notice, at that.

In a very real sense, nothing happened. The elephant stood before the
window for a second, and then he left. "The azaleas," Father whispered,
but loud enough for Mother to hear, and suddenly, after eight years of
marriage, she placed this fellow. She found him out. He could have
sealed her devotion forever simply by leaping for me, covering me with
his body and tearing me, even if it was unnecessary, out of the deadly
range of General Mosby's nose, just as I feel I could have sealed yours if I
hadn't surrendered to K. and her very cold feet. All you ask for is
fidelity, a true heart, and the will not to rise to an occasion like K. That's
all you ever asked of me, and I failed. Jeena, I failed.

Bear with me here, sweet one, please. I have just one more thing to say.
My parents were divorced. You know that. It's no secret. But do you
know when they were divorced? Do you, baby? About ten years after
General Mosby came around, with Father's garden once again in full
bloom, peak condition. I was fifteen. Ten years, Jeena. It took that long.
Our parent's generation took commitment much more seriously than
ours does, even if it meant being commited to misery and disenchantment. Which is what it was. After the General came around, Misery and
Disenchantment were the special ingredients Mother used in all her

meals. You could smell it, you could taste it! For ten years she stuck it out. For ten years she burned his toast. And all that time all my Episcopalian mother was waiting on was a reason good enough to put down on paper, to file without embarrassment, her extreme displeasure with the pencil maker. You can guess what the reason was, Jeena, can't you? I bet you can. And not one woman but many over the years, his head swelled so when he saw his picture on page 6A, I tell you, as he thought about all the other eyes who saw it too. But before that time Mother had neither the guts nor the sense of humor to mention what happened that day the circus came to town. Maybe she didn't know it herself, or maybe, in the end, the elephant had nothing to do with it at all. Maybe I'm making this whole thing up—you decide, or not, it doesn't matter anymore—only don't leave me, my angel, O.K.? *Do not leave me.* I'm a good guy—I really am! I'm more like my father than I ever realized, but I'm young, young enough to learn, and not the worst man in the world. It's warm here, Jeena, and so very cold outside. So warm, and I don't mind the cost paying for it. I will pay this bill in its entirety and I swear, I swear, K. will never happen again. She was my elephant in the garden. Do forgive me, please, please. Jeena, Jeena, Jeena, I may already be a winner!

This Horse
of a Body of Mine

Norbert Blei

Mother is dying of cancer, the doctors say, and I am in a state of remission. I am driving her home from my place in Wisconsin in my father's 1965 Oldsmobile four-door sedan with 35,000 miles on it, original tires, spotless interior and two coats of Simonize he hand-rubbed the day before we left. The chrome bumpers glisten. The engine, valve covers and air cleaner shine. The spare tire, wrapped in plastic, has never touched the ground. My father believes if you take good care of things they will last the rest of your life.

Once a year, when I pick Mother up for a brief vacation with us, I leave my car in his garage and drive the Oldsmobile up north to burn the carbon out. "Look at all that rust on the body," he says. "You don't take care of things." Once a year I always ask him to join Mother and me to visit my wife and kids in Wisconsin, but he has no desire to go anywhere. "It's too far. There's nothing to do. I've got plenty to keep me busy around here," he says.

"How's the car running?" I ask.

"Pretty good. It keeps stopping in wet weather, so I had the guy down the alley tune it up for me."

"That's because you don't use it. It's full of carbon again."

"Once it's warmed up, it's fine. The fellow at the gas station wants to give me five hundred for it. 'Are you kidding?' I said. 'It's like new.' There's nothing like a good heavy car under you in an accident. You don't have a chance in that car of yours.

"You should take yours on the highway once a month. All you do is drive it to the store and church and back.

"And drive your mother around shopping. If it wasn't for her, I

361

wouldn't even have a car. I can walk wherever I go. She can't even walk to the corner."

The Olds is filled with the scent of Estée Lauder, her favorite perfume. "Such an old-fashioned car," she says, sitting beside me on the wide front seat, fumbling with the radio and cigarette lighter. "Look at this ashtray. Did you ever see an ashtray like this? Brand-new. He has a fit if I dirty it. I have to carry my own ashtray in my purse when he drives. Did you ever hear of such a thing? He keeps pennies in there for parking meters. 'What the hell are you saving it for?' I tell him. I tell you, that father of yours!"

She is eating from a bag of Jonathan apples we just purchased at a roadside market. Fresh fruit is good for her, my wife says. Fresh fruit, no white flour, no sugar or salt. Natural vitamins and exercise. "She has got to change her diet," says Sheryl, "or she is going to die. She's too fat. You have to talk to her doctor about megavitamins whether he listens to you or not. Look what they've done for you. Doctors don't know anything about nutrition."

I don't know for sure that vitamins and natural foods did anything for me. I know I took months of radiation treatment for my kind of cancer, and then Doctor Sedlack, the family doctor, said it looks good, and I have been living in a state of remission for over five years now, which Sedlack says is another good sign. Sheryl believes the side effects of radiation are dangerous, that I've been burned, and that I should have never let them do that to me, especially since Sedlack is nothing but a general practitioner.

"Sedlack has been our doctor for as long as I can remember," I tell her. "He speaks my mother's native tongue. She calls him all hours of the day and night. He even comes to the house. She jokes with him. She gives him something to eat. She loves Doctor Sedlack."

"I don't care," says my wife. "If you want her to die, let her keep listening to those people with their radiation and their chemotherapy. They're going to kill her."

"She won't listen to me," I tell her.

"Well, she's your mother," she replies.

"He never plays the radio when he drives," my mother says, biting into another apple, humming with the music.

"You should eat more fruit like that," I tell her. "Lay off all the sweets."

"Everything bothers him. 'Who wants to listen to all that noise?' he moans. What a treat to be able to sit back, light a cigarette, listen to the radio and watch all these beautiful farms go by. He never wants to go anywhere. If it wasn't for me, he'd die in that house. Look at all these

362

small cars on the highway. When I get back I'm going to tell him to buy a new car. What's the name of that small one there? Something like that. Something like yours. Who the hell wants these big monsters anymore?

"I could never get your father to do anything," she says, kicking off her white shoes. "Oh these damn feet keep swelling up. Sedlack says it's all water, it's nothing to worry about. He gave me some pills. I've got more damn pills. Who the hell knows?" She's rummaging through her straw purse for some hard candy and a tube of lipstick. "Your father's always been a stick-in-the-mud. Don't forget I want to stop for some smoked fish and some cheese. You want some candy? They're good. They're hot. Let's stop in one of these small towns for breakfast. I always took my vacation alone. You're better off."

She pulls the sun visor down to arrange her platinum blond wig in the mirror and put on fresh lipstick. She retains an attractiveness that has demanded attention all of her life. Beneath the layers of makeup is an old peasant face, my grandmother's, that I have rarely glimpsed and only noticed emerge for the first time in the hospital the past year. She is wearing a bright floral dress, pink, white, violet and blue. Her wrinkled fingers are thick with costume jewelry. She is wearing an extravagant, gold-looking necklace and bracelet I gave her after her recent operation, fixing it around her neck and upon her wrist while she was dressed in a hospital gown and being fed intravenously. "I hope he remembers to take the pork loin out of the freezer for supper," she says.

She should not be eating pork, according to Sheryl. "All her life she's eaten poisons. Nothing but nitrates. All that homemade sausage from the butcher, tripe soup, lamb, chicken paprika," she says. "Bakery, booze and cigarettes. Then she wonders why she's got cancer. She thinks it's going to go away just like that. Your father doesn't even mention the word in front of her. She doesn't have to eat for two months, with all that fat on her. Tell your father not to buy that stuff. She should be eating more raw vegetables."

"She gets through with supper," says my father, "and after coffee, bakery and cigarettes, she makes herself an ice-cream sundae. She doesn't want people to think she looks sick. What am I going to do with her? Starve her? She won't listen to me. The doctors say all that vitamin business is the bunk. What am I supposed to tell Sedlack? They want to try radiation, so they try it. Then they cut her open again and say they can't do any more surgery, and now chemotherapy is what she should have. The odds are one in five. I don't even tell your mother this. They must know what they're doing. They're doctors. If they cut it all out, why isn't it gone?"

To listen to my wife, I should take my mother to some place out east where they cleanse the body of toxins and prescribe a diet of wheatgrass. The body's metabolism must be turned around to cure its own disease. Or I should get her off chemotherapy immediately and fly her to Mexico for laetrile treatment in some clinic on the Pacific.

"Get out of here," says my mother. "Me on a plane? I'd sooner crawl. So what's supposed to happen to me anyway? Will you tell me? My fingernails are supposed to fall off, my hair's supposed to fall out. Will you please tell me what this stuff is doing to me every week? I've gained fifteen pounds since the last operation. So what am I supposed to do, turn green or something? Nothing phases me. Not this horse of a body of mine."

On Water Street in the town of Kewa Bay we park beside a small corner restaurant. Mother pulls out a pair of pink felt house slippers from her shopping bag and shoves her swollen feet into them. "What the hell do these farmers know?" she says. They are the same style of house slipper my grandmother wore all her life. She pushes the car door open with her knee and bangs it into a parking meter. "Can't they put those damn things somewhere else, out of the way?" Standing in the bright sun, she puts on a pair of dark sunglasses and places a white straw picture hat on the back of her head, fixing it with a pearl hatpin.

"This place is too crowded," she says at the door of the restaurant. The tables and counter are filled with fishermen from all over Wisconsin and Illinois who have come to catch some coho salmon in fall. The bay is smooth and silver in the distance, studded with fishing boats drifting in the early morning mist and sun. "There's a bakery over there," she says. "I'll get some sweet rolls and bread and coffee cake to take home for supper."

I watch the bulk of her shift from side to side in small steps toward the bakery, stopping to peer into a clothing-store window along the way. She is the brightest thing on the street this morning.

Dressed in a blue and white running suit and gray running shoes, I fix a red bandanna on my head and call out to her that I will jog along the lakeshore while she shops. "Don't get all tired out," she says.

Though I married outside of the church, much of my adult life echoes a Catholic upbringing. I am more aware now of abstinence, penance, suffering. When my wife suggested fasting once a week for reasons of health, she could barely comprehend my familiarity with abstinence long ago—fish on Friday, Lenten fasts, never eating on Sundays before taking the sacrament of Holy Communion. Running, in my mind, is penance, suffering and prayer. I fast for her now for reasons of good health. I have lost my priests. The nuns have become indistinguishable from other women.

"Once a week," says my wife, "the body needs a rest. Once a week we will eat nothing." Today is my fast day.

Driving toward Milwaukee, the monotony of the interstate taking hold, I feel my body relaxing, my mind slipping into sleep. "You look tired," she says. "Don't fall asleep now." She turns the radio up louder and offers me a piece of bakery again.

"No thanks," I say. "I'm not eating today. You should try that. Just not eat anything one day a week. You'll feel better."

"Here, try one of these almond crescents. I'll split it with you."

"No. You eat it."

"I don't need it. You look all drawn out. Your face is too thin."

"I feel fine."

"You can't live on nothing. You hardly eat anything in that house of yours."

She takes one bite of the almond crescent and throws the rest back into the bag. "They sure as hell don't know what good bakery is around here."

"Why don't you take a nap, Mother? We still have a few more hours to drive."

"I've got all night to sleep."

"You want to look through some magazines? There are some on the backseat."

"Just drive. Don't worry about me."

"Try the radio near the end of the dial. Maybe you can find some polka music."

She turns her shoulder to me slightly, lights another cigarette and looks out the window, retreating to a stubborn silence I remember as a child.

"Do you still want to stop for some smoked fish? It's up ahead a few miles."

"No, just get me home already, Christ, this is a long ride."

She begins digging into her purse for her rosary and prayer book stuffed with holy cards, all wrapped with one of the wide rubber bands my father saves on the kitchen doorknobs. She turns to the page of indulgenced ejaculations, moving her lips in the words of the last indulgence: *Mother of love, of sorrow, and of mercy, pray for us.* For each utterance, a remission of 300 days of temporal punishment is granted by the church.

I smile at her persistence of such old beliefs, at my own childhood

365

attempts to pile up indulgences at odd moments to lessen my soul's stay in purgatory. She wraps the beads around her hand like old bakery string to be saved and tied and put in the kitchen drawer. It is the same rosary I bought her in Rome, supposedly blessed by her beloved Pope John. She makes the sign of the cross, then works her fingers and lips from the crucifix to the Our Father, the Hail Mary, and the First Joyful Mystery, the Annunciation. She brushes some flakes of frosting from her lap, and beneath the necklace, on her bosom, retrieves a large crumb, which she places in her mouth.

"Your family still believes that eating cures everything," says my wife. "Your aunts are killing their husbands, loading their plates every meal, stuffing them with rye bread and butter, filling their glasses with beer. Then bakery on top of all that. No wonder the whole family suffers from diabetes and heart trouble, and now cancer. Your grandmother could hardly move, she was so huge. Your mother's getting just like her. How can you educate those people? Your mother still believes fat babies are healthy. My children were always too skinny for her."

Our children, slim and supple as young branches, are runners, ten-speed bikers, cross-country skiers, hikers with aluminum-framed backpacks, down vests, jackets and sleeping bags. They dress in bright-colored warm-up gear and survive on small portions of nutritious meals, home-baked wheat bread, fresh juice, raw vegetables, brown rice, vitamins and exercise, and sneak occasional junk food in the company of their friends. They can't wait till they are of age to leave home for the summer, camp in wilderness areas alone, climb mountains and go white-water rafting in the West. They have little to say about their grandmother who embarrasses them with the smelly food she cooks, the perfume she exudes, the queer clothes she wears, the lipstick-smeared kisses she tries to plant on their cheeks. They think she comes from another world.

"All she does is try to stuff them with candy and bakery and salty food," says my wife, "then gives them money to buy anything they want. That's not love. Like married to your father over forty years and always arguing. You call that a marriage?"

At Hanson's Fish and Cheese Shop I leave Mother in the car saying her rosary and buy five pounds of smoked chubs and a pound each of baby swiss, munster and brick. While the woman is wrapping the fish in newspaper, Mother walks in and begins tasting the tiny chunks of cheese set on a tray for customers to sample.

"What is this?" she asks.

"A cheese curd," says the woman.

"That's good. Give us a pound of curds. And a slice of this aged cheddar too. Oh, about that much, a couple of inches. Father likes caraway. You better give us a pound of cheddar with caraway also."

While the woman is weighing and wrapping the cheese, Mother adds a box of crackers, some diet cola, and a handful of hard salami sticks wrapped in plastic.

Back on the highway, she is nibbling on cheese curds with crackers and drinking from a can of diet cola. "I've got crumbs all over. This car's a mess. Your father's going to kill us. The next time you come in, bring a couple cartons of these curds. They're delicious. Your Aunt Milada would like them. Wait till your father sees this smoked fish. Remember how we used to eat smoked fish every Friday?"

A few miles before the expressway through Milwaukee she asks me to stop somewhere so she can use the restroom. There are no rest areas along the interstate or expressway, I tell her. I will have to get off and take the old highway that parallels the new interstate. I remember a small wayside along that stretch.

The old highway is empty and in need of repair. We bump along the tar cracks in the concrete, Mother periodically exclaiming, "Jesus, what kind of a road is this?" Yet the road brings us in closer to the farms, closer to the animals and fields and trees.

"All these beautiful farms with red barns," she says. "Look at those cows, and those baby pigs. Aren't they cute! Remember Grandma's farm in Three Oaks? How she killed the chickens for supper? And the butter she used to make? God, how she worked herself to death on that farm!"

We are the only car in the parking lot of the wayside. While mother trudges toward the restroom, I push the front seat back, stretch and close my eyes.

"Just rest," she says when she returns. "I'm going to get rid of some of this garbage and pump some cold well water over there."

It is early afternoon. I can feel the burning sun on my eyelids. The country smells of drying grasses, cedar, the end of summer. I hear the quick then slow squeaks of the pump handle, then the sudden rush of water. From the corner of my eye I catch a blurry glimpse of her sitting at a green picnic table, her face turned up into the sun, her skirt hiked above her knees, tanning her heavy legs.

I awake to hunger pains, growling sounds. Opening my eyes, I discover my head resting against her thigh, while her head hangs above me in a snoring sleep. The blond wig has fallen to the floor. Gray hair is matted against her forehead and lies bunched above her ears. Her face is as ancient as Grandma's. Rumblings inside her body echo mine, though hers emanate from the pelvic region, where her hands lie clasped, where her cancer lies.

Grasping the steering wheel, I pull myself up slowly.

"What's wrong?" Her eyes flash open.

"Nothing. I want to splash some cold water on my face, then we better get going."

"Here, put some water in this empty soda can for me. I like that iron taste of well water. It reminds me of Grandma's farm and the picnics we used to go on a long time ago in the forest preserves."

I return to find her staring at her face in the mirror behind the visor, her hands vaguely stirring inside her purse. "I look like hell," she says. "Just look at me." She opens a tube of lipstick, then a compact of facial coloring, which she rubs deep into her skin. "Hand me that damn wig," she says. She brushes it with her hand, fluffing the piles of blond curls with her fingers. "There. That's good enough." I hand her the can of cold well water. "Oh, that tastes good," she says. "We should fill up a gallon jug to take home."

All the way back through Milwaukee and over the Illinois state line she talks about her childhood, the picnics they used to go to in the forest preserves. "Grandpa belonged to this club, Ilova, named after some place in Yugoslavia, and they would hold these picnics every year. A truck would come for us early in the morning, and we would all pile on, the kids, the old people, everyone. The trucks were open in the back with those wooden sides, and we would sit there on top of one another and drive all the way to the picnic grounds outside the city.

"Sometimes we would carry blocks of ice with us too in burlap sacks. Grandpa and some of the men would leave even earlier to begin building the fires so they could start roasting lambs and pigs on the spit. They would rub the lambs and pigs both inside and out with handfuls of salt. Sometimes they would stuff the cavities with sausage, and sometimes they would slit the outside skin of the lamb and stick cloves of garlic inside. Grandma would be with the women making coffee, cutting bread, setting out the bakery. Grandpa would later end up with his friends drinking beer and playing cards. The kids would take turns turning the lambs and the pigs on the spit by hand. Then the band would begin playing in the afternoon, and everyone would sing and dance till night. Most of the men would be drunk by then, and the women would be battling with them. Then they would all pile on the trucks and go home, their bellies full.

"You never tasted lamb like that. So juicy. They'd cut and saw and chop it apart. They were no butchers, believe me. You didn't bother with forks. You ate with your hands like a bunch of savages. The skin of the pig was so nice and brown and crispy you could just crack it between your teeth or chew on it all day if you wanted to."

"I ate roast lamb like that in Greece," I tell her. "They still make it that way outside on the spit during Greek Easter."

"Well, they don't have picnics like that anymore," she says. "I don't know what happened to Ilova. They must be all dead."

"Doesn't anyone in the neighborhood roast lambs like that? The Greeks? The Serbs? There must be some Croatian picnics still."

"The young people don't go for that. There's this new Yugoslav butcher, Luka, where I sometimes get my meat. He's supposed to sell lamb and suckling pig he roasts in the back every week. But I don't know if it's against the law nowadays or not."

"Well, ask him when you buy your meat."

"What time is it? Go down Cermak when we get to the neighborhood. I'll just run in and see if he's got anything."

As we approach the outskirts of Chicago, I hear her rummaging through her purse again, her hands tearing the cellophane wrapper off the salami snack. She finishes one. Opens another. Takes a bit out of it and passes it to me. "Here, take a bite. It's good."

I pretend to taste it and pass it back.

"You didn't even try it," she says, crumbling the cellophane into the ashtray.

"Father's probably wondering where we're at," I say to her.

"Let him wonder. All he's going to do is tell me how hard he worked while I was on vacation. How he washed the windows, scrubbed the floor, painted the storm windows. Get the fiddle. Same old stuff. Or he's in the alley. Garbage picking. Bringing home more junk, fixing it, then trying to get rid of it. He can hardly get the car in the garage, he's got so much junk in there. Now he found a guy down the alley throwing out good shoes. He worked for some shoe company or something. Seconds. Shoes people sent back. So your father, you know how he loves to polish shoes and visit the shoemaker. The garage is filled with shoes. He gave five pair to Uncle John last week and one pair to some other guy down the alley. He wants me to ask Sedlack what size shoe he takes. Can you imagine that? 'Like new,' he says. Who the hell wants to wear somebody else's shoes?"

I drive down Cermak, the main drag of the old neighborhood, looking for Luka's butcher shop.

"Slow down," she says. "It's on this block. There. Park in front. Right here. Come in with me."

369

There is an old man ahead of us buying slab bacon and Polish sausage. He is talking with Luka the butcher in a language that sounds like Czech. My mother joins in, making some remark about Wisconsin and fish, and soon the three of them are talking and laughing. I hear her say to Luka something like, "This is my son. He doesn't speak Czech." And Luka smiles, bows, and wipes his hand in his apron before shaking mine.

When the old man leaves, my mother continues the conversation, moving slowly along the meat case, pointing, questioning, buying Bohemian salami (*praski*), hot dogs, *jaternice* and pork chops, while the butcher trims and weighs and wraps and marks each package. She mentions something about roast lamb, and the butcher is silent a moment, then motions for us to come behind the counter and follow him.

He grasps the large, stainless-steel handle of the walk-in cooler and motions to step inside. The door clicks solidly shut behind us. It is cold enough inside to make our breaths visible. A dozen lambs hang from the top hooks along one wall, while five or six suckling pigs hang here and there between sides of beef. There are rabbits, still in their fur, strung around the top of an old wooden barrel filled with fresh bones. And, in the corner near the door, a large buck hangs from the ceiling by its antlers.

I lose the language entirely as Mother and Luka begin to converse in a different tongue, possibly Serbo-Croatian. Though the language sounds harsh, their gestures are warm and benign. Luka, wrapping his arm around the deer, my mother rubbing her hand up and down the blue-white skin of a lamb, then lifting a rabbit's head, puckering her lips, murmuring baby sounds into the eyes, and blowing gently into its fur. Both Luka and she begin laughing, and Luka leads us out of the cooler with his bare arm gently around my mother's waist.

We follow him deeper into the store, where an old man in a dirty white apron watches a lamb turning on a spit powered by an electric motor. In a pan on top a nearby oven lies the hindquarter of another roasted lamb. Luka tears off a piece of the greasy meat with his fingers and places it between my mother's lips.

"Mmmmm," she says, turning to me. "This is delicious. They're all out of pig. I'll have Luka wrap up the rest of this lamb to take home."

My father is waiting at the door. He meets my mother halfway, huffing up the front steps, her arms loaded with packages. "Leave the car in front," he tells me. "I'll put it in the garage later."

"Here," she says, handing him a shopping bag. "I got some roast lamb from the butcher. Put it in a large pan and put it in the oven right away.

We'll have it for supper. And there's smoked fish we brought from Wisconsin, and all kinds of cheese."

"I've already got the pork loin in the oven," he pleads.

"Good. We'll have it for supper tomorrow."

"There's just never enough for you," he says.

"Did you put salt and caraway on the pork? I told you to sprinkle caraway. Leave the door open till he gets the suitcases in. Jesus, that's a long ride. I thought we'd never get home."

He has set the kitchen table for three, in anticipation of our arrival. He has cut the round loaf of Bohemian rye in half and then cut the half into thick slices, stacked neatly on a plate. Three gleaming pilsner glasses stand before the plates, with paper towels folded for napkins. A can of peas and a can of sauerkraut are on the counter near the sink, ready to be opened and emptied into waiting pots.

"Put that stuff in the icebox," says my mother, pulling a housedress over her head, knocking her wig askew. "This damn thing!" She flings the wig into an empty chair. My father looks at me and shakes his head. "I'll make the sauerkraut tomorrow when I make the dumplings," she says. "You've got this oven too damn high."

"How was the car?" asks my father.

"Fine. You should have seen the clouds of black carbon that came pouring out," I tell him.

"It should run like new now," he says.

"Nobody drives cars like that anymore," she tells him, opening the oven door, testing the lamb with her fingers. "Get rid of that relic already."

She unwraps the oily newspaper on the center of the table, revealing a pile of smoked fish the color of old gold. "Look at these, aren't they beautiful?" she says.

"Yeah, but who's going to eat all this?" my father says. "You throw half of it away. Everything ends up in the alley."

Standing before her plate, she breaks the head off a smoked fish with one silent push of the fork, runs her red fingernail underneath and peels back the gold skin as if she were removing a glove. Inserting her fork in the pink-white meat of the back, she loosens entire chunks free of bones. "Wait till you taste this," she tells my father, buttering a slice of rye bread.

He opens three bottles of imported beer from the refrigerator and fills each glass.

"Sit down," she says. "The both of you. Cut some cheese. I'll make some coffee. Where's that bakery I bought?"

"I bought bakery this morning from Vesecky's," Father says. "What did you go and buy bakery for?"

"I bought this up in Wisconsin. Some joint we stopped in. They don't know how to bake up there."

I move the smoked fish out of her way as she sets the pan of roast lamb on a hot plate, tosses the potholders in the sink, and closes the oven door. The kitchen smells of roast pork, caraway, lamb, fish, rye bread, beer and coffee perking.

"Now eat," she says.

The sins of my childhood were small and private. Most of my confessions were appetites: the taste of a candy bar in my closet before taking Holy Communion. My penance was prayer, which came easy. I sought, and now bestow, forgiveness, in the same breath.

The lamb and fish and bread fall apart on my plate. I pick up a fork and taste the lamb, then butter a slab of rye with sweet butter, sprinkling it with salt. The taste of warm lamb and fresh rye in my mouth rekindles old desires. The response is instant: more. There is no time to talk, to think, to see anything but the table of food before me. "Here, try a hunk of this," says my mother with a full mouth, handing me a shank dripping with grease, dropping it on my plate. The fork suddenly feels foreign, in the way. I begin to eat with both hands, to rejoin my family in a ritual of consumption more embracing than the laws of etiquette. The cold glass of pilsner slides in the oil and grease of my fingertips, but I clutch it firmly, raising it to my lips the way a priest would cradle a chalice.

Then Mother is pouring hot coffee, and Father is carrying boxes and bags of bakery from the pantry. "I've got a fruit coffee cake, cherry, pineapple, prune and blueberry," he says. "And a poppy-seed loaf and an almond twist. Which one should I open?"

"Open all of them," she says, breaking the string around the white boxes in both hands. "What's the difference? You can't save bakery, you know that."

While she cuts the coffee cake, my father gathers the loose string, winding it around his hand, slipping it over the back doorknob where he keeps rubber bands.

At six the next morning I rise to drive back to Wisconsin. I see Mother in the light of the kitchen, her robe, her gray hair, saying the rosary at the table. She has a small statue of the Blessed Mother in front of her, along with a votive candle, an ashtray, her cigarettes and coffee.

I move quickly behind her, press my hands into her shoulders, bend down to kiss her on the cheek. "Don't bother with anything," I whisper. "I'm all right."

With the rosary wrapped in her fingers, she squeezes my hand, attempts to rise, and begins to say, "Don't forget . . ." in the midst of her prayers, while I press harder into her flesh for her to continue, to remain just where she is.

My father waits in the garage with the door open. He hands me a lunch bag Mother has packed for me. "You want some shoes?" he says. "They're like new. Here, try these on. Wear something solid on your feet instead of those gym shoes. I had the shoemaker put new soles on this pair. Look at the beautiful job he did. That guy's an artist."

"They're a little too big," I tell him.

"Wear two pairs of socks," he says.

"My car looks great."

"I washed and Simonized it, took all the rust off the bumpers, cleaned the whole inside. Once you learn to take care of things, they'll last forever."

In the Air, Over Our Heads

Amy Herrick

Perhaps Sarah takes the apartment at this rude and disreputable end of
the city as an act of curiosity. In any case, she can't afford much more.
She takes the job, although it doesn't pay well, because she wants to be
on hand to deliver any possible blows of reason to this dark and ignorant age. She knows she will witness much injustice and she expects to
see the miserable and oppressed and mad thrown into dungeons (where
they can have time to grow even more miserable and oppressed and
mad). She recognizes that *she* is as free as one is granted to be – given the
anarchy and disorder that roam the universe like wolves – and she
spends the winter training her reflexes to stop on a dime. However, she
doesn't sleep well, perhaps because she is not sure how much actual
power you get from being free in this great light world.

Early in the spring she is assigned her first murder case. Theresa
Maldonado, after eight years of having her nose broken and her teeth
knocked out, finally picked up a carving knife one night and marched
Luis Maldonado around the kitchen table and stabbed him five times
through the heart. Sarah thinks she is ready for this. She, herself, sick of
love, of raising hopes and watching them dashed, of jumping around
deafened and myopic, kissing people on the mouth and later tripping
over things in their darkened rooms searching for her glasses, throws
herself with deadly seriousness into this case.

Theresa has a small heart-shaped face with sadness as incurably
stamped on it as a postmark. If Sarah can bring in a verdict of temporary
insanity, then Theresa will walk away free. Sarah cannot imagine who
would not agree that stabbing Luis was as innocent and temporarily
insane an act as you're likely to get on this whirling little planet with its
rivers of blood.

Throughout the case the jurors sit up and listen to Sarah like daisies in three straight rows, alert and nervous and eager to please. But on the morning when they finish their deliberations, they shuffle back into the courtroom sheepish as a cloud of butchers. They declare Theresa guilty of murder in the second degree.

After this Sarah starts to experience some imbalance of the inner ear, so that even while she is lying in bed the earth seems ready to finish itself off by a small tip and wrench out of orbit. The trillion tiny heartless voices of the stars rush in her ears until she gets up and stands at the window and looks down at the street. She is standing there one night, trying to catch her breath, when the phone rings and it is Robin announcing that she is going to be released from the hospital tomorrow.

Sarah doesn't know what to do. The next day she waits across the street from the hospital in the shadow of the fruitstand, disguised in an old brown trench coat. While she waits, she watches a man with the brightest, drunkest blue eyes she's ever seen going methodically through the garbage cans. He wears two different shoes and stacked on his head are five or six assorted hats. Who could be such a fool as to look for more hats in a world like this? she wonders.

When Sarah looks across the street again, there is Robin with a little suitcase in her hand, slipping quickly out of the arched and ominous doorway and down the shadowed side of the steps. But as soon as she comes to the bottom and hits the sunlight, she stops stock-still as if she were dazzled or stupified by the sudden brightness. She puts her suitcase down and stands there blinking patiently up at the sky. Her black hair frizzes out around her head as if the last nurse has combed it in a great rush and fury. Sarah couldn't blame this nurse a bit and she stares unhappily from her hiding place at Robin and tries to make up her mind.

When at last she decides, she strides across the street without wasting any more time, almost hungrily. Robin cries out sleepily when she recognizes her and they embrace. Then Sarah pushes her away. "You have exactly a month with me," she says. "Use the time well. After that you're on your own."

"You're the same!" Robin says joyfully. "I talked about you a lot in there, but Carlisle, one of the twins, said you'd forgotten me, just like Martin Burnbauer has forgotten me. Carlisle is in there with his brother because one of them supposedly tried to kill their mother. The doctor told them they couldn't have their street clothes back until they admitted that their mother doesn't really flap around their bedroom at night in the shape of a bat."

375

"And if you act or talk crazy, you're out like a shot."

"I'm just talking about Carlisle."

"Swell," Sarah says, "because your special assignment is to get real and find a job." Grimly, she takes Robin's pack and, shouldering it, sets off without looking back to see if she's following.

They stop on the way for some groceries and as they are toiling up the bread aisle, they pass a man in faded red sweatpants. His arms are loaded with yogurt.

"Too much dairy," Robin says to him as he passes. "It'll give you mucus."

"Mucus is good for you," the man answers. He has a deep, ponderous voice which conceals at the bottom a not-quite-decipherable message. Sarah feels immediately that something has gone wrong. She cannot bring herself to look at him. He wears a tiny gold earring in the shape of a cello in one ear. He is short, she thinks, and fairly tall. My type. He has those kind of eyes that are blue as chunks of sky. No wait—they're brown as mud. She'd better leave. She rolls away up the aisle with her cart.

When he happens to get on line right in back of them at the check-out counter, Sarah is sure that he must have fallen for Robin already. It happens all the time. People fall for her like they are jumping out of planes without parachutes, their eyes wide open. They fall down, down through the blue sky and land on the front stoop bearing roses, telephoning in the middle of the night. Gangsters fall for her and drug addicts and the guys who hand out advertisements on street corners. Robin's part in this seems completely innocent and unconscious. Nevertheless, humming like a hand grenade about to detonate, she sets off the celestial bridegroom in most of the people she passes.

And, indeed, when Sarah turns to look at her, she finds her standing there sleepily, completely wrapped up in reading the headlines on the sensational newspapers:

"IS ELVIS REALLY DEAD?"

Sarah sighs and turns away to gaze with relief and boredom at the palatial, orderly press of the supermarket's treasures, so she is completely unprepared when a fat woman cuts in line in front of them. She is tough and pasty looking, but has balanced a disarmingly tiny pink hat on her head. Sarah does not say anything for a moment. Someone can always pull a knife and, further, she is thinking about the fundamental social inequalities and miseries of which such rudeness is the natural consequence. But since it is necessary at all times to define and make justice, otherwise you might as well be dead, Sarah finally says to this lady, "Excuse me, but I believe we were next in line."

The lady turns and looks at her with one of those huge stone faces which are the result of a life of volcanic rage and says, "I'm in a hurry."

"Well, we're not," she says, "but the fair thing to do would be to ask if we minded if you went ahead."

"Life is tough," the lady snorts and turns her huge back away.

Sarah hears her heart hammering hotly just inside the threshold of her ears. She tries to catch Robin's eye for some sign of fraternity, but Robin, it seems, has noticed nothing. She is still reading the headlines: "DOCTORS SAY HEAD TRANSPLANTS NOW POSSIBLE"

A few minutes later when the time comes for the fat lady to pay for her groceries, she finds that her wallet has been stolen.

Sarah looks up, startled at the squeal of rage. The transformation is wonderful. The stony flesh turns soft and tremulous. The tiny pink hat bobs frantically as the woman wades through her purse again. The fourth or fifth time the woman is going through her purse, her attention is arrested by something. She stops and slowly draws out a small matted black feather, possibly an old pigeon feather that's been dipped in ink. "Where did this come from?" she demands furiously. "Who put this here?"

No one, of course, answers.

Sarah is somewhat startled at the shiver of delight that darts straight across her pulse like a little fish and then disappears. The fat woman throws the feather down on the counter and jolts and jounces out the automatic door.

Sarah prepares to turn and look at the man in red sweatpants accusingly. She sets her face into a stern and unapproachable glare, but is brought up short. He looks even better than he did a few minutes ago. She takes a few steps backward to keep her wits clear, but seeing him gazing speculatively at Robin, she gets a distinct whiff of some spice scent drifting down from the Baking Needs aisle. Nutmeg, is it? Or More-Grief-to-Come?

That night Sarah watches the street below and listens for Robin in the adjoining room, but can hear nothing except The Midnight Hour Social Club, which has put a loudspeaker into its front window in the hopes of drawing new customers. Every night around twelve this loudspeaker bursts into music. Sarah pushes chewing-gum-like earplugs in her ears and watches the two plainclothesmen who have been staking out the storefront next door for heroin traffic. They stir and stretch themselves in the shadows. In this ruined neighborhood it is a slow, cold spring, but still the grass and meadowsweet, the wild clover and dandelion steadily poke up into the vacant lot so that where the broken glass coldly sparked like a field of stars through the winter, now there is a thin creeping veil of green. She hasn't lost a case in weeks. Not since Theresa Maldonado. She is trying to understand this. Everything turns to gold in her hands. Muggers, car thieves, cat burglars exit gayly from the courthouse and melt away into the innocent crowd. She stands there with her earplugs in her ears trying to figure this out and all that comes to mind is a picture of Theresa as she might be right now, lying pale and still in her dark cell, temporarily released from prison by sleep. At that moment a figure in red sweatpants turns the corner and comes jogging slowly down the street. She sees that it is the man from the supermarket. He is pensive and brooding, a little heavy on the feet. She stares help-lessly at his running shoes which, with their outsize, cushioning soles, look like clown shoes to her. As he passes by their window he seems to slow down and look up. She feels a slight burning sensation on her face and the skin of her abdomen, a sweet allergic kind of sensation, like she has eaten one too many strawberries. And she knows that it is nothing much, nothing that won't pass digestively. Still, she is relieved to think that he must be looking for Robin. When he sees Sarah in the window, he falters for just a moment and then raises one hand in greeting, like a traffic cop, perhaps perfectly serene in his faith that this one hand will be powerful enough to keep him from being smashed flat. She watches him as he jogs ponderously down the street and disappears around the corner.

She is up till dawn thinking it out—why the unjust, when the just would do as well? She gazes through her bedroom window and she begins, at last, to believe that in the movements of the clouds, the ups and downs of the sun, the ravings of the birds in the morning, she can see what's going on, that she has started to read some of the secret purposes of nature.

Sarah is not surprised when she comes home one night to find the jogger outside their door on the second-floor landing, playing the cello. She walks by him without a word and lets herself into the apartment.

"Hey!" he calls out to her indignantly as she shuts the door behind her.

Robin is sitting dreamily on a chair in front of the open refrigerator. Every once in a while she leans forward and pulls a little corner off of something and eats it. "Your friend is outside," she says in a muffled voice. "You know, Max, the runner."

"Please don't pick like that," Sarah says. "It makes my skin crawl. Just take something out and eat it. A whole thing of something." Sarah knows that this request will not be honored. Robin needs to pick as a way of getting around her mother who is now dead. But in order to please Sarah she tries. She slowly carries a whole cantaloupe on a blue-and-white plate over to the sofa and lies down and cuts herself a tiny slice. She takes a rest and after that she eats another tiny slice. In the hallway, Max stops to tune his cello and then starts up again. Sarah shifts her gaze and stares in fascination at the pattern of blue-and-white roses marching around the circumference of the chipped plate. She understands that the non-causally-related objects in the area around you will generally confirm the true state of your mind. They might even predict the culmination of things if you know how to pay attention. Sarah imagines that she will be able to read the whole ruthless future here in these roses and she rejoices grimly at the power she thinks she is beginning to muster over all these secret things.

"I hope you looked for a job," Sarah says, certain that Robin has barely moved all day, knowing how easily she is transfixed now by motes of light or little cracks in the wall.

"Actually, I've been very busy, but I can't take just any job, you know. I can't concentrate well and, besides, I have to keep my feet off the ground."

Sarah knows better than to ask why this is so. "Well, then I hope you looked for a job where you can keep your feet off the floor."

"I suppose you mean a paying job. There's lots of ways to get paid, you know. I'd work for certain valuable sorts of information."

Sarah comes and stands behind Robin's head and pulls gently on her long, almost black, hair. "What is it you would consider valuable information?"

Robin looks up at Sarah and says seriously, "Well, for one thing, I'd like to know if there really are accurate records kept of everybody's good and evil deeds and to what use these records are put and I'd also like to know what happens when you die. Though there's other ways to get paid. For instance, Martin Burnbauer, my ex-husband, used to often barter the jewelry he made for things he needed—vegetables or beans. Once he got a wisdom tooth extracted in exchange for a silver bracelet."

Sarah frowns in annoyance and lets go of Robin's hair. "I don't want to hear about that creep, Burnbauer. He's gone now and good riddance. Why do you always want to be talking about him?"

A fat tear, blue against the light of the plate on her chest, slips down Robin's face and dangles clownishly from her chin.

"Oh my God, how can you cry for that worm?" Sarah yells.

"I'm not crying for him!" she shouts. "He wasn't a worm! He rescued me from my mother in the nick of time and he was the moon and the stars to me, but I'm not crying for him anymore. I'm crying because something's been pinching my toes."

Sarah sighs. She checks the floor for any sign of demon hands coming through the linoleum, but can't see any. How had they become friends in the first place? She is irritated by the mystery of this, by what it implies about the limits of what you can know of your own desires and needs. She sits down at the bottom of the sofa by Robin's feet. "But the question is, did you look for a job today?"

Robin is closely examining the air over Sarah's right shoulder. "You think I'm out of my mind, don't you?"

Sarah shrugs. "That's the general idea."

"But you can't imagine what I can see from this vantage point," she says grimly.

Sarah, unable to stop herself, twists her head to see what Robin is staring at. There's nothing there.

"Your friend is out in the hall, you know," Robin says.

"What do you mean, my friend?" Sarah says indignantly. "He's no friend of mine."

"I had a very interesting conversation with him through the peephole. His name is Max and he says he was born with a tail."

"Swell."

"But they operated on it when he was a baby and took it off."

"I hope he put it in a glass jar and preserved it."

"I don't know if he did. He didn't tell me that. But we had quite an interesting conversation and he warned me not to fall in love for a while because it might interfere with my convalescence. He said that people who are in love are the most perishable things in the business."

Sarah cuts herself a slice of cantaloupe from Robin's plate and lifts it to her mouth angrily. The cantaloupe is very ripe and has that pungent, gluey taste, reminiscent of love. She thrusts it away from herself. "One of the best things you could do for yourself is to stop talking to strange men."

"You don't need to worry. His Squatters were talking about food. You never need to worry when they're talking about food."

"What are you talking about? What Squatters?"

"You know what I mean, those invisible things that hang around people's heads. I call them Squatters. Max's were talking about food. He's perfectly safe."

"Oh yeah? Well, what about the tail? 'Never trust anybody with a tail' is my motto."

"Don't worry," Robin says.

The last crab-apple blossoms in the park give up the ghost to a breeze and Sarah and Robin are sitting quietly listening to the cello when the perfume reaches them a few minutes later. Robin stirs restlessly as if she scented her mother's grave, but Sarah takes it without flinching.

Later in the week the heat drops down over the city like a net. Sarah stands at her bedroom window and watches the street. The Midnight Hour Social Club bursts into music and one of the plainclothesmen stretches and goes off and comes back in a little while with an ice-cream cone. She wonders what propitious moment exactly they are waiting for to make their bust. Whether she feels sorry or not for the poor sniffling junkies she cannot tell. Now there is a slow parade of movement down at the corner and soon Max is galloping forlornly by in a pair of red running shorts.

"Faster!" Sarah yells out to him tauntingly and the plainclothesman, who is licking ice cream off his wrist, looks up at her window suspiciously.

Sarah calls the Midnight Hour Social Club and tells them that their loudspeaker is keeping the whole neighborhood awake and that they should turn it down. They ask if she is the person who called last night. If she is, they say, she should be on the lookout for death. Then they hang up.

On Saturday Sarah cajoles Robin into getting up off the sofa and going with her to the laundromat. As soon as they get there Robin promptly sits down and props her feet up on a box of Cheer. She looks on calmly while Sarah loads the clothes into the machines.

When Sarah is done, she comes over to Robin furiously. "Stop being such a lump! You've got to get up and move around and do more. Don't you understand how unhealthy this is?"

"Don't be silly, Sarah. I move around plenty. I have a whole other life you don't see."

Sarah rolls her eyes at the ceiling. "I'm talking about your body. I'm talking about getting your blood moving. You've got to get out there and look for a job."

Robin smiles. "I'm on top of that, Sarah. Really. I'm thinking about trying to get a job in a nursing home. I've wrestled with a lot of fat, greasy devils and I think I might be able to help people prepare for the big-time—dying, I mean."

Sarah pictures Robin going around propping everybody's feet up on boxes and stools. But now Robin is staring fixedly into the back recesses of the laundromat. Sarah turns to follow her gaze, expecting to see nothing, but there is Max. He is explaining to a little boy that he is from outer space and has grown from a benevolent pod. He tells the boy to look inside his ear and see if he can see the blue lights. He says that where he's from, people's heads are full of blue lights, not brains. He leads the boy over to the doorway and points up to the sky where he lives, in case the boy ever wants to visit him. Then he saunters over to Sarah's and Robin's bench and somehow manages to sandwich himself into the space between them.

"Hello, hello. How are you?" he asks, addressing either.

Sarah looks away.

"Sarah isn't sleeping well because of the loud music and I've been plagued by something evil creeping around on the floor lately," Robin says.

"I know just what you're talking about."

Sarah whips around and glares at him, but he seems not to notice. He, too, stares at some invisible spot in the air overhead. His expression is lustful, but kind.

"I found it in my car."

"What?!" Robin shouts.

"It's true. It's true. I know this will sound incredible, but I was driving around late last night and suddenly I had this feeling that there was someone or something inside the car with me."

"Where were you going?" Sarah asks suspiciously.

He looks at her coolly. "That doesn't come into the story. Assume I was joyriding. Assume I was out for a little air or something."

She flushes and drops her gaze to his funny shoes.

"There I was and suddenly I had this feeling there was something in the car with me and I called out, 'Who's there?'—very loudly to put whatever it was on the defensive, but there wasn't any answer. I tried looking over into the back seat, but I couldn't see anything. Finally I panicked and pulled the car over to the curb and jumped out. I waited on the curb for something to happen, but nothing did. I waited a long time, but then finally I walked over to the car and looked inside. There, on the front seat, right next to where I had been sitting, was this watermelon."

Sarah looks up and is startled to find his brown eyes, half-closed, fixed on her. "It was inexplicable," he says sternly. "There was no way it could have gotten into the car. But there it was. What was I supposed to do? If it was a joke, it was the worst sort of joke. I opened the door and rolled it across the seat and let it drop onto the pavement. Then I drove away quickly, but I felt claustrophobic and had difficulty breathing as if the car had filled up with smoke."

The way he's staring at her, she gets the feeling he thinks she's the one who did it.

"I hear you're a lawyer," he says blandly. "It must make it hard to sleep at night seeing the wheels of justice turn so slowly. How do you feel about all those murderers and rapists getting off so lightly?"

She stares at him in disgust.

"Oh, oh," he says. "I've offended you."

"I'm a public defender."

"Don't tell me you're one of those guys who thinks everyone's innocent."

"It's probably more to the point to say that I think no one is innocent."

At this moment, one of Sarah's machines bursts open and everything—soapsuds, water, sheets, towels, underwear and socks—comes spilling out onto the dirty cement floor.

Sarah feels this indignity keenly, as if somehow it were her fault, as if this laundry all over the floor spelled out a secret and grave inadequacy, a lack of sexual poise or knowledge of how to talk smoothly at parties.

Max and Robin help her to shove it all back in. Also the little boy helps eagerly, handing up dripping panties and socks, one by one.

Then the man who owns the laundromat comes in, not a nice person, a densely fleshed man, who obviously holds all these furtive humans with their sacks of dirty laundry in great contempt. Sarah knows just what she must do. She marches over to him and tells him what has happened and that he must make sure the catches on the doors are kept in better repair. He looks at her as if she were a juvenile delinquent.

"You didn't shut the door. If you'd shut the door the way you're supposed to shut it, it wouldn't open in the middle of the cycle."

"I banged the door shut. I shut it as shut as you can shut it."

"You banged the door shut? You banged the door?" He advances on her menacingly. "That's why these machines are always breaking down. People like you banging the doors."

"The door wouldn't shut. I had to bang it."

"This is what I mean. If you don't shut the door properly, it will open in the middle of the cycle. This is not the laundromat's responsibility."

"You should get the doors fixed so that normal human beings can shut them."

"Nothing wrong with the *doors.*"

Sarah sits down on the bench trembling with rage. Robin and Max, leaning up against a spinning washer, look like they've noticed nothing.

When Sarah gets up later to load her clothes into the dryer, she shuts the door and before she even has a chance to put her money in the slot, the dryer begins to turn all by itself.

Furthermore, she's not the only one this is happening to. As she looks around the laundromat she sees that people everywhere are discovering that their dryers have been liberated. Stuck in the round window of each one is a black feather.

Suspicious, she looks around for Max and finds that he is standing right next to her. "How is that done?" she asks angrily.

He shrugs. "Oh, it's easy, I imagine. You just stick a little wire strip in the slot. A bobby pin might do it." He smiles at her lazily, first with just the corners of his wily eyes, then more slowly with his wide mouth. "I know a good place to go dancing," he says. "Would you and Robin like to come with me tonight?"

Sarah's not fooled by this. "You can have her all to yourself. I have a brief to write."

But Robin, of course, will not go either. She says she has plans to make and as soon as she gets back to the apartment, she lies down on the sofa and begins to make them.

For a week Sarah does not see Max and she doubts that Robin could be seeing him either, for she appears entirely disabled by her thoughts. When Sarah leaves in the morning, Robin is lying on the sofa staring spellbound at what appear to be ordinary, empty patches of air. When she arrives home in the evening, she is still there as if she hadn't moved all day.

During this week, as the northern half of the planet tips closer to the sun, the streets and sidewalks appear to shudder and shift with heat. But at night, as Sarah stands at her window and looks at the soft black sky speared on the towers and antennas of the buildings, she feels her other heart, the standing-apart, direct-as-gravity one, the one which even in the midst of anxiety and indigestion and disappointment always remains cool and responsive, takes note of beauty and memorizes it, recognizes justice when it comes, she feels that one coming out more and more certainly, like a pale, far star.

She is on her way home from work on Monday night and just passing the Paris Movie Emporium, where couples are welcome, when Max turns the corner in her direction. She tries to go around him, but he grabs her hand and steps up very close as if he were going to steal her purse.

"Well, did you get him off?"

"What?" Sarah says, standing rigidly, ignoring her own hand in his. "What?"

"Don't be funny. You know what I'm talking about. The one you were writing the brief for the night I asked you guys to go dancing. Did you get him off?"

"Oh him. Yes, I got him off. Did you go dancing?" and, here, she manages to wrench her hand free. She is very relieved, like she has just safely pulled it out of a glass jar filled with bees.

He grabs the other hand. "Don't you ever worry about some of these people getting off scot-free?"

"I've seen many people go to prison who needed something a lot different than several years in a tiny cell to heal them of what ails them. I worry about that a lot more." She takes the other hand back and looks up at the evening sky. It is a clear, darkening green and she has the impression that it is, somewhere, full of stars.

"How's Robin doing?" he asks.

"She leaves in a week. I gave her a month and she has apparently spent that month lying on the sofa. Her time is almost up."

Here he steps forward anxiously and stares into her eyes. She tries to stare back at him without flinching, but feels him poking around in there, searching for God knows what. Afraid that he will look into her heart and see Theresa there in her tiny cell lying on her cot and know how she herself has failed, she closes her eyes and takes a step back.

"You're a real tooth fairy," he says sadly. "What did you want her to get done in one month?"

Sarah is furious, but keeps her composure. "She'll never have any idea of what's going on out there until someone pushes her out. Nothing can get through that fog of hers as long as someone keeps giving her the opportunity to lie on their sofa."

"You don't really know that," he says worriedly. "Sometimes you can't see what friendship is doing for somebody. It works invisibly."

"Ha," she says. "Why, next thing I know you'll be telling me about hardened criminals who suddenly turn into balls of stardust after years of infamy and roll home to make soup for their mothers all because some friend stood by them."

"That wasn't what I meant."

385

The movie this week at the Paris Movie Emporium is *Schoolgirls'*
Recess. As she turns away she sees him staring unhappily at a large poster
photograph of a young girl lifting her blue-and-green Catholic school
uniform to expose her childish rump.

When Sarah gets home she is surprised to find Robin lying on her
back on the sofa grating a carrot over a plate on her stomach.

"What are you doing?" Sarah asks in a threatening voice.

Robin turns to her smiling. Her cheeks are pink with exertion. "I'm
making carrotballs for dinner."

"Carrotballs!"

"Martin Burnbauer, my ex-husband, used to make them. They were
good, but I can't remember what all the ingredients were so I'll have to
improvise."

"Well, I'm not going to eat them, you know. You're just making them
so you can wallow in your memories of that creep, Burnbauer."

"Martin was a king."

"He was a creep and a hustler. He exploited and abused you."

"You're misinterpreting things. You didn't like him. I liked him.
Besides which, you're not getting enough sleep, which clouds your judgment."

"Those are voodoo carrotballs, aren't they? You probably put some of
Martin's leftover hair in there, didn't you?"

Robin laughs.

"I'd like to remind you that you don't have much time left to find some
work."

"I've decided to take the test for the fire department."

"The fire-department test is extremely difficult and they're very selec-
tive. You have to be able to climb hand over hand to the top of a fifty-
foot rope and then slide down, plus a lot of other difficult endurance
tests."

"No problem," Robin says from where she lies on the sofa. "I'm feeling
very strong."

Sarah, reflecting only idly on the injustice that gives Robin so much
love and attention and leaves her with carrotballs, is surprised to find
the thick stem of her own heart snap and flood. She turns away quickly
so Robin will not see, but Robin, quick as a whip, grabs up a pepper
shaker from where it is sitting on the floor nearby, and starts flinging
clouds of pepper into the air over Sarah. "Take off, you demons!" she
shouts. "Don't worry, Sarah, this usually routs them!" Sarah stands
meekly, sneezing and weeping, while Robin wages battle.

386

When Sarah passes by the Paris Movie Emporium the next evening, she notices that the pictures on the billboards have been changed and she looks at them curiously to see what the new movie is to be about. Stuck in the top of one of the billboards is a black feather, and she is taken aback to find that all the new pictures are cutouts from women's magazines: banana-cream pies, brides, babies in diapers.

She and Robin sit out on the stoop that night and, to Sarah's disgust, she finds that all up and down the street, everyone is talking about The Black Feather. On this stoop there is a mother and baby from the third floor and some old ladies who fan themselves with tabloids. On the sidewalk in front of them, four men have just unfolded a folding table and are playing cards.

Sarah is juggling for the baby with an orange, a tennis ball and a small white leather shoe that has dropped off the baby's foot.

At first the conversation here ranges far and wide as if they could look into a glass ball and see all those tiny, sinister Russians lining the streets of Moscow or as if they could zoom right into the living room of that family where the little boy pushed his sister out the fifth-floor window, but eventually it comes round to The Black Feather.

"He makes Sarah want to spit," Robin says confidentially to the old ladies.

"Why's that?" asks the young mother, listening in.

Sarah lets the objects she is juggling fall to the ground and she glares furiously at everyone on the stoop. "Because these are just childish revenges. If you want to make people kinder and better behaved towards each other you have to make them feel welcome in the world. Revenge just makes everybody dig themselves in deeper."

"Well, I don't know," says the young mother, "sometimes I think it cheers people up and lets them get on with things."

"Oh boy," says Sarah. "Don't you see this Black Feather guy is probably just making greedy people greedier and dangerous people more dangerous. And he's certainly not doing anything to further his own course of self-improvement."

"How do you know he's a he?" asks one of the old ladies scornfully.

Sarah shrugs, but the baby, reclining on the stoop in a paper diaper, stares up at her with that perspicaciousness of those who speak no language. Blushing, she picks up the orange, the tennis ball and the baby shoe and begins to juggle again. For a moment, the objects hang shining and suspended in the light of the streetlamp. She sees the plainclothesmen in the shadows staring suspiciously into the air at these flying items.

In the last week Sarah has given her, Robin lies on the sofa counting softly under her breath. Sarah wins three more cases and at night she stands at her window and sees that the city, at heart, is really only constructed out of little dots of light. Toy trains twinkle in the distance around the elevated tracks and disappear. Would I cross that bridge when I came to it? she wonders. That little hammock of fireflies?

By Friday evening she has decided to tell Robin it is time to go. When she gets home Robin is sitting on the sofa with her feet stretched out in front of her on a stool. She is watching them narrowly as if they were an enemy force. Sarah, in the ominous heat, moves around the house irritably, banging and sweeping and dusting.

"Do you remember my mother?" Robin asks. "All she did all day long was squeeze cantaloupes and change toilet-paper rolls and throw out spoiled food. Do you remember what she looked like? Like a big gray squid. That's what's happening to you."

"Oh, I don't think so," Sarah says, distracted by the thought. She insists that Robin get up off the sofa and take a walk with her around the Ukrainian street fair, which is just opening its week of festivities tonight. Before she goes out, Sarah puts on a soft lavender-colored skirt and a white blouse and goes to look at herself in the mirror to see if she does look like a squid. She is taken aback to find that she has entered on one of those unaccountable phases of great beauty and she turns away fast as if she has seen a spook waving at her shyly from a cloud of light over her head.

Robin is in the kitchen inspecting the inside of her sneaker.

"What are you doing?" Sarah asks.

"My shoes feel slippery."

"Well, put some talcum powder on your feet and hurry up about it."

In spite of the heat, there are hundreds of people jammed into the three-block street fair. Stalls lit by strings of colored lanterns line the streets and the summer dark lends to the scene a grim, fairy-like purpose. The smoke from the sausages and deep-fried pastries thickens the air. Religious articles lean over the counters and beckon to them — red-daubed and thorny saints, the Virgin Mary posed as if for a graduation picture in her nimbus of light.

At the end of the street is a raised platform skirted with a cloth decorated in twining birds and flowers. The folk dancers twist around in a speeding circle. Against her will, Sarah feels her hopes rise. If she cannot have love, at least she has within her the power to stand up to the anarchy and disorder of the world, to name what is fair and bear it company.

Behind her she hears Robin cry out as if she saw something coming too. When Sarah turns she sees a little boy, perhaps four years old, standing in front of them, stock still in terror. Obviously lost, he scans the crowd desperately with dark, bright eyes. He seems to feel instinctively, like a bird that has flipped prematurely out of its nest and crashed into the grass, that he had better not move. He whimpers and tries to look around without moving his head. He is dressed to kill with a plastic sword tucked into his black pirate sash and a red bandanna tied around his head.

Sarah is tempted by doubt as she stands there. It seems to her that she sees the expanding and contracting universe replaying this scene, mercilessly, again and again. At last, however, she takes a step towards him. Out of the corner of her eye, she sees Robin step forward too. Before they can reach him, his mother appears.

They know she is the mother because she is holding in her hand a plastic pirate ship. Her pink sundress is too tight and the straps cut into the soft flesh over her breast. She is scanning the crowd desperately and her eyes are strained with fear, but when she sees the child at last, all emotion seems to drain out of her face. It goes dead and white. She rushes over to the boy and grabs his arm and with the back of her hand, slaps his face.

"Didn't I tell you to stay with me?" She slaps him again. "Didn't I?"

The little boy, at the sight of the white, blank face bending over him, closes his eyes. He whimpers each time she hits him, but other than that, stands quite still. The tiny sight of him standing there without resistance drives his mother into a fury and she slaps the side of his head.

"Do you hear me? Do you hear me?"

He nods yes, but doesn't say a word. He is concentrating on some far black sail on the blue horizon.

Sarah hears Robin give a long low hiss, but when all the breath is gone from her lungs, she seems to slump and turn away. Although this scene is taking place right here, off the curb, the space surrounding this mother and child appears theatrically bright and far away, and the great crowd on the street seems to squint and lean forward as if they watched from a high balcony.

Someone has to explain this to me, Sarah thinks. These terrible gaps in the world with no pity in them. How all around the earth tonight there are little rooms noisy with pain where torturers crush their victims' kneecaps and how great a distance we bystanders have to travel before we can open our mouths to say a word.

Sarah sighs and steps towards them. "Excuse me," she says to the woman. "I think maybe you're making a mistake. This little boy was lost and he was looking for you."

The woman stops what she's doing and frowns at Sarah. She writes her off with a glance. "You got any children of your own?" she asks and without waiting for the answer, turns back to her son. She digs her fingers into his arm and shoves the pirate ship into his hands. His fingers curl around it automatically and he is dragged away.

Sarah stands there furious and mortified. The woman seemed to be implying that she could read a secret truth about Sarah. Some hidden barrenness maybe, or inability to hold a man. She walks back through the crowd, her face burning.

She and Robin wander slowly up and down the street examining the things for sale on the tables. They are standing in front of a table overflowing with a jumble of stuff—spatulas and tablecloths, flea collars and key chains—when Max comes up to them. "Very Ukrainian," he says, picking up a plastic cup filled with assorted screws and nails, six for a dollar.

Robin beams at him, but Sarah tries to freeze him out with an icy stare. He tags along with them happily. Sarah, in a fury, decides to leave them behind in the crowd. She weaves her way in and out of knots of people until at last she finds herself alone, standing in front of a lemonade booth. She buys herself a cup. It is freshly squeezed, with honey and ice, and, as sometimes a food or drink can, for a moment it perfectly answers her thirst and loneliness. Recklessly, she buys herself a second cup and, of course, is suddenly struck with the thought of Theresa imprisoned in this heat without the possibility of such succor. She drops the full, sweet cup into a trash can and turns away.

There, in front of her, is the plump child abuser and her pirate son. The woman is examining a potholder in the light of the streetlamp. The child stands next to her, perfectly still, his face swollen with crying, his eyes straining at some invisible spot up in the shadows.

Sarah turns her gaze away for a moment and so misses what happens in the next few seconds. When a whispering and tittering begins in the crowd behind her, she thinks at first it must be for her, that everyone has noticed her immense sadness, but when she turns she sees that after all they are laughing at the pirate boy's mother, who is suddenly standing there in just her panties, her dress lying in a circle around her feet. She is looking in moonlike bewilderment at the laughing and gaping crowd. It is a difficult sight and Sarah understands why everyone laughs. She thinks how the human nude never lends much glory to the landscape, not like a tiger or a python would, or even an everyday horse, standing in a meadow; it's too soft and hairless a thing, too tipsily bipedal. And this human in particular is so pale and biscuit-like in appearance that the crowd cannot help but be convulsed with hilarity.

But when the woman suddenly understands that she is naked, it becomes a different matter. Before their eyes she seems to blow up into a supernaturally huge and furious figure, a crimson-faced banshee or vampire. She shrieks something foul at the crowd in a strange and hellish-sounding tongue and they fall silent waiting for her to burst into flames.

However, what happens after all is that her lower lip begins to tremble and tears spring into her eyes and she leans over to pick up her dress. When she tries to arrange it back over her shoulders she finds that someone has neatly razored open the shoulder straps and neatly razored a long slit down the back.

Here, a man bends down and picks up the black feather where it has fallen and lain covered by the dress and Sarah groans in shame for everyone. When the man tries to hand it to the woman, she knocks it away and it falls back to the ground. She holds the dress around herself as best she can and hustles the little boy in front of her and out of the crowd.

Max, of course, is leaning against a car watching the scene calmly and Robin is standing next to him. In a minute everyone is laughing and chattering again as if the world were after all just an elephant standing on the back of a turtle, a finite and knowable place. The children, grossly, innocent and particularly joyous, pretend to be the fat woman, sketching her breasts in the air and replaying, again and again, her discovery of her nakedness. The adults laugh at the children and the folk dancers swing around very fast. Sarah watches Max closely from the corner of her eye. He looks sleek and content. His eyes are half closed.

She storms over to him in a fury. "And what do you think will happen now?" She watches him carefully for some betraying sign, but he merely opens his eyes a little wider and stares at her in surprise. "Whaddaya mean?" he says.

As his brown eyes meet hers she feels her skin turn pink and then dissolve, no doubt leaving all her internal workings clearly revealed.

"To the child!" she shouts at him and tries to hold his gaze so that he will not look down and see her intestines shining out eagerly. "What do you think will happen to that child now? Why, she'll probably just take him home and beat him up some more, out of pure spite and misery."

391

He frowns and seems to think this over. "Well, that may be true," he says slowly, "but then, on the other hand, people have to tell each other things, don't you think? You can't be a witness to such things and not speak. If you don't, your heart dries up."

"I have blood in my shoes," Robin says suddenly. She has been shifting miserably from one foot to the other for several minutes now.

"What do you mean?" they both say to her sharply.

"Well, I don't know. I've been feeling something slippery in there all evening and now I've realized it's blood."

"Show me," Sarah orders.

Robin bends down obediently and takes off one of her shoes. She holds it up to the light to show them. "See," she says.

The shoe looks slightly sweaty, but there's not a trace of blood.

Sarah stares at Max as if this, too, were his fault. Then she looks at Robin. "Tomorrow your time with me is up, you know," she says gently. "You've got to go."

When they get back home, Robin goes into her room and shuts the door quietly behind her. Sarah stands at the window in the dark and watches the street. She knows what to expect. She's running it wide open and light, aboveboard. She's getting a grasp of the inner nature of things and a street like this holds no secrets from her. At ten-thirty the plainclothesmen appear to take their places in their doorways. At twelve, the Midnight Hour Social Club's loudspeaker comes on. At twelve-thirty, Max goes by.

At twelve thirty-five, the moon appears over the vacant lot, silent and critical, white and cool. Sarah greets it sternly, without even blinking. At twelve-forty, to her astonishment, Max comes galloping back up the street with a bouquet of flowers in his arms. Without even thinking about it, she leans way out to stare at him, unable to make head or tail out of the meaning of this.

He stops at the bottom of her fire escape, smiles up at her and grabs hold of the ladder which someone has foolishly left down. The plainclothesmen stare at him sleepily as he climbs up to her window.

"Well!" he says as he jumps, with a thud, into her room.

She takes a quick step backwards and finds herself in the dark, out of the light of the streetlamp.

"Why aren't you sleeping?" he asks accusingly.

She is certainly furious at this intrusion, but she also feels caught in a curious tight spot — as if at the very brief space where the tide changes, both helpless and langorous, about to be thrown back up on the beach.

"Insomnia," she says briefly.

"Aaah," he says. "That would explain several things. I suppose the music from across the street doesn't help either, does it?"

She doesn't answer him.

The streetlamp hovers at his back like a pink alien spaceship, so while his outline glows brightly, he is otherwise dark and faceless. She breathes very deliberately, wanting to keep her reflexes sharp, but this plan backfires. The air is filled with an overpowering scent of summer leaves and pollen and her head swims. When, at last, she takes a step forward, she sees that it is because of the big, feathery, plucked-looking bouquet of flowers.

Well, he is surely in love, she thinks wistfully. He is standing there looking smug and yet defenseless, the way you look when you undertake to crawl up out of the sea onto land for the first time.

Sarah hears Robin open her bedroom door and step into the hallway. "Well, go ahead," Sarah sighs. "There she is."

Sarah goes over to the window and looks out. The moon is now riding high over the tenements and the street is caught in its steady, penetrating light. Nothing will escape. It holds everything transfixed with its baleful, white glance. It seems to her she's been standing here looking out this window into the moonlight for a long, long time, when Max, whom she'd thought years gone, says sadly, "You've been misunderstanding me, I think. I brought these flowers for you."

At first these words only get to her in the way small matters do, like flies at a picnic or a shoelace coming undone or someone saying, "Please pass the pepper." And even as she realizes, with a lurch, what they must mean, and even as she is wondering, with that curious thrill with which one wonders such matters, what his kisses will be like, she knows that this will come and this will go, and maybe it will be a sweet matter, but it won't be of much importance.

Sarah is pleased to find herself so lightly snared and she thinks about how not only is the world no longer considered to be a finite place, lodged solidly in the heart of a bright-faced God, it is also no longer considered to be an infinite place, constructing itself endlessly out of an endless variety of chances and accidents. No, nowadays, it's supposedly the organization itself of the world which is so magical, which throws off stars and gases, which creates its own energy and falls into dust and then rises up out of the dust even more terrible and complicated. She is eager to win as much power and influence as she can over the secret nature of these things.

Plainclothesman Number One shakes himself and walks off to get his nightly ice-cream cone. Plainclothesman Number Two saunters over to the vacant lot to take a pee. He wades into the tall grasses and the moment he disappears, a dark figure detaches itself from the shadows below and races lightly across the street towards the Midnight Hour Social Club. This hooded figure, sure of itself and fast, has in its hand a long, pointed instrument and, for a second, Sarah's heart stops, thinking she recognizes Theresa's bloody knife, but then she sees it is a screwdriver.

Sarah wants to yell out some warning, but doesn't dare for fear of adding any more dangers to the situation. And, indeed, in a moment a couple emerges from the club. The hooded figure hesitates only briefly and then steps back into the shadows. The couple is not dancing now, but that they have been dancing recently is easy to tell for their feet skip a little and the man is snapping his fingers. The woman is dressed in a full, red skirt which is only now beginning to deflate slowly. Sarah holds her breath in terror lest they turn around, but their eyes and ears must still be ringing and they walk happily to the corner through the loud music and disappear.

Instantly the hooded figure leaps from the shadows again and dashes towards the loudspeaker, which is propped high in the window just out of reach. It leaps up and stabs the speaker once, twice, three times in the guts with the screwdriver and suddenly the street is silent. The figure pauses for a moment, hand in pocket, then drops a black feather to the ground and turns and races back across the street.

Suddenly Sarah finds herself urgently sleepy and yawns a big yawn. "Did you realize it was her all along?" she asks him irritably. She can barely keep her eyes open.

"Sure," he whispers and now he leans forward and touches her cheek with just the tips of his fingers. They feel cool and smell sweet from the stolen roses and foul from the daisies plucked out of vacant lots. "I saw her take that lady's wallet in the supermarket. Besides, who else could it have been?"

Sarah just manages to reach out and brush his cheek lightly with her sleepy fingers.

In a minute they hear Robin reenter the apartment and close the door to her room.

"You're not really going to throw her out tomorrow, are you?" he asks.

Then, only mildly astounded to find that *this* is the place she gets caught, she says, "No, of course not."

"I knew you wouldn't," he says gently.

She yawns right in his face and, smiling, pushes him out the window onto the fire escape.

Even before he has reached the bottom, she has fallen into bed, knowing that this may be the last holy moment for a long time and that it is not given to her to know just where the next will come from.

She acknowledges grumblingly to whoever hovers in the air over her head that although she may have within her the power to stand up to the anarchy and disorder of the world, she actually has only the most limited authority over that power. It will choose its own times and will behave erratically in accordance with some impenetrable plan. All she can do is be as ready as possible to make good.

Then, turning her face against the cool pillow, she is swept out towards the far morning on a wide, untracked river of sleep.

A Sudden Story
Robert Coover

Once upon a time, suddenly, while it still could, the story began. For the hero, setting forth, there was of course nothing sudden about it, neither about the setting forth, which he'd spent his entire lifetime anticipating, nor about any conceivable endings, which seemed, like the horizon, to be always somewhere else. For the dragon, however, who was stupid, everything was sudden. He was suddenly hungry and then he was suddenly eating something. Always, it was like the first time. Then, all of a sudden, he'd remember having eaten something like that before: a certain familiar sourness . . . And, just as suddenly, he'd forget. The hero, coming suddenly upon the dragon (he'd been trekking for years through enchanted forests, endless deserts, cities carbonized by dragonbreath, for him "suddenly" was not exactly the word), found himself envying, as he drew his sword (a possible ending had just loomed up before him, as though the horizon had, with the desperate illusion of suddenness, tipped), the dragon's tenseless freedom. Freedom? the dragon might have asked, had he not been so stupid, chewing over meanwhile the sudden familiar sourness (a memory . . . ?) on his breath. From what? (Forgotten.)

In Proportion

Lynn Grossman

She is small and it is smaller, but it isn't the smallest it has been. The smallest had been when she was three and had started. Then, when she put it under her chin and drew the bow across it, the sound was not like music. Music-to-be, is what I called it.

The teacher had said it was in proportion. Proportion was the thing that counted, the teacher had said.

At three, it was a miniature in complete detail, a tiny version of a perfect thing. She was that, too, when she was three.

At eight it is bigger, but still in proportion, for she is bigger, too.

There is a right way and a wrong way, and I want to do it right for her. For me, it is hard to tell, right and wrong. Proportion, I mean. When I carry it for her, it is too small in my hand. Out of my hand it looks even smaller to me, but I think it might look bigger to her. Proportion is easier to see when you are eight.

In the taxi she is too small for the seat belt. She is looking out the window, but it looks to me like she cannot see the street. It looks to me like she can see sky and tops of buildings. When you are her size, up is where you are always looking.

There is no partition in the taxi. The driver points to the case and asks if it's a small machine gun. Everyone asks that question, but I laugh anyway, to be polite. She doesn't laugh. She has only learned polite up to Please and Thank You.

She snaps the snaps on the case with her index finger and her thumb. When she was born, I spread her fingers and traced her hand. When she got older, she traced my hand next to hers. Last year, both our hands could not fit on the same piece of paper. This year, she would not let me trace her hand at all.

The driver drums the steering wheel. His hands are big, bigger than hers and mine put together. He guesses her age, eight.

Right, I say.

Eight and a quarter, she says. She seems to know the value of time.

We are in the park when I see them. We are at the place in between where you can't see the buildings on the East Side and you can't see the buildings on the West Side. That is an unlucky place in the middle, I think. That place in the park is like being lost. I don't like being in between, and I have always felt relieved to be past it, to know what side of the city I am on. But that is where we are.

She can balance it under her chin without holding on. Her small face fits perfectly on the ebony cup. When I play it to show her how, my face does not fit at all. My face hides the bridge and the tuning pins. When it was the smallest it had been, I would try to show her on the strings. I would press one string, but two would go down. My hand was too big. It was an impossibility, for me, anyway, like wearing a mitten and picking up a dime.

She had to show me. She would put her fingers on the strings and I would talk them into position. I would talk and they would move. We could do this so quickly we were like one person, really, half-big and half-small.

They are attached to the visor with rubber bands stretched so tight over the vinyl they are as thin as violin strings. They start small and go big, bigger, biggest in steps, like nesting dolls. Only these are not identical, even though they seem to be the same child, even though the backgrounds are identical—light blue and mottled the way paper looks when you crumple it and spread it out again. These are different poses. These pictures are in special frames under the rubber bands, special plastic frames with fancy edges.

The boy in the pictures has big, dark eyes, like my kid's eyes. The smallest is when he is a baby. The biggest looks about my kid's age. The other one is someplace in between.

The driver talks to my kid, but she does not answer him. She is not a friendly kid, and that is all right with me. But I do not want to be rude to him, at least not in front of her. Everything you do in front of them is a lesson, I think, and I want to do it right for her.

So I talk to him. Small talk. I say, Is that your kid? and I see her eyes look up in the direction of the visor. So what comes next is my fault. My fault for asking.

That is my son, he says. He is eight. He is dead, is what the driver says to us.

We get off at Fifth and walk the big block. I do not speak because I cannot do it right for her. This is one I cannot do right for me. I think death is not out of proportion, it has just always seemed that way to me. I am as small as she is when it comes to this, but I would rather she not know, so I do not talk at all.

She walks close to my leg and the violin hits the small place behind my knee. She looks like she is thinking. I can see her index finger on the handle of the case picking the cuticle on her thumb. That is what she does when she thinks, picks.

Here are the deaths I think she knows about: death by ray gun, death by meteor shower, death by pricking a finger on a bobbin, death by poisoned apple.

The deaths I know about, I don't want to say.

Maybe she is thinking of her deaths. I know I am thinking of mine. I know I am thinking of the child he kept in the present tense.

Why do they put machine guns in violin cases? is the question she asks when she crosses our silence, but she doesn't wait for the answer. She drops my hand and walks on ahead of me, and she swings the violin against her own leg.

We walk the two flights when we get there, and I cannot catch my breath. It is not the stairs, I think, but because she is in the present tense, too.

The day she was born, when she was the smallest she had been, I could not imagine a time when I would not be bigger than she was.

I am too slow for her now. She takes the stairs two at a time, and beats me to the top. She looks big on the landing when I am looking up.

The Blue Baby

Leon Rooke

There was a time down in North Carolina when nothing ever happened.

There was the time up north in the Yukon when a man I knew locked up another man I knew inside a freezer and the man froze.

There were those times and there were other times.

I don't know which times to tell you about.

There was the time when I was twelve and riding a bicycle around and around a small shrub in the backyard and the front tire hit a brick and the bicycle crumpled beneath me and I broke a tooth and she did not care.

I am convinced she did not care.

So there was that time too.

There were the times she would bounce me on her knees and ask, Who do you love most, him or me? You didn't remember him or anything about him, but there were those times she asked that. He was like your nickel which rolled between the floorboards into the utter, unreachable darkness of the world. He was like that. Who do you love most, him or me? And though you knew the answer you never said a word, not one. You would only hang your head and wait for the knee-ride to begin again. She would stop the ride to take your face in her hands and ask that. And though you knew the answer, knew it to the innermost ache of your heart, you never said a word, not one.

You couldn't say, Ride me, Mama. You could only squint at the thin darkness between the floorboards and wonder what else over the long years had fallen between those cracks.

Him or me?

For years and years she asked this and you always knew but never answered, and now you are here by her bedside and still you can't.

400

So there were those times. Some of the times were good times, but they do not belong here. I don't know where they belong.

Here is another one. Sometimes on a dark night you could stand under a tree in front of your house and see two naked fat people in the upstairs room in the house across the street.

I thought, If only they knew how ugly they are.

I thought, Why do they do that?

I thought, Why don't they turn off that light?

The fat man up there lived in another place, lived across the river, and I thought he should stay in the place he came from.

My friends on that street would gather under that tree and they would say, Oh baby, look at them go, and you never could get your friends away from that tree. Shut up, they would say, what's eating you?

My mother was a friend of this woman. She was to be seen in this woman's company, in this fat woman's company, she was to be seen with them. I wondered whether my mother knew what went on up there with this fat couple, and why, when she went out on double dates, she had to go out with people like this.

He had a car, that's why.

On Saturday nights they went to dances together in a place called Edgewater, Virginia.

I stand corrected on this one small matter. I said "car" but it was not a car. His was a stingy little truck, dusty and black, with narrow, balding tires and corncobs and empty fertilizer sacks in the rear. When they went out to these dances the fat woman would sit up under the fat man's arms and my mother would sit in the cab on her date's lap, her head folded up against the ceiling, and all four would be hooting with laughter.

That was one time.

There was that time I broke a tooth falling against a brick while riding my bicycle around and around this little shrub and my mother said, Now no girl will ever marry you, but I knew she didn't care. She hardly even looked, scarcely even glanced at me, because I wasn't bleeding.

I got hit in the jaw once with a baseball, there was that time.

I pulled long worms out of my behind, there were those times, and I didn't tell her.

There was the time a dentist, my first dentist, took out an aching tooth, the wrong tooth, with a pair of garage pliers and charged two dollars.

You could see those worms up in white circles on my cheeks and across my shoulders and people would look at you, they'd say, Look at that boy, he has worms.

You took a folded note to the store one time which you were not supposed to read, but you read it and it said, Give him head lice powder, I will pay you later.

You stole a nickel from her purse one time and it rolled between the floorboards and you have not yet confessed that.

You were such a nice little boy, so sweet and good.

You had to sit on a board when you got a haircut. You'd see the barber pick up the board and sling it up over the arms of the chair and you wanted to hit him.

You put a penny in the weight machine in front of the drugstore and got your fortune told. You would put in the penny or one of your friends would, and then that friend would step up on the scale with you or you would step up beside him, step up carefully, not to jiggle or the red cover would slam down over the numbers, and then one of you would step off, step carefully off, not to jiggle, and the numbers would roll back to reveal your own true weight, although both of you had the same fortune.

For two years I never weighed more or less than eighty-seven pounds. There was that time.

Women—young girls, ladies—would come to the door and they would ask, Is So-and-So here? Where is So-and-So? But you weren't supposed to tell them, even if you knew, because So-and-So had washed his hands of these women, was done with them, yet they wouldn't leave him alone.

Policemen knocked on the door, too, they too wanted to know where So-and-So was.

So-and-So was in trouble with women, with the law, with the family and with everyone else, and what you heard was he was no good, he was mean, he cared about no one, he would as soon hit you as look at you, but he was my mother's brother and she was ever defending him and hiding him and if anyone didn't like it they could go climb a pole.

You had to go to the store to buy your mother's Kotex, because no one else would or no one else was around, and that was terrible. The storekeeper would say, Speak up, boy, and you would again grumble the word. He would put the Kotex up on the counter and everyone would stare at it, would say this or that, they'd look at me, look me over closely, then the storekeeper would wrap the box in brown paper like a slab of meat and take your money and go away rubbing it between his fingers.

Sometimes a strange dog would come up and follow you for a bit,

402

follow you home even, even stand scratching at the door, but you never knew whose dog it was or what name you could call it except Dog or what means you could devise to make it stay.

Mrs. Whitfield next door refused to return any hit ball which landed in her yard.

The one pecan tree in this place I am talking about was surrounded by a high fence and you could not reach the limbs even with poles and no matter how hard or long you tried.

At night you threw rocks at the light hanging from a cable supported by poles at either side of the gravel street and when you hit it you ran, because Mrs. Whitfield would be calling the law.

The policemen patrolled these streets like beings from another side of the world.

A boy my age jumped or fell from the water tower at the edge of town, there was that time.

There was the time a car was parked in the same alley that ran behind our house, with a hose hooked up from the exhaust to a window, but only the woman died. The man with her had awakened in the night, had changed his mind and fled. She was some other man's wife and her blouse was open and below the waist she had nothing on except her green shoes. My mother said to us all, she said, What kind of scum would leave her like that?

The town smelled. It smelled because of the paper mills and sometimes a black haze would cover the sky and you would have to hold your nose.

Those fat, naked people in the room upstairs, you would see them drink from a bottle sometimes. You would see them with their arms around each other and then a hand would reach down to the windowsill and pick up the bottle.

You would see the light bulb hanging from their ceiling and a fly strip dangling to catch the flies.

A body was discovered one summer in a stream called the Dye Ditch, the stream you had to cross to reach grammar school, but you went down to look at that place in the ditch where the body was discovered but no one was there, no corpse was there, and after a while you didn't hear anyone speak of it and you never knew who it was had been stabbed in that ditch. The ditch was deep, with steep clay walls, the walls always wet, wet and smooth and perfect, but clay was not a thing you knew to do anything with. You found a shoe in the woods just up from the bank, a shoe with the tongue missing, and you said, This was the stabbed man's shoe and you asked yourself why So-and-So had done it, because of some woman, most likely.

Some days the ditch water was one color, some days another color, vile colors, and at other times it was a mix of many.

You couldn't dam up that stream although you spent endless days trying, and you put your bare foot in the stabbed man's shoes but you still didn't know why or how it had happened.

You were such a nice little boy. You were so nice. You tried making biscuits once, as a surprise for your mother when she came in from work, but you forgot to mix lard in, and the salt and baking powder, and the biscuits didn't rise, and when she came in you'd forgotten to wipe up the flour from the table and floor.

She would sit you on her knees and hold your shoulders as she bounced you up and down and she would say, Which do you love best, him or me?

You were swinging on a tree-rope by the Dye Ditch, swinging high, into the limbs, and you let go and flew and when you landed a rusty nail came up all the way through your foot and as you hobbled the half-mile home you were amazed that it hurt so little and bled so little, and when you got home your brother pulled out the nail with pliers and your mother rubbed burning iodine over the wound and said, Be sure you wear clean socks for the next little while.

Three streets were paved, all others were gravel, and all of the streets were named after U.S. presidents. There was an uptown called Rosemary and a downtown called Downtown, and uptown was bigger, while Downtown was dying, was dead, but was the place you had to go through if you wanted for whatever reason to cross the river.

Across the river was nothing, it was death across the river. The fat man had come from across the river, so had my mother when she was fourteen and fleeing death, which was exactly how she spoke of it. Oh, honey, it was death on that farm.

He was down between the cracks, my father was, that's where he was.

There was another time, an early time, when I walked with my grandfather across the fields and when he stopped to pick up soil and crumble it and let it sift between his fingers I would pick up soil and do the same.

Your grandfather let you walk down the rows with him, he let you hold the plow, and he said, Just let the mule do the work, but you couldn't hold the plow handles and the reins at the same time and the plow blade kept riding up out of the ground. When you came to the end of a row the mule would stop and your grandfather would look at both of you, look and flap his hat against his leg, and say, Now let's see which of you have the better sense. You stood behind your grandfather's chair in the evenings and combed his balding head, but your grandmother said, I've got enough plates to get to the table, why should I get theirs? Why can't she come and take away these that are hers and leave me with those that are mine?

No one asked her to marry that drinker.

Didn't we tell her sixteen was too young?

She made her own bed. There ain't one on their daddy's side ever had pot to pee in or knew what pot was for.

So there was the time she came and packed your goods, your brother and sister's goods, in a paper sack, and took you to town for the first time. The town was only seven miles away, but it was the first time and it was quite a town. It had a downtown called Downtown and an uptown called Rosemary, and she had two upstairs rooms downtown on Monroe Street, and you had to be very quiet up there because the woman who lived below lived alone below and she was so stupid she thought every sound meant a thief was coming to steal her money.

She had a blue baby, this baby with an enormous blue head, and all of the light bulbs in her rooms were blue so that you wouldn't know she had a blue baby.

Every day for five days in the week, sometimes six, your mother left for work before daylight, you would hear the car out on the street honk for her, you would hear the car door slam, hear the engine, the roll of tires, and she would be gone. You would hear her moving softly about you, you would feel her tucking you in, then she would be gone. You went to school that first week and for five days stood in the woods watching the children at play outside, then the bell would ring and they would go inside, and when the yard had cleared you would tramp through the woods back home, you would dawdle at the Dye Ditch and check where you could and could not jump it and be amazed at all the vile colors, you would sit on the bank and grieve and tell yourself that tomorrow you would go inside with them. Then you would sneak up the stairs and never make a sound all day, just you and the blue baby and the baby's mother in that silent house. You would sit at the table drawing rings of water on the yellow top. At the end of the day your mother would come in with a bag of groceries, come in with a sweater looped over one arm, come in with cotton fuzz in her hair, and she would say, How do you like your new school, is it a nice school? How do you like your new friends?

She would sit you on her knees and bounce you and say, How is my handsome man today?

You were such a good little boy.

On Fridays you got up early to deliver the local paper and the people would not pay, they would say, It is not worth my nickel, and you kept returning but they rarely would pay, although they did not tell you to stop delivering their paper and if you did stop they would call the editor, they would say, Where's my paper?

There was the time I knocked on one door and my Uncle So-and-So answered without his clothes on and he said, You haven't seen me, you don't know where I am, and he gave me a dollar.

The blue baby died and went to heaven, but the woman downstairs did not change her light bulbs.

On Mondays you would take your mother's white blouse and black skirt to the cleaners and on Saturdays you would see her wearing these. You would see her in heels, her legs in nice stockings, her mouth red, and she would say, How do I look?

She would say, Say Hello to Monty, but you wouldn't.

She would say, He's so cute when he's pouting, and that would make you grin.

She would say, I'll be home early, but you stayed up late with your head pressed against the window and she never came, no, she never.

There was the time she said, You smell like four dead cats in a trunk, why don't you wash? And she flung your clothes off and scraped at your knees, elbows and heels, she twisted a cloth up in your ears, she said, This crust will never come off, and when she had your skin pink and burning she said, Your father is coming, you want to look nice for him, don't you?

But he didn't come, and I put back on my dirty clothes and hid under the house until past bedtime, until past the time she'd stopped walking the street and calling my name, and then I went in and would talk to no one.

There was the time she said, I want the three of you out of this house, I want you out this minute, if I don't get a minute's peace I will stab myself with these scissors. So she dressed you and your brother in identical Little Boy Blue short-pant suits with straps that came over the shoulder, and she washed your faces and necks and ears and slicked your hair down with water. She gave your sister thirty-six cents from her red purse and she said, Take them to see the moving picture show at the Peoples Theater and don't you dare come back until the picture is over. My sister said, Mama, how will we know when the picture is over? and my mother said, When the rest of the audience gets up to leave that's when you leave, and not a second before. So we trouped down to the movie, hurrying to get there because we couldn't imagine what it might be like to see a moving picture show. We entered in the dark and sat in seats at the very rear, while up on the screen you saw the back of a man's head and a woman with her head thrown back and they were kissing. We sat on the edge of our seats, holding hands, my sister in the middle and telling us not to kick our legs, as the man got into a jeep and drove off, not returning the wave of the woman who was running after him, and he got smaller and smaller in his jeep as the music got louder, and then we saw tears slide down the woman's face and she collapsed to her knees in the muddy road and in the next second the theater lights were rising and everyone was getting up. They were getting up, they were all leaving.

On the way home the three of us bawled and my sister said it wasn't worth thirty-six cents, it wasn't worth nothing and Mama must be crazy.

So that was that time and that is why I have hated movies to this day.

You weighed eighty-seven pounds for so many of those years.

You wore socks so stiff with filth you could barely work your feet into them in the morning. Your nose ran, always ran, and you wiped the snot on your sleeves until they turned stiff also, from cuff to elbow.

You would feel this tickling movement, this wriggling motion, while you sat on the toilet, and you'd stand up and wrench yourself over and there would be this long worm coming out of your behind. You couldn't believe it that first time, but here it was, proof that worms were living inside you, and it made you ache with the shame that if worms did, lived inside you, then what else could?

You will tell no one. You would be walking down the street and you'd feel it, feel the worm, and you'd reach a hand inside your britches and pull the worm all the way out and you'd think it never was going to stop coming.

Who do you love best, him or me?

There was the time all this ended, but you never knew when it was that time was, so it was as though that time never ended, which is one reason to think about it. I think about it because it ended, but never really ended, that is why I think about it.

They were always washing your ears.

They were always saying, Tie your shoelaces.

You were always being shoved one way or another by one person or another and you never gained an ounce through so many years.

We got home from the moving picture show fifteen minutes after we left and our mother was sitting in her slip in the kitchen chair, with her eyes closed and both wrists up white in her lap and her feet in a pan of water.

Cotton fluff was in her hair.

One year you asked your mother whatever happened to that fat old guy with the truck who went with that woman across the street, and she didn't know who you meant. Some days later, while washing her hair over a white bowl, she suddenly clapped her hands and said, Oh him, they are not going together any longer, it was never serious anyhow. It's just that he treated her decently and he wasn't a tightwad, and he liked good fun. Why are you asking about something like that?

Why are you? Sometimes I find myself thinking you are a strange little boy.

You're odd. That's how you strike me sometimes.

I think about it now because now she lies in this bed with tubes up her nose and tubes attached to her shaved head and she's holding my hand, or rather her hand is limp in mine and you can't hear her breathe. You can't see her chest rise and her lids never move. Her fingers are silent in mine.

You think of the man you knew who was locked up in the freezer in the Yukon and how he froze.

You think of the freezer and of opening the door, but when the door is opened after all of these years all you see is the freezer empty and the frosty tumble of air.

You think of these things and of those times.

She has been this way for an hour or more, not moving, and so have I, the two of us here, neither of us moving and nothing happening, her hand cold in mine and the night darkening and I still haven't answered.

Yarrow

Joyce Carol Oates

He was afraid to borrow the money from a bank.

It was a Saturday morning in early April, still winter, soft wet snow falling, clumps the size of blossoms.

A messy season, flu season, dirt-raddled snow drifted against the edges of things, mud thawing on the roads. A cavernous-clouded sky and blinding sunshine and it was the longest drive he'd made in his truck in memory, three miles to his cousin Tyrone Clayton's house.

Tyrone saw it in his face. Asked him inside, asked him did he want an ale? — Irene and the children were in town shopping.

The radio was turned up loud: Fats Domino singing "Blueberry Hill."

Mud on Jody's boots, so he said he wouldn't come all the way into the house, he'd talk from the doorway. Didn't want to track up Irene's clean floor.

He could only stay a minute, he said. He had a favor to ask.

"Sure," Tyrone said. Laying his cigarette carefully in an ashtray.

"I need to borrow some money."

"How much?"

"Five hundred dollars."

Jody spoke in a low quick voice just loud enough for Tyrone to hear. Then exhaled as if he'd been holding his breath in for a long time.

Tyrone said, keeping his voice level and easy, "Guess I can manage that."

"I'll pay you back as soon as I can," Jody said. "By June at the latest."

"No hurry," Tyrone said.

Then they were silent. Breathing hard. Excited, deeply embarrassed. Tyrone knew that Jody needed more than five hundred dollars — much more than five hundred dollars — but the way things were right now he couldn't afford to lend him more. He just couldn't afford it and even five hundred dollars was going to be hard. He knew that Jody knew all this but Jody had had to come to him anyway, knowing it, asking the favor, knowing that Tyrone would say yes but knowing that Tyrone could barely afford it either. Because Jody was desperate and if Tyrone hadn't quite wanted to understand that until this minute he had to understand it now.

His cousin's young, aggrieved, handsome face inside that sallow face blurred and pocked by fatigue. Three days' growth of whiskers on his chin and he wouldn't meet Tyrone's eyes—he was that ashamed.

Tyrone said he could get to the bank Monday noon, would that be soon enough?

Jody said as if he hadn't been listening that he wanted to pay the going rate of interest on the loan. "Ask them at the bank, will you?—and we'll work it out."

"Hell no," Tyrone said, laughing, surprised. "I don't want any interest."

"Just find out," Jody said, an edge to his voice, "and we'll work it out."

Tyrone asked how was Brenda these days, he'd heard from Irene she was getting better? But his voice came out weak and faltering.

Jody said she *was* getting better, she rested a lot during the day, the stitches from the surgery had come out but she still had a lot of pain and the doctor warned them about rushing things, so she had to take it slow.

He did the grocery shopping, for instance. All the shopping. Not that he minded—he didn't—he was damned glad Brenda was alive—but it took time and he only had Saturdays really.

Then this afternoon if the snow didn't get worse he was hoping to put in a shift at the quarry, three or four hours. Shoveling mainly, some clean-up—

He was speaking faster, with more feeling. A raw baffled voice new to him and his eyes puffy and red-rimmed as if he'd been rubbing at them.

All this while Jody's truck was idling in the driveway, spewing out clouds of exhaust. He'd left the key in the ignition, which Tyrone thought was a strange thing to do, almost rude.

Snowflakes were falling thicker now, blown in delicate skeins by the wind. Twisting and turning and looping like narrowing your eyes to shift your vision out of focus so that it's your own nerve-endings you see out there.

Wet air, colder than the temperature suggested. Flu season and everybody was passing it around to everybody else.

Something more needed to be said before Jody left but Tyrone couldn't think what it was.

410

He stood in the doorway watching Jody maneuver the truck out onto the road. It was a heavy-duty dump truck, Jody's own truck, a '49 Ford he'd have to be replacing soon. Tyrone was thinking they should have shaken hands or something but it wasn't a gesture that came naturally or easily to them. He couldn't remember when he had last shaken hands with somebody close to him as Jody and this morning wasn't the time to start.

He watched Jody drive away. He hadn't gotten around to shaving yet that morning himself and he stood vague and dazed, rubbing his stubbled jaw, thinking how much it had cost Jody McIllvanney to ask for that five hundred dollars, and how much it would cost him.

For the past year or more Jody's wife Brenda had been sick. Twenty-eight years old, thin, nervous, red-haired, pretty, she'd had four children now ranging in age from Dawn, who was thirteen years old and said to be troublesome, to the baby boy, who was only eighteen months. In between were two more boys, ten years and six years. Brenda had never quite recovered from the last pregnancy, came down with a bladder infection, had to have an operation just after Christmas—at a city hospital forty miles away, which meant people in Yarrow had to drive eighty miles round-trip to see her. Which meant, too, more medical bills the McIllvanneys couldn't afford.

The day before she was scheduled to enter the hospital, Brenda spoke with Irene Clayton on the phone and said she was frightened she was going to die.

"Don't talk that way," Irene said sharply.

Brenda was crying as if her heart were broken and Irene was afraid she too would start to cry.

"I just don't think Jody could manage without me," Brenda was saying. "Him and the children—and all the bills we owe—I just don't think he could keep going."

"You know better than to talk that way," Irene said. "That's a terrible thing to say." She listened to Brenda crying and felt helpless and frightened herself. She said, "You hadn't better let Jody hear you going on like that."

The McIllvanneys lived in Brenda's parents' old farmhouse, which wasn't by choice but all they could afford. Some years ago Jody had started building his own house at the edge of town but he ran out of money shortly after the basement was finished—Jody was a trucker, self-employed; his work tended to be local, seasonal, not very reliable—and for more than a year the family lived in the basement, below-ground.

411

(The roof was tar-papered over and there were windows but still the big single room was damp, chilly, depressing—the children were always coming down with colds. Dawn called it a damn dumb place to live, no wonder the kids on the school bus laughed at them all. Living like rats in a hole!) After Brenda's mother died they moved into the old farmhouse, which was free and clear, no mortgage, except it had been built in the 1880's and was termite-ridden and needed repairs constantly. Rotting shingles—leaky roof—earthen cellar that flooded when it rained: you name it. Bad as the Titanic, Jody said. He wished the damn thing *would* sink.

When Brenda got pregnant for the fourth time Jody began working part-time at the limestone quarry in Yarrow Falls: hard, filthy, backbreaking work he hated but it paid better than anything else he could find and he didn't have to join a union. Jody handled a shovel, he climbed ladders, he operated drills and tractors and wire-saws; when it rained he stood in the pit water to his knees. Coughing up phlegm, his feet aching as if they were on fire. Just temporary work he hoped wouldn't kill him.

Worse yet, he told Tyrone, he might develop a taste for the quarry. Like most of the quarriers. The limestone, the open fresh air, the weird machines that were so noisy and dangerous—it was work not just anybody could do. You had to have a strong back and the guts for it and anything like that, it tended to get under your skin if you weren't careful. It brought some pride with it after all.

The Clayton children Janice and Bobby were fond of their Uncle Jody—as they were taught to call him: Janice knew he was really a cousin of theirs, just as he was a cousin of their father's—except when he was in one of his bad moods. Then he wouldn't really look at them, he'd just mutter hello without smiling. He had a worse temper than their father and he was a bigger man than their father—muscled arms and shoulders that looked as if they were pumped up and that the flesh would hurt, ropy veins and skin stretched tight. But he could be funny—loud-laughing as a kid—with a broad side-slanting grin and a way of teasing that left you breathless and excited as if you'd been tickled with quick hard fingers. Their own father was lean and hard and soft-spoken; an inch or two shorter than his cousin. He worked at the Allis-Chalmers plant in town and never had anything interesting to say about it—just that it was *work*, and it *paid*—while Jody had all sorts of tales, some believable and some not, about driving his truck. Never a dull minute

412

with Jody around! Irene always said. Tyrone said that was true but—
"You know how he exaggerates."

One summer when Janice was a small child her Uncle Jody came over to the house with a half-dozen guinea chicks in a cardboard box, a present for them, and Janice had loved the chicks tiny enough to stand in the palm of her hand—they didn't weigh anything! No feathers like the adults, just fuzzy blond down, stubby wings and legs disproportionately long for their bodies. They were fearless, unlike the adults that were so suspicious and nerved-up all the time.

"They're pretty birds," Jody said. "I like seeing them around the place—you get kind of used to them."

The Claytons tried to raise the guinea fowl according to Jody's instructions but they died off one by one and in the end even Janice lost her enthusiasm for them. She'd given them special names—Freckles, Peewee, Queenie, Bathsheba—but they disappointed her because all they wanted to do was eat.

They only liked her, she said, because she fed them.

After Jody borrowed the five hundred dollars from Tyrone he didn't drop by the house for a long time. And Tyrone didn't seek him out, feeling embarrassed and uncomfortable: he didn't want Jody to think he was waiting to be paid back or even that he was thinking about the money.

(Was he thinking about it? Only occasionally, when it hit him like a blow to the gut.)

Irene didn't hear from Brenda very often either, which was strange, she said, and sad, and she hoped the money wouldn't come between them because Brenda was so sweet and such a good friend and needed somebody to talk to, what with Jody and Jody's moods—and that Dawn was a handful too, judging from what Janice said. (Dawn was a year older than Janice but in her class at school.) Irene said, "Why don't we invite them over here for supper or something?—we haven't done that in a long time." But Tyrone thought the McIllvanneys might misunderstand. "He'll think I'm worried about that money," Tyrone said.

It wasn't until midsummer that Jody made what he called the first payment on the loan, one hundred and seventy-five dollars he gave Tyrone in an envelope, and Tyrone was relieved, and embarrassed, and tried to tell him why not keep it for a while since probably he needed it—didn't he need it?—and there wasn't any hurry anyway. But Jody insisted. Jody said it was the least he could do.

Then: word got back to Tyrone that Jody had borrowed money from a mutual friend of theirs at about the time he'd borrowed the five hundred dollars from Tyrone *and he had paid all of it back.* Three hundred and fifty dollars and he'd paid all of it back in a lump sum and Tyrone was damned mad to hear about it and Irene tried to tell him it didn't mean anything, only that Jody knew Tyrone better, was closer to Tyrone, like a brother; also if he'd only borrowed three hundred and fifty dollars from the other man it was easier to pay it all back and close out the debt. Sure, said Tyrone. That makes me the chump.

But he didn't mean it and when a few days later, or a week later, Irene brought the subject up again, wondering when Jody was going to pay the rest of the money, he cut her off short saying it was his money, not hers, and it was between him and Jody and hadn't anything to do with her, did she understand that?

Janice didn't want to tell her mother but: when they went back to school in the fall Dawn McIllvanney began to behave mean to her. And Dawn could be really mean when she wanted to be.

She was a chunky, thickset girl, swarthy skin like her father's, sly eyes, a habit of grinning so it went through you like a sliver of glass—not a bit of friendliness in it. Called Janice "*Jan-y*" in a sliding whine and shoved her on the school bus or when they were waiting in the cafeteria line, "Oh excuse me, *Jan-y!*" she'd say, making anyone who was listening laugh. Dawn was the center of a circle of four or five girls who were rough and pushy and loud, belligerent as boys; she got poor grades in school not because she was stupid—though she might have been a little slow—but because she made a show of not trying, not handing in homework, wising off in class and angering her teachers. Janice thought it was unfair that Dawn McIllvanney had such a pretty red-haired mother while she had a mother who was like anybody's mother—plain and pleasant and boring. She'd always thought, before the trouble started, that Brenda McIllvanney would rather have had *her* for a daughter than Dawn.

Janice soon understood that Dawn hated her and she'd better keep her distance from her but it happened that in gym class she couldn't and that was where Dawn got her revenge: threw a basketball right into Janice's face one time, broke Janice's pink plastic glasses, claimed afterward it was an accident—"*Jan-y*" got in her way. Another time, when the girls were doing gymnastics, Dawn stuck her big, sneakered foot out in front of Janice as Janice—who was wiry and quick, one of the best

414

gymnasts in the class—did a series of cartwheels the full length of the mat, and naturally Janice fell, fell sideways, fell hard, seeing as she fell her cousin's face pinched with hatred, the rat-glittering little eyes. Pain shot like a knife, like many knives, through Janice's body and for a long time she couldn't move—just lay there sobbing, hearing Dawn McIllvanney's mock-incredulous voice as the gym instructor reprimanded her, *Hey I didn't do anything, what the hell are you saying, look it was her, she's the one, it was her own damn fault, the little crybaby—*

Janice never told her mother about the incident. She tried not to think that Dawn, who was her cousin after all, had wanted to hurt her really—break her neck or her backbone, cripple her for life. She tried not to think that.

One warm autumn day Irene Clayton met Brenda McIllvanney in the A&P in town—Brenda whom she hadn't seen in months—Brenda who was thin, almost gaunt, but wearing a flowery print dress—red lipsticked lips and hard red nails and a steely look that went through Irene like a razor. And Irene just stood there staring as if the earth had opened at her feet.

In her parked car in the lot Irene leaned her forehead against the steering wheel and began to cry. She made baffled sobbing sounds that astonished and deeply embarrassed the children—Janice and Bobby had never seen their mother cry in such a public place, and for so little reason they could understand. She usually wept in a rage at them!

Bobby threw himself against the back seat, pressing his hands over his ears. Janice, in the passenger's seat, looked out the window and said, "Momma, you're making a fool of yourself," in the coldest voice possible.

Tyrone wasn't accustomed to thinking about such things, poking into his own motives, or other people's. But he'd known, he said. As soon as he'd handed Jody the money, that was it.

Irene said she didn't believe it.

She knew Brenda, and she knew Jody, and she didn't believe it.

Jody had thanked him but he hadn't wanted to look at him, Tyrone said. Took the money 'cause he couldn't not take it but that was that.

"I don't believe it *really*," Irene said, wiping at her eyes.

Tyrone said nothing, lighting up a cigarette, shaking out the match. His movements were jerky and angry these days, these many days. Often it looked as if he was quarreling with someone under his breath. Irene said, "I don't believe it *really*."

Jody sold his truck, gave up trucking for good, worked full-time now at the limestone quarry, still in debt, and that old house of theirs looked worse than ever—chickens and guinea fowl picking in the grassless front yard amid tossed-out trash, Brenda's peony beds overgrown with weeds as if no woman lived in the house at all—but still—somehow—Jody managed to buy a '53 Chevrolet up in Yarrow Falls; and he and Brenda were going out places together again, roadhouses and taverns miles away where no one knew them. Sometimes they were alone and sometimes they were with another couple. Their old friends rarely saw them now.

Tyrone was always hearing from relatives that the McIllvanneys couldn't seem to climb out of their bad luck though Jody was working ten, twelve hours a day at the quarry, et cetera; poor Brenda had some kind of thyroid condition now and had to take medicine so expensive you couldn't believe it, et cetera; and Tyrone listened ironically to all this and said, "O.K. but what about me?—*what about me?*" And there never seemed to be any answer to that.

If Tyrone ran into Jody in town it was sheerly by accident. And damned clumsy and embarrassing: Jody pretended he didn't see Tyrone, turned nonchalantly away, whistling, hands in his pockets, turned a corner and walked fast and disappeared.

Asshole. As if Tyrone didn't see *him.*

Tyrone complained freely of his cousin to anyone who would listen: old friends, mutual acquaintances, strangers. He was baffled and bitter and hurt and furious, wondering aloud when he'd get his money back. And would he get it *with interest* as Jody had promised.

When he'd been drinking a bit Tyrone said that nobody had ever thought Jody McIllvanney would turn out the way he had—a man whose word wasn't worth shit—not much better than a common crook—a man who couldn't even support his wife and children. "Anybody that bad off, he might as well hang himself," Tyrone would say. "Stick a shotgun barrel into his mouth and pull the trigger."

He had to stop thinking about Jody all the time, Irene said. She was getting scared he'd make himself sick.

She'd lain awake too many nights herself thinking about the McIllvanneys—Brenda in particular—and she wasn't going to think about them any longer. "It isn't healthy," she said, pleaded. "Ty?—it eats away at your heart."

But Tyrone ignored her, he was calculating (sitting at the kitchen table, a sheet of paper before him, pencil in hand, bottle of Molson's Ale at his elbow) how much Jody was probably earning a week up at the

Falls now that he'd been promoted from shoveler to drill-runner. It made him sick to think that—subtracting union dues, Social Security and the rest—Jody was probably making a few more dollars a week than he made at Allis-Chalmers. And if Jody could get an extra shift time-and-a-half on Saturdays he'd be making a damn sight more.

When Tyrone stood he felt dizzy and panicky, as if the floor was tilting beneath his feet.

Most people in Yarrow were on Tyrone's side but he sensed there were some on Jody's side and lately he'd begun to hear that Jody was saying things about *him*—bad-mouthing him so you'd almost think it was Tyrone Clayton who owed Jody McIllvanney money and not the other way around. Hadn't Jody helped him put asbestos siding on his house when he and Irene had first moved in—? (Yes but he, Tyrone, had helped Jody with that would-be house of his, helping to put in the concrete, lay the beams for the basement ceiling, tar-paper the god-damned roof in the middle of the summer.) Tyrone went out drinking to the places he'd always gone and there were the men he'd been seeing for years, men he'd gone to school with, but Jody wasn't there, there was a queer sort of authority in Jody's absence, as if, the more *he* said, the more his listeners were inclined to believe *Jody*. "I know things are still bad for Jody and Brenda," he'd say, speaking passionately, conscious of the significance of his words—which might be repeated after all to Jody—"and I don't even want the fucking money back but I do want respect. I do want respect from that son of a bitch."

(Though in fact he did want the money back: every penny of it.)

(And he tended to think Jody still owed him five hundred dollars, the original sum, plus interest, no matter he'd insisted at the time of the loan that he didn't want "interest" from any blood relation.)

There were nights he came home drunk, other nights he was so agitated he couldn't sit still to eat his supper because he'd heard something at work that day reported to him and Irene tried to comfort him, Irene said he was frightening the children, Irene said in a pleading voice, Why not try to forget?—forgive?—like in the Bible?—wasn't that real wisdom?—and just not lend anybody any money ever again in his life. "What the hell was I supposed to do?" Tyrone would say, turning on her furiously. "Tell my own cousin that I grew up with that I wouldn't help him out? Tell him to get out of that doorway there?" Irene backed off saying, "Ty, I don't know what you were supposed to do but it turned out a mistake, didn't it?" And Tyrone said, his face contorted with rage and his voice shaking, "It wasn't a mistake at the time, you stupid bitch. *It wasn't a mistake at the time.*"

One night that fall the telephone rang at nine p.m. and Irene answered and it was Jody McIllvanney, whose voice she hadn't heard in a long time, drunk and belligerent, demanding to speak to Tyrone—who luckily wasn't home. So Jody told Irene to tell him he'd been hearing certain things that Tyrone was saying behind his back and he didn't like what he'd heard and if Tyrone had something to say to him why not come over to the house and tell it to his face and if Tyrone was afraid to do that he'd better keep his mouth shut or *he'd* come over *there* and beat the shit out of Tyrone.

Jody was shouting, saying he'd pay back the goddamn money when he could, that was the best he could do, he hadn't asked to be born, that was the best he could do, goddamn it— And Irene, speechless, terrified, slammed down the receiver.

Afterward she said she'd never heard anyone anywhere sounding so crazy. Like he'd have killed her if he'd been able to get hold of her. . . .

A chilly breezy November day but there was Jody McIllvanney in coveralls and a T-shirt, no jacket, bareheaded, striding along the sidewalk, not looking where he was going: and Janice Clayton stared at him, shocked at how he'd changed—my God he was big now! almost what you'd call *fat!*—weighing maybe two hundred sixty pounds, barrel-chested, big jiggly stomach pressing against the fabric of his coveralls, his face bloated too and his skin lumpy. It was said that stone quarriers ate and drank like hogs, got enormous, and there was Jody the shape of a human hog, even his hair long and shaggy, greasy, like a high-school kid or a Hell's Angel. Janice stood frozen on the sidewalk, her schoolbooks pressed against her chest, hoping, praying, her Uncle Jody wouldn't glance up and see her or if he did he wouldn't recognize her though her heart kicked and she thought *I don't hate him like I'm supposed to.*

But he looked up. He saw her. Saw how she was shrinking out toward the curb to avoid him and so he let her go, just mumbled a greeting she couldn't hear, and the moment was past, she was safe, she pushed her glasses up her nose and half-ran up the street to escape. She remembered how he used to call out "How's it going?" to her and Bobby instead of saying hello—winking to show that it was a joke (what did any adult man care about how things were going for children) but serious in a way too. And she'd never known how to answer, nor had Bobby. "O.K.," they'd say, embarrassed, blushing, flattered. "All right I guess."

(Janice had no anticipation, not the mildest of premonitions, that that would be the last time she'd see her Uncle Jody but long afterward the

418

sight of him would remain vivid in her memory, powerful, reproachful, and the November day too of gusty winds and the smell of snow in the air, a texture like grit. Waiting for the bus she was dreamy and melancholy watching how the town's south-side mills gave off smoke that rose into the air like mist. Powdery, almost iridescent, those subtle shifting colors of the backs of pigeons – iridescent gray, blue, purple shading into black.

The guinea fowl had long since died off but Janice had snapshots of her favorites, their names carefully recorded.)

*   *   *

Shortly after the New Year Tyrone was driving to town when he saw a man hitchhiking by the side of the road, and sure enough it was Jody McIllvanney – Jody in his sheepskin jacket, a wool cap pulled low over his forehead, thumb uplifted. His face looked closed-in as a fist; he might have recognized Tyrone but gave no sign just as Tyrone, speeding past, gave no sign of recognizing him. It had all happened so swiftly Tyrone hadn't time to react. He wondered if Jody's new car had broken down and he laughed aloud harshly, thinking, Good. Serve him right. Serve them all right.

He watched his cousin's figure in the rearview mirror, diminishing with distance.

Then: for some reason he'd never be able to explain he decided to turn his car around, drive back to Jody; maybe he'd slow down and shout something out the window, or maybe – just maybe – he'd give the son of a bitch a ride if it looked like that might be a good idea. But as he approached Jody it was clear that Jody intended to stand his ground, didn't want any favors from him, you could see from his arrogant stance that he'd rather freeze his ass off than beg a ride from Tyrone: he'd lowered his arm and stood there in the road, legs apart, waiting. A big beefy glowering man you could tell wanted a fight even without knowing who he was.

Tyrone's heart swelled with fury and righteousness.

Tyrone hit the horn with the palm of his hand to scare the son of a bitch off the road.

He was laughing, shouting, *thief! liar! lying betraying bastard!*

What did he do then but call Jody's bluff, aim the car straight at him, fifty miles an hour and he'd lost control even before he hit a patch of cobbled ridged ice and began to skid – hardly had time before the impact to turn the wheel, pump desperately at the brakes – and he saw his

419

cousin's look of absolute disbelief, not even fear or surprise, as the left fender slammed into him, the chassis plowed into his body and threw it aside and out of Tyrone's sight.

The steering wheel caught Tyrone in the chest. But he was all right. He was coughing, choking, but he was all right, gripping the wheel tight and pumping the brakes as the car leveled out of its wild swerve and came to a bumpy rest in a ditch. Scrub trees and tall grasses clawing at the windshield and Jesus his nose was bleeding and he couldn't see anything in the rearview mirror but he knew Jody was dead: that sickening thud, that enormous impact like a man-sized boulder flung against the car, that's what it meant.

"Jesus . . ."

Tyrone sat panting in his car, the motor racing, clouds of exhaust lifting behind; he was terrified, his bladder contracted, heart pumping like crazy and it couldn't have happened, could it?—that quickly?—hairline cracks on his windshield and his nose clogged with blood?—except he'd felt the body snapping beneath the car, it wasn't something you were likely to mistake as anything but death.

He didn't have to drive back another time. Didn't have to see the bright blood on the snow.

He pressed his forehead against the steering wheel. A terrible hammering in his chest he'd have to wait out.

"Damn you fuck you *Jody* . . ."

He'd done it on purpose, hadn't he!

Tyrone busied himself maneuvering his car out of the ditch, rocking the chassis, concentrating on the effort which involved his entire physical being; he was panting, grunting, whispering *C'mon baby c'mon for Christ's sweet sake*, then he was free and clear and back on the road and no one knew.

He'd begun to shiver convulsively. Though he was sweating too inside his clothes. And his bladder pinched in terror as he hadn't felt it in a long, long time.

But he was all right, wasn't he? And the car was operating.

That was the main thing.

He drove on, slowly at first, then panic hit him in a fresh wave and he began to drive faster, thinking he was going in the wrong direction but had had to get somewhere—where?—had to get help.

Police, ambulance. He'd go home and telephone.

There's a man dead on the road. Hitchhiker and he'd stepped in front of the car and it was over in an instant.

Blood dripping from his nose onto his fucking jacket and those hairline cracks in the windshield, like cracks in his own skull. He was crying, couldn't stop.

He'd tell Irene to make the call. Wouldn't tell her who it was he'd hit. Then he'd drive back to Jody, *Hey you know I didn't mean it why the hell didn't you get out of the way I was just kidding around then the ice, why the hell didn't you get out of the way goddamn you you did it on purpose didn't you—*

But maybe it would be better if he stopped at the first house, a neighbor's house.

Police, or the ambulance? Or both? There was an emergency number he'd never memorized the way you were supposed to. . . .

His mind was shifting out of focus, going blank in patches empty and white-glaring as the snowy fields.

Those fields you could lose yourself in at this time of year. Staring and dreaming, stubbled with grass and grain and tracked over with animal prints but you couldn't see that at a distance—everything clean and clear, dazzling blinding white. At a distance.

It was a secret no one knew: Jody McIllvanney was dead.

Bleeding his life out in a ditch. In the snow.

He hadn't survived the impact of the car, Tyrone knew that. No chance of it, plowing into a human being like that full in the chest and the gut, he'd felt the bones being crushed, the backbone snapped—*felt* it.

He'd feel it all his life!

He'd seen bodies crumpled, Jesus he'd seen more than his fair share. Kids his own age, Americans, Japs, in uniform, near-naked, bleeding, broken bones, eyes rolled up into their skulls. But mostly he'd been lucky enough to come upon them after death had come and gone and only the body was left.

No witnesses.

No one on the road this time of day.

He had to get help but help was a long way off.

His foot pressing down hard on the accelerator then letting up when the tires began to spin, it was dangerous driving in the winter along these roads, dangerous driving any time the roads were likely to be slippery, now approaching a single-lane bridge crashing over the bridge the floorboards bouncing and kicking and the car trembling, Oh sweet Jesus help me.

Explaining to someone, a patrolman on the highway, how it wasn't his fault. The hitchhiker standing flat-footed in the road not dodging out of the way even when the car began to skid.

He'd lost control of the car. But then he'd regained it.

No witnesses.

How could he be held to blame?

If Jody had paid in installments for instance twenty-five dollars, even ten dollars every month or so. Paring back on the debt just to show his good faith. His gratitude.

He couldn't be held responsible. He'd kill himself if they came to arrest him.

Except: no witnesses.

Except: his car was damaged.

The fender crushed, the bumper, part of the hood—that's how they would know. Blood splashed on the grill.

That's how they would find him.

That's how they would arrest him.

He and Jody used to go deer hunting farther north; you sling the carcass over the fender unless it's too big—then you tie it to the roof of the car. Twine tied tight as you can tie it.

He'd known without having to look.

Asshole. Bleeding his life out back in a ditch.

But who would know? If he kept going.

If he drove on past his house—just kept driving as if it weren't any house he knew, any connection to him—drive and drive up into the northern part of the state until something happened to stop him. Until his gas gave out.

Death of a Son
Njabulo S. Ndebele

At last we got the body. Wednesday. Just enough time for a Saturday funeral. We were exhausted. Empty. The funeral still ahead of us. We had to find the strength to grieve. There had been no time for grief, really. Only much bewilderment and confusion. Now grief. For isn't grief the awareness of loss?

That is why when we finally got the body, Buntu said: "Do you realize our son is dead?" I realized. Our awareness of the death of our first and only child had been displaced completely by the effort to get his body. Even the horrible events that caused the death: we did not think of them, as such. Instead, the numbing drift of things took over our minds: the pleas, letters to be written, telephone calls to be made, telegrams to be dispatched, lawyers to consult, "influential" people to "get in touch with," undertakers to be contacted, so much walking and driving. That is what suddenly mattered: the irksome details that blur the goal (no matter how terrible it is), each detail becoming a door which, once unlocked, revealed yet another door. Without being aware of it, we were distracted by the smell of the skunk and not by what the skunk had done.

We realized something too, Buntu and I, that during the two-week effort to get our son's body, we had drifted apart. For the first time in our marriage, our presence to each other had become a matter of habit. He was there. He'll be there. And I'll be there. But when Buntu said: "Do you realize our son is dead?" he uttered a thought that suddenly brought us together again. It was as if the return of the body of our son was also our coming together. For it was only at that moment that we really began to grieve; as if our lungs had suddenly begun to take in air when just before, we were beginning to suffocate. Something with meaning began to emerge.

We realized. We realized that something else had been happening to us, adding to the terrible events. Yes, we had drifted apart. Yet, our estrangement, just at that moment when we should have been together, seemed disturbingly comforting to me. I was comforted in a manner I did not quite understand.

The problem was that I had known all along that we would have to buy the body anyway. I had known all along. Things would end that way. And when things turned out that way, Buntu could not look me in the eye. For he had said: "Over my dead body! Over my dead body!" as soon as we knew we would be required to pay the police or the government for the release of the body of our child.

"Over my dead body! Over my dead body!" Buntu kept on saying.

Finally, we bought the body. We have the receipt. The police insisted we take it. That way, they would be "protected." It's the law, they said.

I suppose we could have got the body earlier. At first I was confused, for one is supposed to take comfort in the heroism of one's man. Yet, inwardly, I could draw no comfort from his outburst. It seemed hasty. What sense was there to it when all I wanted was the body of my child? What would happen if, as events unfolded, it became clear that Buntu would not give up his life? What would happen? What would happen to him? To me?

For the greater part of two weeks, all of Buntu's efforts, together with friends, relatives, lawyers and the newspapers, were to secure the release of the child's body without the humiliation of having to pay for it. A "fundamental principle."

Why was it difficult for me to see the wisdom of the principle? The worst thing, I suppose, was worrying about what the police may have been doing to the body of my child. How they may have been busy prying it open "to determine the cause of death"?

Would I want to look at the body when we finally got it? To see further mutilations in addition to the "cause of death"? What kind of mother would not want to look at the body of her child? people will ask. Some will say: "It's grief." She is too grief-stricken.

"But still . . . ," they will say. And the elderly among them may say: "Young people are strange."

But how can they know? It was not that I would not want to see the body of my child, but that I was too afraid to confront the horrors of my own imagination. I was haunted by the thought of how useless it had been to have created something. What had been the point of it all? This body filling up with a child. The child steadily growing into something that could be seen and felt. Moving, as it always did, at that time of day when I was all alone at home waiting for it. What had been the point of it all?

How can they know that the mutilation to determine "the cause of death" ripped my own body? Can they think of a womb feeling hunted? Disgorged?

And the milk that I still carried. What about it? What had been the point of it all?

Even Buntu did not seem to sense that that principle, the "fundamental principle," was something too intangible for me at that moment, something that I desperately wanted should assume the form of my child's body. He still seemed far from ever knowing.

I remember one Saturday morning early in our courtship, as Buntu and I walked hand-in-hand through town, window-shopping. We cannot even be said to have been window-shopping, for we were aware of very little that was not ourselves. Everything in those windows was merely an excuse for words to pass between us.

We came across three girls sitting on the pavement, sharing a packet of fish and chips after they had just bought it from a nearby Portuguese café. Buntu said: "I want fish and chips too." I said: "So seeing is desire." I said: "My man is greedy!" We laughed. I still remember how he tightened his grip on my hand. The strength of it!

Just then, two white boys coming in the opposite direction suddenly rushed at the girls, and, without warning, one of them kicked the packet of fish and chips out of the hands of the girl who was holding it. The second boy kicked away the rest of what remained in the packet. The girl stood up, shaking her hand as if to throw off the pain in it. Then she pressed it under her armpit as if to squeeze the pain out of it. Meanwhile, the two boys went on their way laughing. The fish and chips lay scattered on the pavement and on the street like stranded boats on a river that had gone dry.

"Just let them do that to you!" said Buntu, tightening once more his grip on my hand as we passed on like sheep that had seen many of their own in the flock picked out for slaughter. We would note the event and wait for our turn. I remember I looked at Buntu, and saw his face was somewhat glum. There seemed no connection between that face and the words of reassurance just uttered. For a while, we went on quietly. It was then that I noticed his grip had grown somewhat limp. Somewhat reluctant. Having lost its self-assurance, it seemed to have been holding on because it had to, not because of a confident sense of possession.

It was not to be long before his words were tested. How could fate work this way, giving to words meanings and intentions they did not carry when they were uttered? I saw that day, how the language of love could so easily be trampled underfoot, or scattered like fish and chips on the pavement, and left stranded and abandoned like boats in a river that suddenly went dry. Never again was love to be confirmed with words. The world around us was too hostile for vows of love. At any moment, the vows could be subjected to the stress of proof. And love died. For words of love need not be tested.

On that day, Buntu and I began our silence. We talked and laughed, of course, but we stopped short of words that would demand proof of action. Buntu knew. He knew the vulnerability of words. And so he sought to obliterate words with acts that seemed to promise redemption.

On that day, as we continued with our walk in town, that Saturday morning, coming up towards us from the opposite direction, was a burly Boer walking with his wife and two children. They approached Buntu and me with an ominously determined advance. Buntu attempted to pull me out of the way, but I never had a chance. The Boer shoved me out of the way, as if clearing a path for his family. I remember, I almost crashed into a nearby fashion display window. I remember, I glanced at the family walking away, the mother and the father each dragging a child. It was for one of those children that I had been cleared away. I remember, also, that as my tears came out, blurring the Boer family and everything else, I saw and felt deeply what was inside of me: a desire to be avenged.

But nothing happened. All I heard was Buntu say: "The dog!" At that very moment, I felt my own hurt vanish like a wisp of smoke. And as my hurt vanished, it was replaced, instead, by a tormenting desire to sacrifice myself for Buntu. Was it something about the powerlessness of the curse and the desperation with which it had been made? The filling of stunned silence with an utterance? Surely it ate into him, revealing how incapable he was of meeting the call of his words.

And so it was, that that afternoon, back in the township, left to ourselves at Buntu's home, I gave in to him for the first time. Or should I say I offered myself to him? Perhaps from some vague sense of wanting to heal something in him? Anyway, we were never to talk about that event. Never. We buried it alive deep inside of me that afternoon. Would it ever be exhumed? All I vaguely felt and knew was that I had the keys to the vault. That was three years ago, a year before we married.

The cause of death? One evening I returned home from work, particularly tired after I had been covering more shootings by the police in the East Rand. Then I had hurried back to the office in Johannesburg to piece together on my typewriter the violent scenes of the day, and then to file my report to meet the deadline. It was late when I returned home, and when I got there, I found a crowd of people in the yard. They were those who could not get inside. I panicked. What had happened? I did not ask those who were outside, being desperate to get into the house. They gave way easily when they recognized me.

Then I heard my mother's voice. Her cry rose well above the noise. It turned into a scream when she saw me. "What is it, mother?" I asked, embracing her out of a vaguely despairing sense of terror. But she pushed me away with an hysterical violence that astounded me.

"What misery have I brought you, my child?" she cried. At that point, many women in the room began to cry too. Soon, there was much wailing in the room, and then all over the house. The sound of it! The anguish! Understanding, yet eager for knowledge, I became desperate. I had to hold onto something. The desire to embrace my mother no longer had anything to do with comforting her; for whatever she had done, whatever its magnitude, had become inconsequential. I needed to embrace her for all the anguish that tied everyone in the house into a knot. I wanted to be part of that knot, yet I wanted to know what had brought it about.

Eventually, we found each other, my mother and I, and clasped each other tightly. When I finally released her, I looked around at the neighbors and suddenly had a vision of how that anguish had to be turned into a simmering kind of indignation. The kind of indignation that had to be kept at bay only because there was a higher purpose at that moment: the sharing of concern.

Slowly and with a calmness that surprised me, I began to gather the details of what had happened. Instinctively, I seemed to have been gathering notes for a news report.

It happened during the day, when the soldiers and the police that had been patrolling the township in their Casspirs began to shoot in the streets at random. Need I describe what I did not see? How did the child come to die just at that moment when the police and the soldiers began to shoot at random, at any house, at any moving thing? That was how one of our windows was shattered by a bullet. And that was when my mother, who looked after her grandchild when we were away at work, panicked. She picked up the child and ran to the neighbors. It was only when she entered the neighbor's house that she noticed the wetness of the blanket that covered the child she held to her chest as she ran for the sanctuary of neighbors. She had looked at her unaccountably bloody hand, then she noted the still bundle in her arms, and began at that moment to blame herself for the death of her grandchild. . .

427

Later, the police, on yet another round of shooting, found people gathered at our house. They stormed in, saw what had happened. At first, they dragged my mother out, threatening to take her away unless she agreed not to say what had happened. But then they returned and, instead, took the body of the child away. By what freak of logic did they hope that by this act their carnage would never be discovered?

That evening, I looked at Buntu closely. He appeared suddenly to have grown older. We stood alone in an embrace in our bedroom. I noticed, when I kissed his face, how his once lean face had grown suddenly puffy.

At that moment, I felt the familiar impulse come upon me once more, the impulse I always felt when I sensed that Buntu was in some kind of danger, the impulse to yield something of myself to him. He wore the look of someone struggling to gain control of something. Yet, it was clear he was far from controlling anything. I knew that look. Had seen it many times. It came at those times when I sensed that he faced a wave that was infinitely stronger than he, that it would certainly sweep him away, but that he had to seem to be struggling. I pressed myself tightly to him as if to vanish into him; as if only the two of us could stand up to the wave.

"Don't worry," he said. "Don't worry. I'll do everything in my power to right this wrong. Everything. Even if it means suing the police!" We went silent.

I knew that silence. But I knew something else at that moment: that I had to find a way of disengaging myself from the embrace.

Suing the police? I listened to Buntu outlining his plans. "Legal counsel. That's what we need," he said. "I know some people in Pretoria," he said. As he spoke, I felt the warmth of intimacy between us cooling. When he finished, it was cold. I disengaged from his embrace slowly, yet purposefully. Why had Buntu spoken?

Later, he was to speak again, when all his plans had failed to work: "Over my dead body! Over my dead body!"

He sealed my lips. I would wait for him to feel and yield one day to all the realities of misfortune.

Ours was a home, it could be said. It seemed a perfect life for a young couple: I, a reporter; Buntu, a personnel officer at an American factory manufacturing farming implements. He had traveled to the United States and returned with a mind fired with dreams. We dreamed together. Much time we spent, Buntu and I, trying to make a perfect home. The occasions are numerous on which we paged through *Femina*, *Fair Lady*, *Cosmopolitan*, *Home Garden*, *Car*, as if somehow we were going to surround our lives with the glossiness in the magazines. Indeed, much of our time was spent window-shopping through the magazines. This time, it was different from the window-shopping we did that Saturday when we courted. This time our minds were consumed by the things we saw and dreamed of owning: the furniture, the fridge, TV, videocassette recorders, washing machines, even a vacuum cleaner and every other imaginable thing that would ensure a comfortable modern life.

Especially when I was pregnant. What is it that Buntu did not buy, then? And when the boy was born, Buntu changed the car. A family, he would say, must travel comfortably.

The boy became the center of Buntu's life. Even before he was born, Buntu had already started making inquiries at white private schools. That was where he would send his son, the bearer of his name.

Dreams! It is amazing how the horrible findings of my newspaper reports often vanished before the glossy magazines of our dreams, how I easily forgot that the glossy images were concocted out of the keys of typewriters, made by writers whose business was to sell dreams at the very moment that death pervaded the land. So powerful are words and pictures that even their makers often believe in them.

Buntu's ordeal was long. So it seemed. He would get up early every morning to follow up the previous day's leads regarding the body of our son. I wanted to go with him, but each time I prepared to go he would shake his head.

"It's my task," he would say. But every evening he returned, empty-handed, while with each day that passed and we did not know where the body of my child was, I grew restive and hostile in a manner that gave me much pain. Yet Buntu always felt compelled to give a report on each day's events. I never asked for it. I suppose it was his way of dealing with my silence.

One day he would say: "The lawyers have issued a court order that the body be produced. The writ of *habeas corpus*."

On another day he would say: "We have petitioned the Minister of Justice."

On yet another he would say: "I was supposed to meet the Chief Security Officer. Waited the whole day. At the end of the day they said I would see him tomorrow if he was not going to be too busy. They are stalling."

Then he would say: "The newspapers, especially yours, are raising the hue and cry. The government is bound to be embarrassed. It's a matter of time."

And so it went on. Every morning he got up and left. Sometimes alone, sometimes with friends. He always left to bear the failure alone.

How much did I care about lawyers, petitions and Chief Security Officers? A lot. The problem was that whenever Buntu spoke about his efforts, I heard only his words. I felt in him the disguised hesitancy of someone who wanted reassurance without asking for it. I saw someone who got up every morning and left not to look for results, but to search for something he could only have found with me.

And each time he returned, I gave my speech to my eyes. And he answered without my having parted my lips. As a result, I sensed, for the first time in my life, a terrible power in me that could make him do anything. And he would never ever be able to deal with that power as long as he did not silence my eyes and call for my voice.

And so, he had to prove himself. And while he left each morning, I learned to be brutally silent. Could he prove himself without me? Could he? Then I got to know, those days, what I'd always wanted from him. I got to know why I have always drawn him into me whenever I sensed his vulnerability.

I wanted him to be free to fear. Wasn't there greater strength that way? Had he ever lived with his own feelings? And the stress of life in this land: didn't it call out for men to be heroes? And should they live up to it even though the details of the war to be fought may often be blurred? They should.

Yet it is precisely for that reason that I often found Buntu's thoughts lacking in strength. They lacked the experience of strife that could only come from a humbling acceptance of fear and then, only then, the need to fight it.

Me? In a way, I have always been free to fear. The prerogative of being a girl. It was always expected of me to scream when a spider crawled across the ceiling. It was known I would jump onto a chair whenever a mouse blundered into the room.

Then, once more, the Casspirs came. A few days before we got the body back, I was at home with my mother when we heard the great roar of truck engines. There was much running and shouting in the streets. I saw them, as I've always seen them on my assignments: the Casspirs. On five occasions they ran down our street at great speed, hurling tear-gas canisters at random. On the fourth occasion, they got our house. The canister shattered another window and filled the house with the terrible pungent choking smoke that I had got to know so well. We ran out of the house gasping for fresh air.

So, this was how my child was killed? Could they have been the same soldiers? Now hardened to their tasks? Or were they new ones being hardened to their tasks? Did they drive away laughing? Clearing paths for their families? What paths?

And was this our home? It couldn't be. It had to be a little bird's nest waiting to be plundered by a predator bird. There seemed no sense to the wedding pictures on the walls, the graduation pictures, birthday pictures, pictures of relatives, and paintings of lush landscapes. There seemed no sense anymore to what seemed recognizably human in our house. It took only a random swoop to obliterate personal worth, to blot out any value there may have been to the past. In desperation, we began to live only for the moment. I do feel hunted.

It was on the night of the tear gas that Buntu came home, saw what had happened, and broke down in tears. They had long been in the coming. . .

My own tears welled out too. How much did we have to cry to refloat stranded boats? I was sure they would float again.

A few nights later, on the night of the funeral, exhausted, I lay on my bed, listening to the last of the mourners leaving. Slowly, I became conscious of returning to the world. Something came back after it seemed not to have been there for ages. It came as a surprise, as a reminder that we will always live around what will happen. The sun will rise and set, and the ants will do their endless work, until one day the clouds turn gray and rain falls, and even in the township, the ants will fly out into the sky. Come what may.

My moon came, in a heavy surge of blood. And, after such a long time, I remembered the thing Buntu and I had buried in me. I felt it as if it had just entered. I felt it again as it floated away on the surge. I would be ready for another month. Ready as always, each and every month, for new beginnings.

And Buntu? I'll be with him, now. Always. Without our knowing, all the trying events had prepared for us new beginnings. Shall we not prevail?

The Amanuensis

Wayne Assam

It has long been a source of surprise to me that, even in the present age of progress at any cost, a scientific defense of prejudice has yet to see the light.

The eminent philosopher and thinker Dr. Y at last agreed to grant me an interview. I hope it is good form to say philosopher *and* thinker. Since making the acquaintance of that great man I have become more heedful of contradictions, paradoxes, neoplasms, pleonasms and tautologies. Not that I, of course, an unworthy dilettante, presume to distinguish among these mysteries with the histological punctiliousness of the deep doctors of metaphysics.

May I say, doctor, I said as I shook his hand, what an honor it is at last to meet you, so to speak, in the flesh. He grimaced and at once withdrew his hand, impatient, I suppose, of the body, as no doubt befits a great spirit. It was a spectacle awesome, humbling and surprising, such as is not given one to witness every day. Confirmed at last, in my own experience, was a phenomenon which I, as a common man among common men, would not otherwise seriously have imagined possible. Though with me grossly, in the body, he had, in the mind or spirit— assuming that they are one and the same—taken flight. How many of us can afford such luxuries?

I coughed. This proved inefficacious. Might we not begin? I ventured. He seemed lost within himself, if that adequately expresses the facts. I repeated myself. Fortunately the room did not echo. I consoled myself with the silence.

It appeared he would be thus withdrawn no little while. I seized upon this opportunity to examine a great man's room at my leisure. It was remarkable, the room, for a combination of roominess and sparse furnishing that did not however communicate to one—I mean to me—an atmosphere of empty isolation, a clear sign, this, I supposed, of the uncluttered efficiency of the philosopher's mind. Let me hasten to add that I am well aware of the present anti-hermeneutical vogue. I think I may say, however, that, in this instance, I was provoked.

What can I do for you? said Dr. Y. I must have looked puzzled. *I* should be the one to look puzzled here, said he severely. The nature of your business? You have an appointment? Well, in that case. He waved me to a chair.

His secretary entered with some tea. See that we are not disturbed, said Dr. Y. She nodded, and left as quietly as she had come. I thought that injunction unfortunate. Even my first impressions of her were favorable.

Now then, he said, pouring. You have some questions? How many sugars? Sweet tooth, I see. Fire away then.

I thought it best to have a sip of tea before beginning. Yes? he said, yes? How is it, I said, beginning, that science has not kept step with the march of prejudice? Metaphors come in very handy to people like me.

I was not in the least insulted when he flung himself backwards into his chair. But the answer, the answer, said Dr. Y., is locked in the very terms of the question. I remained in the dark, anxious for illumination. Examine if you will, said Dr. Y, your terms. Take science, there's a term for you. I don't doubt it, my dear Dr. Y, said I, but I remain firmly in the dark. I am, my dear fellow, said he, drawing himself erect, a philosopher, not a candlemaker. I resume. Would you not say or rather incline to the proposition that science consists in selecting, from a multitude of possible causes of a particular phenomenon, that cause or conjunction of causes—or shall I say rather reasons, causes having fallen, in our age, mysteriously into disfavor—Where am I? Er was all I could manage. Ah yes, said he. Which accounts for it with the greatest symmetry and economy? I saw no immediate advantage in dissent. And would you not denominate the faculty which performs this act—I intend no frivolous dramatical allusion—would you not designate it, said he, to make an end, judgment? If pressed, I said, I would. Science, then, said Dr. Y., is a question of judgment.

433

The secretary entered for the tea-things. What a stroke of luck! I was just able to gulp down my last drop. I was able, also, to note, in passing—that is to say as she passed—her stirring figure and entrancing gait.

A question, said Dr. Y, of judgment. Consider, now, with me, prejudice. I am speaking of the word. Attend very closely, now, while I give a demonstration of the modern analysis.

My alarm must have been evident. He tried in vain to reassure me. However, I lacked not only pen and paper but also that well-known mechanism for projecting abstractions upon some inner screen. Dr. Y dismissed my fears, as I recall, with a swish of his tie. Even if I myself were unable to follow, he would, he said, so to speak, bring me back word of any discoveries he might make. I was desperate and this reassured me. He waited courteously a moment while I dug myself into my seat, and began.

The point I wish to make, said the doctor, becomes clear when we generate from the substantive "prejudice" an hypothetical transitive variant form "prejudge." He paused, and continued. Now "pre-" means "before"; it signifies antecedency. He invited me to ponder, for my own edification, a sprinkling of confirmatory examples from personal experience. I thought of "prestidigitator," "premonstratensian," "preputial," "pretzel" and "prestissimo." Accordingly, said Dr. Y, we now have—if I may appropriate a much-vaunted metaphor from contemporary mythology—the two atomic forms "pre"—equivalent to "before"—and "judgment." Now these two forms, as separate particles, suggest no sure meaning to the mind. From this fact we infer that what we have before us here is no less than a missing third term, a preterition, a conceptual elision—the law, in short, of the excluded middle.

I sat silent, blank and breathless. I confess I considered excusing myself, as I used to do many years ago at school when it all got beyond me, under pretext of ill health. But the good doctor had a look of such intellectual delight that it would have convulsed me with guilt to abandon him.

We are now in a position, said Dr. Y, to survey, in schematic form, our present position. I cannot deny I was extremely glad of the chance to take my ease, as it were, at last, and survey the aforementioned position. He scribbled the following schema high on the topmost sheet of a thick wad of notepaper:

434

$$\text{Let "pre"} + \text{"judge"} = 0$$
$$\text{then } 0 = \text{"pre"} + \text{"judge"}$$
but this is absurd
$$\text{therefore "pre"} + \text{"judge"} + \text{"x"} = \text{non-0}$$
this yields:
$$\text{"pre"} + \text{"x"} + \text{"judge"} = \text{non-0}$$

I hope sincerely that I have remembered well. I was never one for symbols, there may be omissions. Perhaps there was a Q.E.D. All the same, I must say, without meaning to boast of it, that I do read rather well upside-down. The way in which I acquired this little art is quite detaining. But perhaps some other time.

My schooldays seem distant to me now. I have a vague memory of the image, in a textbook, of some ancient ponderer deep in meditation, with a moving finger in the mud or sand. In those days, I suppose, writing-pads were harder to come by. It is charitable to assume that he had a bath or wash afterwards. At any rate, I endeavor still, even at this late date, to emulate his expression of sublime oblivion, so far as I am able, in memory or imagination, to reconstitute it.

That is all very well, said Dr. Y, but let us now ask ourselves what it is exactly that precedes judgment, since that is the point we have reached. He repeated the question. I, enchanted once again by sandcastles and mudbaths, heard its echo dreamily within. Ponder it at your leisure, urged Dr. Y, mull it over. What is it that might and very likely does precede judgment?

I had not reckoned with such demands upon my concentrative faculties. That which is not judgment? I ventured in desperation. Excellent! cried Dr. Y, excellent! My dear, dear fellow! Ah, the austere satisfaction of clarity and logical thinking, the inexorable march of reason valiantly onwards against the citadel of comprehension!

I am a man of no great gifts, I say it without shame. It is merely a piece of ill-fortune, I hold no one accountable, least of all my forebears, whom well I might. And yet, I may say truly that I have tried time and time again, by availing myself of every opportunity to acquaint myself with the works of men and women my superiors in intellectual and imaginative power, as well as by such independent thinking as a man of my modest courage and capacities is capable of, to, to—I say it with some trepidation—to better myself. However, this matter is delicate and by no means to be rushed.

435

Dr. Y buzzed for his secretary. Yes, doctor? she said. A glass of water for my guest, said he. I drank it down in one great gulp. She really seemed a most delightful creature.

I think, said Dr. Y, that a second interview would be quite in order. Next week? Make a note, my dear. The same day and hour? In that case goodbye.

And he bent to his work.

*   *   *

When the time for the second interview had come I found myself much fortified after a week of Scrabble and crossword puzzles. If I mention this it is only that those inclined to sneer at such pastimes might bethink themselves.

The secretary led me in. No occasion had, so far, arisen for me to learn her name. I admit I considered throwing propriety to the winds. But the very sensuous austerity which attracted me to her left me, for the moment, utterly, utterly – how shall I say?

Dr. Y regarded me warily as we shook hands, but I kept my lips sealed. Perhaps smiling would have lessened the effort. Sit down, sit down, my dear chap, said Dr. Y. You are well? Much better, I said. No thank you, my dear, said Dr. Y, that will be all, for the moment.

What a superb figure! It seemed to me she had noticed my interest and, what is more, so I felt persuaded, was not displeased by it. She closed the door softly after her.

Ah yes, said Dr. Y, looking up from his notes, ah yes. Now then.

It is likely, I said, dear doctor, that science might, one day, provide evidence that prejudice is a fact? Oh it undoubtedly exists, he said. Ah, ah, I see what you mean. No, no, I deem it improbable.

I rose, thinking the interview at an end. But to my surprise he went on.

You remember our previous discussion of course? I remembered vaguely, from my schooldays, from my classical lessons to be exact – unless I am greatly mistaken – the figure of the rhetorical question. But I am reminiscing.

436

It will do no great harm, nonetheless, said Dr. Y, to speculate upon the matter. It seemed a capital idea. A paronomasiac, I see, said Dr. Y distantly. But do sit down, won't you, my dear chap. Let's not stand on ceremony. I expressed my concurrence in action.

It *is* odd, at any rate, to resume, this, how shall I say, said Dr. Y, deficiency, call it that, of or in science. I waited quietly in polite ignorance. When you consider how long it has been among us—I refer, said he, to prejudice—you might almost call—that is to say denominate—it by the designation tradition. It was at this point in particular that I remember being struck by the good doctor's peculiar originality of conception. The more I think about it, said Dr. Y, the more I am almost persuaded that progress such as we know it would have been inconceivable without it. I agreed and begged him for an illustration. I am a philosopher, sir, said he, not a draughtsman. I craved his pardon. After a moment of silence he went on.

Consider if you will the following. Would you not say that there exist— let us, for convenience, leave out of account the outer nebulae and confine ourselves to our own—I intend a secular sense—parish—that there exist, to make an end, persons superior, to other persons, in, for instance, artistic dexterity and intensity of feeling, in bureaucratic ambidexterity and professional condolence, in analytical profundity and a capacity for sustained concentration? It was painful, but I saw no way to deny it. Is concentration, however, I begin to wonder, a faculty in its own right? But that is merely by the way. Accordingly, said Dr. Y, we are blessed as it were with fine painters, composers, writers, even, with great administrators and military tacticians, with superb thinkers—which includes, I suppose, the mathematicians and logicians—and, last but by no means least, with—I speak in all humility—outstanding philosophers.

Would you not say, then, doctor, I said, that as in individuals, so, too, in nations? Your formulation, said he, is obscure, or perhaps merely clumsy, or indeed, perhaps, the one on account of the other. Which shows that everything is related. To everything else, I mean. But I think I take your meaning. The nature of things being what it is and not, so far as the present state of knowledge enables us to ascertain, otherwise, I express myself, on this question, in the following manner.

You admit, of course, said Dr. Y, that there have been, on the tellurian sphere, at various times, battles and wars, and that these have been fought and waged between and against different nations, alliances apart? So, roughly, I had always been taught. And that there have been, in these engagements, both victor and vanquished, master and maimed, dead and living? I hesitated. He was gracious. I make no apologies for my constitution. However, eager to continue, I ventured, Doctor, may we not *assume* the affirmative, and see what follows? Ah, my dear fellow, said he, my dear, dear fellow, you have begun at last to imbibe the true philosophical spirit. I thanked him for his kindness, and, returning the favor, bade him resume.

I resume, then, said Dr. Y. Now it is clear that he who is victor is victor, in many instances, by virtue of superiority, to him who is vanquished, that is. Even if we admit destiny I cannot see how this would change or rather permute anything. For it is patent that destiny would of necessity select only superior agents to transmit its intentions.

I was glad he mentioned destiny, an enigma I have never been able, if you will permit me the expression, to penetrate to my satisfaction. Dr. Y, however, spoke no more of destiny.

But do not for a moment think, said Dr. Y, that I imagine or would have you imagine victory to be merely a question of keeping one's fingers crossed. Oh no, my dear fellow, said he, you must, in addition, mark you, be constantly on your toes. At any rate, the fact remains that there necessarily exist, as a convincing working hypothesis, superior and inferior races.

Yet are there not those who say, said I, not that I say it, that in reality it is all but a single great race? By Blunderbuss! cried Dr. Y, what a rash assumption! Will they insinuate, without a shred of evidence, that we were all going in the same direction to begin with? He rose to the full height of his great argument. Let us, said he, have an end at last to all such and suchlike lunacies, and concern ourselves with the facts. And where the facts are as yet undisclosed or misconceived or, indeed, unspeakable, let us fix our gaze in consolation upon the great eternal truths!

The secretary entered with the tea. How enchanting she looked as she bent over and set down the tray! Dr. Y raised his eyebrows. Perhaps I did, too, in sympathy. Why three? said he. Professor Q is here, said she. Why then show him in, said he. Professor Q entered quietly behind her. But, doctor, she began. Desist, said Dr. Y, he is among us. Ah! what a glorious—She shut the door.

Professor Q drew up a chair in eager anticipation. Dr. Y signaled to him from the eminence so far attained, tracing the path of discovery that had led to it. I hope I may be pardoned for such figures. We are not all of us intelligent enough to think without their aid.

I see, said Professor Q in quiet rapture, I see, I see. Yes, said Dr. Y from a great distance, yes, yes. Shall I pour? I ventured. I poured regardless. We sipped in silence, save for the sound of the sipping.

And yet how is it, cried Professor Q, spilling his tea, how is it that there irrefragably exists a class of entities M, such that the proposition p "the members m', m'', m''' . . . of class M are constituted such that an impartial observer O, at a coign of vantage C, fixed by a set of coordinates (Θ, ϕ, h), would, in surveying a random section of M, experience that section not as particulate, but as a continuum" is, in many instances, completely satisfied? The good doctor and I agreed that it was incomprehensible.

Professor Q withdrew a large pipe, blew down its shaft, filled and lit it, and sat back vaporously in his high chair. Dr. Y produced from a drawer in his great desk a silver box richly ornamented with curious designs. I am trying to give up, thank you, I said, declining a cigar. Sheer hypocrisy—I abhor smoking.

Yes, indeed, cried Professor Q, puffing, what we require above all are clear distinctions. Precisely, said Dr. Y, spitting. Where there is distinction, said he, there also will you find classification. Quite so, cried Professor Q, together they constitute one of the hallmarks of our great democracy. Yet how, I ventured, might any distinctions hold where all are equal? The two great scholars shuddered behind a pall of smoke.

I see here, do I not, cried Professor Q, an affinity with the matter—if you will forgive me for being obvious—with the matter of smoking, in our day, among the young. Dr. Y drew deeply at his cigar. I thought with nostalgia of my schooldays. I allude of course, cried Professor Q, to the question of blurred distinctions. Hence the affinity. I see what you're driving at, said Dr. Y. I waited politely in silence, lost in a fumy haze.

The secretary entered and left at once, coughing and clattering away charmingly upon her high heels. I myself took full advantage of this opportunity to cough once or twice unnoticed.

For consider, cried Professor Q, childhood is all very pleasant and so forth, a kind of abandoned idyll sought once more in vain in song and sermon. But we outgrow it, do we not, we attain, in time, to be brief, the raised plateau of maturation. You say how is the precise moment of this attainder—that is to say attainment—to be recognized? I say again, consider. We deploy once more our great fleet of distinctions, we gird our loins for war and victorious conquest, we await a wind of inspiration, and analysis is once more in full swing.

Now, cried Professor Q, what is thus revealed? Dr. Y withdrew delicately his cigar. Briefly, cried Professor Q, this. There exist, do there not, at the poles of childhood and adulthood, the—if I may thus express myself—the lollipop and the cigarette. Naturally, I pass over here in silence, for the sake of symmetry, convenience and refinement, the maternal breast and other succedanea. I resume. Thus do we find in the sweetness of childhood much that is rotten, whereas—

But are you not, my dear Q, said Dr. Y, are you not now wandering just a little? My dear Y, cried Professor Q, am I not, as are you, a wanderer, an explorer, a voyager, a journeyman of the intellectual realm, the noetic sphere? Indeed, said Dr. Y. Well then, cried Professor Q. Quite, said Dr. Y.

Whereas the smoker in his maturity draws into himself, so that they are borne in him much like tremendous problems, the customary inhalations, and then after a moment's thought, releases them once again into the nameless void. Dr. Y nodded in approval. I began to wonder whether I was not out of my element, or at least out of my depth. Indeed, it is only thanks to an ingenious cassette-recorder concealed on my person that these interviews can be given here, for the edification and instruction of posterity, more or less in their original form, as close in tone and wealth of incident as was possible in transcription. But of this more later.

I confess I fail entirely, my dear professor, I said, to recognize the precise affinity to which you have alluded, if you will forgive my ignorance. I am a scientist, cried Professor Q, not a saint. However, consider if you will the following.

Smoking is everywhere adjudged by those qualified to do so, to wit smokers, a mark of superiority, elegance and good breeding. This is not the moment for going more deeply into the sound and sundry reasons for such a judgment, adumbrated earlier on in my lecture. Now, and here we find ourselves at the crux, the core, the—how shall I say?— heart, the hub, the nub, the very *noli me tangere* of the matter—how is classification on this head to retain its precision, when, in our age, regardless of years, sex or race, all the world and his wife have begun to smoke?

Dr. Y drew desolately at his cigar. The inference, said he, though manifestly fallacious, that people are today maturing far more rapidly than they used to, seems inescapable.

While the two majestic savants drew and puffed in silent anguish I began, despite myself, to consider these matters more closely. The following hypothesis, which, I have since learnt, I did not originate— though this will trouble only those of primogenitary humor—occurred to me. It still seems to me now, upon mature reflection, to have retained its first appeal. I see in it the clear elegance, the symmetry, the ordered inevitability, of a simple though unifying fundamental truth. Moreover it is entirely reasonable.

But what are the facts? Let us contrast civilized man with the primitive races.

We observe, first, that, among us, generally, men show facial hair.

Next, that, among them, generally, men lack facial hair.

And, again, that universally, with few exceptions, boys lack facial hair.

The inference is clear. Thus is the general validity of our theory conclusively demonstrated.

Let me not, however, deny that several asymmetries have since, in this connection—entirely involuntarily, I must emphasize—occurred to me. Among these is the fact, very probably no less so than any other, that, universally, women of advanced age, so far as circumstances enable them to attain it, display, on occasion, facial hair. Concerning the precise effects of vanity and modern technology upon the frequency of this phenomenon I do not pretend to be qualified to pronounce an opinion Indeed, if truth be told—and I am one of those who hold that it must, in many cases – I have been unable to resolve this entire perplexity to my satisfaction. Who is so bold, however, as to declare it wholly beyond the ingenuity of man?

But I come now to a grave difficulty. Those rash enough to oppose the General Law enunciated above will perhaps endeavor to prove it wrong by, say, *reductio ad nauseam*. They might, accordingly, reason as follows.

You say that pilosity is a mark of civilization.

And yet the ape is distinguished by hirsutism.

Reply.

I will not deny that this argument carries a certain force. But I intend to show that such cogency as it has it borrows more from sentiment than logical acuity. I see no more advantage in denying the hirsutism of the ape than in denying the pilosity of civilized man. Accordingly, I shall deny neither. However, let me say this to our opponents, and let them never forget it, that – or rather, since I have digressed horribly, let me resume this matter at the earliest opportunity.

Nothing could be seen but smoke, nothing felt but a stinging of the senses and the urge for flight. I was far too desperate to seek reasons for my going. Finding the door at last I opened it a little, but no light penetrated the haze. I slipped out and, without fear of disapprobation, coughed to my heart's content.

The secretary sat, as it seemed to me, with an air almost of expectancy at her typewriter. The smoke, I gasped, pointing, coughing, adjusting to the oxygen. She offered to type up my notes. I revealed to her my ingenious machine. We arranged to meet later at her flat, where we would transcribe together quietly over a light meal and some good wine.

A superb woman in many respects. In all, very probably. I myself think her unique, in the sense – how shall I put it? – in the sense that there is, in the world, so far as my experience goes, none other quite like her.

Her influence upon me is certainly growing. Soon, perhaps, she will suggest that I dispense with my slaves. What should I say? What do? What right have I now, at this late date, I ask you, to change the whole

442

course of my life? And does not even she, now, enjoy, through association with me, benefits whose provenance she might well—how shall I say?

I trust these are not frivolous questions.

It cannot now be long before at last I learn her name.

Buddah

Susan Straight

"Look at this little Buddha-head dude, man," one of them said. He pushed closer. "He got them Chinese eyes."

"He got a big old head, too, man. I think we should make him say somethin. He don't respect us," another voice said from behind him. Buddah kept his lips pressed warm together and felt the voices slide forward, tighter, taking away the air. He couldn't breathe, and woke from the dream with the dry heat pressing through the walls; hot air seemed to waft into the room as if a giant mouth were hovering around it. A tickle of sweat curled around the skin behind his ear. He lay still, listening for the snores of Rodriguez and Sotelo, the two boys who shared his room. But their beds were empty, he saw, and fear pulled at his ribs. *Did Gaines and TC make them guys leave so they could jump me?* he thought, and when he turned his head and felt the rough pillowcase against his neck he remembered that Sotelo and Rodriguez had gone home to L.A. on a week pass.

It was his seventh day. *I can't go on home pass till I been in this place for a month,* he said to himself. *They gon talk me to death, bout behavior and pattern of your life, and them Crips gon try and dog me every time I turn around.* He opened the door and looked out at the bare land, the stiff yellow grass like dog fur in patches, that surrounded St. Jude's School for Boys. *Now everybody on they home pass, and ain't nobody left but me and them guys that messed up or don't got nowhere to go,* he thought. The gray-green weeds close to the fence shivered in the wind. Every day he thought of the miles of desert and boulders he had seen when the social worker drove him in from L.A. "Your program is six months," the man had said.

No one else was awake yet; none of the other boys were roaming the

444

walks in front of the buildings, hanging over the balconies, waiting for an overheated car to pull in off the highway. If a woman ever got out to look for help, they would swarm like dust toward her. Buddah listened to the wind. *Must be lettin us sleep cause nobody goin home.* He looked down the railing to the other end of the building to see if Jesse, the counselor for the thirteen-to-fifteen-year-olds, was awake, but his door was still closed. A long row of doorknobs glinted in the sun. *Third door Gaines and TC. Sotelo said they ain't got no home pass. They gon be on me all the time, talkin bout am I gon buy Gaines some pants with my state money. Am I gon give up the ducats.*

He thought of the dream, the shapes pressing forward, and he touched the trunk on the floor by his bed. That circle of voices was how he had gotten his name, months ago. A delegation of Bounty Hunters stood around him when he neared the project. "Fuckin Buddha-head, can't even see out them eyes, they so slanty." He'd been waiting for it, and had gifts ready for them: a car stereo, sunglasses from the Korean store, and himself. "I can pull for you," he whispered to them.

At St. Jude's, he had covered the scarred top of his trunk with a sheet of white paper, the way the others had, and written his name in curved letters:

BUDDAH
SOUL GARDENS BOUNTY HUNTER'S

He thought the name might protect him here, but it had been a mistake. He wanted to be left alone, to collect his things invisibly, not to speak. That first night, when they were asked, Sotelo and Rodriguez read the trunk and told the other boys, "New baby? He's red, man." Bounty Hunters wore red bandannas, called each other "Blood." Crips were blue-raggers, and shouted "Cuzz" before they shot someone.

But there were only two other red rags at St. Jude's, and they were in the oldest group. In Buddah's group there were two Crips. Gaines and TC Harris had flashed their hands at him, their fingers and thumbs contorted in the signals Buddah had always run from. Gaines fanned his fingers out over his biceps and said, "Oh, yeah."

Now it ain't nobody in the room but me, six more days. Buddah looked at the low wide windows and imagined the shapes he would see at night, blocking the light from the parking lot when they walked past the curtains; he saw the room as dark and gold-toned as if it were night now, and the crack of light that would cut in as they opened the door.

He let the lock clink against the metal edging of the trunk. It contained everything he had at St. Jude's: the jeans, white T-shirts and cheap canvas shoes Jesse took him to buy with part of the state money. "You got to lock your shit up all the time if you want to keep it," Jesse had said, and Buddah laughed through his nose. Locks ain't about nothin. Shit. They tellin *me* bout locks.

Buddah opened Sotelo's nightstand and saw only paper covered with drawings of heavy-eyed girls. He bent and looked under Sotelo's bed; he'd seen him drop something behind the head one night. This was the first time he been alone, able to look. He saw a blunt shape against the wall, lying in the folds of green bedspread. It was a short length of pipe, dull heavy iron. Shit, everybody must got one a these, he thought. He bent to Rodriguez's side and heard Jesse's voice, heard him banging on doors with the flat of his hand, calling, "Get up, hardheads, we got places to go."

Montoya's clipped words came from the doorway next to Buddah's. "Hey, man, Jesse, you wake up so early? You miss me already, man?"

"Yeah, Montoya, I couldn't wait," Jesse said. "Get ready for breakfast."

Buddah slipped to his trunk quickly and dropped the pipe behind it. He heard it land, muffled, on the edge of his bedspread, and then Jesse swung open the door, saying, "Five minutes, Smith. How you like this heat?"

Buddah looked at Jesse's long feet on the hump of the doorway. Ain't here to be likin it.

"Still can't speak, huh?" Jesse said. "Maybe you'll talk at the beach if we cool you off." He turned and Buddah saw the flash of a bird diving to the parking lot for potato-chip crumbs.

They waited for Jesse near the long white van. Montoya, his hair combed smooth and feather-stiff, walked his boxer's walk in baggy *cholo* khakis. Carroll, a white boy, leaned against the van, arms folded under the "Highway to Hell" that crossed his T-shirt. Buddah stood apart from them, in the shade of a squat palm tree, preparing to be invisible. His arms were folded too, and he pushed down on his feet, feeling the long muscles in his thighs tighten. The ghostly bushes past the fence turned in the wind.

Won't nobody see me. Them Crips be busy talkin shit to Jesse, and I ain't gotta worry bout nobody else. I'ma get me somethin at the beach. It'll be somethin there.

The sound of electric drums, sharp as gunfire, came from the balcony. Buddah waited until they approached. TC wore new razor-creased Levis and a snow-white T-shirt, a blue cap set high and slanted on his sunglasses. He carried the radio, a box of cassettes and a can of soda, singing loudly, "It shoulda been *blue*" over the words of the woman who sang, "It shoulda been you."

Gaines followed him, pointing at Buddah when TC sang "blue." "If we was at home, nigger, it be a .357 to the membrane," he whispered to Buddah, taking the pointing finger and running it around his ear.

Buddah pulled in the sides of his cheeks, soft and slippery when he bit them with his back teeth. Yeah, but I wouldn't be wearin no red rag, cause I ain't no Bounty Hunter. I'm a independent. Red, blue, ain't about shit to me. He was careful not to let his lips move; he had to be conscious of it, because when he spoke to himself, he would feel his lips touching each other sometimes and falling away as soft and slight as tiny bubbles popping. Probably look like I'm fixin to cry, he thought.

No bandannas were allowed at St. Jude's, no careless hand signals, nothing to spark gang fights. Gaines looked carefully for Jesse, and smiled close to Buddah's face. "The red rag is stained with the blood of disrespectful Hunters, slob. You gon respect us." He got one a them devil peaks, Buddah thought, like Mama say when people's hair all in a point on they forehead. Mama say them some evil people with peaks. He glanced away, at TC, who was uninterested, popping his fingers and singing.

You don't never stop talkin. You always runnin your mouth, that way everybody look at you, know where you are. He saw Jesse appear from the office, and Gaines moved away. Not like me. I'm bad cause you don't see me.

It was easy because he was so small and quiet; he walked into the stores imagining that everything in his face blended together, skin, lips, eyes all the same color. He wasn't hungry with hard rings around his stomach, like when he didn't eat anything for a long time, but he wanted something else in his mouth, a solid taste like he had chosen whatever he wanted. When they still lived in a house, when he was eleven, his mother left pots of red beans on the stove when she went to work in the afternoon. Sometimes she left greens and a pan of corn-bread, or three pieces of chicken, one each for him, Danita and Donnie.

He used to walk with her to the bus stop, saying nothing, watching her skin begin to shine from the heat, like molasses, with a liquid red sheen underneath the color. Her mouth moved all the time, to smile, to tell him to hurry and get back to the house and damn it, don't be hangin out in the street. Say somethin, David! All right, now. Lock the door.

He always waited until five o'clock had passed and then left the house,

447

saying sternly to his younger brother and sister, "Y'all watch TV. Don't move. I be back."

He stepped over the jagged hole in the wooden porch and walked past children riding bicycles, thin knees angling like iron pipes. The store was five blocks away, a small grocery store with a Korean man behind the register. Women crowded the store then, shopping before they went home from work. They walked around the stacks of cans blocking the aisle, picked over the bright, shiny vegetables and fruit.

Fingering the quarter in his pocket, he brushed past the women near the bread and potato chips. He bent next to one woman, watching, and slid bags of potato chips into the pit of his dark blue windbreaker; they rested silent and light against his stomach. For Danita. He imagined his eyes were like ball bearings, greased, so that he didn't move enough of anything else to rustle. Zingers for himself. At the counter loaded with candy, he knelt to look at the bottom row and beside his knee, pushed a Butterfinger up the sleeve of his jacket. He paid for Donnie's pack of gum, watching the Korean man's eyes, comparing them to his own, holding his plastic-like jacket very still. I got somethin, he thought, looking at the man's hands. I got your stuff.

Walking home quickly, he always touched the food with the same pride. The store was different. He had slipped in and out and something was changed, missing.

"Oh, man, look who comin, Loco Lopez," TC said. "He done lost his home pass cause they busted him with that paint thinner. My man was *high*."

"*Qué paes?*" Lopez said to Montoya.

"Shut up, TC," Jesse said. "Let's go. Only reason I'm takin you to the beach is cause it's so damn hot out here I can't think."

"I got shotgun," TC said.

Jesse looked at him hard and said, "Who are you, ghetto child goes to the beach? Where's your lawn chair and picnic basket?"

TC opened the van's front door and said, "I left the caviar at my crib, homes. Too Cool only takin the essentials. And I *been* to the beach, O.K.? Me and my set went to Venice, and it was jammin, all them bikinis and shit."

"Yeah, well, don't expect to pick up any girls at this beach, not dressed like that," Jesse said. He looked at them. Buddah watched Gaines sit alone in the long seat behind TC. Montoya and Lopez sat together in the back seat; Carroll and Buddah sat far from each other in the middle of the van.

448

"Anybody gets out of my sight, we go back," Jesse started, turning onto the highway. "Anybody talks shit, like you guys did at the skating rink last week, TC, we're gone, right back to the Jude's." Jesse paused to look in the rearview mirror. "I'm takin you guys to Laguna. It's not the closest, but it's small, so I can keep an eye on you."

The back of Gaines's neck glittered with sweat. Buddah felt the hot wind from the window scour his face; he watched TC rest his hand on the radio and pop his shoulders so they rippled. Buddah felt a tremor in his chest, a settling of his spine, and he touched the window.

The low purplish mountains that rimmed the desert were wrinkled in strange thin folds and trenches, like his grandmother's neck. He saw her, sitting in her tiny yard in Long Beach the way she'd been the only time he'd ever visited her. She was silent like him, her body rocking slightly all the time, watching her greens and peas grow against the chain link fence. The velvety skin near her hairline was still tight, and her eyes were slanted upward like his. The mountains came closer as the van began to leave the desert, and soon they were smoother, covered with burnt gold grass and stunted trees. Buddah was thinking that he hadn't seen a beach in Long Beach when the music began to beat through the van. TC drew circles with his hands in the air, and Jesse reached over and turned the radio off. "Man, you ain't got *no* soul," TC complained.

"I'm gonna tell you guys, no blasting the box when we get there," Jesse began again. "And something else. Montoya, Lopez, Smith, I don't want you guys even *looking* at anybody's stuff. Montoya, you see what happened to your buddy Jimenez when he took that jacket at the skating rink. Two months added to his program."

"So, man, I been a good boy," Montoya said, and Lopez laughed.

"That's why your mother said she didn't want you home this time, right?" Jesse said. "Last home pass you took twenty dollars from her purse."

Now he gon start all this talk about behavior and why do you steal, Buddah thought. But Jesse said, "Smith," and looked into the mirror again. "You been doin pretty good, but this is your first off-ground, so don't blow it." Buddah felt them all look at him, and he turned his face to the window, angry, tasting the inside of his cheeks again. Bunk you, man. Don't be tellin me shit. A wine-colored Thunderbird pulled past the van. The faces inside were green behind their windows, staring at the name painted on the van door, at the boys. What y'all lookin at? He felt the glass against his lips. You lookin at me, and I had your T-Bird. Woulda been set.

They had moved to the seventh building of the Solano Gardens housing project, an island run by Bounty Hunters in an ocean of Crips, just after his eleventh birthday. At the welter of railroad tracks behind the junior high, he walked rapidly, seeing the blue bandannas, the watching faces.

But he lived in Soul Gardens; the Bounty Hunters owned him. He had to be occasionally valuable to them, because no one could step outside the project alone, without a protective cadre of red rags. He watched them gather in the courtyard and then walked slightly behind. They left him alone until they needed something.

The dent-puller, long and thin, pierced into car locks easily and pulled the entire silver circles out for him. The cars were like houses, each with its own smell and a push of air that he felt against his face for an instant when he bent to pull the stereo, someone else's smell that he let escape. He learned to start the car if Ellis told him to, and the feel of each steering wheel under his fingers for a moment made his stomach jump. Soft, leather-bound he'd felt once, but cold and ridged usually.

They hadn't gotten caught when they stripped or stole cars in the neighborhood, but Ellis decided he wanted a T-Bird. At the house he finally chose in Downey, where the 7–11 they passed had only white faces inside, a wine-red Thunderbird was parked. Ellis looked at Buddah with a strange smile on his face. Buddah had been waiting for this, too. "Ain't doin no house," Buddah said, and Ellis pushed him. "You know they got a VCR. You better be *down*," Ellis said.

Buddah loved the cars, their metallic shine like crystal sugar on the fruit candy that was his mother's favorite. Some of them even smelled sweet. But the house, even when he stood under the eaves moving the lock, smelled heavy and wrong, and when the door opened and the foreign air rushed at him, he heard the screaming of the alarm and then running.

The ocean glinted like an endless stretch of blue flake on a hood. Buddah had never seen so much water, so many white people. Jesse said, "What you guys think, huh?"

"None a these women got booty," TC said. "No ass to hold onto."

Jesse drove down a street that curved toward the water. Clean, shining cars lined both sides: Mercedeses, BMW's, station wagons, a Porsche. Buddah looked at the cars, at the chalky clean sidewalks and smooth grass. Jesse circled twice before he found a parking space, and then he said, "Damn, we don't have quarters. We're gonna have to walk to a store to get some, cause if I pull out we won't find another space."

They trailed behind him like fish, swerving and shifting. "Where we goin, man?" Lopez asked. "I don't see no 7–11 or nothin."

Up close, the cars looked even better, a gleaming line unbroken by a parking space as far as they walked, the perfect doors and weak round locks. Ellis would tell me to pull the Mercedes, Buddah thought, and just then Gaines said, "Mercedes, the ladies, when I get one they gon be crazy." Buddah slowed; he'd been thinking about telling Ellis where the cars were, but when he heard Gaines's voice, the same one that had been whispering to him every day for a week, he thought, shit, I don't even know where we are. Ain't tellin Ellis shit when he ax me where I been. Think everything for him.

They walked through an art show that lined the sidewalk, and had to go single file to get past. Buddah watched TC rock his shoulders in step to the beat inside his head, passing closely by people to brush them with air, making them move and look at him. Jesse pulled them inside a restaurant lobby and went to get change. "I ain't seen *no* brothers, man," Gaines said to TC.

"I'm tellin you," TC said. "We gon be specks like on a sheet."

At the start of the steep asphalt trail down to the crescent-shaped beach, a large sign read:

Glenn E. Vedder Ecological Reserve
PLEASE DO NOT REMOVE
Shells, Rocks, Plants, Marine Life, or Game Fish
so that others may see and enjoy them
TAKE OUT ONLY THAT WHICH YOU BROUGHT IN

Jesse stopped and read the sign silently for a moment; TC said, "Man, it ain't school time," when he read it out loud. After Jesse finished, TC said, "Thank you, Mr. Man. How people suppose to know you went to the beach if you don't got no souvenir?"

"You suppose to come back with a suntan, man," Lopez said. "Big problem for you, huh?"

"Man, I'll kick your ass," TC said, and Jesse pushed him away.

Buddah stared at the shifting colors, felt the sand against his palm when he sat down. Green plants cascaded from the cliffs behind them, and the bathing suits and water were in motion. He saw a sea gull overhead, hovering. It was clean, thick white, like his T-shirts after his mother bleached them. The gull glided, circled, dipping slightly to turn; it never moved its hard, sharp wings, just bore down on the crowd of

451

people and suddenly pulled up to place its feet on a rock ten feet away. He look just like TC, Buddah thought. Think he bad, showin off.

TC had been watching, too. "That's how we is in the set, man, be swoopin, just like that bird, ain't never move false," he said. "We see what we want and we on it, cool." Buddah looked at Gaines. His shoulders were hunched uncomfortably, like loaves of bread against his neck, and he stared out at the water. "What we suppose to do?" he said to Jesse. "Just sit here?"

"I didn't say you guys couldn't move, I just said you can't disappear," Jesse answered. "Do whatever you want. Look at the scenery. Don't drown." No one moved. "Can any of you swim?"

Carroll said, "I used to know. I went to a lake one time." They looked at him. "A goddamn lake ain't no ocean," Gaines said. He looked back at the water.

"Just go touch it," Jesse said. "It won't kill you." He took off his shoes and his long feet were ashy gray and rough. Walking toward the water, he said, "Come on, I'll save you if you trip and get your hair wet."

Somebody else gotta move first, Buddah thought. Not me. We specks for sure, like them rocks. TC turned up his radio; he and Gaines watched girls walk by and stare. Carroll, Montoya and Lopez had gone to the water's edge, where they stood near Jesse. Buddah saw Jesse gesturing to boats far out on the ocean.

"Forget this shit, man, I ain't sittin with no slob red-ragger," TC said. "Ain't shit to do here." He stood over Buddah. Gaines was watching the waves; he seemed to have forgotten Buddah.

You ain't bad now, Too Cool. Nobody payin good attention to you like you want. You just a speck. TC picked up the radio and pushed Gaines's foot. "Dude down there sellin sodas, homes. Come on, man, fore I have to fuck this red boy up." Buddah waited. Gaines looked at him and said, "When you givin me my money, punk? I ain't playin." He stood up. It ain't your money. Buddah got up and walked forward slightly, waiting until he heard the music leave.

He looked at the tangle of wet black rocks on the left end of the beach, about twenty yards away, the spray flying from behind them. He felt eyes on him, from the blankets and towels. Now I'm botherin you, cause I ain't movin, I ain't swimmin or nothin. How you know I ain't come to this beach all the time and it's boring?

Three kids made a sand castle, looking up at him now and then. It was plain and round, and the walls sagged because the sand was too wet, too close to the waves. See, I woulda had that castle sharp. Have me some

452

shells line up on the outside, have a whole fence made outta shells. Jesse and the others walked back to the blankets. "Where's Gaines and TC?" Jesse said. Buddah lifted his chin toward the soda seller. "Don't get too happy about bein here, man," Jesse said impatiently. "You could be sweatin back at the Jude's."

"I'm goin over here," Buddah said.

Jesse raised his eyebrows. "He says. Don't go past the rocks."

When he made it to the first rock, it was dry and grayish; he ran his hand over the hard warmth. Tiny broken shells were jammed inside the rock's holes. Buddah walked toward the wet, glistening black closer to the ocean. He stood on the edge of the wet sand, feeling his feet sink, and saw the smallest waves, the tiny push of water just at the edge, after the wave had washed up on the beach and before the water pulled back. The dying waves lined the sand with circlets of bright white. He walked forward and smeared the lines with his shoe.

The tall square rock in front of him had a smooth side, from which a fat pale boy climbed down. Buddah stopped, turning away from the boy's staring face. When he had passed, Buddah walked to the wet part and sat on one of the low, flat rocks. From far away it had looked deep black, but he saw that it was only slightly wet. Green feathery plants hung near the bottom, and he was surprised at the shells and animals clinging to the top. The shells clamped down tightly when he touched them. Lockin up, like you a house. But I could get you if you didn't stay inside.

I could get some a these shells, like them big pretty ones. I go out on them rocks and people only see black, not me. The rocks led to a long formation—a pier, almost, out into the water. Buddah pulled himself up the face of the first rock; at the top, white foam spilled over the end. Small pools of water, still as plastic, were everywhere around him as he walked, picking his way past clumps of seaweed, until he found a dry spot to sit on.

I'm gone. Can't nobody see nothin. He felt his skin warm to the rock. Snails and long insects that looked like roaches dotted the rock. Buddah saw a small snail near his hand; its shell was dull and dry, ashy like Jesse's feet. He touched it with his finger and it didn't move or tighten down like the round shells. He must be dyin, too dry. Must of got left here when the water dried up from one a his holes. A pool of water nearby was empty. He pulled at the snail lightly, wincing at the sucking resistance. Let go. You know you can't be out here all dry. It's some water for you right here. He turned the shell up to look at it; the rim was pink,

453

and a blank, hard eye covered the snail inside. You can open up, let me check you out. But you probably ugly like any other snail.

He dropped the shell into the shallow pool and it was suddenly vivid under the water—the pale dull purple darkened to green, and brighter purple markings showed in a spiral pattern. The snail came out after a second and rocked its shell. Buddah pulled it from the water. You done lived dry that long. I'ma take you back, get some salt from the kitchen, make you some good water like you need. He waited for the snail to right itself in his palm, but it stayed inside. Cool, stay locked till we get back. Gently, he pushed the shell into his jeans pocket.

The darkness of the rocks made him secure. He turned around slowly, squinting until he could see Jesse and the others. They were drinking sodas. Carroll stood with his feet in the water, arms folded, watching the boats.

Buddah walked farther down the rocks. He sat again near the largest pool of water; whole and broken shells and round, smooth stones waited on the bottom, their colors clear and glossy like red beans soaking in a bowl.

"Slob, man, you been out there playin with yourself?" Gaines said when Buddah approached.

"Shut up, Gaines. That's why we gotta go, cause you guys get bored and talk too much shit," Jesse said. He turned to Buddah. "I was hopin you would see us packin up, Smith."

Jesse started up the beach, talking to Carroll. TC and Gaines waited to walk behind Buddah. He felt the shells in his pockets, hard weight against his thighs like money. "You lettin us get behind you, slob, so watch out," Gaines whispered. "You all alone."

Buddah let his head fall back a little so that he looked up the sandy trail. I got something from here. Y'all could be lyin bout bein here, but not me. He felt himself out on the rock, in the spray, listening to the power of the waves, and Gaines's and TC's voices were like bird cries, far away. "Why you look at the water? You can't hide in no water. I'm tired of waitin for my money, pussy."

Buddah fingered the sharpest of the shells and smiled with his head turned toward the cliff.

It was almost ten o'clock, lights out. The noises circled around the courtyard and flew up to his room; through the window screen, Buddah could hear the older boys in the next building shouting something to their counselor and Gaines and TC talking out on the balcony, the radio still playing from their doorway. Jesse would come by in a few minutes and make sure they all went into their rooms. Buddah listened in the dark.

"Inside, guys. If you didn't run your mouths so much today, I was thinking of takin you to the Stallone flick next weekend."

"What flick?" TC said.

"*First Blood*," Jesse answered.

"Shit, man, why you gotta say that word in my *presence* and shit," TC said. Buddah imagined his head jerking violently. "*First Cuzz*, I told you. You disrespectin me."

"You see, TC? I'm so tired of that shit. It ain't the real world. You got table clean-up all week."

"Man, Jesse, you the one don't know. You could die for that shit."

"Inside, punks."

Jesse stopped at Montoya's door, and then Buddah heard the feet slide to his. Jesse was wearing house shoes; he'd be going to bed now, and the night man would watch St. Jude's.

Light flashed in the doorway. Buddah sat motionless, but Jesse didn't leave. He walked to the trunk suddenly, where the white paper was brightly lit. He see the pipe, Buddah thought, and pushed hard with his feet on the floor. "Bounty Hunters, shit," Jesse said. "What bounty did you get? Nothin valuable to you, just shit to sell and all this red rag crap. Soon as you start talkin you'll probably bore me with all that shit, too." He waited, and then closed the door.

Uh uh, cause I ain't workin no job for the blue, like TC and them. But now Jesse got them mad, and they probably come. Buddah got the shells out, arranging them in lines, in fences. He leaned forward and touched the cool pipe on the floor. I could wait and wait, and then what? He went to the sink, where the snail was in the soap dish, and pushed at the tightly-closed shell. You waitin, too, for me to leave you alone. But you could wait forever.

The night man's hard shoes cracked the grit on the balcony when he opened the doors every hour in the beginning. Buddah knew he would quit checking after he heard no noise; he would sit in the room downstairs and watch TV. Buddah waited until the moonlight shifted in the window. He sat, still listening, until the brightest part had gone over the roof. He took off his shirt and opened his door.

His bare feet pressed into the sharp sand. He imagined himself on the black rocks, invisible as he pressed close to the stucco wall. TC and Gaines were breathing hard and long, he could hear through their screen. The doorknob turned easily, since it was turned so many times every day and night. Buddah stood in the close air by the wall and listened to them breathe. He had stood by his mother every time, hearing her throat vibrate, before he went out to meet Ellis and the rest of them. Buddah moved away from the wall. The cassettes were on top of TC's trunk, in neat stacks. Buddah lifted off the top four from the closest stack and held them tightly together so they wouldn't click. He pulled the door slowly, straight toward him, and turned the knob. On the balcony, he stood for a moment, looking down the dark tunnel of the overhanging roof to the edge of the stairway and then the flat land past the fence that was exposed, lit silver as flashbulbs by the moonlight coming from behind the buildings, from behind his back.

Broder's Loves

Sidney Sulkin

Muttering to himself in fake argument to avoid cracked-coconut good-morning smiles, Milford Broder, seventy-three but dapper still, unlike the gaping carcasses all about him, propelled his chair toward the cross-roads of the corridors and found the nurse he was looking for perched on the hall desk talking earnestly, somewhat heatedly, into the telephone. Her small chest, white and puffed as a dove's breast in the snug uniform, lifted and subsided. "I told you about him, Richard. Yes, I did. Well, you try." Broder pulled back and braked. Her voice, lowered, had the husky whisper of a brush on metal. "Very old. And alone. Remember? Yes, nice, very nice. And rich." A laugh, pebbles jostling, and she hung up and sat for a meditative moment on the corner of the desk swinging a white-stockinged leg.

Broder waited, a couple of systolic beats, and then rolled around to encounter her as if by chance. "Good morning." He detected an exhalation as of weariness as she turned. She was extremely young, yet often, fleetingly, appeared old, fatigued with the living still to come. Glitter entered the eyes as she recognized him and smiled. "The bed has another lump," he said. "The one in green wanted to fix it. I told her never mind."

The eyes creased at him, mocking. "You look to me like you had a fine night's sleep." She tapped his wrist—"I'll come look at it in a little while"—and tripped off, the pliant soles of her white wedge shoes sighing along the corridor.

Broder, disgusted with himself, swung in an arc and wheeled back toward his room. Milford Broder, whiner. Crude gambit out of distant schoolboyhood—"My book has a torn page," holding up the volume to lure lilac-fragrant Miss Rooney close for the sperm-stirring brush of flesh or hair. He halted in mid-corridor, invaded abruptly by a feeling of emptiness and loss. How much of the love he had received in his life had been educed by whining? Even the love—the one among the many—that still beat, like the wings of a dying moth, in a cobwebby corner of his consciousness? He shuddered, seized the wheels of his chair and rolled into his room to a squishing halt alongside the narrow bed. Now he was Milford King David of the chilled old bones requiring solace and warming. He smiled and felt a soft constriction in the loose-hanging scrotum.

Broder waited. He scanned the newspaper lying on his bed; he rose from his chair to examine his teeth, brushed a second time, flossed, rinsed with Lavoris blowing out the cheeks, wiped, sat back in his chair and rolled to the doorway. He sniffed, turning his nostrils in the air like a moose. No sound or smell of her; only the endless hum and murmur of television floating through the corridors like the solipsistic muttering of a schizophrenic; and the usual chemical smells: liniments, solvents, sweetly menacing anesthetics, and—lacing the brew—the urinous odor of yellowing flesh.

Then he heard her, the walk like a humming.

"Well, Mr. Broder." She came in brisk as a breeze, touched him, smiling—broad mouth for so small a face—always touched him, arm, shoulder, wrist. He watched from his chair while she pushed a hand under the blanket, testing for the lump in the mattress. "This is awful, I'm amazed you slept at all." Fingers on his arm. "We'll get you a new mattress. Today. Don't you worry. That's a nice robe. Silk? You had a different one the other day."

"I like to switch, pep things up."

"You always look good."

"You look pretty good yourself."

She aimed a laugh toward her shoes. "Always in white. And wedgies."

"It doesn't matter with someone like you. Any color. White. Blue. Sunny yellow. Smart brown. Elegant black. Your boyfriend must be proud when you step out together."

Laughter tossed about like blossoms, another tap on the shoulder and she carried her fragrance away. He sat still, watching her go. The narrow shoulders, seen from the back, sagged. She needed to be rescued from tedium. She needed a liberating companion, someone to enlarge her life, intelligent, animating. As Milford Broder used to be. He turned back into the room and sat gazing through the window.

He had come to the nursing home to recuperate after an operation, conveyed in a taxi by his daughter who had flown in from the other

458

coast to perform the minimum obligatory attendance and flown back at once to resume her frantic pursuit of tranquility. His son had telephoned from Mexico to express filial concern and explain in a voice cheerful with dissemblement that he could not possibly come at this time, perhaps later. What was he involved in down there—marijuana? opium? Perhaps he was in jail. Broder stared out at the heavy clouds racing steadily away, always away, into nothing. He had come to stay until the wound in his stomach, jagged as a coastal map, healed; soon he would return to his small apartment and settle back into the placid existence he had become used to: read, listen to his beloved Mozart, observe, ponder and molder. And now, suddenly, astonishingly, in this place, the nearly forgotten sensation of the genitals stirring. Phoenix rising from the ashes. Broder erupted a grin toward the fleeing clouds, swung his chair and headed down the corridor.

There she was shining in the hall light, floating from side to side, a white-and-yellow butterfly, pausing to touch, quip, laugh along the column of ambulators that shuffled up and down the corridors like a *passeggiata* of the damned. Dr. Bracken, pink lips showing moistly through his beard, stopped to joke with her; the husky laugh broke from her and her hand went to his arm. The stethoscope on his chest glittered. But it was Broder she would come to in the end: her eyes squinted down the hall toward him and she waved and he knew that it would be so. She would come and they would smile, secret with understanding, and go into his room. And then. But all things slowly.

It was some hours before she appeared; she came to inquire whether the new mattress had arrived—it had, surprisingly—and lingered to adjust the blind, shift the water pitcher, glance at the book on his table—*Tales of Edgar Allan Poe*—straighten the blankets. He began to talk.

"I read Poe long ago. He had deep psychological understanding, a brilliant mind, perhaps a little bit cracked, maybe that's where the genius flows through." He looked at her to see if she was listening and saw the deep-set eyes, suddenly familiar, gazing at him and a tremor of recollected joy and of guilt passed through him; her gaze shifted.

She rubbed the silk piping of his robe. "Another one," she teased. "Lovely."

"I confess. Extravagance. A weakness." Her fingers, just below his lips, moved sensuously on the blue silk. "I'll tell you a secret. Every time I spend five hundred dollars on myself I send twenty-five dollars to the Children's Hospital or the Old Folks' Home or the Society Against Torture in a Civilized World. Not fifty dollars, I admit, twenty-five. Still. Appeasement of the conscience, the soul, whatever it is that sits deep inside making us feel guilty. Not out there somewhere. Inside. I've tried various religions—" Lies, all lies. An adolescent grappling for attention. Was she bored? She was listening; talk the old seducer.

"I don't bother much with religion," she said. "My mother used to go on about a church wedding but after she died I don't know. I remember Poe in high school. 'Quoth the Raven, "Nevermore." ' " She picked up the book and riffled the pages. A white button closed the short sleeve on the upper arm. The rest of the arm was bare.

Broder began to talk about Dr. Bracken: Beware of him, a man with little flecks of spittle at the corners of his mouth, the libido salivating, a predator. Her amused glance told him that she was wise to the doctor and that she knew what he was up to, too. He smiled back. For that matter, he knew what she was up to. He reached for an envelope on his side table. "Could you do me a little favor? I need to be sure this is postmarked before the end of the week." He watched as she glanced at the address: Metropolitan Life Insurance. He laughed. "Not that it matters. I won't be the one to collect." "Oh, now—" she said reproachfully, pushing a lip at him. She slipped the envelope into her pocket. "There's a post office on the next block." She left, one hand still resting on the envelope in her pocket.

He would like sometime, Broder said when she dropped by again, to tell her about his travels, and about his records and maybe someday play them for her, did she enjoy music?

"I don't know, I've never listened much." Grave dark-fringed eyes, gelatin lips; one tooth, glistening, tipped inward. "I would like to."

"I came to it late, myself. I came to everything late, everything that matters to me now, including the realization of what should have mattered to me when I was younger," he said. He would tell her one day about his loves. "Do you never wear a mask?"

"Mask?"

He laughed. "Pretense. Bluff. False front. I used to pretend I loved music. But it was long after the pretense that it really happened. I used to pose as an intellectual though I possessed no ideas, read nothing, knew nothing of politics, history, philosophy, art, music, theater, economics. An hour with the Sunday *Times* and I was ready to go to a party and make clever statements. I presented myself for a time as a businessman. Even that was bluff. Luck sustained me. And a few connections. Yes, and women." He smiled. "I have worn many masks. And you?"

She laughed. "All the time." She sat near the window; the autumn light, dimming, fell in a silvery sheen on her cheek and barely parted

460

lips—a figure, contemplative, contented, in one of the lovely Dutch pictures that he had come to enjoy; he had melted the weariness from her.

She dropped in at every possible moment, it appeared, and he found himself talking without stop; and pretty soon she was talking, too; and it seemed to him that he was in a continuous state of excitation. She would like to read, she said, if only she had the time, and to do things like go to museums, perhaps. But she was always exhausted, she confided, laughing. "My boyfriend is—you know—very demanding." She eyed him. "Does it shock you?" Broder wet his lips. Would it shock her, he asked, to hear that even in his day they did such things? In fact, he plunged, he had celebrated the noble conjunction with all his wives before marriage, and indeed with many another without marriage, loved and unloved. "It begins early, much earlier than we like to admit, and never stops even in old age. You may not believe it but it's true. Stokowski. Picasso. Justice Douglas. Casals. King David." She smiled. "I believe it."

She was small, small-boned but full-fleshed, with light amber hair, thick, cut short and worn airily loose; the mouth broad and sensual; the eyes, under strong brows, deep-set and close to the nose-bridge, brown, flecked with sunlight; the skin sun-warmed. He had guessed, perhaps because of her name—Wennerman, Lissa Wennerman—that she was out of Netherlander forebears, perhaps she had said something. When she was nearby he saw her precisely; no detail, it seemed to him, escaped his absorption of her; the slope of the narrow shoulders (the fatigue, he came to believe, was partly bad posture; perhaps in time he would be able to clasp the upper arms affectionately—resilient flesh through the soft dress, the bird-like bones within—and show her before a mirror what bearing, as if a vase were being carried on the head, could accomplish); the one eyelid slightly lower than the other; the moist, nearly pouting underlip; the rhythmic movement of the narrow hips, the small buttocks. When she was not present he sketched her to himself as if she were an amalgam of recollected images bringing back bits and pieces of all his other women now refocused in fading light: the pointed chin of one, the mobile eyebrows of another—one a perfect tulip, straight, firm, polished; another the wounded swallow, defeated, weary, tempting the hawk. And Carla. Broder contemplated the water glass, the vials of pills, on his nightstand. Deep-eyed Carla, most loved and most lost as if she had floated in and out of his life on a breeze or a fantasy.

461

"All my life I kept avoiding the life I intended to live," he told Lissa Wennerman sitting in his chair beside her while she tended the small desk in the hall, filling out papers, answering the telephone, returning the smiles and greetings of strollers.

"I know what you mean," she said, "that's been true of me."

"I chose the wrong careers," he went on, turning his back to avoid a septuagenarian using an aluminum walker who, assuming that Broder was several years younger, had chosen him as repository for his oral memoirs. "Loved the wrong women," he continued, "—oh, touched my real life once or twice, stuck my nose in to see what it would be like and got scared at the risk—"

She glanced up. "What was your real life?" Mocking? No, empathetic; they had disappointments in common.

"Seeking," he said.

"Seeking?" The deep gaze, childlike—tell me a story—rose toward him.

"Yes," he began—

"How is my favorite nurse today?"

The oleaginous voice, the talc odor staining the air, announced lecherous Dr. Bracken.

Broder swung his chair sharply and handpedaled down the corridor. The terrace door was open, the small enclosure empty; he wheeled bumpily onto the flagstones and sucked, snorting, at the night air until his annoyance subsided. She had been listening to him. What would he have told her? Seeking. Risk. Betrayal. He stared into the moist gloom that curled like dragon's teeth over the lawn. In the Yucatan there was a well among the trees covered by mists at night into which young maidens had been thrown; the bones were still there, they said, but the blood had seeped into the earth and given rise to the profusion of starflowers all around. Tourists tiptoed to the edge and stared down at the rancid darkness.

I went to Mexico one time—had he told her this, it seemed to him that he had, he could hear his voice saying it, and see her listening; perhaps not—with my first wife. Georgiana. Yes, a lovely name. They all had pretty names. Yours is a pretty one, too. We went to see the sandstone temples ornamented with jaguars and serpents and rows of skulls and starflowers, and to visit the pyramids that hide deep caves no one has yet penetrated. We stood looking at a curved stone sacrifice table and were suddenly drawn to each other. We ought to make love on that slab, we said. We were young. I remember how we looked at each other sadly. Instead we went back to the hotel and did it in the shaded room with the heat crawling in like a reptile. It was the last time we were drawn to

462

each other. We both went looking elsewhere. Maybe we were infected by the Mayas, who used to abandon everything they built and go in search of another place to start again. No one knows why.

He climbed out of his chair and walked along the cement balustrade. He was supposed to be out of the chair by now. The surgeon had telephoned twice. Young, earnest, capable, with a large nose and pinched mouth, eager to save. Let him and he would implant new parts and have you galumphing around forever. Why not? We the semi-living are less danger to the world than the vigorously energetic. He shuffled to his chair and wheeled himself back into the interior warmth.

Wounded Georgiana: her hair was glossy black, worn in straight bangs. He had betrayed her long before Mexico. They were young and publicly engaged to be married. He went to Paris on a business trip for three months, an apprentice design engineer, and met the daughter of one of the company's customers and made love at once. Georgiana back home is the one I will marry, he said to himself, I am pledged to her, this is an interlude, the kind of thing that goes on in Paris, it will pass, a young man's way of maturing. And how could it matter? The world was tumbling, Paris was already gray with the coming shame. He watched the street skirmishes of the right and the left from a safe café, pretended an earnest devotion to the language by reading, trying to read, Romains, Du Gard, Malraux, wrote long letters about sullen taxi drivers, the collapse of civilization, and made love without cessation. Then he went home and married Georgiana but the marriage was poisoned. It was a wrong marriage from the start. The girl in Paris was the one he should have married. Broder paused at the threshold to his room. What did that girl look like? He could no longer remember.

He saw the Praxitelean boyfriend one afternoon from his second-story window over the parking lot. Lissa in a yellow raincoat, yellow hat, ran to him in the light rain where he stood bareheaded beside his small pickup truck, his thick curls shining; he was large, he leaned to engulf her. Did she talk to him about old Mr. Broder, rich, alone? About the stalking doctor? About what? Going to bed. He was exhausting her.

Broder turned from the window and saw himself in the mirror on his closet door. Not tall. Never was, though never so short as this. Perhaps in the new era of life-prolongation the body will shrink into nothingness instead of dying. He sighed at the pale eyes studying him. Once he did love. Carla. Carla, now suddenly back in the mind, penetratingly, after decades. Why had he betrayed even her? Why? Because when he was with her the longing would not cease. How does that sound? Grandiose.

But it's true. Do you know the poem *Ich weiss nicht was soll es bedeuten das ich so traurig bin*—I don't know what has come over me that makes me so melancholy? When I was in high school we used to recite it to each other. The vision of the siren combing her golden hair, drawing men toward her. Even when I was with Carla—and she had golden hair, like yours, lighter, with a little red in it, yours has some too—even then I felt that melancholy. Perhaps it was because she possessed something she would not surrender. Would it be different today, with young people able to release themselves to each other without inhibition or taboo? But what was taboo between Carla and him except duplicity?

Broder, gazing disapprovingly at himself in the mirror, pushed his narrow shoulders back, hollow chest out. The cranium was large for the frail body; a noble head, Roman: strong cheekbones and jaw, high temples made higher by the bald skull, pinkish but blotched; small ears; small fish-like mouth, too small for the head—the weakness showed there, the unreliability, and showed in the gray eyes, once clear and lively, now vacant like the eyes of one of those seated old men on a Roman gravestone. The hair had been luxuriant and was now almost gone except for the feathery gray collar at the back and above the ears. Nothing prepossessing here. And yet he had been attractive to women once, a slim blondish young man, always young-looking even with the moustache that he wore for some years, straw-colored and thick. Women saw promise in me; I made promises to them. Now the faces came crowding back, all of them, like old letters floating down on him out of a forgotten closet.

What I told you about Carla is a lie. I was faithless to her not because of Heine's poem but because there is a beast in us, men and women, that betrays. Yes, we long for and need and love each other; and we lie to and betray each other. And we do worse, much much worse. Don't we? Why do I say we? I. I.

"I don't see anybody visiting you," Lissa said. "Don't you have anyone?"

He took her gaze: the eyes were innocent.

"No one I care about."

"I'm sorry."

"No, it's all right. They've written me off, and I've written them off." Broder looked down at his small fingers. "I'm an independent man. Comfortably situated. And without encumbrances. It's a good way to be." He shrugged. "Pretty soon I'll go back to my apartment and resume a pleasant enough life. A bit lonely, I admit—" He smiled at her. "After all, most of my life I have had the company of pretty women."

"I don't think you ever stay lonely very long. You're too interesting."

"Well, thank you. I'll return the compliment. You are too pretty and gentle not to have many suitors. I hope you have picked one who will be good to you. You deserve it."

"This has been a flattery contest," she laughed.

"I am serious," he said. "I know what life can be."

I see all my life in you, he went on, thought he did, or was it another day? I see all I have loved and been loved by and all I have ruined, and the latter far outweighs the former. It happened often that he spoke and realized afterwards that it had been only to himself while she was talking about something else, or that he had been speaking to the clouds from the terrace or to the television screen while it maundered on about football and denture cleansers or simpered that the next question would bring the jackpot if the contestant could say—listen carefully—What comes after *here?* Giggle. The answer is *after. Hereafter,* get it? Screaming laughter, dollars spilling. And now, he thought, the question is where. Where is hereafter? In the grave. Yes, in the grave to which the animals carry the corpse of the hunter while gypsies play the heart-riven composer's sad sardonic tunes.

Did the composer break his own heart? I did mine. Broder looked out at a stone sky.

We met, Carla and I, and immediately others began pairing us. We belonged together. We became one of those couples in the movies running in the fields, splashing through water—though I think we were too old for that kind of bubbling. She was serious, and at the same time exuberant; she used to gaze at me for long moments as if in disbelief of her happiness, and then burst into talk and laughter. We loved, had sex. And immediately—why?—I began to look around restlessly; held her hand, kissed her and began thinking of I don't know what. We got married. Success began. We were both working. We went together to buy fashionable clothes, admiring each other, forcing extensions of ourselves onto each other. She was lovely: golden hair pulled straight back from the forehead and coiled; thin nose, oval face. I was trained as an industrial engineer—I won't go into all the doubts to do with that. She was a teacher in a small private school. She was pleased with her work; she loved teaching young people. It was a prosperous time. The big war, the good war, was over. We had looked at the pictures of the camps and shuddered and murmured, "My God, my God," and begun to hide the ghastly details away in some untroubled part of ourselves. I had had two

465

disastrous marriages before I went to do my brief war stint sitting in an office in southern England calculating weights and densities of various combinations of cement, wood, metal. I was ready now for true love, true happiness. And it came and I was not satisfied with it. You must understand that Carla was a gifted person. I don't mean in the usual ways of voice or hand or brain or talent. She was gifted in the faculty for love. It came from her naturally, as fragrance comes from a flower. Once, early in our love, suddenly afraid—premonitions, I guess—she put her hands around my throat. "I'm practicing strangleholds." Then she laughed and kissed me and took her long cool fingers from my throat and put them elsewhere. She was in love, and was loved, and preferred to believe that once that had happened to her, that was the way things ought to be and were going to be. She loved with the part of her that was Carla, that remained Carla; and that was what I was invited to love, and did love, and betrayed.

"I would like to see Stockholm," Lissa said.

"Stockholm?"

"You told me you lived there for a while. As a matter of fact you were in love there. You forget the things you tell me."

"Too many things perhaps."

"I hope you'll continue, I enjoy listening." Laughing, touching his arm. He expected the fingers to come up and comb through his fringe of hair. "I would like to go there with someone like you."

"Would you? Yes, you would like it. The winters are very cold, everything glitters. In summer the day lasts all night, turns into a magical silver dusk, and at midsummer everyone eats crayfish and drinks schnapps and makes love." Broder's eyes blurred; he felt a warming of the skin. "I would like to take you there."

"That would be nice."

"Yes, I was in love there."

Broder lay soaking in the morning, an old man, in eighteen gallons of bathwater. Steam rose and condensed on the white tile walls. He tried to think about his son in Mexico, his daughter in California. But his mind was occupied by the persistent lapping of the feminine water against his genitals. He closed his eyes. How long ago—who was it, yes, he remembered, plain, they were no longer beautiful. The attendant, a stubby black man, cheerful, helped him from the tub. He turned his back, shamed, and toweled himself.

He was out of his chair now, walking. He roamed the long low building, staying away from the others, especially the old guy trying to dump his memoirs on him. There would soon be no excuse for staying. Come home with me. We will have pleasant times together. I am still vigorous, as you see, and there is something in you that responds. You are young and will still be young when I am gone. What I have will be left to you. What would she say? Blue mists curled over the lawn.

The calculating doctor was closing on her. Maybe they had already had a rendezvous. He saw them laughing down near the laundry. She was sizing him up, a better catch certainly than her curly-haired boyfriend, if he wasn't already married.

She spoke abruptly one day about her boyfriend. She hadn't cared for him at the start, he was too handsome, the body too perfect—ah, she sees that. But he was not a conceited young man, in fact he pitied himself, his good looks had isolated him and that had drawn her to him. Now she was unsure. He was weak, often changed jobs, talked very little—she smiled at that; all he seemed to know about was hunting and sex. He spent money on guns and boots. What would life be like with him? He really was not very interesting, nice as he was.

"Do you find Dr. Bracken interesting?"

"No," she laughed, "the most interesting person I know is you."

"Is that so?"

"Yes, it is. Really."

"In that case, I ought to be your boyfriend."

"All right, you are." She came toward him laughing and he lifted his face. But it was the top of his forehead that she kissed.

"I can't stay," she said moving to the door, "they watch me, they say I spend too much time with patients. They mean you. We ought to run away to Stockholm."

He saw her again with the blond giant. They stood in the parking lot looking back toward his window. Talking about him? Plotting? And if it was a plot what would it matter? If she came to him once, just once. Who was the old king who offered his kingdom?

Broder walked in the far corners of the building, alone, shambling, feeling the pull of the wound in his belly. A heavy loneliness opened in him.

Yes, he had been in love in Stockholm. "They were doing interesting things in design in Scandinavia," he told Lissa, "and I was sent to learn about it." Had he told her everything? Carla was to come a couple of months later to join me after arranging for a leave of absence from her job. We had been married about a year, much in love, as I told you, happy. Two weeks after I arrived—low skies, long double ranks of firelogs lining the streets, ice floes already visible from the quais—I fell in

467

love with another woman, a Swedish woman married to a Jewish doctor, a Pole, who had spent five years in the Nazi camps. They were devoted to each other just as Carla and I were devoted to each other. It just happened. It happens all the time, this reshuffling of love. Is anyone to blame? Of course.

The husband was a gentle man, soft-eyed. He worked in one of the bookstores. I don't know why he was not practicing medicine, perhaps language difficulties or restrictions on foreigners. Perhaps he was more comfortable among books; he liked to hold them and touch them but with an odd detached look in his eyes as if even they could no longer be trusted. He quizzed me at length, anxiously, about the Congress and Senator McCarthy who was riding high in those days—do you know about him? I made up stories about friends who had spoken up to the Senator though I knew no one who had. It never occurred to him that his lovely wife was betraying him. Or perhaps it did. I don't know. I never saw the look in his eyes when he learned; I had by then begun my retreat; perhaps he never learned; I hope not. I am not proud of the episode; I only tell about it because it happened. A loving wife, a good man—she was wrong to hurt him. (I suspect he was already beyond hurt.) I was wrong to hurt Carla. Carla knew at once. The set of the mouth told me, a beautiful wide mouth, like yours. She had had premonitions, now confirmed: I would dissemble, betray; evil flowed through me on its way to its ultimate depredations. "I love you, Milford darling," she had said, delighted with the sound. "I love you, Carla sweet." As if saying it unabashedly, as in an old tale, would unlock the center of it. "I want to love you forever." "And I you." Squeezing hands, we had watched Tamara Toumanova dance *Phèdre*.

Thirty years, and for twenty of them he had managed to think of her rarely. How else does one survive?

"My intention," Lissa said, "was to be a nurse. I couldn't stay with it."

"You are a nurse."

"No, only a helper. It's better than being a salesgirl. I tried typing but I was awful. I thought the solution to everything was to find a good-looking man and get married. Maybe it is, I don't know. Sometimes I feel like all I want is to have a man for a while and then no one and then maybe another for a while. It would be easier. I wouldn't feel pushed. Sometimes I even envy the girls on the street." She tossed her head back in a throaty laugh.

If he had known her when he was younger: the delicious unraveling of the possibilities, the longings.

"Once on one of my vacations I told my boyfriend I was going back

468

home to see an uncle who was dying. Actually I went to a resort club in the Caribbean for a week. I wasn't looking for another man but just to see what others were doing. It was nothing but people trying to act the way people do in credit-card advertisements on television. I was terribly disappointed. I hoped they had found something that would be revealed to me." She gazed dreamily toward the window and he thought of the way she looked after she had been talking on the telephone to her boyfriend, sitting on the edge of the desk swinging her foot. "I had a heavy tan when I came back so I said I stayed with a cousin and spent the time under her sunlamp while I was waiting for my uncle to die. I knew he didn't believe me. And even though I was lying I was angry at him for not having faith in me."

The voice was Georgiana's for a moment; but mostly it was the honey-husky voice of Carla; and the mouth and the hair were Carla's. "You keep reminding me of someone I knew."

"One of your wives, your many wives," she laughed.

"Yes. Carla."

"The one you loved most."

"Yes."

The aching under the heart had been there all the time, lying in wait.

"The most beautiful of them."

"Yes."

I destroyed my Carla. She had been light, airy; warm to the touch; content to be in love, to be loved. She changed; thinned; the deep eyes grew heated, the hands dry. The lovely oval face grew long and, some-how, heavy. A curl grew on the lips. I lost her. Why did I do it? Kleptomania of the rich. Love came too easily, needed testing. No. Psychological claptrap. A flaw then, a quirk of nature. A twisted zygote in my making. More. Vessel of sin. For is it not true, say the preachers, that man cannot accept love, that love is given and denied, that man (and woman) is loved and betrays? And God? God also betrays. Ask the Stockholm husband. Now we're entering the whirlpool. Settle for the twisted zygote.

Early in the morning his daughter telephoned. She had been thinking about him; actually, she had had her attention called to him by a communication from the institution informing her that he would soon be able to leave and it was hoped the family et cetera. He was disgusted with himself. What had possessed him to give them her name as next of kin? A moment of sentimental absurdity. Now she had it in mind to come and help him settle back into his apartment, or perhaps if he liked she could take him to California with her, it was a place devoted to giving solace to the body, not to speak of the spirit. She went on and on. She must have risen at dawn to beat the daytime rates. Perhaps she had been having an all-night session with her swami or preceptor or mystagogue or priest, he was not sure what kind of soul-washing rituals she was engaged in these days. She had been married twice, or was it three times, it was not quite clear whether the third was ever a marriage or whether she was still with him, or, considering the fashion, was it a her? In many ways she was not unlike her father with his multiple marriages. It was the second of his that produced her and her brother, quickly, as if the union had a desperate need to justify itself, had to atone for the catastrophe of the first marriage (Georgiana) and to accomplish something productive before it, too, collapsed. After it was loudly over, the wounded wife, Andrea, poor bleeding Andrea—beautiful, they were all beautiful, she as a Dresden figurine, same glaze, same impenetrability, except for the nursed vulnerability under the sheen—conveniently, blessedly, died. It was hard to believe that he had been to bed with her at all, let alone twice, the fired hardness of that flesh. One thing the daughter copied from the mother, the little self-congratulatory smile: La Gioconda, thought the mother; Buddha, dreamed the daughter.

The bread-soft voice on the telephone continued; the guru had certainly been stirring among the ashes last night. "You still have many years, Father," she said. Father? A new word in her mouth. Perhaps it had suddenly occurred to her that he might still have some money. "Peace and quiet and love," she said. If he made no response maybe she would run out of sentiment and that would be the end of it. He examined his fingers curled around the telephone. Absurd little fingers. He had more than once pressed them against Georgiana's mouth to silence her, in vain. Georgiana, too, used to talk feeling to death. "I am sorry for you, Milford, I wish I could forgive you, I wish I could have seen earlier what was happening." "My God," he told her, "you talk like an English novel." "That's too bad, it's my feelings I'm talking about." "They don't exist." "You strangled them," she bleated. "Oh my God, now we're writing a play." Later, with Carla, none of the foolish things they said to each other seemed artificial.

My first wife Georgiana looked a little bit like you, he told Lissa, the very fine skin and small bones. "I could do nothing with her, we never connected. We tried traveling. It was a failure. So we quit. Then, at once, I tumbled into the second marriage, anxious, I suppose, to show I could make something work. It didn't. Having children made it worse

470

than the other. The third, to Carla, was the best but I destroyed—" no, he didn't put it like that to Lissa—"it failed, too."

After Carla he was a loose-roaming bachelor, perhaps in penance; also a hard-driving careerist, perhaps to conceal hurt: long hours, sharp deals, fast trips, conspicuous spending, exhausting and exhausted couplings. For a time, Broder became an ambitious reader: Mann, James, Wilson, Sartre. ("Am I not myself a wave of chilled air? To have neither blood, nor lymph, nor flesh. To be only part of the cold.")

Henrietta appeared; slim, proficient in bed, considerate; and still, though he was given everything he needed or ought to need, he commenced at once to look around and found someone else, and then someone else again—Gilda, Zoe, Charlotte. And Henrietta, betrayed, caring no longer, faded, a tulip in winter, and the zest was gone even out of faithlessness. And he grew old.

The telephone wire, Broder realized, had fallen silent. "I'm going to stay here," he said. "I have friends. There is no need for you to come. You can't afford it and I certainly cannot. I appreciate your offer." As a matter of fact, I have met someone who will take good care of me and for whom I, for my part, care a good deal. My body has come alive again since I first saw her; and, if I may say so, I think she too, especially her mind, but also the body, I believe, in spite of the great difference of age— all history, after all, all literature is replete with examples—she too has come alive since she met me. Had he said that? Would it bring the born-again daughter running to save the old man from folly? But the line was dead. Perhaps she had concluded long ago that he had hung up and had done the same.

The boyfriend appeared twice in the lot standing beside his small blue pickup truck—"TOYOTA" emblazoned on its front and back like a football jersey—gazed up toward the building for long moments, and went away; the eyes, Broder guessed, hot with anger and longing and guilt, the male self-exiled, abandoned.

"I saw your boyfriend looking for you and leave without you. Twice."

"He'll be all right. He has his hunting. He'll be going to the woods soon. North Carolina. Ducks, I think. Someone has a hunting cabin. They drink and play cards and bring in girls."

"Have you given him up?"

"I thought it would be good to calm down for a little while and see."

"Reassessment."

"Yes."

"He won't want to lose you. You're a very attractive woman. But he's a handsome and virile young man. Aren't you afraid of losing him?"

Silence. "Yes, I am." Pause. "Maybe I will."

"And then?"

And then all possibility. She was smiling. "I don't know. Perhaps I'll find another boyfriend. I think I would like a little time. Maybe I could spend an hour or two at night reading. Or listening to music." Laughing now at her own pretensions. "I'd like to leave this place."

She was standing near the window in his room. The pale, dusty rose lips. A moist expectancy in the eyes. It could happen, she wished it. She wished to be lifted into his fullness. A rippling passed over his skin; his bones, it seemed to him, were dissolving. Broder sat down.

"I leave here myself in a few days," he said.

"I know."

"Perhaps you. I would like."

"If I can help."

Were they saying it? Adolescents stumbling.

"Yes. I. Yes. If you would be willing. I will pay."

"Oh no, not pay."

It was happening. Was it possible? Or was the boyfriend out there—? No, she had fallen in love with the wise old man. A few life-enhancing years. How could the mind-impoverished duck-hunter compare? Or the talc-smelling doctor with the goat eyes? A sweet exultation flowed through Broder.

She had come to stand near him, fingering his collar. "I do like this robe especially." A fragrance, as of spices, settled over him; the remembered pangs of love passed searing through him.

"Then you will come," Broder said to the beautiful woman smiling at him. He began to rise; he would, at her *Yes*, brush with his lips the parting of the silken hair.

Her fingers lay on his sleeve. "You'll be fine, once you've settled in, I know you will. You have lots of interests, and friends, too, I'm sure."

"You."

"I'm going home for a little while." She laughed tapping his arm. "To see an uncle."

The sky, thick as ice, came crashing through the window at him. "I thought." His throat clogged. "I have a little money." A noise like the shuffling of a thousand slippered feet crowded his ears. "Records. Books." Was she listening? Mocking? "You would like the records. And the books. There's a little restaurant. Did I tell you? Fixed up with bric à brac of Normandy. Sole à Dieppoise. Not real, not the real thing, but they try. An occasional film. A concert. Insurance. Something to leave." The cave of his chest filled, he was drowning; in his abdomen, in the lower colon, a vengeful aching spread. He had been betrayed, she had been leading him on. All she had meant was kindness.

"Maybe I won't let him go to North Carolina," she said from the doorway, winking, and disappeared, leaving behind the tintinnabulation of her laugh.

He saw her with the doctor. He saw her below his window racing across the lot to the armspreading charioteer with the golden curls.

She came to bid him farewell and offered to accompany him to the taxi and to telephone him at home from time to time to see if he was comfortable but he declined.

Broder climbed the dim-lit stairwell to his tiny apartment: a sitting room, a sleeping alcove, a sink and a couple of cooking coils, a dripping shower, a toilet with cracked seat. On one wall shelves supported by brackets held a couple of dozen books, a dozen records, a turntable, two speakers; opposite hung a photograph of Broder standing alone before the ruins at Selinunte, and over the sofa a reproduction of the *Window at Collioure* of Matisse, its warm oranges and pinks emitting the only color in the room.

Broder laid out his medicines alongside the sink. He examined his supply of canned soups. He boiled water and made himself a cup of instant decaffeinated coffee and sat at his own window and looked out at the gray skyless street. On her upper arm, the small white button closing the sleeve against the flesh. He smiled. He rose and put on one of his bathrobes and placed a flute quartet on the turntable and sat and listened. A haze grew in the room; and now he felt them all around him, all the lovely women he had known, like flights of birds gusting from the trees at dusk, brushing against him, murmuring his name, accusing and forgiving.

Something Big

Robert S. Nelsen

With her hand, the mother pulled the boy toward the bathtub. The boy felt as though he were a bull, a bull being dragged by the horns through the yellow ooze of the fly dip out back beside the bulls' corral. This was the boy's first bath in this new house; he had arrived just a week ago. The boy had walked up the lane to the house and had stared into the house through the screen door until the mother opened the door and motioned for him to enter. At the screen door, the boy had been silent, and there before that bathtub, the boy was silent still.

The boy looked at that bathtub perched on top of iron eagles' feet. Looking at the bathtub and its eagles' feet moved the boy closer to the mother. The mother walked around behind the boy, and the boy could feel the mother squeeze herself between the boy and that bathtub. The boy could feel the mother press her body against his back, wedging him between her soft legs, wedging the boy from his feet to where his head fit into where the mother's legs stopped. The boy was five years old.

"Off with your clothes," the mother said in a singsong voice. "That's law number one of the bathtub laws."

The mother quickly stripped the boy of his shirt and stockings and threw the shirt and stockings toward the clothes hamper. One stocking missed going into the clothes hamper and stuck to the outside of the clothes hamper. The boy's eyes moved from the stocking back to the bathtub, and he knew that this time he would do something more than lighting a fire, maybe stealing something big.

With the boy wedged between the mother's legs from his feet to where his head fit into where the mother's legs stopped, the mother undid the buttons on the boy's pants. Her hand stopped as it reached into the inside of the boy's pants, slid over his bare penis, and discovered that he

474

was wearing no underwear. The mother quickly withdrew her hand and coughed, or at least the boy thought that it was a cough he heard. The boy felt the mother pry his body from her body.

The mother turned the boy to face her. The boy could see red in the moon-shaped cheeks and thick neck of the mother. The boy did not know how many bathtub laws existed, but he was certain that one of the laws, just like the laws at the other six houses in which he had lived, would say wear underwear. With his pants still unsnapped, the boy looked up at the mother's round face framed by her home-cut gray hair, and he smiled at her. The mother did not frown, but the mother did not smile either. The boy continued smiling. Smiles usually worked for him.

"Take off your pants, and turn on the cold water," the mother said.

The boy obediently took off his pants and turned on the cold water. Naked, the boy sat down on the edge of the bathtub, his bare feet dangling in the air above the bathtub's eagles' feet. The boy looked around the bathroom for something to steal, for something big. Finding nothing except for a half-empty bottle of perfume that could not possibly be worth stealing, the boy looked to see if the mother wore a ring that he could steal, but he saw that she did not.

"Feel how deep the water is," the mother said, her voice cutting through the noise of the water squirting from the cold-water spigot and splashing against the cold water colored yellow by the bathtub's rust-stained porcelain. "An inch of cold water is all you need. That's what law number two of the bathtub laws says."

The boy turned and sniffed at the yellowed water. The water smelled to him as though it were stewed-cabbage water. The boy stuck his two hands in the water, and with the two hands flat on top of each other, the cold water lapped over the top of them. The water, the boy guessed, must be close to an inch deep. The boy took his hands from the yellow water and showed the mother one finger, meaning that the water was one inch deep.

"That's perfect," the mother said. "Turn it off. It's time for law number three. Add an inch of hot water to the cold water."

The boy bent down and turned on the hot water. With the hot water splashing against the cold water already in the bathtub, the boy stared at the mother, and the mother stared back at the boy. Since the day that the boy had stared into the house through the screen door, the mother had referred to herself as Mother; the boy, on the other hand, had never offered a name or any other words for that matter. The boy dropped his stare from the mother's eyes to the swirling water in the bathtub. As soon as he saw the water, the boy looked once more around the bathroom for something big to steal. Again seeing nothing worth stealing, the boy knew that he would have to go outside to steal something big, something like a horse or a bull or a tractor or a dog or maybe one of the neighbor's sheep.

The boy's hands, feeling the depth of the water, moved down and then up the cracked, yellowed porcelain of the bathtub. The boy held up two fingers this time for the mother and turned off the hot water.

"Get in and lie down," the mother said, "and get yourself good and wet. That's law number four. Five says stand up and soap your body, every inch of it. Then, after you are all soaped up, six says lie back down in the water and wash all that soap off your body. I've got some washing of my own to do. You're on your own till I get back."

Lying there in the yellowed bathtub water, the boy watched the mother leave the bathroom and listened to the door close behind her. Quickly, the boy stood up and lathered his body with soap. Then the boy lay down in the bathtub and spread his legs wide. With soap bubbles from his body floating in the water around him in what looked to the boy like soap islands, the boy took hold of his penis and pretended that his penis was a bull's horn, and he shoved his bull's horn up and through one soap island after another. Again and again the boy shoved the bull's horn up through the water, ramming it clean through, bursting the soap islands into disappearing pieces.

The boy heard what he thought was a cough again and turned to see the mother beside the bathtub. The boy saw the red in the round cheeks and stout neck of the mother, the red that the boy had seen in the cheeks and neck of the mother when she discovered that he wore no underwear. The boy sunk into the yellow water to be out of sight of the mother, but the yellow water seemed to the boy to make his naked body even bigger.

The mother said, "What do you think you're doing? Stop. Stop it right now. Not in my house you don't."

The boy watched the mother take a step toward him and then turn and leave the bathroom without saying anything more. The boy listened to the door close, hearing it close softer than he expected. The boy rolled over in the bathtub and felt as though now he were a bull stranded in the yellow ooze of the fly dip out back beside the bulls' corral. The boy gripped his bull's horn and rammed the horn against the bottom of the bathtub. In return, or so it seemed to the boy, the bathtub rammed back at the bull's horn. Again, even harder, the boy rammed the bull's horn against the bottom of that bathtub. The bathtub rammed back against the boy so hard that he hurt all the way from his

476

horn to his spine. Faster and faster, the boy rammed the bottom of the bathtub, and faster and faster the bath rose up and rammed itself against the boy. With tears in his eyes, the boy rolled over back upright in the bathtub. Today, the boy decided, today had to be the day to steal something big.

The boy decided that he could not steal a horse or a bull or a tractor or a dog or even one of the neighbor's sheep today because he could not think of a place where he could hide anything that big, not today. But the boy did think of the neighbor's raspberries, and the neighbor's strawberries, and the neighbor's tomatoes that he could steal today, things that he could eat and would not have to hide.

The boy stared at the bathtub that had hurt the boy from his bull's horn to his spine. The boy doubled his fist, and, just as he was about to punch the bathtub, he heard the bathroom door open and the mother begin talking.

"O.K., only two more bathtub laws to go," the mother said, "and you are going to like both of them. Law number seven says baths don't have to last more than ten minutes, and law number eight says you only have to take one bath a week. See, you're done and you didn't even drown."

Smiling, the mother turned and left the bathroom, this time without closing the door. The boy jumped out of the bathtub and wiped the towel once over his hair, once over his front and once over his back. Freed from the yellow water of the bathtub, the boy thought only of the neighbor's garden with its raspberries and its strawberries and its tomatoes. From the clothes hamper, the boy took his shirt, pants and stockings, pulling the one stocking from where it was still stuck on the outside of the clothes hamper. The boy did not bother with underwear. Outside the screen door, the boy grabbed his boots, and he stamped his feet into his boots there on the front porch in front of the screen door where he had first looked inside the house.

In his boots, the boy ran to the horse's pen next to the bulls' corral and the fly dip. The boy climbed into the horses' pen and I laid himself down in the dust hole that the horses used to dry themselves off. Over and over the boy rolled in the dust hole, just as he had seen the horses roll around in the dust hole after being unsaddled. The boy stood up, and he spat into his hands and rubbed the spit into the dust covering his face.

"Bathtub," the boy shouted, "die! Stay away from me and my dirt, or I'll cut your eagles' feet off."

The boy ran to the barn and he unhooked two of the milk buckets that hung on nails pounded into a wooden beam in the room where the mother separated the cream from the milk. The separating machine beside the boy glittered as spotless stainless steel glitters. The boy, the boy ready to steal from the neighbor at the other end of the lane, looked at the separating machine and dashed out of the barn.

Outside, the boy swung the milk buckets over his head. The milk buckets glittered at the boy as the mother's separating machine in the barn had glittered at the boy. The boy put the milk buckets close to his legs to stop the buckets from glittering, and he walked down the lane. The heels of his boots raised no sound, but looking behind himself, the boy saw the heels kick spurts of dust into the air. Seeing the spurts of dust and then looking back down the lane toward the neighbor's garden and seeing one of the neighbor's black sheep grazing right next to the garden made the boy laugh.

The top strand of barbed-wire fence in front of the neighbor's garden buzzed when the boy touched it. The boy tossed the mother's two milk buckets over the barbed-wire fence, and, on his back, the boy began wiggling under the barbed-wire fence. Halfway between the mother's land and the neighbor's land, the boy's shirt caught on one of the wire barbs, unsnapping the snaps on his shirt and opening the shirt up. The boy's bare chest shone there before his eyes, a clean bare chest, a bare chest cleaned by that bathtub and its bathtub laws. The boy twisted his head, looked at the neighbor's garden, unhooked his shirt from the barbed wire and wiggled the rest of his body onto the neighbor's land.

The boy grabbed the milk buckets and ran to the raspberry bushes. The raspberry bushes were bare. The strawberry plants were bare too, and even the tomato vines were bare. The boy sat the milk buckets in the garden's dirt and dropped quickly to his hands and knees. On all fours, the boy searched for something big to steal. Up and down the rows he went on his hands and knees until he finally found a partial row of cabbages and a small patch of unweeded radishes. The boy pulled up a handful of radishes, looked at them, and tossed them to the ground. Then the boy straddled a cabbage plant and wiggled back and forth until, with a popping sound, the cabbage tore loose in the boy's hands. The boy placed the cabbage in one of the milk buckets. The cabbage covered the shiny bottom of the bucket and came halfway up the sides. The boy straddled another cabbage, wiggling it, pulling on it until it tore loose in his hands, and then he tossed the cabbage into the other milk bucket. The boy threw the milk buckets with the cabbages in them over the barbed wire fence, and he wiggled underneath the bottom strand of barbed wire back onto the mother's land. The boy took hold of the stainless-steel handles of the milk buckets, and, swaying from side to side

478

and swinging the buckets out in front of him, he walked back up the lane to the bulls' corral next to the yellow ooze of the fly dip.

With the cabbages in his hands, the boy used his elbows to climb the pole fence. On top, the boy hooked his boots under the pole below him and took his pocketknife from his pocket. The boy cut into one of the cabbages and laid the pieces of cabbage on the pole that he was sitting on, squeezing the pieces with his legs so that they would not fall to the ground. The boy stabbed his hand and fingers with the pocketknife, and the boy dripped the blood from his hand and fingers onto the cabbage between his legs, turning the cabbage red with blood. With his bloodied hand, the boy tossed the blood-red cabbage to the bulls. The bulls sniffed at the blood-red cabbage and soon began eating the red pieces. The boy cut into the other cabbage and placed it between his legs on the pole and stabbed his other hand and fingers and dripped the new blood onto that cabbage, turning it the same blood red. The boy tossed the blood-red cabbage to the bulls, and placing his bloodied hands on top of his head as though they were bull's horns, he watched the bulls below him fight over the cabbage.

Story of My Weight

Anne Calcagno

Until the other day, I did not know my feet had become so crookedly misshapen and wide. I told myself my socks were unnecessarily thick; the weather too hot; it stood to reason my shoes were squeezing me. That wasn't true. The things I owned or faced hadn't twisted on me: it was me. I had changed without knowing it because I hadn't looked my way for a long time. With my eyes focused away from me, I've lived out my days in an interlude. Because when I suddenly saw the width of my warped feet, my eyes next traveled up the length of my legs, noticing mottled bruises like disheveled leaves rotting on my legs—I have distractedly smashed into things. I moved to cover them, saw the back of my hand, vein-swelled and colorful, too, like a cabbage leaf. In surprise, I touched my face, the skin slack as silk. I was stunned; as if it all happens in one day, the pieces lined up: I am not young.

It feels as if I have always been fat. I married twenty-three years ago, have been overweight for twenty. Over time, I lost all personal perspective, grew overwhelmed in reaction to wide-eyed glances: when you're fat you're a focus. In public places, like the supermarket, they observe you until you can't get away from being your own prisoner. Wheeling my cart around, I peered at as much as I could, before fleeing. I've been an exaggeration of cells, a reduced woman. My short blond hair curls into squat corkscrews, tips up; sometimes, when the perm is running out, I look bristling. Yet, when the harried supermarket cashier glances up, I'm the one whose eyes roll into her lap. This is how it is to be an anomaly. Yet, the point is: the other day I looked at my feet, which are gnarled by widening corns, and it became terribly clear: like other women, conclusively mortal, I am going by degrees. No one is a constant picture.

My disfigurement was a private affair. I ate and many things became mine. My consumption accumulated, giving me the appearance of having more years than my actual age. For many years, with a lot of effort, I still could have peeled off these layers and reached a young person. But it is too late. Time went ahead and did some real altering. I am forty-one and look like hell. I've watched my failure. But my feet, the other day, weren't a continuation of this exaggerated flesh that haunts me. They were life and the broad response of time. I don't know why I saw this.

Age is an invisible train charging through the dark, wearing down the rails. Gradually, I'd been feeling in need of repair. I grew to have more bent space inside. I thought: what should I call this? What have I done?

My husband, perhaps two weeks before I looked at my feet, became aware of his own wearing-down. He began to feel his life erasing, tried to leap back from the movement of the train, the foreshortening of horizons. He grappled to stop losing things. He remembered me differently; supple, eighteen, my eyes on the gravel, lifting up very quickly to notice he was there. I was like a leaf. He could have picked me up and taken me anywhere, kept me in his pocket, or pressed in a book.

The other week, a martini in his hand, he said, "You were sweet and your ankles were thin, hon'. Now you're close to a heart attack."

"What's happened now?" I asked.

"For Chrissake, Susan, you're wasting your life. Listen, I don't want to watch you do this any more. Lose some weight. I'll buy you dresses. We'll make you into a star, the star of my life, Susan. We've been waiting too long to do this."

"Harry, how did this come out of the blue?" I ventured.

"Don't you understand what I'm saying?" he replied.

Harry is growing bald and his remaining disconnected hairs stood straight up with the lamplight gleaming behind them. He had finished his drink. He stared at me. We were in the middle of a movie episode and I was a girl in bright dresses, and he was a young dapper ready to love. But he was catching on fire with the lamplight gleaming around his head and shoulders.

Harry invested himself in this rejuvenative idea, insistent. He had not talked to me much in a long time, yet now he repeated himself. "You lose some weight. I'll buy you dresses. What about the good old days?" These must have been in the beginning of our marriage. Being a salesman, he started going away. Absence became a pattern. I sought company in food. I grew into a wide plateau; crushing the good old days, he says. I can't remember the good old days.

Five years ago, I did start to work. The newspaper ad looked for someone "willing to learn." I am a secretary for an escort service, on the top floor of an old undecorated building. They call it a modeling agency. This is the way it's done: hidden and glorified. I believed the disguise for a long time because that's what you see looking up at you in the yellow pages. You have to read the fine print to figure out the code. And I didn't see it. Strangers in town get lonely, perhaps greedy. They call my boss, Rose, willing to pay. I file the accounts. An array of girls in tight colorful dresses and hose, with foreign accents or long hair, always in high heels, comes to the office dependent and warm, wanting more than they have. I give them applications and they preen themselves in front of me as if I am neutral practice for a man. I watch silent but accustomed. I keep thinking I'm to give them something, but I can't find it. I have come to believe in the heart of every woman there is a secretary; she wants to assist. These women are so different from me in their way of serving; each is a bird full of plumes and her red fingernails hand me back the forms. But she is a secretary. And I am.

I tried to explain this idea to Harry a while back. "Hell, call them something better than secretaries. You can't get help like that from Kelly Girls!" His hand slaps his knee with gusto. In the beginning, I was happy because of the way he enjoyed his own jokes.

"It's serious," I said. "So many servants in the world."

"We all need people to rely on, sweet cakes. That's what you forgot about when you decided to become tight as a rock."

When I found out the girls weren't models, I was amazed. Harry visited me at the office a couple of times to peek at photos. "Act like I'm an important account," he said.

In the meantime he had a few salesman's affairs, things in motels he lately informed me of. He was explaining his decision to help me regain the shape he met. Upset, he confessed, he could not make love to shapeless flesh; he pursued women with angles and curves until it bored him. "I can't remember one face," he said. "You know that's pretty sad."

"Why did you tell me that?" I said.

"Because when you try to understand yourself you need a confidante. When you tell someone else your sins, you've got a responsibility to change. Now you'll make me change, hon'."

"I never wanted to know everything about you," I said. "Can't you see what I do to keep myself protected?"

Harry has always wanted the woman he loves to be so riveting that the envious stares of others around him will, like a magnetic force, keep him gravitated to her. I grew into a monstrosity. But the way they stared at me spun him away.

After Harry confessed, I couldn't get rid of what he had told me, and how my weight had ruined my life. Two weeks later, on a glazed and flat day, my feet caught my attention. I stared. Minute by minute I grew amazed, because my realization was unprecedented. I paused for some time. Looking at my feet, I saw that age had bitten into them. It didn't appear hesitant to finish its meal. And I don't know why but then I knew that my hands, my eyes, my cartilage—all of me—was tied close to the same sounds and ways of others, held to the globe. I am what always happens in time, and it's so magnanimously unlike my own failings. I know now I am in common. The only thing is: I do not want to become the shape of a woman Harry chased.

If I am ever thin I will not have thrown off dead weight; my husband will have pressed it into a thin red lining right under my skin; that is what memory is like. Harry stormed into our house with yesterday's picture in mind and stuck it on me. I am very full and he has decided I'm just beginning. But no one can be emptied out. Never before has my aloneness been made so clear. There are other fat women like me; I see them in the pastry aisles. But I am in myself alone.

Harry has been out of town, on a job, for three days. At lunchtime, I went to the Red Cross shoe store and selected bright green comfort-fit pumps. Their sharp little heels protruded like horns from two tender cocoons. It was me and the geriatric ladies all belonging in the store together, relishing our colorful spoiling of our troubled feet. Things have blown open around me as if I had suddenly stepped over the horizon into a rushing wind: it lifts my hem, pulls my hair into disorder, swirls up my sleeves. Walking to work in this pictured disorder I've realized I want someone to talk to, to explain this disarray. I feel newly in existence, terribly sensitive, sick of confinement. What is this? An older woman. Unlike before, I'm impelled to watch myself as a part of everyone.

I know the women Harry slept with were likely to spend an hour getting ready to go out for coffee. He looked for this, having found me incapable of it. It wasn't for him to see that their ardent self-description is an embroidery of hunger. When these women are as young as the escorts I work with, they feel the pulse of their generation clicking in their heels, and they toss and turn looking for something. They stretch into life like branches, to grow. My husband, I am sure, never sensed this feeling in them; instead, he felt out his advantage. Their limbs were octopus tentacles he could feast on. And when they were older didn't the women still seem to be looking for an answer? By habit, they allow their men to imagine that they are waiting to be shown life. The men become accustomed mostly to devouring them blind. The women don't ask for change. They don't like change. They want to remain beautiful and wanted. Over the years it takes more and more time.

Today, a girl walked into the office, rather tall in a red coat. Her hair was bleached, curling down her shoulders, her nose pointed, her mouth plump as a rosebud. She reminded me of a picture of the women at Louis XVI's court in France, women in high hair and lace, with red cheeks, women decadent in their life, who at the end of the world said: "Let them eat cake."

I wondered if she knew about any of this. "You think women understand the world less than men?" I asked.

She looked at me and her eyes turned very thin. "Are you kidding? Every one of those men had a mom, and if those moms hadn't been preparing men for the world the men wouldn't be able to handle anything." She looked at her red fingernails. "It takes a woman to know," she said. Then she leaned close to me. "I know how to baby men, too," she said.

"Don't do it," I said.

"Shit. I don't have much time. Is this an interview?" She pulled her hose up, tightening them, first up her ankles, then along her thighs.

"They look at photos before the interview," I said.

"I look good," she said. Then Rose called the girl into her office.

I made a collect call to my friend Rema, whom I've known since childhood. She listens without needing preliminaries though she lives far away. "Rema, thank God you're home. Can you listen now?"

"Well, tell me."

"It just hit me like a ton of bricks that I haven't given myself a look in years. Who've I been?"

"You've been living, honey," Rema says. "Where did you get this idea you have to stare at yourself all the time, to live? That can hold you up. Plenty of people go nuts."

"No. We don't have this idea straight, most of us: you have gold running in your veins, up to your heart; if you see that, you begin to catch it."

"Some people might feel that way," she says. "Sure some do. What's been happening?" Her voice is patient as lake water.

"I can't understand myself why everything has changed," I say. "Everything seems on fire. It makes me so nervous." I just looked at my feet.

Rema says, "That's how it is: you can't tell when the next thing is going to happen."

After work I like to walk a few extra blocks to the bus for exercise.

People are so busy running home, I'm unnoticed. Today, the yellow leaves were falling and breathing themselves into the wind, mingling a bitter scent of regret. I've noticed each winter comes by advance of many tantrums; the trees toss their heads, the grasses shake, disheveled, blown up, turned brown. Today, the leaves scurried over, wildly dancing between my feet while an endless blue blanket looked down, self-contained. All at once, something darted at my feet. I pressed myself up against a wall. My heart nearly leapt out of my mouth. It was a squirrel now staring at me, flicking its tail, a yard away, raising itself on its hindquarters. It began to gesture at me by way of masticating though it had nothing in its jaw. Two others ran up and all three performed this communication, chewing a mock meal, under the understanding that I had something to give them. And I do understand hunger. But I had nothing for them. On the bus going home I saw animals in people's faces: a lynx, goats, the flamingo, a saddened spaniel. But they won't show their hunger.

It saddens me to know I walked around for years in trepidation of myself without knowing or remembering about this hunger in others. I tried to hide my own but they saw it on my body. I peered out a small window which never opened. Every day circled me like gauze, and I was mummified into the years. My husband called it a disgrace. My heart closed like a little stone. Harry is ravenous for taut flesh yet now age flicks him around in its large jaw, tugs at his skin, decomposes his bones. He is amazed, denying so much hunger.

I never had the brazen confidence to deny life's big appetite, but I never thought I'd understand it, either. Yet life and time are always tapping in your ear to confide in you. Occasionally, I would be startled by sounds like a foreign song; vague, remarkable music. I placed it far away. But chords were rising through me, to describe me. This is how potential approaches you: in no one else's language. If you grasp it, other people sense it. It begins to announce itself. Like a song, you can't exactly say you see it. Mine rose up through my feet.

I looked down at myself and saw the silent onslaught of years, the wide general thing represented in my feet. This isn't my failure. I have a double dimension of weight: one fat made me hide, but this can have grace because it's everyone's mirror.

The night before Harry left on his present trip, he visited the super-market. Lettuce, trim-fit dinners, broccoli, tomatoes, celery and crackers returned with him. He looked as happy as an auctioneer. He slapped his hands together, grinned: "Here we go! Now we're ready, aren't we?"

It was as if a beetle began crawling inside my stomach.

"The thing I want to tell you, honey, is that this isn't just about taking off pounds; it's about building a whole new spirit. A spic-and-span streamlined one, Susie. I can hardly wait."

I looked straight at him. "What I'm concerned with is my spirit. But you can't get it with celery. How could you go looking in the supermarket?"

Harry's eyes retracted quick as crabs. "You're a coward?" he asked me. "Are you? Shit, you're the biggest disappointment in my life." He turned around to the kitchen sink and spat in it. Then he grabbed the porcelain edge as if he was saving it from falling off the wall. "You're going to ruin our life," he shouted.

I have my age. It climbs around my hips and pulls them down into more and more chairs. All my veins are pulsing more fiercely, and this work, through time, has slackened my skin, interspersed it with magnets and marbles. This is an accumulation I must tend to. Life surreptitiously crowded in me. I want to walk through my markings, to pick them up as on a cafeteria line, then to have so full a dish I'll be stunned by it. Age is a sort of overeating.

I've noticed many of the escorts from my office fear life will pass them by. They fling themselves into the world to be touched. Life has walked through me and, like a town square, I have been mute through the walkings, have been the vessel, not the subject. I see that though I did not pay attention to the way life was changing me, I cannot say it passed me by. It passes no one by. I must try to tell them this. Age draws itself on the flesh and time becomes palpable. You can tell yourself certain things did not happen and let your mind become a blank slate, but the flesh won't play chameleon. It stabilizes you, and imprints the artifacts of your route; they're yours.

I am rising, heavy and powerful as an old seal, independent in my digestion, awake.

The Sweater

Norman Manea

She would leave Monday and return on Friday. She would leave crying as if it were for the last time. Next time she would not have the strength to leave us alone—so much can happen in a week. Or at the end of her days away a miracle would occur; she would not have to leave us anymore.

The sky would suddenly open; we would find ourselves in a real train, not like the one they unloaded us from, like cattle to slaughter, in this empty place at the end of the world. A warm, brightly lit train with soft seats . . . kind, polite ladies would serve us any kind of food we wanted, as is the right of travelers returning from the other world. Or by Friday, when she should come back, this endless ashen sky, which we kept waiting with dread to enter at last, and have done with everything, would come crashing down and swallow us up.

She returned hurriedly, panting, bent under the weight of her sack, which bulged with the days and nights she labored for us. She looked like a shadow; she had withered; she had turned black. We waited at the window for her to rise slowly out of the smoke of the plain as she approached feverishly, a phantom. She had fought, we knew, she had begged; finally they had allowed her to go to the foreign village nearby. She had nowhere to run, and we stayed where we were. They paid for Father's work with a quarter loaf of bread a day. Without her, we would have died at the beginning.

So they had let her go, with their cynical goodwill accepting her pleas as a game worth playing a while longer, if only to interrupt it suddenly with an abundance of cruelty and pleasure.

Monday to Friday she knitted for those local peasants whose language she did not know.

487

The game could be interrupted at any time, we knew, in the hovel where she left us, or in the warm houses where she worked mutely to earn her potatoes, beans, flour too, sometimes even cheese, dried prunes, apples. She alone still believed that we would survive, and so she held fast to anything that might save us.

Friday meant, then, a kind of new beginning, as if we had received yet another reprieve. She staggered toward us, crushed by the weight, as she dragged herself along, bent under the sack. The joy of seeing each other again became so sharp that none of us could speak. She would move about for a long time like a madwoman, as if she could not believe that she had found us and was seeing us again. She ran helplessly from one wall to the other, frightened, without coming near us. She came to her senses with difficulty, looking for enough strength to open the sack she had thrown down when she entered the room. When she bent over to divide up the contents, it meant that she had calmed down.

She had taken out and set on the floor, as she always did, six mounds for the following six days: potatoes, beets; she set aside three apples. None of us expected anything different from what we were used to. She passed her hand over her forehead and huddled exhausted beside the sack. "I've brought something else, too"; this did not necessarily mean a surprise. We were not expecting anything new; we had forgotten how to wish for any other kinds of gifts and were amazed that she was able to do even this much.

With difficulty she pulled it out from the bottom of the sack, as if she were lifting it by its ears or its big front paws. She did not have the strength to hold it in her arms and show it to us. She let it slip down from her skeletal hands, to fall onto the opening of the sack. There it looked even thicker, stuffed.

It could only be for Father, of course, but it seemed too beautiful, perhaps for the very reason that it would have tempted anyone who saw it to simply take it for himself, even if it were not meant for him. It brightened everything with its colors, as if a magician who would save us wanted to show what he was capable of. At night only smoke, cold and darkness breathed around us; we heard nothing but explosions, screams, the barks of the guards, crows and frogs—we had long ago forgotten about glitter.

She had not opened it up so we could see it whole, but it no longer mattered. Clearly it was something real. Even our rescue now seemed closer, or at least possible, if we could see and touch such a miracle.

I could not resist it; I had come close to stroke it. It looked fluffy, obedient; you could wrap yourself in it and not care about anyone

488

anymore. I brushed my hand against its sleeves, its neck. I held it tight, turned it this way and that, and it submitted to my will. I laid it down and unfolded it; then I folded it back together and picked it up to take to Father. I would have forgotten about everything had her voice not stopped me in time, as I was waiting for her to do: to hear that it was really mine.

But if it could be desired at all, he deserved it most of all; he had been the first, long ago, to lose all hope.

It was thick; it looked big; it had been made for him, without a doubt. I had to give it to him; there was no reason for me to delay any longer.

"No, it's not for Father," she managed to whisper, as if she were guilty of something.

I stopped, bewildered, still holding it in my arms and blinded by its colors and warmth. I realized that I should have kept out of it or at least have known how things stood from the very beginning.

At last the poor woman had made something for herself. On the snow-covered roads of the steppe, she would have more use for it than we. I should have thought of it myself; I should remind myself how she always left—wrapped in a sack, her feet swathed in rags. Such blindness, such stupidity was inexcusable. I almost wept with mortification. I would not have wanted to let go of it; it looked soft and obedient, but if it was hers, I no longer had anything to say. I unfolded it to look at it one more time. Now it did not look so big. She had made it for herself; for once she had thought about her own needs. I turned toward the good fairy huddled in the corner of the room where it seemed to be warmer.

"The sweater is for Mara," she smiled, or wept, I do not know.

It had gotten dark, and I could no longer see her. I could not tell if she had smiled at me as I had thought, or whether she had collapsed, as sometimes happened. A purple haze fell over and around me; perhaps evening was setting in.

I should not have done it, but I remained still for a long time, with my head buried in the softness of the sleeves and body, nestled in with no intention of leaving. Through the thick layer of wool, however, the icy silence, which they could no longer stand, grew heavier; I could not even hear their breathing anymore.

I turned around and walked resolutely toward Mara. In the end I went in the direction I was supposed to, I maintain this, and deposited it in the girl's arms.

Only the next day did I look at it more carefully. It no longer looked so marvelous, first because it had been knitted only out of knots, you could see that. I turned it inside out and showed Mara to convince her, knot next to knot, as though it had grown only out of odds and ends barely tied together. Then the color. It seemed to have some more red here and there, it is true, but beyond that it was a mixture; you couldn't make anything out of it. White with gray, black, a trace of yellow, a remnant of green and another, darker green; a gray stripe, a bit of rotten earth brown next to a purple plum; over there a tip of pink ham, next to it a bird's red-and-yellow beak. Of course it had not been fashioned for a girl; anybody could have seen that. But I did not tell her. Mara's position, they told me, was special, and had to be preserved at all cost.

We loved her too much; we protected her more vigorously than ourselves—that is what they always told us. I could not show her that it was too big for her, and with a crew neck like a boy's. She could have seen that for herself, after all—she was old enough—but to do that she would have had to take it off again and look at it. She was allowed everything, of course. When she asked to keep it on they let her. The first few days at least she even slept in it, completely dressed. The cold froze us both day and night, it is true, especially at night. But if you tried to dress more warmly, the same plague befell you every time: lice. Undress, wash, cover yourself with other rags, clean ones; we boiled them and checked all their seams; otherwise it was disaster. I know very well that they would not have allowed *me* to sleep with all my clothes on three nights in a row. Even if she was the one they watched over most diligently. The moment they heard that someone had gotten sick at the other end of the pavilions, they would start to examine her. Obsessed, they felt her forehead, her neck; they would peer into her eyes, at her hair, her nails. What panic if she should have a hot forehead or warm hands . . .

She had to go back alive at all cost, they would whisper. She had ended up among us by mistake. What would be said if she of all people were lost, and we returned, as if we had been careful to save only our own skins? Perhaps her mother had already found out where we were and was on her way here with proof to establish the truth. The little girl had nothing to do with our curse; she was innocent. Her mother had sent her to stay with an old friend for a few weeks, far away from the hospital where she had been admitted. Caught in the fury, taken together with us, she had come as far as this. Protests convinced no one; they did not have time for clarifications. They did not believe us. Of course we too, in our own way, were innocent; everyone shouted it to keep hope alive. But the case of this guest of ours seemed much more serious to us all. If the situation were not cleared up and the unfortunate girl had to be held with us longer, she had to be the last to go, in any case—everyone agreed—to outlive us all. They would whisper in corners when the little girl did not hear them; they vied with each other over who watched over her, not knowing what to do to please her and protect her from harm. I should have guessed from the beginning that the gift could only be for her, that they would let her do with it as she pleased.

Only now, on the fourth day, could I look at it calmly. A miracle, I could no longer deny it. I might have asked for it for one night at least. She would have let me have it; she would have even let me keep it, had I asked her. She was always kind to me. But it was not allowed, I knew. I could admire it without embarrassment for hours on end, however. Not even the most clever magician would have been capable of something more wonderful. The knots made it stronger, concentrating and increasing the warmth beneath while allowing the sweater to look light and smooth on the surface. As for the colors, strange islands of dye, black, green, blue, to run your fingers and eyes over and sink them deeply wherever you pleased until you came across a red palm of African sand, an ashen tip of a cloud touched by golden stripes, the sun or flowers. A whole day would not have been enough for all these continents that grew one from the other, bewildering you.

I did not have time to get bored looking at it. Nor to borrow it or wear it until I became indifferent to it. The following week Mara had cheeks red from fever, and she abandoned it, leaving it to lie alone in the corner next to the window. I looked at it; I thought about it, but I did not touch it, although I longed to.

Mara was feeling worse and worse; she was dying. Since the time my grandparents had taken ill, I knew what would happen at the beginning and later. She would die soon; they would not be able to help her. The hours when she revived, happy and talkative once more, were plain deceptions, I knew.

She would not have had any reason, then, not to give it to me. The disease would progress. The days became longer; death was drawing near, I could feel it. Frightened, I waited to see the beloved little girl suddenly freeze. I do not know if by offering it to me now . . . as if reclaiming it could alter the natural course of events. They would have given it to me to save her, though it was not my fault that she was ill and they would not find the medicines to save her.

I was not involved in their words or sobs when they decided to bury her, together with all the things that had been hers, at the edge of the forest beside my grandparents.

I waited, trembling, still hoping they would forget. But Mother snatched it out of the corner and threw it savagely on top, over the other things.

They stood near the little girl a few moments more, sobbing, suffocating, holding one another close. Although she was not one of us, Mara was the first to follow my grandparents. She had become ours. When they were ready to carry the coffin out of the house, Father put his big hand above it, felt around, found it, pulled it to one side and let it fall behind him. Mother had seen; she looked at him long but said nothing. She agreed to save it.

Shivering, we returned late from the forest. It was raining, the mud stuck to our rags. Clods of earth full of water had covered Mara. I knew, since what had happened with my grandparents, that she would not return. I remembered how she used to huddle up against the cold with her arms around my neck. Her sudden full laugh had charmed us. Silent, we stretched out on the mud floor, where night found each of us.

I had not gone near it, did not touch it. I only stole a few glances at it, as it lay abandoned and numb in the approaching darkness. Nor did anyone tell me to take it the next day, although the room seemed to have become even colder and damper. Monday, Mother left again; that afternoon when we were alone, Father put it on my shoulders. I felt the sleeves slide over my chest; I pulled them on and put my head in its warmth. It fit snugly, as if it had been made especially for me. I would have gone out in the yard to show myself or would have walked around the room with it at least, but I did not dare. I crouched; at last I had what I had wanted for so long. I was trembling, I could no longer suppress it.

My joy, however, was short-lived. The very next day I felt it hanging limply on my shoulders. This was the signal, I remembered. It had started the same way with my grandparents and then with Mara. The sickness was stalking near; it crept in slowly, unnoticed; seeping in little by little, only to break out suddenly toward evening when those who were attacked shook, dizzy with fever, and collapsed, unable to say even a word.

The agitation would start: asking the neighbors for medicine, an aspirin at least, or a little alcohol. In the end the thermometer appeared. It was the only one in the entire camp, always kept in the same dirty patch of blanket by an old madwoman. The thermometer was hard to obtain; you had to demand it loudly. It passed carefully from hand to hand, like a talisman, until it reached the sick person. If it had broken, our last ties with the normal world would have disappeared, and we still wished to be tied to it.

This time too the doctor would follow. The distinguished gentleman with slender glasses and confidence in his cures had been replaced by a tired, ragged, hunched-over consumptive. We called him doctor also; he too had small white hands, although he did not wash them at the beginning and end of his visit, as in the past. His gestures and consultations were as short as possible.

He had laid his hand on the little girl's forehead, he had looked at her fingers; then he had felt for her veins and counted the number of pulsations with his lips. He had uncovered her thin yellowish body and turned it to this side and that to show the spots, more and more of them: the disease had completely taken over the body of the little patient. There was nothing else to do but raise his hands and mutter the name of the agony, which would last only a few days more. Only if a miracle, only a miracle . . . he raised his hands once more, limply, to beg, as did everyone, for the miracle; then he slipped out, bent and ashamed, just as he had come.

Evening was approaching; I felt the light growing more and more tired, ready to give up, and especially the bitter cold that suddenly pierced me. The evening chill had begun to settle in when I felt something strange; it was as if it had abandoned me, as if it were no longer protecting me; inert and cold, it now hung exhausted over me. It must have been carrying the disease within it the whole time. It had betrayed Mara too, but she had not been able to take it with her when she died. My turn had come. I would have taken it off and burned it, thrown it out, but it was too late; that would serve no purpose now.

I would not have wanted to end up in that dark wet grave where you did not know what would follow. I admitted guiltily that I should not have pursued the colors and the warmth so impatiently. I should have controlled myself, waited; I should not have followed Mara's suffering so shamelessly, and afterward, not content until I felt it cover me. I should not have been so weak and blind, so impatient that when I had it I was overcome by tears of joy. I must have been seen, noticed for my base behavior and greed. Had I given it up, if not at the beginning, at least after Mara's death, the punishment might have been avoided.

I could take it no longer; I went to the window. Father as usual was looking through the narrow aperture of light for a miracle or a disaster. Toward evening hopelessness would overcome him; he no longer knew how to suppress it.

"The disease. The disease, I'm sick." But at first he did not hear me. He turned suddenly, put his hand on my forehead, my neck. He pulled me in front of the window and asked me to count, to stick out my tongue and to open my eyes. "You're pale, very pale, but you'll be all right," he said and picked me up in his big arms to sleep.

I did not have the strength to speak. I pointed a few times to the poisoned sleeves and raised my hand toward the diseased collar, but he did not notice. It had become very dark. I was covered by his big smile as he bent over me and put his palm on my moist brow.

I woke up in a coffin being lowered into a grave next to Mara; then I forgot everything. I was shivering; day had come; I wanted to tell them that I would not make it to Friday, so there would be no one to save me. Night came; I saw nothing except a thick cloud, ever thicker, and I heard the frightened voice above.

I felt the puff of hurried breathing. "Good that I've come, I've come in time," she said. I also heard the high voice of the doctor gasping nearby. "He doesn't have spots; there are no symptoms," that is what he said: "symptoms." It sounded nice, "symptoms." I dragged the word after me; I was falling, tumbling down; symptoms, it was almost a caress. I was sliding, going down; I no longer knew anything. Wet slippery fish passed over my burning lips; they licked my ears, and I flowed with them. Now and then I shook the waves from my chest and tried to open my eyes. I saw Mara, transparent, made of wax; the sharp yellow teeth of the doctor, the grave again.

The drowning probably lasted several days, until I again heard that familiar voice. "I feel better about leaving; I'm glad it's over." I had escaped the arms of death; coming to, I staggered as I attempted my first steps along the walls, with Father's arm to support me, to the window facing the steppe, which had swallowed everything.

I managed to ask if I still had spots.

"You never had them. You weren't sick. Only a scare, that's what the doctor said. You were delirious, raving the whole time. 'It's stuck to me,' you kept saying. 'It's stuck to me,' and you tried to raise your hands."

He lifted me under my arms so I could look out the window. He gave me hot gruel. Friday morning, the steppe gave Mother back to us. "I came earlier; I told them you were sick. They gave me some lard to give you strength."

And so I gained strength; I could look at it again. Defeated, diminished, obedient in a corner, ready to serve me. But I had become someone else. I let it wait; I no longer looked at it. They had covered me with a thick blanket; I no longer felt even a trace of cold. Everyone revolved around me, determined not to abandon me again.

It had shrunk smaller and smaller. I allowed it finally to embrace me, and it proved not to be so dangerous. In the time it had lain thrown rolled-up next to the humid walls, its prickly uneven hairs had softened somewhat. I put my nose, my whole face in the roughness of the sweater, once so soft and good, to be intoxicated with its warmth, like that of toasted bread or baked potatoes, or fresh sawdust, or the fragrance of milk, rain, leaves, the longing for pencils and apples. But it was not like that; it was more like a strange odor, of mold. Something rotten and heavy. Or only sharp, choking, I don't remember. It had blackened and dried; it was becoming a weary stranger.

We got more used to each other in the next few days; we were beginning to recognize each other. We were slowly finding each other again. It was becoming its old self, more and more fluffy and warm. The colors had come alive; again there was a world of dyes. Still, its nearness frightened me, oppressed me. I had wanted it to be mine alone. My impatience had hastened Mara's death! I shuddered although no one but it had found me out. I approached it without courage, weak. My arms would get tangled in it; I could not get it over my head. When at last it clung to me, already too tight, it seemed to choke me. I was no longer afraid of the sickness. Mara had taken away its power, I knew; it could not give me the sickness. Only the guilt, the terror, the embrace of the hot sleeves around my neck as the little girl tried every night to huddle next to me against the cold.

But I was getting used to it, and it had also calmed down. It no longer caught my eye to keep reminding me. It obeyed me; it served me as it faded, adapted. Often I forgot about myself; I had acquired a certain confidence.

But I did not take it to the doctor's burial; that would have been too much. It was during a terrible snowstorm; I trembled with horror and bitter cold. I had hidden it well so no one would find it. I forgot about it for quite a few days and set it free only much later, when the burials had multiplied to several every day. There were no more reprieves anywhere; there was no longer any reason to be careful. They died by the dozens; the curse fell at random, exactly on those who least expected it. They no longer had time for me, nor I for myself; the terror had become everyone's, huge, ready to swallow us all. We shrank stunned; we forgot about ourselves and everyone else.

Baseness, guilt, nothing counted anymore. It had understood that too. Its color and smell faded, allowing it to pass unobserved. It was merely functional: I took it with me every day; it protected me, that was all. It stretched out perfectly, a shield, without a hint of our former glorious

495

intimacy. We did not see each other; we defended ourselves the best we could although there was no defense. The winds of the steppes kept coming nearer to take their pick of us. Their greedy roar covered all terrors. No one could have heard a single sob, guilty and base.

Each day stalked us. We forgot the days; we waited, listening for the maddening screech of the night. Time pursued us; there was nothing left to be done. Time itself had sickened, and we belonged to it.

Translated from the Romanian by Cornelia Golna

A Committee of the Whole

Carol Bly

Since her middle-aged daughter had died before she did, Alice Malley expected only sorrow, increasing solitude, and eventual decrepitude. Instead, she found herself in the midst of twenty-three friendly people enthusiastically bent on any number of projects, one right after another. While Linda was alive, Alice had paid no attention to the other residents at St. Aidan's: they were simply vague background—people you saw greeting one another at the elevators, people accusing each other of cheating at checkers or hearts, people forever coming up with smiles, handing her computer graphics called "Housekeeping Update" or "Our Week's Events" or "This Week in the Duluth Area."

There was a happy, rather drunken couple among them, Charles and Martha. There was a loner, who kept himself to the one third-floor room St. Aidan's had. There was the community paranoid, LeRoy Beske, who had a strange conviction that all the world was divided into the lucky Shattuck School graduates and the unlucky, who were principally LeRoy and his grandson. When Charles or anyone else tried to explain to LeRoy what a small part of the world's population was made up of Shattuck graduates, he snarled, "You can call 'em what you want—Andover, St. Paul's, whoever—they're all Shattuck in my book, with their feet on the neck of the poor!"

As long as Linda was alive, Alice Malley's world shook and woke itself at the moment when Linda swung into her room, grinning with her great fair fifty-year-old health, her bluff manner, her armsful of organic-gardening treatises. In the spring she generally had a cardboard box or two of cuttings or bare roots. The last time Alice saw her she had brought dwarf-pear stock to try espalier on the parking-lot wall. Meals, nights, walks were simply the distance between Linda's visits. Sometimes

497

Linda telephoned from K.C. or Atlanta to explain she was stuck. She told Alice exactly when she could get home, and visited Alice exactly at the time mentioned.

One day Petra, a woman who lived next-door to Linda, came. It happened to be a Wednesday morning, when St. Aidan's residents were gathered in the Fellowship Lounge, so Petra sorted her way through people folding up chairs, finding canes, taking turns using the elevators. At last she found Alice trying to drive a beanpole firmly into the gravelly soil of the residents' garden. Petra told her that Linda's plane had struck another plane.

After that, Alice noticed her surroundings. She had grown up in Duluth, so Lake Superior, with its spit of land making the harbor, its queer aerial bridge, the wavy cold water strung across with whitecaps, the harsh, curiously medieval rooftops of the West End, were all familiar to her. Now she saw them inwardly for the first time.

She joined everything going on at St. Aidan's. She saw that people pretended to be much more interested in one another than could possibly be true. They smiled at one another a good deal. They were patient with LeRoy Beske. Linda had been killed in late spring: by midsummer Alice was secretary of the Group which a social-work student convened each Wednesday. She donated her daughter's library to the Seamen's Mission. By autumn she joined the protests against the St. Aidan's manager's various schemes to remove the residents' privileges.

Nearly all meetings and programs were well attended. Everyone except Jack Laresstad went to everything. A few people, especially Martha, who drank in the mornings, nodded off during slide shows of Third World countries, but they politely woke themselves during the "Question Period" and tried to have eye contact with the speaker when they could. Mr. Binner, the manager, brought in a good many fourth-rate speakers for them. Each one was introduced as a "very very special person," whom they were lucky to have right there, as a rich resource person. Someone told them how cruelly used the Third World sailors were on the ocean-going boats. A marine biologist told them what could live and what could not live at the deepest levels of Lake Superior.

Each Tuesday Mr. Binner held house meetings which he liked to call "Housekeeping Updates." Everybody tried to pay close attention at the "Updates," in order to catch and halt any loss of privilege in the early stages, if possible. LeRoy Beske was sure that Mr. Binner invested their monthly payments, as well as the grant money St. Aidan's got, in gigantic firms whose fingers went deep into all the money-pots of the world and delivered the booty into Mr. Binner's personal account. Each

498

Wednesday they had "Group." Nearly every day they had a cocktail hour of sorts, in Charles's and Martha's room, where Malcolm the minibus driver left off cases of vodka and beer, wrapped in Eddie Bauer camping bags. They had parties, everyone holding a toothbrush glass or a glass taken from the Fellowship Lounge. Charles called their parties "celebrations": they celebrated defeating the manager in his attempt to plow over their gardens. They celebrated defeating the manager in his plan to authorize Malcolm to drive them into downtown Duluth only twice a week instead of three times a week. They celebrated after the "Housekeeping Update" in which they voted that Mr. Binner take the sunflower seed for St. Aidan's ten bird-feeding stations out of his operating expenses instead of insisting the residents pay for it themselves. Charles was forever shouting, "Celebration, folks! Martha and I want you all to come to our room! Five sharp!" as if life were a succession of marches under the Arc de Triomphe.

They had one recluse, Jack Laresstad, who mainly stayed in his third-floor room, monitoring the harbor with his binoculars. They had one bellicose member, LeRoy Beske. Like most paranoids, Beske made strong use of *Robert's Rules*, bringing them in even when the meeting was not formal. "Call the question!" LeRoy would shout. "Call the god-damned question!" in just the mix of fury and expertise to waken even Martha, who generally had her head on Charles's shoulder throughout any meeting. She would raise herself gently, like a mermaid trying the air. She would cry out charmingly, "Yes—O yes! Call the question!"

"We need to adjourn the goddamned meeting," LeRoy said. "We need to reconvene as a Committee of the Whole!"

"So the chair can't stop you from talking! Not a chance, my boy!" Charles said with a laugh.

"I am sick of being pushed around by a bunch of snobbish old Shat-tuck grads!" LeRoy flung back at Charles. "My grandson's trying to get started in business and who cheats him clean? Gentlemen! Shattuck graduates who think they're so good they don't have to pay their bills!"

Everyone knew about LeRoy's grandson. Everyone knew about every-one else except Jack Laresstad.

Alice, amazed at the folly of her life, took part in everything. She did not cultivate a friendship with Jack because he was solitary. He was the only chance of a serious friendship so she saved him for last, whatever last should be. The grief of St. Aidan's was that you ran through any one person's repertoire of wit and wisdom in two weeks. You knew the names and circumstances of their relations, you knew whether or not a harsh wind off Lake Superior would make them complain or talk about neuralgia. You knew of all the blizzards they and their friends or family had nearly died in. Alice was saving Jack, therefore, so there should be something other than LeRoy Beske's tantrums to differentiate each day.

She knew he had taken it in that she was now among them all, in a way she had not been before. He greeted her, and she responded, in the odd, almost uniform imported raillery that most St. Aidan's residents used with each other: it was a slightly unnatural formality, which seemed to say, At some point in my life I lived a little more elegantly than I do now, and the elegance remains inside me.

At the elevators Jack said, smiling, "Madam!"

"Sir!" Alice said.

"May I ask what your energetic group have on for this frigid blustery day?" he said. The elevators of St. Aidan's did not go to the third floor where his room was, so he had come down a flight of stairs, and now waited with Alice to descend to the Fellowship Lounge for breakfast. He was very neat in his white shirt, open at the neck, not a lumberjack shirt. He had just a bit of white hair. He had the habit of bending towards anyone he spoke to, actually seeming to listen.

She told him, "We constantly fight against crime. Last week it was Mr. Binner's crooked deal with some landscape company that wanted to do away with our gardens. Today we have to save Helen's job."

Jack said, "Who's Helen?"

"Our social worker. She helped us fight Mr. Binner about the landscaping so he left in a temper. Now he has asked her supervisor to come be at our meeting. We know that he intends to disgrace her. She is doing something called a 'practicum'."

"You garden, don't you?" Jack said. The elevator slowly lowered them.

Alice turned the conversation away from gardening. Her instinct was not to talk about the subject of greatest interest.

"What's out on the lake so far today?" she asked him.

"Something big moored sternwise to us, sailing under a Libyan flag. And fourteen hundred gulls at last count."

No sooner did they emerge on the main floor than Charles came rapidly forward. "Oh Alice!" he cried. "Hello, Jack. Oh Alice! LeRoy is saying he won't go through with it!"

She had to follow him over to the window, where a few of the residents had set their trays. Beyond their heads the November day looked rather bright, whitey and fragile: there was a slight frosty lick on the rock outcropping just below St. Aidan's, a slight shine to the steep-pitched roofs on the hillside. The lake still lay motionless under its morning fog.

LeRoy looked up. "I'm not going to do it," he said. "It's goddamned humiliating. Besides, it's blackmail. What do I care if Helen loses her job or her practicum or whatever it is? Lots of people lose lots of things! Look how many people have cheated my grandson!"

Charles tapped LeRoy's hand with his fork. "We know about your grandson, you know. Cheated by Shattuck graduates!"

"Sneer all you like!" LeRoy shouted.

One of the maids came over. "Can I help with anything, Mr. Beske?" she said.

"O hell!" LeRoy said. "Why should all you city slicks care about one poor kid trying to make a living at a wrecking business?"

Alice said, "Doing our best, LeRoy. *You* work this morning, *we* all work to help your grandson this afternoon! We do care!"

People always went to their rooms after breakfast. Then the elevators clicked and clicked over their safety catches as the residents returned in twos and threes and fours to the Fellowship Lounge for Group. Helen Pool, their young social-work student, got the chairs set around in a circle. This morning a sensible, kindly-faced woman of fifty or so stood talking to the manager near the Fellowship Lounge doorway.

When everyone sat down, Helen said in her terribly young, not particularly resonant voice: "Before we *check in* I would like to introduce a very very special person to you."

Everyone who came to St. Aidan's was introduced as a very very special person, so now the Group waited, unaffected.

"This is my supervisor, Ms. Dietrich," Helen said.

Charles leaned over and said to Alice, "This is it!"

Alice couldn't decide whether she felt pleasantly excited at the adventures they had planned for the day or if she felt extraordinarily depressed at the stupidity of all their agendas. Since Helen had introduced Ms. Dietrich to Group, they were to go with Plan B. LeRoy was very red in the face, but he swung into his first speech:

"Hi, Ms. Dietrich!" he shouted.

"Good to have you with us," Charles said.

"Before we *check in* can I say something, Helen?" cried LeRoy. Now he was on his feet.

"You know you don't have to stand up to speak out at Group, LeRoy," Helen said.

LeRoy sat down. "Helen," he said very loudly, "I want to say what a difference it makes that you come have these sessions with us. Before you started Group with us, we never shared any of our personal concerns. We had negative feelings and nowhere to go with them. We acted out. The bottom line is, we didn't bring anything out into the open."

LeRoy paused. Alice heard Charles say very low: "I know that I myself had trouble with . . ."

LeRoy manfully took it up: "I know that I myself had trouble with how I conducted myself in this room. I would feel angry that my grandson Terry didn't visit me more. Or I'd feel angry the way this place is run. It always seemed crazy to me that people accused me of cheating at checkers when I always felt that Mr. Binner, over there, was cheating the residents here in any way he thought he could get away with. Of course that was just a feeling of mine. I had angry feelings."

Helen was not a very bright worker. "It is O.K. to have angry feelings, LeRoy. We've talked about that," she said.

LeRoy was grinding forward. "I'd be still feeling angry that someone had cheated my grandson, see, Helen, there is this optometrist downtown that cheated my grandson—"

Helen cut in: "We've talked about the optometrist, LeRoy."

LeRoy cut back in: "And I'd think about that and have angry feelings and if the person I was playing chess with got up and went out sometimes I would move one or two of their pawns off. If the person was a dumbbell or if they were some rich Shattuck School type I'd try to slide their knight, maybe, off, too, and then stand it up with the other pieces which had been taken."

Charles did not forget his cue. "You cheat, LeRoy! You cheat! That was my knight you took and when I said so you denied it, and in front of the whole Group, too!"

Helen said, "Did you want to respond to Charles, LeRoy?"

LeRoy said, "So I cheated sometimes. In hearts, too. If there were three, I would look at the kitty. I think I was under a lot of pressure but didn't realize it."

Charles: "Why are you telling us all this *now*, LeRoy?"

Martha, who had no assigned part, suddenly said very clearly in a silvery voice, "How come LeRoy Beske is wearing a tie when he never wears a tie? I think it looks very sweet." Her head slid back down onto Charles's shoulder.

LeRoy said: "Helen makes it possible for us to work out this kind of stuff," he said. "Somehow I feel so much more in . . . in control of my life now."

Charles said, with his hand steadying Martha so she didn't sink into his lap, "I must say, I feel the same thing, Helen. I feel as if we can all get together and make the changes we want to make in our lives. I used to

502

get depressed. Now, when I feel depressed by something, I let it have its space, but I don't let it climb all over me."

"Like all my cursing and dirty language," LeRoy said. "I am cutting down on it, making a track record like you said, Helen. But I am going to need help with this. So the rest of you can help some."

The ten who were in the Project kept a straight face, but a few of the others looked stunned. One woman, who had firmly slept through every St. Aidan's program ever offered, was not only wide awake but on her feet, half her weight square over the four points of her cane. She studied the face of each speaker.

Alice Malley thought, Well, it stands to reason. When you are nine years old a skillful liar can fool you. But when you've lived another eighty or ninety years you have heard a good many people lie in a good many different kinds of circumstances, so most likely you can tell when you wake up in a room where four people are lying steadily.

LeRoy had one more speech, if Alice recalled the rehearsals right, then Charles, then she herself was to say, "I don't know if I can take in anything more right now, Helen—I think I'm winding down!" and then Martha was supposed to follow the two social workers out to the parking lot to overhear their reactions to everything. But Martha obviously had not obeyed Charles's request that she not drink anything just this one day when they had so much to do: Alice decided she would go to the parking lot herself.

She got past LeRoy, who was shouting at Charles: "How'd I do, big boy? How'd I do? Not it's *your* turn, big boy!"

It was bright and cold outside. Alice found Helen and Ms. Dietrich leaning against one of their cars. They had lighted cigarettes and were laughing and talking, not, Alice noticed, bothering to make eye contact. Eye contact was a bloodletting issue at St. Aidan's Group: everyone hated being told by the twenty-three-year-old social worker they must make eye contact.

They smiled as she came up. Alice was delighted when Ms. Dietrich shook hands with her. She caught herself just in time before saying, "You remind me so much of my daughter—I noticed it all through the Group meeting! You remind me so very much of her! How much you remind me of her! It is the same rather hearty, frank face! I should not mention this perhaps—but you remind me so much of Linda! Did you know that my Linda was killed?"

She did not say any of that.

Helen, who had a trick of not just looking at people but rather poring over them, said, "Don't cry, Alice: it came out all right this morning! Really it did!"

Ms. Dietrich, still holding Alice's hand, smiled. "I have been telling Helen here," she said, "that she must be doing something right in her practicum I have overseen a lot of practicums but I have never yet seen a whole roomful of people lie themselves blue in the face in order to make a master-of-social work degree candidate look good in front of her supervisor!"

They all laughed and Alice wiped her nose.

"I gather Mr. Binner is a jerk," Ms. Dietrich offered.

They talked about the sleazy manager for a while, they shook hands again, and Alice spent a couple of minutes studying the parking-lot wall. She would need to furr out from the stone, with bamboo or other sticks, so she could progressively train the pear-tree branches as they came along. Now the little roots of them were curled, spineless still, safe under the gravelly dirt and mulch.

After a while she went in: for a half hour she had been lost in thought about the baby pear trees. She felt happy about it.

Charles caught her arm in the hallway. "Bad news," he said.

He led her over to the checkers table, away from people who were beginning to line up for the luncheon trays.

"LeRoy is very sick. Right after Group he apparently sat down on the carpet by the elevators and wouldn't get up. People thought he was having one of his paranoid tantrums. It turned out he was in a coma, and they've taken him to St. Mary's."

Charles paused. "I guess that's the end of the afternoon plan."

Alice said, "Nonsense. Let's go ahead with it!"

"But what good will it do? What difference will it make to LeRoy? He's probably had a stroke! We'll go downtown and make fools of ourselves — and all for nothing!"

Alice said, "It's true we will make fools of ourselves. Let's go through it, anyway. If LeRoy recovers, think how he'll feel!"

When the Special Committee of Ten gathered by the minibus, Malcolm checked their names on his clipboard. "LeRoy's not here yet," he said. They explained he was sick.

Alice went around to each person and made sure he or she had the right typed sheet: half the sheets had little else but figures on them: the other half had a couple of paragraphs of neat typing. Mr. Binner's secretary had let Alice use the copier, but she had had to pay fifteen cents for each copy because Mr. Binner had told her if they ever let the

504

residents start making copies free, next thing everybody would do a whole book.

Malcolm drove them sedately down the Skyline Drive, then steeply down one of the avenues to Superior Street, and then east.

"I'll be right here in an hour!" Malcolm told each person climbing out. To Alice, who got out last, he said, "Don't spend everything you got in one place!"

Alice had not lived in a jovial community for two years for nothing. "Spend all *what* in one place!" she jeered back in the right tone.

"Come on," Charles said, "We're on."

The man who owed LeRoy Beske's grandson $215 was Dr. Royce Salaco, an optometrist with an office facing Lake Superior on one side, the ground-floor of a business building on another, and Superior Street on the north side. Charles and Molly and Alice had been past it so many times they felt as if they knew it inch by inch.

No one wanted to get started: all ten clustered together on the windy sidewalk, longing to be like the passersby – just private citizens not committed to some dreadful project.

Charles whispered, "Keep your spirits up! Here we go! Big celebration afterward in Molly's and my room, O.K.? O.K! Let's go! O.K., Alice. From now on, you're LeRoy."

She knew his lines well enough. With Charles hanging about a few feet behind, she went into the foyer of the building and turned left into Dr. Salaco's office. Out of the corner of her eye she saw the residents divide themselves into those who were to stay on Superior Street and those who were to stand about in the building. Charles waited at the office door, without coming in.

Throughout both rehearsals she had found Dr. Salaco simply another Scandinavian-looking Minnesota optometrist: he had his rather coarse, neat, pale hair, expressionless eyes behind the rimless glasses. Now, as Alice crept over towards his counter with its swivel seat for customers being fitted, Dr. Salaco looked like a film-version Abwehr officer – pale, blond, gigantic, with the snappy look of someone with a lifelong commitment to pure evil.

He said, "Can I help you this afternoon?"

"I've come about your account with Terence Beske," Alice said.

"How's that?"

"I've come to regularize your account with Terence Beske," Alice said.

"Lady, I haven't got the least idea what you're talking about!"

"Terence Beske," Alice explained, "is the young man who pulled your car out of the ditch you put it in on August 16, 1987. It was three-fifteen

505

in the morning. Then he drove you and your lady friend to where you needed to go. He did it as a personal favor, charging you only for the gas, although you promised, at the time, to 'make it worth his while.' Then, as contracted for by you, he replaced your Michelins with some old tires, since you told him that was all right with State Farm. He presided over the assessment by the claims officer. He has sent you a total of four billings since then which—"

"Lady," Dr. Salaco said, "I don't know who or what you are talking about but I'm afraid I am going to have to ask you to leave. As you see, I have a busy day and there is a customer waiting."

Alice did not look back. "The man in the doorway?" she said. "He's with me."

As LeRoy and Charles had planned it, there would be nice sass in the scene if LeRoy did not even look over his shoulder to check if it *was* Charles who had come in. They had reckoned that if someone else happened into the doorway just then, that person wouldn't hear LeRoy's "he's with me" and if he or she did, wouldn't believe it had any application. If worse came to worst, Charles could elbow in front of someone.

"Yes," Alice said, actually drawling now, warming to the part. "He's with me. And those ones out in the street now—if you'd look. Those people out there passing out sheets to passersby? They are handouts explaining how you didn't pay your bill to a twenty-year-old entrepreneur. And the people in the building lobby now. . ."

Alice waited while Dr. Salaco spun around and glared through the lobby window of his shop. A few people were waiting for the elevators. Four senior citizens were handing sheets of paper to the others. A man stooped over the fountain: when he straightened up, an old person smiled at him and handed him a sheet.

"Those people," Alice now said, "are handing out just the figures—billing dates—a breakdown of Terry's service to you. We thought people who do business right in the same building with you should know the level of ethical unconcern you operate on."

Alice moved over to the wall full of tiny shelves: each little brace held a model piece of eyewear. She ran her hand over a few of the nose-sections, then picked one up and put on the frames. They had no prescription, of course, which gave her an odd feeling: when she put the glasses on, even though she *knew* they had no glass in them, she unconsciously expected to see better.

She wandered over to the window that overlooked the harbor.

"You're good at your trade," she said, loudly, so Dr. Salaco would hear although she was looking at the lake. "With these glasses of yours I can see so well I can see right into the portholes of that ship way out there. Libyan, I see she is. Right—and lying on the bunk is a guy from some African country who has been two hundred and twenty days aboard and can't even go ashore here because one of the ship's officers cheated him. You know," Alice said conversationally, "it is amazing how if someone doesn't have someone to look out for them, they get cheated by the rich. That poor sap in his bunk there, reading some book he probably got at the Seamen's Mission—yes—wait a second!" Alice took the glasses off, and tipped them in front of her eyes, as if to sharpen the lens angle. "Yes," she said. "A book on land stewardship, how do you like *that*! Anyway—Third World, no union, no ombudsman—no advocate!"

She came back over to the middle of the shop. "What surprises me is that someone of your luck and prestige and wealth should decide to cheat a helpless young person! Now why would that be?"

She could feel Charles fidgeting in the door.

Dr. Salaco went round behind the counter. "How much do you want?" he said.

Alice thought fast. "Your account with Terry is two hundred and fifteen. If I were you I'd make it two fifty. You've given the man trouble."

The optometrist handed her up the check and said very levelly, "I want both of you out of here in one second flat. Get out."

Alice turned to go. There stood Charles, with his raincoat collar up, looking pleased as punch, exactly like the kind of man who explains to traffic cops that he is with the CIA. She felt happy as a girl that the whole job was over. She spun around and said, "Do you want us to explain to the people out there on Superior Street that you decided to pay up and be fair after all?"

"That's all right, doc," Charles said. "We're leaving."

Alice escaped from the celebration in Charles's and Martha's room. When she knocked at Jack's door he called "Come in!" but turned to look at her with his binoculars still up to his eyes. It made her feel as if she had entered a tree shrew's apartment—and this ancient, owly creature was welcoming her.

"I understand all your day's projects went very well," he said. "Would you like some insty-pot tea?"

Yes she would.

They drank the hot, mindless-tasting stuff.

Jack looked at her carefully. "There's lots to be depressed about," he said. "I understand that LeRoy Beske is seriously sick?"

507

She told Jack what she knew about LeRoy. She thought of him in the brilliant lighting of an intensive-care unit.

Jack said, "I only know two tricks against feeling sad. And neither one of them works perfectly. Here's the first. What you do is—you shut off the lights in your room at this time of day." He got up and turned off his light. "Most people try to brighten up the dusk—great mistake! Turn the lights *off*, and then the lights and everything else from the outside will come *in*."

They looked at the shadowy, chilled city. The last of the afternoon sun still lighted the lake some: it gave its surface a rounded, smooth look, as if the very surface of it were strong enough to support life. Alice and Jack couldn't see the slight chop which reminds one of what lies on the bottom of even inland seas.

"When the light outside is stronger than the light inside, you aren't so aware of your self as something at all," Jack said. "All you have is nature, so to speak.

"O.K. so far?"

"Better than O.K.!" said Alice.

"Then here is the second idea," he said. "Let's say a person feels the life leaking out of them. Day by day, here at St. Aidan's. Now here is what you do: you had better go on imagining the leak all right, like imagining yourself a leaky cup. But instead of imagining your life leaking out of the cup, what you do is, you imagine the universe out there slowly, slowly leaking into you."

Alice nodded.

"Those are two very very terrific ideas," she told him.

"I think so too," Jack said. "I think they're terrific. But they don't work completely. I have been going around and around about it," he said. "There are a couple of things that just keep coming and coming and coming, and you can put all the philosophy you like up against them, they get through like dust. One of them is death, of course, and then the other one is just pure idiocy. That's what it is, just pure human idiocy."

Coupon for Blood

Sandy Huss

For a brain, Phin had to cope with hard baked clay. This he owed to his maker, who—though he had blown Phin up tight as a rubber raft, inspiring every chamber of his body with pure and lucid air—hadn't thought to give Phin much of anything else. In the beginning, moist and infused with oxygen, the lush gritty clay of his cerebrum had been good enough to eat, rich in salubrious minerals—food, indeed, for thought. But from the time Phin turned thirteen he had tried to jazz it up, had bled out the air, had baked and fired, with the result that now his head rattled with potsherds and jagged bits of roofing tile. Occasionally his inner eye, working like the mirrors of a kaleidoscope, trained itself upon this chaos, reflecting some seeming order out of this substance for thinking that could no longer support a thought. But the mirrors too had been damaged over the years, their silver scratched and charred, so that the images they presented were crazed and dim, and what passed in this brain for memories, information or ideas were often chimerical—and sometimes alien even to Phin who had given them birth.

But he had no doubts about what he saw just then. Even from the box canyon of the bus's back seats, Phin could tell that a coupon for blood waited to board. While the driver (out on the street, babysitting her children over the phone) held the pay-phone's metal cord to her heart, the coupon for blood kept its tail to the wind. While the passengers already aboard the idling bus clucked to each other about company time, the coupon for blood stamped its feet and pressed its great hooked fingers to its lips. Phin, temporarily out of the late November cold and agog that a coupon for blood was headed his way, hugged himself and clapped the soles of his sneakered feet.

Everyone waited while the driver changed a diaper over the phone.

She wiped her fingers over and over through the hair at her temple, explaining to her daughter how to charge the safety pin with static, so that the pin–filmed with deposits of urea or not–would glide. Phin didn't mind the delay: as long as a nine-year-old struggled to pierce layered folds of diaper without stabbing her infant sister, as long as she fumbled against the tension of the gaping pin, Phin could picture himself stretched out on a narrow table, tethered only by dreams of what his pint of blood (worth two bucks more than usual, once he got his hands on the coupon) would buy.

Next to lying on the table itself, nothing made Phin more lighthearted than imagining himself there, his blood draining through a rubber tube that lay in a loop across his forearm like an out-of-body vein, the loop counter-balancing the drag of gravity that sucked his red and white cells into a little plastic pouch. At the same time that the loop's weight kept the end of the hollow needle buried in his skin, its precise curve prevented the tube from kinking and impeding the flow. Every technician at every blood bank made the same loop, as regular as a coil in a handwriting exercise, as practiced and legible (even to Phin for whom sentences had become a chore) as an *l* or an *e*, rising and backtracking across his forearm, one after another, for as many months and years as his marrow could crank the hemoglobin out. Phin reveled in the regeneration of his blood. It was a wonderful world, he thought, that would give him money for something he couldn't hold in his hand.

When Phin slapped his feet together, Deedee, catty-corner across the aisle, had been startled and relieved. Until then she had read in his face prostitution and unrelenting pain. Phin was ravishingly poor: his skin, the color of a tarnished penny, clung to his cheekbones, and his sparse curly lashes tossed diaphanous veils before his eyes. His cheap tight pants bound his thighs and genitals, and his skimpy T-shirt, its pieces stamped out haphazardly along the bias by machine, hung in a skewed line that barely covered him. He was nineteen, Deedee's age, and his remaining beauty had the fragility of a pear ripe too long by a day, a pear whose skin is still thin and promising, still so primed to yield that the gentlest thumb-smear can skim it away, but whose flesh beneath is pocked with rotting translucence so that it no longer tempts the tongue, so that its only use is as a matrix for seed. Sitting modestly upright, his tapered fingers caging his knees, Phin had seemed to Deedee to be awaiting absolution, to be dogged by regret for having loosed all evil upon the world. Deedee (white, enrolled in one of the better state universities, and hungry for her lunch) had been glum, having recently

510

been taught how she caused Phin's poverty, how it profited her. She took heart at his little leap.

She was so relieved that she unzipped the knapsack propped between her feet and felt through it until something crackled in her hand. With both hands buried in the knapsack she forced apart stubborn cellophane welds. Casually she lifted a barbecued chip to her lips. Even as she broke its back with her teeth she knew she was rude, but now that Phin wasn't starving there was only one other person near enough for Deedee to offend—a woman of fifty, straight across the aisle—who probably already thought of Deedee as a slob: the older woman was magnificent. Black as basalt with a cast of blue, her skin seemed to have just lately cooled, and the light in her eyes suggested that she yet smoldered within. Katy (for that was her name) had anchored herself in her seat with her severe Etta Jenicks, with her own sense of worth.

Even when a bus is idling, its backmost passengers brace themselves. In the bench seats above the wheels, they, like Deedee and Katy, like Deedee and Phin, face each other—usually there are mothers with strings of children (and strollers that won't collapse), indigents and evangelists, high-school kids with graffitied notebooks, sometimes a bold unattended child—and they brace themselves against their own sidelong hurtling, unrestrained by each other's arms (even if arms were offered, there'd be too much open space in which to fall). They brace themselves against their roll to the front like so many thudding cabbages, where they would lie in a heap beneath a box of shifting coins.

This bus made its last stop within two blocks of the Greyhound station, and Katy—like Deedee—was headed there: beneath her seat a gray cardboard suitcase lay, ancient and ungainly, like something beached and stoically smothering beneath its own weight. Deedee, untucked and overslept, her student pallor unvaried by any blush of health, her own luggage a collection of knapsacks and canvas bags splotched with coffee and ballpoint ink—felt she must seem a flibbertigibbet in Katy's eyes. The woman was a monolith. How had she made that of herself? Deedee wanted her approval, but saw no chance of it, so pulled the little cellophane bag out into the open and munched away. The chips were stale, but Deedee accepted their staleness as a punishment: they were half gone by the time the driver and the coupon for blood climbed aboard.

Deedee, not in the market herself, naturally didn't realize that a coupon for blood was about to enter her life. She saw only middle-aged Harper in his green all-weather coat, clamping the *Post-Dispatch* under his arm. He must habitually have carried a paper there: a smeary stain

511

had swallowed his armpit and spread halfway down his side. Deedee had the meanness of spirit to be ashamed of him, being guilty of such carelessness herself: she often left a thumbprint of chocolate or cheese dust on a library page. She sometimes felt that at any moment she too could become a walking stain.

For the length of the aisle Harper ducked his head, one hand lifting his green plaid hat by the crown—in obeisance to the ladies, it seemed. Yet he swaggered at the same time, trilled unselfconsciously, and flapped his hand in the pocket of his coat so violently that the hem knocked away Deedee's little cellophane bag. She said, "Hey!"—but as she spoke, Harper heedlessly punted the chips all the way to the back of the bus, and as Deedee said, "Hey!" again, Harper stepped on the bag, pivoting as he sat down on the bench that faced the front. Barbecued crumbs spilled from the bag's mouth beneath his shoe.

Deedee rolled her eyes and gave out an exaggerated sigh. She saw Katy turn her face toward the back of the driver's head. At least they were finally on their way.

Harper dropped his paper next to himself on the seat within reach of Phin, who—oblivious to Deedee's little disaster—bent toward the newsprint dotingly. He'd been prepared to change his seat if necessary, but the coupon had come straight to him.

"So sorry." Harper lifted his hat to Deedee, higher than before, revealing an oily baldness marked by parallel tracks of surgical scar. They ran from his eyebrows across his crown toward his nape as if he were a waxwork whose pate had served as a toy truck's proving ground. His hat back on, he bent over and with fastidious fingers swept the broken chips, a cigarette filter and a scrap of religious tract into the bag. Meanwhile, Phin's hand hovered above the neglected paper, but he did not touch.

Harper held the little bag out to Deedee, who took it, though she pinched it by a corner, dangling it away from herself like someone else's trash. She looked over at Katy. Katy looked down.

"Shit." Deedee glowered at the floor.

Harper raised a disciplinary finger in the air. "No smoking, food or drink," he said, ticking his finger toward the posted rule. Ignoring the covetous Phin, Harper selected a section of his paper and snapped it open with a sharp crack, sealing himself away behind it as if the bus were his own living room. Poor Phin, the drudge wife, inclined toward the newsprint, his eyes bashful and full of need, one hand with its long fingers just barely raised.

Behind that paper Harper's flesh was pulpy, his skin squamous, and his chemical sweat might have come straight from the embalmer's gun, but he thought of himself as oozing vitality. Living either on the street or in the bin, he rarely saw himself in anything besides window glass or bumper chrome, but even if Harper's world had been filled with highly polished mirrors, his clamminess would have registered with himself as a glow. Harper had been repeatedly doctored: he almost always felt good.

Now that he had taught that girl a lesson he felt wonderful, and his face flushed with righteous blood—some of which (as you might expect) had once streamed (though with different perceptions) through poor Phin's arteries and veins. Last summer Harper had lectured a less docile mark than Deedee: a hospital attendant bearing Harper's dinner on a tray. The young man had taken offense at the word *Jigaboo*, and couldn't be persuaded to approve it even after Harper explained that he had been set down on the planet expressly to assign the lower animals their names. The attendant likewise could not credit *Shine*, *Smoke*, *Junglebunny* or *Coon*, and didn't give a rat's ass what Harper had been taught in Sunday School. By the time the other workers separated the attendant from his heavy tray, Harper had lain in a coma and a slick of gore.

Harper remembered none of this, had even momentarily forgotten his mission to name (which he usually forgot when he took his Mellaril instead of trading it for sex or food), but that was how it had come to be that Harper had been transfused, that it was in part Phin's blood that Harper's heart now pumped, first to his lungs, then to his spackled brain, giving him a magnanimous idea.

"Here's the sports page, buddy," he said to Phin. "You can keep it, I'll just throw it away." He went back behind the business section, which he pretended to read.

Phin held the paper up in front of himself at arm's length as if it were sheet music and he would momentarily begin to sing. But he spoke, instead, in a voice that was soft and musical. "Does this here have a coupon for blood?"

Harper feigned absorption in the world of commerce for a moment, but then folded down the paper. "Well, I don't know . . . a coupon for blood?"

"Yeah. For two dollars."

"What do you want to buy blood for?"

Katy and Deedee looked for a heartless instant at each other, then away.

"Not buy. Sell."

"With a coupon they give you two dollars?"

513

"They give you eight dollars, but with a coupon they give you two more."

"Ten dollars?"

Phin poked around in his broken brain, looking first at eight dollars, then at two. He couldn't bring them together in any way, but he didn't want to disagree. He smiled slowly, keeping his lids down for a moment, then raising them languidly. Phin had sold sex as well as plasma, and could say yes wordlessly.

Harper didn't smile in return. "Well, you can look." He withdrew behind his paper and sat very still.

Phin peeled open his allotted section, still holding it at arm's length, still sitting expectantly straight. As he paged through, the bell rang, and an old woman in the middle of the bus who had been facing the front stood up, walked toward the back, and waited in the stairwell near the back door. She held a sack of groceries against her hip, and took a long look at the two raised walls of newsprint that were Harper and Phin. "Huh," she said, and got off.

Just as she closed the door behind the woman, the driver perceived a presence in her womb. From the time she'd been an adolescent she had set her inner ear to listen for change, so that even sleeping her body had always known when to wake itself with the news that she was about to bleed. And now she heard a familiar burgeoning, the forbidding sound of the division that is multiplication, and she knew what she had known for several days. For a long while this sound would only get louder, its frequency higher, until the train of transformations that would bring her new baby to her had passed. For a moment she allowed tears to gather, but by the time she had pulled back out into traffic and begun to inventory the cupboards at home (planning what her eldest could fix for lunch), her eyes were dry.

Phin had some ideas about the coupon: a shape, some dotted lines, its location on the page: someone, he was sure, had recently shown him one. There would be a cross in each corner of a rectangle, he thought. Crosses hung before his mind's eye as if he had just sped past a family plot on the open road, could still see tracers of gold and blue.

He studied every page. The fine print of the box scores snaked before his bloodshot eyes. He squinted for some time at a photograph wherein a man holding a soccer ball seemed to be sitting on another man's head, a flagpole growing out of his own. Phin forgot for a horrible moment what he was looking for, but then he remembered, and felt a glow of good fortune returning to surround him like a divine cloud that would protect him and show him the way. A clip-and-save box in the classi-

514

fieds gave his heart a little thrill, but there were no crosses, and the bold
WORD PROCESSING meant, Phin was positive, that the coupon had
nothing to do with him. There were pages of cars for sale, and Phin's
eyes sucked the names of some of them into his crumbling brain: Phoenix, Aries, Delta 88. Electra . . . Electra . . . Phin had ridden once in a
midnight-blue Electra—or had he just leaned on it in a blue and midnight street?

The coupon wasn't here. Phin took his bearings by looking through a
film of pomade on the window: they hadn't yet reached the numbered
streets. He had seen Harper somewhere before, he was sure, maybe on
this very bus. He bet that Harper would ride with him to the end of the
line. There was plenty of paper still to check, and he had five—maybe
six—more miles. Phin trued up the corners of the sports section, folded it
precisely and balanced it on his knees, waiting for Harper to notice him.

And Harper lowered his paper as if he had not been reading at all.

With Harper's eye on him, Phin spoke again, a music box in Harper's
hands. This was as clear to Harper as it was to Deedee and Katy, more
clear perhaps, because polluted by chemicals he was free to see the
delicate porcelain ballerina twirling in Phin's throat. It gave him great
pleasure to arouse such attentiveness and modesty in Phin, as if he were,
by tiny increments, leading him from barbarism to light. Phin sounded
more and more angelic to Harper's ear: "Would you mind if I just
checked those?"

Phin pointed to the stack of paper on the seat, but Harper knew better
than to relinquish anything. "I'll see if it's in here," he said, and flipped
through the business section so fast that the back of the bus filled with
the flapping of gigantic wings. "There's no coupon for blood in here,
buddy. There's nothing in here but the Dow Jones." Harper shrugged his
shoulders with a crackling of paper and withdrew again.

Phin brought the pads of his fingers together in imitation of the
Praying Hands. Very slowly he turned his head away from Harper to
look outside. Twenty-first street. When he checked back, Harper was
watching him. "What about those?"

Harper, affected by Phin's pretty smile—a smile that Harper would like
to keep on Phin's face if he could—graciously picked through the paper
at his side and handed one more section over. "I guess you can have this,
buddy. I'll just throw this away."

Deedee opened her mouth with a click of her tongue and a quick
intake of breath, but closed it again and turned red.

Katy covertly kept an eye on her. Deedee had a pointed chin and two
dark moles—one above each corner of her mouth—that gave her face a

catlike triangularity. Her slit-eyed twitching heightened the effect: she seemed as tortured as a house cat spying on a pair of warring toms from the wrong side of a screen—the stink of hot fur, the sight of backs bristling and humped cause her heart to pound, oxygen to crowd her cells, and blood to stream, messianic, through her veins. But she sits, contained, on a windowsill, slapping at it with her tail, raising nothing but backlit, floating motes. Once the fight moves down the block she'll throw herself down from the window and charge—dishing throw rugs one after another out of her way—as far in one direction as the walls of her house will permit, then wheel and take another tack, crash behind the couch and end tables, bruise herself against the furniture.

Deedee for now was still at the window, and the poor stymied thing kept sneaking looks at Katy, wanting Katy to nanny her, wanting Katy to nanny the whole bus. But Katy intended to let those nasty boys run *each other* ragged—she had problems of her own.

Phin began to page through a thick sheaf of department-store ads as daintily as he had waded through the sports, and Deedee's heart went out to him. Someone who could read ought to step in. Phin, scrawny as he was, probably shouldn't be peddling drop one, but Deedee wanted him to do—to have—whatever he desired, for reasons even she was suspicious of: his blackness, his wasted beauty, that bastard Harper's lunacy. Deedee still clutched her trashed bag of chips out of a horror of littering. Yes, she wanted that smug son-of-a-bitch—crazy or not—to do the generous thing. She imagined herself commandeering the paper, finding—or not finding, definitively—the damn coupon. But every reaction she anticipated from Harper was withering. She couldn't bear to give him an opening.

If Deedee's mother had still been alive, Deedee would have had more to offer than the heroics of a busybody. If Deedee's mother had still been alive, Deedee wouldn't have been headed back to school the day after Thanksgiving with nothing in her luggage but half a round-trip bus ticket and a desiccated, bloodless meal: she had rice cakes and peanut butter left, stuff suited to the fitful stomach of chemotherapy. (The barbecued chips, Deedee figured, must have been a whim, mentioned by her mother wistfully, fetched by husband or son in a hell-bent car, then rejected from a pit of nausea.)

If Deedee's mother had still been alive, Deedee would have had a couple pounds of turkey in tow, half an apple-cake and a fistful of cold hard cash—the price of her bus ticket and then some. But though Deedee had cooked the holiday meal, she had left it all behind, sure that control over the family larder didn't transfer to the temporary help.

Taking the leavings of her mother's restricted diet couldn't possibly offend – no one still living in her father's house considered it food.

If Deedee had asked her father for groceries, for cash, he doubtless would have given her enough to tide her over until her check for work-study came in Monday's mail. But unless she asked, her father seemed to assume that she could chow down on the intellectual breeze. Her mother had been dead now for months, it was not as if her father were still hazy with grief. Deedee was simply out of sight – even when *in* sight – out of mind. She felt too insubstantial to ask for a loan. Deedee had expected to miss her mother when she died, but she hadn't expected that her mother's death would give birth to her own poverty.

Musing in this vein, Deedee hid from herself the fact that she had what Phin was looking for: in the shape of a two-dollar bill, a bill so new and crisp it could have held knife pleats. She kept it folded within a concealed compartment in her wallet, safe from even her own emergency. As far as Deedee was concerned it was a relic that wouldn't spend.

By the time her mother died, the sick woman's purse had long been out of her control, her cash spent on grieving people's groceries, her lists of things to do ticked off by grieving people's hands. Deedee had often carried the purse itself from house to hospital to market; her brothers had taken out their mother's wallet and crammed it into their jacket pockets; everyone in the family had had occasion to dig through the linen and leather bag: tallying check stubs, tracking down rolls of film and dry-cleaning or reading off strings of numbers from insurance cards. Her mother's purse had been an open book. So when Deedee, boxing things for the Goodwill, had discovered a stash of two-dollar bills wedged in the wallet's plastic album between a list of clinic phone numbers and an organ donor card, she had been annoyed with herself that she hadn't noticed it before. The little lump of cash wasn't so little that it shouldn't have been obvious all along.

With the lump unfolded and four two-dollar bills laid out on the floor, Deedee had felt contempt for her mother as she had suddenly felt contempt for all people who refuse to honor a certain kind of currency – then end up holding it all. People with caches of fifty-cent pieces and Susan B. Anthony coins, people whose imagination limited money to denominations for which there were slots in cash registers and vending machines. But at the same time she had felt a loopy joy that her mother had left this weird legacy. Like the marvelous irrelevancy of the donor card, the money seemed a symbol to Deedee that her mother had intended to save her own life – but Deedee blushed at the thought of

517

saying as much to her father or to his sons. So she kept a single bill for herself and stuffed the rest inside the stand for her mother's best wig, which she hid in an attic trunk.

Everyone on that bus but Phin had at least two dollars, but everyone's money was already spent. The driver's roll of quarters was destined for pay-phones, and the woman wearing a sweatsuit would need the four ones in her pocket for a box of tampons—soon. The woman with blue hair, who had just gotten on, and who was painstakingly threading her gauzy headscarf through the top buttonhole of her coat, had only her weekly allowance from her sister for Bingo cards. The guy carrying a new fire extinguisher was saving to straighten his kid's teeth, and the couple reading the Bible together wanted someday to have furniture in their living room. Even Harper's three dollars from selling his Elavil (which was supposed to counteract his Mellaril) had been budgeted for lunch at Burger King. Phin may have had no cash, but then he had only a few needs that he could remember, and he took solace in what Deedee found appalling: he was a walking factory of sex and blood. He was always on line. And he knew he would get the coupon, it was meant to be.

Katy had more money on her than the rest of the riders combined—and it never occurred to her to share it with Phin. She needed it to put up her daughter's bail. Their phone conversation had been unsatisfactory because they'd been whispering on both ends of the line—her daughter to thwart her guard, Katy to let her husband sleep—but Katy knew for sure that her daughter had been picked up driving a stolen car, a car she had thought belonged to her new boyfriend. Her daughter had known he was AWOL—had even, she admitted, mostly approved—but she had never once doubted that the car was his. That much she had promised Katy, in an insistent whisper Katy had to believe.

Even from two states away, her daughter could fill Katy with disappointment and self-reproach, from two states away she could make Katy's wallet gurgle like an open drain. In the past year Katy had bought eyeglasses when her daughter's prescription changed, neutered her adopted cats, kept up the insurance on her car. Now this.

Her daughter seemed to have been spun out of her, but never to have detached from her, seemed in fact to contain *her* now, like a cocoon. As her daughter grew older, it was Katy who changed, who was forced to embrace her daughter's chaos if she were to embrace her daughter at all. Katy supposed it was inevitable that her daughter would lead a fitful and struggling life, having spent her childhood in Katy's steady shade. For her daughter Katy could leave her husband this once. He would survive: he loved the pork-chop sandwiches they made at the neighborhood bar.

Phin's progress through the paper went more and more slowly; he had to look repeatedly over his shoulder out the window—they were nearing the end of the line. The more the fragments of crockery in Phin's head tried to piece together a vessel that could contain Harper, the more Phin remembered Harper saying he loved him, saying that Phin was a beautiful bitch. Phin remembered Harper's pulse quickening, Harper's fingers at Phin's nape kneading Phin's hair. Harper had never *had* such raunchy sex before, he had said, that had been the *most lewd* experience of his entire life, Phin was a Grade A, floor-licking, cock-sucking whore.

Even if Harper hadn't tipped Phin while he still knelt at Harper's feet (without Phin having to dogtrot after him, flirting and begging just a bit), Phin would have remembered Harper fondly, would have preened himself over being called Grade A. It was what he had always thought about himself, when he could still think—that he was choice.

And here again was that smitten man.

That it might have been someone other than Harper who had been so good to him, Phin had no reason to believe. It seemed likely enough, as likely as the coupon itself, as likely as its ultimate transfer to his own hands. Phin had the optimism of bad memory. He shifted his seat next to Harper and looked up into his face. Harper had loved him once, he was sure. "Look," Phin said, thumping a health-club ad, "it looks something like this here."

Harper let the business section crumple in his lap as if his weary arms couldn't support it any more. "Buddy," he said, "it ain't in here, I looked."

Harper felt the high drama of his beleaguerment, of his duty to be magnanimous and kind. He looked around for an audience. The girl and the nigger woman both looked at their hands, but the bus driver had an eyebrow cocked at him in the rearview mirror. Harper panicked: they were at the end of the line. Harper hated to give the driver a reason to cast her evil eye his way. "Sorry, buddy," he said, and scooped together his paper, including the sections he'd given to Phin. He lurched out the back door, holding onto his hat as he stepped into the wind. He heard Phin's footsteps behind him, rubber soles as hard as old erasers clunking on the stairs, but Harper didn't look back.

With the men's departure, Deedee roused herself, folded her chip bag over and over at one end, and stuffed it into the pocket of her parka where it slowly opened, making tiny rustles and pops as she gathered her book bags. With the men's departure, she had a little trouble believing what she'd just heard and seen. If she'd only done something, she'd know how it all turned out. When she got to the stairwell, she saw that in her bending and leaning she'd been hogging the aisle, making Katy wait to draw her suitcase from beneath her seat. Deedee might not be able to help anyone, but at least she shouldn't be getting in their way. She sighed and shrugged piteously, but refused to let herself wait for any look of tolerance—let alone forgiveness—in Katy's eyes.

She started down the stairs, and there was Phin in the street, bouncing up and down, a parade-struck child, one moment craning his head to watch Harper zigzag down the street like a pigeon, the next moment eyeing the door of the bus. He was waiting, it turned out, for her.

He looked up at her and showed his teeth, but his eyes were flat and expressionless, their color that of raw liver, of clotted menstrual blood. "Help me, baby," he said.

Deedee couldn't understand what Phin wanted from her, it was too late, she had nothing, she was no match for Harper after all. But as she stood in the stairwell struggling with an answer for him, she became transfixed by the sudden knowledge of the two-dollar bill in her wallet, by the sound of her mother's hands folding it, by the image of the full white moons rising on the horizons of her mother's fingernails. Deedee felt that she could never step off the bus into the stream of trouble that was Phin: he was a sluice of one-way valves. She would pool forever in the loggy legs of the universe if she gave him anything.

But how could she refuse? Phin waited with the confidence of someone people loved.

All Deedee's life she would remain uncertain whether it was Katy's hand or the curved edge of Katy's suitcase in the small of Deedee's back that pushed Deedee from the bus and kept on pushing until she was well past Phin. She felt she deserved only the suitcase, the suitcase accidentally, at that, but she hoped for Katy's hand. When the pushing stopped, Deedee looked lovingly at the side of Katy's face, but the older woman surged by, her eyes on the sign that read *BUS*, one shoulder dipped to balance the suitcase in the opposite hand.

The bus's door closed, and in the driver's womb a blastula of cells implanted itself. The driver could give it only divided attention, being—always—otherwise occupied. She closed her doors, checked her mirrors, and began her shuttle back to the other end of the line.

Deedee, her lumpy luggage banging around her knees, followed a respectful distance behind Katy, and slipped forever through the dross of Phin's brain. He fixed his eyes on something at the end of a long city block: that hat and that dirty coat, that pale bald neck would be easy to track. Phin ambled along in his sneakers, waiting for Harper to throw the coupon away.

The Eleventh Edition

Leo E. Litwak

I came to Detroit from Iron Mountain, Michigan, a poor boy with nothing to lose and a world to gain. Iron Mountain winters were terrible but no season gave me relief. I escaped as soon as I finished high school. I left nothing behind. There was only Dad, who was bitter and alcoholic, and by the time I left we had exhausted each other. We were no longer even joined by dislike. He shrugged when I told him I was taking off.

"You can always come back, but that's nothing to look forward to."

I arrived in Detroit, eighteen years old, entirely free, eager for a new life. And there it was, at Wayne University, available to all comers.

Two nights a week I entered a private home converted to college use. A once-elegant parlor had been painted light green and unsparingly illuminated with overhead fluorescent lighting. I listened to the scraping of iron and plywood chairs, the squeal of wooden arms unfolded, brief-cases unsnapping, notebooks and texts thumped down. We waited for the magician who would transform this plain room and its ordinary sounds into our land of dreams.

His coming was heralded by the brisk rap of his cane on the outside stairs. He began lecturing while at the parlor door. He hung his cane on the lip of the blackboard and kept talking while arranging his notes on Renaissance Florence.

Professor Diekman was a bent little man. He was slightly twisted to the right, as if he were lecturing on the run, hurling words back at his pursuers.

We learned about Guelphs, Ghibellines, Dante, Machiavelli, the painters, the sculptors, the craftsmen, the poets, the guilds.

He operated in great swoops. He lighted on a detail, developed it, then

521

leaped elsewhere. Over the weeks the direction of his narrative became clear.

The Florentine bankers lent to monasteries, took the sheep as collateral, traveled Europe without regard for boundaries, and finally controlled the wool market. Diekman followed the vagaries of capitalism from its beginnings in fourteenth-century Florence to its consummation on the Detroit assembly line.

There was nothing so odd that he couldn't find a link to our experience. He clarified what was opaque, made coherent what seemed alien and terrifying.

I studied with Diekman for three years, then entered the graduate program. I enrolled in whatever he taught. I took his three-semester history of philosophy sequence, his course in esthetics, dabbled at Homeric Greek to become eligible for his *Iliad* seminar, learned German in preparation for his lectures on Goethe.

During those years I was employed at Brant's Import and Export. Each morning I reported to the warehouse and checked inventory. I counted slabs of Italian marble. I unwrapped delicate wall sconces, examined them for defects, rewrapped them. I counted boxes of cut crystal to make sure that Brant had received the full order. I measured bolts of English linen, stacked Polish carpets, opened crates of Mexican glassware. By late afternoon I had finished. The rest of my time belonged to Diekman.

*   *   *

I lost all connection to Iron Mountain. I was no longer that boy. But who was I and where was I? I was out of touch. I didn't allow myself to touch. There was no ground under my feet. I felt that I belonged nowhere until I established myself on campus.

I moved whenever I found a cheaper room and finally ended at Tuchler's place, a few blocks from the Wayne campus. I had a room on the second floor, next to the bath. I was utterly concentrated on my studies. My vision narrowed. My hearing, though, became omnivorous. I devoured sound, greedy for it, straining like a hungry fledgling for any word that could bring me ease.

All I heard was old Walsh coughing in the room next to mine. He desperately harrumphed, trying to clear his throat of a death that was already beyond his throat.

His memory was erratic and he sometimes forgot that we'd met. The wispy old fellow would knock on my door to introduce himself again.

"Hi, there. My name is Frank Walsh. I'm your neighbor."

We met regularly but no use clarifying matters, so once more I'd say, "Russell Hansen."

"What?"

"Hansen."

"Hansen. That's a good simple name. I didn't catch the first name."

"Russell."

"Russell? I had a partner named Russell. I was in the seed business, you know. Volunteer Seed." And he was off. Till the moment when he could again describe the one agony that remained fresh and unforgotten. "My wife died last year. We were married fifty-three years. And when you lose a companion of fifty-three years, oh golly," he said, "oh, golly. You don't get over it in a day."

More than a day had elapsed; in fact, more than a year. His wife was long dead. The old man couldn't distinguish days and years. He was a retired pensioner. He slept when sleep came. He once knocked at my door after midnight. "Sorry, sir. I thought I heard you dining. I wonder if you could use this bottle of wine. It was a gift to me but I don't touch the stuff." It was an ancient bottle, opened years ago, and long since become vinegar. I thanked him, took the bottle, but didn't allow him to stay.

His radio sputtered out at night and then self-ignited in a jarring burst of breakfast music at five in the morning. I heard the confused old man call out, "Yes? Yes? What time is it?"

He wasn't the neighbor I'd have chosen. I avoided distraction. Professor Gerard Diekman ruled my life. The austere little man didn't suffer fools. I labored to stay in his good graces. When he mentioned a text during class, I checked it out. At his beckoning I entered deep waters. I floundered but learned to swim. When he wrote a critique of my paper and concluded, "Very good," I felt confirmed. But his disapproval, displayed in that same precise, crabbed script, could take the ground from under my feet. Four years his student and I was still unacknowledged. He called my name at the beginning of each semester but there was no further recognition. I had no idea where I stood, and there were times when I choked on books.

I was as desperate as Walsh for human connection. Even the old man would sometimes serve.

I knocked on his door, beat hard to penetrate the sound of his radio. He finally called out, "Hello? Is someone there?"

When he opened up I reminded him that I was his neighbor, Russell Hansen.

"Of course you're Russell Hansen. I know that."

523

His room was crammed with furnishings gathered over a lifetime. I noticed a Seth Thomas pendulum clock, a massive oak wardrobe, a glass-enclosed bookcase containing a leatherbound edition of the *Encyclopedia Britannica*. The room was dominated by a radio phonograph console, tuned to the news.

He invited me to sit. He told me again of his arrival in Detroit at the turn of the century. He came by steamer from Buffalo with his bride, Louise. He landed at a slip later occupied by an excursion boat. He rented a duplex on Bagley Street and started the Volunteer Seed Company.

Everyone loved Louise, he said. She had the best heart in the world. This was the preliminary of a story I heard him tell more than once. They were young. Louise was expecting. The business struggled but prospects were good. It would have been paradise except for the man next door who had converted a backyard toolshed into a machine shop. He made a terrific racket but Walsh was reluctant to complain. The fellow was skinny as death and clanged away with intimidating earnestness. Louise urged her husband to talk to the man.

" 'Tell the gentleman I can't get to sleep, Frank. He's disturbing the neighborhood.' "

Walsh told Louise it was his policy to live and let live and he did nothing about the noise until one night the racket went on and on— steel on steel—and it was too much. He put on a buffalo-plaid robe over his pajamas. The man was in his garage, working at his lathe. Walsh pleaded with him.

" 'Have a heart, sir. I have to be up at five in the morning and it's already ten-thirty.'

"This fellow pulls away from the lathe. He pushes back his goggles. 'Ten-thirty, you say? It can't be ten-thirty. Only a loony would be out at ten-thirty in his pajamas. And you don't look like a loony to me.' I didn't want to make a fuss. I admired his industry. If it was only a case of my pleasure I'd say, 'Go on till the rooster crows.' But I told him my Louise was expecting and she wasn't having an easy time of it.

" 'Well, sir,' this skinny gentleman said to me, 'I know your missus and if she wants me to shut down business—' He turned off the lathe, took off his gloves, stuck out his hand and introduced himself.

" 'Henry Ford of the Edison Illuminating Company.'

"Yessir! Henry Ford. Isn't that a piece of history, young man? He was working on a model of the internal combustion engine in that shed. We became friends. Not so much me and Henry—no one ever called him Hank—but his wife Clara and my Louise. Everyone loved Louise. It was

524

the easiest thing in the world. Henry told me, 'You got yourself a princess. More than a dumb mick has a right to.' And I said to him, 'Mr. Ford, I couldn't agree with you more.'

"Oh, golly," Frank Walsh said. "Oh, golly. When you lose a companion of fifty-three years you don't get over it in a day."

I once asked about the *Encyclopedia Britannica*, Eleventh Edition. Was he aware of its achievement?

"A salesman came to our door. Louise was at home. She miscarried, you see, and we tried again. But the years went by and we knew we couldn't have kids. She handled the correspondence for Volunteer Seed. The best secretary in the world. Still, that wasn't her life. That salesman told her the *Encyclopedia* was the way out. It was an education. 'How can we afford it, honey?' We were trying to make a go of it and it was no cinch. Who was going to read it? Twenty-nine volumes. I'm not much of a reader. We publish a seed catalog, you know. One of the largest in the Midwest. But she'd set her heart on the *Encylopedia*. He was a darned fine salesman. With an item as expensive as his, why cut corners?"

He bought the leatherbound version, not the cloth. And not the diminutive Handy Volume Issue, but the full-sized deluxe set, easy on the eyes. For a time she would come home from Volunteer and fix dinner and afterwards sit with the *Encyclopedia* and unfold the delicate tissue maps and, for instance, consider the state of Michigan. Population in 1900, 90 percent white. About 15,000 Negroes. 6,000 Indians. And exactly 9 Japanese. The state of Michigan produced the bulk of the peppermint crop in the United States. "Did you know that, Russ?" The statistics read to him by Louise were never forgotten. But she gave up reading after a few tries. The *Encyclopedia* wasn't what she expected. Volunteer Seed went bankrupt in 1930. Louise took a job as a saleslady at Hudson's, Walsh as a bookkeeper for the Briggs Bodyworks in Highland Park.

They never owned a home. They could have bought a Chicago Boulevard mansion in the days when the seed company flourished. But they had no need for it without kids. They always rented fine, large apartments until the last. Now one room was enough. He had a decent landlady and good neighbors.

But, oh, golly, to lose a companion of fifty-three years—

Mrs. Tuchler had to remind him each week to pay the rent. She retained a German accent and delivered her cautions to Walsh with the spirit of a Prussian sergeant. I heard her repeat the rules with special addenda for Walsh. Prompt payment on Monday. Clean the tub after you bathe. Each resident was responsible for his own room. She did the hallways and bathroom. No loud music. No loud parties. All calls reported on the pad by the phone. She warned that excessive use of electricity or gas would bring a rent increase.

The rules, hand-lettered on green matting paper, were mounted next to the phone. She told us she didn't apologize for being strict. It was a declining neighborhood and she meant to hold the fort. She kept after the old man. He was hard of hearing, his memory dimmed. She spoke at full-volume in an accent that refused to acknowledge *w*'s. She came upstairs, hitting every tread with authority, disciplining the wood beneath her.

"Mr. Walsh? Mr. Walsh?" (Pronounced "Valsch.") Hard raps, then letting herself in. I heard her clearly through the wall. "You must raise the toilet seat. The other roomers complain." I hadn't complained, nor, I'm sure, had Betty McCarthy. "You get the seat dirty, you get the floor dirty. You don't clean the tub neither."

Walsh was abject. "Sorry," he said. Sorry wasn't enough. He said again, "I'm sorry, Missus." She occupied an apartment directly below. When she heard the nighttime pacing and the radio at full-volume she stepped into the vestibule, braced on the newel post, and shouted, "Quiet!" Then the trek upstairs to discipline him face-to-face.

She called me "Professor." I corrected her a few times. "Only a student, Mrs. Tuchler." Perhaps she imagined that if a professor were in residence the encroaching ghetto would stop a block away and not incorporate her house.

"The Professor is preparing his lessons," she warned Walsh. "He wants quiet."

I told her the old man didn't bother me. "Old age is our destiny, too, Mrs. Tuchler."

"Ah," she said. "What would you know from old age? You learn it in books? You think I am the hard-hearted landlady, but do you know, for three months that man has not paid his rent? His pension check doesn't come. I write for him and they promise to send new checks. Maybe it will come. Maybe not. My bills come for sure."

He'd been with her for five years. His wife was already dead when he arrived. He said she died last year but his memory was jumbled. He had no one. Who was he to Mrs. Tuchler? Not her kin. She knew there was no pleasure growing old. She knew far better than I that there were no happy endings. She was preparing for her own bad time. She began by hardening her heart. If he didn't pay the rent—out! If he continued bothering other tenants, he had to go.

Walsh usually managed to soften her. When she stomped upstairs to demand quiet and to threaten eviction, he endured the scolding. Sorry, he said. Sorry. And when her anger ebbed he reminded her that Louise was also of German origin. He insisted that she sit while he played a favorite record of Louise's, Richard Tauber singing, "*Du, du liegst mir im Herzen.*" The song always touched her. She urged the old man to stay alert. If he lost his wits he was doomed.

"Don't you worry, Missus. I'm fine. Don't you worry."

He sometimes lured me to his room to hear his records. He had an old recording of Bing Crosby singing "Pennies from Heaven." He played a scratchy record of a thin tenor voice singing "Poor Butterfly" and "Ramona." He turned up the volume, his ear pressed to the speaker. "They sure knew how to write songs in those day, Russ."

Betty McCarthy was the other lodger on our floor. She had the room across the hall. She was a new tenant, a Wayne drama student. She worked nights in a cabaret. She was plump and attractive, a cheerful, busy young woman but it was fortunate for my peace of mind that she didn't spend much time at Tuchler's. She was always in hurried transitions. She moved at full speed and set off waves of turbulence. Her high heels click-clicked on the outer stone stairs. She rattatattatted up the wooden stairway. When she reached the first landing the phone invariably began ringing. She came down full force in her rush to be there and then a breathless, "Hiiii," and I overheard the dumb, flirty exchange that followed. "I can't," she said, drawing out the "can't" so that it meant she wanted to, she'd love to, but, regrettably, she was unable to. "Maybe next week. If I can get away. No, I can't say for sure." Then an almost orgasmic, "Me, too! Oh, yes!"

Then rush, rush, rush. I heard the frantic sound of her across the hall. Drawers jerked open and slammed shut, a rush to the bath ahead of me, a chipper, "Be right out!" and the sound of faucets, the toilet flushing, emerging with hair in pink rollers, "All yours!" Back to her room, the rattle of hangers, all that scurrying in behalf of projects I couldn't imagine as anything but trivial. When she finally slammed the door on her way out (Tuchler yelled, "Don't slam the door!") and Walsh was, for the moment, subdued, I could again pursue my obligations to Professor Diekman without distraction. I wanted nothing more.

*   *   *

Diekman weeded his classes ruthlessly and it was a triumph to survive his selection. If you didn't have the prerequisites he said, "Sorry." If you came to class unprepared, he invited you to drop the course. If you were loyal but without promise, he let you know—in a generous manner, true—that it made no sense for you to persist. But if you persisted, as I did, you might find the everyday world transformed into Homer's or Goethe's.

I was in the last year of the MA program when I summoned up the nerve to approach him. I asked him to supervise my thesis. I should have consulted him at an earlier stage. I waited for him to choose me, but he gave no sign. I couldn't stall off the interview and finally made the appointment.

He was a small man, further diminished by a spinal curvature arrested at an eleven-degree tilt to the right. The slant was a perfect orientation for a point of view always on the bias toward irony.

"What are you after, Mr. Hansen?"

I hoped for an academic career.

"Surely not in philosophy."

Did he think that was so absurd? I knew I was too young to have that large an ambition. Still, I hoped some day to be worthy.

"You hope. . ." His off-center look spared me a direct gaze but lent emphasis to the sardonic tone. "Mr. Hansen, I am obliged to try to discourage you. You impose a terrible responsibility on me."

"How is that, sir?"

No doubt I was bright enough. He liked my written work. I would probably make a decent teacher. "But to what purpose, Mr. Hansen? What reward do you expect?" Honor? Who would honor me? Students would pass out of my life. The university had no more regard for a professor's achievement than a landlord had for his lodger's. What reward then? Association with the wise? Was that the basis for my hope? I'd discover knuckleheaded colleagues, venal superiors, moronic students. Did I have the illusion of a handsome salary? It was his duty to thwart the philosopher and encourage the entrepreneur. Better a car dealer or a realtor than a philosopher.

All I wanted, I said, was the good opinion of Professor Diekman. That was reward enough.

"Are you of sound mind, Mr. Hansen? Do you know my reputation? A martinet. Notorious for holding students back for unacceptable thesis work. You'll have an easier road with others in the department." If I insisted on working with him he'd hold me to a high level of performance. There would be no perfunctory acceptance of a manuscript. Nothing shoddy would pass his supervision.

I wanted to stretch and he was the man to draw me out. I would accept no one but Professor Diekman.

528

It was then he used my first name. "What is your topic, Russell?"

" 'Descartes's Dream of a Demon.' "

I was, of course, familiar with Descartes's famous dreams that preceded the Meditations, wasn't I?

I was.

There was no dream of a demon.

I referred to the demon whom Descartes invited us to dream, the subverter of the material world.

Wasn't that too labored a topic? Did I have something new to add? But we would talk, he said, and agreed to supervise my thesis.

He invited me to join a circle of students who met at his home Friday nights. "It means giving up more robust Friday night pleasures, Russell. I'll understand perfectly if you find that's too great a sacrifice."

I was delighted to make the sacrifice. I was more than delighted. Ecstatic. And I joined the Diekman circle.

There were six of us, all graduate students, all male. I was the youngest and the least schooled. We met in Diekman's apartment Friday evening for supper. A topic emerged while we were eating, apparently at random. Then for several hours Diekman guided us along the path we had chosen.

We read for him. We adopted his aloof ironic style. Perhaps I even began tilting to the right.

On Friday night I'd leave my barren, mildewed room and the sound of Walsh harrumphing and the cascade of Betty's heels and enter the formality of Diekman's apartment off Jefferson Avenue. Diekman was heir to a Grand Rapids stove factory and very well off. There was a uniformed doorman in the plush lobby. I rose in a gilded elevator to the fifth floor. The apartment was furnished with old family pieces—eighteenth-century pine cabinets, hefty armoires, leather-topped desks, copper lamps hooded by steeply sloped silk shades with beaded fringes. Everything was placed with a precision that was the signature of one ordering sensibility. No wife, no mother, no decorator, only Diekman. There were walls of graphics, one room specializing in Orientals, elsewhere Rembrandt miniatures, Italian views, French contemporaries.

He prepared careful suppers. He himself ate little. Eating was for him a matter of discipline rather than appetite.

One night he watched a portly graduate student, Jules Vincenti, lavish preserves on Breton crepes then take the pancakes in a few massive bites, his chewing thoughtful and bovine. Diekman asked, "Do you like sweets, Mr. Vincenti?"

"They're my undoing."

Vincenti stopped eating while Diekman mused on sweets. Could a world open on a tea-softened madeleine? A coffee-dunked cruller? He didn't think so. Sugar wasn't a thoughtful food. The gratification was too immediate and conclusive. A subtle cuisine carried with it the threat of decay, an ambiguous texture, the tongue made cautious, the pace of eating slowed, all our senses marshalled as we carefully ventured into the next bite. The French and Chinese offered a metaphysical cuisine whose purpose wasn't merely to gratify the palate but to chasten it. The sauces that lingered on the edge of decay reminded the palate that it masticated death, not only the death of what was ingested, but the death of the chewing machine itself—teeth, tongue, palate.

"When we're children we have the blissful conviction that there is nothing beyond the heaven of distilled sweetness. But as we age, Mr. Vincenti, we begin to taste our dying and our appetite matures. We are on the treadmill of generation and decay and if we are to become wise there's no return to the simple connection to sugar."

He formalized the needs of his body. He transformed such necessities as eating into an artful practice. He dressed with great care, not to hide his crookedness—that was out of the question—but to make it irrelevant, to establish that he was the author of himself and not the mere effect of his scoliosis.

Stripped of his tailored tweeds and striped shirt and red bow tie and built-up oxfords he would have appeared as grotesque as a crab without its carapace. He didn't allow himself to be stripped. He maintained austere control. He called us by first name. We would never think of calling him "Gerard." It was always "Sir" or "Professor Diekman."

His aloofness veiled a passionate nature that he could expose in the safety of the Diekman circle.

He once began a reading from Faust. He was powerfully moved. He trembled, the verse barely audible. He was obviously having trouble continuing. There were only the six of us to see him make a fool of himself, but these six were his entire dominion. He stopped, closed his eyes, then rushed for his Baldwin Grand. He weaved back and forth as he played, and sang.

Meine Ruhe ist hin
Mein Herz ist schwer
Ich finde sie nimmer
Und nimmer
Und nimmermehr

A high tenor voice. He was first Marguerite, then stepped into the shoes of Faust. He observed the mad Gretchen. He grieved, but there was no going back. The compact was made. Her madness was the price he paid en route to power.

I was at first embarrassed by the release of his voice. He stretched to the breaking point to accommodate the final *NIMmermehr*, hovering near an uncontrolled tremolo. What idea did he have of himself? But then, entirely composed, he went on to observe how Faust, shaken by pity, is tempted to give up the struggle for transcendence. He is kept on track by the necessary devil.

> *So lang man auf die Erde lebt,*
> *So lang sei dir nichts verboten.*
> *Es irrt der Mensch so lang er strebt.*

The risk must be taken. The striving will not be arrested. Poor lunatic Gretchen is the sacrifice to the God he serves.

> *Er bedient euch in besondere Weise.*

He came from Grand Rapids. His origins were Dutch Reform. He'd long since abandoned the creed but retained a sense of a grievous past and an apocalyptic future. This was the position that structured his courses: we were inextricably embedded in history, fixed there by our station and its duties, doomed whatever our struggles to consummate the destinies of our fathers. The past was fossilized in our character and language: nothing new under the sun. And then, for those elected, a release from bondage through the miracle of art. Grace conferred, not by God in heaven, but by Homer and Mozart and Rembrandt and Goethe.

Our crooked Mephisto led us to the Detroit Institute of Art, prepared to go to any length to open our eyes. He once stood in front of a Mondrian, tucked his cane under his arm and made surprising staccato motions like an East Indian dancer. A group of passing teenagers giggled. A museum guard moved toward us. The dapper little man, tilted off-center, flapped his arms, shuffled his feet, danced his response to Mondrian, scorning a dogmatic formalism that insisted on the sufficiency of the painting within its frame. He didn't care who saw or heard. He spoke in full voice.

"I reflect the force in the painting. The tension between line and color is in me. I experience the stress. It is resolved inside me. The harmony in

531

the Mondrian I find in myself. Where it is hot, I am hot. Where the line thickens, I thicken. I experience the thickening."

He broke into a peculiar jig, his cane fell, his arms mimed vectors working through the Mondrian checkerboard, his pace regulated by the intensity of color. He ignored the gigglers. He didn't allow the possibility of our embarrassment. The guard saw that it was Professor Diekman and withdrew.

"When you face the work of art your obligation is to experience the work, not make judgments. Risk yourselves. Be fools if necessary."

I was tremendously excited by these sessions. The ordinary world seemed illuminated and transformed.

Wasn't the luminous vision worth any sacrifice? Even family? Even Gretchen's? There was no Gretchen for Diekman. He had his Rembrandt lithographs, his Utamaros, his Wunderlichs, his Hundertwassers. Above all, his library.

He had turned a large parlor into a cylinder of books. A 180-degree arc was occupied by philosophy. There was a large segment for classics. There were leather-bound collections and massive art books. The middle shelf above his desk featured the *Encyclopedia Britannica*, Eleventh Edition.

I mentioned that my neighbor owned the same edition.

One of the grand human achievements, Diekman said. The world orchestrated by an extraordinary assembly of scholars, acting in concert, as if there were a single author with a single vision and a single voice and that voice offered a universal design, history unrolling, purposefully directed. Was there any need for updating? All that had happened since the 1911 publication could be extrapolated. Was there any novelty? The scale of events had changed. Otherwise the Eleventh Edition was sufficient.

From the fifth floor at Diekman's, I glimpsed Canada across the Detroit River. At this height—the windows closed—we couldn't hear traffic. We had no inkling of neighborhoods in convulsion. When Diekman went to his piano and illustrated Apollonian grace with a phrase of Mozart, the turbulence below disappeared. I forgot my mornings at Brant's warehouse and the sound of death in Frank Walsh's throat.

But then down the elevator, out into the street, winter coming, a sharp edge in the air, and back to the commonplace world of Tuchler's rooming house.

One night, returning from Diekman's, traffic seemed especially dense. There was a tie-up at the intersection of Woodward and Warren. Horns were blaring. And there was Frank Walsh at the center of it. He had stepped off the curb. Instead of crossing he turned in every direction. Drivers stopped to allow the old man to fix on a course. Those who couldn't see what caused the tie-up blew their horns. I led him to the walk. He wasn't dressed for the weather. He wore a summer suit of black poplin. He was too disoriented to recognize me.

"Russ Hansen," I said. "Your neighbor."

"Russ!" He caught my hand. "This is terrible! I've lost my car!"

I didn't know he had a car.

"A 1940 Plymouth coupe, a two-seater. You can't miss it. Dark green, a big trunk, whitewalls. She's old but she's never failed me. I seem to have lost her." He'd gone to the neighborhood grocery earlier in the day. Parked his car on Forest near Cass. And somehow forgotten it. He'd walked home, listened to the radio, opened a can of soup for dinner. Dozed off. Then, suddenly awakened, he remembered his car. He couldn't find it. He feared it had been stolen. He walked down Forest to Second. He returned via Warren. "It must be stolen."

"Did you leave your keys in the car?"

He searched his pockets. He flapped his arms in dismay. "I'm sorry, Russ."

I told him we'd have to awaken Mrs. Tuchler. He pleaded with me not to wake her up. But he couldn't find his license or registration and she might have the information.

"Don't wake the poor lady. Morning is soon enough."

She was still up and despite his pleading I knocked on her door. Orange hair in curlers, a robe over a flannel nightie, chins gathering, thin lips pursed in outrage.

"Are you crazy, Mr. Walsh? You don't have a car for three years now. They took away your license." She explained to me that he'd had a series of accidents. "One after another. He bumps the car in front. He bumps the car in back. He bumps the car on the side. Then he drives away." She said to Walsh, "And what do you mean, a Plymouth? It was a Buick you owned. A big car. Don't you remember? They took away your license and you sold it to the Russian housepainter who lived on the third floor. Georgie. You don't remember Georgie, for godsakes, Mr. Walsh?"

"He had a wife Masha."

"Yes, Masha. You sold him your Buick. The Plymouth was your car maybe when your missus was alive. You're losing your head, Mr. Walsh. You made the professor walk up and down the street for nothing."

"Oh, dear, I'm sorry." It must have been a dream. He'd awakened suddenly, recalling that he'd gone to the grocery and left his car. He hurriedly dressed, rushed over, and it was gone. Of course. He sold his car to the Russian housepainter who lived upstairs with Masha. Georgie. Completely forgotten. Could it have been a dream? It was so vivid. He was so sure. The Buick and not the Plymouth? The Plymouth long gone?

He came to my door before dawn and woke me up. "Something's happening, Russ. I'm sure I parked the Plymouth outside the A&P. I know it's there."

He faded fast. Not even memories held him in place. A week later I heard him cry out in the hall. "No," he shouted. "Oh, no!" He shrunk away from me. He was in his pajamas, a trail from the middle of the hallway to his door. The hall carpet was a mess. I smelled death in his spoor. It was an awful smell. "I'm sorry," he groaned, "I'm so sorry," then started weeping and ran to his room.

I knocked on the door. "It's O.K., Mr. Walsh. Anybody can have an accident. Let me help you clean up."

I walked in. He was standing with his pajama bottoms around his ankles. He begged me to leave.

"It could happen to anyone. We'll clean up before Mrs. Tuchler finds out."

"Please! Please!"

I stooped to get his pajama bottoms. He tried to push me away.

"No reason to be embarrassed," I told him. There was every reason and I struggled to keep disgust out of my voice. I bundled his pajama bottoms and lifted them gingerly.

"I got lost," he mourned.

I assured him it could happen to anyone.

I led him to the bathroom and ran a tub. His legs were smeared. I helped him into the tub. I talked to keep down the disgust. "It's O.K. It's not so terrible." And, in fact, as I worked it stopped being terrible.

His feet and hands seemed huge because the rest of him had dwindled to skin and bones. He leaned on my shoulder. I held him around the waist and mopped him with a washcloth hanging on the rack, probably Betty McCarthy's. I drained the tub, then filled it again. I told him to sit and relax while I cleaned the hallway.

I went downstairs to the utility closet beneath the stairs, looking for a mop and bucket. Mrs. Tuchler heard and came out in her robe. I told her there had been an accident.

"What kind of accident?"

"Mr. Walsh got lost on the way to the toilet."

She charged upstairs. I heard her shout, "*Gott im Himmel!* You were lost? From your room to the toilet?"

"I was lost." He imagined himself in another home, another time, utterly confused. A few feet from succor, but lost.

"You cannot be lost! They'll put you in the crazy house!" She looked at the mess. "*Schrecklich! Schrecklich!*" She warned Walsh he was on thin ice. If he didn't take care he was done for. "Do you understand? Can you hear me?"

"I was lost."

"Ach. It's no use."

I offered to clean the floor.

"Don't trouble yourself, Mr. Hansen. The old fellow is no good anymore."

I told her not to be hard on him. He was only confused.

"Only confused? Only? He got nothing. He got nobody. He'll end in the crazy house."

She toweled the old man and we led him to bed. She insisted that I go to my room. She was still working at midnight, scrubbing the carpet, mopping the floor, the bucket clanging. I heard her, "*Gott im Himmel!*" out in the hallway.

Betty McCarthy, returning from her late stint as a cabaret waitress, knocked on my door.

"I saw your light. Listen. Mr. Walsh is crying."

I told her what happened.

"Oh, gee, the poor old guy."

She knocked but he refused to answer. She coaxed him to open the door. Did he need anything? Wasn't he hungry? She bet he hadn't eaten.

"Please, Miss. Don't trouble yourself. I'm fine."

"It's no trouble. There's an all-night place only a couple blocks away."

He didn't mean us to hear his weeping. He meant to swallow his death without troubling anyone but couldn't remember his resolve for courage.

She located a Chinese restaurant that was open and brought him a container of wonton soup. "It's delicious. You'll feel better if you eat."

We found the container still untouched when we entered his room several days later.

*　　*　　*

Betty McCarthy suggested we meet to discuss arrangements for Mr. Walsh. We went downstairs to see Mrs. Tuchler. She had just finished eating and was still in her apron. Her living room smelled of onions and chicken.

"Arrangements? What do you mean arrangements?"

"The old man needs help," Betty said. "We could see to it that he gets regular meals. We could take care of his laundry, help with his bath."

"His bath? We should wash him and dry him? Like his baby-sitters?"

"I wouldn't put it that way."

"A baby-sitter is part-time. The parents show up. They pay the sitter. They drive the sitter home. Who is it that drives me home, Miss McCarthy?"

"That's not what I had in mind."

"Even if he was my own family I would have problems. I got something more to do with my time than to be a baby-sitter. Maybe you can afford such charity—"

"I don't look at it as charity."

"What else? You give up your time for a man who is nobody to you."

"He's a human being, Mrs. Tuchler."

"I am also a human being. You'll take care of me, also?"

"I hope there'll be someone for you, Mrs. Tuchler."

"I don't count on it. I take care of myself."

I suggested we think of our obligation to Mr. Walsh as a temporary arrangement while we inquired about relatives.

"You don't think I asked? There is nobody. He is alone. I warned him—you heard me, Professor—he shouldn't lose his head, it will be the end for him."

Betty said she could bring food before she left for work.

"Tell me. How long will you keep up such an arrangement? One week, maybe? I give it no more."

"Don't you have any feeling for him, Mrs. Tuchler?"

"Feelings I got. Feelings I got plenty. Feelings cost nothing."

I went to his room in the morning.

The container of soup was unopened on his table.

I asked if he wanted breakfast.

He shook his head.

No orange juice? No coffee?

He shook his head.

Toast?

536

He didn't answer.

He sat in his Morris chair.

"Do you want me to read you the morning paper?"

He shook his head.

"Shall I read something from the *Encyclopedia?*"

He looked up.

"Shall I find something to read?"

He nodded.

Only the pages of Volume 18 were cut, MED to MUM, where Louise had read the statistics of Michigan and found nine forlorn Japanese in that peppermint-growing state.

I pulled out the tissue map of Michigan.

I brought him his spectacles. I drew my finger up Lake Erie and the Detroit River into Lake St. Clair. I traveled up Lake Huron through the Straits of Mackinac into Lake Michigan. We hugged the shore all the way to Chicago. I called out the beach towns and offshore islands.

"Leland," he repeated after me.

"Do you know Leland?"

He spoke in a rusty, abraded voice. "We stayed in Leland one summer. There was an Indian family. Potawatomies. One of them named Archie brought us white fish. They treated them like colored people."

I offered him juice and toast and a banana and he ate with good appetite.

I opened POL-REE and cut pages with a paring knife.

Potawatomi, derived from the Indian word for fire-maker. Algonquian stock. Settled in lower Michigan. They were allied with the French in their wars against the Iroquois and took part in the conspiracy of Pontiac.

Pontiac. A chief of the Ottawas. On May 7, 1763 he tried to occupy Fort Detroit and failed. He besieged the fort until October 30th.

The city of Pontiac, named in honor of the Indian chief, is the county seat of Oakland County, Michigan, on the Clinton River, about 26 miles N.W. of Detroit. The Eastern Michigan Asylum for the Insane (1878), with grounds covering more than 500 acres, is located in Pontiac. The name "Eloise" was derived from the official name.

MOTOR VEHICLES.

In 1910. The total number in the United Kingdom was 183,000. There were 46,000 vehicles in France and 42,000 in Germany. The United States of America with 225,000 cars was foremost.

"Old Henry," he said. "Good old Henry. Nobody ever called him Hank."

537

There was no mention of Ford in 1910. The invention of the internal combustion engine was attributed to a German, Gottlieb Daimler.

"Henry worked on the internal combustion engine in a garage on Bagley Street. He was with the Edison Illuminating Company."

I opened DEM-EDW and located Detroit, founded in 1701 by Antoine de la Mothe Cadillac (c.1661–1730). Cadillac arrived on the 24th of July with about 1600 followers. They at once built a palisade fort about 200-feet-square south of what is now Jefferson Avenue between Griswold and Shelby Street. Cadillac named it Fort Pontchartrain in honor of the French Colonial Minister.

Betty called to say she might be late and I told her not to rush. The old man seemed back to his ordinary state of unworldliness.

"I'll bring him a bite to eat."

"No wonton soup," I told her. "He's well-stocked."

I checked again that evening before leaving for Diekman's and he was in his chair, nodding off with the radio on.

*   *   *

At Diekman's that night I mentioned the old man and the tragedy of old age and the apparent failure of community.

There was a time, Diekman said, when old age was no tragedy.

The monastery town of St. Gall thrived in an age of walls. Walls around the monastery, walls around the castle, walls around the town. And beyond the walls a girdle of fields and then forest. Everything necessary for the complete life was inside the walls or just beyond.

There were goldsmiths, silversmiths, blacksmiths, potters, weavers, bakers, brewers. The monks had flocks of sheep and goats and herds of cattle and horses. Their gardens were designed for year-around sustenance. The ten thousand people within the walls served under the benign rule of the abbot. It was a way of life that came about as a consequence of the Saracen invasion. The barbarians had destroyed all connections. Language itself was at risk. Spoken utterance coarsened. The written language became exclusively the province of clerics. The abbot stood at the center of a world that had otherwise lost its center.

The discipline imposed by the abbot secured the walled paradise.

How tentative was our link to the past. How easy to break the chain of tradition that bound us to our origins and safeguarded the knowledge needed for survival.

The good father was the salvation. The abbot supervised life within

538

the walls. Every moment had its definition. Time was marked by the seasons and the sacraments and the holy days. There was no confusion of estates. Every position was clear and distinct.

Diekman said that if he could have arrested history he would have chosen a time before Henry Ford bound us together in a chain of highways and made us one. Divisions were overcome, boundaries removed. Making us one, Ford made us nothing. Letting everyone in, he breached the walls of community, destroyed the distinction between inside and outside, hastened the entropy that would in its final stage bring us again to chaos.

The university should have been our tower, our fortress, our St. Gall. But Wayne was penetrated by city streets, everyone allowed to enter, the university turned from its vocation to safeguard the life of the spirit.

Diekman saw himself, I suppose, as our abbot and Friday nights in his apartment a recreation of St. Gall.

I was ready to settle for a good father.

*   *   *

I put my ear to the wall and didn't hear any coughing or rattling. The radio was off. I knocked on his door and he didn't answer. I called Mrs. Tuchler.

I feared what we might find when she opened his door but he wasn't in. We waited past midnight and he didn't show up and Mrs. Tuchler called the police.

Betty returned at two in the morning.

"You said he was back to normal and there was no reason to stick to the schedule."

"Normal in his case does not mean in full possession of his wits."

The next morning we walked the neighborhood and asked if anyone had seen Frank Walsh. The old man was well-known. Everyone seemed to know he'd been married for fifty-three years and was a friend of Henry Ford. The postman reported seeing Walsh get on the Woodward streetcar at Warren.

A couple days later Mrs. Tuchler received a call from a social worker at the Eastern Michigan Asylum, once explicitly designated for the insane and known as Eloise. The old man had somehow managed the twenty-six miles to Pontiac and checked himself in. He was unable to identify himself but Mrs. Tuchler's phone number was in his wallet.

Perhaps he'd gone there because the name sounded like "Louise,"

Betty borrowed a 1950 powder-blue Ford coupe and we drove to Pontiac to visit Walsh.

I didn't find out until we were underway that she was a novice driver with only a temporary permit. She leaned forward, clenched the wheel.

"Are you sure you can drive?"

"What's to it?"

I had never learned, myself.

Her chatter ebbed and flowed with the conditions of traffic. She became more confident as we drove out Woodward beyond the zoo. We passed the Wigwam restaurant, the Shrine of the Little Flower where Father Coughlin once presided. She relaxed as traffic diminished. Her conversation steadied. She was a drama student at Wayne. She had played Irina in *The Three Sisters*. She had been Miriam in *Winterset*. She'd been enthusiastically reviewed in the college newspaper. Philosophy wasn't her thing and she'd never heard of Professor Diekman.

She rattled on and I pretended to listen.

The asylum came into view off the road, a red-brick castle, steep pitched roof clutched by gables, towers with witches' hats. It was the kind of redness you'd get if the brick clay never dried. Inside that red building you felt as if you were underground, even on the top floor in the tiny rooms beneath the plunging roof.

"Well, we're here. Shall we go in?"

Smoke curled from the chimneys of Eloise. The day was cold and the brittle grass cracked when we stepped on it.

The smell of the place must have come from a desperate effort to purge what had been in the red clay from the beginning and could never be removed unless the site were leveled and the remains either carted off or buried.

We were stopped at Reception and told we couldn't see the old man since we weren't relatives but Betty led the way down a corridor. We drifted with visitors and crazy people and old folks. We mingled with the robed and the pajama-ed and those in overcoats and mufflers. We walked up broad stairways illuminated by dull globes, past red lights marking exits, through wards of the ambulant. We came to a corridor where the old folks were seated on cane benches in a glassed-in porch. We found old Walsh in a wheelchair. He wore a threadbare robe. He was so faded and withered we would have passed without recognizing him. A custodian told us, "That's him. That's your grandpa."

"It's Russ Hansen," I told him, "and Betty McCarthy." His lips fluttered, his eyes wouldn't focus.

Betty, who had hardly spoken more than words of greeting to the old man, tried to prod him into response.

"How do you like it here, Mr. Walsh? Do they feed you O.K.? I bet the food's terrible. Do you remember that soup I brought you, Mr. Walsh?" On and on, as if she imagined she could talk him out of senility.

I think he said, "Russ?" The voice was unused and choked and the sound not coherent. I'm not sure he spoke my name.

"We're holding your things for you."

The pale blue eyes didn't record a thing.

I asked if he wanted the picture of Louise in his room. It might make the room more like home. He didn't respond.

I held his hand for a few moments then placed it on the arm of the chair. He took no further notice and I had nothing to say.

Betty whispered, "Let's go."

Outside her breath frosted. Her long muffler came loose. She furled it securely. She tugged down on her green tam-o'-shanter. "Well," she said, "at least someone saw him."

"What did we see? There's no one there."

* * *

He bequeathed Eloise his shadow. The substance remained with Mrs. Tuchler.

There was the Seth Thomas pendulum clock, the wardrobe with the lion's claw feet, his Zenith console, an oak highboy, a gilt-framed photo of himself as a young Irishman—tinted blond, red-cheeked—a companion photo of a corseted Louise with splendid curls and a firm sensible mouth. There were other items that Mrs. Tuchler disposed of—a paperweight with a Currier and Ives snow scene, a signed Maxfield Parrish "Dawn," a hand-crocheted bedspread. And so on. The treasure for me was the Eleventh Edition, in pristine condition.

An Eloise doctor said that Walsh would never be back. He walked when set in motion but the spirit had left the machine. Tuchler said she'd have to get rid of his things. She had no place to store them. Betty wanted the old man's room with its exterior windows. There was already a prospective tenant for the vacancy. There weren't any relatives to assume debts or assets. He owed Mrs. Tuchler several months' back rent. A lawyer advised her she could sell the "junk"—the clock, the wardrobe, the bedstead, the chest of drawers, the dresser with the oval mirror. The sale would cover her expenses. As for the *Encyclopedia*, any dealer would be glad to pay a few dollars, but why not keep it in the family?

"You take it, Professor. Give me ten dollars and it is done."

We stalked his dying, and now closed in to feed.

I arranged the *Encylopedia* on my windowsills, ten volumes to a window and entered its pages.

REF-SAI was still uncut.

The town of St. Gall owes its origin to St. Gall, an Irish hermit, who in 614, built his cell in the thick forest which then covered the site of the future monastery, and lived there, with a few companions, till his death in 640. Many pilgrims later found their way to his cell, and about the middle of the eighth century the collection of hermits' dwellings was transformed into a regularly organized Benedictine monastery. For the next three centuries this was one of the chief centers of learning and education in Europe. About 954 the monastery and its buildings were surrounded by walls as a protection against the Saracens, and this was the origin of the town.

The Encyclopedia offered whatever anyone wanted in the way of towns, cities, continents, even the starry universe. Walsh wanted nothing. He only claimed a bed in a ward at Eloise.

Mrs. Tuchler gave Betty the photographs of Walsh and Louise, valuable for the elaborate, gilt frames.

The poor old guy, Betty said. No one cared. And we were already divvying up the spoils.

* * *

I came across the final words imputed to Descartes, dying in Sweden of pneumonia. I offered them to the Diekman circle:

" 'My soul, you have been captive for a long time, now the hour has come when you must leave your prison, this body; you must bear this separation with joy and courage.' "

The words were reported by Ambassador Charcut, who was in attendance.

I found the speech repellent.

"Why?"

"It's too rehearsed."

Diekman didn't take Descartes's statement at face-value. "My soul? This body?" Whose voice was it that addressed the soul and referred to the body? Someone named René Descartes who distinguished himself from his soul and body? "Where is the voice housed that speaks to 'my soul'? Who is the third man who intrudes between body and soul?"

Vincenti suggested that the voice of Ego occurs at a higher level of language than the mention of body and soul and so doesn't intrude between them.

Diekman dismissed this solution. "It's simpler to not accept the speech at its face-value. Though clearness and distinctness are everything to Descartes, he doesn't have time to make his meaning clear when he's dying. His language becomes condensed, ambiguous, poetic. Surely he doesn't mean to say that the soul of René Descartes will survive disembodiment as a ghost of himself. Who would the ghost resemble? There is no single Descartes. He has passed—as we all do—through a series of transformations, from youth to age, from health to illness. So even if there were cameras available, no single representation would serve. There's no fixing him once and for all. Isn't he simply foretelling what in fact turns out to be the case? Descartes tells us, as he's dying, that he welcomes his disembodiment and his coming immortality. Cartesianism will survive, he tells us."

I offered a simpler explanation. Descartes didn't make the deathbed speech. A man dying of pneumonia wouldn't have had enough wind for that speech. It must have been composed by Charcut, an avid Cartesian.

"That, too," Diekman said, "is irrelevant. The separation of body and soul is a fable. The fable holds that we are victims of our appetites and only free when appetite diminishes. Glaucon, for example, welcomes old age and the ebbing of desire. We have other uses for a fable than to question its truth."

"The truth about dying," I said, "is that it leaves you speechless."

I was hooted down for offering "the truth about dying." They weren't tempted to move the discussion in a morbid direction. It was raining; snow was on the way; we were cozy inside, dining by candlelight, a fire crackling in a frame of ceramic tiles.

The supper that night featured a seafood pasta, served in a porcelain tureen. Prawns and scallops and crabmeat were added to each portion of pasta and the dish topped with sautéed peas and carrots.

Vincenti asked for grated cheese but the Professor told him grated cheese was not served with seafood pasta.

Diekman's bathroom was a large, tiled room, entered through a dressing alcove. I opened a cabinet and saw thick towels rolled in the shape of loaves of bread in hues of red, blue, green, yellow. Above the double basin of pink porcelain there was a large mirror circled by flourescence

The medicine cabinet revealed a man who must have suffered in every part. There were capsules for muscle spasm. He used sedatives and laxatives. There were medicines for eyes, skin, feet, rectum.

He clearly took great care before presenting himself. There was a tub with an aluminum railing and a separate shower stall. A shelf, straddling the bath, contained bath oil, skin lotion, pumice stone. On the lip of the tub there were shampoos and moisturizers. On the marble commode there were soaps in a variety of shapes, little balls in gaudy wrappers, rounds of soap, rectangles of soap, a green-flecked soap in the form of a fish, another shaped from transparent, pink gel into the form of a cupid. A basket of potpourri on the water tank shed a cinnamon, ginger odor.

* * *

There was little evidence of shit in that room and hardly any evidence in the Eleventh Edition. I opened SAI-SHU and didn't find a listing. There were no entries for excreta or feces in EVA-FRA.

The encyclopedia contained the world in almost every feature but only a Latinate mention of shit under sewage where there was a discussion of the use of "excreta" as manure and the storing of excreta in middens and cesspools. The method for disposing of feces in 1910 was the same as ours today, dilution and defecation through pipes four to six inches in diameter.

* * *

I shoved open the bathroom door. Either the latch didn't hold or she was neglectful. Betty was poised at the sink in an open kimono, her left leg extended, foot in the basin, leaning forward soaping painted toes, red hair floating down over her eyes, a glimpse of freckled breasts, the rusty thatch below, the tensed right leg sturdy and muscular. "Sorry," I said and shut the door.

I apologized when she came out.

"No problem. I should have made sure the door was locked."

"Anyway," I said, "it's a gorgeous view."

She moved into Walsh's room, her bed against the wall dividing us. We were separated by six inches of lathe and air and plasterboard. I could hear the rustle of her sheets and the squeal of springs.

One early morning before dawn I knocked at her door.

"Who is it?"

I whispered, "Russ," and she opened to me.

*   *   *

I knew that the charges I brought against Diekman in the court of my mind wouldn't hold. Was his john too lavish? Was he to blame for the way Vincenti ate, for Descartes's foolish death, for the absence of any reference to Iron Mountain or lost fathers or shit in the Eleventh Edition? The grievances were trivial but suddenly his walled city closed in on me and I felt entombed and couldn't bear listening to him tidy up the world.

I dropped out of the Diekman circle. I left without saying a word to Diekman. I had nothing to say. I couldn't give an account of a defection I didn't understand. I abandoned campus. I didn't answer Vincenti's messages. I prepared to move from the neighborhood. I was with Betty so it's not entirely true that I was in despair.

I met him again, possibly for the last time, shortly after Christmas. Trees were still up, stars still in windows, there was new snow on the ground. I was shopping at the Kroger's market. I walked down the soup aisle and there he was in overcoat, muffler, gloves, a basket in his hand, his cane hooked on an arm, wearing a Russian-style fur hat.

It wasn't his neighborhood or his kind of store and I didn't expect to meet him there.

Yes, he said, a surprising place to meet. He didn't ordinarily shop here. He was careful about food, as he was sure I knew, but he felt a cold coming on and didn't have time or energy for refined shopping. At any rate, the objects he carried were only apparently trivial. He held up the soup can glorified by Andy Warhol. He spoke in full voice, no evidence of a cold. He praised Warhol for transforming banality and demonstrating that food had become something other than food. A citizen of mid-twentieth-century America was free of the necessity imposed by brute hunger and didn't have to spend a major effort tracking down the next meal. The package was now more important than the soup.

He had once scorned salesmen as purveyors of kitsch and schlock. Now he understood that they were, in fact, visionaries of the commonplace, true esthetes who awakened us to neglected beauty and enlarged our world. We could enter Kroger's as we once entered a gallery of art.

He denied the food he craved and passed off the denial as art.

I was outraged by the show he put on for random shoppers who had stopped traffic in the aisle to listen. He didn't ask me where I'd been. He didn't give me a chance to make excuses.

"Food isn't a priority with me and I don't care how it comes wrapped."

He nodded, smiled. It was the betrayal he expected. He offered me a slanted, mocking look. "We welcome the moment when our children instruct us so we can cut them free."

He acknowledged me as his child and there are times when I can imagine pleading, "Take me back. I've lost my way."

*   *   *

She's pinned photos of stars to the walls. Dietrich and Hepburn and Harlow and Gable nourish her dream of stardom. I saw her at the World Theater in "My Sister Eileen." She played perky Eileen. It was herself she played, without subterfuge, almost artlessly. She was charming and likable and received an ovation from the mainly college audience.

I told her, "Everyone pulls for you. You're really liked."

She wanted honest feedback that would help in her work. What didn't I like about her performance?

I enjoyed the evening. She was a fine Eileen. Still, I wasn't sure about her range. Her voice lacked timbre and occasionally faded. There was actually something appealing in this, something naive and childlike that disarmed criticism. But how deep could she go?

"I'm not deep, Russ. I never said I was."

Her dream of stardom will pass. She's buoyant and good-hearted and believes any condition is alterable, even grievous old age. It's typical that she would offer Frank Walsh wonton soup.

I've said goodbye to the Diekman circle and it terrifies me when I think I've set myself on the trail of Frank Walsh, headed toward a red-brick grave among the living dead. I warn Betty—no mausoleums, no walls, no ill health, no old age. We live young and die happy. I want that in the contract.

Agreed, she says, confident that enthusiasm and buoyancy can manage anything.

Alvin Jones's Ignorant Wife

Margaret Broucek

I work with a young gal who don't think her husband is gon fool around, hmmm? She's not a stupid gal, just ignorant. I know he will. But she ain't married yet, not even a boyfriend around, so she's got this vision, see, how it's gonna be for her.

She cornered me and Alice and Yvonne in the emulsion room one day and I knew she was gon bring it up again. She says to us, "Hey now, here's my point—you all haven't fooled around on your husbands, have you?" She didn't get an answer right off, so she asked Yvonne—"Yvonne, see I know you haven't fooled around." Yvonne was standing at the counter next to me and I see her pocked chin's hanging lower than usual. Well, Alice pipes right up. "Let's all say we have!" And me and Yvonne didn't have a choice, had to go along with that. Girl's eyes peeled open, slow, and she looked so she like to had a baby! I sure felt bad for her—just dropped her big lip, turned around and left. And I know what'll happen to her. She'll be running round in her yard; she'll draw a crowd, like that woman we all saw dancing with the gun.

I messed with Alvin Jones a while back, when my kids was young. He lived across the street with his string bean, Carla? Karen?, don't know what it was. Alvin was a big man, see, and built so nice. I could make an afternoon watching him wax his car in his small shorts and nothing else. And he always had a good word for me. Well it didn't last long, now, and really I just wanted to smell him up close (didn't Yvonne laugh when I told her that). He helped me in with my grocery bags one day. That was the start. I told him "just set them on the kitchen counter and thanks a lot." But he wanted a powdered doughnut out of one of those long boxes with the cellophane window. *That* was the start.

547

Those months we carried on I don't guess I ever asked him about his skin-and-bones wife. I just remember it was a summer of flies, hot houses and hot car seats, and a summer you could never get the film off your skin. God knows why Alvin wanted my doughnuts. I had been with my husband seven years then. I smelled like my husband, wore his shirts since I never left the house. I looked like *my husband*, but Alvin gave me open-mouth kisses. He'd come over midday with those five-pound bags of ice that he'd dump in the bathtub. Then we'd run a bit of cool water over them and slide in howling. Yes I do remember that ice-clinking around and bumping 'gainst my numb skin, and Alvin rubbing me warm after. I figured his wife was at work, and he wasn't gon be no worse for wear when she got home, not that big old man, naah.

Mondays, in August, Alvin would pull in my drive with his top down and I'd come out the door with my head silk-wrapped and sunglasses on with rhinestones set in. "Why Miss Aretha Franklin!" he'd say. He'd put a towel on the seat where I was to sit. Once we drove in the country, and it was all steam. And the only trees, there, were the ones what sat in rows on both sides of the road and hung over you with those humming bugs nesting thick in the leaves. Gawd! I was scared they was gonna drop in the car with Alvin and me. That day he was singing blues, "I wish it would rain." Felt like we was sitting in front of one of those big clothes dryers with the door open, only not really, because our clothes was wringing wet and my scarf was ruint. Sounds like a bad day, hmm? I liked the time Alvin was singing.

Wasn't long then — Uh uuh. Two days, three days, a few days passed — before he was mowing Widow Timm's yard. He even bagged all the grass and set it by the drive real nice. Got so I missed him quite a bit around mid-morning. I'm shamed to admit it, but I'd linger by the front window about an hour a day. He'd stop me in the street every once in a while, tell me, "Why Mrs. Otis, every time I see you I'm falling in love again, prettier every day." Once, when he happened to have a glass of tea along, he fished around in it and brought out a small ice piece to slip in the neck of my dress. It slid so slow down my back, and I stood there till I couldn't feel it sting, and he was back at his door.

Now, I did envy the man's wife. She got to see his big teeth all the time and live in that split-level with the iceman. After a while, half the women on the block had been with her husband and we didn't none of us pity her. We marveled at her, how she was so quiet — not ranting and raving like so many do, you know. Every time I laid eyes on his gal she was to and from the car, kind of running up on her toes and not looking to see what the neighbors was about.

This one evening, late, I was picking up bits of cake out the backyard 'cause James, my husband, threw half his dinner onto the grass, didn't want that corn bread that come in a box and tossed the pan out the kitchen door. It was too sweet, see, got to make it all by hand. Well, I got about all the pieces back in the pan when I heard a radio blasting across the street. Wasn't like Alvin to turn his music up so I walked around to see. I was hearing someone singing along too and I thought, "Lord, that wife of his sure can't carry a tune." First person I saw was Widow Timms pressed up against her window, sliding herself around to get a good look at something, then Ginny Meyer and all her children sitting in their parked car, rolling up the windows, poking the locks down. Then I make it around to see the show: Alvin's gal swinging her hair, leaping about that yard with a gun above her head. She fired the whole round off before the police came, put her in their car.

Well, she didn't kill Alvin. He was gone, with some woman from two blocks down who won money suing the police. And either Alvin left a note or somebody told his wife what she never suspected. She hadn't known any of it, see.

And this young gal I work with had two men in mind that she was sure would never fool around. Her father, she said, and her brother-in-law, that was her list, and she nodded as if to say the case was closed. She'd met my husband at a company picnic and wanted to add him to her list too, asked me, "Uh, does your husband go out on you?"

Girl, we're lucky to see him home one night a week, and his women call the house.

I didn't tell her that about him, 'cause I'm not one to be pitied, you know. She's the one. She'll be running around in her yard, draw a crowd—entire families watching her from the car.

Fishbone

Donna Trussell

The other girls from my senior class were off at college or working. Not me. I stayed alone in my room and played The Game of Life. Mama didn't like it.

"Wanda, are you on drugs?" she said.

I shook my head. I spun the plastic wheel—it made a ratchet sound—and moved the blue car two spaces, up on a hill. The great thing about The Game of Life was all the plastic hills and valleys. No other game had such realism.

"You need a change," Mama said. "You're going to Meemaw's."

My bus was leaving early the next morning, so I had to pack in a hurry. But I took the time to put a matchbook in my purse. I don't smoke, but I thought it might come in handy if I needed to send a message to the bus driver: Hijacker, ninth row, submachine gun under his coat.

The sky was overcast, and it was a slow, pale trip. The only rest stop was in Centerville, where I got a fish sandwich at the Eat It and Beat It.

Meemaw was waiting for me at the station. She smelled of cold cream and lilacs.

Ed grabbed my suitcase. "Yo," he said.

"Yo," I said back.

Ed's pickup was full of old *Soldier of Fortunes*. I rested my feet on top of a picture of a tank. Meemaw's life sure had changed since she married Ed.

"My little girl," she said. She patted my knee the way a kid flattens Play-Doh.

"She's not your girl," Ed said. "She's your granddaughter."

"She *is* my little girl."

550

A chain link fence now surrounded Meemaw's garden. "Keeps dogs out," she said. The fence made her farm look even less farmish than it had, with its green shack for a barn and refrigerator toppled on its side out back and giant new house modeled after the governor's mansion.

Meemaw fussed over me at supper: Wanda, can I get you some more roast, would you like another helping of butter beans, how about some corn bread?

Ed had three cups of coffee with supper. He poured the coffee into his saucer and blew on it. I asked him why he drank his coffee that way.

He didn't answer. Finally Meemaw said, "To cool it down."

Ed's cup and saucer were monogrammed in gold. My plate too.

"Meemaw, where's your dishes?" I asked. "The ones with purple ribbons and grapes?"

"Well, we have Ed's china now."

He slurped his coffee, staring straight ahead. He might as well have been talking to the curtains when he said, "I'm glad you're here, Wanda, because I've been wanting to ask you something. All day I've been wondering—who paid the hospital when you had that baby? The taxpayers?"

I smashed a butter bean with my fork. "Excuse me," I said and went outside.

I looked out across the pine trees, dark green. I used to believe trees had people inside them. I wished some God would change me into a tree. That wouldn't be a bad life—sun, rain, birds. Kids looking for pine cones. Me shaking my branches for them.

The peat moss in the garden was warm. I lay down and pulled a watermelon close.

After a while Meemaw came out and sat down near my head, in the snapdragons and cucumbers. Meemaw planted vegetables and flowers together, except for the gladiolas, off by themselves. Pink, peach, yellow, white—a million baby shoes, shifting in the wind.

She smoothed my hair and talked about exercise and how important it was.

"Meemaw, what happened to your strawberries?"

"Birds. But that's all right. Plenty for the birds too."

Every morning we'd go out to pull weeds, and she'd tell me uplifting stories about people she knew. Trials they'd had. A young man wanted to commit suicide because law school was so hard. Once a week his mother wrote him letters full of encouraging words.

"What kind of encouraging words?"

"Oh, 'Don't give up.' That sort of thing."

When he graduated he found out she'd been dead for a month. She'd known she was dying, and had written the last letters ahead of time.

Meemaw knew lots of stories about people who "took the path of least resistance" and ended up sick or poor. I got back at her by asking personal questions.

"Meemaw, have you ever had an orgasm?"

Yes, she said. Once. "I was glad to know what it is that causes so much of human behavior." She smiled and handed me a bunch of gladiolas.

Afternoons I stayed in my room. Mama wouldn't let me bring The Game of Life. I lay on the bed a lot. The light fixture had leaves and berries molded in the glass. Once I wrapped my arms around the chest of drawers and put my head down on the cool marble top.

Meemaw would call me to supper. There wasn't much discussion at the table. If anyone said anything, it was Ed talking to Meemaw or Meemaw talking to me. Except for once, when I went to the stove to get some salt. Ed told me I'd done it all wrong. "You don't bring the *plate* to the salt. You bring the *salt* to the plate."

After supper Meemaw and I went down to the barn. She milked Sissy. I fed the chickens. I'd throw a handful of feed and they'd move in at eighty miles an hour.

Ed never came with us. He hates Sissy, Meemaw told me. "He's jealous."

"Jealous of a cow?"

"Why, of course. I spend so much of my time with her."

Evenings Ed watched *Walking Tall* on his VCR. Or he went inside his toolshed. He never worked on anything. He looked at catalogs and ordered tools, and when they came he hung them on the walls. He read books about the end of the world: the whole state of Colorado was going to turn into Jell-O, and people will drown. "You've got five years to live, young lady," he told me. "*Five years.*"

He had guns—a whole case-full. Once I saw him polishing them when I was standing in the hall by his study.

"What do you think you're doing?" he said.

I walked away. He shut the door.

One day when I was watching Meemaw through a little diamond shape made of my thumbs and two fingers, Ed said, "You planning on sitting on your butt all summer?"

"I haven't thought about it."

"Start thinking."

Meemaw knew a man in town who was looking for help. She knew everybody in town.

"It's a photography studio," Meemaw said.

"I don't know anything about photography."

"He's willing to train someone. It's a nice place. There's another studio in town, but everybody says Mr. Lamont's is the one that puts on the finishing touch."

She made the phone call. Ed was smiling behind his magazine. I *knew* he was.

I drove Meemaw's old Fairmont into town. First Ed showed me all the things I had to do to it, because "service stations don't do a damned thing anymore." He showed me the oil stick and the radiator. He told me to check the windshield-wiper blades once a week. He was just about to make me measure the air in the tires when I said I'd be late for my interview if I didn't get going.

Mr. Lamont wore glasses and a pair of green doubleknit pants that were stretched about as far as they could go.

"Wanda, you put here that your last job was back in December. What have you been doing since then?"

"Nothing."

"Nothing?"

"Nothing you'd want to know about."

"But I would like to know."

"O.K. I was in love with this guy. We were going to get married, but then we didn't. And then I had a baby boy."

"Oh."

"He's been adopted."

"I see." Mr. Lamont tried to look neutral, but I could see little bursts of energy flying from the corners of his mouth.

"I can't pay minimum wage," he said.

"Whatever." I might as well be here, I thought, as out on the farm with Ed.

After supper Ed gave me a lecture about jobs and responsibility and attitude. People don't think, they just don't *think*. World War III is coming, and no one's prepared. All the goddamned niggers will try to steal their chickens.

"But I'm ready for them," he said. "I've been stocking up on hollow points. They blow a hole in a man as big as a barrel." He punched his fist in the air. Meemaw sort of jumped, but she didn't say anything. She clanked the dishes and sang "Rock of Ages" a little louder.

553

I went to bed with the pamphlet Mr. Lamont gave me, *The Fine Art of Printing Black and White*. The paper is very sensitive, it said.

The next day Mr. Lamont showed me the safelight switch. "See that gouge? I did that so I could feel for it in the dark."

He did a test strip. "Agitate every few seconds," he said, rocking the developer tray.

He let me print a picture of a kid holding a trophy. "Make it light," he said. "The newspaper adds contrast. Look how this one came out." He showed me a clipping of a bunch of Shriners. They looked like they had some kind of skin disease.

After a week I got the hang of it, and Mr. Lamont left me in charge of black and white. I liked the darkroom. No phones. No people, except for the faces that slowly developed before me. Women and their fiancés. Sometimes the man stood behind the woman and put both arms around her waist.

Jimmy used to do that.

He held me like that at the senior picnic. It was windy. Big rocks nailed down the corners of each tablecloth. Blue gingham. The white tablecloths had to be returned because the principal thought they'd remind the students of bedsheets. Jimmy and I laughed; we'd been making love for weeks. We got careless, in the tall grasses by Cedar Creek Lake. Night birds called across the water.

When I was two weeks late, I told him. He looked away. There's a clinic, he said, in Dallas. I covered his lips with my fingers.

At Western Auto they said they'd take him on, weekends and nights. At the Sonic, too, for the morning shift. Jimmy and I looked at an apartment on Burning Tree Drive, southwest of town. A one-bedroom. He stared at the ceiling. Jimmy? I said.

Goodbye, goodbye, I told the mirror long before I really said it.

I read every book I could find about babies and their tadpole bodies. I gave up Coke and barbecue potato chips. My breasts swelled. I felt great. Hormones, the doctor said.

At first my baby was just a rose petal, sleeping, floating. At eight months I played him records, Mama's *South Pacific* and Daddy's "Seventy-six Trombones." I stood right next to the stereo, and he talked to me with thumps of his feet.

You want to feel him kick? I asked. Mama shook her head and kept on ironing. Daddy left the room.

I didn't get a baby shower. Mama told everyone I was putting it up for adoption. "It," she called him. I made up different names for him. Fishbone, one week. Logarithm, the next.

Mama bought me a thin gold wedding band to wear to the hospital. Girls don't do that anymore, I told her. Some girls even keep their babies, these days.

Not here in Grand Saline, she said. Not girls from good families.

My little Fishbone got so big two nurses had to help push him out. Breathe, they said. Pant hard.

Please let me hold him, I said. *Please.*

Now, Wanda, Mama said. You know what's best.

He cried. Then he slipped away, down the hall. The room caved in on me, with its green walls and white light. Mama held me down, saying, we've been through this. We decided.

At the nurse's station Jimmy left me a get-well card. Good luck, he wrote. That's all.

Mama took me home to a chocolate cake, and we never talked about Fishbone again. She never mentioned Jimmy's name.

Sometimes now, before driving home to Meemaw, I stopped at the trailer court at the edge of town. I watched people. A woman would frown and I'd think: that's me heating up a bottle for Fishbone and the formula got too hot. A man takes off his cowboy boots and props his feet on the coffee table. A woman tucks herself next to him. He kisses her hair, her neck.

I remembered love. I remembered it all. Now I felt thick and dull, something to be tossed away in the basement.

"How's the passport picture coming?" Mr. Lamont asked, knocking on my door.

"Don't come in. Paper exposed."

"That man going to New Guinea is back."

The man had worried about his eyes. I've got what they call raccoon eyes, he'd said, is there any way you can lighten it up around the eyes?

He looked disappointed when I gave him the picture. "I know you did the best you could," he said. He smiled. He didn't look like a criminal when he smiled.

When I got home, Meemaw was cutting up chicken wire and putting it over holes in the coop. Making it "snake proof," she said. I took over the cutting. I'd never used wire cutters before. Everything is just paper in their path.

"It's so bare in the chicken coop," I said. "Why don't you put down an old blanket or something?"

"You know, Wanda, I did that very thing one time, when I had a batch of baby chicks. I put down a carpet scrap, so they'd be warm. And they died. Every single one! I was just heartbroken. And do you know what I found out? They'd eaten the carpet."

"How'd you find that out?"

"I did an autopsy."

"Ooooo, Meemaw! How awful."

She shrugged. "Nothing awful about it. I wanted to know."

"I could never be a doctor," I said.

I read somewhere that these psychologists asked a bunch of surgeons why they became doctors, and they all said they wanted to help people. And then they did psychological tests on them and found out they were part sadists. They liked knives.

"How about a photographer?" Meemaw said. "I hear they teach photography in college now. I would pay for you to go."

I rolled up the leftover chicken wire and put it away in the barn. Meemaw came in after me.

"Time to milk Sissy, isn't it?" I said. I went to get the milk pail.

"What do you want to do with your life, Wanda?"

"You promised not to ask me that anymore."

She laughed and patted me on the back. "Yes, I did." She set the pail under Sissy, and then turned to face me again. "But what *are* you going to do?"

"I don't know, Meemaw."

Lately I'd been thinking about the homeless on TV, and how they live. I live in the gutter, I could say. It has a nice ring to it.

"Wanda, I once read a book where the first page had a quotation from the Bible. I thought it was the most beautiful of any Bible verse I'd ever read. It said the Lord will restore unto you the years the locusts have eaten."

She paused. When I didn't say anything, she waved her arms, saying, "Isn't that beautiful?"

"Uh huh."

The barn door swung open. Ed.

"How many times do I have to tell you not to leave the wheelbarrow out? It's been sitting there in the garden since morning."

"I told her it was O.K.," Meemaw said. "It doesn't hurt anything."

"The hell it doesn't. If you leave it out, it rusts. If it rusts, you have to buy a new one."

"I don't think it'll rust for ten years at least."

"Either you use the tools or they use you. That's all I have to say about it."

He stomped off.

Meemaw rubbed my arm. "Don't worry about it. Ed's just upset because yesterday you left his mail in the glove compartment instead of bringing it in to him. He's afraid somebody could have stolen his pension check."

"Who would steal it out here in the middle of nowhere? Who'd even know it's there?"

Meemaw went back to milking Sissy. I always thought milking a cow would be fun, till I tried it. The milk comes out in tiny streams, about the size of dental floss. It takes forever.

"You know how Ed is."

"Yeah, I know. Why did you marry him, anyway?"

"He needed me."

"But why not marry someone you needed?"

"I don't need anybody. I just need to be needed. They say money is the root of all evil, but I say selfishness is. Selfishness, and lack of exercise."

That got her started.

"Sweetie," she said, "I once read about a mental hospital for rich movie stars. It costs a powerful lot of money to go there. And you know what the doctors make those ladies do? Run in circles. Why, one movie star had to cut wood for two hours."

I thought about that on the way back to the house, but I couldn't see how cutting wood would make a difference.

That night I wrote a letter to Jimmy: "I hope you like it at college. Do you ever think about our baby? Whenever I take a shower, I think I hear him crying. Do you have this problem?"

I signed it, "Your friend, Wanda," and sent the letter in care of his parents.

"Let sleeping dogs lie," Mama wrote. "Think of the future. Pastor Dobbins will be needing a new receptionist at the church, and he told me he's willing to interview you. It's very big of him, considering."

I dropped the letter into the pigpen. The next day I could only see one corner, and after that it was gone.

I did Dwayne Zook, his sister Tracy Zook, and then I was finally done with the high-school-annual pictures. Mr. Lamont asked me to sit at the front desk to answer the phone and give people their proofs.

"Lovely," they'd say. Or, "Your boss surely does a fine job." Mr. Lamont told me to answer everything with: "He had a lot to work with." There was this one girl, though, who looked like Ted Koppel. I didn't know what to say to her.

We had lots of brides, even in August. I patted their faces dry and gave

557

them crushed ice to eat. I spread their dresses in perfect circles around their feet.

One day Mr. Lamont asked if I'd like to come into his darkroom to see how he did color.

"It looks like pink," he said, "but we call it magenta." He held up another filter. "What would you call that?"

"Turquoise?"

"Cyan," he said.

"Sigh-ann."

He let me do one, a baby sitting with its mother on the grass. The picture turned out too yellow, so I did another one.

"Perfect," he said. "You learn real quick."

"Thanks."

We goofed off the rest of the day. He showed me some wedding pictures that were never picked up. "A real shame," he said. "That's the best shot of the getaway car I've ever done."

He started going down to Food Heaven to get lunch for both of us. We'd eat Crescent City Melts and talk. He teased me about Ed, asking if it was true that he got kicked in the head by a mule when he was a kid.

"Does he really have two Cadillacs?"

"Three. They just sit out back. He drives his pickup truck everywhere."

Sometimes Mr. Lamont would come into my darkroom. He'd check on my supply of stop bath or Panalure. Then he'd lean in the corner and watch me work. He never touched me. We'd just stand there in the cool darkness.

He told me about his mother and why he couldn't leave her. "Cataracts," he said. "I read to her."

I told him about the book I got at the library, *The Songwriter's Book of Rhymes*. Also-ran rhymed with Peter Pan, Marianne, caravan, Yucatan, lumberman and about two hundred other words.

In *Discovering Your America* every state was pale pink, green or yellow. Nebraska had tiny bundles of wheat in one corner, and New Mexico had Indian headdresses. That night I dreamed I was high above Texas, watching the whole pink state come alive. Oil wells gushed. Fish flopped high in the air. Little men in hard hats danced around.

"I don't want to go to photography school," I told Meemaw the next morning. "I want to buy a car and drive to West Texas. Or maybe California."

"You can't do that," Meemaw said. "A young girl, alone."

"Why not?"

"It's just not done."

"Why can't I be the first to do it?"

"Oh, Wanda."

Meemaw believes in Good and Evil. She doesn't understand how lonely people are. Anyone who tried to hurt me, I would talk to him. I would listen to his tales of old hotels and wide-hipped women who left him.

On my seventy-seventh day at Meemaw's I came home and found Ed filling up the lawnmower.

"It's about time you earned your keep," he said.

"What about supper?"

"Forget supper. You're going to mow the lawn."

"Oh, is that so?"

"Yes, ma'am, you betcha that's so." He sat down on a lawn chair. "Get started."

A vat of green Jell-O swallowed him up, chair and all.

While I mowed, I thought of another fate for him — a giant cheese grater with arms and legs. Ed ran and ran, and then stumbled. The cheese grater stood over him and laughed as Ed tried to crawl away.

I didn't get to the big finale because the lawnmower made a crunching sound and stopped. Ed came running over, asking how come I didn't comb the yard first, how come I can't do anything right? "You're as lazy as a Mexican housecat."

His red, puffy face pushed into mine. In the folds of his skin I could see the luxury Meemaw had given him, her flowers and food and love. He just lapped it up.

He followed me into the house. Young people! Welfare! Good-for-nothings!

"You're a fine one to talk," I said, turning to face him. "I've never seen you lift a finger around here."

He moved towards me, and then stopped. He was so close I could see his eyes roll up into his head, and his eyelids quiver. The room was silent. I heard the hands on the clock move.

"You ungrateful bitch," he said. "Your grandmother thinks you're different, but I told her. I told her what you are."

It got dark while he told me what I was. He must have been rehearsing. I heard words I knew he got out of a dictionary. Meemaw twirled yarn and cried.

He got my suitcase and threw it at my feet.

559

"Get out. Now." He turned to Meemaw. "If she's here when I come back, I'll send for my things."

He slammed the door. His truck roared out, spitting gravel into the night.

"He's a child," Meemaw said. "A grown-up child, and I can't do anything about it." She held my face in her hands. "My little girl. My sweetie. What are we going to do?"

She put my head on her shoulder. We stood there, rocking.

"I named my baby Fishbone," I said. "Did you know that?" She shushed me and patted my back.

He'd be eight months old now. In twenty years he'll come looking for me. We'll have iced tea and wonder how to act. I wanted you, I'll tell him, but I was young. I didn't know I was strong.

"There's a bus to Grand Saline in the morning," Meemaw said. "I'll call your mother."

We rode a taxi into town. Meemaw got me a room at the motel. She brushed my hair and put me in bed.

"You can go home now, Meemaw."

"Yes, I suppose I can."

She wouldn't leave until I pretended I was asleep. But I couldn't sleep at all. I found a *Weekly World News* under the bed. I read every story in it. Then the ads, about releasing the secret power within you and True Ranches for sale and the Laffs Ahoy Klown Kollege in Daytona Beach.

At five A.M. I went for a walk. The air was cool and clear as October. I breathed deep.

Waffle Emporium was open. Something about dawn at a coffee shop gets to me. Pink tabletops, and people too sleepy to talk. New things around the corner. Carlsbad Caverns. White Sands.

I thought about what I was going to do next. I had eight hundred dollars inside my shoes. I could go anywhere. San Francisco, to work at the Believe It or Not Museum. Or Miami—I could take care of dolphins. I thought about Indian reservations. Gas stations in the desert. Snake farms. The owner would be named Chuck, probably, or Buzz.

I walked to the bus station and read the destination board. I said each city twice, to see how it felt on my tongue.

560

Rodriguez's Myopia

Leo Masliah

Rodriguez came into the waiting room. Its only furnishings consisted of some long sofas and a small table, on top of which there stood a lighted lamp; the lamp was topped by a pale yellow lampshade featuring a picture of a boat. In the picture four rough-looking men each held an oar; three of the oars were largely submerged. The fourth, which stood out most clearly in the picture, appeared to be made of cedar. In its lower section—where it was widest—someone had made some fairly deep cuts that resembled a human face, albeit somewhat confusedly; it was difficult to determine whether that form had been sought intentionally or whether it was a mere figment of the imagination, evident only to the observer inclined to see it. The face seemed to be that of an Indian—most notably in the region of the cheeks, from the center of which there emerged groups of bluish lines, like tattoos. The lines on the left cheek depicted a Portuguese or a Spanish galleon, with its sail strained to the breaking point, as if by the force of a strong wind. A tiny lookout, stationed at his observation post, seemed to wave his arms, eager to advise the crew of their possible proximity to land. The captain, standing on the deck, remained absorbed in his own thoughts, oblivious to the gesticulation of the lookout. Nor did he seem to notice a map that lay close by one of his boots, strangely unaffected by the wind which persisted in its struggle to break the resistance of the solid sails. It was a map of Africa surrounded by long lines indicating the circumnavigational routes. One of these routes, marked in bright red, ended at a spot on the coast of what is today known as Nigeria. The tiny piece of continent designated by the end of the red line was occupied by a minuscule drawing in colors, almost certainly typical of a village in the region. It portrayed a hut from which a native was emerging in squatting

561

position, due to the scant height of the space not obstructed by the thatched roof and walls. Next to the hut a woman, seated and with her legs crossed, could be seen inserting a fish into an almost cylindrical opening in the earth. A few inches away was a ceramic jug containing some leftover food that failed to obscure entirely the folk scene adorning the interior surface of the receptacle. It pictured a hunting party: a group of aborigines chasing a deer. Their weapons were surely the same ones they used for intertribal combat; otherwise there was no possible explanation for the large shields they carried, all of them bearing colorful illustrations on their external surfaces. Some of these illustrations had been damaged, perhaps by enemy lances in recent skirmishes; but on one of the shields the layer of pigments derived from plant matter had apparently survived intact. The painted areas, the outlines of which were not very sharp, at a distance nevertheless took on the exact shape of a metal saber. Though this weapon surely belonged to a civilization of invaders and not to the civilization of the creator of the shield, its design had been reproduced to perfection: the handle featured a golden cross, on which a Christ of pallid complexion lay dying. A soldier of the Empire, who seemed to spring from the handle of the saber, stood gallantly at the side of the Redeemer; in his right hand he held a parchment containing incomprehensible annotations, no doubt purely a product of the painter's imagination. The only decipherable element on the parchment was a drawing at the top, comparable to a letterhead. It represented the mythological character Perseus, his eyes fixed on a mirror to avoid the icy gaze of the Gorgon, who stood behind him. However, the image in the mirror was not Medusa's face but a landscape, perhaps the environs of the temple, reflected on the shiny surface through one of the rare openings in its main facade. The landscape consisted of an endless expanse of open field, devoid of trees or any other form of vegetation, topped by a slightly grayish-blue sky in which there appeared only the majestic figure of a gigantic bird, its wings fully spread. The bird was in every respect similar to an airplane; its small eye—the only one visible—could easily have been the side window of a cockpit. Additionally, the creature's small pupil, which contained a blemish at the top perhaps as a result of some eye infection, was the very picture of a pilot's head covered by a visored helmet, in the center of which a golden glimmer evoked the insignia of the air force of a neighboring country. This insignia was comprised of three juxtaposed logotypes, shaped respectively like a ship, an airplane and a railroad—the concomitance of those three objects symbolizing recognition of the brotherhood of all the national transportation networks. The locomotive standing on the railroad tracks displayed the emblem of the state-run company to which it belonged: the sketchy shape of a building behind big letters spelling out the company's name. Without a doubt, the building was the first central railroad station in the country's history, but the schematic quality of the design failed to express that too clearly. One window on the top floor of the edifice was scarcely visible. Judging by what little could be seen, it didn't belong to an office or to any room; it only opened onto a corridor, dotted with two rows of doors of diffuse outlines. One of the doors appeared to be open, although it was still possible to discern on the brass plaque identifying it the name and position of a high-ranking public official. Inside the room, the only thing Rodriquez could make out—and that with great effort—was a painting that occupied almost a third of the surface of the wall. But it was impossible to see what that painting contained. Disappointed, he directed his gaze elsewhere.

Translated from the Spanish by Louise B. Popkin

Retreat

Arthur Morey

Matty agreed that Thursday night Otis could return to pack his clothes and books; he had to be gone for good by Friday. His lawyer assured him that this was the best deal they could cut.

Dead broke, Otis moved out of the motel and began to spend nights in his office at the radio station. Each evening, he stayed at his desk after the others left, listening to the taped broadcasts. At eleven or so, just as his own show began, he would turn out the lights and stretch out on the carpet, staring into dark corners, as the old do, neither dreaming nor thinking. The rigging of the venetian blind in his window had rotted and snapped. Otis stuck a box of quarter-inch tape edgewise between the louvers to hold them apart. The glow from the mercury streetlamps suffused the room like fog. The white noise of the city was like the surf of a dead sea. He wondered if the boy heard it too. Otis would never again miss Matty but he would miss the idea of her, the form in which he imagined her. There is hurting and there is pain and Otis had passed them somewhere up the coast and gone beyond to deeper water.

Come morning he would find himself, as in a jump cut, exactly where he had lain down on the floor, the daylight oozing through the chink in the blinds. He would try to read meaning into the watermarks on the ceiling or he would pick at pieces of chewing gum, black as old pitch, in the carpet, rubbing at them until they came out in little mouse-turd balls under his fingertips. He would breakfast on graham crackers and coffee from yesterday and hit the streets before the secretary arrived.

Matty opened the door herself Thursday. She grimaced, turned, and strode back into the kitchen. She was as she had been for most of the two years since she became pregnant: Something was going to get hit. A moment later he heard the screen door slam and her heavy steps going down the back stairs. To Edward's, he thought, for tea. Otis felt only the memory of sorrow. He had lost his wife long since, even before she'd begun visiting Edward or disappeared with him, before her success as a merchant, even before the weekend she packed her belongings and announced she was taking the baby to live on some kind of communal farm. He'd lost her as you lose a cat who wants to be petted but claws when you hold it close.

He heard Edward's door shut. Rita, Matty's daughter, fourteen, entered on cue. "Miles is still awake," she said, her delivery wooden. "You can sit with him."

"Do you want to talk?"

"I'm staying with friends, thanks."

They were not good actors, Matty and Rita. They confused themselves with their roles and they changed roles often. But they had a natural instinct for melodrama that Otis admired.

When Rita left too, man and boy were alone. On the sun porch, Miles was working out in his crib, talking to himself. The sun was nearly down and he must have seen the man as a shadow at first because he cried out in alarm and then giggled at the smell or sound of his father. *Omphalos*, Otis thought. The laugh came from the navel of the universe. Hearing it, he was drawn into the baby's world of perfect benignity, knew the sun was the eye of God looking with tender concern over all aching creation, smiling, even, on tormented Matty and abraded Rita as on this sweet child and on Otis himself for all his mistakes. For a few minutes he and the baby bit chin and then Otis changed him and rocked him until he submerged in sleep, nearly sinking his father with him.

This was one of the things Otis would not give up, the sight of the boy sleeping, the terrestrial nirvana radiating out from him. He would fight to keep this, though he was not a talented fighter. Laying his son down in the crib, Otis imagined he heard from his own heart a gasp like the wheeze of a punctured accordion. There was a pain, too, like that of an abscessed tooth above his throat, back of his eyes, where tears lodge. Had he needed to speak, he knew his voice would be strangled and screened, like the voice of a shipwrecked movie alien whimpering to return to the ammonia seas of its native planet.

Matty and Rita had apparently spent the week streamlining. Otis's gear, making room for theirs, had been tossed into giant, damp, use-softened cartons. All were half-empty and there was no order in the arrangement: ties snaked through paperbacks, sweatshirts held flower-pots, chopsticks were stubbed into audio cassettes. His file folders were empty, their viscera removed as in autopsy for evidence of something or other Matty had given her lawyer. One carton in particularly violent confusion held the few books he cared about, commentaries, dictionaries and stories about the old heroes in the dead language Otis had studied in school. The boxes had been shoved up against the fireplace in a loose heap. It looked like a Mayan temple ravaged by time, vines and monkeys.

After a couple of hours of packing he was too tired to move. Hunkered down on the dhurrie, his back against the sofa, Otis watched the late news. The weatherman, one of those types who begins his career playing messengers in college Shakespeare, was predicting the onset of a heat wave tomorrow, the day of his one-man diaspora.

By nine the next morning it was ninety degrees. The sky was the gray of aluminum pans filled with water to humidify winter and then forgotten on radiators. Day and night in the hazy city were like the first and second days of creation in the old story—evenings and mornings without sun and moon. Otis walked out and down the street past the newsstand, the café, the auto lots, the train yard, signed out his U-Haul, bought a carton of Coke and drove back past the cemetery, singing.

His voice was impeccable. It was not that he sounded like Willie Nelson, now, or Muddy Waters or even Tom Waits; he had no talent. But you might have known, hearing him, that they'd all been on the same tour.

Otis Perrault was a loner by instinct, a radio announcer by trade, a man with very little luck. Twice in his life he had done something for love: he had taken a degree in classical Greek and married a woman he met in a new-age coffee shop after six weeks of courtship. Now, at forty, by trying to set up house with his son, he was about to strike one last off-balance blow for sentiment.

He parked the truck near the back stairway. The apartment upstairs was quiet; Rita had taken the boy to the park. Otis closed up the last of the boxes. About ten, Matty, Rita and Miles came up the front steps.

"Here, kid," Matty said, "say hi to your dad." Had they owned any crystal, Matty's voice, either by pitch or by volume, would have cracked it. Rita ducked into her room.

Matty was dressed in a professional's gray suit with a large bow at the shirt collar. Her running shoes were worn over a half sock with a pompom sewn at the heel.

"I don't appreciate having to come back from work," Matty said.

"You had to?"

"How do I know you won't take the silver?" she said. "Rita's afraid to stand up to you." She handed over the baby. Otis made a face at the boy, who smiled.

"Be here now, Otis," Matty instructed. "He needs changing."

Otis rediapered the boy in the crib in the sun-room. As usual the change made the kid playful but Otis was distracted. Matty, he knew, really was fearful of losing the silver. He couldn't remember where it was stored.

He balanced the boy on his arm and walked into the living room. Matty was reading a report, fanning herself with a copy of *Interview*. "You've got five hours," she said, never taking her eyes from the page. "You gonna make it?"

"The truck's in the back," he said. "I could take the crib now."

"You'd take Miles today?"

"Why not?"

"How will you work?"

"I can still make my own hours."

Matty chewed it over. "I can't risk it," she said, looking at him for the first time, to see if he flinched.

"Sure you can," he said, neutral.

"You're not responsible," she said. "You're a drifter. An artsy vagrant is what my lawyer called you." And then, overstating her case, she added, "And you're a man, after all."

Hell isn't some place we're taught about. We anticipate it by nature. When it doesn't appear in everyday life we cobble together some surrogate out of marriage, family, work—whatever is handy. Calcutta, Jonestown, Soweto, the death camps, My Lai, Beirut, Dublin were as far beyond Otis's imagination as bliss, wealth and death. But for a healthy man in an easy time and country, Otis felt—after the struggle over the boy began—that he had seen the back alleys of the netherworld. He would like to set up in his new flat in austerity—hard beds, uncooked food, only candles for light—and to spend his time meditating the basic questions. He was learning faith in his way; he understood, now, that the universe is governed by a few simple laws: whatever is painful, stupid, convoluted or vain is bound to prevail. Simplicity, integrity and beauty lose every time, world without end. Such patterns to life, Otis thought, prove there must be a God. But what is He driving at? Otis hoped that if his life got real simple, He might shed some light.

He would have to act cautiously. Austerity isn't considered a virtue in caregivers. Ms. Hernandez, the court-appointed social worker Otis was obliged to see, would not approve of him taking his son on retreat; she'd want something conventional. Otis needed to establish his respectability.

With some such intention in mind, he went down to the basement and began loading in the second-best furniture: the Swedish chairs, the puke-taupe rug, the wood-grain, formica table with the leaf rusted in place, the phone stand, a bookshelf, a mattress. Mildewed and bleached by the damp, much of the stuff was halfway to driftwood, the color of cave fish, not worth saving. Otis kept it in the hope that she'd accept it, the social worker. There is always a woman to please, he thought. That is a basic law also.

By the time he was ready to finish upstairs it was noon and the blinding gray sky made his skin ooze. Miles slept. Matty talked on the phone in the air-conditioned bedroom. The boxes that the women had packed weren't heavy but they were too big to lift. He dragged them down the steps and along the pavement to the truck. Several times he thought he was finished and then Matty found bedding or books that were his and tossed them off the back porch.

Otis had taken a flat on Mill Street. It was in a courtyard building six blocks away from the one he had shared with Matty. The buildings faced opposite directions, like repelling magnets.

About two Otis turned off Mill Street and parked in the alley. Five Cokes were gone and his skin felt clammy. His back had begun locking and he Grouchoed his way from the truck to the apartment, not bothering to force himself all the way upright. He was consoled by the pain, which made it easier not to think.

As he pulled one of the cartons down the sidewalk, it began to distend, like a cell dividing, opening and then inexorably spilling his clothes onto the pavement. They were, like most of his things, hand-me-downs, gifts, found objects, bargains. Many were shades of never-fashionable avocado and mustard, polyester blends, odd weaves. A few were vivid plaid flannels. Buttons were gone and elbows and cuffs were fraying. The shapeless wool shirt had been made by his grandmother twenty-five years earlier. Seeing them exposed in the sunlight, Otis felt ashamed, as if they were his nakedness and not its camouflage. He wanted to believe (it was untrue) that he wouldn't be caught dead in three-quarters of them, that he only saved them against the time he decided to paint the kitchen. But he stuffed them all back into the boxes, even the hideous turtlenecks with holes. He reminded himself that old clothes would be useful for wrapping wounds, if nothing else, when industry was wiped out by the next war or the long-overdue (according to him) collapse of the West. At least he could wear the rags rolling through puddles he and Miles would find when the cool rains came at last.

Even with furniture and cartons, the new rooms looked empty. There were three of them, and Otis took a long time deciding which should be which. He would drag his bed from one to another depending on his mood, the expectations of visitors, the direction and force of the wind. When a friend gave him a fat couch with a bad leg, Otis left it in the dining room and slid his bed into the next one over, where he had set up a playpen and sleeping mat for Miles.

Less than a week after the move, Matty stopped by without warning one day to drop off the boy and the cockatiel. She was terribly busy, she said.

"Working?"

"Networking," she answered darkly. Reformatting her life. She knew Otis wouldn't mind about Miles.

When Otis had first met Matty she was wearing an Indian-print dress and audible jewelry at the ankle. She had a tasteful stud in her nostril and an informed interest in prisms and crystals. She had tried marriages, photography, therapy, politics, performance art, meditation, channelling and computers. It was only afterwards, when she went to work for an importing firm, that all of her aspects began, in her words, to resonate harmoniously. She was a businessman, through and through. What she wanted was executive responsibility for Miles. Whatever happened she could never concede he was living with his father. The boy was in her care, merely delegated to Otis; she had her eye on things. Miles was Matty's means of reminding Otis who was boss, of punishing him for loving the child more than he had loved the mother.

Their first day together in the new flat, the man and his son sat on the floor, rolling balls and film canisters back and forth to each other. Then they wrestled, made sandwiches, napped. Days with the boy had always been as simple as this, hourless, encompassed by dawn and dusk, interrupted only by rainstorms, firetrucks and brilliant star turns by the sun.

Matty didn't come back for several days. In the following weeks she only visited, taking the boy with her on weekends. When it suited her schedule, two or three times a week, Matty would pick the boy up afternoons. Otis would bring him back evenings.

Otis learned to take the walk home slowly. In the twilight, crumpled on his father's shoulder, the baby seemed to slip into a kind of dream-time. He cooed and waved, flirting with streetlights, the moon and the stars. He was enraptured by the flickering reflections of television sets, which made the bay windows of the two-flats look like aquariums. At home, too, Miles wooed light. Naked bulbs and candles sent spasms of joy through his whole body. Otis attached a long pullcord to the fixture in his closet. Sitting on Otis's arm, the boy clowned, did takes, looked for photo opportunities as he turned the light on and off.

Their life in the first weeks on Mill Street began to fall into a routine. Lunch, for example, had its liturgy. They sang their way through it—a small man-and-boy's choir—adding their own percussive imitations of animals, backhoes and locomotives. The boy made faces and Otis mimicked them. Or vice versa. He teased, offering and then pulling back crumbs when his father went for them. Miles's cheerful egotism seemed innate and essential. He insisted on sitting in doorways to play and Otis stumbled over his toys every time he passed. The boy refused to be ignored and Otis, as though acting on instinct, could not help but pay attention.

They walked everywhere together, the boy on the man's arm, face to face. Otis could see his own features in the boy's expressions. But when Miles fell asleep, his face, with its plummy mouth and his thin, half-closed eyelids, was entirely his own. He's imprinting on you, someone said, but Otis thought it might be the other way around. After a few months, Otis began to feel sure that he and the baby were not distinct. He couldn't reconstruct the time, not much more than a year ago, when Miles wasn't present. His son seemed always to have been somewhere, laughing, observing, diverting, gurgling in Otis's ear, waiting in the wings. Their ideas (one using words, one not) marched lockstep. The two were matched: Friday and Crusoe marooned, Lennon and McCartney, Bergen and McCarthy, Jules and Jim, Butch and Sundance, Quixote and Sancho. Each was the other's best audience. They were a circular *folie à deux*. Only when they were at odds did Miles seem a baby.

The boy was becoming his father's perfect master. Otis studied: how does he grow? Do I teach him or is the person he is meant to be simply blooming? Using tools like a spoon or a ball, the boy imitated the man. But at the tap, for example, he handled the cup his own way, learning about water from water itself.

Otis held to the idea that he was on retreat. He had no direct experience of the contemplative life, but in the seventies he had known a couple of gurus socially. Meg, who ran the toy store—an attractive,

570

fortyish, Episcopalian lady – instructed him a little. She took occasional weekends with friends from her church and returned pensive and soothed, like a woman who has come from a tryst. Otis imagined a retreat as a kind of research without books. The hermit, he assumed, moved logically from one insight to the next, progressing systematically towards some essential truth. It was not working out that way for him. Unlike most hermits, Otis had gone into his wilderness with a small boy. Learning from Miles, Otis's understanding of things grew the way a tree does, in every direction at once, with epiphanies blooming, without warning, at no predictable place. After all the advice given him by lawyers and friends, he would have liked – though he made his livelihood from talk – to take a vow of silence. But it would have been dishonest. He had been in conversation with the boy since the day he was born.

The social worker, Ms. Hernandez – an exhausted woman who had truly seen everything – was not sympathetic to Otis. "When he's older," she said, "you can teach him to play ball. That's not enough?" Late in September, man and wife appeared in court. Miles, reluctantly, stayed with the sitter. The judge agreed that Matty should be listed as primary caretaker. Details were to be resolved. The lawyers obligingly returned to their offices and labored on in their lonely, unappreciated calling, communicating with Otis and Matty only through runic bills, drawing up a schedule for the boy – largely fictitious – that would look good to the judge and the social workers.

Two weeks later, Otis's radio show was canceled. No one noticed. Fallen from grace on the airwaves, he was put to work selling advertising time to local businessmen. Many were flattered to be called by a low-magnitude celebrity who knew how very special their establishments were. Otis went to his office only a few days a week. He contacted clients during the boy's naps, always pretending to be calling from a pay phone at O'Hare, on his way to an important meeting.

Otis and son spent their daylight hours that autumn on the circuit of local playgrounds, deciding which swings swung most smoothly, which slides had the finest views. Miles liked best playing hunter-gatherer, loping across the grasslands of a nearby field on his stubby legs, looking for dogs, airplanes, rabbits. Routines came and went, were conceived, tested and then discarded unsentimentally. For three days in a row, for example, the boy galloped everywhere, always right foot first. Then he stopped and never did it again. In the rows of great dying elms that stood watch over the streets, their leaves thinning in the cold and rain,

571

man and boy played hide-and-seek endlessly, reenacting the fears each had of being alone. Over and over they lost and were lost and then each, suddenly and joyfully, found and was restored.

Their favorite playground sat across from a baseball diamond next to the elevated train track. Two lines ran there, one a diesel commuter train, the other a trolley. Each time one passed Miles stopped all play and watched in awe. Otis bought copies—wooden and plastic trains, trains with and without batteries, music boxes shaped like locomotives, books about trains. Miles learned the sequence of cars. He would lie down with the toys, his head against the floor to make them seem big as possible and shunt them back and forth on a more orderly schedule than his own.

At night, while the boy slept, Otis swept, mopped and then sat at the sawhorse desk in the empty big room. As he wrote copy for ads he had sold during the day, he could almost hear the dirty laundry composting in the closet. The unanswered letters from friends in New York and elsewhere faded and blurred, whining without conviction as they disintegrated in the blue folder. The books swelled and mildewed in stacks on the floor beneath the sill where the houseplants dried out. When the boy's breathing became very regular (Otis could tune in from any room) he would try to make notes on the day. It astonished him that the most memorable and significant hours were made up of such ordinary stuff. They were like the mind-blowing experiences of college roommates, you would have to have been there to get the point. Otis recorded the fall into the puddle at the end of the slide, the return of the cats to the pretty blond nurse's window, the afternoon that the siren was set off in the backyard next-door by the man in the funny felt hat, the last sprinkler of the season.

As the fall receded, Matty spent more and more time in the city. The weather had grown changeable then cruel; Matty followed suit. For several days one week in October, Miles bawled at seeing his mother. One night after supper she returned him, pushing her way through the door. Otis noticed she was wearing an earclip and her coat bore the scent of patchouli that he would forever associate with sex.

She entered talking. Matty's cadences, the very fact that his parents were face to face with each other, made the boy edgy. Otis paced. Miles clung to his knees, trying to climb. "See what I mean?" she said, interrupting herself. "He's insecure, I know what I'm talking about. He follows me everywhere, he won't leave me alone, it's making me crazy. Rita was never like that. You don't notice these things. That's something we have to take up with what's-her-name, the therapist." She began, then, to list more of the boy's shortcomings, tracing them all to Otis. Otis was, she said, a deadbeat and idiot, spiritually bankrupt, primitive. He was turning her own son against her, she said. She told him how much Rita hated him, how much Miles would come to hate him—she'd see to that. . . .

When she attained the level of cursing in complete sentences, Otis got Miles to bed. Matty continued to talk in the next room, listening to nothing but the private melody of her rage—implacable, uninterruptible. Otis didn't know what had provoked her. But he knew she'd leave more quickly if he waited her out.

For Matty, words had no innate meaning. They were merely what you use to get what you want—not precision instruments, that is, but something more like church keys, chisels, screwdrivers, to pry lids off, poke holes, drive points home, crack things open.

When Otis emerged from the boy's bedroom Matty suggested that they sleep together. Otis told her to leave. She left. She came back, ringing the doorbell in longer and longer bursts. She shouted at him from the street. But it was cold and as Otis watched through the window she got into her car and leaned on the horn. The horn stuck. By the time the police answered the neighbors' complaints, Matty was gone.

In the small hours afterwards, Otis sat by the window smoking and watching the sky lighten. He wanted to surrender, to find a quiet curb in a foreign city—a city where they spoke a language he did not understand—and to sit there through cold and heat, winter and summer, until his time was up.

By the next midday, listless, feverish, oppressed, Otis had metamorphosed into Despair. Exhausted, sure he had ulcers, he collapsed on the bed and stared at the ceiling. Miles grasped the situation immediately. Taking his favorite pillows, one in each hand, he began to practice entrances from the kitchen. Here he came as a cheerleader! As the Pink Panther! As Maurice Chevalier! As Mr. Bojangles! He made a false start. He sneaked in, hiding his face in pillows. He backed in, giggling maniacally. There was no room in Miles's cosmos for surrender or even slowing down. He was a pulsar.

Trying to understand what was troubling Matty, Otis made inquiries. She was neither at home nor at work for two days. Edward didn't answer his phone. Rita had quit her job at the coffeehouse; someone there thought she was moving. It did not surprise Otis when his lawyer called to say he'd heard from Matty's. Matty wanted a meeting to

573

change the custody arrangements. But what with vacations, holidays, schedules, it would have to be put off for weeks. The lawyer meant well: "I'll do us a favor and try to delay until after Christmas, O.K.? Maybe it'll blow over. Buy her a present. How's the boy? You keeping him healthy? That's important."

Towards mid-November, the cold coming down from the north curled under itself and a wind called the Hawk began to blow in from the lake over the cemetery, through the tunnel under the train-tracks and down Mill Street. Otis had no car and was out of cash. They would be trapped indoors soon. Miles would learn to speak inside, as all people had once, perhaps, during the ice ages. The language of hunters and gatherers doesn't need details: words for direction and distance, the name of the prey. Bees can dance you a message like that. But meanly sheltered, cold, poor and waiting for big game to happen along, that was a time, surely, when storytelling and the love of stories was what kept the strong ones going.

In the division of spoils, Otis had salvaged a scuffed-up clock radio. As the summer faded they'd listened to Cubs games. The digital numbers on the radio were scrambled so they looked like an indecipherable alphabet—Hebrew, perhaps—and they flashed on and off continually. Miles loved them. Once baseball season was over, they lost contact with the outside. Otis tuned in the news occasionally, though there was no real news anymore, no watershed events, only evidences of familiar downtrends—the decline of charity, new peaks of meanness, vanity and idiocy.

Miles discovered how to tune the dial. Sitting on the bed, fiddling wildly, he could regularly find six or seven clear channels for every one of Otis's. Jazz, he found, old blues, folk singing, sermons. Occasionally he'd stop to dance or to let the cockatiel listen to Bach (the bird whistled classical). Otis heard snatches of ethereal melodies but lost them every time; the boy tuned too quickly. Eagerly, Otis would take the radio from him and try to hold onto the music, but in his hands the box was good only for continuous news, talk shows, jingles and static.

But when the bird and boy were covered and asleep, Otis, tuning carefully as a safecracker, found the station that broadcast to truckers nationwide. And he daydreamed he was in a rig on Interstate 80 heading east out of the Poconos across New Jersey to the George Washington Bridge and into Manhattan where the friends of his springtime still lived.

574

On 17 November, his 525th day, Miles walked into the kitchen, where Otis was scrambling an egg. The boy sat down on the floor, and distinctly said, for the first time in his father's hearing, "juice" then "shoe" and "eye." He pointed to each. Later he said "down" when he wanted to get down from his chair. He learned "tea" at lunch and "cheese" at dinner. Otis wondered, Do kids everywhere learn nouns first? Or do ours start with things because things is what we care about? Miles also said "Thank you" this first day. Rita reported on the nineteenth that he said the cat was "nice" (or perhaps claimed that he was being nice to the cat).

Miles's new words were not always pronounced with perfect clarity. But Otis knew that they were words because of the expression of glee, even of power, the giggle of command, that went along with speaking them. They were distorted by the joy of accomplishment and his astonishment at the things themselves. Having watched him talk for a few days, Otis realized that whenever Miles had seen a streetlamp or walked into a courtyard or lit a jack-o-lantern or passed a naked bulb in a hallway, it was not "aieee" that he cried out, but "light." It was his excitement at seeing the light that he had to master to become a speaking being. If he never pronounces the word as we do, Otis thought, it's all right. Lights are worth going nuts over.

A week after Miles began to speak English or, as he later said, Human, the day after Thanksgiving, Matty dropped by in the evening "to chat." Otis and the boy continued the game they were playing and she resented that. Within minutes she had started to recite her litany of epithets. Otis kept his ears open. He thought if he let her continue, Matty might, inadvertently, touch down in reality somehow, tell him the plans she and her lawyer were making, give him a clue whether she aimed to get the boy back. But after a time he began to listen to what she was saying, as if it meant something. It made him uneasy. Maybe, he thought, she will say things like this in court. Maybe, even, some of the things she's saying are true. After all, she had been his wife. He once loved her. Could she be entirely wrong?

In the pandemonium, Miles began to fall apart. He crawled into his father's lap. Matty snatched him away. He began to shout. Otis reached for him. Matty set the baby down on the couch, punched Otis and then began to console the kid. Something about the routine seemed funny to Otis. She did it with such fluidity—the baby drop, the right hook, the Madonna position—that he could only conclude she now had a modern dance master in addition to one for her spirit. He became cautious. He was afraid if he kicked her out she'd take the boy.

Could he trust her to drive, even, mad as she was? He didn't have the grit it takes to stand in the doorway playing tug-of-war with the baby. It was one of his serious shortcomings.

As if the boy were treasure trove, the Maltese falcon, say, Matty wrapped him up in a blanket, put him down in the middle of the couch and continued her siege. She went on until the boy was asleep and the man numb, until, at last, she made herself cry.

At 1:00 or so Otis lay back on the couch and let the world go dark. The boy was asleep beside him. Matty was in the chair by the window, sobbing.

A half-hour after dawn Miles was awake. Ready to go. Otis picked up the boy and walked through the house. It was eerily silent, still as a forest hushed by a snowfall. The boy only smacked his mouth; even the bird was calm. Matty, motionless as a rolled carpet, lay on the bed against the wall. Otis went back to the living room. He watched the boy play with a truck on the floor. Hungry but helpless, he wondered how long it would take to teach Miles to cook. Only one of his eyes seemed to transmit properly so he saw the world in soft focus as if they were living a cinema romance.

Slowly and delicately, like a man with a thousand-pound hangover, Otis made pancakes. He and the boy knocked down blocks. Miles was curious at the sight of his mother in bed. But he made no attempt to wake her.

They needed airing out. Man and boy took a long walk around the neighborhood. Miles was hugely amused watching a dog take a pee, concerned about the trees, which were bare and tossed by wind, eager to ride the one swing left by the city hanging in the playground.

Riding on his father's arm like a puppet, Miles began to entertain. He imitated Otis's imitations of animals. He invented his own. He did a good small dog, a kitty, a believable donkey, a terrific though soft-spoken pig. They began to work up a version of "Old MacDonald"—adding to the animals a few renditions of farm machinery. And through the E-I-E-I-O's Otis thought he felt the inquiring presence of his paradoxical God: Why not give the kid back to his mother, he wondered, and go back to New York? Was it worth putting Miles through more nights like last night? If Matty did go to court in a month or so, she would probably win the boy back and take him away. Could Otis stop her when he couldn't face her down at the doorway, when he couldn't pay lawyers? If he left, would he really be deserting the kid? Miles knew him. Given the innate charity and faith of chil-

dren, Miles would go on loving him in his absence, as children of
soldiers try to make themselves as brave as their imaginary fathers.
Who was Otis helping by staying? Miles? Himself? How could he
know?

When Otis returned to the apartment, determined to have a show-
down, Matty was gone.

She did not call. Sunday, man and boy were together alone. Otis
took the phone off the hook. The sight of his father reading the paper
grieved the boy and Otis put his head beside his son's and bellowed
with him, as cattle and whales do, exploring how it feels to be a beast,
unconscious in the hands of Nature.

They grew restless as the day wore on. It was unseasonably balmy.
After nap the two went to the playground and stayed all afternoon.
Otis brought along a camera to keep himself occupied.

The swings were empty. Otis struck up a conversation with the only
adult in the playground, a young mother with a whiny, small, three-
year-old boy. They talked for a few minutes, as mothers do at the
periphery of sandboxes, about toys and shoes and stages of
development.

It was while he and Miles were playing on the slide that he began to
hear Matty's voice again:

"You have no talent. You're a laughingstock with your radio people
and with those so-called intellectuals, too. What did you do? Take a
degree in Greek and then not want to teach? Not that teachers have it
great but it's a living at least and you haven't ever had a profession.
Not anything solid at all, nothing of integrity."

He had remained silent the first time. "I studied Homer because I
liked it," Otis answered now.

"But you have a son, and you're forty. Why didn't you do something
with your degree? Because you're a fuck-up, that's why. You couldn't
cut it. You got a radio show. . . . You don't even have that anymore.
You're embarrassing."

"I like storytelling," Otis had said, falling back on his old defense. "If
Homer were alive today, he'd be in radio."

Matty's voice continued in his head. It didn't seem to Otis as if she
were present, he was only remembering what she said. But he had no
power to stop the memories. It was as though they had become his own
train of thought. Every one of his mistakes and rash acts wounded
him. He knew now what Odysseus must have felt in Hades, blood

577

spread everywhere to attract the shades who swarmed to the smell of it like sharks.

"You are a joke as a provider. Me marry you as a meal-ticket? That's a laugh! But that's what Rita thought. We were much better off before you."

The snows would come before Christmas and the Hawk in off the lake would blow for weeks at a time. His newest boots were five years old and cracking. The heavy fur on squirrel tails and the law of averages suggested that winter might be cold this year.

"You're a coward and you lie, you're dishonest—well, Rita always had your number there. She hated you and she hated your attitude from the beginning. She wrote letters to her friends—and they begged her not to say anything to hurt me—but she despised you. She knew you were a phony. . . ."

He didn't say to Matty what she must have begun to see already, that because he loved his father Miles was already sure to become like him, as Otis was like father and grandfather. It was already too late for anyone to train out of the boy his talent as an animal imitator or his sense of timing, entering with pillows.

From the sandbox Miles shouted and ran up to his father, making a mock-terrifying expression. Otis grinned back but it felt all wrong, contrived, as if his face were a second-rate rubber mask: Richard Nixon, Dracula, Elmer Fudd. The boy hugged him anyway.

"You are an asshole," Matty droned on in his memory. "And that makes me an asshole too, because I married an asshole. And that little kid, that wonderful little boy, deserves better than an asshole for a father. . . ."

Otis was with the boy at the merry-go-round when he began to argue with the voice. It was as if a chorus of his own shades rallied to him. He remembered Sundays almost forty years earlier when he was very small. His grandfather, Old Perrault, then seventy, was working full-time in Vancouver, Washington, building Liberty ships. The old man must have been exhausted, but on Sunday visits, because Otis loved it so much, he would clap his aluminum hard hat on the boy, set him down in the wheelbarrow, and roll him up and down the back roads, not yet built up, near Battleground, in the shadow of Mount St. Helens.

Otis loved his grandmothers, his sweet and stern Aunt Rosalind and his mother. But now, walking in circles, holding Miles on the back of the plastic horse, he remembered his father, grandfather and uncles in incident after incident, as though his upbringing had been undertaken only by men. He remembered following his Uncle Nelson to the barn where the cow awaited them—how he would stretch his stride and swing his arms copying the man, proud in the certainty that someday he, too, would take on Dawn this way, in single combat. He could smell again the dew and dung, the hay and engine oil. He remembered the New Year's night when he threw a paper streamer at his father, knocking off and breaking his glasses and how his father cuffed him and the utter contrition in his voice when he came with Otis's mother into the bedroom to apologize.

Matty said in his ear, "You play Mommy to him, you diaper him because he's all you've got and you think he'll love you but he'll never love you, not after he finds out who you are and what you've done to me. And I'll be sure he finds out, don't you worry. I won't cover for you. He'll feel nothing but contempt."

He remembered his Uncle Canby, the marine home on leave, chasing away the bad boys who threw snowballs with rocks inside at Otis's father's new sedan. He remembered the cabin built by his one-armed Uncle Bill, one of the handsomest and funniest men of the century. Otis the boy would visit him there and try to learn to build fires while the old man did his best to tease him gently into a sense of irony.

Miles had quit spinning the merry-go-round and was undertaking a small excavation in the sandbox near the swings. He looked at his father with an expression of disdain. The sand was sticky. He smacked his hands together so they would be clean when he began to dig again. Otis picked him up to put him in a swing. The boy held tight, for fun, around Otis's neck and the man remembered how kissing his grandfather was a risky business because of his prickly beard. Pushing Miles back and forth, grabbing at his toes or making faces to see if he would laugh, Otis remembered his father reading *Wind in the Willows* to his sister and him. And though it was his mother who packed the good lunch of sandwiches and oranges in the neat little white cardboard box, Matty's voice had drowned out his mother's part in that adventure and Otis remembered mostly his father, a sportscaster, driving the 100 miles back from the basketball game he had taken his boy to see. Otis remembered himself, the boy, drowsing on the seat beside his father, his head on his father's thigh, half asleep, trying to make his wriggly body comfortable on the car seat, kicking again and again at the dashboard and at the tall, green-knobbed floor shift of the Nash. He could remember the safeness he felt then and felt now from the other side, from Miles as he clung to his father with arms, legs, chin in

579

that perfect fit that had evolved over tens of thousands of generations of parents and children at play.

And it had never occurred to Otis until this moment to wonder how the man stayed awake in the downpour and drove so patiently up the old Willamette Valley highway. It was only now, when he could see his father was a man as he himself is a man and not something much, much greater, that the son knew how tired the father must have been from work and from his kid and his hide-and-seek and his testing of echoes and his proving how hard he could punch.

Dusk came on abruptly. Up the street was a raw-brick, fairly new apartment building. In front of it had been planted a flowering cherry tree. Someone had put up white Christmas lights in the bare branches. The boy, riding the horse-shaped swing, spotted them over his father's shoulder. Fast as a serial cowboy he slipped off the horse and set off towards the lights. No obstacle broke his stride. Before Otis could catch up he was past the edge of the sandbox and halfway across the bumpy surface of the playground. The man caught him and, carried by momentum, scissored his way over the low cyclone fence, carrying the boy up the street.

"Daight," said Miles, grinning at his father.

In front of the apartment building the boy got down and charged, Teddy Roosevelt fashion, up the hill. The dim photograph shows him studying the lights in the tree with respect close to reverence. He glanced at his father only a second and pointed:

"Daight!"

Not even the train, which was passing just beyond, distracted him now. He approached the tree looking at the Christmas bulbs and through them to the sky where a brother star or two had appeared. From the boy's angle, the wedge of moon should have been visible above the branches. The bulbs were artifice, the stars and moon essence of his world of lights. The imitation mixed with the real thing and to the boy, if they were different at all, they must have seemed equally wonderful: nice copies, nice originals.

"Noom," he said with pleasure, looking at the crescent. He knew it from a book.

Behind the two the young mother passed, pulling a fancy wagon in which her son sat uncomfortably. He was staring at his mittens and whining something to her in a nasal singsong which she didn't acknowledge. As they passed, Otis heard the kid asking for cookies.

Miles walked to the tree trunk, his head tilted back to look at the

580

lights and beyond to deep space. The tree that supported the lights must have seemed to support the real stars, the moon, the clouds and the airplanes as well. Almost solemnly – with goodwill and fellow feeling – the boy reached out and patted the bark, showing his admiration and offering encouragement. He called to his father and after a moment the man walked up the hill and stood next to the boy looking up at the lights for himself.

Gwenan Wilbur has joined the *TriQuarterly* staff as Assistant to the Editor, replacing Janet E. Geovanis, who left *TQ* to enter the field of technical writing. Gwenan will assist in publicity and distribution for *TriQuarterly* magazine as well as for TriQuarterly Books/Another Chicago Press. She is also a student of Russian language and literature in the Slavic Department at Northwestern University.

Leo L. Litwak's story "The Eleventh Edition," which originally appeared in *TriQuarterly* #74 and is reprinted in the present volume, also appears as the first-prize winner in *Prize Stories 1990: The O. Henry Awards*, edited by William Abrahams. The anthology was recently issued by Doubleday in both hardcover and paperback editions.

THE EXPENDABLES

By
ANTONYA NELSON

Winner of the Flannery O'Connor Award for
Short Fiction

"In The Expendables by Antonya Nelson...we see clearly what it is that the
best young writers have to offer — a kind of pizazz, the love of undercurrent, of
voyeuristic intensity, a bewildered fascination with ritual as it has been under-
mined in our time, yet sustained, too, in an oddly moving way. We also witness
familial relationships from the bottom up."
—Ray Carver in AMERICAN FICTION 88

"...a vivid and exciting debut...a fresh and distinctive talent."
—PUBLISHERS WEEKLY

"Nelson dissects conflict between contemporary men and women, the hapless
derailment of traditions intended to honor birth, marriage and death...With an
unsentimental eye and honed passion, Antonya Nelson leads us through the
disonant tumult of contemporary society, where 'fragility and durability are
equal,' and faith in love's transformative power prevails over persistent irony
and contradiction. This is a fine collection of stories."
—Melissa Pritchard in THE CHICAGO TRIBUNE

"In these piercing stories, Ms. Nelson flings off the cloak of conventionality
that her characters wrap around themselves for protection against others, and
against their own shame over the vehemence of their feelings. Then they retreat,
as Daniel says of his father in The Expendables, back 'into his unfathomable self
once again.' Ms. Nelson makes the unfathomable selves of her characters
fathomable in this superb collection of stories."
—Sherie Posesorski in THE BALTIMORE SUN

"The stories...are candid snapshots of the lifestyle and mind set of
Americans...They are studies of people trapped inside themselves, struggling to
deal with love, death, and disaffection."
—LIBRARY JOURNAL

"These are stories written with searing honesty and compassion, with
remarkable understanding of the human condition. It's been a long time since
I've read a collection of stories that moved me as much as this did."
—Mary Elsie Robertson, author of WHAT I HAVE TO TELL YOU

"These are fine, vibrant stories — tough-minded and delicate at the same time.
They show a rare gift for creating characters that are both fully clear and fully
surprising. Antonya Nelson is a superbly talented writer."
—Joan Silber, author of IN THE CITY

The University of Georgia Press
Athens, Georgia 30602

ISBN 0-8203-1156-1 $15.95

It was a Thursday when I lifted the phone and called my agent. I said, "Gabe, I'm going to be sixty-six tomorrow, Friday, January 13, 1978, and I've been writing fiction all my life and no one's ever published a word of it and I'd give my left pinkie to get into *The Paris Review*." And I did because Gabriel was interested at once and told me that he'd get in touch with me the next day because he thought he might find a buyer. He did. . . . When my story came out, I went to Dr. Dodypol and had the finger removed surgically and under anesthesia. His head nurse, Kate Crackernuts, wrapped the finger in cotton bandages and in red tissue paper with a yellow ribbon around it and I walked out a published author and weighing three ounces less than when I walked in.

—Dallas Wiebe, "Night Flight to Stockholm," Issue 73

THE PARIS REVIEW

"A Prestigious Launching Pad for Young Writers."
—The Boston Globe

35

TriQuarterly

Fiction • Poetry • Art • Criticism
Three times a year

The New York Times has called **TriQuarterly** "perhaps the pre-eminent journal for litera[ry] fiction" in the nation. **Chicago** magazine describes it as " one of the best, issue after issue." B[ut] see for yourself—subscribe now . . .

TriQuarterly thanks the following life subscribers:

David C. Abercrombie
Amin Alimard
Lois Ames
Richard H. Anderson
Roger Anderson
Sandy Anderson
University of Arizona Poetry Center
Gayle Arnzen
Michael Attas
Asa Baber
Tom G. Bell
Carol Bly
Kay Bonetti
Robert Boruch
Van K. Brock
Gwendolyn Brooks
Timothy Browne
Paul Bundy
Eric O. Cahn
David Cassak
Stephen Chapman
Anthony Chase
Freda Check
Michael Chwe
Andrew Cyr
Doreen Davie
Kenneth Day
Mark W. DeBree
Alan Distler
Anstiss Drake
John B. Elliott
Christopher English
Carol Erickson
Steven Finch
David R. Fine
Paul Fjelstad
Torrence Fossland
Jeffrey Franklin
Peter S. Fritz
Mrs. Angela M. Gannon
Kathy M. Garness
Lawrence J. Gorman
Maxine Groffsky
Rev. Dr. Elliott Hagle
Jack Hagstrom
Ross B. Heath
Charles Hedde
Donald Hey
Donald A. Hillel
Craig V. Hodson
Irwin L. Hoffman
Irwin T. Holtzman
P. Hosier
Charles Huss

Curtis Imrie
Helen Jacob
Del Ivan Janik
Dr. Alfred D. Klinger
Loy E. Knapp
Sydney Knowlton
Mr. and Mrs. Carl A. Kroch
Judy Kunz
Conrad A. Langenberg
John Larroquette
Isaac Lassiter
Dorothy Latiak
Patricia W. Linton
Philip Lister
Mr. and Mrs. W. J. Lorentz de Haas
Prof. Kubet Luchterhand
Ellen L. Marks
Richard Marmulstein
James Marquardt
Kevin McCanna
Robert D. McChesney
Charles Gene McDaniel
Robert McMillan
Michael Meaney
George Meredith
Lois Adele Meyer
C. R. Michel
University of Michigan Hopwood Room
Ralph Miller
Kenneth Monroe
James E. Morrison IV
Max Nathan
Dean Neprud
Catherine Ohs
Paul Peters and Rosemarie Kozdron
Scott Peters
Jane Petro
Evelyn Pine
Doyle Pitman
Barbara Polikoff
Alex T. Primm
Richard Prinz, M.D.
Honora Rankine-Galloway
Anne Katheryn Ream
J. M. Reese
Peter Reich
Susan Reiners
Don Reynolds
Christopher Richter
Diane Rider
Rivier College
Sam Rosenthal
David Roth, M.D.
Jim Rowe